GW01606573

THE ESSENTIAL JAMES BOND

by the same author

The adventures of James Bond

DIAMONDS ARE FOREVER
DR NO
GOLDFINGER
FOR YOUR EYES ONLY
CASINO ROYALE
THE SPY WHO LOVED ME
LIVE AND LET DIE
MOONRAKER
FROM RUSSIA, WITH LOVE

also by Ian Fleming

THE DIAMOND SMUGGLERS
THRILLING CITIES

for children

CHITTY-CHITTY-BANG-BANG: THE MAGICAL CAR

THE ESSENTIAL JAMES BOND

Thunderball
On Her Majesty's Secret Service
You Only Live Twice
The Man With the Golden Gun
Octopussy and The Living Daylights

IAN FLEMING

JONATHAN CAPE
LONDON

This edition first published 1994

1 3 5 7 9 10 8 6 4 2

First published in the United Kingdom in 1994 by Jonathan Cape
Random House, 20 Vauxhall Bridge Road, London SWIV 2SA

Random House Australia (Pty) Limited
20 Alfred Street, Milsons Point, Sydney,
New South Wales 2061, Australia

Random House New Zealand Limited
18 Poland Road, Glenfield,
Auckland 10, New Zealand

Random House South Africa (Pty) Limited
PO Box 337, Bergvlei, South Africa

Random House UK Limited Reg. No. 954009

A CIP catalogue record for this book
is available from the British Library

ISBN 0-224-03756-0

Typeset by Pure Tech Corporation, Pondicherry, India
Printed in Great Britain by
Mackays of Chatham PLC, Chatham, Kent

CONTENTS

THUNDERBALL

Bond reached in his pocket for another cigarette. It couldn't be, yet it was so. Just what his Service and all the other intelligence services in the world had been expecting to happen. The anonymous little man in the raincoat with a heavy suitcase — or golf bag, if you like. The left luggage office, the parked car, the clump of bushes in a park in the centre of a big town. And there was no answer to it. In a few years' time, if the experts were right, there would be even less answer to it. Every tin-pot little nation would be making atomic bombs in their backyards, so to speak.

Apparently there was no secret now about the things. It had only been the prototypes that had been difficult — like the first gunpowder weapons for instance, or machine-guns or tanks. Today these were everybody's bows and arrows. Tomorrow, or the day after, the bows and arrows would be atomic bombs. And this was the first blackmail case. Unless SPECTRE was stopped, the word would get round and soon every criminal scientist with a chemical set and some scrap iron would be doing it. If they couldn't be stopped in time there would be nothing for it but to pay up. Bond said so.

To
ERNEST CUNEO
Muse

I

'TAKE IT EASY, MR BOND'

IT WAS ONE of those days when it seemed to James Bond that all life, as someone put it, was nothing but a heap of six to four against.

To begin with he was ashamed of himself — a rare state of mind. He had a hangover, a bad one, with an aching head and stiff joints. When he coughed — smoking too much goes with drinking too much and doubles the hangover — a cloud of small luminous black spots swam across his vision like amoebae in pond water. The one drink too many signals itself unmistakably. His final whisky and soda in the luxurious flat in Park Lane had been no different from the ten preceding ones, but it had gone down reluctantly and had left a bitter taste and an ugly sensation of surfeit. And, although he had taken in the message, he had agreed to play just one more rubber. Five pounds a hundred as it's the last one? He had agreed. And he had played the rubber like a fool. Even now he could see the queen of spades, with that stupid Mona Lisa smile on her fat face, slapping triumphantly down on his knave — the queen, as his partner had so sharply reminded him, that had been so infallibly marked with South, and that had made the difference between a grand slam redoubled (drunkenly) for him, and four hundred points above the line for the opposition. In the end it had been a twenty-point rubber, £100 against him — important money.

Again Bond dabbed with the bloodstained styptic pencil at the cut on his chin and despised the face that stared sullenly back at him from the mirror above the washbasin. Stupid, ignorant bastard! It all came from having nothing to do. More than a month of paper-work – ticking off his number on stupid dockets, scribbling minutes that got spikier as the weeks passed, and snapping back down the telephone when some harmless section officer tried to argue with him. And then his secretary had gone down with the flu and he had been given a silly, and, worse, ugly bitch from the pool who called him 'sir' and spoke to him primly through a mouth full of fruit stones. And now it was another Monday morning. Another week was beginning. The May rain thrashed at the windows. Bond swallowed down two Phensics and reached for the Enos. The telephone in his bedroom rang. It was the loud ring of the direct line with Headquarters.

James Bond, his heart thumping faster than it should have done, despite the race across London and a fretful wait for the lift to the eighth floor, pulled out the chair and sat down and looked across into the calm, grey, damnably clear eyes he knew so well. What could he read in them?

'Good morning, James. Sorry to pull you along a bit early in the morning. Got a very full day ahead. Wanted to fit you in before the rush.'

Bond's excitement waned minutely. It was never a good sign when M addressed him by his Christian name instead of by his number. This didn't look like a job — more like something personal. There was none of the tension in M's voice that heralded big, exciting news. M's expression was interested, friendly, almost benign. Bond said something noncommittal.

'Haven't seen much of you lately, James. How have you been? Your health, I mean.' M picked up a sheet of paper, a form of some kind, from his desk, and held it as if preparing to read.

Suspiciously, trying to guess what the paper said, what all this was about, Bond said, 'I'm all right, sir.'

M said mildly, 'That's not what the M.O. thinks, James. Just had your last Medical. I think you ought to hear what he has to say.'

Bond looked angrily at the back of the paper. Now what the hell! He said with control, 'Just as you say, sir.'

M gave Bond a careful, appraising glance. He held the paper closer to his eyes. ' "This officer",' he read, ' "remains basically physically sound. Unfortunately his mode of life is not such as is likely to allow him to remain in this happy state. Despite many previous warnings, he admits to smoking sixty cigarettes a day. These are of a Balkan mixture with a higher nicotine content than the cheaper varieties. When not engaged upon strenuous duty, the officer's average daily consumption of alcohol is in the region of half a bottle of spirits of between sixty and seventy proof. On examination, there continues to be little definite sign of deterioration. The tongue is furred. The blood pressure a little raised at 160/90. The liver is not palpable. On the other hand, when pressed, the officer admits to frequent occipital headaches and there is spasm in the trapezius muscles and so-called 'fibrositis' nodules can be felt. I believe these symptoms to be due to this officer's mode of life. He is not responsive to the suggestion that over-indulgence is no remedy for the tensions inherent in his professional calling and can only result in the creation of a toxic state which could finally have the effect of reducing his fitness as an officer. I recommend that No.007 should take it easy for two to three weeks on a more abstemious regime, when I believe he would make a complete return to his previous exceptionally high state of physical fitness." '

M reached over and slid the report into his OUT tray. He put his hands flat down on the desk in front of him and looked sternly across at Bond. He said, 'Not very satisfactory is it, James?'

Bond tried to keep impatience out of his voice. He said, 'I'm perfectly fit, sir. Everyone has occasional headaches. Most week-end golfers have fibrositis. You get it from sweating and then sitting in a draught. Aspirin and embrocation get rid of them. Nothing to it, really, sir.'

M said severely, 'That's just where you're making a big mistake, James. Taking medicine only suppresses these symptoms of yours. Medicine doesn't get to the root of the trouble. It only conceals it. The result is a more highly poisoned condition which may become chronic disease. All drugs are harmful to the system. They are contrary to nature. The same applies to most of the food we eat — white bread with all the roughage removed, refined sugar with all the goodness machined out of it, pasteurized milk which has had most of the vitamins boiled away, everything overcooked and denaturized. Why,' M reached into his pocket for his notebook and consulted it, 'do you know what our bread contains apart from a bit of over-ground flour?' M looked accusingly at Bond. 'It contains large quantities of chalk, also benzol peroxide powder, chlorine gas, sal ammoniac, and alum.' M put the notebook back in his pocket. 'What do you think of that?'

Bond, mystified by all this, said defensively, 'I don't eat all that much bread, sir.'

'Maybe not,' said M impatiently. 'But how much stone-ground whole wheat do you eat? How much yoghurt? Uncooked vegetables, nuts, fresh fruit?'

Bond smiled. 'Practically none at all, sir.'

'It's no laughing matter.' M tapped his forefinger on the desk for emphasis. 'Mark my words. There is no way to health except the natural way. All your troubles' — Bond opened his mouth to protest, but M held up his hand — 'the deep-seated toxaemia revealed by your Medical, are the result of a basically unnatural way of life. Ever heard of Bircher-Brenner, for instance? Or Kneipp, Preissnitz, Rikli, Schroth, Gossman, Bilz?'

'No, sir.'

'Just so. Well those are the men you would be wise to study. Those are the great naturopaths — the men whose teaching we have foolishly ignored. Fortunately,' M's eyes gleamed enthusiastically, 'there are a number of disciples of these men practising in England. Nature cure is not beyond our reach.'

James Bond looked curiously at M. What the hell had got into the old man? Was all this the first sign of senile decay? But M looked fitter than Bond had ever seen him. The cold grey eyes were clear as crystal and the skin of the hard, lined face was luminous with health. Even the iron-grey hair seemed to have new life. Then what was all this lunacy?

M reached for his IN tray and placed it in front of him in a preliminary gesture of dismissal. He said cheerfully, 'Well, that's all, James. Miss Moneypenny has made the reservation. Two weeks will be quite enough to put you right. You won't know yourself when you come out. New man.'

Bond looked across at M, aghast. He said in a strangled voice, 'Out of where, sir?'

'Place called Shrublands. Run by quite a famous man in his line — Wain, Joshua Wain. Remarkable chap. Sixty-five. Doesn't look a day over forty. He'll take good care of you. Very up-to-date equipment, and he's even got his own herb garden. Nice stretch of country. Near Washington in Sussex. And don't worry about your work here. Put it right out of your mind for a couple of weeks. I'll tell 009 to take care of the Section.'

Bond couldn't believe his ears. He said, 'But, sir. I mean, I'm perfectly all right. Are you sure? I mean, is this really necessary?'

'No,' M smiled frostily. 'Not necessary. Essential. If you want to stay in the Double-O Section, that is. I can't afford to have an officer in that section who isn't one hundred per cent fit.' M lowered his eyes to the basket in front of him and took out a signal file. 'That's all, 007.' He didn't look up. The tone of voice was final.

Bond got to his feet. He said nothing. He walked across the room and let himself out, closing the door with exaggerated softness.

Outside the door, Miss Moneypenny looked sweetly up at him.

Bond walked over to her desk and banged his fist down so that the typewriter jumped. He said furiously, 'Now what the hell, Penny? Has the old man gone off his rocker? What's all this bloody nonsense? I'm damned if I'm going. He's absolutely nuts.'

Miss Moneypenny smiled happily. 'The manager's been terribly helpful and kind. He says he can give you the Myrtle room, in the annex. He says it's a lovely room. It looks right over the herb garden. They've got their own herb garden, you know.'

'I know all about their bloody herb garden. Now look here, Penny,' Bond pleaded with her, 'be a good girl and tell me what it's all about. What's eating him?'

Miss Moneypenny, who often dreamed hopelessly about Bond, took pity on him. She lowered her voice conspiratorially. 'As a matter of fact, I think it's only a passing phase. But it *is* rather bad luck on you getting caught up in it before it's passed. You know he's always apt to get bees in his bonnet about the efficiency of the Service. There was the time when all of us had to go through that physical exercise course. Then he had that head-shrinker in, the psycho-analyst man — you missed that. You were somewhere abroad. All the Heads of Section had to tell him their dreams. He didn't last long. Some of their dreams must have scared him off or something. Well, last month M got lumbago and some friend of his at Blades, one of the fat, drinking ones I suppose,' Miss Moneypenny turned down her desirable mouth, 'told him about this place in the country. This man swore by it. Told M that we were all like motor-cars and that all we needed from time to time was to go to a garage and get decarbonized. He said he went there every year. He said it only cost twenty guineas a week which was less than what he spent in Blades in one day and it made him feel wonderful. Well, you know M always likes trying new things, and he went there for ten days and came back absolutely sold on the place. Yesterday he gave me a great talking-to all about it and this morning in the post I got a whole lot of tins of treacle and wheat germ and heaven knows what all. I don't know what to do with the stuff. I'm afraid my poor poodle'll have to live on it. Anyway, that's what happened and I must say I've never seen him in such wonderful form. He's absolutely rejuvenated.'

'He looks like that blasted man in the old Kruschen Salts advertisements. But why does he pick on me to go to this nut-house?'

Miss Moneypenny gave a secret smile. 'You know he thinks the world of you — or perhaps you don't. Anyway, as soon as he saw your Medical he told me to book you in.' Miss Moneypenny screwed up her nose. 'But, James, do you really drink and smoke as much as that? It can't be good for you, you know.' She looked up at him with motherly eyes.

Bond controlled himself. He summoned a desperate effort at nonchalance, at the throwaway phrase. 'It's just that I'd rather die of drink than of thirst. As for the cigarettes, it's really only that I don't know what to do with my hands.' He heard the stale, hangover words fall like clinker in a dead grate. Cut out the schmaltz! What you need is a double brandy and soda.

Miss Moneypenny's warm lips pursed into a disapproving line. 'About the hands — that's not what I've heard.'

'Now don't you start on me, Penny.' Bond walked angrily towards the door. He turned round. 'Any more ticking-off from you and when I get out of this place I'll give you such a spanking you'll have to do your typing off a block of Dunlopillo.'

Miss Moneypenny smiled sweetly at him. 'I don't think you'll be able to do much spanking after living on nuts and lemon juice for two weeks, James.'

Bond made a noise between a grunt and a snarl and stormed out of the room.

2

SHRUBLANDS

JAMES BOND SLUNG his suitcase into the back of the old chocolate-brown Austin taxi and climbed into the front seat beside the foxy, pimpled young man in the black leather windcheater. The young man took a comb out of his breast pocket, ran it carefully through both sides of his duck-tail hair-cut, put the comb back in his pocket, then leaned forward and pressed the self-starter. The play with the comb, Bond guessed, was to assert to Bond that the driver was really only taking him and his money as a favour. It was typical of the cheap self-assertiveness of young labour since the war. This youth, thought Bond, makes about twenty pounds a week, despises his parents, and would like to be Tommy Steele. It's not his fault. He was born into the buyers' market of the Welfare State and into the age of atomic bombs and space flight. For him, life is easy and meaningless. Bond said, 'How far is it to Shrublands?'

The young man did an expert but unnecessary racing change round an island and changed up again. ''Bout half an hour.' He put his foot down on the accelerator and neatly but rather dangerously overtook a lorry at an intersection.

'You certainly get the most out of your Bluebird.'

The young man glanced sideways to see if he was being laughed at. He decided that he wasn't. He unbent fractionally. 'My dad won't spring me something better. Says this old crate was okay for him for twenty years so it's got to be okay for me for another twenty. So I'm putting money by on my own. Half way there already.'

Bond decided that the comb-play had made him over-censorious. He said, 'What are you going to get?'

'Volkswagen Minibus. Do the Brighton races.'

'That sounds a good idea. Plenty of money in Brighton.'

'I'll say.' The young man showed a trace of enthusiasm. 'Only time I ever got there, a couple of bookies had me take them and a couple of tarts to London. Ten quid and a fiver tip. Piece of cake.'

'Certainly was. But you can get both kinds at Brighton. You want to watch out for being mugged and rolled. There are some tough gangs operating out of Brighton. What's happened to the Bucket of Blood these days?'

'Never opened up again after that case they had. The one that got in all the papers.' The young man realized that he was talking as if to an equal. He glanced sideways and looked Bond up and down with a new interest. 'You going into the Scrubs or just visiting?'

'Scrubs?'

'Shrublands — Wormwood Scrubs — Scrubs,' said the young man laconically. 'You're not like the usual ones I get to take there. Mostly fat women and old geezers who tell me not to drive so fast or it'll shake up their sciatica or something.'

Bond laughed. 'I've got fourteen days without the option. Doctor thinks it'll do me good. Got to take it easy. What do they think of the place round here?'

The young man took the turning off the Brighton road and drove westwards under the Downs through Poynings and Fulking. The Austin whined stolidly through the inoffensive countryside. 'People think they're a lot of crackpots. Don't care for the place. All those rich folk and they don't spend any money in the area. Tea-rooms make a bit out of them — specially out of the cheats.' He looked at Bond. 'You'd be surprised. Grown people, some of them pretty big shots in the City and so forth, and they motor around in their Bentleys with their bellies empty and they see a tea-shop and go in just for their cups of tea. That's all they're allowed. Next thing, they see some guy eating buttered toast and sugar cakes at the next table and they can't stand it. They order mounds of the stuff and hog it down just like kids who've broken into the larder — looking round all the time to see if they've been spotted. You'd think people like that would be ashamed of themselves.'

'Seems a bit silly when they're paying plenty to take the cure or whatever it is.'

'And that's another thing,' the young man's voice was indignant. 'I can understand charging twenty quid a week and giving you three square meals a day, but how do they get away with charging twenty quid for giving you nothing but hot water to eat? Doesn't make sense.'

'I suppose there are the treatments. And it must be worth it to the people if they get well.'

'Guess so,' said the young man doubtfully. 'Some of them do look a bit different when I come to take them back to the station.' He sniggered. 'And some of them change into real old goats after a week of nuts and so forth. Guess I might try it myself one day.'

'What do you mean?'

The young man glanced at Bond. Reassured and remembering Bond's worldly comments on Brighton, he said, 'Well, you see we got a girl here in Washington. Racy bird. Sort of local tart if you see what I mean. Waitress at a place called the Honey Bee Tea Shop — or was, rather. She started most of us off, if you get my meaning. Quid a go and she knows a lot of French tricks. Regular sport. Well, this year the word got round up at the Scrubs and some of these old goats began patronizing Polly — Polly Grace, that's her name. Took her out in their Bentleys and gave her a roll in a deserted quarry up on the Downs. That's been her pitch for years. Trouble was they paid her five, ten quid and she soon got too good for the likes of us. Priced her out of our market, so to speak. Inflation, sort of. And a month ago she chucked up her job at the Honey Bee, and you know what?' The young man's voice was loud with indignation. 'She bought herself a beat-up Austin Metropolitan for a couple of hundred quid and went mobile. Just like the London tarts in Curzon Street they talk about in the papers. Now she's off to Brighton, Lewes — anywhere she can find the sports, and in between whiles she goes to work in the quarry with these old goats from the Scrubs! Would you believe it!' The young man gave an angry blast on his klaxon at an inoffensive couple on a tandem bicycle.

Bond said seriously, 'That's too bad. I wouldn't have thought these people would be interested in that sort of thing on nut cutlets and dandelion wine or whatever they get to eat at this place.'

The young man snorted. 'That's all you know. I mean' — he felt he had been too emphatic — 'that's what we all thought. One of my pals, he's the son of the local doctor, talked the thing over with his dad — in a roundabout way, sort of. And his dad said no. He said that this sort of diet and no drink and plenty of rest, what with the massage and the hot and cold Sitz baths and what have you, he said that all clears the blood-stream and tones up the system, if you get my meaning. Wakes the old goats up — makes 'em want to start cutting the mustard again, if you know the song by that Rosemary Clooney.'

Bond laughed. He said, 'Well, well. Perhaps there's something to the place after all.'

A sign on the right of the road said ' *"Shrublands". Gateway to Health. First right. Silence please.'* The road ran through a wide belt of firs and evergreens in a fold of the Downs. A high wall appeared and then an imposing, mock-battlemented entrance with a Victorian lodge from which a thin wisp of smoke rose straight up among the quiet trees. The young man turned in and followed a gravel sweep between thick laurel bushes. An elderly couple cringed off the drive at a blare from his klaxon and then on the right there were broad stretches of lawn and neatly flowered borders and a sprinkling of slowly moving figures, alone and in pairs, and behind them a red brick Victorian monstrosity from which a long glass sun-parlour extended to the edge of the grass.

The young man pulled up beneath a heavy portico with a crenellated roof. Beside a varnished, iron-studded arched door stood a tall glazed urn above which a notice said: '*No smoking inside. Cigarettes here please.*' Bond got down from the taxi and pulled his suitcase out of the back. He gave the young man a ten-shilling tip. The young man accepted it as no less than his due. He said, 'Thanks. You ever want to break out, you can call me up. Polly's not the only one. And there's a tea-shop on the Brighton road has buttered muffins. So long.' He banged the gears into bottom and ground off back the way he had come. Bond picked up his suitcase and walked resignedly up the steps and through the heavy door.

Inside it was very warm and quiet. At the reception desk in the big oak-panelled hall a severely pretty girl in starched white welcomed him briskly. When he had signed the register she led him through a series of sombrely furnished public rooms and down a neutral-smelling white corridor to the back of the building. Here there was a communicating door with the annex, a long low cheaply built structure with rooms on both sides of a central passage. The doors bore the names of flowers and shrubs. She showed him into Myrtle, told him that 'The Chief' would see him in an hour's time, at six o'clock, and left him.

It was a room-shaped room with furniture-shaped furniture and dainty curtains. The bed was provided with an electric blanket. There was a vase containing three marigolds beside the bed and a book called *Nature Cure Explained* by Alan Moyle, M.N.B.A. Bond opened it and ascertained that the initials stood for 'Member: British Naturopathic Association'. He turned off the central heating and opened the windows wide. The herb garden, row upon row of small nameless plants round a central sundial, smiled up at him. Bond unpacked his things and sat down in the single armchair and read about eliminating the waste products from his body. He learned a great deal about foods he had never heard of, such as Potassium Broth, Nut Mince, and the mysteriously named Unmalted Slippery Elm. He had got as far as the chapter on massage and was reflecting on the injunction that this art should be divided into Effleurage, Stroking, Friction, Kneading, Petrissage, Tapotement, and Vibration, when the telephone rang. A girl's voice said that Mr Wain would be glad to see him in Consulting Room A in five minutes.

Mr Joshua Wain had a firm, dry handshake and a resonant, encouraging voice. He had a lot of bushy grey hair above an unlined brow, soft, clear brown eyes, and a sincere and Christian smile. He appeared to be genuinely pleased to see Bond and to be interested in him. He wore a very clean smock-like coat with short sleeves from which strong hairy arms hung relaxed. Below were rather incongruous pin-stripe trousers. He wore sandals over socks of conservative grey and when he moved across the consulting room his stride was a springy lope.

Mr Wain asked Bond to remove all his clothes except his pants. When he saw the many scars he said politely, 'Dear me, you do seem to have been in the wars, Mr Bond.'

Bond said indifferently, 'Near miss. During the war.'

'Really! War between peoples is a terrible thing. Now, just breathe in deeply, please.' Mr Wain listened at Bond's back and chest, took his blood pressure, weighed him and recorded his height, and then, after asking him to lie face down on a surgical couch, handled his joints and vertebrae with soft, probing fingers.

While Bond replaced his clothes, Mr Wain wrote busily at his desk. Then he sat back. 'Well, Mr Bond, nothing much to worry about here, I think. Blood pressure a little high, slight osteopathic lesions in the upper vertebrae — they'll probably be causing your tension headaches, by the way — and some right sacroiliac strain with the right ilium slightly displaced backwards. Due to a bad fall some time, no doubt.' Mr Wain raised his eyebrows for confirmation.

Bond said, 'Perhaps.' Inwardly he reflected that the 'bad fall' had probably been when he had had to jump from the Arlberg Express after Heinkel and his friends had caught up with him around the time of the Hungarian uprising in 1956.

'Well now.' Mr Wain drew a printed form towards him and thoughtfully ticked off items on a list. 'Strict dieting for one week to eliminate the toxins in the blood-stream. Massage to tone you up, irrigation, hot and cold Sitz baths, osteopathic treatment, and a short course of Traction to get rid of the lesions. That should put you right. And complete rest, of course. Just take it easy, Mr Bond. You're a civil servant, I understand. Do you good to get away from all that worrying paper-work for a while.' Mr Wain got up and handed the printed form to Bond. 'Treatment rooms in half an hour, Mr Bond. No harm in starting right away.'

'Thank you.' Bond took the form and glanced at it. 'What's Traction, by the way?'

'A mechanical device for stretching the spine. Very beneficial.' Mr Wain smiled indulgently. 'Don't be worried by what some of the other patients tell you about it. They call it "The Rack". You know what wags some people are.'

'Yes.'

Bond walked out and along the white-painted corridor. People were sitting about, reading or talking in soft tones in the public rooms. They were all elderly, middle-class people, mostly women, many of whom wore unattractive quilted dressing-gowns. The warm, close air and the frumpish women gave Bond claustrophobia. He walked through the hall to the main door and let himself out into the wonderful fresh air.

Bond walked thoughtfully down the trim narrow drive and

smelled the musty smell of the laurels and the laburnums. Could he stand it? Was there any way out of this hell-hole short of resigning from the Service? Deep in thought, he almost collided with a girl in white who came hurrying round a sharp bend in the thickly hedged drive. At the same instant as she swerved out of his path and flashed him an amused smile, a mauve Bentley, taking the corner too fast, was on top of her. At one moment she was almost under its wheels, at the next, Bond, with one swift step, had gathered her up by the waist and, executing a passable Veronica, with a sharp swivel of his hips had picked her body literally off the bonnet of the car. He put the girl down as the Bentley dry-skidded to a stop in the gravel. His right hand held the memory of one beautiful breast. The girl said 'Oh!' and looked up into his eyes with an expression of flurried astonishment. Then she took in what had happened and said breathlessly, 'Oh, thank you.' She turned towards the car. A man had climbed unhurriedly down from the driving seat. He said calmly, 'I am so sorry. Are you all right?' Recognition dawned on his face. He said silkily, 'Why, if it isn't my friend Patricia! How are you, Pat? All ready for me?'

The man was extremely handsome — a dark bronzed woman-killer with a neat moustache above the sort of callous mouth women kiss in their dreams. He had regular features that suggested Spanish or South American blood and bold, hard brown eyes that turned up oddly, or, as a woman would put it, intriguingly, at the corners. He was an athletic-looking six foot, dressed in the sort of casually well-cut beige herring-bone tweed that suggests Anderson and Sheppard. He wore a white silk shirt and a dark red polka-dot tie, and the soft dark brown V-necked sweater looked like vicuna. Bond summed him up as a good-looking bastard who got all the women he wanted and probably lived on them — and lived well.

The girl had recovered her poise. She said severely, 'You really ought to be more careful, Count Lippe. You know there are always patients and staff walking down this drive. If it hadn't been for this gentleman,' she smiled at Bond, 'you'd have run me over. After all, there *is* a big sign asking drivers to take care.'

'I am so sorry, my dear. I was hurrying. I am late for my appointment with the good Mr Wain. I am as usual in need of decarbonization — this time after two weeks in Paris.' He turned to Bond. He said with a hint of condescension, 'Thank you, my dear sir. You have quick reactions. And now, if you will forgive me —' He raised a hand, got back into the Bentley, and purred off up the drive.

The girl said, 'Now I really must hurry. I'm terribly late.' Together they turned and walked after the Bentley.

Bond said, examining her, 'Do you work here?' She said that she did. She had been at Shrublands for three years. She liked it. And how long was he staying? The small-talk continued.

She was an athletic-looking girl whom Bond would have casually associated with tennis, or skating, or show-jumping. She had the sort of firm, compact figure that always attracted him and a fresh open-air type of prettiness that would have been commonplace but for a wide, rather passionate mouth and a hint of authority that would be a challenge to men. She was dressed in a feminine version of the white smock worn by Mr Wain, and it was clear from the undisguised curves of her breasts and hips that she had little on underneath it. Bond asked her if she didn't get bored. What did she do with her time off?

She acknowledged the gambit with a smile and a quick glance of appraisal. 'I've got one of those bubble cars. I get about the country quite a lot. And there are wonderful walks. And one's always seeing new people here. Some of them are very interesting. That man in the car, Count Lippe. He comes here every year. He tells me fascinating things about the Far East — China and so on. He's got some sort of a business in a place called Macao. It's near Hong Kong, isn't it?'

'Yes, that's right.' So those turned-up eyes were a dash of Chinaman. It would be interesting to know his background. Probably Portuguese blood if he came from Macao.

They had reached the entrance. Inside the warm hall the girl said, 'Well, I must run. Thank you again.' She gave him a smile that, for the benefit of the watching receptionist, was entirely neutral. 'I hope you enjoy your stay.' She hurried off towards the treatment rooms. Bond followed, his eyes on the taut swell of her hips. He glanced at his watch and also went down the stairs and into a spotlessly white basement that smelled faintly of olive oil and aerosol disinfectant.

Beyond a door marked 'Gentlemen's Treatment' he was taken in hand by an indiarubbery masseur in trousers and singlet. Bond undressed and with a towel round his waist followed the man down a long room divided into compartments by plastic curtains. In the first compartment, side by side, two elderly men lay, the perspiration pouring down their strawberry faces, in electric blanket-baths. In the next were two massage tables. On one, the pale, dimpled body of a youngish but very fat man wobbled obscenely beneath the pummelling of his masseur. Bond, his mind recoiling from it all, took off his towel and lay down on his face and surrendered himself to the toughest deep massage he had ever experienced.

Vaguely, against the jangling of his nerves and the aching of muscles and tendons, he heard the fat man heave himself off his table and, moments later, another patient take his place. He heard the man's masseur say, 'I'm afraid we'll have to have the wrist-watch off, sir.'

The urbane, silky voice that Bond at once recognized said with authority, 'Nonsense, my dear fellow. I come here every year and I've always been allowed to keep it on before. I'd rather keep it on, if you don't mind.'

'Sorry, sir.' The masseur's voice was politely firm. 'You must have had someone else doing the treatment. It interferes with the flow of blood when I come to treat the arm and hand. If you don't mind, sir.'

There was a moment's silence. Bond could almost feel Count Lippe controlling his temper. The words, when they came, were spat out with what seemed to Bond ludicrous violence. 'Take it off then.' The 'Damn you' didn't have to be uttered. It hung in the air at the end of the sentence.

'Thank you, sir.' There was a brief pause and then the massage began.

The small incident seemed odd to Bond. Obviously one had to take off one's wrist-watch for a massage. Why had the man wanted to keep it on? It seemed very childish.

'Turn over, please sir.'

Bond obeyed. Now his face was free to move. He glanced casually to his right. Count Lippe's face was turned away from him. His left arm hung down towards the floor. Where the sunburn ended, there was a bracelet of almost white flesh at the wrist. In the middle of the circle where the watch had been there was a sign tattooed in red on the skin. It looked like a small zigzag crossed by two vertical strokes. So Count Lippe had not wanted this sign to be seen! It would be amusing to ring up Records and see if they had a line on what sort of people wore this little secret recognition sign under their wrist-watches.

3
THE RACK

AT THE END of the hour's treatment Bond felt as if his body had been eviscerated and then run through a wringer. He put on his clothes and, cursing M, climbed weakly back up the stairs into what, by comparison with the world of nakedness and indignities in the basement, were civilized surroundings. At the entrance to the main lounge were two telephone booths. The switchboard put him through to the only Headquarters number he was allowed to call on an outside line. He knew that all such outside calls were monitored. As he asked for Records, he recognized the hollowness on the line that meant the line was bugged. He gave his number to Head of Records and put his question, adding that the subject was an Oriental probably of Portuguese extraction. After ten minutes Head of Records came back to him.

'It's a Tong sign.' His voice sounded interested. 'The Red Lightning Tong. Unusual to find anyone but a full-blooded Chinaman being a member. It's not the usual semi-religious organization. This is entirely criminal. Station H had dealings with it once. They're represented in Hong Kong, but their headquarters are across the bay in Macao. Station H paid big money to get a courier service running into Pekin. Worked like a dream, so they gave the line a trial with some heavy stuff. It bounced, badly. Lost a couple of H's top men. It was a double-cross. Turned out that Redland had some sort of a deal with these people. Hell of a mess. Since then they've cropped up from time to time in drugs, gold smuggling to India, and top-bracket White Slavery. They're big people. We'd be interested if you've got any kind of a line.'

Bond said, 'Thanks, Records. No, I've got nothing definite. First time I've heard of these Red Lightning people. Let you know if anything develops. So long.'

Bond thoughtfully put back the receiver. How interesting!

Now what the hell could this man be doing at Shrublands? Bond walked out of the booth. A movement in the next booth caught his eye. Count Lippe, his back to Bond, had just picked up the receiver. How long had he been in there? Had he heard Bond's inquiry? Or his comment? Bond had the crawling sensation at the pit of his stomach he knew so well — the signal that he had probably made a dangerous and silly mistake. He glanced at his watch. It was seven thirty. He walked through the lounge to the sun-parlour where 'dinner' was being served. He gave his name to the elderly woman with a wardress face behind a long counter. She consulted a list and ladled hot vegetable soup into a plastic mug. Bond took the mug. He said anxiously, 'Is that all?'

The woman didn't smile. She said severely, 'You're lucky. You wouldn't be getting as much on Starvation. And you may have soup every day at midday and two cups of tea at four o'clock.'

Bond gave her a bitter smile. He took the horrible mug over to one of the little café tables near the windows overlooking the dark lawn and sat down and sipped the thin soup while he watched some of his fellow inmates meandering aimlessly, weakly, through the room. Now he felt a grain of sympathy for the wretches. Now he was a member of their club. Now he had been initiated. He drank the soup down to the last neat cube of carrot and walked abstractedly off to his room, thinking of Count Lippe, thinking of sleep, but above all thinking of his empty stomach.

After two days of this, Bond felt terrible. He had a permanent slight nagging headache, the whites of his eyes had turned rather yellow, and his tongue was deeply furred. His masseur told him not to worry. This was as it should be. These were the poisons leaving his body. Bond, now a permanent prey to lassitude, didn't argue. Nothing seemed to matter any more but the single orange and hot water for breakfast, the mugs of hot soup, and the cups of tea which Bond filled with spoonfuls of brown sugar, the only variety that had Mr Wain's sanction.

On the third day, after the massage and the shock of the Sitz baths, Bond had on his programme 'Osteopathic Manipulation and Traction'. He was directed to a new section of the basement, withdrawn and silent. When he opened the designated door he expected to find some hairy H-man waiting for him with flexed muscles. (H-man, he had discovered, stood for Health-man. It was the smart thing to call oneself if you were a naturopath.) He stopped in his tracks. The girl, Patricia something, whom he had not set eyes on since his first day, stood waiting for him beside the couch. He closed the door behind him and said, 'Good lord. Is this what you do?'

She was used to this reaction of the men patients and rather touchy about it. She didn't smile. She said in a businesslike voice, 'Nearly twenty per cent of osteopaths are women. Take off your clothes, please. Everything except your pants.' When Bond had amusedly obeyed she told him to stand in front of her. She walked round him, examining him with eyes in which there was nothing but professional interest. Without commenting on his scars she told him to lie face downwards on the couch and, with strong, precise, and thoroughly practised holds, went through the handling and joint-cracking of her profession.

Bond soon realized that she was an extremely powerful girl. His muscled body, admittedly unresistant, seemed to be easy going for her. Bond felt a kind of resentment at the neutrality of this relationship between an attractive girl and a half-naked man. At the end of the treatment she told him to stand up and clasp his hands behind her neck. Her eyes, a few inches away from his, held nothing but professional concentration. She hauled strongly away from him, presumably with the object of freeing his vertebrae. This was too much for Bond. At the end of it, when she told him to release his hands, he did nothing of the sort. He tightened them, pulled her head sharply towards him, and kissed her full on the lips. She ducked quickly down through his arms and straightened herself, her cheeks red and her eyes shining with anger. Bond smiled at her, knowing that he had never missed a slap in the face, and a hard one at that, by so little. He said, 'It's all very well, but I just had to do it. You shouldn't have a mouth like that if you're going to be an osteopath.'

The anger in her eyes subsided a fraction. She said, 'The last time that happened, the man had to leave by the next train.'

Bond laughed. He made a threatening move towards her. 'If I thought there was any hope of being kicked out of this damn place I'd kiss you again.'

She said, 'Don't be silly. Now pick up your things. You've got half an hour's Traction.' She smiled grimly. 'That ought to keep you quiet.'

Bond said morosely, 'Oh, all right. But only on condition you let me take you out on your next day off.'

'We'll see about that. It depends how you behave at the next treatment.' She held open the door. Bond picked up his clothes and went out, almost colliding with a man coming down the passage. It was Count Lippe, in slacks and a gay windcheater. He ignored Bond. With a smile and a slight bow he said to the girl, 'Here comes the lamb to the slaughter. I hope you're not feeling too strong today.' His eyes twinkled charmingly.

The girl said briskly, 'Just get ready, please. I shan't be a moment putting Mr Bond on the Traction table.' She moved off down the passage with Bond following.

She opened the door of a small anteroom, told Bond to put his things down on a chair, and pulled aside plastic curtains that formed a partition. Just inside the curtains was an odd-looking kind of surgical couch in leather and gleaming aluminium. Bond didn't like the look of it at all. While the girl fiddled with a series of straps attached to three upholstered sections that appeared to be on runners, Bond examined the contraption suspiciously. Below the couch was a stout electric motor on which a plate announced that this was the Hercules Motorized Traction Table. A power drive in the shape of articulated rods stretched upwards from the motor to each of the three cushioned sections of the couch and terminated in tension screws to which the three sets of straps were attached. In front of the raised portion where the patient's head would lie, and approximately level with his face, was a large dial marked in lbs.-pressure up to 200. After 150 lbs. the numerals were in red. Below the headrest were grips for the patient's hands. Bond noted gloomily that the leather on the grips was stained with, presumably, sweat.

'Lie face downwards here, please.' The girl held the straps ready.

Bond said obstinately, 'Not until you tell me what this thing does. I don't like the look of it.'

The girl said patiently, 'This is simply a machine for stretching your spine. You've got some mild spinal lesions. It will help to free those. And at the base of your spine you've got some right sacroiliac strain. It'll help that too. You won't find it bad at all. Just a stretching sensation. It's very soothing really. Quite a lot of patients fall asleep.'

'This one won't,' said Bond firmly. 'What strength are you going to give me? Why are those top figures in red? Are you sure I'm not going to be pulled apart?'

The girl said with a touch of impatience, 'Don't be silly. Of course if there was too much tension it might be dangerous. But I shall be starting you only at 90 lbs. and in a quarter of an hour I shall come and see how you're getting on and probably put you up to 120. Now come along. I've got another patient waiting.'

Reluctantly Bond climbed up on the couch and lay on his face with his nose and mouth buried in a deep cleft in the headrest. He said, his voice muffled by the leather, 'If you kill me, I'll sue.'

He felt the straps being tightened round his chest and then round his hips. The girl's skirt brushed the side of his face as she bent to reach the control lever beside the big dial. The motor began to whine. The straps tightened and then relaxed, tightened and relaxed. Bond felt as if his body was being stretched by giant hands. It was a curious sensation, but not unpleasant. With difficulty Bond raised his head. The needle on the dial stood at ninety. Now the machine was making a soft iron hee-hawing, like a mechanical donkey, as the gears alternately engaged and disengaged to produce the rhythmic traction.

'Are you all right?'

'Yes.' He heard the girl pass through the plastic curtains and then the click of the outer door. Bond abandoned himself to the soft feel of the leather at his face, to the relentless intermittent haul on his spine and to the hypnotic whine and drone of the machine. It really wasn't too bad. How silly to have had nerves about it!

A quarter of an hour later he heard again the click of the outside door and the swish of the curtains.

'All right?'

'Fine.'

The girl's hand came into his line of vision as she turned the lever. Bond raised his head. The needle crept up to 120. Now the pull was really hard and the voice of the machine was much louder.

The girl put her head down to his. She laid a reassuring hand on his shoulder. She said, her voice loud above the noise of the gears, 'Only another quarter of an hour to go.'

'All right.' Bond's voice was careful. He was probing the new strength of the giant haul on his body. The curtains swished. Now the click of the outside door was drowned by the noise of the machine. Slowly Bond relaxed again into the arms of the rhythm.

It was perhaps five minutes later when a tiny movement of the air against his face made Bond open his eyes. In front of his eyes was a hand, a man's hand, reaching softly for the lever of the accelerator. Bond watched it, at first fascinated, and then with dawning horror as the lever was slowly depressed and the straps began to haul madly at his body. He shouted — something, he didn't know what. His whole body was racked with a great pain. Desperately he lifted his head and shouted again. On the dial, the needle was trembling at 200! His head dropped back, exhausted. Through a mist of sweat he watched the hand softly release the lever. The hand paused and turned slowly so that the back of the wrist was just below his eyes. In the centre of the wrist was the little red sign of the zigzag and the two bisecting lines. A voice said quietly, close up against his ear, 'You will not meddle again, my friend.' Then there was nothing but the great whine and groan of the machine and the bite of the straps that were tearing his body in half. Bond began to scream, weakly, while the sweat poured from him and dripped off the leather cushions on to the floor.

Then suddenly there was blackness.

4

TEA AND ANIMOSITY

IT IS JUST as well that the body retains no memory of pain. Yes, it hurt, that abscess, that broken bone, but just how it hurt, and how much, is soon forgotten by the brain and the nerves. It is not so with pleasant sensations, a scent, a taste, the particular texture of a kiss. These things can be almost totally recalled. Bond, gingerly exploring his sensations as life came flooding back into his body, was astonished that the web of agony that had held his body so utterly had now completely dissolved. It was true that his whole spine ached as if it had been beaten, each vertebra separately, with wooden truncheons, but this pain was recognizable, something within his knowledge and therefore capable of control. The searing tornado that had entered his body and utterly dominated it, replacing his identity with its own, had gone. How had it been? What had it been like? Bond couldn't remember except that it had reduced him to something lower in the scale of existence than a handful of grass in the mouth of a tiger.

The murmur of voices grew more distinct.

'But what told you first that something was wrong, Miss Fearing?'

'It was the noise, the noise of the machine. I had just finished a treatment. A few minutes later I heard it. I'd never heard it so loud. I thought perhaps the door had been left open. I wasn't really worried but I came along to make sure. And there it was. The indicator up to 200! I tore down the lever and got the straps off and ran to the surgery and found the coramine and injected it into the vein — one c.c. The pulse was terribly weak. Then I telephoned you.'

'You seem to have done everything possible, Miss Fearing. And I'm sure you bear no responsibility for this terrible thing.' Mr Wain's voice was doubtful. 'It really is most unfortunate. I suppose the patient must have jerked the lever, somehow. Perhaps he was experimenting. He might easily have killed himself. We must tell the company about this and have some safety arrangement installed.'

A hand gingerly clasped Bond's wrist, feeling for his pulse. Bond thought it was time to re-enter the world. He must quickly get himself a doctor, a real one, not one of these grated-carrot merchants. A sudden wave of anger poured through him. This was all M's fault. M was mad. He would have it out with him when he got back to Headquarters. If necessary he would go higher — to the Chiefs of Staff, the Cabinet, the Prime Minister. M was a dangerous lunatic — a danger to the country. It was up to Bond to save England. The weak, hysterical thoughts whirled through his brain, mixed themselves up with the hairy hand of Count Lippe, the mouth of Patricia Fearing, the taste of hot vegetable soup and, as consciousness slipped away from him again, the diminishing voice of Mr Wain: 'No structural damage. Only considerable surface abrasion of the nerve ends. And of course shock. You will take personal charge of the case, Miss Fearing. Rest, warmth, and effleurage. Is that under . . .?'

Rest, warmth, and effleurage. When Bond came round again, he was lying face downward on his bed and his whole body was bathed in exquisite sensation. Beneath him was the soft warmth of an electric blanket, his back glowed with the heat from two large sun lamps, and two hands, clad in what felt to be some particularly velvety fur, were rhythmically passing, one after the other, up and down the whole length of his body from his neck to the backs of his knees. It was a most gentle and almost piercingly luxurious experience, and Bond lay and bathed himself in it.

Presently he said sleepily, 'Is that what they call effleurage?'

The girl's voice said softly, 'I thought you'd come round. The whole tone of your skin suddenly changed. How are you feeling?'

'Wonderful. I'd be still better for a double whisky on the rocks.'

The girl laughed. 'Mr Wain did say dandelion tea would be best for you. But I thought a little stimulant might be good, I mean just this once. So I brought the brandy with me. And there's plenty of ice as I'm going to give you an ice-pack presently. Would you really like some? Wait, I'll put your dressing-gown over you and then you can see if you can turn over. I'll look the other way.'

Bond heard the lamps being pulled away. Gingerly, he turned on his side. The dull ache returned, but it was already wearing off. He cautiously slipped his legs over the side of the bed and sat up.

Patricia Fearing stood in front of him, clean, white, comforting, desirable. In one hand was a pair of heavy mink gloves, but with the fur covering the palm instead of the back. In the other was a glass. She held out the glass. As Bond drank and heard the reassuring, real-life tinkle of the ice, he thought: this is a most splendid girl. I will settle down with her. She will give me effleurage all day long and from time to time a good tough drink like this. It will be a life of great beauty. He smiled at her and held out the empty glass and said, 'More.'

She laughed, mostly with relief that he was completely alive again. She took the glass and said, 'Well, just one more then. But don't forget it's on an empty stomach. It may make you dreadfully tight.' She paused with the brandy bottle in her hand. Suddenly her gaze was cool, clinical. 'And now you must try and tell me what happened. Did you accidentally touch the lever or something? You gave us all a dreadful fright. Nothing like that has ever happened before. The Traction table's really perfectly safe, you know.'

Bond looked candidly into her eyes. He said reassuringly, 'Of course. I was just trying to get more comfortable. I heaved about and I do remember that my hand hit something rather hard. I suppose it must have been the lever. Then I don't remember any more. I must have been awfully lucky you came along so quickly.'

She handed him the fresh drink. 'Well, it's all over now. And thank heavens nothing's badly strained. Another two days of treatment and you'll be right as rain.' She paused. She looked rather embarrassed. 'Oh, and Mr Wain asks if you could possibly keep all this, all this trouble, to yourself. He doesn't want the other patients to get worried.'

I should think not, thought Bond. He could see the headlines. 'PATIENT TORN NEARLY LIMB FROM LIMB AT NATURE CLINIC. RACK MACHINE GOES BERSERK. MINISTRY OF

HEALTH STEPS IN.' He said, 'Of course I won't say anything. It was my fault anyway.' He finished his drink, handed back the glass, and cautiously lay back on the bed. He said, 'That was marvellous. Now how about some more of the mink treatment. And by the way. Will you marry me? You're the only girl I've ever met who knows how to treat a man properly.'

She laughed. 'Don't be silly. And turn over on your face. It's your back that needs treatment.'

'How do you know?'

Two days later, Bond was once more back in the half-world of the nature cure. The routine of the early morning glass of hot water, the orange, carefully sliced into symmetrical pigs by some ingenious machine wielded, no doubt, by the wardress in charge of diets, then the treatments, the hot soup, the siesta, and the blank, aimless walk or bus ride to the nearest tea-shop for the priceless strength-giving cups of tea laced with brown sugar. Bond loathed and despised tea, that flat, soft, time-wasting opium of the masses, but on his empty stomach, and in his febrile state, the sugary brew acted almost as an intoxicant. Three cups he reckoned had the effect, not of hard liquor, but of just about half a bottle of champagne in the outside world, in real life. He got to know them all, these dainty opium dens — Rose Cottage, which he avoided after the woman charged him extra for emptying the sugar bowl; The Thatched Barn, which amused him because it was a real den of iniquity — large plates of sugar cakes put on one's table, the piercing temptation of the smell of hot scones — the Transport Café, where the Indian tea was black and strong and the lorry drivers brought in a smell of sweat and petrol and the great world (Bond found that all his senses, particularly his palate and nose, had miraculously become sharpened), and a dozen other cottagey, raftery nooks where elderly couples with Ford Populars and Morris Minors talked in muted tones about children called Len and Ron and Pearl and Ethel, and ate in small mouthfuls with the points of their teeth and made not a sound with the tea things. It was all a world whose ghastly daintiness and propriety would normally have sickened him. Now, empty, weak, drained of all the things that belonged to his tough, fast, basically dirty life, through banting, he had somehow regained some of the innocence and purity of childhood. In this frame of mind, the naivety and total lack of savour, surprise, excitement, of the dimity world of the Nice-Cup-of-Tea, of the Home-made Cakes, and the One-Lump-or-Two, were perfectly acceptable.

And the extraordinary thing was that he could not remember when he had felt so well — not strong, but without any aches and pains, clear of eye and skin, sleeping ten hours a day and, above all, without that nagging sense of morning guilt that one is slowly wrecking one's body. It was really quite disturbing. Was his personality changing? Was he losing his edge, his point, his identity? Was he losing the vices that were so much part of his ruthless, cruel, fundamentally tough character? Who was he in process of becoming? A soft, dreaming, kindly idealist who would naturally leave the Service and become instead a prison visitor, interest himself in youth clubs, march with the H-bomb marchers, eat nut cutlets, try and change the world for the better?

James Bond would have been more worried, as day by day the H-cure drew his teeth, if it had not been for three obsessions which belonged to his former life and which would not leave him — a passionate longing for a large dish of Spaghetti Bolognese containing plenty of chopped garlic and accompanied by a whole bottle of the cheapest, rawest Chianti (bulk for his empty stomach and sharp tastes for his starved palate), an overwhelming desire for the strong, smooth body of Patricia Fearing, and a deadly concentration on ways and means to wring the guts of Count Lippe.

The first two would have to wait, though tantalizing schemes for consuming both dishes on the day of his release from Shrublands occupied much of his mind. So far as Count Lippe was concerned, work had started on the project from the moment Bond took up again the routine of the cure.

With the cold intensity he would have employed against an enemy agent, say in a hotel in Stockholm or Lisbon during the war, James Bond set about spying on the other man. He became garrulous and inquisitive, chatting with Patricia Fearing about the various routines at Shrublands. 'But when do the staff find time to have lunch?' 'That man Lippe looks very fit. Oh, he's worried about his waist-line! Aren't the electric blanket-baths good for that? No, I haven't seen the Turkish Bath Cabinet.

Must have a look at it some time.' And to his masseur: 'Haven't seen that big chap about lately, Count something — Ripper? Hipper? Oh yes, Lippe. Oh, noon every day? I think I must try and get that time as well. Nice being clear for the rest of the day. And I'd like to have a spell in the Turkish Bath thing when you've finished the massage. Need a good sweat.' Innocently, fragment by fragment, James Bond built up a plan of operations — a plan that would leave him and Lippe alone among the machinery of the sound-proof treatment rooms.

For there would be no other opportunity. Count Lippe kept to his room in the main building until his treatment time at noon. In the afternoons he swished away in the violet Bentley — to Bournemouth it seemed, where he had 'business'. The night porter let him in around eleven each night. One afternoon — in the siesta hour — Bond slipped the Yale lock on Count Lippe's room with a straight piece of plastic cut off a child's aeroplane he had bought for the purpose in Washington. He went over the room meticulously and drew a blank. All he learned — from the clothes — was that the Count was a much travelled man — shirts from Charvet, ties from Tripler, Dior, and Hardy Amies, shoes from Peel, and raw silk pyjamas from Hong Kong. The dark red morocco suitcase from Mark Cross might have contained secrets, and Bond eyed the silk linings and toyed with the Count's Wilkinson razor. But no! Better that revenge, if it could be contrived, should come out of a clear sky.

That same afternoon, drinking his treacly tea, Bond scraped together the meagre scraps of his knowledge of Count Lippe. He was about thirty, attractive to women, and physically, to judge from the naked body Bond had seen, very strong. His blood would be Portuguese with a dash of Chinaman and he gave the appearance of wealth. What did he do? What was his profession? At first glance Bond would have put him down as a tough *maquereau* from the Ritz bar in Paris, the Palace at St Moritz, the Carlton at Cannes — good at backgammon, polo, water-skiing, but with the yellow streak of the man who lives on women. But Lippe had heard Bond making inquiries about him and that had been enough for an act of violence — an inspired act that he had carried out swiftly and coolly when he finished his treatment with the Fearing girl and knew, from her remark, that Bond would be alone on the Traction table. The act of violence might only have been designed to warn, but equally, since Lippe could only guess at the effect of a 200-lb. pull on the spine, it might have been designed to kill. Why? Who was this man who had so much to hide? And what were his secrets? Bond poured the last of his tea on to a mound of brown sugar. One thing was certain — the secrets were big ones.

Bond never seriously considered telling Headquarters about Lippe and what he had done to Bond. The whole thing, against the background of Shrublands, was so unlikely and so utterly ridiculous. And somehow Bond, the man of action and resource, came out of it all as something of a ninny. Weakened by a diet of hot water and vegetable soup, the ace of the Secret Service had been tied to some kind of a rack and then a man had come along and just pulled a lever up a few notches and reduced the hero of a hundred combats to a quivering jelly! No! There was only one solution — a private solution, man to man. Later perhaps, to satisfy his curiosity, it might be amusing to put through a good Trace on Count Lippe — with S.I.S. Records, with the C.I.D., with the Hong Kong Station. But for the time being Bond would stay quiet, keep out of Count Lippe's way, and plan meticulously for just the right kind of pay-off.

By the time the fourteenth day, the last day, came, Bond had it all fixed — the time, the place, and the method.

At ten o'clock, Mr Joshua Wain received Bond for his final check-up. When Bond came into the consulting room, Mr Wain was standing by the open window doing deep-breathing exercises. With a final thorough exhalation through the nostrils he turned to greet Bond with an Ah! Bisto! expression on his healthily flushed face. His smile was elastic with good-fellowship. 'And how's the world treating you, Mr Bond? No ill effects from that unhappy little accident? No. Quite so. The body is a most remarkable piece of mechanism. Extraordinary powers of recovery. Now then, shirt off, please, and we'll see what Shrublands has managed to do for you.'

Ten minutes later, Bond, blood pressure down to 132/84, weight reduced by ten pounds, osteopathic lesions gone, clear of eye and tongue, was on his way down to the basement rooms for his final treatment.

As usual, it was clammily quiet and neutral-smelling in the

white rooms and corridors. From the separate cubicles there came an occasional soft exchange between patient and staff, and, in the background, intermittent plumbing noises. The steady whir of the ventilation system created the impression of the deep innards of a liner in a dead calm. It was nearly twelve thirty. Bond lay face down on the massage table and listened for the authoritative voice and the quick slap of the naked feet of his prey. The door at the end of the corridor sighed open and sighed shut again. 'Morning, Beresford. All ready for me? Make it good and hot today. Last treatment. Three more ounces to lose. Right?'

'Very good, sir.' The gym shoes of the chief attendant, followed by the slapping feet, came down the corridor outside the plastic curtain of the massage room and on to the end room of all, the electric Turkish bath. The door sighed shut and a few minutes later sighed again as the attendant, having installed Count Lippe, came back down the corridor. Twenty minutes went by. Twenty-five. Bond rolled off the table. 'Well, thanks, Sam. You've done me a power of good. I'll be back to see you again one of these days I expect. I'll just go along and have a final salt rub and a Sitz bath. You cut along to your carrot cutlets. Don't worry about me. I'll let myself out when I've finished.' Bond wrapped a towel round his waist and moved off down the corridor. There was a flurry of movement and voices as the attendants got rid of their patients and made their way through the staff door for the luncheon break. The last patient, a reformed drunk, called back from the entrance, 'See you later, Irrigator!' Somebody laughed. Now the petty-officer voice of Beresford sounded down the corridor, making certain that everything was shipshape: 'Windows, Bill? Okay. Your next is Mr Dunbar at two sharp. Len, tell the laundry we shall need more towels after lunch. Ted . . . Ted. You there, Ted? Well, then, Sam, look after Count Lippe, would you, Turkish bath.'

Bond had listened to this routine for a whole week, noting the men that cut minutes off their duty and got off early to lunch, noting the ones that stayed to do their full share of the last chores. Now, from the open door of the empty shower room, he called back, in Sam's deep voice, 'Okay, Mr Beresford,' and waited for the crisp squeak of the gym shoes on the linoleum. There it was! The brief pause half way down the corridor and then the double sigh as the staff door opened and shut. Now there was dead silence save for the hum of the fans. The treatment rooms were empty. Now there was only James Bond and Count Lippe.

Bond waited a moment and then came out of the shower room and softly opened the door to the Turkish bath. He had had one session in the place, just to get the geography clear in his mind, and the scene was exactly as he remembered.

It was a white cubicle treatment room like all the others, but in this one the only object was a big cream metal and plastic box about five feet tall by four feet square. It was closed on all sides but the top. The front of the big cabinet was hinged to allow a patient to climb in and sit inside and there was a hole in the top with a foam rubber support for the nape of the neck and the chin, through which the patient's head emerged. The rest of his body was exposed to the heat from many rows of naked electric bulbs inside the cabinet and the degree of heat was thermostatically controlled by a dial at the back of the cabinet. It was a simple sweat-box, designed, as Bond had noticed on his previous visit to the room, by the Medikalischer Maschinenbau G.m.b.H., 44 Franziskanerstrasse, Ulm, Bavaria.

The cabinet faced away from the door. At the hiss of the hydraulic fastener, Count Lippe said angrily, 'Goddammit, Beresford. Let me out of this thing. I'm sweating like a pig.'

'You said you wanted it hot, sir.' Bond's amiable voice was a good approximation to the chief attendant's.

'Don't argue, goddammit. Let me out of here.'

'I don't think you quite realize the value of heat in the H-Cure, sir. Heat resolves many of the toxins in the blood-stream and for the matter of that in the muscle tissue also. A patient suffering from your condition of pronounced toxaemia will find much benefit from the heat treatment.' Bond found the H-lingo rattling quite easily off the tongue. He was not worried about the consequences to Beresford. He would have the solid alibi of luncheon in the staff canteen.

'Don't give me that crap. I tell you, let me out of here.'

Bond examined the dial on the back of the machine. The needle stood at 120. What should he give the man? The dial ran up to 200 degrees. That much might roast him alive. This was only to be a punishment, not a murder. Perhaps 180 would be a just retribution. Bond clicked the knob up to 180. He said: 'I think just half an hour of real heat will do you the world of good, sir.' Bond dropped the sham voice. He added sharply, 'And if you catch fire you can sue.'

The dripping head tried to turn, failed. Bond moved towards the door. Count Lippe now had a new voice, controlled but desperate. He said woodenly, concealing the knowledge and the hate, 'Give you a thousand pounds and we're quits.' He heard the hiss of the opening door. 'Ten thousand. All right then, fifty.'

Bond closed the door firmly behind him and walked quickly down the corridor to put on his clothes and get out. Behind him, deeply muffled, came the first shout for help. Bond closed his ears. There was nothing that a painful week in hospital and plenty of Gentian Violet or Tannic Acid jelly wouldn't cure. But it did cross his mind that a man who could offer a bribe of fifty thousand pounds must be either very rich or have some very urgent reason for needing freedom of movement. It was surely too much to pay just for avoidance of pain.

James Bond was right. The outcome of this rather childish trial of strength between two extremely tough and ruthless men, in the bizarre surroundings of a nature clinic in Sussex, was to upset, if only in a minute fashion, the exactly timed machinery of a plot that was about to shake the governments of the Western world.

5

S.P.E.C.T.R.E.

THE BOULEVARD HAUSSMANN, in the VIIIth and IXth Arrondissements, stretches from the Rue du Faubourg St Honoré to the Opéra. It is very long and very dull, but it is perhaps the solidest street in the whole of Paris. Not the richest — the Avenue d'Iéna has that distinction — but rich people are not necessarily solid people and too many of the landlords and tenants in the Avenue d'Iéna have names ending in 'escu', 'ovitch', 'ski', and 'stein', and these are sometimes not the endings of respectable names. Moreover, the Avenue d'Iéna is almost entirely residential. The occasional discreet brass plate giving the name of a holding company in Liechtenstein or in the Bahamas or the Canton de Vaud in Switzerland are there for tax purposes only — the cover names for private family fortunes seeking alleviation from the punitive burden of the Revenue, or, more briefly, tax-dodging. The Boulevard Haussmann is not like that. The massive, turn-of-the-century, bastard Second Empire buildings in heavily ornamented brick and stucco are the 'sièges', the seats, of important businesses. Here are the head offices of the *gros industriels* from Lille, Lyons, Bordeaux, Clermont Ferrand, the 'locaux' of the *grosses légumes*, the 'big vegetables' in cotton, artificial silk, coal, wine, steel, and shipping. If, among them, there are some fly-by-nights concealing a lack of serious capital — *des fonds sérieux* — behind a good address, it would only be fair to admit that such men of paper exist also behind the even solider frontages of Lombard and Wall Streets.

It is appropriate that among this extremely respectable company of tenants, suitably diversified by a couple of churches, a small museum and the French Shakespeare Society, you should also find the headquarters of charitable organizations. At No. 136 bis, for instance, a discreetly glittering brass plate says '*F.I.R.C.O.*' and, underneath, '*Fraternité Internationale de la*

Résistance Contre l'Oppression'. If you were interested in this organization, either as an idealist or because you were a salesman of, say, office furniture, and you pressed the very clean porcelain bell button, the door would in due course be opened by an entirely typical French concierge. If your business was serious or obviously well-meaning, the concierge would show you across a rather dusty hall to tall, bogus Directoire double doors adjoining the over-ornamented cage of a shaky-looking lift. Inside the doors you would be greeted by exactly what you had expected to see — a large dingy room needing a fresh coat of its café-au-lait paint, in which half a dozen men sat at cheap desks and typed or wrote amidst the usual accoutrements of a busy organization — In and Out baskets, telephones, in this case the old-fashioned standard ones that are typical of such an office in this part of Paris, and dark green metal filing cabinets in which drawers stand open. If you were observant of small details, you might register that all the men were of approximately the same age-group, between thirty and forty, and that in an office where you would have expected to find women doing the secretarial work, there were none.

Inside the tall door you would receive the slightly defensive welcome appropriate to a busy organization accustomed to the usual proportion of cranks and time-wasters but, in response to your serious inquiry, the face of the man at the desk near the door would clear and become cautiously helpful. The aims of the Fraternity? We exist, monsieur, to keep alive the ideals that flourished during the last war among members of all Resistance groups. No, monsieur, we are entirely unpolitical. Our funds? They come from modest subscriptions from our members and from certain private persons who share our aims. You have perhaps a relative, a member of a Resistance group, whose whereabouts you seek? Certainly, monsieur. The name? Gregor Karlski, last heard of with Mihailovitch in the summer of 1943. Jules! (He might turn to a particular man and call out.) Karlski, Gregor. Mihailovitch, 1943. Jules would go to a cabinet and there would be a brief pause. Then the reply might come back, Dead. Killed in the bombing of the General's headquarters, October 21st, 1943. I regret, monsieur. Is there anything further we can do for you? Then perhaps you would care to have some of our literature. Forgive me for not having time to spare to give you more details of FIRCO myself. But you will find everything there. This happens to be a particularly busy day. This is the International Refugee Year and we have many inquiries such as yours from all over the world. Good afternoon, monsieur. *Pas de quoi.*

So, or more or less so, it would be and you would go out on to the Boulevard satisfied and even impressed with an organization that was doing its excellent if rather vague work with so much dedication and efficiency.

On the day after James Bond had completed his nature cure and had left for London after, the night before, scoring a most satisfactory left and right of Spaghetti Bolognese and Chianti at Lucien's in Brighton and of Miss Patricia Fearing on the squab seats from her bubble car high up on the Downs, an emergency meeting of the Trustees of FIRCO was called for seven o'clock in the evening. The men, for they were all men, came from all over Europe, by train or car or aeroplane, and they entered No. 136 bis singly or in pairs, some by the front door and some by the back, at intervals during the late afternoon and evening. Each man had his allotted time for arriving at these meetings — so many minutes, up to two hours, before zero hour — and each man alternated between the back and the front door from meeting to meeting. Now there were two 'concierges' for each door and other less obvious security measures — warning systems, closed circuit television scanning of the two entrances, and complete sets of dummy FIRCO minutes, backed up one hundred per cent by the current business of the FIRCO organization on the ground floor. Thus, if necessary, the deliberations of the 'Trustees' could, in a matter only of seconds, be switched from clandestine to overt — as solidly overt as any meeting of principals in the Boulevard Haussmann could possibly be.

At seven o'clock precisely the twenty men who made up this organization strode, lounged or sidled, each according to his character, into the workmanlike boardroom on the third floor. Their chairman was already in his seat. No greetings were exchanged. They were ruled by the chairman to be a waste of breath and, in an organization of this nature, hypocritical. The men filed round the table and took their places at their numbers, the numbers from one to twenty-one that were their only names and that, as a small security precaution, advanced round the rota by two digits at midnight on the first of every month. Nobody smoked — drinking was taboo and smoking frowned upon — and nobody bothered to glance down at the bogus FIRCO agenda on the table in front of him. They sat very still and looked up the table at the chairman with expressions of the sharpest interest and what, in lesser men, would have been obsequious respect.

Any man seeing No. 2, for that was the chairman's number of the month, even for the first time would have looked at him with some degree of the same feelings, for he was one of those men — one meets perhaps only two or three in a lifetime — who seem almost to suck the eyes out of your head. These rare men are apt to possess three basic attributes — their physical appearance is extraordinary, they have a quality of relaxation, of inner certainty, and they exude a powerful animal magnetism. The herd has always recognized the other-worldliness of these phenomena and in primitive tribes you will find that any man singled out by nature in this fashion will also have been chosen by the tribe to be their chief. Certain great men of history, perhaps Genghis Khan, Alexander the Great, Napoleon, among the politicians, have had these qualities. Perhaps they even explain the hypnotic sway of an altogether more meagre individual, the otherwise inexplicable Adolf Hitler, over eighty million of the most gifted nation in Europe. Certainly, No. 2 had these qualities and any man in the street would have recognized them — let alone these twenty chosen men. For them, despite the deep cynicism ingrained in their respective callings, despite their basic insensitivity towards the human race, he was, however reluctantly, their Supreme Commander — almost their god.

This man's name was Ernst Stavro Blofeld and he was born in Gdynia of a Polish father and a Greek mother on May 28th, 1908. After matriculating in economics and political history at the University of Warsaw he studied engineering and radionics at the Warsaw Technical Institute and at the age of twenty-five obtained a modest post in the central administration of the Ministry of Posts and Telegraphs. This would seem a curious choice for such a highly gifted youth, but Blofeld had come to an interesting conclusion about the future of the world. He had decided that fast and accurate communication lay, in a contracting world, at the very heart of power. Knowledge of the truth before the next man, in peace or war, lay, he thought, behind every correct decision in history and was the source of all great reputations. He was doing very well on this theory, watching the cables and radiograms that passed through his hands at the Central Post Office and buying or selling on margin on the Warsaw Bourse — only occasionally, when he was absolutely certain, but then very big — when the basic nature of the postal traffic changed. Now Poland was mobilizing for war and a spate of munition orders and diplomatic cables poured through his department. Blofeld changed his tactics. This was valuable stuff, worth nothing to him, but priceless to the enemy. Clumsily at first, and then more expertly, he contrived to take copies of cables, choosing, for the ciphers hid their contents from him, only those prefixed 'MOST IMMEDIATE' or 'MOST SECRET'. Then, working carefully, he built up in his head a network of fictitious agents. These were real but small people in the various embassies and armament firms to whom most of the traffic was addressed — a junior cipher clerk in the British Embassy, a translator working for the French, private secretaries — real ones — in the big firms. These names were easily obtained from the diplomatic lists, by ringing up a firm and asking Enquiries for the name of the chairman's private secretary. He was speaking for the Red Cross. They wished to discuss the possibility of a donation from the chairman. And so on. When Blofeld had all his names right, he christened his network TARTAR and made a discreet approach to the German Military Attaché with one or two specimens of its work. He was rapidly passed on to the representative of AMT IV of the Abwehr, and from then on things were easy. When this pot was bubbling merrily, and the money (he refused to accept payment except in American dollars) coming in (it came in fast; he explained that he had so many agents to pay off), he proceeded to widen his market. He considered the Russians but dismissed them, and the Czechs, as probable non-, or at any rate slow, payers. Instead he chose the Americans and the Swedes, and money positively showered in on him. He soon realized, for he was a man of almost mimosaic sensibility in matters of security, that the pace could not possibly last. There would be a leak: perhaps between the Swedish and German secret services, who he knew (for through his contacts with their spies he was picking up the gossip of his new trade) were working closely together in some territories; or through Allied counter-espionage or their cryptographic services; or else one of his national agents would die or be transferred without his knowledge while he continued to use the name as a source. Anyway, by now he had two hundred thousand dollars and there was the added spur that the war was getting too close for comfort. It was time for him to be off into the wide world — into one of the safe bits of it.

Blofeld carried out his withdrawal expertly. First he slowly petered off the service. Security, he explained, was being tightened up by the English and the French. Perhaps there had been a leak — he looked with mild reproof into the eyes of his contact — this secretary had had a change of heart, that one was asking too much money. Then he went to his friend on the Bourse and, after sealing his lips with a thousand dollars, had all his funds invested in Shell Bearer Bonds in Amsterdam and thence transferred to a Numbered Safe Deposit box with the Diskonto Bank in Zurich. Before the final step of telling his contacts that he was *brûlé* and that the Polish Deuxième Bureau was sniffing at his heels, he paid a visit to Gdynia, called on the Registrar and on the Church where he had been baptized and, on the pretext of looking up details of an invented friend, neatly cut out the page recording his own name and birth. It remained only to locate the passport factory that operates in every big seaport and purchase a Canadian seaman's passport for 2,000 dollars. Then he was off to Sweden by the next boat. After a pause in Stockholm for a careful look round the world and some cool thinking about the probable course of the war, he flew to Turkey on his original Polish passport, transferred his money from Switzerland to the Ottoman Bank in Istanbul, and waited for Poland to fall. When, in due course, this happened, he claimed refuge in Turkey and spent a little money amongst the right officials in order to get his claim established. Then he settled down. Ankara Radio was glad to have his expert services and he set up RAHIR, another espionage service built on the lines of TARTAR, but rather more solidly. Blofeld wisely waited to ascertain the victor before selling his wares, and it was only when Rommel had been kicked out of Africa that he plumped for the Allies. He finished the war in a blaze of glory and prosperity and with decorations or citations from the British, Americans, and French. Then, with half a million dollars in Swiss banks and a Swedish passport in the name of Serge Angstrom, he slipped off to South America for a rest, some good food, and a fresh think.

And now Ernst Blofeld, the name to which he had decided it was perfectly safe to return, sat in the quiet room in the Boulevard Haussmann, gazed slowly round the faces of his twenty men, and looked for eyes that didn't squarely meet his. Blofeld's own eyes were deep black pools surrounded — totally surrounded, as Mussolini's were — by very clear whites. The doll-like effect of this unusual symmetry was enhanced by long silken black eyelashes that should have belonged to a woman. The gaze of these soft doll's eyes was totally relaxed and rarely held any expression stronger than a mild curiosity in the object of their focus. They conveyed a restful certitude in their owner and in their analysis of what they observed. To the innocent, they exuded confidence, a wonderful cocoon of confidence in which the observed one could rest and relax knowing that he was in comfortable, reliable hands. But they stripped the guilty or the false and made him feel transparent — as transparent as a fishbowl through whose sides Blofeld examined, with only the most casual curiosity, the few solid fish, the grains of truth, suspended in the void of deceit or attempted obscurity. Blofeld's gaze was a microscope, the window on the world of a superbly clear brain, with a focus that had been sharpened by thirty years of danger and of keeping just one step ahead of it, and of an inner self-assurance built up on a lifetime of success in whatever he had attempted.

The skin beneath the eyes that now slowly, mildly, surveyed his colleagues was unpouched. There was no sign of debauchery, illness, or old age on the large, white, bland face under the square, wiry black crew-cut. The jawline, going to the appropriate middle-aged fat of authority, showed decision and independence. Only the mouth, under a heavy, squat nose, marred what might have been the face of a philosopher or a scientist. Proud and thin, like a badly healed wound, the compressed, dark lips, capable only of false, ugly smiles, suggested contempt, tyranny, and cruelty. But to an almost Shakespearian degree. Nothing about Blofeld was small.

Blofeld's body weighed about twenty stone. It had once been all muscle — he had been an amateur weightlifter in his youth — but in the past ten years it had softened and he had a vast belly that he concealed behind roomy trousers and well-cut double-breasted suits, tailored, that evening, out of beige doeskin. Blofeld's hands and feet were long and pointed. They were quick-moving when they wanted to be, but normally, as now, they were still and reposed. For the rest, he didn't smoke or drink and he had never been known to sleep with a member of either sex. He didn't even eat very much. So far as vices or physical weaknesses were concerned, Blofeld had always been an enigma to everyone who had known him.

The twenty men who looked up the long table at this man and waited patiently for him to speak were a curious mixture of national types. But they had certain characteristics in common. They were all in the thirty-to-forty age-group, they all looked extremely fit, and nearly all of them — there were two who were different — had quick, hard, predatory eyes, the eyes of the wolves and the hawks that prey upon the herd. The two who were different were both scientists with scientists' otherworldly eyes — Kotze, the East German physicist who had come over to the West five years before and had exchanged his secrets for a modest pension and retirement in Switzerland, and Maslov, formerly Kandinsky, the Polish electronics expert who, in 1956, had resigned as head of the radio research department of Philips AG of Eindhoven and had then disappeared into obscurity. The other eighteen men consisted of cells of three (Blofeld accepted the Communist triangle system for security reasons) from six national groups and, within these groups, from six of the world's great criminal and subversive organizations. There were three Sicilians from the top echelon of the Unione Siciliano, the Mafia; three Corsican Frenchmen from the Union Corse, the secret society, contemporary with and similar to the Mafia, that runs nearly all organized crime in France; three former members of SMERSH, the Soviet organization for the execution of traitors and enemies of the State that had been disbanded on the orders of Khrushchev in 1958 and replaced by the Special Executive Department of the M.W.D.; three of the top surviving members of the former Sonderdienst of the Gestapo; three tough Yugoslav operatives who had resigned from Marshal Tito's Secret Police, and three highland Turks (the Turks of the plains are no good), formerly members of Blofeld's RAHIR and subsequently responsible for KRYSTAL, the important Middle East heroin pipeline whose outlet is Beirut. These eighteen men, all experts in conspiracy, in the highest ranges of secret communication and action and, above all, of silence, also shared one supreme virtue — every man had a solid cover. Every man possessed a valid passport with up-to-date visas for the principal countries in the world, and an entirely clean sheet with Interpol and with their respective national police forces. That factor alone, the factor of each man's cleanliness after a lifetime in big crime, was his highest qualification for membership of S.P.E.C.T.R.E. — The Special Executive for Counterintelligence, Terrorism, Revenge, and Extortion.

The founder and chairman of this private enterprise for private profit was Ernst Stavro Blofeld.

6

VIOLET-SCENTED BREATH

BLOFELD COMPLETED HIS inspection of the faces. As he had anticipated, only one pair of eyes had slid away from his. He had known he was right. The double-checked reports had been entirely circumstantial, but his own eyes and his intuition had to be the seal. He slowly put both hands under the table. One hand remained flat on his thigh. The other went to a side-pocket and drew out a thin gold vinaigrette and placed it on the table in front of him. He prised open the lid with his thumbnail, took out a violet-scented cachou, and slipped it into his mouth. It was his custom, when unpleasant things had to be said, to sweeten his breath.

Blofeld tucked the cachou under his tongue and began to talk in a soft, resonant, and very beautifully modulated voice.

'I have a report to make to members about The Big Affair, about Plan Omega.' (Blofeld never prefixed his words with 'Gentlemen', 'Friends', 'Colleagues', or the like. These were fripperies.) 'But before I proceed to that matter, for security's sake I propose to touch upon another topic.' Blofeld looked mildly round the table. The same pair of eyes evaded his. He continued in a narrative tone of voice: 'The Executive will agree that the first three years of our experience have been successful. Thanks in part to our German section, the recovery of Himmler's jewels from the Mondsee was successfully accomplished in total secrecy and the stones disposed of, by our Turkish section, in Beirut. Income: £750,000. The disappearance of the safe with its contents intact from the M.W.D. headquarters in East Berlin has never been traced to our Russian section, and the subsequent sale to the American Central Intelligence Agency yielded 500,000 dollars. The interception of one thousand ounces of heroin in Naples, the property of the Pastori circuit, when sold to the Firpone interests in Los Angeles, brought in 800,000 dollars. The British Secret Service paid £100,000 for the Czech germ warfare phials from the State chemical factory in Pilsen. The successful blackmail of former S.S. Gruppenführer Sonntag, living under the name of Santos in Havana, yielded a meagre 100,000 dollars — unfortunately all the man possessed — and the assassination of Peringue, the French heavy-water specialist who went over to the Communists through Berlin, added, thanks to the importance of his knowledge and the fact that we got him before he had talked, one billion francs from the Deuxième Bureau. In round sums, as the Special Executive knows from our accounts, the total income to date, not counting our last and undistributed dividend, has amounted to approximately one and a half million pounds sterling in the Swiss francs and Venezuelan bolivars in which for reasons of prudence — they continue to be the hardest currencies in the world — we convert all our takings. This income, as the Special Executive will be aware, has been distributed in accordance with our charter as to ten per cent for overheads and working capital, ten per cent to myself, and the remainder in equal shares of four per cent to the members — a profit to each member of approximately £60,000. This amount I regard as a barely adequate remuneration for members' services — £20,000 a year is not in accordance with our expectations — but you will be aware that Plan Omega will yield sufficient to provide each of us with a considerable fortune and will allow us, if we wish to do so, to wind up our organization and transfer our respective energies to other pursuits.' Blofeld looked down the table. He said amiably, 'Any questions?'

The twenty pairs of eyes, on this occasion all of them, gazed stolidly, unemotionally back at their chairman. Each man had made his own calculation, knew his own mind. There was no comment to be extracted from these good, though narrow, minds. They were satisfied, but it was not a part of their harsh personalities to say so. These were known things that their chairman had spoken. It was time for the unknown.

Blofeld slipped a second cachou into his mouth, manœuvred it under his tongue, and continued.

'Then so be it. And now to the last operation, completed a month ago and yielding one million dollars.' Blofeld's eyes moved down the left-hand rank of members to the end of the row. He said softly, 'Stand up No. 7.'

Marius Domingue of the Union Corse, a proud, chunky man with slow eyes, who was wearing ready-made, rather sharp clothes that probably came from the Galeries Barbès in Marseilles, got slowly to his feet. He looked squarely down the table at Blofeld. His big, rough hands hung relaxed at the seam of his trousers. Blofeld appeared to answer his gaze, but in fact he was noting the reaction of the Corsican next to No. 7, No. 12, Pierre Borraud. This man sat directly facing Blofeld at the far end of the long table. It was his eyes that had been evasive during the meeting. Now they were not. Now they were relaxed, assured. Whatever the eyes had feared had passed.

Blofeld addressed the company. 'This operation, you will recall, involved the kidnapping of the seventeen-year-old daughter of Magnus Blomberg, owner of the Principality Hotel in Las Vegas and participant in other American enterprises through his membership of the Detroit Purple Gang. The girl was abducted from her father's suite in the Hotel de Paris in Monte Carlo and taken by sea to Corsica. This part of the operation was executed by the Corsican section. One million dollars ransom was demanded. Mr Blomberg was willing and, in accordance with the instructions of SPECTRE, the money, in an inflated life raft, was dropped at dusk off the Italian coast near San Remo. At nightfall the raft was recovered by the ship operated by our Sicilian section. This section is to be commended for detecting the transistorized radio transmitter concealed in the raft which it was intended should allow a unit of the French Navy to direction-find our ship and hunt it down. On receipt of the ransom money, and in accordance with our undertaking, the girl was returned to her parents apparently suffering from no ill effects except for the hair-dye that had been necessary to transfer her from Corsica to a wagon-lit in the Blue Train from Marseilles. I say "apparently". From a source in the police commissariat at Nice, I now learn that the girl was violated during her captivity in Corsica.' Blofeld paused to allow this intelligence time to sink in. He continued. 'It is the parents who maintain that she was violated. It is possible that only carnal knowledge, with her consent, was involved. No matter. This organization undertook that the girl would be returned undamaged. Without splitting hairs about the effect of sexual knowledge on a girl, I am of the opinion that, whether the act was voluntary or involuntary on the girl's part, she was returned to her parents in a damaged, or at least used, condition.' Blofeld rarely employed gestures. Now he slowly opened the left hand that lay on the table. He said, in the same even tone of voice, 'We are a large and very powerful organization. I am not concerned with morals or ethics, but members will be aware that I desire, and most strongly recommend, that SPECTRE shall conduct itself in a superior fashion. There is no discipline in SPECTRE except self-discipline. We are a dedicated fraternity whose strength lies entirely in the strength of each member. Weakness in one member is the death-watch beetle in the total structure. You are aware of my views in this matter, and on the occasions when cleansing has been necessary you have approved my action. In this case, I have already done what I considered necessary vis-à-vis this girl's family. I have returned half a million dollars with an appropriate note of apology. This despite the matter of the radio transmitter which was a breach of our contract with the family. I dare say they knew nothing of the ruse. It was typical police behaviour — a pattern that I was expecting. The dividend for all of us from this operation will be correspondingly reduced. Regarding the culprit, I have satisfied myself that he is guilty. I have decided on the appropriate action.'

Blofeld looked down the table. His eyes were fixed on the man standing — on No. 7. The Corsican, Marius Domingue, looked back at him steadily. He knew he was innocent. He knew who was guilty. His body was still with tension. But it was not fear. He had faith, as they all had, in the rightness of Blofeld. He could not understand why he had been singled out as a target for all the eyes that were now upon him, but Blofeld had decided, and Blofeld was always right.

Blofeld noted the man's courage and sensed the reasons for it. He also observed the sweat shining on the face of No. 12, the man alone at the head of the table. Good! The sweat would improve the contact.

Under the table, Blofeld's right hand came up off his thigh, found the knob, and pulled the switch.

The body of Pierre Borraud, seized in the iron fist of 3,000 volts, arced in the armchair as if it had been kicked in the back. The rough mat of black hair rose sharply straight up on his head and remained upright, a gollywog fringe for the contorted, bursting face. The eyes glared wildly and then faded. A blackened tongue slowly protruded between the snarling teeth and remained hideously extended. Thin wisps of smoke rose from under the hands, from the middle of the back, and from under the thighs where the concealed electrodes in the chair had made contact. Blofeld pulled back the switch. The lights in the room that had dimmed to orange, making a dull supernatural glow, brightened to normal. The roasted meat and burned fabric smell spread slowly. The body of No. 12 crumpled horribly. There was a sharp crack as the chin hit the edge of the table. It was all over.

Blofeld's soft, even voice broke the silence. He looked down the table at No. 7. He noted that the staunch, impassive stance had not quavered. This was a good man with good nerves. Blofeld said, 'Sit down No. 7. I am satisfied with your conduct.' (Satisfaction was Blofeld's highest expression of praise.) 'It was necessary to distract the attention of No. 12. He knew that he was under suspicion. There might have been an untidy scene.'

Some of the men round the table nodded their understanding. As usual, Blofeld's reasoning made good sense. No one was greatly perturbed or surprised by what they had witnessed. Blofeld always exercised his authority, meted out justice, in full view of the members. There had been two previous occasions of this nature, both at similar meetings and both on security or disciplinary grounds which affected the cohesion, the inner strength, of the whole team. In one, the offender had been shot by Blofeld through the heart with a thick needle fired from a compressed air pistol — no mean feat at around twelve paces. In the other, the guilty man, who had been seated next to Blofeld on his left hand, had been garrotted with a wire noose casually flicked over his head and then, with two swift steps by Blofeld, pulled tight over the back of the man's chair. Those two deaths had been just, necessary. So had this death, the third. Now, the members, ignoring the heap of death at the end of the table, settled in their chairs. It was time to get back to business.

Blofeld snapped shut the gold vinaigrette and slipped it into a waistcoat pocket. 'The Corsican section,' he said softly, 'will put forward recommendations for a replacement for No. 12. But that can wait until after completion of Plan Omega. On this matter, there are certain details to be discussed. Sub-operator G, recruited by the German section, has made an error, a serious error which radically affects our time-table. This man, whose membership of the Red Lightning Tong in Macao should have made him expert in conspiracy, was instructed to make his headquarters at a certain clinic in the south of England, an admirable refuge for his purposes. His instructions were to keep intermittent contact with the airman Petacchi at the not-far-distant Boscombe Down airfield where the bomber squadron is under training. He was to report at intervals on the airman's fitness and morale. His reports have been satisfactory, and the airman, by the way, continues to be willing. But Sub-operator G was also required to post The Letter on D plus One, or three days from now. Unfortunately this foolish man took it upon himself to become embroiled in a hotheaded fashion with some fellow patient at the clinic, as a result of which, and I need not go into details, he is now in Brighton Central Hospital suffering from second-degree burns. He is thus out of action for at least a week. This will involve an irritating but fortunately not a serious delay in Plan Omega. Fresh instructions have been issued. The airman Petacchi has been provided with a phial of influenza virus of sufficient strength for him to remain on the sick list for one week during which he will be unable to accept his test flight. He will take the first flight after his recovery and alert us accordingly. The date of his flight will be communicated to Sub-operator G and he will by that time be recovered and will post The Letter according to plan. The Special Executive,' Blofeld glanced round the table, 'will readjust their flight schedules to Area Zeta in accordance with the new operational schedule. As for Sub-operator G' — Blofeld bent his gaze, one by one, on the three ex-Gestapo men — 'this is an unreliable agent. The German section will make arrangements for his elimination within twenty-four hours of the posting of The Letter. Is that understood?'

The three German faces stood unanimously to attention. 'Yes, sir.'

'For the rest,' continued Blofeld, 'all is in order. No. 1 has solidly established his cover in Area Zeta. The treasure-hunting myth continues to be built up and has already gained full credence. The crew of the yacht, all hand-picked sub-operators, are accepting the discipline and the security regulations better than had been expected. A suitable land base has been secured. It is remote and not easily accessible. It belongs to an eccentric Englishman, the nature of whose friends and personal habits demands seclusion. Your arrival in Area Zeta continues to be minutely planned. Your wardrobe awaits you in Areas F and D, according to your various flight plans. This wardrobe, down to the smallest detail, will be in accordance with your identities as financial backers of the treasure hunt who have demanded to visit the scene and take part in the adventure. You are not gullible millionaires. You are the kind of rich, middle-class rentiers and businessmen who might be expected to be taken in by such a scheme. You are all shrewd, so you have come to watch over your investment and ensure that not one doubloon goes astray.' (Nobody smiled.) 'You are all aware of the part you have to play and I trust that you have studied your respective roles with close attention.'

There was a careful nodding of heads round the table. These men were all satisfied that not too much had been asked of them in the matter of their cover. This one was a rich café proprietor from Marseilles. (He had been one. He could talk to anyone about the business.) That one had vineyards in Yugoslavia. (He had been brought up in Bled. He could talk vintages and crop-sprays with a Calvet from Bordeaux.) That one had smuggled cigarettes from Tangier. (He had done so and would be just sufficiently discreet about it.) All of them had been given covers that would stand up at least to second-degree inspection.

'In the matter of aqualung training,' continued Blofeld, 'I would like reports from each section.' Blofeld looked at the Yugoslav section on his left.

'Satisfactory.' 'Satisfactory,' echoed the German section, and the word was repeated round the table.

Blofeld commented, 'The safety factor is paramount in all underwater operations. Has this factor received sufficient attention in your respective training schedules?' Affirmative. 'And exercises with the new CO_2 underwater gun?' Again all sections reported favourably. 'And now,' continued Blofeld, 'I would like a report from the Sicilian section on the preparations for the bullion drop.'

Fidelio Sciacca was a gaunt, cadaverous Sicilian with a closed face. He might have been, and had been, a schoolmaster with communist leanings. He spoke for the section because his English, the compulsory language of the Special Executive, was the best. He said, in a careful, expository tone of voice, 'The chosen area has been carefully reconnoitred. It is satisfactory. I have here,' he touched the briefcase on his lap, 'the plans and detailed time-table for the information of the Chairman and members. Briefly, the designated area, Area T, is on the north-west slopes of Mount Etna, above the tree line — that is to say between the altitudes of 2,000 and 3,000 metres. This is an uninhabited and uncultivated area of black lava on the upper slopes of the volcano more or less above the small town of Bronte. For the purpose of the drop, an area approximately two kilometres square will be marked out by the torches of the recovery team. In the centre of this area will be positioned a Decca Aircraft Homing Signal as an additional navigational aid. The bullion flight, which I estimate conservatively will consist of five Mark IV Transport Comets, should make their run in at ten thousand feet at an air speed of 300 m.p.h. Having regard to the weight of each consignment, multiple parachutes will be needed, and, owing to the harsh nature of the terrain, very careful packing in foam rubber will be essential. The parachutes and the packings should be coated in Dayglo or some phosphorescent paint to assist recovery. No doubt,' the man opened his hands, 'the SPECTRE memorandum of dropping instructions will include these and other details, but very careful planning and co-ordination by those responsible for the flight will be necessary.'

'And the recovery team?' Blofeld's voice probed softly but with an urgent edge to it.

'The Capo Mafiosi of the district is my uncle. He has eight grandchildren, to whom he is devoted. I have made it clear that the whereabouts of these children is known to my associates. The man understood. At the same time, as instructed, I made him the offer of one million pounds for total recovery and safe delivery to the depot at Catania. This is a most important sum for the funds of the Unione. The Capo Mafiosi agreed to these terms. He understands that the robbery of a bank is in question. He wishes to know no more. The delay that has been announced will not affect the arrangements. It will still be within the full moon period. Sub-operator 52 is a most capable man. He has been provided with the Hallicraftor set issued to me for the purpose and he will listen on 18 megacycles in accordance with the schedule. Meanwhile he remains in touch with the Capo Mafiosi, to whom he is related by marriage.'

Blofeld was silent for a long two minutes. He slowly nodded. 'I am satisfied. So far as the next step is concerned, the disposal of the bullion, this will be in the hands of Sub-operator 201, of whom we have had full experience. He is a man to be trusted. The M.V. *Mercurial* will load at Catania and proceed through the Suez Canal to Goa, in Portuguese India. En route, at a designated cross-bearing in the Arabian Gulf, she will rendezvous with a merchant ship owned by a consortium of the chief Bombay bullion brokers. The bullion will be transferred to this ship in exchange for the equivalent value, at the ruling gold bullion price, in used Swiss francs, dollars, and bolivars. These large amounts of currency will be broken up into the allotted percentages and will then be transferred from Goa by chartered plane to twenty-two different Swiss banks in Zurich, where they will be placed in deposit boxes. The keys to these numbered boxes will be distributed to members after this meeting. From that moment on, and subject of course to the usual security regulations regarding injudicious spending and display, these deposits will be entirely at the disposal of members.' Blofeld's slow, calm eyes surveyed the meeting. 'Is this procedure considered satisfactory?'

There were cautious nods. No. 18, Kandinsky, the Polish electronics expert, spoke up. He spoke without diffidence. There was no diffidence between these men. 'This is not my province,' he said seriously. 'But is there not danger that one of the navies concerned will intercept this ship, the *Mercurial*, and remove the bullion? It will be clear to the Western powers that the bullion will have to be removed from Sicily. Various patrols of the air and sea would be an easy matter.'

'You forget,' Blofeld's voice was patient, 'that neither the first, nor if need be the second, bomb will be rendered safe until the money is in the Swiss banks. There will be no risk on that score. Nor, another possibility that I had envisaged, is there likely to be danger of our ship being pirated on the high seas by some independent operator. I envisage that complete secrecy will be enforced by the Western powers. Any leakage would result in panic. Any other questions?'

Bruno Bayer, one of the German section, said stiffly, 'It is fully understood that No. 1 will be in immediate control in Area Zeta. Is it correct that he will have full powers delegated by yourself? Is it that he will, so to speak, be Supreme Commander in the field?'

How typical, thought Blofeld. The Germans will always obey orders, but they wish to be quite clear where final authority resides. The German generals would only obey the Supreme Command if they knew Hitler approved the Supreme Command. He said firmly, 'I have made it clear to the Special Executive, and I repeat: No. 1 is already, by your unanimous vote, my successor in case of my death or incapacity. So far as Plan Omega is concerned, he is deputy Supreme Commander of SPECTRE, and since I shall remain at Headquarters to keep watch over reactions to The Letter, No. 1 will be Supreme Commander in the field. His orders will be obeyed as if they were my own. I hope we are fully agreed in this matter.' Blofeld's eyes, sharply focused, swept the meeting. Everyone signified his agreement.

'So,' said Blofeld. 'Then the meeting is now closed. I will instruct the disposal squad to take care of the remains of No. 12. No. 18, please connect me with No. 1 on 20 megacycles. That waveband will have been unoccupied by the French Post Office since eight o'clock.'

7

'FASTEN YOUR LAP-STRAP'

JAMES BOND SCRAPED the last dregs of yoghurt out of the bottom of the carton that said '*Goat-milk culture. From our own Goat Farm at Stanway, Glos. The Heart of the Cotswolds. According to an authentic Bulgarian recipe.*' He took an Energen roll, sliced it carefully — they are apt to crumble — and reached for the black treacle. He masticated each mouthful thoroughly. Saliva contains ptyalin. Thorough mastication creates ptyalin which helps to convert starches into sugar to supply energy for the body. Ptyalin is an enzyme. Other enzymes are pepsin, found in the stomach, and trypsin and erepsin found in the intestine. These and other enzymes are chemical substances that break up the food as it passes through the mouth, the stomach, and the digestive tract and help absorb it directly into the blood-stream. James Bond now had all these important facts at his finger-tips. He couldn't understand why no one had told him these things before. Since leaving Shrublands ten days before, he had never felt so well in his life. His energy had doubled. Even the paper-work he had always found an intolerable drudgery was now almost a pleasure. He ate it up. Sections, after a period of being only surprised, were now becoming slightly irritated by the forceful, clear-headed minutes that came shooting back at them from the Double-O Section. Bond awoke so early and so full of beans that he had taken to arriving at his office early and leaving late, much to the irritation of his secretary, the delectable Loelia Ponsonby, who found her own private routines being put seriously out of joint. She also was beginning to show signs of irritation and strain. She had even taken upon herself to have a private word with Miss Moneypenny, M's private secretary and her best friend in the building. Miss Moneypenny, swallowing her jealousy of Loelia Ponsonby, had been encouraging. 'It's all right, Lil,' she had said over coffee in the canteen. 'The Old Man was like that for a couple of weeks after he had got back from that damned nature cure place. It was like working for Gandhi or Schweitzer or someone. Then a couple of bad cases came up and rattled him and one evening he went to Blades — to take his mind off things I suppose — and the next day he felt awful, and looked it, and from then on he's been all right again. I suppose he got back on the champagne cure or something. It's really the best for men. It makes them awful, but at least they're human like that. It's when they get godlike one can't stand them.'

May, Bond's elderly Scottish treasure, came in to clear the breakfast things away. Bond had lit up a Duke of Durham, kingsize, with filter. The authoritative Consumers Union of America rates this cigarette the one with the smallest tar and nicotine content. Bond had transferred to the brand from the fragrant but powerful Morland Balkan mixture with three gold rings round the paper he had been smoking since his teens. The Dukes tasted of almost nothing, but they were at least better than Vanguards, the new 'tobaccoless' cigarette from America that, despite its health-protecting qualities, filled the room with a faint 'burning leaves' smell that made visitors to his office inquire whether 'something was on fire somewhere'.

May was fiddling about with the breakfast things — her signal that she had something to say. Bond looked up from the centre news page of *The Times*. 'Anything on your mind, May?'

May's elderly, severe features were flushed. She said defensively, 'I have that.' She looked straight at Bond. She was holding the yoghurt carton in her hand. She crumpled it in her strong fingers and dropped it among the breakfast things on the tray. 'It's not my place to say it, Mister James, but ye're poisoning yersel'.'

Bond said cheerfully, 'I know, May. You're quite right. But at least I've got them down to ten a day.'

'I'm not talking about yer wee bitty smoke. I'm talking 'bout this,' May gestured at the tray, 'this pap.' The word was spat out with disdain. Having got this off her chest, May gathered steam. 'It's no recht for a man to be eating bairns' food and slops and suchlike. Ye needn't worry that I'll talk, Mister James, but I'm knowing more about yer life than mebbe ye were wishing I did. There's been times when they've brought ye home from hospital and there's talk you've been in a motoring accident or some such. But I'm not the old fule ye think I am,

Mister James. Motoring accidents don't make one small hole in yer shoulder or yer leg or somewhere. Why, ye've got scars on ye the noo — ach ye needn't grin like that, I've seen them — that could only be made by buellets. And these guns and knives and things ye carry around when ye're off abroad. Ach!' May put her hands on her hips. Her eyes were bright and defiant. 'Ye can tell me to mind my ain business and pack me off back to Glen Orchy, but before I go I'm telling ye, Mister James, that if ye get yerself into anuither fight and ye've got nothing but yon muck in yer stomach, they'll be bringing ye home in a hearse. That's what they'll be doing.'

In the old days, James Bond would have told May to go to hell and leave him in peace. Now, with infinite patience and good humour, he gave May a quick run through the basic tenets of 'live' as against 'dead' foods. 'You see, May,' he said reasonably, 'all these denaturized foods — white flour, white sugar, white rice, white salts, whites of egg — these are dead foods. Either they're dead anyway like whites of egg or they've had all the nourishment refined out of them. They're slow poisons, like fried foods and cakes and coffee and heaven knows how many of the things I used to eat. And anyway, look how wonderfully well I am. I feel absolutely a new man since I took to eating the right things and gave up drink and so on. I sleep twice as well. I've got twice as much energy. No headaches. No muscle pains. No hangovers. Why, a month ago there wasn't a week went by but that on at least one day I couldn't eat anything for breakfast but a couple of aspirins and a prairie oyster. And you know quite well that that used to make you cluck and tut-tut all over the place like an old hen. Well,' Bond raised his eyebrows amiably, 'what about that?'

May was defeated. She picked up the tray and, with a stiff back, made for the door. She paused on the threshold and turned round. Her eyes were bright with angry tears. 'Well, all I can say is, Mister James, that mebbe ye're right and mebbe ye're wrong. What worries the life out of me is that ye're not yersel' any more.' She went out and banged the door.

Bond sighed and picked up the paper. He said the magical words that all men say when a middle-aged woman makes a temperamental scene, 'change of life', and went back to reading about the latest reasons for not having a Summit meeting.

The telephone, the red one that was the direct line with Headquarters, gave its loud, distinctive jangle. Bond kept his eyes on the page and reached out a hand. With the Cold War easing off, it was not like the old days. This would be nothing exciting. Probably cancelling his shoot at Bisley that afternoon with the new F.N. rifle. 'Bond speaking.'

It was the Chief of Staff. Bond dropped his paper on the floor. He pressed the receiver to his ear, trying, as in the old days, to read behind the words.

'At once please, James. M.'

'Something for me?'

'Something for everyone. Crash-dive, and Ultra Hush. If you've got any dates for the next few weeks, better cancel them. You'll be off tonight. See you.' The line went dead.

Bond had the most selfish car in England. It was a Mark II Continental Bentley that some rich idiot had married to a telegraph pole on the Great West Road. Bond had bought the bits for £1,500 and Rolls had straightened the bend in the chassis and fitted new clockwork — the Mark IV engine with 9.5 compression. Then Bond had gone to Mulliners with £3,000, which was half his total capital, and they had sawn off the old cramped sports saloon body and had fitted a trim, rather square convertible two-seater affair, power-operated, with only two large-armed bucket seats in black leather. The rest of the blunt end was all knife-edged, rather ugly, boot. The car was painted in rough, not gloss, battleship grey and the upholstery was black morocco. She went like a bird and a bomb and Bond loved her more than all the women at present in his life rolled, if that were feasible, together.

But Bond refused to be owned by any car. A car, however splendid, was a means of locomotion (he called the Continental 'The Locomotive' . . . 'I'll pick you up in my locomotive') and it must at all times be ready to locomote — no garage doors to break one's nails on, no pampering with mechanics except for the quick monthly service. The locomotive slept out of doors in front of his flat and was required to start immediately, in all weathers, and, after that, stay on the road.

The twin exhausts — Bond had demanded two-inch pipes; he hadn't liked the old soft flutter of the marque — growled solidly as the long grey nose topped by a big octagonal silver bolt instead of the winged B, swerved out of the little Chelsea square and into King's Road. It was nine o'clock, too early for the bad traffic, and Bond pushed the car fast up Sloane Street and into the park. It would also be too early for the traffic police, so he did some fancy driving that brought him to the Marble Arch exit in three minutes flat. Then there came the slow round-the-houses into Baker Street and so into Regents Park. Within ten minutes of getting the Hurry call he was going up in the lift of the big square building to the eighth and top floor.

Already, as he strode down the carpeted corridor, he smelled emergency. On this floor, besides M's offices, was housed Communications, and from behind the grey closed doors there came a steady zing and crackle from the banks of transmitters and a continuous machine-gun rattle and clack from the cipher machines. It crossed Bond's mind that a General Call was going out. What the hell had happened?

The Chief of Staff was standing over Miss Moneypenny. He was handing her signals from a large sheaf and giving her routing instructions. 'CIA Washington, Personal for Dulles. Cipher Triple X by Teleprinter. Mathis. Deuxième Bureau. Same prefix and route. Station F for Head of NATO Intelligence. Personal. Standard route through Head of Section. This one by Safe Hand to Head of M.I.5, Personal, copy to Commissioner of Police, Personal, and these,' he handed over a thick batch, 'Personal to Heads of Stations from M. Cipher Double X by Whitehall Radio and Portishead. All right? Clear them as quick as you can, there's a good girl. There'll be more coming. We're in for a bad day.'

Miss Moneypenny smiled cheerfully. She liked what she called the shot-and-shell days. It reminded her of when she had started in the Service as a junior in the Cipher Department. She leant over and pressed the switch on the intercom. '007's here, sir.' She looked up at Bond. 'You're off.' The Chief of Staff grinned and said, 'Fasten your lap-strap.' The red light went on above M's door. Bond walked through.

Here it was entirely peaceful. M sat relaxed, sideways to his desk, looking out of the broad window at the distant glittering fretwork of London's skyline. He glanced up. 'Sit down, 007. Have a look at these.' He reached out and slid some foolscap-sized photostats across the desk. 'Take your time.' He picked up his pipe and began to fill it, absent-minded fingers dipping into the shell-base tobacco jar at his elbow.

Bond picked up the top photostat. It showed the front and back of an addressed envelope, dusted for fingerprints, which were all over its surface.

M glanced sideways. 'Smoke if you like.'

Bond said, 'Thanks, sir. I'm trying to give it up.'

M said, 'Humpf,' put his pipe in his mouth, struck a match, and inhaled a deep lungful of smoke. He settled himself deeper in his chair. The grey sailor's eyes gazed through the window introspectively, seeing nothing.

The envelope, prefixed 'PERSONAL AND MOST IMMEDIATE', was addressed to the Prime Minister, by name, at No. 10, Downing Street, Whitehall, London, SW1. Every detail of the address was correct down to the final 'P.C.' to denote that the Prime Minister was a Privy Councillor. The punctuation was meticulous. The stamp was postmarked Brighton, 8.30 a.m. on June 3rd. It crossed Bond's mind that the letter might therefore have been posted under cover of night and that it would probably have been delivered some time in the early afternoon of the same day, yesterday. A typewriter with a bold, rather elegant type had been used. This fact together with the generous 5-by-7½-inch envelope and the spacing and style of the address gave a solid, businesslike impression. The back of the envelope showed nothing but fingerprints. There was no sealing wax.

The letter, equally correct and well laid-out, ran as follows:

> Mr Prime Minister,
>
> You should be aware, or you will be if you communicate with the Chief of the Air Staff, that, since approximately 10 p.m. yesterday, 2nd June, a British aircraft carrying two atomic weapons is overdue on a training flight. The aircraft is Villiers Vindicator O/NBR from No. 5 R.A.F. Experimental Squadron based at Boscombe Down. The Ministry of Supply Identification Numbers on the atomic weapons are MOS/bd/654/Mk V. and MOS/bd/655/Mk V. There are also U.S.A.F. Identification Numbers in such profusion and of such prolixity that I will not weary you with them.

This aircraft was on a NATO training flight with a crew of five and one observer. It carried sufficient fuel for ten hours' flying at 600 m.p.h. at a mean altitude of 40,000 feet.

This aircraft, together with the two atomic weapons, is now in the possession of this organization. The crew and the observer are deceased and you have our authority to inform the next-of-kin accordingly, thus assisting you in preserving, on the grounds that the aircraft has crashed, the degree of secrecy you will no doubt wish to maintain and which will be equally agreeable to ourselves.

The whereabouts of this aircraft and of the two atomic weapons, rendering them possible of recovery, will be communicated to you in exchange for the equivalent of £100,000,000 in gold bullion, one thousand, or not less than nine hundred and ninety-nine, fine. Instructions for the delivery of the gold are contained in the attached memorandum. A further condition is that the recovery and disposal of the gold will not be hampered and that a free pardon, under your personal signature and that of the President of the United States, will be issued in the name of this organization and all its members.

Failure to accept these conditions within seven days from 5 p.m. G.M.T. on June 3rd, 1959 — i.e. not later than 5 p.m. G.M.T. on June 10th, 1959 — will have the following consequences. Immediately after that date a piece of property belonging to the Western Powers, valued at not less than the aforesaid £100,000,000, will be destroyed. There will be loss of life. If, within 48 hours after this warning, willingness to accept our terms is still not communicated, there will ensue, without further warning, the destruction of a major city situated in an undesignated country of the world. There will be very great loss of life. Moreover, between the two occurrences, this organization will reserve to itself the right to communicate to the world the 48-hour time limit. This measure, which will cause widespread panic in every major city, will be designed to hasten your hand.

This, Mr Prime Minister, is a single and final communication. We shall await your reply, every hour on the hour G.M.T., on the 16-megacycle waveband.

Signed
S.P.E.C.T.R.E.
The Special Executive for Counterintelligence,
Terrorism, Revenge, and Extortion

James Bond read through the letter again and put it carefully down on the desk in front of him. He then turned to the second page, a detailed memorandum for the delivery of the gold. 'North-western slopes of Mount Etna in Sicily . . . Decca Navigational Aid transmitting on . . . Full moon period . . . between midnight and 0100 G.M.T. . . . individual quarter-ton consignments packed in one-foot-thick foam rubber . . . minimum of three parachutes per consignment . . . nature of planes and flight schedule to be communicated on the 16-megacycle waveband not later than 24 hours before the operation . . . Any counter measures initiated will be considered a breach of contract and will result in the detonation of Atomic Weapon No. 1 or No. 2 as the case may be.' The typed signature was the same. Both pages had one last line: 'Copy to the President of the United States of America, by Registered Airmail, posted simultaneously.'

Bond laid the photostat quietly down on top of the others. He reached into his hip-pocket for the gunmetal cigarette case that now contained only nine cigarettes, took one and lit it, drawing the smoke deep down into his lungs and letting it out with a long, reflective hiss.

M swivelled his chair round so they were facing each other. 'Well?'

Bond noticed that M's eyes, three weeks before so clear and vital, were now bloodshot and strained. No wonder! He said: 'If this plane, and the weapons, really are missing, I think it stands up, sir. I think they mean it. I think it's a true bill.'

M said, 'So does the War Cabinet. So do I.' He paused. 'Yes, the plane with the bombs is missing. And the stock numbers on the bombs are correct.'

8

'BIG FLEAS HAVE LITTLE FLEAS . . .'

BOND SAID, 'What is there to go on, sir?'

'Damned little, practically speaking nothing. Nobody's ever heard of these SPECTRE people. We know there's some kind of independent unit working in Europe — we've bought some stuff from them, so have the Americans, and Mathis admits now that Goltz, that French heavy-water scientist who went over last year, was assassinated by them, for big money, as a result of an offer he got out of the blue. No names were mentioned. It was all done on the radio, the same 16 megacycles that's mentioned in the letter. To the Deuxième Communications section. Mathis accepted on the off-chance. They did a neat job. Mathis paid up — a suitcase full of money left at a Michelin road sign on N1. But no one can tie them in with these SPECTRE people. When we and the Americans dealt, there were endless cutouts, really professional ones, and anyway we were more interested in the end product than the people involved. We both paid a lot of money, but it was worth it. If it's the same group working this, they're a serious outfit and I've told the P.M. so. But that's not the point. The plane is missing and the two bombs, just as the letter says. All details exactly correct. The Vindicator was on a NATO training flight south of Ireland and out into the Atlantic.' M reached for a bulky folder and turned over some pages. He found what he wanted. 'Yes, it was to be a six-hour flight leaving Boscombe Down at eight p.m. and due back at two a.m. There was an R.A.F. crew of five and a NATO observer, an Italian, man called Petacchi, Giuseppe Petacchi, squadron leader in the Italian Air Force, seconded to NATO. Fine flyer, apparently, but they're checking on his background now. He was sent over here on a normal tour of duty. The top pilots from NATO have been coming over for months to get used to the Vindicator and the bomb-release routines. This plane's apparently going to be used for the NATO long-range striking force. Anyway,' M turned over a page, 'the plane was watched on the screen as usual and all went well until it was west of Ireland at about 40,000 feet. Then, contrary to the drill, it came down to around 30,000 and got lost in the transatlantic air traffic. Bomber Command tried to get in touch, but the radio couldn't or wouldn't answer. The immediate reaction was that the Vindicator had hit one of the transatlantic planes and there was something of a panic. But none of the companies reported any trouble or even a sighting.' M looked across at Bond. 'And that was the end of it. The plane just vanished.'

Bond said, 'Did the American DEW line pick it up — their Distant Early Warning system?'

'There's a query on that. The only grain of evidence we've got. Apparently about five hundred miles east of Boston there was some evidence that a plane had peeled off the inward route to Idlewild and turned south. But that's another big traffic lane — for the northern traffic from Montreal and Gander down to Bermuda and the Bahamas and South America. So these DEW operators just put it down as a B.O.A.C. or Trans-Canada plane.'

'It certainly sounds as if they've got the whole thing worked out pretty well, hiding in these traffic lanes. Could the plane have turned northwards in the middle of the Atlantic and made for Russia?'

'Yes, or southwards. There's a big block of space about 500 miles out from both shores that's out of radar range. Better still, it could have turned on its tracks and come back in to Europe on any of two or three air-lanes. In fact it could be almost anywhere in the world by now. That's the point.'

'But it's a huge plane. It must need special runways and so on. It must have come down somewhere. You can't hide a plane of that size.'

'Just so. All these things are obvious. By midnight last night the R.A.F. had checked with every single airport, every one in the world, that could have taken it. Negative. But the C.A.S. says of course it could be crash-landed in the Sahara for instance, or on some other desert, or in the sea, in shallow water.'

'Wouldn't that explode the bombs?'

'No. They're absolutely safe until they're armed. Apparently even a direct drop, like that one from the B-47 over North

Carolina in 1958, would only explode the T.N.T. trigger to the thing. Not the plutonium.'

'How are these SPECTRE people going to explode them then?'

M spread his hands. 'They explained all this at the War Cabinet meeting. I don't understand it all, but apparently an atomic bomb looks just like any other bomb. The way it works is that the nose is full of ordinary T.N.T. with the plutonium in the tail. Between the two there's a hole into which you screw some sort of a detonator, a kind of plug. When the bomb hits, the T.N.T. ignites the detonator and the detonator sets off the plutonium.'

'So these people would have to drop the bomb to set it off?'

'Apparently not. They would need a man with good physics knowledge who understood the thing, but then all he'd have to do would be to unscrew the nose cone on the bomb — the ordinary detonator that sets off the T.N.T. — and fix on some kind of time fuse that would ignite the T.N.T. without it being dropped. That would set the thing off. And it's not a very bulky affair. You could get the whole thing into something only about twice the size of a big golf bag. Very heavy, of course. But you could put it into the back of a big car, for instance, and just run the car into a town and leave it parked with the time fuse switched on. Give yourself a couple of hours' start to get out of range — at least 100 miles away — and that would be that.'

Bond reached in his pocket for another cigarette. It couldn't be, yet it was so. Just what his Service and all the other intelligence services in the world had been expecting to happen. The anonymous little man in the raincoat with a heavy suitcase — or golf bag, if you like. The left luggage office, the parked car, the clump of bushes in a park in the centre of a big town. And there was no answer to it. In a few years' time, if the experts were right, there would be even less answer to it. Every tin-pot little nation would be making atomic bombs in their backyards, so to speak. Apparently there was no secret now about the things. It had only been the prototypes that had been difficult — like the first gunpowder weapons for instance, or machine-guns or tanks. Today these were everybody's bows and arrows. Tomorrow, or the day after, the bows and arrows would be atomic bombs. And this was the first blackmail case. Unless SPECTRE was stopped, the word would get round and soon every criminal scientist with a chemical set and some scrap iron would be doing it. If they couldn't be stopped in time there would be nothing for it but to pay up. Bond said so.

'That's about it,' commented M. 'From every point of view, including politics, not that they matter all that much. But neither the P.M. nor the President would last five minutes if anything went wrong. But whether we pay or don't pay, the consequences will be endless — and all bad. That's why absolutely everything has got to be done to find these people and the plane and stop the thing in time. The P.M. and the President are entirely agreed. Every intelligence man all over the world who's on our side is being put on to this operation — Operation Thunderball they're calling it. Planes, ships, submarines — and of course money's no object. We can have everything, whenever we want it. The Cabinet have already set up a special staff and a war-room. Every scrap of information will be fed into it. The Americans have done the same. Some kind of a leak can't be helped. It's being put about that all the panic, and it is panic, is because of the loss of the Vindicator — bombs included, whatever fuss that may cause politically. Only the letter will be absolutely secret. All the usual detective work — fingerprints, Brighton, writing paper — these'll be looked after by Scotland Yard with the F.B.I., Interpol, and all the NATO intelligence organizations helping where they can. Only a segment of the paper and the typing will be used — a few innocent words. This will all be quite separate from the search for the plane. That'll be handled as a top espionage matter. No one should be able to connect the two investigations. M.I.5 will handle the background to all the crew members and the Italian observer. That will be a natural part of the search for the plane. As for the Service, we've teamed up with the C.I.A. to cover the world. Allen Dulles is putting every man he's got on to it and so am I. Just sent out a General Call. Now all we can do is sit back and wait.'

Bond lit another cigarette, his sinful third in one hour. He said, putting unconcern into his voice, 'Where do I come in, sir?'

M looked vaguely at Bond, as if seeing him for the first time. Then he swivelled his chair and gazed again through the window at nothing. Finally he said, in a conversational tone of voice, 'I have committed a breach of faith with the P.M. in telling you all this, 007. I was under oath to tell no one what I have just told you. I decided to do what I have done because I have an idea, a hunch, and I wish this idea to be pursued by a' — he hesitated — 'by a reliable man. It seemed to me that the only grain of possible evidence in this case was the DEW radar plot, a doubtful one I admit, of the plane that left the East–West air channel over the Atlantic and turned south towards Bermuda and the Bahamas. I decided to accept this evidence, although it has not aroused much interest elsewhere. I then spent some time studying a map and charts of the Western Atlantic and I endeavoured to put myself in the minds of SPECTRE — or rather, for there is certainly a mastermind behind all this, in the mind of the chief of SPECTRE: my opposite number, so to speak. And I came to certain conclusions. I decided that a favourable target for Bomb No. 1, and for Bomb No. 2, if it comes to that, would be in America rather than in Europe. To begin with, the Americans are more bomb-conscious than we in Europe and therefore more susceptible to persuasion if it came to using Bomb No. 2. Installations worth more than £100,000,000, and thus targets for Bomb No. 1, are more numerous in America than in Europe, and finally, guessing that SPECTRE is a European organization, from the style of the letter and from the paper, which is Dutch by the way, and also from the ruthlessness of the plot, it seemed to me at least possible that an American rather than a European target might have been chosen. Anyway, going on these assumptions, and assuming that the plane could not have landed in America itself or off American shores — the coastal radar network is too good — I looked for a neighbouring area which might be suitable. And,' M glanced round at Bond and away again, 'I decided on the Bahamas, the group of islands, many of them uninhabited, surrounded mostly by shoal water over sand and possessing only one simple radar station — and that one concerned only with civilian air traffic and manned by local civilian personnel. South, towards Cuba, Jamaica, and the Caribbean, offers no worthwhile targets. Anyway it is too far from the American coastline. Northwards towards Bermuda has the same disadvantages. But the nearest of the Bahama group is only 200 miles — only six or seven hours in a fast motorboat or yacht — from the American coastline.'

Bond interrupted. 'If you're right, sir, why didn't SPECTRE send their letter to the President instead of the P.M.?'

'For the sake of obscurity. To make us do what we are doing — hunting all round the world instead of only in one part of it. And for maximum impact. SPECTRE would realize that the arrival of the letter right on top of the loss of the bomber would hit us in the solar plexus. It might, they would reason, even shake the money out of us without any further effort. The next stage of their operation, attacking target No. 1, is going to be a nasty business for them. It's going to expose their whereabouts to a considerable extent. They'd like to collect the money and close the operation as quickly as possible. That's what we've got to gamble on. We've got to push them as close to the use of No. 1 bomb as we dare in the hope that something will betray them in the next six and three-quarter days. It's a slim chance. I'm pinning my hopes on my guess' — M swung his chair round to the desk — 'and on you. Well,' he looked hard at Bond, 'any comments? If not you'd better get started. You're booked on all New York planes from now until midnight. Then on by B.O.A.C. I thought of using an R.A.F. Canberra, but I don't want your arrival to make any noise. You're a rich young man looking for some property in the islands. That'll give you an excuse to do as much prospecting as you want. Well?'

'All right, sir.' Bond got to his feet. 'I'd rather have had somewhere more interesting — the Iron Curtain beat for instance. I can't help feeling this is a bigger operation than a small unit could take on. For my money this looks more like a Russian job. They get the experimental plane and the bombs — they obviously want them — and throw dust in our eyes with all this SPECTRE ballyhoo. If SMERSH was still in business, I'd say they'd got a finger in it somewhere. Just their style. But the Eastern Stations may pick up something on that if there's anything in the idea. Anything else, sir? Who do I co-operate with in Nassau?'

'The Governor knows you're coming. They've got a well-trained police force. C.I.A. are sending down a good man, I gather. With a communications outfit. They've got more of that sort of machinery than we have. Take a cipher machine with the Triple X setting. I want to hear every single detail you turn up. Personal to me. Right?'

'Right, sir.' Bond went to the door and let himself out. There was nothing more to be said. This looked like the biggest job the Service had ever been given and, in Bond's opinion, for he didn't give much for M's guess, he had been relegated to the back row of the chorus. So be it. He would get himself a good sunburn and watch the show from the wings.

When Bond walked out of the building, carrying the neat leather cipher case, an expensive movie camera perhaps, slung over his shoulder, the man in the beige Volkswagen stopped scratching the burn-scab under his shirt, loosened, for the tenth time, the long-barrelled forty-five in the holster under his arm, started the car and put it in gear. He was twenty yards behind Bond's parked Bentley. He had no idea what the big building was. He had simply obtained Bond's home address from the receptionist at Shrublands and, as soon as he got out of the Brighton hospital, he had carefully tailed Bond. The car was hired, under an assumed name. When he had done what had to be done he would go straight to London Airport and take the first plane out to any country on the Continent. Count Lippe was a sanguine individual. The job, the private score he had to settle, presented no problem to him. He was a ruthless, vengeful man and he had eliminated many obstreperous and perhaps dangerous people in his life. He reasoned that, if they ever came to hear of this, SPECTRE would not object. The overheard telephone conversation on that first day at the clinic showed that his cover had been broached, however slightly, and it was just conceivable that he could be traced through his membership of the Red Lightning Tong. From there to SPECTRE was a long step, but Sub-operator G knew that once a cover began to run, it ran like an old sock. Apart from that, this man must be paid off. Count Lippe had to be quits with him.

Bond was getting into his car. He had slammed the door. Sub-operator G watched the blue smoke curl from the twin exhausts. He got moving.

On the other side of the road, and a hundred yards behind the Volkswagen, SPECTRE No. 6 slipped his goggles down over his eyes, stamped the 500-c.c. Triumph into gear and accelerated down the road. He swerved neatly through the traffic — he had been a test rider for D.K.W. at one time in his post-war career

— and stationed himself ten yards behind the off rear wheel of the Volkswagen and just out of the driver's line of vision in the windscreen mirror. He had no idea why Sub-operator G was following the Bentley, nor who the Bentley belonged to. His job was to kill the driver of the Volkswagen. He put his hand into the leather satchel he carried slung over his shoulder, took out the heavy grenade — it was twice the normal military size — and watched the traffic ahead for the right pattern to allow his getaway.

Sub-operator G was watching for a similar pattern. He also noted the spacing on the lamp-posts on the pavement in case he might be blocked and have to run off the road. Now the cars ahead were sparse. He stamped his foot into the floor and, driving with his left hand, drew out the Colt with his right. Now he was up with the Bentley's rear bumper. Now he was alongside. The dark profile was a sitting target. With a last quick glance ahead, he raised the gun.

It was the cheeky iron rattle of the Volkswagen's air-cooled engine that made Bond turn his head, and it was this minute reduction of the target area that saved his jaw. If he had then accelerated, the second bullet would have got him, but some blessed instinct made his foot stamp the brake at the same time as his head ducked so swiftly that his chin hit the horn button, nearly knocking him out. Almost simultaneously, instead of a third shot, there came the roar of an explosion and the remains of his windshield, already shattered, cascaded around him. The Bentley had stopped, the engine stalled. Brakes screamed. There were shouts and the panicky screams of horns. Bond shook his head and cautiously raised it. The Volkswagen, one wheel still spinning, lay on its side in front and broadside to the Bentley. Most of the roof had been blown off. Inside, and half sprawling into the road, was a horrible, glinting mess. Flames were licking at the blistered paintwork. People were gathering. Bond pulled himself together and got quickly out of his car. He shouted, 'Stand back. The petrol tank'll go.' Almost as he said the words there came a dull boom and a cloud of black smoke. The flames spurted. In the distance, sirens sounded. Bond edged through the people and strode quickly back towards his headquarters, his thoughts racing.

The inquiry made Bond lose two planes to New York. By the

time the police had put out the fire and had transported the bits of man and the bits of machinery and bomb casing to the morgue it was quite clear that they would have nothing to go on but the shoes, the number on the gun, some fibres and shreds of clothing, and the car. The car-hire people remembered nothing but a man with dark glasses, a driver's licence in the name of Johnston, and a handful of fivers. The car had been hired three days before for one week. Plenty of people remembered the motorcyclist, but it seemed that he had no rear number plate. He had gone like a bat out of hell towards Baker Street. He wore goggles. Medium build. Nothing else.

Bond had not been able to help. He had seen nothing of the Volkswagen driver. The roof of the Volkswagen had been too low. There had only been a hand and the glitter of a gun.

The Secret Service asked for a copy of the police report and M instructed that this should be sent to the Thunderball war-room. He saw Bond briefly again, rather impatiently, as if it had all been Bond's fault. Then he told Bond to forget about it — it was probably something to do with one of his past cases. A hangover of some kind. The police would get to the bottom of it in time. The main thing was Operation Thunderball. Bond had better get a move on.

By the time Bond left the building for the second time, it had begun to rain. One of the mechanics from the car pool at the back of the building had done what he could, knocking out the remains of the Bentley's windscreen and cleaning the bits out of the car, but when he got home at lunch time Bond was soaked to the skin. He left the car in a near-by garage, telephoned Rolls and his insurance company (he had got too close to a lorry carrying steel lengths, for reinforced concrete presumably. No, he had not got the lorry's number. Sorry, but you know how it is when these things happen all of a sudden), and then went home and had a bath and changed into his dark blue tropical worsted. He packed carefully — one large suitcase and a holdall for his underwater swimming gear — and went through to the kitchen.

May was looking rather contrite. It seemed as if she might make another speech. Bond held up his hand. 'Don't tell me, May. You were right. I can't do my work on carrot juice. I've got to be off in an hour and I need some proper food. Be an angel and make me your kind of scrambled eggs — four eggs.

Four rashers of that American hickory-smoked bacon if we've got any left, hot buttered toast — your kind, not wholemeal — and a big pot of coffee, double strength. And bring in the drink tray.'

May looked at him, relieved but aghast. 'Whatever happened, Mister James?'

Bond laughed at the expression on her face. 'Nothing, May. It just occurred to me that life's too short. Plenty of time to watch the calories when one gets to heaven.'

Bond left May tut-tutting at this profanity, and went off to look to his armament.

9

MULTIPLE REQUIEM

SO FAR AS SPECTRE was concerned, Plan Omega had gone exactly as Blofeld had known it would and Phases I to III in their entirety had been completed on schedule and without a hitch.

Giuseppe Petacchi, the late Giuseppe Petacchi, had been well chosen. At the age of eighteen he had been co-pilot of a Focke-Wulf 200 from the Adriatic anti-submarine patrol, one of the few hand-picked Italian airmen who had been allowed to handle these German planes. The group was issued with the latest German pressure mines charged with the new Hexogen explosive just when the tide had turned in the Allied battle up the spine of Italy. Petacchi had known where his destiny lay and had gone into business for himself. On a routine patrol, he had shot the pilot and the navigator, very carefully, with one 38 bullet in the back of the head for each of them, and had brought the big plane skimming in, just above the waves to avoid the anti-aircraft fire, to the harbour of Bari. Then he had hung his shirt out of the cockpit as a token of surrender and had waited for the R.A.F. launch. He had been decorated by the English and the Americans for this exploit and had been awarded £10,000 from special funds for his presentation to the Allies of the pressure mine. He had told a highly coloured story to the intelligence people of having been a one-man resistance ever since he had been old enough to join the Italian Air Force, and he emerged at the end of the war as one of Italy's most gallant resistance heroes. From then on life had been easy — pilot and later captain in Alitalia when it got going again, and then back into the new Italian Air Force as colonel. His secondment to NATO followed and then his appointment as one of the six Italians chosen for the Advance Striking Force. But he was now thirty-four, and it occurred to him that he had had just about enough of flying. He especially did not care for the idea of being part of the spearhead of NATO defences. It was time for younger men to provide the heroics. And all his life he had had a passion for owning things — flashy, exciting, expensive things. He had most of what he desired — a couple of gold cigarette cases, a solid gold Rolex Oyster Perpetual Chronometer on a flexible gold bracelet, a white convertible Lancia Gran Turismo, plenty of sharp clothes, and all the girls he wanted (he had once been briefly married but it had not been a success). Now he desired, and what he desired he often got, a particular Ghia-bodied 3,500 G.T. Maserati he had seen at the Milan motor show. He also wanted Out — out of the pale green corridors of NATO, out of the Air Force and, therefore, off to new worlds with a new name. Rio de Janeiro sounded just right. But all this meant a new passport, plenty of money, and 'organismo' — the vital 'organismo'.

The organismo turned up, and turned up bearing just those gifts that Petacchi lusted for. It came in the shape of an Italian named Fonda who was at that time No. 4 in SPECTRE and who had been casing the personnel of NATO, via Versailles and Paris night-clubs and restaurants, for just such a man. It had taken one whole very careful month to prepare the bait and inch it forward towards the fish and, when it was finally presented, No. 4 had been almost put off by the greed with which it had been gobbled. There was delay while the possibility of a double-cross was probed by SPECTRE, but finally all the lights were green and the full proposition was laid out for inspection. Petacchi was to get on the Vindicator training course and hijack the plane. (There was no mention of atomic weapons. This was a Cuban revolutionary group who wanted to call attention to its existence and aims by a dramatic piece of self-advertisement. Petacchi closed his ears to this specious tale. He didn't mind in the least who wanted the plane so long as he was paid.) In exchange, Petacchi would receive one million dollars, a new passport in any name and nationality he chose, and immediate onward passage from the point of delivery to Rio de Janeiro. Many details were discussed and perfected, and when, at eight o'clock in the evening of that June 2nd, the Vindicator screamed off down the runway and out over St Alban's Head, Petacchi was tense but confident.

For the training flights, a couple of ordinary civil aircraft seats had been fixed inside the roomy fuselage just back of the large cockpit, and Petacchi sat quietly for a whole hour and watched the five men at work at the crowded dials and instruments. When it came to his turn to fly the plane he was quite satisfied that he could dispense with all five of them. Once he had set George, there would be nothing to do but stay awake and make certain from time to time that he was keeping exactly at 32,000 feet, just above the transatlantic air-channel. There would be a tricky moment when he turned off the East–West channel on to the North–South for the Bahamas, but this had all been worked out for him and every move he would have to make was written down in the notebook in his breast pocket. The landing was going to need very steady nerves, but for one million dollars the steady nerves would be summoned.

For the tenth time Petacchi consulted the Rolex. Now! He verified and tested the oxygen mask in the bulkhead beside him and laid it down ready. Next he took the little red-ringed cylinder out of his pocket and remembered exactly how many turns to give the release valve. Then he put it back in his pocket and went through into the cockpit.

'Hullo, Seppy. Enjoying the flight?' The pilot liked the Italian. They had gone out together on one or two majestic thrashes in Bournemouth.

'Sure, sure.' Petacchi asked some questions, verified the course set on George, checked the air speed and altitude. Now everyone in the cockpit was relaxed, almost drowsy. Five more hours to go. Rather a bind missing *North by North-West* at the Odeon. But one would catch up with it at Southampton. Petacchi stood with his back to the metal map rack that held the log and the charts. His right hand went to his pocket, felt for the release valve, and gave it three complete turns. He eased the cylinder out of his pocket and slipped it behind him and down behind the books.

Petacchi stretched and yawned. 'Is time for a zizz,' he said amiably. He had got the slang phrase pat. It rolled easily off the tongue.

The navigator laughed. 'What do they call it in Italian — "Zizzo"?'

Petacchi grinned cheerfully. He went through the open hatch, got back to his chair, clamped on his oxygen mask, and turned the control regulator to 100 per cent oxygen to cut out the air bleed. Then he made himself comfortable and watched.

They had said it would take under five minutes. Sure enough, in about two minutes, the man nearest to the map rack, the navigator, suddenly clutched his throat and fell forward, gargling horribly. The radio operator dropped his earphones and started forward, but with his second step he was down on his knees. He lurched sideways and collapsed. Now the three other men began to fight for air, briefly, terribly. The co-pilot and the flight engineer writhed off their stools together. They clawed vaguely at each other and then fell back, spreadeagled. The pilot groped up towards the microphone above his head, said something indistinctly, got half to his feet, turned slowly so that his bulging eyes, already dead, seemed to stare through the hatchway into Petacchi's, and then thudded down on top of the body of his co-pilot.

Petacchi glanced at his watch. Four minutes flat. Give them one more minute. When the minute was up, he took rubber gloves out of his pocket, put them on and, pressing the oxygen mask tight against his face and trailing the flexible tube behind him, he went forward, reached down into the map rack, and closed the valve on the cylinder of cyanide. He verified George and adjusted the cabin pressurization to help clear the poison gas. He then went back to his seat to wait for fifteen minutes.

They had said fifteen would be enough, but at the last moment he gave it another ten and then, still with his oxygen mask on, he went forward again and began slowly, for the oxygen made him rather breathless, to pull the bodies back into the fuselage. When the cockpit was clear, he took a small phial of crystals out of his trousers pocket, took out the cork, and sprinkled the cabin floor with them. He went down on his knees and watched the crystals. They kept their white colour. He eased his oxygen mask away and took a small cautious sniff. There was no smell. But still, when he took over the controls and began easing the plane down to 32,000 and then slightly north-west-by-west to get into the traffic lane, he kept the mask on.

The giant plane whispered on into the night. The cockpit, bright with the yellow eyes of the dials, was quiet and warm. In the deafening silence in the cockpit of a big jet in flight there was only the faint buzz of an invector. As he verified the dials, the click of each switch seemed as loud as a small-calibre pistol-shot.

Petacchi again checked George with the gyro and verified each fuel tank to see that they were all feeding evenly. One tank pump needed adjustment. The jet pipe temperatures were not overheating.

Satisfied, Petacchi settled himself comfortably in the pilot's seat and swallowed a benzedrine tablet and thought about the future. One of the headphones scattered on the floor of the cockpit began to chirrup loudly. Petacchi glanced at his watch. Of course! Boscombe Air Traffic Control was trying to raise the Vindicator. He had missed the third of the half-hourly calls. How long would Air Control wait before alerting Air Sea Rescue, Bomber Command, and the Air Ministry? There would first be checks and double-checks with the Southern Rescue Centre. They would probably take another half-hour and by that time he would be well out over the Atlantic.

The chirrup of the headphones went quiet. Petacchi got up from his seat and took a look at the radar screen. He watched it for some time, noting the occasional 'blip' of planes being overhauled below him. Would his own swift passage above the air corridor be noted by the planes as he passed above them? Unlikely. The radar on commercial planes has a limited field of vision in a forward cone. He would almost certainly not be spotted until he crossed the Defence Early Warning line, and DEW would probably put him down as a commercial jet that had strayed above its normal channel.

Petacchi went back to the pilot's seat and again minutely checked the dials. He weaved the plane gently to get the feel of the controls. Behind him, the bodies on the floor of the fuselage stirred uneasily. The plane answered perfectly. It was like driving a beautiful quiet motor-car. Petacchi dreamed briefly of the Maserati. What colour? Better not his usual white, or anything spectacular. Dark blue with a thin red line along the coachwork. Something quiet and respectable that would fit in with his new, quiet identity. It would be fun to run her in some of the trials and road races — even the Mexican '2,000'. But that would be too dangerous. Supposing he won and his picture got into the papers! No. He would have to cut out anything like that. He would only drive the car really fast when he wanted to get a girl. They melted in a fast car. Why was that? The sense of surrender to the machine, to the man whose strong, sunburned hands were on the wheel? But it was always so. You turned the car into a wood after ten minutes at 150 and you would almost have to lift the girl out and lay her down on the moss, her limbs would be so trembling and soft.

Petacchi pulled himself out of the daydream. He glanced at his watch. The Vindicator was already four hours out. At 600 m.p.h. one certainly covered the miles. The coastline of America should be on the screen by now. He got up and had a look. Yes, there, 500 miles away, was the coastline map already in high definition, the bulge that was Boston, and the silvery creek of the Hudson River. No need to check his position with weather ships Delta or Echo that would be somewhere below him. He was dead on course and it would soon be time to turn off the East–West channel.

Petacchi went back to his seat, munched another benzedrine tablet, and consulted his chart. He got his hands to the controls and watched the eerie glow of the gyro compass. Now! He eased the controls gently round in a fairly tight curve, then he flattened out again, edged the plane exactly on to its new course, and re-set George. Now he was flying due south, now he was on the last lap, a bare three hours to go. It was time to start worrying about the landing.

Petacchi took out his little notebook. 'Watch for the lights of Grand Bahama to port, and Palm Beach to starboard. Be ready to pick up the navigational aids from No. 1's yacht — dot-dot-dash; dot-dot-dash, jettison fuel, lose height to around 1,000 feet for the last quarter of an hour, kill speed with the air brakes, and lose more height. Watch out for the flashing red beacon and prepare for the final approach. Flaps down only at the check altitude with about 140 knots indicated. Depth of water will be forty feet. You will have plenty of time to get out of the escape hatch. You will be taken on board No. 1's yacht. There is a Bahamas Airways flight to Miami at 8.30 on the next morning and then Braniff or Real Airlines for the rest of the way. No. 1 will give you the money in 1,000-dollar bills or in traveller's cheques. He will have both available, also the passport in the name of Enrico Valli, Company Director.'

Petacchi checked his position, course, and speed. Only one

more hour to go. It was three a.m. G.M.T., nine p.m. Nassau time. A full moon was coming up and the carpet of clouds 10,000 feet below was a snowfield. Petacchi dowsed the collision lights on his wing tips and fuselage. He checked the fuel: 2,000 gallons including the reserve tanks. He would need 500 for the last four hundred miles. He pulled the release valve on the reserve tanks and lost 1,000 gallons. With the loss of weight the plane began to climb slowly and he corrected back to 32,000. Now there was twenty minutes to go — time to begin the long descent . . .

Down through the cloud base, the moments of blindness and then, far below, the sparse lights of North and South Bimini winked palely against the silver sheen of the moon on the quiet sea. There were no whitecaps. The met. report he had picked up from Vero Beach on the American mainland had been right: 'Dead calm, light airs from the north-east, visibility good, no immediate likelihood of change' and a check on the fainter Nassau Radio had confirmed. The sea looked as smooth and as solid as steel. This was going to be all right. Petacchi dialled Channel 67 on the pilot's command set to pick up No. I's navigational aid. He had a moment's panic when he didn't hit it at once, but then he got it, faint but clear — dot-dot-dash, dot-dot-dash. It was time to get right down. Petacchi began to kill his speed with the air brakes and cut down the four jets. The great plane began a shallow dive. The radio altimeter became vocal, threatening. Petacchi watched it and the sea of quicksilver below him. He had a moment when the horizon was lost. There was so much reflection off the moonlit water. Then he was on and over a small dark island. It gave him confidence in the 2,000 feet indicated on the altimeter. He pulled out of the shallow dive and held the plane steady.

Now No. 1's beacon was coming in loud and clear. Soon he would see the red flashing light. And there it was, perhaps five miles dead ahead. Petacchi inched the great nose of the plane down. Any moment now! It was going to be easy! His fingers played with the controls as delicately as if they were the erotic trigger points on a woman. Five hundred feet, four hundred, three, two . . . there was the pale shape of the yacht, lights dowsed. He was dead on line with the red flash of the beacon.

Would he hit it? Never mind. Inch her down, down, down. Be ready to switch off at once. The belly of the plane gave a jolt. Up with the nose! Crash! A leap in the air and then . . . Crash again!

Petacchi unhinged his cramped fingers from the controls, and gazed numbly out of the window at the foam and small waves. By God he had done it! He, Giuseppe Petacchi, had done it!

Now for the applause! Now for the rewards!

The plane was settling slowly and there was a hiss of steam from the submerging jets. From behind him came the rip and crack of tearing metal as the tail section gaped open where the back of the plane had broken. Petacchi went through into the fuselage. The water swirled around his feet. The filtering moonlight glittered white on the upturned face of one of the corpses now soggily awash at the rear of the plane. Petacchi broke the perspex cover to the handle of the port-side emergency exit and jerked the handle down. The door fell outwards and Petacchi stepped through and walked out along the wing.

The big jolly-boat was almost up with the plane. There were six men in it. Petacchi waved and shouted delightedly. One man raised a hand in reply. The faces of the men, milk-white under the moon, looked up at him quietly, curiously. Petacchi thought: these men are very serious, very businesslike. It is right so. He swallowed his triumph and also looked grave.

The boat came alongside the wing, now almost awash, and one man climbed up on to the wing and walked towards him. He was a short, thick man with a very direct gaze. He walked carefully, his feet well apart and his knees flexed to keep his balance. His left hand was hooked in his belt.

Petacchi said happily, 'Good evening. Good evening. I am delivering one plane in good condition.' (He had thought the joke out long before.) 'Please sign here.' He held out his hand.

The man from the jolly-boat took the hand in a strong grasp, braced himself, and pulled sharply. Petacchi's head was flung back by the quick jerk and he was looking full into the eyes of the moon as the stiletto flashed up and under the offered chin, through the roof of the mouth, into the brain. He knew nothing but a moment's surprise, a sear of pain, and an explosion of brilliant light.

The killer held in the knife for a moment, the back of his hand feeling the stubble on Petacchi's chin, then he lowered the body on to the wing and withdrew the knife. He carefully rinsed the knife in the sea water and wiped the blade on Petacchi's back and put the knife away. Then he hauled the body along the wing and thrust it underwater beside the escape hatch.

The killer waded back along the wing to the waiting jolly-boat and laconically raised a thumb. By now four of the men had pulled on their aqualungs. One by one, with a last adjustment of their mouthpieces, they clumsily heaved themselves over the side of the rocking boat and sank in a foam of small bubbles. When the last man had gone, the mechanic at the engine carefully lowered a huge underwater searchlight over the side and paid out the cable. At a given moment he switched the light on and the sea and the great sinking hulk of the plane were lit up with a mist of luminescence. The mechanic slipped the idling motor into gear and backed away, paying out cable as he went. At twenty yards, out of range of the suction of the sinking plane, he stopped and switched off his engine. He reached into his overalls and took out a packet of Camels. He offered one to the killer, who took it, broke it carefully in half, put one half behind his ear and lit the other half.

The killer was a man who rigidly controlled his weaknesses.

10

THE *DISCO VOLANTE*

ON BOARD THE yacht, No. 1 put down his night glasses, took a Charvet handkerchief out of the breast pocket of his white shark-skin jacket and dabbed gently at his forehead and temples. The musky scent of Schiaparelli's Snuff was reassuring, reminding him of the easy side of life, of Dominetta who would now be sitting down to dinner — everyone kept Spanish hours in Nassau and cocktails would not have finished before ten — with the raffish but rather gay Saumurs and their equally frivolous guests; of the early game that would already be under way at the Casino; of the calypsos thudding into the night from the bars and night-clubs on Bay Street. He put the handkerchief back in his pocket. But this also was good — this wonderful operation! Like clockwork! He glanced at his watch. Just ten fifteen. The plane had been a bare thirty minutes late, a nasty half-hour to have to wait, but the landing had been perfect. Vargas had done a good quick job on the Italian pilot — what was his name? — so that now they were running only fifteen minutes late. If the recovery group didn't have to use oxy-acetylene cutters to get out the bombs, they would soon make that up. But one mustn't expect no hitch at all. There was a good eight hours of darkness to go. Calm, method, efficiency, in that order. Calm, method, efficiency. No. 1 ducked down off the bridge and went into the radio cabin. It smelled of sweat and tension. Anything from the Nassau control tower? Any report of a low-flying plane? Of a possible crash into the sea off Bimini? Then keep watching and get me No. 2. Quick, please. It's just on the quarter.

No. 1 lit a cigarette and watched the yacht's big brain get to work, scanning the ether, listening, searching. The operator played the dials with insect fingers, pausing, verifying, hastening on through the sound waves of the world. Now he suddenly stopped, checked, minutely adjusted the volume. He raised his thumb. No. 1 spoke into the little sphere of wire mesh that rose in front of his mouth from the base of the headset. 'No. 1 speaking.'

'No. 2 listening.' The voice was hollow. The words waxed and waned. But it was Blofeld, all right. No. 1 knew that voice better than he remembered his father's.

'Successful. Ten fifteen. Next phase ten forty-five. Continuing. Over.'

'Thank you. Out.' The sound waves went dead. The interchange had taken forty-five seconds. No conceivable fear of interception in that time, on that waveband.

No. 1 went through the big stateroom and down into the hold. The four men of B team, their aqualungs beside them, were sitting around smoking. The wide underwater hatch just above the keel of the yacht was open. Moonlight, reflected off the white sand under the ship, shone up through the six feet of water in the hold. Stacked on the grating beside the men was the thick pile of tarpaulin painted a very pale café-au-lait with occasional irregular blotches of dark green and brown. No. 1 said, 'All is going very well. The recovery team is at work. It should not be long now. How about the chariot and the sled?'

One of the men jerked his thumb downwards. 'They are down there. Outside on the sand. So it will be quicker.'

'Correct.' No. 1 nodded towards a crane-like contraption fastened to a bulkhead above the hold. 'The derrick took the strain all right?'

'That chain could handle twice the weight.'

'The pumps?'

'In order. They will clear the hold in seven minutes.'

'Good. Well, take it easy. It will be a long night.' No. 1 climbed the iron ladder out of the hold and went up on deck. He didn't need his night glasses. Two hundred yards away to starboard the sea was empty save for the jolly-boat riding at anchor above the golden submarine glow. The red marker light had been taken in to the boat. The rattle of the little generator making current for the big searchlight was loud. It would carry far across a sea as still as this. But accumulators would have been too bulky and might have exhausted themselves before the work was finished. The generator was a calculated risk and a small one at that. The nearest island was five miles away and uninhabited unless someone was having a midnight picnic on it. The yacht had stopped and searched it on the way to the rendezvous. Everything had been done that could be done, every precaution taken. The wonderful machine was running silently and full out. There was nothing to worry about now except the next step. No. 1 went through the hatch into the enclosed bridge and bent over the lighted chart table.

Emilio Largo, No. 1, was a big, conspicuously handsome man of about forty. He was a Roman and he looked like a Roman, not from the Rome of today, but from the Rome of the ancient coins. The large, long face was sunburned a deep mahogany brown and the light glinted off the strong rather hooked nose and the clean-cut lantern jaw that had been meticulously shaved before he had started out late that afternoon. In contrast to the hard, slow-moving brown eyes, the mouth, with its thick, rather down-curled lips, belonged to a satyr. Ears that, from dead in front, looked almost pointed, added to an animalness that would devastate women. The only weakness in the fine centurion face lay in the overlong sideburns and the too carefully waved black hair that glistened so brightly with pomade that it might almost have been painted on to the skull. There was no fat on the big-boned frame – Largo had fought for Italy in the Olympic foils, was almost an Olympic-class swimmer with the Australian crawl, and only a month before had won the senior class in the Nassau water-ski championships — and the muscles bulged under the exquisitely cut shark-skin jacket. An aid to his athletic prowess were his hands. They were almost twice the normal size, even for a man of his stature, and now, as they walked across the chart holding a ruler and a pair of dividers, they looked, extruding from the white sleeves that rested on the white chart, almost like large brown furry animals quite separate from their owner.

Largo was an adventurer, a predator on the herd. Two hundred years before, he would have been a pirate — not one of the jolly ones of the story books, but a man like Blackbeard, a bloodstained cut-throat who scythed his way through people towards gold. But Blackbeard had been too much of a bully and a roughneck and wherever he went in the world he left behind a telltale shambles. Largo was different. There was a cool brain and an exquisite finesse behind his actions that had always saved him from the herd's revenge — from his post-war debut as head of the black market in Naples, through five lucrative years smuggling from Tangier, five more masterminding the wave of big jewel robberies on the French Riviera, down to his last five with SPECTRE. Always he got away with it. Always he had seen the essential step ahead that would have been hidden from lesser men. He was the epitome of the gentleman crook — a man of the world, a great womanizer, a high liver, with the entrée to café society in four continents, and the last survivor, conveniently enough, of a once famous Roman family whose fortune, so he said, he had inherited. He also benefited from having no wife, a spotless police record, nerves of steel, a heart of ice, and the ruthlessness of a Himmler. He was the perfect man for SPECTRE, and the perfect man, rich Nassau playboy and all, to be Supreme Commander of Plan Omega.

One of the crew knocked on the hatch and came in. 'They have signalled. The chariot and sled are on the way.'

'Thank you.' In the heat and excitement of any operation, Largo always created calm. However much was at stake, however great the dangers and however urgent the need for speed and quick decisions, he made a fetish of calm, of the pause, of an almost judo-like inertia. This was an act of will to which he had trained himself. He found it had an extraordinary effect on his accomplices. It tied them to him and invoked their obedience and loyalty more than any other factor in leadership. That he, a clever and cunning man, should show unconcern at particularly bad, or, as in this case, particularly good news, meant that he already knew that what had happened would happen. With Largo, consequences were foreseen. One could depend on him. He never lost balance. So now, at this splendid news, Largo deliberately picked up his dividers again and made a trace, an imaginary trace, on the chart for the sake of the crew member. He then put down the dividers and strolled out of the air-conditioning into the warm night.

A tiny worm of underwater light was creeping out towards the jolly-boat. It was a two-man underwater chariot identical with those used by the Italians during the war and bought, with improvements, from Ansaldo, the firm that had originally invented the one-man submarine. It was towing an underwater sled, a sharp-prowed tray with negative buoyancy used for the recovery and transport of heavy objects under the sea. The worm of light merged with the luminescence from the searchlight and, minutes later, re-emerged on its way back to the ship. It would have been natural for Largo to have gone down to the hold to witness the arrival of the two atomic weapons. Typically, he did nothing of the sort. In due course the little headlight reappeared, going back over its previous course. Now the sled would be loaded with the huge tarpaulin, camouflaged to merge in with just this piece of underwater terrain, with its white sand and patches of coral outcrop, that would be spread so as to cover every inch of the wrecked plane and pegged all round with corkscrew iron stanchions that would not be shifted by the heaviest surface storm or groundswell. In his imagination, Largo saw every move of the eight men who would now be working far below the surface on the reality for which there had been so much training, so many dummy exercises. He marvelled at the effort, the incredible ingenuity, that had gone into Plan Omega. Now all the months of preparation, of sweat and tears, were being repaid.

There came a bright blink of light on the surface of the water not far from the jolly-boat — then another and another. The men were surfacing. As they did so, the moon caught the glass of their masks. They swam to the boat — Largo verified that all eight were there — and clumsily heaved up the short ladder and over the side. The mechanic and Brandt, the German killer, helped them off with their gear, the underwater light was switched off and hauled inboard and, instead of the rattle of the generator, there came the muffled roar of the twin Johnstons. The boat sped back to the yacht and to the waiting arms of the derricks. The couplings were made firm and verified and, with a shrill electric whine, the boat, complete with passengers, was swung up and inboard.

The captain came and stood at Largo's side. He was a big, sullen, rawboned man who had been cashiered from the Canadian Navy for drunkenness and insubordination. He had been a slave to Largo ever since Largo had called him to the stateroom one day and broken a chair over his head on account of a questioned command. That was the kind of discipline he understood. Now he said, 'The hold's clear. Okay to sail?'

'Are both the teams satisfied?'

'They say so. Not a hitch.'

'First see they all get one full jigger of whisky. Then tell them to rest. They will be going out again in just about an hour. Ask Kotze to have a word with me. Be ready to sail in five minutes.'

'Okay.'

The eyes of the physicist, Kotze, were bright under the moon. Largo noticed that he was trembling slightly as if with fever. He tried to instil calm into the man. He said cheerfully, 'Well, my friend. Are you pleased with your toys? The toy-shop has sent you everything you want?'

Kotze's lips trembled. He was on the verge of excited tears. He said, his voice high, 'It is tremendous! You have no idea. Weapons such as I had never dreamed of. And of a simplicity — a safety! Even a child could handle these things without danger.'

'The cradles were big enough for them? You have room to do your work?'

'Yes, yes.' Kotze almost flapped his hands with enthusiasm. 'There are no problems, none at all. The fuses will be off in no time. It will be a simple matter to replace them with the time mechanism. Maslov is already at work correcting the threads. I am using lead screws. They are more easy to machine.'

'And the two plugs — these ignitors you were telling me about? They are safe? Where did the divers find them?'

'They were in a leaden box under the pilot's seat. I have verified them. Perfectly simple when the time comes. They will of course be kept apart in the hiding place. The rubber bags are splendid. Just what was needed. I have verified that they seal completely watertight.'

'No danger from radiation?'

'Not now. Everything is in the leaden cases.' Kotze shrugged. 'I may have picked up a little while I was working on the monsters but I wore the harness. I will watch for signs. I know what to do.'

'You are a brave man, Kotze. I won't go near the damned things until I have to. I value my sex-life too much. So you are satisfied with everything? You have no problems? Nothing has been left on the plane?'

Kotze had got himself under control. He had been bursting with the news, with his relief that the technical problems were within his power. Now he felt empty, tired. He had voided himself of the tensions that had been with him for weeks. After all this planning, all these dangers, supposing his knowledge had not been enough! Supposing the bloody English had invented some new safety device, some secret control, of which he knew nothing! But when the time came, when he unwrapped the protective webbing and got to work with his jeweller's tools, then triumph and gratitude had flooded into him. No, now there were no problems. Everything was all right. Now there was only routine. Kotze said dully, 'No. There are no problems. Everything is there. I will go and get the job finished.'

Largo watched the thin figure shamble off along the deck. Scientists were queer fish. They saw nothing but science. Kotze couldn't visualize the risks that still had to be run. For him the turning of a few screws was the end of the job. For the rest of the time he would be a useless supercargo. It would be easier to get rid of him. But that couldn't be done yet. He would have to be kept on just in case the weapons had to be used. But he was a depressing little man and a near hysteric. Largo didn't like such people near him. They lowered his spirits. They smelled of bad luck. Kotze would have to be found some job in the engine room where he would be kept busy and, above all, out of sight.

Largo went into the cockpit bridge. The captain was sitting at the wheel, a light aluminium affair consisting only of the bottom half of a circle. Largo said, 'Okay. Let's go.' The captain reached out his hand to the bank of buttons at his side and pressed the one that said '*Start Both*'. There came a low, hollow rumble from amidships. A light blinked on the panel to show that both engines were firing properly. The captain pulled the electro-magnetic gear shift to '*Slow Ahead Both*' and the yacht began to move. The captain made it '*Full Ahead Both*' and the yacht trembled and settled a little in the stern. The captain watched the revolution counter, his hand on a squat lever at his side. At twenty knots the counter showed 5,000. The captain inched back the lever that depressed the great steel scoop below the hull. The revolutions remained the same, but the finger of the speedometer crawled on round the dial until it said forty knots. Now the yacht was half-flying, half-planing across the glittering sheet of still water, the hull supported four feet above the surface on the broad, slightly uptilted metal skid and with only a few feet of the stern and the two big screws submerged. It was a glorious sensation and Largo, as he always did, thrilled to it.

The motor yacht, *Disco Volante*, was a hydrofoil craft, built for Largo with SPECTRE funds by the Italian constructors, Leopoldo Rodrigues, of Messina, the only firm in the world to have successfully adapted the Shertel-Sachsenberg system to commercial use. With a hull of aluminium and magnesium alloy, two Daimler-Benz four-stroke diesels supercharged by twin Brown-Boveri turbo superchargers, the *Disco Volante* could move her 100 tons at around fifty knots, with a cruising range at that speed of around four hundred miles. She had cost £200,000, but she had been the only craft in the world with the speed, cargo- and passenger-space, and with the essential shallow draught for the job required of her in Bahamian waters.

The constructors claim of this type of craft that it has a particular refinement that SPECTRE had appreciated. Having high stability and a shallow draught, *Aliscafos*, as they are called in Italy, do not determine magnetic field variation, nor do they cause pressure waves — both desirable characteristics, in case the *Disco Volante* might wish, some time in her career, to escape detection.

Six months before, the *Disco* had been shipped out to the Florida Keys by the South Atlantic route. She had been a sensation in Florida waters and among the Bahamas, and had vastly helped to make Largo the most popular 'millionaire' in a corner of the world that crawls with millionaires who 'have everything'. And the fast and mysterious voyages he made in the *Disco*, with all those underwater swimmers and occasionally with a two-seater Lycoming-engined folding-wing amphibian mounted on the roof of the streamlined superstructure, had aroused just the right amount of excited comment. Slowly, Largo had let the secret leak out — through his own indiscretions at dinners and cocktail parties, through carefully primed members of the crew in the Bay Street bars. This was a treasure hunt, an important one. There was a pirates' map, a sunken galleon thickly overgrown with coral. The wreck had been located. Largo was only waiting for the end of the winter tourist season and for the calms of early summer and then his shareholders would be coming out from Europe and work would begin in earnest. And two days before, the shareholders, nineteen of them, had duly come trickling into Nassau by different routes

— from Bermuda, from New York, from Miami. Rather dull-looking people to be sure, just the sort of hard-headed, hard-working businessmen who would be amused by a gamble like this, a pleasant sunshine gamble with a couple of weeks' holiday in Nassau to make up for it if the doubloons were after all not in the wreck. And that evening, with all the visitors on board, the engines of the *Disco* had begun to murmur, just when they should have, the harbour folk agreed, just when it was getting dark, and the beautiful dark blue and white yacht had slid out of harbour. Once in the open sea, the engines had started up their deep booming that had gradually diminished to the south-east, towards, the listeners agreed, an entirely appropriate hunting ground.

The southerly course was considered appropriate because it is among the Southern Bahamas that the great local treasure troves are expected to be found. It was through the southerly passages through these islands — the Crooked Island, the Mayaguana and the Caicos passages — that the Spanish treasure ships would try to dodge the pirates and the French and British fleets as they made for home. Here, it is believed, lie the remains of the *Porto Pedro*, sunk in 1668, with a million pounds of bullion on board. The *Santa Cruz*, lost in 1694, carried twice as much, and the *El Capitan* and *San Pedro*, both sunk in 1719, carried a million, and half a million, pounds of treasure respectively.

Every year, treasure hunts for these and other ships are carried out among the Southern Bahamas. No one can guess how much, if anything, has been recovered, but everyone in Nassau knows of the 72-lb. silver bar recovered by two Nassau businessmen off Gorda Cay in 1950, and since presented to the Nassau Development Board, in whose offices it is permanently on view. So all Bahamians know that treasure is there for the finding, and when the harbour folk of Nassau heard the deep boom of the *Disco*'s engines dying away to the south, they nodded wisely.

But once the *Disco* was well away and the moon had not yet risen, with all lights dowsed, she swung away in a wide circle towards the west and towards the rendezvous point she was now leaving. Now she was a hundred miles, two hours, away from Nassau. But it would be almost dawn when, after one more vital call, Nassau would again hear the boom of her engines coming in from the false southern trail.

Largo got up and bent over the chart table. They had covered the course many times and in all weathers. It was really no problem. But Phases I and II had gone so well that double care must be taken over Phase III. Yes, all was well. They were dead on course. Fifty miles. They would be there in an hour. He told the captain to keep the yacht as she was, and went below to the radio room. Eleven fifteen was just coming up. It was call time.

The small island, Dog Island, was no bigger than two tennis courts. It was a hunk of dead coral with a smattering of seagrape and battered screw palm that grew on nothing but pockets of brackish rainwater and sand. It was the point where the Dog Shoal broke the surface, a well-known navigational hazard that even the fishing boats kept well away from. In daylight, Andros Island showed to eastwards, but at night it was as safe as houses.

The *Disco* came up fast and then slowly lowered herself back into the water and slid up to within a cable's length of the rock. Her arrival brought small waves that lapped and sucked at the rock and then were still. The anchor slipped silently down forty feet and held. Down in the hold, Largo and the disposal team of four waited for the underwater hatch to be opened.

The five men wore aqualungs. Largo held nothing but a powerful underwater electric torch. The four others were divided into two pairs. They wore webbing slung between them and they sat on the edge of the iron grating with their frogmen's feet dangling, waiting for the water to swirl in and give them buoyancy. On the webbing, between each pair, rested a six-foot-long tapering object in an obscene grey rubber envelope.

The water seeped, rushed, and then burst into the hold, submerging the five men. They slipped off their seats and trudged out through the hatchway, Largo in the lead and the two pairs behind him at precisely tested intervals.

Largo did not at first switch on his torch. It was not necessary and it would bring stupid, dazed fish that were a distraction. It might even bring shark or barracuda and, though they would be no more than a nuisance, one of the team, despite Largo's assurances, might lose his nerve.

They swam on in the soft moonlit mist of the sea. At first there was nothing but a milky void below them, but then the coral shelf of the island showed up, climbing steeply towards the surface. Sea fans, like small shrouds in the moonlight, waved softly, beckoning, and the clumps and trees of coral were grey and enigmatic. It was because of these things, the harmless underwater mysteries that make the skin crawl on the inexperienced, that Largo had decided to lead the disposal teams himself. Out in the open, where the plane had foundered, the eye of the big searchlight made, with the known object of the plane itself, the underwater world into the semblance of a big room. But this was different. This grey-white world needed the contempt of a swimmer who had experienced these phantom dangers a thousand times before. That was the main reason why Largo led the teams. He also wanted to know exactly how the two grey sausages were stored away. It could happen, if things went wrong, that he would have to salvage them himself.

The underpart of the small island had been eroded by the waves so that, seen from below, it resembled a thick mushroom. Under the umbrella of coral there was a wide fissure, a dark wound in the side of the stem. Largo made for it and, when he was close, switched on his torch. Beneath the umbrella of coral it was dark. The yellow light of the torch showed up the minute life of an inshore coral community — the pale sea urchins and the fierce black spines of sea eggs, the shifting underbrush of seaweeds, the yellow and blue seeking antennae of a langouste, the butterfly and angel fish, fluttering like moths in the light, a coiled bêche de mer, a couple of meandering sea caterpillars and the black and green jelly of a sea hare.

Largo lowered the black fins on his feet, got his balance on a ledge, and looked round, shining his torch on the rock so that the two teams could get a foothold. Then he waved them on and into the smooth broad fissure that showed a glimmer of moonlight at its far end inside the centre of the rock. The underwater cave was only about ten yards long. Largo led the teams one after the other through and into the small chamber that might once perhaps have been a wonderful repository for a different kind of treasure. From the chamber a narrow fissure led to the upper air and this would certainly become a fine blow-hole in a storm, though it would be unlikely that fishermen would be close enough to the Dog Shoal in a storm to see the water fountaining out of the centre of the island. Above the present waterline in the chamber, Largo's men had hammered stanchions into the rock to form cradles for the two atomic weapons with leather straps to hold them secure against any weather. Now, one by one, the two teams lifted the rubber packages up on to the iron bars and made them secure. Largo examined the result and was satisfied. The weapons would be ready for him when he needed them. In the meantime such radiation as there was would be quarantined within this tiny rock a hundred miles from Nassau and his men and his ship would be clean and innocent as snow.

The five men trudged calmly back to the ship and into the hold through the hatch. To the boom of the engines the bows of the *Disco* lifted slowly out of the water and the beautiful ship, streamlined like the gondola of some machine of the air rather than of the sea, skimmed off on the homeward journey.

Largo stripped off his equipment and, with a towel round his slim waist, went forrard to the radio cabin. He had missed the midnight call. It was now one fifteen — seven fifteen in the morning for Blofeld.

Largo thought of this while contact was being made. Blofeld would be sitting there, haggard perhaps, probably unshaven. There would be coffee beside him, the last of an endless chain of cups. Largo could smell it. Now Blofeld would be able to take a taxi to the Turkish baths in the Rue Aubert, his resort when there were tensions to be dissipated. And there, at last, he would sleep.

'Number 1 speaking.'

'Number 2 listening.'

'Phase III completed. Phase III completed. Successful. One a.m. here. Closing down.'

'I am satisfied.'

Largo stripped off the earphones. He thought to himself, So am I! We are more than three-quarters home. Now only the devil can stop us.

He went into the stateroom and carefully made himself a tall glass of his favourite drink — crème de menthe frappé with a maraschino cherry on top.

He sipped it delicately to the end and ate the cherry. Then he took one more cherry out of the bottle, slipped it into his mouth, and went up on the bridge.

11

DOMINO

THE GIRL IN the sapphire-blue MG two-seater shot down the slope of Parliament Street and at the junction with Bay Street executed an admirable racing change through third into second. She gave a quick glance to the right, correctly estimated the trot of the straw-hatted horse in the shafts of the rickety cab with the gay fringe, and swerved out of the side street left-handed. The horse jerked back his head indignantly and the coachman stamped his foot up and down on the big Bermuda bell. The disadvantage of the beautiful deep ting-tong, ting-tong of the Bermuda carriage bell is that it cannot possibly sound angry, however angrily you may sound it. The girl gave a cheerful wave of a sunburned hand, raced up the street in second, and stopped in front of The Pipe of Peace, the Dunhills of Nassau.

Not bothering to open the low door of the MG, the girl swung one brown leg and then the other over the side of the car, showing her thighs under the pleated cream cotton skirt almost to her waist, and slipped to the pavement. By now the cab was alongside. The cabby reined in. He was mollified by the gaiety and beauty of the girl. He said, 'Missy, you done almost shaved de whiskers off of Old Dreamy here. You wanna be more careful.'

The girl put her hands on her hips. She didn't like being told anything by anyone. She said sharply, 'Old Dreamy yourself. Some people have got work to do. Both of you ought to be put out to grass instead of cluttering up the streets getting in everyone's way.'

The ancient Negro opened his mouth, thought better of it, said a pacifying 'Hokay, Missy. Hokay', flicked at his horse and moved on, muttering to himself. He turned on his seat to get another look at the she-devil, but she had already disappeared into the shop. 'Dat's a fine piece of gal,' he said inconsequentially, and put his horse into an ambling trot.

Twenty yards away, James Bond had witnessed the whole scene. He felt the same way about the girl as the cabby did. He also knew who she was. He quickened his step and pushed through the striped sun-blinds into the blessed cool of the tobacconist's.

The girl was standing at a counter arguing with one of the assistants. 'But I tell you I don't want Senior Service. I tell you I want a cigarette that's so disgusting that I shan't want to smoke it. Haven't you got a cigarette that stops people smoking? Look at all that.' She waved a hand towards the stacked shelves. 'Don't tell me some of those don't taste horrible.'

The man was used to crazy tourists and anyway the Nassavian doesn't get excited. He said, 'Well, Mam . . .' and turned and languidly looked along the shelves.

Bond saïd sternly to the girl, 'You can choose between two kinds of cigarette if you want to smoke less.'

She looked sharply up at him. 'And who might you be?'

'My name's Bond, James Bond. I'm the world's authority on giving up smoking. I do it constantly. You're lucky I happen to be handy.'

The girl looked him up and down. He was a man she hadn't seen before in Nassau. He was about six feet tall and somewhere in his middle thirties. He had dark, rather cruel good looks and very clear blue-grey eyes that were now observing her inspection sardonically. A scar down his right cheek showed pale against a tan so mild that he must have only recently come to the island. He was wearing a very dark blue lightweight single-breasted suit over a cream silk shirt and a black knitted silk tie. Despite the heat, he looked cool and clean, and his only concession to the tropics appeared to be the black saddle-stitched sandals on his bare feet.

It was an obvious attempt at a pick-up. He had an exciting face, and authority. She decided to go along. But she wasn't going to make it easy. She said coldly, 'All right. Tell me.'

'The only way to stop smoking is to stop it and not start again. If you want to *pretend* to stop for a week or two, it's no good trying to ration yourself. You'll become a bore and think about nothing else. And you'll snatch at a cigarette every time the hour strikes or whatever the intervals may be. You'll behave greedily. That's unattractive. The other way is to have cigarettes that are either too mild or too strong. The mild ones are probably the best for you.' Bond said to the attendant, 'A carton of Dukes, kingsize with filter.' Bond handed them to the girl. 'Here, try these. With the compliments of Faust.'

'Oh, but I can't. I mean . . .'

But Bond had already paid for the carton and for a packet of Chesterfields for himself. He took the change and followed her out of the shop. They stood together under the striped awning. The heat was terrific. The white light on the dusty street, the glare reflected back off the shop fronts opposite and off the dazzling limestone of the houses made them both screw up their eyes. Bond said, 'I'm afraid smoking goes with drinking. Are you going to give them both up or one by one?'

She looked at him quizzically. 'This is very sudden, Mr — er — Bond. Well, all right. But somewhere out of the town. It's too hot here. Do you know The Wharf out beyond the Fort Montague?' Bond noticed that she looked quickly up and down the street. 'It's not bad. Come on. I'll take you there. Mind the metal. It'll raise blisters on you.'

Even the white leather of the upholstery burned through to Bond's thighs. But he wouldn't have minded if his suit had caught fire. This was his first sniff at the town and already he had got hold of the girl. And she was a fine girl at that. Bond caught hold of the leather-bound safety grip on the dashboard as the girl did a sharp turn up Frederick Street and another one on to Shirley.

Bond settled himself sideways so that he could look at her. She wore a gondolier's broadrimmed straw hat, tilted impudently down over her nose. The pale blue tails of its ribbon streamed out behind. On the front of the ribbon was printed in gold 'M/Y DISCO VOLANTE'. Her short-sleeved silk shirt was in half-inch vertical stripes of pale blue and white and, with the pleated cream skirt, the whole get-up reminded Bond vaguely of a sunny day at Henley Regatta. She wore no rings and no jewellery except for a rather masculine square gold wrist-watch with a black face. Her flat-heeled sandals were of white doeskin. They matched her broad white doeskin belt and the sensible handbag that lay, with a black and white striped silk scarf, on the seat between them. Bond knew a good deal about her from the immigration form, one among a hundred, which he had been studying that morning. Her name was Dominetta Vitali. She had been born in Bolzano in the Italian Tyrol and therefore probably had as much Austrian as Italian blood in her. She was twenty-nine and gave her profession as 'actress'. She had arrived six months before in the *Disco* and it was entirely understood that she was mistress to the owner of the yacht, an Italian called Emilio Largo. 'Whore', 'tart', 'prostitute' were not words Bond used about women unless they were professional streetwalkers or the inmates of a brothel, and when Harling, the Commissioner of Police, and Pitman, Chief of Immigration and Customs, had described her as an 'Italian tart' Bond had reserved judgment. Now he knew he had been right. This was an independent, a girl of authority and character. She might like the rich, gay life but, so far as Bond was concerned, that was the right kind of girl. She might sleep with men, obviously did, but it would be on her terms and not on theirs.

Women are often meticulous and safe drivers, but they are very seldom first-class. In general Bond regarded them as a mild hazard and he always gave them plenty of road and was ready for the unpredictable. Four women in a car he regarded as the highest danger potential, and two women as nearly as lethal. Women together cannot keep silent in a car, and when women talk they have to look into each other's faces. An exchange of words is not enough. They have to see the other person's expression, perhaps in order to read behind the other's words or to analyse the reaction to their own. So two women in the front seat of a car constantly distract each other's attention from the road ahead and four women are more than doubly dangerous, for the driver not only has to hear, and see, what her companion is saying but also, for women are like that, what the two behind are talking about.

But this girl drove like a man. She was entirely focused on the road ahead and on what was going on in her driving mirror, an accessory rarely used by women except for making up their faces. And, equally rare in a woman, she took a man's pleasure in the feel of her machine, in the timing of her gear changes, and the use of her brakes.

She didn't talk to Bond or seem to be aware of him, and this allowed him to continue his inspection without inhibition. She had a gay, to-hell-with-you face that, Bond thought, would become animal in passion. In bed she would fight and bite and then suddenly melt into hot surrender. He could almost see the proud, sensual mouth bare away from the even white teeth in a snarl of desire and then, afterwards, soften into a half-pout of loving slavery. In profile the eyes were soft charcoal slits such as you see on some birds, but in the shop Bond had seen them full face. Then they had been fierce and direct with a golden flicker in the dark brown that held much the same message as the mouth. The profile, the straight, small uptilted nose, the determined set of the chin, and the clean-cut sweep of the jawline were as decisive as a royal command, and the way the head was set on the neck had the same authority — the poise one associates with imaginary princesses. Two features modified the clean-cut purity of line — a soft, muddled Brigitte Bardot haircut that escaped from under the straw hat in an endearing disarray, and two deeply cut but soft dimples which could only have been etched by a sweet if rather ironic smile that Bond had not yet seen. The sunburn was not overdone and her skin had none of that dried, exhausted sheen that can turn the texture of even the youngest skin into something more like parchment. Beneath the gold, there was an earthy warmth in the cheeks that suggested a good healthy peasant strain from the Italian Alps and her breasts, high-riding and deeply V-ed, were from the same stock. The general impression, Bond decided, was of a wilful, high-tempered, sensual girl — a beautiful Arab mare who would only allow herself to be ridden by a horseman with steel thighs and velvet hands, and then only with curb and saw-bit — and then only when he had broken her to bridle and saddle. Bond thought that he would like to try his strength against hers. But that must be for some other time. For the moment another man was in the saddle. He would first have to be unhorsed. And anyway, what the hell was he doing fooling with these things? There was a job to be done. The devil of a job.

The MG swept out of Shirley Street on to Eastern Road and followed the coast. Across the wide harbour entrance were the emerald and turquoise shoals of Athol Island. A deep-sea fishing boat was passing over them, the two tall antennae of her twelve-foot rods streaming their lines astern. A fast motorboat came hammering by close inshore, the water-skier on the line behind her executing tight slaloms across the waves of her wake. It was a sparkling, beautiful day and Bond's heart lifted momentarily from the trough of indecision and despondency created by an assignment that, particularly since his arrival at dawn that day, seemed increasingly time-wasting and futile.

The Bahamas, the string of a thousand islands that straggle five hundred miles south-east from just east of the coast of Florida to just north of Cuba, from latitude 27° down to latitude 21°, were, for most of three hundred years, the haunt of every famous pirate of the Western Atlantic, and today tourism makes full use of the romantic mythology. A road sign said '*Blackbeard's Tower 1 mile*' and another '*Gunpowder Wharf. Sea Food. Native Drinks. Shady Garden. First Left*'.

A sand track showed on their left. The girl took it and pulled up in front of a ruined stone warehouse against which leant a pink clapboard house with white window-frames and a white Adam-style doorway over which hung a brightly painted inn sign of a powder keg with a skull and crossbones on it. The girl drove the MG into the shade of a clump of casuarinas and they got out and went through the door and through a small dining-room with red and white checked covers and out on to a terrace built on the remains of a stone wharf. The terrace was shaded by sea-almond trees trimmed into umbrellas. Trailed by a shuffling coloured waiter with soup stains down his white coat, they chose a cool table on the edge of the terrace looking over the water. Bond glanced at his watch. He said to the girl, 'It's exactly midday. Do you want to drink solid or soft?'

The girl said, 'Soft. I'll have a double Bloody Mary with plenty of Worcester sauce.'

Bond said, 'What do you call hard? I'll have a vodka and tonic with a dash of bitters.' The waiter said, 'Yassuh,' and mooched away.

'I call vodka on the rocks hard. All that tomato juice makes it soft.' She hooked a chair towards her with one foot and stretched out her legs on it so that they were in the sun. The position wasn't comfortable enough. She kicked off her sandals and sat back, satisfied. She said, 'When did you arrive? I haven't seen you about. When it's like this, at the end of the season, one expects to know most of the faces.'

'I got in this morning. From New York. I've come to look for a property. It struck me that now would be better than in the season. When all the millionaires are here the prices are hopeless. They may come down a bit now they're gone. How long have you been here?'

'About six months. I came out in a yacht, the *Disco Volante*. You may have seen her. She's anchored up the coast. You probably flew right over her coming in to land at Windsor Field.'

'A long low streamlined affair? Is she yours? She's got beautiful lines.'

'She belongs to a relative of mine.' The eyes watched Bond's face.

'Do you stay on board?'

'Oh no. We've got a beach property. Or rather we've taken it. It's a place called Palmyra. Just opposite where the yacht is. It belongs to an Englishman. I believe he wants to sell it. It's very beautiful. And it's a long way away from the tourists. It's at a place called Lyford Key.'

'That sounds the sort of place I'm looking for.'

'Well, we'll be gone in about a week.'

'Oh.' Bond looked into her eyes. 'I'm sorry.'

'If you've got to flirt, don't be obvious.' Suddenly the girl laughed. She looked contrite. The dimples remained. 'I mean, I didn't really mean that — not the way it sounded. But I've spent six months listening to that kind of thing from these silly old rich goats and the only way to shut them up is to be rude. I'm not being conceited. There's no one under sixty in this place. Young people can't afford it. So any woman who hasn't got a harelip or a moustache — well not even a moustache would put them off. They'd probably like it. Well I mean absolutely any girl makes these old goats get their bifocals all steamed up.' She laughed again. She was getting friendly. 'I expect you'll have just the same effect on the old women with pince-nez and blue rinses.'

'Do they eat boiled vegetables for lunch?'

'Yes, and they drink carrot juice and prune juice.'

'We won't get on then. I won't sink lower than conch chowder.'

She looked at him curiously. 'You seem to know a lot about Nassau.'

'You mean about conch being an aphrodisiac? That's not only a Nassau idea. It's all over the world where there are conchs.'

'Is it true?'

'Island people have it on their wedding night. I haven't found it have any effect on me.'

'Why?' She looked mischievous. 'Are you married?'

'No.' Bond smiled across into her eyes. 'Are you?'

'No.'

'Then we might both try some conch soup some time and see what happens.'

'That's only a little better than the millionaires. You'll have to try harder.'

The drinks came. The girl stirred hers with a finger, to mix in the brown sediment of Worcester sauce, and drank half of it. She reached for the carton of Dukes, broke it open, and slit a packet with her thumbnail. She took out a cigarette, sniffed it cautiously, and lit it with Bond's lighter. She inhaled deeply and blew out a long plume of smoke. She said doubtfully, 'Not bad. At least the smoke looks like smoke. Why did you say you were such an expert on giving up smoking?'

'Because I've given it up so often.' Bond thought it time to get away from the small-talk. He said, 'Why do you talk such good English? Your accent sounds Italian.'

'Yes, my name's Dominetta Vitali. But I was sent to school in England. To the Cheltenham Ladies' College. Then I went to RADA to learn acting. The English kind of acting. My parents thought that was a ladylike way to be brought up. Then they were both killed in a train crash. I went back to Italy to earn my living. I remembered my English but' — she laughed without bitterness — 'I soon forgot most of the rest. You don't get far in the Italian theatre by being able to walk about with a book balanced on your head.'

'But this relative with the yacht.' Bond looked out to sea. 'Wasn't he there to look after you?'

'No.' The answer was curt. When Bond made no comment she added, 'He's not exactly a relative, not a close one. He's a sort of close friend. A guardian.'

'Oh yes.'

'You must come and visit us on the yacht.' She felt that a bit of gush was needed. 'He's called Largo, Emilio Largo. You've probably heard. He's here on some kind of a treasure hunt.'

'Really?' Now it was Bond's turn to gush. 'That sounds rather fun. Of course I'd like to meet him. What's it all about? Is there anything in it?'

'Heaven knows. He's very secretive about it. Apparently there's some kind of a map. But I'm not allowed to see it and I have to stay ashore when he goes off prospecting or whatever he does. A lot of people have put up money for it, sort of shareholders. They've all just arrived. As we're going in a week or so, I suppose everything's ready and the real hunt's going to start any moment now.'

'What are the shareholders like? Do they seem sensible sort of people? The trouble with most treasure hunts is that either someone's been there before and sneaked off with the treasure or the ship's so deep in the coral you can't get at it.'

'They seem all right. Very dull and rich. Terribly serious for something as romantic as treasure hunting. They seem to spend all their time with Largo. Plotting and planning I suppose. And they never seem to go out in the sun or go bathing or anything. It's as if they didn't want to get sunburned. As far as I can gather, none of them have ever been in the tropics before. Just a typical bunch of stuffy businessmen. They're probably better than that. I haven't seen much of them. Largo's giving a party for them at the Casino tonight.'

'What do you do all day?'

'Oh, I fool around. Do a bit of shopping for the yacht. Drive around in the car. Bathe on other people's beaches when their houses are empty. I like underwater swimming. I've got an aqualung and I take one of the crew out or a fisherman. The crew are better. They all do it.'

'I used to do it a bit. I've brought my gear. Will you show me some good bits of reef some time?'

The girl looked pointedly at her watch. 'I might do. It's time I went.' She got up. 'Thanks for the drink. I'm afraid I can't take you back. I'm going the other way. They'll get you a taxi here.' She shuffled her feet into her sandals.

Bond followed the girl through the restaurant to her car. She got in and pressed the starter. Bond decided to risk another snub. He said, 'Perhaps I'll see you at the Casino tonight, Dominetta.'

'P'raps.' She put the car pointedly into gear. She took another look at him. She decided that she did want to see him again. She said, 'But for God's sake don't call me Dominetta. I'm never called that. People call me Domino.' She gave him a brief smile, but it was a smile into the eyes. She raised a hand. The rear wheels spat sand and gravel and the little blue car whirled out along the driveway to the main road. It paused at the intersection and then, as Bond watched, turned right-handed towards Nassau.

Bond smiled. He said, 'Bitch,' and walked back into the restaurant to pay his bill and have a taxi called.

12

THE MAN FROM THE C.I.A.

THE TAXI TOOK Bond out to the airport at the other end of the island by the Interfield Road. The man from the Central Intelligence Agency was due in by Pan American at 1.15. His name was Larkin, F. Larkin. Bond hoped he wouldn't be a muscle-bound ex-college man with a crew-cut and a desire to show up the incompetence of the British, the backwardness of their little Colony, and the clumsy ineptitude of Bond, in order to gain credit with his chief in Washington. Bond hoped that at any rate he would bring the equipment he had asked for before he left London through Section A, who looked after the liaison with C.I.A. This was the latest transmitter and receiver for agents in the field, so that the two of them could be independent of cable offices and have instant communication with London and Washington, and the most modern portable Geiger counters for operating both on land and underwater. One of the chief virtues of C.I.A., in Bond's estimation, was the excellence of their equipment, and he had no false pride about borrowing from them.

New Providence, the island containing Nassau, the capital of the Bahamas, is a drab sandy slab of land fringed with some of the most beautiful beaches in the world. But the interior is nothing but a waste of low-lying scrub, casuarinas, mastic, and poison-wood with a large brackish lake at the western end. There are birds and tropical flowers and palm trees, imported fully grown from Florida, in the beautiful gardens of the millionaires round the coast, but in the middle of the island there is nothing to attract the eye but the skeleton fingers of spidery windmill pumps sticking up above the pine barrens, and Bond spent the ride to the airport reviewing the morning.

He had arrived at seven a.m. to be met by the Governor's A.D.C. — a mild error of security — and taken to the Royal Bahamian, a large old-fashioned hotel to which had recently been applied a thin veneer of American efficiency and tourist gimmicks — iced water in his room, a Cellophane-wrapped basket of dingy fruit 'with the compliments of the Manager', and a strip of 'sanitized' paper across the lavatory seat. After a shower and a tepid, tourist breakfast on his balcony overlooking the beautiful beach, he had gone up to Government House at nine o'clock for a meeting with the Commissioner of Police, the Chief of Immigration and Customs, and the Deputy Governor. It was exactly as he had imagined it would be. The MOST IMMEDIATES and the TOP SECRETS had made a superficial impact and he was promised full co-operation in every aspect of his assignment, but the whole business was clearly put down as a ridiculous flap and something that must not be allowed to interfere with the normal routine of running a small, sleepy colony, nor with the comfort and happiness of the tourists. Roddick, the Deputy Governor, a careful, middle-of-the-way man with a ginger moustache and gleaming pince-nez, had put the whole affair in a most sensible light. 'You see, Commander Bond, in our opinion — and we have most carefully debated all the possibilities, all the, er, angles, as our American friends would say — it is inconceivable that a large four-engined plane could have been hidden anywhere within the confines of the Colony. The only airstrip capable of taking such a plane — am I right, Harling? — is here in Nassau. So far as a landing on the sea is concerned, a, er, ditching I think they call it, we have been in radio contact with the Administrators on all the larger outer islands and the replies are all negative. The radar people at the meteorological station . . .'

Bond had interrupted at this point. 'Might I ask if the radar screen is manned round the clock? My impression is that the airport is very busy during the day, but that there is very little traffic at night. Would it be possible that the radar is not so closely watched at night?'

The Commissioner of Police, a pleasant, very military-looking man in his forties, the silver buttons and insignia on whose dark blue uniform glittered as they only can when spit and polish is a main activity and there are plenty of batmen around, said judiciously, 'I think the Commander has a point there, sir. The airport commandant admits that things do slacken off a bit when there's nothing scheduled. He hasn't got all that amount of staff and of course most of them are locals, sir. Good men, but hardly up to London Airport standards. And the radar at the met. station is only a G.C.A. set with a low horizon and range — mostly used for shipping.'

'Quite, quite.' The Deputy Governor didn't want to be dragged into a discussion about radar sets or the merits of Nassavian labour. 'There's certainly a point there. No doubt Commander Bond will be making his own inquiries. Now there was a request from the Secretary of State,' the title rolled sonorously forth, 'for details and comments on recent arrivals in the island, suspicious characters, and so forth. Mr Pitman?'

The Chief of Immigration and Customs was a sleek Nassavian with quick brown eyes and an ingratiating manner. He smiled pleasantly. 'Nothing out of the ordinary, sir. The usual mixture of tourists and businessmen and local people coming home. We were asked to have details for the past two weeks, sir.' He touched the briefcase on his lap. 'I have all the immigration forms here, sir. Perhaps Commander Bond would care to go through them with me.' The brown eyes flicked towards Bond and away. 'All the big hotels have house detectives. I could probably get him further details on any particular name. All passports were checked in the normal manner. There were no irregularities and none of these people was on our Wanted List.'

Bond said, 'Might I ask a question?'

The Deputy Governor nodded enthusiastically. 'Of course. Of course. Anything you like. We're all here to help.'

'I'm looking for a group of men. Probably ten or more. They probably stick together a good deal. Might be as many as twenty or thirty. I guess they would be Europeans. They probably have a ship or a plane. They may have been here for months or only a few days. I gather you have plenty of conventions coming to Nassau — salesmen, tourist associations, religious groups, heaven knows what all. Apparently they take a block of rooms in some hotel and hold meetings and so forth for a week or so. Is there anything like that going on at the moment?'

'Mr Pitman?'

'Well, of course we do have plenty of those sort of gatherings. Very welcome to the Tourist Board.' The Chief of Immigration smiled conspiratorially at Bond as if he had just given away a closely guarded secret. 'But in the last two weeks we've only had a Moral Rearmament group at the Emerald Wave and the Tiptop Biscuit people at the Royal Bahamian. They've gone now. Quite the usual convention pattern. All very respectable.'

'That's just it, Mr Pitman. The people I'm looking for, the people who may have arranged to steal this plane, will certainly take pains to look respectable and behave in a respectable fashion. We're not looking for a bunch of flashy crooks. We think these must be very big people indeed. Now, is there anything like that on the island, a group of people like that?'

'Well,' the Chief of Immigration smiled broadly, 'of course we've got our annual treasure hunt going on.'

The Deputy Governor barked a quick, deprecating laugh. 'Now steady on, Mr Pitman. Surely we don't want them to get mixed up in all this, or heaven knows where we shall end. I can't believe Commander Bond wants to bother his head over a lot of rich beachcombers.'

The Commissioner of Police said doubtfully, 'The only thing is, sir — they do have a yacht, and a small plane for the matter of that. And I did hear that a lot of shareholders in the swindle had come in lately. Those points do tally with what the Commander was asking about. I admit it's ridiculous, but this man Largo's respectable enough for Commander Bond's requirements and his men have never once given us trouble. Unusual to have not even one case of drunkenness in a ship's crew in nearly six months.'

And Bond had leapt at the flimsy thread and had pursued it for another two hours — in the customs building and in the Commissioner's office — and, as a result, he had gone walking in the town to see if he could get a look at Largo or any of his party or pick up any other shreds of gossip. As a result he had got a good look at Domino Vitali.

And now?

The taxi had arrived at the airport. Bond told the driver to wait and walked into the long low entrance hall just as the arrival of Larkin's flight was being announced over the Tannoy. He knew there would be the usual delay for customs and immigration. He went to the souvenir shop and bought a copy of the *New York Times*. In its usual discreet headlines it was still leading with the loss of the Vindicator. Perhaps it knew also about the loss of the atom bombs, because Arthur Krock, on the leader page, had a heavyweight column about the security aspects of the NATO alliance. Bond was half way through this when a quiet voice in his ear said, '007? Meet No. 000.'

Bond swung round. It was! It was Felix Leiter!

Leiter, his C.I.A. companion on some of the most thrilling cases in Bond's career, grinned and thrust the steel hook that was his right hand under Bond's arm. 'Take it easy, friend. Dick Tracy will tell all when we get out of here. Bags are out front. Let's go.'

Bond said, 'Well God damn it! You old so-and-so! Did you know it was going to be me?'

'Sure. C.I.A. knows all.'

At the entrance Leiter had his luggage, which was considerable, put aboard Bond's taxi, and told the driver to take it to the Royal Bahamian. A man standing beside an undistinguished-looking black Ford Consul saloon left the car and came up. 'Mr Larkin? I'm from the Hertz company. This is the car you ordered. We hope she's what you want. You did specify something conventional.'

Leiter glanced casually at the car. 'Looks all right. I just want a car that'll go. None of those ritzy jobs with only room for a small blonde with a sponge bag. I'm here to do property work — not jazz it up.'

'May I see your New York licence, sir? Right. Then if you'll just sign here . . . and I'll make a note of the number of your Diner's Club card. When you go, leave the car anywhere you like and just notify us. We'll collect it. Have a good holiday, sir.'

They got into the car. Bond took the wheel. Leiter said that he'd have to practise a bit on what he called 'this Limey southpaw routine' of driving on the left, and anyway he'd be interested to see if Bond had improved his cornering since their last drive together.

When they were out of the airport Bond said, 'Now go ahead and tell. Last time we met you were with Pinkertons. What's the score?'

'Drafted. Just damned well drafted. Hell, anyone would think there was a war on. You see, James, once you've worked for C.I.A., you're automatically put on the reserve of officers when you leave. Unless you've been cashiered for not eating the codebook under fire or something. And apparently my old Chief,

Allen Dulles that is, just didn't have the men to go round when the President sounded the fire alarm. So I and twenty or so other guys were just pulled in — drop everything, twenty-four hours to report. Hell! I thought the Russians had landed! And then they tell me the score and to pack my bathing trunks and my spade and bucket and come on down to Nassau. So of course I griped like hell. Asked them if I shouldn't brush up on my Canasta game and take some quick lessons in the Cha-cha. So then they unbuttoned and told me I was to team up with you down here and I thought maybe if that old bastard of yours, N or M or whatever you call him, had sent you down here with your old equalizer, there might be something cooking in the pot after all. So I picked up the gear you'd asked for from Admin., packed the bow and arrows instead of the spade and bucket, and here I am. And that's that. Now you tell, you old sonofabitch. Hell, it's good to see you.'

Bond took Leiter through the whole story, point by point from the moment he had been summoned to M's office the morning before. When he came to the shooting outside his headquarters, Leiter stopped him.

'Now what do you make of that, James? In my book that's a pretty funny coincidence. Have you been fooling around with anybody's wife lately? Sounds more like around The Loop in Chicago than a mile or so from Piccadilly.'

Bond said seriously, 'It makes no sense to me, and none to anyone else. The only man who might have had it in for me, recently that is, is a crazy bastard I met down at a sort of clinic place I had to go to on some blasted medical grounds.' Bond, to Leiter's keen pleasure, rather sheepishly gave details of his 'cure' at Shrublands. 'I bowled this man out as a member of a Chinese Tong, one of their secret societies, the Red Lightning Tong. He must have heard me getting the gen on his outfit from Records — on an open line from a call box in the place. Next thing, he damned near managed to murder me. Just for a lark, and to get even, I did my best to roast him alive.' Bond gave the details. 'Nice quiet place, Shrublands. You'd be surprised how carrot juice seems to affect people.'

'Where was this lunatic asylum?'

'Place called Washington. Modest little place compared with yours. Not far from Brighton.'

'And the letter was posted from Brighton.'

'That's the hell of a long shot.'

'I'll try another. One of the points our chaps brought up was that if a plane was to be stolen at night and landed at night, a full moon would be the hell of an aid to the job. But the plane was taken five days after the full. Just supposing your roast chicken was the letter-sender. And supposing the roasting forced him to delay sending the letter while he recovered. His employers would be pretty angry. Yes?'

'I suppose so.'

'And supposing they gave orders for him to be rubbed for inefficiency. And supposing the killer got to him just as he got to you to settle his private account. From what you tell me he wouldn't have lain down under what you did to him. Well, now. Just supposing all that. It adds up, doesn't it?'

Bond laughed, partly in admiration. 'You've been taking mescalin or something. It's a damned good sequence for a comic strip, but these things don't happen in real life.'

'Planes with atom bombs don't get stolen in real life. Except that they do. You're slowing down, James. How many people would believe the files on some of the cases you and I have got mixed up in? Don't give me that crap about real life. There ain't no such animal.'

Bond said seriously, 'Well, look here, Felix. Tell you what I'll do. There's just enough sense in your story, so I'll put it on the machine to M tonight and see if the Yard can get anywhere with it. They could check with the clinic and the hospital in Brighton, if that's where he was taken, and they may be able to get on from there. Trouble is, wherever they get, there's nothing left of the man but his shoes, and I doubt if they'll catch up with the man on the motorbike. It looked a real pro job to me.'

'Why not? These hijackers sound like pros. It's a pro plan. It all fits all right. You go ahead and put it on the wire and don't be ashamed of saying it was my idea. My medal collection has got to looking a bit thin since I left the outfit.'

They pulled up under the portico of the Royal Bahamian and Bond gave the keys to the parking attendant. Leiter checked in and they went up to his room and sent for two double dry Martinis on the rocks and the menu.

From the pretentious dishes, 'For Your Particular Consideration', printed in Ornamental Gothic, Bond chose Native Seafood Cocktail Suprême followed by Disjointed Home Farm Chicken, Sauté au Cresson, which was described in italics as 'Tender Farm Chicken, Broiled to a Rich Brown, Basted with Creamery Butter and Disjointed for Your Convenience. Price 38/6 or dollars 5.35.' Felix Leiter went for the Baltic Herring in Sour Cream followed by 'Chopped Tenderloin of Beef, French Onion Rings (Our Renowned Beef is Chef Selected from the Finest Corn-fed, Mid-Western Cattle, and Aged to Perfection to Assure you of the Very Best). Price 40/3 or dollars 5.65.'

When they had both commented sourly and at length about the inflated bogosity of tourist hotel food and particularly the mendacious misuse of the English language to describe materials which had certainly been in various deep-freezes for at least six months, they settled down on the balcony to discuss Bond's findings of the morning.

Half an hour and one more double dry Martini later, their luncheon came. The whole thing amounted to about five shillings' worth of badly cooked rubbish. They ate in a mood of absent-minded irritation, saying nothing. Finally Leiter threw down his knife and fork. 'This is Hamburger and bad Hamburger. The French onion rings were never in France and what's more,' he poked at the remains with a fork, 'they're not even rings. They're oval.' He looked belligerently across at Bond. 'All right, Hawkshaw. Where do we go from here?'

'The major decision is to eat out in future. The next is to pay a visit to the *Disco* — now.' Bond got up from the table. 'When we've done that, we'll have to decide whether or not these people are hunting pieces of eight or £100,000,000. Then we'll have to report progress.' Bond waved at the packing cases in a corner of the room. 'I've got the loan of a couple of rooms on the top floor of police headquarters here. The Commissioner's co-operative and a solid character. These Colonial police are good, and this one's a cut above the rest. We can set up the radio there and make contact this evening. Tonight there's this party at the Casino. We'll go to that and see if any of these faces mean anything to either of us. The first thing's to see if the yacht's clean or not. Can you break that Geiger counter out?'

'Sure. And it's a honey.' Leiter went to the cases, selected one, and opened it. He came back carrying what looked like a Rolleiflex camera in a portable leather case. 'Here, give me a hand.' Leiter took off his wrist-watch and strapped on what appeared to be another watch. He slung the 'camera' by its strap over his left shoulder. 'Now run those wires from the watch up my sleeve and down inside my coat. Right. Now these two small plugs go through these holes in my coat pocket and into the two holes in the box. Got it? Now we're all fixed.' Leiter stood back and posed. 'Man with a camera and a wrist-watch.' He unbuttoned the flap of the camera. 'See? Perfectly good lenses and all that. Even a button to press in case you have to seem to take a picture. But in back of the make-believe there's a metal valve, a circuit, and batteries. Now take a look at this watch. And it is a watch.' He held it under Bond's eyes. 'Only difference is that it's a very small watch mechanism and that sweep second-hand is a meter that takes the radio-active count. Those wires up the sleeve hitch it on to the machine. Now then. You're still wearing that old wrist-watch of yours with the big phosphorous numerals. So I walk round the room for a moment to get the background count. That's basic. All sorts of things give off radiation of some sort. And I take an occasional glance at my watch — nervous type, and I've got an appointment coming up. Now here, by the bathroom, all that metal is giving off something and my watch is registering positive, but very little. Nothing else in the room and I've established the amount of background interference I'll have to discount when I start to get hot. Right? Now I come close up to you and my camera's only a few inches away from your hand. Here, take a look. Put your watch right up against the counter. See! The sweephand is getting all excited. Move your watch away and it loses interest. It's those phosphorous numerals of yours. Remember the other day one of the watch companies withdrew an air-pilots' watch from the market because the Atomic Energy people got fussy? Same thing. They thought this particular pilots' watch, with the big phosphorescent numerals, was giving off too much radiation to be good for the wearer. Of course,' Leiter patted the camera case, 'this is a special job. Most types give off a clicking sound and if you're prospecting for uranium, which is the big market for these machines, you wear earphones to try and pick up the stuff underground. For this job we don't need anything so sensitive. If we get near where those bombs are hidden, this damned sweephand'll go right off the dial. Okay? So let's go hire ourselves a sixpenny sick and pay a call on the ocean greyhound.'

13

'MY NAME IS EMILIO LARGO'

LEITER'S 'SIXPENNY SICK' was the hotel launch, a smart Chrysler-engined speedboat that said it would be 20 dollars an hour. They ran out westwards from the harbour, past Silver Cay, Long Cay and Balmoral Island, and round Delaporte Point. Five miles further down the coast, encrusted with glittering seashore properties the boatman said cost £400 per foot of beach frontage, they rounded Old Fort Point and came upon the gleaming white and dark blue ship lying with two anchors out in deep water just outside the reef. Leiter whistled. He said in an awestruck voice, 'Boy, is that a piece of boat! I'd sure like to have one of those to play with in my bath.'

Bond said, 'She's Italian. Built by a firm called Rodrigues at Messina. Thing called an *Aliscafo*. She's got a hydrofoil under the hull and when she gets going you let this sort of skid down and she rises up and practically flies. Only the screws and a few feet of the stern stay in the water. The Police Commissioner says she can do 50 knots in calm water. Only good for inshore work of course, but they can carry upwards of a hundred passengers when they're designed as fast ferries. Apparently this one's been designed for about forty. The rest of the space is taken up with the owner's quarters and cargo space. Must have cost damned near a quarter of a million.'

The boatman broke in, 'They say on Bay Street that she goin' go after the treasure these next few days or so. All the people that own share in the gold come in a few days ago. Then she spen' one whole night doin' a final recce. They say is down Exhuma way, or over by Watlings Island. Guess you folks know that's where Columbus make him first landfall on this side of the Atlantic. Around fourteen ninety somethin'. But could be anywhere down there. They's always been talk of treasure down 'mongst the Ragged Islands — even as far as Crooked Island. Fact is she sail out southward. Hear her myself, right until her engines died away. East by south-east I'da say.' The boatman spat discreetly over the side. 'Must be plenty heap of treasure with the cost of that ship and all the money they throwing 'way. Every time she go to the hoiling wharf they say the bill's five hundred pound.'

Bond said casually, 'Which night was it they did the final recce?'

'Night after she hoiled. That'd be two nights ago. Sail round six.'

The blank portholes of the ship watched them approach. A sailor polishing brass round the curve of the enclosed dome that was the bridge walked through the hatch into the bridge and Bond could see him talking into a mouthpiece. A tall man in white ducks and a very wide-mesh singlet appeared on deck and observed them through binoculars. He called something to the sailor, who came and stood at the top of the ladder down the starboard side. When their launch came alongside, the man cupped his hands and called down, 'What is your business please? Have you an appointment?'

Bond called back, 'It's Mr Bond, Mr James Bond. From New York. I have my attorney here. I have an inquiry to make about Palmyra, Mr Largo's property.'

'One moment please.' The sailor disappeared and returned accompanied by the man in white ducks and singlet. Bond recognized him from the police description. He called down cheerfully, 'Come aboard, come aboard.' He gestured for the sailor to go down and help fend the launch. Bond and Leiter climbed out of the launch and went up the ladder.

Largo held out a hand. 'My name is Emilio Largo. Mr Bond? And . . .?'

'Mr Larkin, my attorney from New York. Actually I'm English, but I have property in America.' They shook hands. 'I'm sorry to bother you, Mr Largo, but it's about Palmyra, the property I believe you rent from Mr Bryce.'

'Ah yes, of course.' The beautiful teeth gleamed warmth and welcome. 'Come on down to the stateroom, gentlemen. I'm sorry I am not properly dressed to receive you.' The big brown hands caressed his flanks, the wide mouth turned down in deprecation. 'My visitors usually announce themselves on the ship-to-shore. But if you will forgive the informality . . .' Largo allowed the phrase to die on the air and ushered them through a low hatch and down a few aluminium steps into the main cabin. The rubber-lined hatch hissed to behind him.

It was a fine large cabin panelled in mahogany with deep wine-red carpet and comfortable dark blue leather club chairs. The sun shining through the slats of venetian blinds over the broad square ports added a touch of gay light to an otherwise rather sombre and masculine room, its long centre table littered with papers and charts, glass-fronted cabinets containing fishing gear and an array of guns and other weapons, and a black rubber underwater diving suit and aqualung suspended, almost like the skeleton in a sorcerer's den, from a rack in one corner. The air-conditioning made the cabin deliciously cool, and Bond felt his damp shirt slowly freeing itself from his skin.

'Please take a chair, gentlemen.' Largo carelessly brushed aside the charts and papers on the table as if they were of no importance. 'Cigarettes?' He placed a large silver box between them. 'And now what can I get you to drink?' He went to the loaded sideboard. 'Something cool and not too strong perhaps? A Planter's Punch? Gin and tonic? Or there are various beers. You must have had a hot journey in that open launch. I would have sent my boat for you if only I had known.'

They both asked for a plain tonic. Bond said, 'I'm very sorry to barge in like this, Mr Largo. No idea I could have got you on the telephone. We just got in this morning and as I've only a few days I have to get a move on. The point is, I'm looking for a property down here.'

'Oh yes?' Largo brought the glasses and bottles of tonic to the table and sat down so that they formed a comfortable group. 'What a good idea. Wonderful place. I've been here for six months and already I'd like to stay for ever. But the prices they're asking —' Largo threw up his hands. 'These Bay Street pirates. And the millionaires, they are even worse. But you are wise to come at the end of the season. Perhaps some of the owners are disappointed not to have sold. Perhaps they will not open their mouths so wide.'

'That's what I thought.' Bond sat comfortably back and lit a cigarette. 'Or rather what my lawyer, Mr Larkin, advised.' Leiter shook his head pessimistically. 'He had made some inquiries and he frankly advised that real estate values down here have gone mad.' Bond turned politely towards Leiter to bring him into the conversation. 'Isn't that so?'

'Daft, Mr Largo, quite daft. Worse even than Florida. Out of this world. I wouldn't advise any client of mine to invest at these prices.'

'Quite so.' Largo obviously didn't want to get drawn too deeply into these matters. 'You mentioned something about Palmyra. Is there anything I can do to help in that respect?'

Bond said, 'I understand you have a lease of the property, Mr Largo. And there is talk that you may be leaving the house before long. Only gossip of course. You know what they are in these small islands. But it sounds more or less what I'm looking for and I gather the owner, this Englishman, Bryce, might sell if he got the right price. What I was going to ask you,' Bond looked apologetic, 'was whether we might drive out and look the place over. Some time when you weren't there of course. Any time that might suit you.'

Largo flashed his teeth warmly. He spread his hands. 'But of course, of course, my dear fellow. Whenever you wish. There is no one in residence but my niece and a few servants. And she is out most of the time. Please just call her up on the telephone. I shall tell her that you will be doing so. It is indeed a charming property — so imaginative. A beautiful piece of design. If only all rich men had such good taste.'

Bond got to his feet and Leiter followed suit. 'Well that's extraordinarily kind of you, Mr Largo. And now we'll leave you in peace. Perhaps we may meet again in the town some time. You must come and have lunch. But,' Bond poured admiration and flattery into his voice, 'with a yacht like this, I don't suppose you ever want to come ashore. Must be the only one on this side of the Atlantic. Didn't one used to run between Venice and Trieste? I seem to remember reading about it somewhere.'

Largo grinned his pleasure. 'Yes, that is right, quite right. They are also on the Italian lakes. For passenger traffic. Now they are buying them in South America. A wonderful design for coastal waters. She only draws four feet when the hydrofoil is operating.'

'I suppose accommodation's the problem?'

It is a weakness of all men, though not necessarily of all women, to love their material possessions. Largo said, with a trace of pricked vanity, 'No, no. I think you will find that is not so. You can spare five minutes? We are rather crowded at the moment. You have heard no doubt of our treasure hunt?' He looked sharply at them as a man would who expects ridicule. 'But we will not discuss that now. No doubt you do not believe in these things. But my associates in the affair are all on board. With the crew, there are forty of us. You will see that we are not cramped. You would like?' Largo gestured to the door in the rear of the stateroom.

Felix Leiter showed reluctance. 'You know, Mr Bond, that we have that meeting with Mr Harold Christie at five o'clock?'

Bond waved the objection aside. 'Mr Christie is a charming man. I know he won't mind if we are a few minutes late. I'd love to see over the ship if you're sure you can spare the time, Mr Largo.'

Largo said, 'Come. It will not take more than a few minutes. The excellent Mr Christie is a friend of mine. He will understand.' He went to the door and held it open.

Bond had been expecting the politeness. It would interfere with Leiter and his apparatus. He said firmly, 'Please go first, Mr Largo. You will be able to tell us when to duck our heads.'

With more affabilities, Largo led the way.

Ships, however modern, are more or less the same — the corridors to port and starboard of the engine room, rows of cabin doors, which Largo explained were occupied, the large communal bathrooms, the galley, where two cheerful-looking Italians in white smocks laughed at Largo's jokes about the food and seemed pleased with the visitors' interest, the huge engine room where the chief engineer and his mate, Germans it seemed, gave enthusiastic information about the powerful twin diesels and explained the hydraulics of the hydrofoil depressor — it was all exactly like visiting any other ship and saying the right things to the crew, using the right superlatives to the owner.

The short space of afterdeck was occupied by the little two-seater amphibian, painted dark blue and white to match the yacht, its wings now folded and its engine cowled against the sun, a big jolly-boat to hold about twenty men, and an electric derrick to hoist them in- and outboard. Bond, estimating the ship's displacement and her free-board, said casually, 'And the hold? More cabin space?'

'Just storage. And the fuel tanks of course. She is an expensive ship to run. We have to carry several tons. The ballast problem is important with these ships. When her bows come up, the fuel shifts aft. We have to have big lateral tanks to correct these things.' Talking fluently and expertly Largo led them back up the starboard passageway. They were about to pass the radio room when Bond said, 'You said you had ship-to-shore. What else do you carry? The usual Marconi short and long wave, I suppose. Could I have a look? Radio has always fascinated me.'

Largo said politely, 'Some other time, if you don't mind. I'm keeping the operator full time on met. reports. They're rather important to us at the moment.'

'Of course.'

They climbed up into the enclosed dome of the bridge, where Largo briefly explained the controls and then led them out on to the narrow deck space. 'So there you are,' said Largo. 'The good ship *Disco Volante* — the Flying Saucer. And she really does fly, I can assure you. I hope you and Mr Larkin will come for a short cruise one of these days. For the present,' he smiled with the hint of a secret shared, 'as you may have heard, we are rather busy.'

'Very exciting, this treasure business. Do you think you've got a good chance?'

'We like to think so.' Largo was deprecating. 'I only wish I could tell you more.' He waved an apologetic hand. 'Unfortunately, as they say, my lips are sealed. I hope you will understand.'

'Yes of course. You have your shareholders to consider. I only wish I was one so that I could come along. I suppose there's not room for another investor?'

'Alas no. The issue, as they say, is fully subscribed. It would have been very pleasant to have had you with us.' Largo held out a hand. 'Well, I see that Mr Larkin has been looking anxiously at his watch during our brief tour. We must not keep Mr Christie waiting any longer. It has been a great pleasure to meet you, Mr Bond. And you, Mr Larkin.'

With a further exchange of courtesies they went down the ladder to the waiting launch and got under way. There was a last wave from Mr Largo before he vanished through the hatch to the bridge.

They sat in the stern well away from the boatman. Leiter shook his head. 'Absolutely negative. Reaction around the engine room and the radio room, but that's normal. It was all normal, damnably normal. What did you make of him and the whole set-up?'

'Same as you — damned normal. He looks what he says he is, and behaves that way. Not much crew about, but the ones we saw were either ordinary crew or wonderful actors. Only two small things struck me. There was no way down to the hold that I could see, but of course it could have been a manhole under the passage carpet. But then how do you get the stores he talked of down there? And there's the hell of a lot of space in that hold even if I don't know much about naval architecture. I'll do a check with the oiling wharf through the customs people and see just how much fuel he does carry. Then it's odd that we didn't see any of these shareholders. It was around three o'clock when we went on board and most of them may have been having siestas. But surely not all nineteen of them. What do they do in their cabins all the time? Another small thing. Did you notice that Largo didn't smoke and that there was no trace of tobacco smell anywhere in the ship? That's odd. Around forty men and not one of them is a smoker. If one had anything else to go on one would say that wasn't coincidence but discipline. The real pros don't drink or smoke. But I admit it's a damned long shot. Notice the Decca Navigator and the echo-sounder? Pretty expensive bits of equipment both of them. Fairly normal on a big yacht of course, but I'd have expected Largo to point them out when he was showing us the bridge. Rich men are proud of their toys. But that's only clutching at straws. I'd have said the whole outfit's as clean as a whistle if it wasn't for all that missing space we weren't shown. That talk about fuel and ballast sounded a bit glib to me. What do you think?'

'Same as you. There's at least half of that ship we didn't see. But then again there's a perfectly good answer to that. He may have got a stack of secret treasure-hunting gear down there he doesn't want anyone to see. Remember that merchant ship off Gibraltar during the war? The Italian frogmen used it as a base. Big sort of trap door affair cut in the hull below the waterline. I suppose he hasn't got something like that?'

Bond looked sharply at Leiter. 'The *Olterra*. One of the blackest marks against Intelligence during the whole war.' He paused. 'The *Disco* was anchored in about forty feet of water. Supposing they'd got the bombs buried in the sand below her. Would your Geiger counter have registered?'

'Doubt it. I've got an underwater model and we could go and have a sniff round when it gets dark. But really, James,' Leiter frowned impatiently, 'aren't we getting a bit off beam — seeing burglars under the bed? We've got damn-all to go on. Largo's a powerful-looking piratical sort of chap, probably a bit of a crook where women are concerned. But what the hell have we got against him? Have you put a Trace through on him and on these shareholders and the crew members?'

'Yes. Put them all on the wire from Government House, Urgent Rates. We should get an answer by this evening. But look here, Felix,' Bond's voice was stubborn, 'there's a damned fast ship with a plane and forty men no one knows anything about. There's not another group or even an individual in the area who looks in the least promising. All right, so the outfit looks all right and its story seems to stand up. But just supposing the whole thing was a phoney — a damned good one of course, but then so it ought to be with all that's at stake. Take another look at the picture. These so-called shareholders all arrive just in time for June 3rd. On that night the *Disco* goes to sea and stays out till morning. Just supposing she rendezvous'd that plane in shallow water somewhere. Just suppose she picked up the bombs and put them away — in the sand under the ship, if you like. Anyway, somewhere safe and convenient. Just suppose all that and what sort of a picture do you get?'

'A B picture so far as I'm concerned, James.' Leiter shrugged resignedly. 'But I guess there's just enough to make it a lead.' He laughed sardonically. 'But I'd rather shoot myself than put it in tonight's report. If we're going to make fools of ourselves, we'd better do it well out of sight and sound of our Chiefs. So what's on your mind? What comes next?'

'While you get our communications going, I'm going to check with the oiling wharf. Then we'll call up this Domino girl and try and get ourselves asked for a drink and have a quick look at Largo's shore base — this Palmyra. Then we go to the Casino and look over the whole of Largo's group. And then,' Bond looked stubbornly at Leiter, 'I'm going to borrow a good man from the Police Commissioner to give me a hand, put on an aqualung and go out and have a sniff round the *Disco* with your other Geiger machine.'

Leiter said laconically, 'Destry Rides Again! Well, I'll go along with that, James. Just for old times' sake. But don't go and stub your toe on a sea urchin or anything. I see there are free Cha-cha lessons in the ballroom of the Royal Bahamian tomorrow. We've got to keep fit for those. I guess there'll be nothing else in this trip for my memory book.'

Back in the hotel, a dispatch rider from Government House was waiting for Bond. He saluted smartly, handed over an O.H.M.S. envelope and got Bond's signed receipt in exchange. It was a cable from the Colonial Office 'Personal to the Governor'. The text was prefixed PROBOND. The cable read: 'YOUR 1107 RECORDS HAVE NOTHING REPEAT NOTHING ON THESE NAMES STOP INFORMATIVELY ALL STATIONS REPORT NEGATIVELY ON OPERATION THUNDERBALL STOP WHAT HAVE YOU QUERY.' The message was signed 'PRISM', which meant that M had approved it.

Bond handed the cable to Leiter.

Leiter read it. He said, 'See what I mean? We're on a bum steer. This is a thumb-twiddler. See you later in the Pineapple Bar for a dry Martini that's half a jumbo olive. I'll go send a postcard to Washington and ask them to send down a couple of WAVES. We're going to have time on our hands.'

14
SOUR MARTINIS

AS IT TURNED OUT, the first half of Bond's programme for the evening went by the board. On the telephone, Domino Vitali said that it would not be convenient for them to see the house that evening. Her guardian and some of his friends were coming ashore. Yes it was indeed possible that they might meet at the Casino that evening. She would be dining on board and the *Disco* would then sail round and anchor off the Casino. But how would she be able to recognize him in the Casino? She had a very poor memory for faces. Would he perhaps wear a flower in his buttonhole or something?

Bond had laughed. He said that would be all right. He would remember her by her beautiful blue eyes. They were unforgettable. And the blue rinse that matched them. He had put the receiver down half way through the amused, sexy chuckle. He suddenly wanted to see her again very much.

But the movement of the ship altered his plans for the better. It would be much easier to reconnoitre her in the harbour. It would be a shorter swim and he would be able to go into the water under cover of the harbour police wharf. Equally, with her anchorage empty, it would be all the easier to survey the area where she had been lying. But if Largo moved the yacht about so nonchalantly was it likely the bombs, if there were any, would be hidden at the anchorage? If they were, surely the *Disco* would stand watch over them. Bond decided to put a decision aside until he had more, and more expert, information about the ship's hull.

He sat in his room and wrote his negative report to M. He read it through. It would be a depressing signal to get. Should he say anything about the wisp of a lead he was working on? No. Not until he had something solid. Wishful intelligence, the desire to please or reassure the recipient, was the most dangerous commodity in the whole realm of secret information. Bond could imagine the reaction in Whitehall where the Thunderball war-room would be ready, anxious to grasp at straws. M's careful 'I think we may conceivably have got a lead in the Bahamas. Absolutely nothing definite, but this particular man doesn't often go wrong on these things. Yes, certainly I'll check back and see if we can get a follow-up.' And the buzz would get around: 'M's on to something. Agent of his thinks he's got a lead. The Bahamas. Yes, I think we'd better tell the P.M.' Bond shuddered. The MOST IMMEDIATES would pour in to him: 'Elucidate your 1806.' 'Flash fullest details.' 'Premier wants detailed grounds for your 1806.' There would be no end to the flood. Leiter would get the same from C.I.A. The whole place would be in an uproar. Then, in answer to Bond's tatty little fragments of gossip and speculation, there would come the blistering: 'Surprised you should take this flimsy evidence seriously.' 'Futurely confine your signals to facts,' and, the final degradation, 'View speculative nature your 1806 and subsequents comma future signals must repeat must be joint and countersigned by CIA representative.'

Bond wiped his forehead. He unlocked the case containing his cipher machine, transposed his text, checked it again and went off to police headquarters where Leiter was sitting at his keyboard, the sweat of concentration pouring down his neck. Ten minutes later Leiter took off his earphones and handed over to Bond. He mopped his face with an already drenched handkerchief. 'First it's sunspots and I had to swap over to the emergency wavelength. There I found they'd put a baboon on the other end — you know, one of the one that can write the whole of Shakespeare if you leave him at it long enough.' He angrily waved several pages of cipher groups. 'Now I've got to unscramble all this. Probably from Accounts about how much extra income tax this sunshine trip will cost me.' He sat down at a table and began cranking away at his machine.

Bond put his short message over quickly. He could see it being punched out on the tapes in one of those busy rooms on the eighth floor, going to the supervisor, being marked 'Personal for M, copy to OO Section and Records', then another girl hurrying off down the passage with the flimsy yellow forms on a clip file. He queried whether there was anything for him and signed off. He left Leiter and went down to the Commissioner's room.

Harling was sitting at his desk with his coat off, dictating to a police sergeant. He dismissed him, pushed a box of cigarettes over his desk to Bond and lit one himself. He smiled quizzically. 'Any progress?'

Bond told him that the Trace on the Largo group had been negative and that they had called on Largo and gone over the *Disco* with a Geiger counter. This also had been negative. Bond still wasn't satisfied. He told the Commissioner what he wanted to know about the fuel capacity of the *Disco* and the exact location of the fuel tanks. The Commissioner nodded amiably and picked up the telephone. He asked for a Sergeant Molony of the harbour police. He cradled the receiver and explained, 'We check all fuelling. This is a narrow harbour crammed with small craft, deep-sea fishing boats and so on. Quite a fire hazard if something went wrong. We like to know what everyone is carrying and whereabouts in the ship. Just in case there's some fire-fighting to be done or we want a particular ship to get out of range in a hurry.' He went back to the telephone. 'Sergeant Molony?' He repeated Bond's questions, listened, said thank-you, and put the receiver down. 'She carries a maximum of 500 gallons of diesel. Took that amount on on the afternoon of June 2nd. She also carries about forty gallons of lubricating oil and a hundred gallons of drinking water — all carried amidships just forrard of the engine room. That what you want?'

This made nonsense of Largo's talk of lateral tanks and the difficult ballast problem and so forth. Of course he could have wanted to keep some secret treasure-hunting gear out of sight of the visitors, but at least there *was* something on board he wanted to hide, and, for all his show of openness, it was now established that Mr Largo might be a rich treasure hunter, but he was also an unreliable witness. Now Bond's mind was made up. It was the hull of the ship he wanted to have a look at. Leiter's mention of the *Olterra* had been a long shot, but it just might pay off.

Bond passed on a guarded version of his thoughts to the Commissioner. He told him where the *Disco* would be lying that night. Was there on the force a totally reliable man who could give him a hand with his underwater recce, and was there a sound aqualung, fully charged, available?

Harling gently asked if this was wise. He didn't exactly know the laws of trespass, but these seemed to be good citizens and they were certainly good spenders. Largo was very popular with everyone. Any kind of scandal, particularly if the police was involved, would create the hell of a stink in the Colony.

Bond said firmly, 'I'm sorry, Commissioner. I quite see your point. But these risks have to be run and I've got a job to do. Surely the Secretary of State's instructions are sufficient authority,' Bond fired his broadside, 'I could get specific orders from him, or from the Prime Minister for the matter of that, in about an hour if you feel it's necessary.'

The Commissioner shook his head. He smiled. 'No need to use the big guns, Commander. Of course you shall have what you want. I was just giving you the local reaction. I'm sure the Governor would have given you the same warning. This is a small puddle here. We're not used to the crash treatment from Whitehall. No doubt we'll get used to it if this flap lasts long enough. Now then. Yes, we've got plenty of what you want. We've got twenty men in the Harbour Salvage Unit. Have to. You'd be surprised how often a small boat gets wrecked in the fairway, just where some cruise ship's going to anchor. And of course there's the occasional body. I'll have Constable Santos assigned to you. Splendid chap. Native of Eleuthera, where he used to win all the swimming prizes. He'll have the gear you want where you want it. Now just give me the details . . .'

Back in his hotel, Bond took a shower, swallowed a double Bourbon Old Fashioned and threw himself down on his bed. He felt absolutely beat — the plane trip, the heat, the nagging sense that he was making a fool of himself in front of the Commissioner, in front of Leiter, in front of himself, added to the dangers, and probably futile ones at that, of this ugly night swim, had built up tensions that could only be eased by sleep and solitude. He went out like a light — to dream of Domino being pursued by a shark with dazzling white teeth that suddenly became Largo, Largo who turned on him with those huge hands. They were coming closer, they reached slowly for him, they had him by the shoulder . . . But then the bell rang for the end of the round, and went on ringing.

Bond reached out a drugged hand for the receiver. It was Leiter. He wanted that Martini with the jumbo olive. It was nine o'clock. What the hell was Bond doing? Did he want someone to help with the zip?

The Pineapple Room was panelled in bamboo carefully varnished against termites. Wrought-iron pineapples on the tables and against the wall contained segments of thick red candle, and more light was provided by illuminated aquaria let into the walls and by ceiling lights enclosed in pink glass starfish. The Vinylite banquettes were in ivory white and the barman and the two waiters wore scarlet satin calypso shirts with their black trousers.

Bond joined Leiter at a corner table. They both wore white dinner jackets with their dress trousers. Bond had pointed up his rich, property-seeking status with a wine-red cummerbund. Leiter laughed. 'I nearly tied a gold-plated bicycle chain round my waist in case of trouble, but I remembered just in time that I'm a peaceful lawyer. I suppose it's right that you should get the girls on this assignment. I suppose I just stand by and arrange the marriage settlement and later the alimony. Waiter!'

Leiter ordered two dry Martinis. 'Just watch,' he said sourly.

The Martinis arrived. Leiter took one look at them and told the waiter to send over the barman. When the barman came, looking resentful, Leiter said, 'My friend, I asked for a Martini and not a soused olive.' He picked the olive out of the glass with the cocktail stick. The glass, that had been three-quarters full, was now half full. Leiter said mildly, 'This was being done to me while the only drink you knew was milk. I'd learned the basic economics of your business by the time you'd graduated to Coca-Cola. One bottle of Gordon's gin contains sixteen true measures — double measures that is, the only ones I drink. Cut the gin with three ounces of water and that makes it up to twenty-two. Have a jigger glass with a big steal in the bottom and a bottle of these fat olives and you've got around twenty-eight measures. Bottle of gin here costs only two dollars retail, let's say around a dollar sixty wholesale. You charge eighty cents for a Martini, one dollar sixty for two. Same price as a whole bottle of gin. And with your twenty-eight measures to the bottle, you've still got twenty-six left. That's a clear profit on one bottle of gin of around twenty-one dollars. Give you a dollar for the olives and the drop of vermouth and you've still got twenty dollars in your pocket. Now, my friend, that's too much profit, and if I could be bothered to take this Martini to the management and then to the Tourist Board, you'd be in trouble. Be a good chap and mix us two large dry Martinis without olives and with some slices of lemon peel separate. Okay? Right, then we're friends again.'

The barman's face had run through indignation, respect and then the sullenness of guilt and fear. Reprieved, but clutching at his scraps of professional dignity, he snapped his fingers for the waiter to take away the glasses. 'Okay, suh. Whatever you says. But we've got plenty overheads here and the majority of customers they doan complain.'

Leiter said, 'Well, here's one who's dry behind the ears. A good barman should learn to be able to recognize the serious drinker from the status-seeker who wants just to be seen in your fine bar.'

'Yassuh.' The barman moved away with Negro dignity.

Bond said, 'You got those figures right, Felix? I always knew one got clipped, but I thought only about a hundred per cent — not four or five.'

'Young man, since I graduated from Government service to Pinkertons, the scales have dropped from my eyes. The cheating that goes on in hotels and restaurants is more sinful than all the rest of the sin in the world. Anyone in a tuxedo before seven in the evening is a crocodile, and if he couldn't take a good bite at your pocketbook he'd take a good bite at your ear. The same goes for the rest of the consumer business, even when it's not wearing a tuxedo. Sometimes it gets me real mad to have to eat and drink the muck you get and then see what you're charged for it. Look at our damned lunch today. Six, seven bucks with fifteen per cent added for what's called service. And then the waiter hangs about for another fifty cents for riding up in the elevator with the stuff. Hell,' Leiter ran an angry hand through his mop of straw hair, 'just don't let's talk about it. I'm fit to bust a gut when I think about it.'

The drinks came. They were excellent. Leiter calmed down and ordered a second round. He said, 'Now let's get angry about something else.' He laughed curtly. 'Guess I'm just sore at being back in Government service again watching all the taxpayers' money going down the drain on this wild goose chase. Mark you, James,' there was apology in Leiter's voice, 'I'm not saying this whole operation isn't a true bill, hell of a —— mess in fact, but what riles me is that we should be a couple of arse-end Charlies stuck down on this sand-spit while the other guys have got the hot spots — you know, places where something really may be happening — or at least likely to happen. Tell you the truth, I felt like a damned fool gumshoeing round that feller's yacht this afternoon with my little Geiger toy.' He looked keenly at Bond. 'You don't find you grow out of these things? I mean it's all right when there's a war on. But it seems kinda childish when peace is bustin' out all over.'

Bond said doubtfully, 'Of course I know what you mean, Felix. Perhaps it's just that in England we don't feel quite as secure as you do in America. The war just doesn't seem to have ended for us — Berlin, Cyprus, Kenya, Suez, let alone these jobs with people like SMERSH that I used to get tangled up in. There always seems to be something boiling up somewhere. Now this damned business. Dare say I'm taking it all too seriously, but there's something fishy going on around here. I checked up on that fuel problem and Largo certainly told us a lie.' Bond gave the details of what he had learned at police headquarters. 'I feel I've got to make sure tonight. You realize there's only about seventy hours to go? If I find anything, I suggest tomorrow we take a small plane and really run a search over as much of the area as we can. That plane's a big thing to hide even under water. You still got your licence?'

'Sure, sure.' Leiter shrugged his shoulders. 'I'll go along with you. Of course I will. If we find anything, perhaps the signal I got this evening won't look so damned silly after all.'

So this was what had put Leiter into such a vile temper! Bond said, 'What was that?'

Leiter took a drink and gazed morosely into his glass. 'Well, for my money it's just so much more attitudinizing by those power-struck fatcats at the Pentagon. But that sheaf of stuff I was waving about was a circular to all our men on this job to say that the Army and the Navy and the Air Force are holding themselves ready to give full support to C.I.A. if anything turns up. Think of that, dammit!' Leiter looked angrily at Bond. 'Think of the waste of fuel and manpower that must be going on all over the world keeping all these units at readiness! Just to show you, know what I've been allocated as my striking force?'

Leiter gave a harsh, derisive laugh. 'Half-squadron of Super Sabre fighter bombers from Pensacola, and —' Leiter stabbed at Bond's forearm with a hard finger. 'And, my friend, the *Manta*! The —— *Manta*! Our latest —— atomic submarine!' When Bond smiled at all this vehemence, Leiter continued more reasonably: 'Mark you, it's not quite so idiotic as it sounds. These Sabres are on anti-submarine sweep duties anyway. Carrying depth charges. They have to be at readiness. And the *Manta* happens to be on some sort of a training cruise in the area, getting ready to go under the South Pole for a change I suppose, or some other damned promotion job to help along the Navy Estimates. But I ask you! Here's all these million dollars' worth of material on instant call from Ensign Leiter, commanding Room 201 in the Royal Bahamian Hotel! Not bad!'

Bond shrugged his shoulders. 'Seems to me your President is taking all this a bit more seriously than his Man in Nassau. I suppose our Chiefs of Staff have weighed in with our stuff on the other side of the Atlantic. Anyway, no harm in having the big battalions in the offing just in case Nassau Casino happens to be Target No.1. By the way, what ideas have your people got about these targets? What have you got in this part of the world that fits in with SPECTRE's letter? We've only got the joint rocket base at a place called North-West Cay at the eastern end of the Grand Bahamas. That's about 150 miles north of here. Apparently the gear and prototypes we and your people have got there would easily be worth £100,000,000.'

'The only possible targets I've been given are Cape Canaveral, the naval base at Pensacola and, if the party really is going to take place in this area, Miami for Target No. 2, with Tampa as a possible runner-up. SPECTRE used the words "a piece of property belonging to the Western Powers". That sounds like some kind of installation to me — something like the uranium mines in the Congo, for instance. But a rocket base would fit all right. If we've got to take this thing seriously, I'd lay odds on Canaveral or this place on Grand Bahama. Only thing I can't understand, if they've got these bombs, how are they going to transport them to the target and set them off?'

'A submarine could do it — just lay one of the bombs offshore through a torpedo tube. Or a sailing dinghy for the matter of that. Apparently exploding these things is no problem so long as they recovered all the parts from the plane. Apparently you'd just have to insert some kind of fuse thing in the right place between the T.N.T. and the plutonium, and screw the impact fuse off the nose and fit a time fuse that would give you time to get a hundred miles away.' Bond added casually, 'Have to have an expert who knows the drill of course, but the trip would be no problem for the *Disco*, for instance. She could lay the bomb off Grand Bahama at midnight and be back at anchor off Palmyra by breakfast time.' He smiled. 'See what I mean? It all adds up.'

'Nuts,' said Leiter succinctly. 'You'll have to do better than that if you want my blood pressure to go up. Anyway, let's get the hell out of here and go have ourselves some eggs and bacon in one of those clip joints on Bay Street. It'll cost us twenty dollars plus tax, but the *Manta* probably burns that every time her screws turn full circle. Then we'll go along to the Casino and see if Mr Fuchs or Signor Pontecorvo is sitting beside Largo at the blackjack table.'

15

CARDBOARD HERO

THE NASSAU CASINO is the only legal casino on British soil anywhere in the world. How this is justified under the laws of the Commonwealth no one can quite figure. It is leased each year to a Canadian gambling syndicate and their operating profits in the smart winter season are estimated to average around $100,000. The only games played are roulette, with two zeros instead of one, which increases the take to the house from the European 3.6 to a handsome 5.4; blackjack, or 21, on which the house makes between six and seven per cent; and one table of chemin de fer, whose cagnotte yields a modest five per cent. The operation is run as a club in a handsome private house on West Bay Street and there is a pleasant dance and supper room with a three-piece combo that plays old favourites in strict time, and a lounge bar. It is a well-run, elegant place that deserves its profit.

The Governor's A.D.C. had presented Bond and Leiter with membership cards, and after they had had coffee and a stinger at the bar they separated and went to the tables.

Largo was playing chemin de fer. He had a fat pile of hundred-dollar plaques in front of him and half a dozen of the big yellow thousand-dollar biscuits. Domino Vitali sat behind him chain-smoking and watching the play. Bond observed the game from a distance. Largo was playing expansively, bancoing whenever he could and letting his own banks run. He was winning steadily, but with excellent manners, and by the way people joked with him and applauded his coups he was obviously a favourite in the Casino. Domino, in black with a square-cut neckline and with one large diamond on a thin chain at her throat, was looking morose and bored. The woman on Largo's right, having bancoed him three times and lost, got up and left the table. Bond went quickly across the room and slid into the empty place. It was a bank of eight hundred dollars — the round sum being due to Largo making up the cagnotte after each play.

It is good for the banker when he has got past the third banco. It often means the bank is going to run. Bond knew this perfectly well. He was also painfully aware that his total capital was only 1,000 dollars. But the fact that everyone was so nervous of Largo's luck made him bold. And, after all, the table has no memory. Luck, he told himself, is strictly for the birds. He said, 'Banco.'

'Ah, my good friend Mr Bond.' Largo held out a hand. 'Now we have the big money coming to the table. Perhaps I should pass the bank. The English know how to play at railway trains. But still,' he smiled charmingly, 'if I have to lose I would certainly like to lose to Mr Bond.'

The big brown hand gave the shoe a soft slap. Largo eased out the pink tongue of playing card and moved it across the baize to Bond. He took one for himself and then pressed out one more for each of them. Bond picked up his first card and flicked it face up into the middle of the table. It was a nine, the nine of diamonds. Bond glanced sideways at Largo. He said, 'That is always a good start — so good that I will also face my second card.' He casually flicked it out to join the nine. It turned over in mid-air and fell beside the nine. It was a glorious ten, the ten of spades. Unless Largo's two cards also added up to nine or nineteen, Bond had won.

Largo laughed, but the laugh had a hard edge to it. 'You certainly make me try,' he said gaily. He threw his cards to follow Bond's. They were the eight of hearts and the king of clubs. Largo had lost by a pip — two naturals, but one just better than the other, the cruellest way to lose. Largo laughed hugely. 'Somebody had to be second,' he said to the table at large. 'What did I say? The English can pull what they like out of the shoe.'

The croupier pushed the chips across to Bond. Bond made a small pile of them. He gestured at the heap in front of Largo: 'So, it seems, can the Italians. I told you this afternoon we should go into partnership.'

Largo laughed delightedly. 'Well, let's just try once again. Put in what you have won and I will banco it in partnership with Mr Snow on your right. Yes, Mr Snow?'

Mr Snow, a tough-looking European who, Bond remembered, was one of the shareholders, agreed. Bond put in the eight hundred and they each put in four against him. Bond won again, this time with a six against a five for the table — once more by one point.

Largo shook his head mournfully. 'Now indeed we have seen the writing on the wall. Mr Snow, you will have to continue alone. This Mr Bond has green fingers against me, I surrender.'

Now Largo was smiling only with his mouth. Mr Snow suivied and pushed forward 1,600 dollars to cover Bond's stake. Bond thought: I have made 1,600 dollars in two coups, over five hundred pounds. And it would be fun to pass the bank and for the bank to go down on the next hand. He withdrew his stake and said, 'La main passe.' There was a buzz of comment. Largo said dramatically, 'Don't do it to me! Don't tell me the bank's going to go down on the next hand! If it does I shoot myself. Okay, okay, I will buy Mr Bond's bank and we will see.' He threw some plaques out on to the table — 1,600 dollars' worth.

And Bond heard his own voice say banco! He was bancoing his own bank — telling Largo that he had done it to him once, then twice, and now he was going to do it, inevitably, again!

Largo turned round to face Bond. Smiling with his mouth, he narrowed his eyes and looked carefully, with a new curiosity, at Bond's face. He said quietly, 'But you are hunting me, my dear fellow. You are pursuing me. What is this? Vendetta?'

Bond thought, I will see if an association of words does something to him. He said, 'When I came to the table I saw a spectre.' He said the word casually, with no hint at double meaning.

The smile came off Largo's face as if he had been slapped. It was at once switched on again, but now the whole face was tense, strained, and the eyes had gone watchful and very hard. His tongue came out and touched his lips. 'Really? What do you mean?'

Bond said lightly, 'The spectre of defeat. I thought your luck was on the turn. Perhaps I was wrong.' He gestured at the shoe. 'Let's see.'

The table had gone quiet. The players and spectators felt that a tension had come between these two men. Suddenly there was the smell of enmity where before there had been only jokes. A glove had been thrown down, by the Englishman. Was it about the girl? Probably. The crowd licked its lips.

Largo laughed sharply. He stitched gaiety and bravado back on his face. 'Aha!' His voice was boisterous again. 'My friend wishes to put the evil eye upon my cards. We have a way to deal with that where I come from.' He lifted a hand, and with only the first and little fingers outstretched in a fork, he prodded once, like a snake striking, towards Bond's face. To the crowd it was a playful piece of theatre, but Bond, within the strong aura of the man's animal magnetism, felt the ill-temper, the malevolence behind the old Mafia gesture.

Bond laughed good-naturedly. 'That certainly put the hex on me. But what did it do to the cards? Come on, your spectre against my spectre!'

Again the look of doubt came over Largo's face. Why again the use of this word? He gave the shoe a hefty slap. 'All right, my friend. We are wrestling the best of three falls. Here comes the third.'

Quickly his first two fingers licked out the four cards. The table had hushed. Bond faced his pair inside his hand. He had a total of five — a ten of clubs and a five of hearts. Five is a marginal number. One can either draw or not. Bond folded the cards face down on the table. He said, with the confident look of a man who has a six or a seven, 'No card, thank you.'

Largo's eyes narrowed as he tried to read Bond's face. He turned up his cards, flicked them into the middle of the table with a gesture of disgust. He also had a count of five. Now what was he to do? Draw or not draw? He looked again at the quiet smile of confidence on Bond's face — and drew. It was a nine, the nine of spades. By drawing another card instead of standing on his five and equalling Bond, he had drawn and now had a four to Bond's five.

Impassively Bond turned up his cards. He said, 'I'm afraid you should have killed the evil eye in the pack, not in me.'

There was a buzz of comment round the table. 'But if the Italian had stood on his five . . . ' 'I always draw on a five.' 'I never do.' 'It was bad luck.' 'No, it was bad play.'

Now it was an effort for Largo to keep the snarl off his face. But he managed it, the forced smile lost its twist, the balled fists relaxed. He took a deep breath and held out his hand to Bond.

Bond took it, folding his thumb inside his palm just in case Largo might give him a bone-crusher with his vast machine-tool of a hand. But it was a firm grasp and no more. Largo said, 'Now I must wait for the shoe to come round again. You have taken all my winnings. I have a hard evening's work ahead of me just when I was going to take my niece for a drink and a dance.' He turned to Domino. 'My dear, I don't think you know Mr Bond, except on the telephone. I'm afraid he has upset my plans. You must find someone else to squire you.'

Bond said, 'How do you do. Didn't we meet in the tobacconist's this morning?'

The girl screwed up her eyes. She said indifferently, 'Yes? It is possible. I have such a bad memory for faces.'

Bond said, 'Well, could I give you a drink? I can just afford even a Nassau drink now, thanks to the generosity of Mr Largo. And I have finished here. This sort of thing can't last. I mustn't press my luck.'

The girl got up. She said ungraciously, 'If you have nothing better to do.' She turned to Largo: 'Emilio, perhaps if I take this Mr Bond away, your luck will turn again. I will be in the supper room having caviar and champagne. We must try and get as much of your funds as we can back in the family.'

Largo laughed. His spirits had returned. He said, 'You see, Mr Bond, you are out of the frying pan into the fire. In Dominetta's hands you may not fare so well as in mine. See you later, my dear fellow. I must now get back to the salt mines where you have consigned me.'

Bond said, 'Well, thanks for the game. I will order champagne and caviar for three. My spectre also deserves his reward.' Wondering again whether the shadow that flickered in Largo's eyes at the word had more significance than Italian superstition, he got up and followed the girl between the crowded tables to the supper room.

Domino made for a shadowed table in the farthest corner of the room. Walking behind her, Bond had noticed for the first time that she had the smallest trace of a limp. He found it endearing, a touch of childish sweetness beneath the authority and blatant sex appeal of a girl to whom he had been inclined to award that highest, but toughest, French title — a *courtisane de marque*.

When the Clicquot rosé and fifty dollars' worth of Beluga caviar came — anything less, he had commented to her, would be no more than a spoonful — he asked her about the limp. 'Did you hurt yourself swimming today?'

She looked at him gravely. 'No. I have one leg an inch shorter than the other. Does it displease you?'

'No. It's pretty. It makes you something of a child.'

'Instead of a hard old kept woman. Yes?' Her eyes challenged him.

'Is that how you see yourself?'

'It's rather obvious isn't it? Anyway, it's what everyone in Nassau thinks.' She looked him squarely in the eyes, but with a touch of pleading.

'Nobody's told me that. Anyway, I make up my own mind about men and women. What's the good of other people's opinions? Animals don't consult each other about other animals. They look and sniff and feel. In love and hate, and everything in between, those are the only tests that matter. But people are unsure of their own instincts. They want reassurance. So they ask someone else whether they should like a particular person or not. And as the world loves bad news, they nearly always get a bad answer — or at least a qualified one. Would you like to know what I think of you?'

She smiled. 'Every woman likes to hear about herself. Tell me, but make it sound true, otherwise I shall stop listening.'

'I think you're a young girl, younger than you pretend to be, younger than you dress. I think you were carefully brought up, in a red-carpet sort of way, and then the red carpet was suddenly jerked away from under your feet and you were thrown more or less into the street. So you picked yourself up and started to work your own way back to the red carpet you had got used to. You were probably fairly ruthless about it. You had to be. You only had a woman's weapons and you probably used them pretty coolly. I expect you used your body. It would be a wonderful asset. But in using it to get what you wanted, your sensibilities had to be put aside. I don't expect they're very far underground. They certainly haven't atrophied. They've just lost their voice because you wouldn't listen to them. You couldn't afford to listen to them if you were to get back on that red carpet and have the things you wanted. And now you've got the things.' Bond touched the hand that lay on the banquette between them. 'And perhaps you've almost had enough of them.' He laughed. 'But I mustn't get too serious. Now about the smaller things. You know all about them, but just for the record, you're beautiful, sexy, provocative, independent, self-willed, quick-tempered, and cruel.'

She looked at him thoughtfully. 'There's nothing very clever about all that. I told you most of it. You know something about Italian women. But why do you say I'm cruel?'

'If I was gambling and I took a knock like Largo did and I had my woman, a woman, sitting near me watching and she didn't give me one word of comfort or encouragement I would say she was being cruel. Men don't like failing in front of their women.'

She said impatiently, 'I've had to sit there too often and watch him show off. I wanted you to win. I cannot pretend. You didn't mention my only virtue. It's honesty. I love to the hilt and I hate to the hilt. At the present time, with Emilio, I am half way. Where we were lovers, we are now good friends who understand each other. When I told you he was my guardian, I was telling a white lie. I am his kept woman. I am a bird in a gilded cage. I am fed up with my cage and tired of my bargain.' She looked at Bond defensively. 'Yes, it is cruel for Emilio. But it is also human. You can buy the outside of the body, but you cannot buy what is inside — what people call the heart and the soul. But Emilio knows that. He wants women for use. Not for love. He has had thousands in this way. He knows where we both stand. He is realistic. But it is becoming more difficult to keep to my bargain — to, to, let's call it sing for my supper.'

She stopped abruptly. She said, 'Give me some more champagne. All this silly talking has made me thirsty. And I would like a packet of Players —' she laughed — 'Please, as they say in the advertisements. I am fed up with just smoking smoke. I need my hero.'

Bond bought a packet from the cigarette girl. He said, 'What's that about a hero?'

She had entirely changed. Her bitterness had gone, and the lines of strain on her face. She had softened. She was suddenly a girl out for the evening. 'Ah, you don't know! My one true love! The man of my dreams. The sailor on the front of the packet of Players. You have never thought about him as I have.' She came closer to him on the banquette and held the packet under his eyes. 'You don't understand the romance of this wonderful picture — one of the great masterpieces of the world. This man,' she pointed, 'was the first man I ever sinned with. I took him into the woods, I loved him in the dormitory, I spent nearly all my pocket money on him. In exchange, he introduced me to the great world outside the Cheltenham Ladies' College. He grew me up. He put me at ease with boys of my own age. He kept me company when I was lonely or afraid of being young. He encouraged me, gave me assurance. Have you never thought of the romance behind this picture? You see nothing, yet the whole of England is there! Listen,' she took his arm eagerly, 'this is the story of Hero, the name on his cap badge. At first he was a young man, a powder monkey or whatever they called it, in that sailing ship behind his right ear. It was a hard time for him. Weevils in the biscuits, hit with marlinspikes and ropes' ends and things, sent up aloft to the top of all that rigging where the flag flies. But he persevered. He began to grow a moustache. He was fair-haired and rather too pretty,' she giggled, 'he may even have had to fight for his virtue, or whatever men call it, among all those hammocks. But you can see from his face — that line of concentration between his eyes — and from his fine head, that he was a man to get on.' She paused and swallowed a glass of champagne. The dimples were now deep holes in her cheeks. 'Are you listening to me? You are not bored having to listen about my hero?'

'I'm only jealous. Go on.'

'So he went all over the world — to India, China, Japan, America. He had many girls and many fights with cutlasses and fists. He wrote home regularly — to his mother and to a married sister who lived at Dover. They wanted him to come home and meet a nice girl and get married. But he wouldn't. You see, he was keeping himself for a dream girl who looked rather like me. And then,' she laughed, 'the first steamships came in and he was transferred to an ironclad — that's the picture of it on the right. And by now he was a bosun, whatever that is, and very important. And he saved up from his pay and instead of going out fighting and having girls he grew that lovely beard, to make himself look older and more important, and he set to with a needle and coloured threads to make that picture of himself. You can see how well he did it — his first windjammer and his last ironclad with the lifebuoy as a frame. He only finished it when he decided to leave the Navy. He didn't really like steamships. In the prime of life, don't you agree? And even then he ran out of gold thread to finish the rope round the lifebuoy, so he just had to tail it off. There, you can see on the right where the rope crosses the blue line. So he came back home on a beautiful golden evening after a wonderful life in the Navy and it was so sad and beautiful and romantic that he decided that he would put the beautiful evening into another picture. So he bought a pub at Bristol with his savings and in the mornings before the pub opened he worked away until he had finished and there you can see the little sailing ship that brought him home from Suez with his duffel bag full of silks and seashells and souvenirs carved out of wood. And that's the Needles Lighthouse beckoning him in to harbour on that beautiful calm evening. Mark you,' she frowned, 'I don't like that sort of bonnet thing he's wearing for a hat, and I'd have liked him to have put "H.M.S." before the "*Hero*", but you can see that would have made it lop-sided and he wouldn't able to get all the "*Hero*" in. But you must admit it's the most terrifically romantic picture. I cut it off my first packet, when I smoked one in the lavatory and felt terribly sick, and kept it until it fell to pieces. Then I cut off a fresh one. I carried him with me always until things went wrong and I had to go back to Italy. Then I couldn't afford Players. They're too expensive in Italy and I had to smoke things called Nazionales.'

Bond wanted to keep her mood. He said, 'But what happened to the hero's pictures? How did the cigarette people get hold of them?'

'Oh well, you see one day a man with a stove-pipe hat and a frock coat came into the hero's pub with two small boys. Here,' she held the packet sideways, 'those are the ones, "John Player & Sons". You see, it says that their Successors run the business now. Well they had one of the first motor-cars, a Rolls-Royce, and it had broken down outside the hero's pub. The man in the stove-pipe hat didn't drink of course — those sort of people didn't, not the respectable merchants who lived near Bristol. So he asked for ginger beer and bread and cheese while his chauffeur mended the car. And the hero got it for them. And Mr John Player and the boys all admired the two wonderful tapestry pictures hanging on the wall of the pub. Now this Mr Player was in the tobacco and snuff business and cigarettes had just been invented and he wanted to start making them. But he couldn't for the life of him know what to call them or what sort of a picture to put on the packet. And he suddenly had a wonderful idea. When he got back to the factory he talked to his manager and the manager came along to the pub and saw the hero and offered him a hundred pounds to let his two pictures be copied for the cigarette packet. And the hero didn't mind and anyway he wanted just exactly a hundred pounds to get married on.' She paused. Her eyes were far away. 'She was very nice, by the way, only thirty and a good plain cook and her young body kept him warm in bed until he died many years later. And she bore him two children, a boy and a girl. And the boy went into the Navy like his father. Well, anyway, Mr Player wanted to have the hero in the lifebuoy on one side of the packet and the beautiful evening on the other. But the manager pointed out that that would leave no room for all this' — she turned over the packet — 'about "Rich, Cool", and "Navy Cut Tobacco" and that extraordinary trade mark of a doll's house swimming in chocolate fudge with Nottingham Castle written underneath. So then Mr Player said, "Well then, we'll put one on top of the other." And that's just exactly what they did and I must say I think it fits in very well, don't you? Though I expect the hero was pretty annoyed at the mermaid being blanked out.'

'The mermaid?'

'Oh yes. Underneath the bottom corner of the lifebuoy where it dips into the sea, the hero had put a tiny mermaid combing her hair with one hand and beckoning him home with the other. That was supposed to be the woman he was going to find and marry. But you can see there wasn't room and anyway her breasts were showing and Mr Player, who was a very strong Quaker, didn't think that was quite proper. But he made it up to the hero in the end.'

'Oh, how did he do that?'

'Well you see the cigarettes were a great success. It was really the picture that did it. People decided that anything with a wonderful picture like that on the outside must be good and Mr

Player made a fortune and I expect his Successors did too. So when the hero was getting old and hadn't got long to live, Mr Player had a copy of the lifebuoy picture drawn by the finest artist of the day. It was just the same as the hero's except that it wasn't in colour and it showed him very much older, and he promised the hero that this picture too would always be on his cigarette packets, only on the inside bit. Here.' She pushed out the cardboard container. 'You see how old he looks? And one other thing, if you look closely, the flags on the two ships are flying at half mast. Rather sweet of Mr Player, don't you think, to ask the artist for that. It meant that the hero's first and last ships were remembering him. And Mr Player and his two sons came and presented it to him just before he died. It must have made it much easier for him don't you think?'

'It certainly must. Mr Player must have been a very thoughtful man.'

The girl was slowly returning from her dreamland. She said in a different, rather prim voice, 'Well thank you anyway for having listened to the story. I know it's all a fairy tale. At least I suppose it is. But children are stupid in that way. They like to have something to keep under the pillow until they're quite grown up — a rag doll or a small toy or something. I know that boys are just the same. My brother hung on to a little metal charm his nanny had given him until he was nineteen. Then he lost it. I shall never forget the scenes he made. Even though he was in the Air Force by then and it was the middle of the war. He said it brought him luck.' She shrugged her shoulders. There was sarcasm in her voice as she said, 'He needn't have worried. He did all right. He was much older than me, but I adored him. I still do. Girls always love crooks, particularly if they're their brother. He did so well that he might have done something for me. But he never did. He said that life was every man for himself. He said that his grandfather had been so famous as a poacher and a smuggler in the Dolomites that his was the finest tombstone among all the Petacchi graves in the graveyard at Bolzano. My brother said he was going to have a finer one still, and by making money the same way.'

Bond held his cigarette steady. He took a long draw at it and let the smoke out with a quiet hiss. 'Is your family name Petacchi then?'

'Oh yes. Vitali is only a stage name. It sounded better so I changed it. Nobody knows the other. I've almost forgotten it myself. I've called myself Vitali since I came back to Italy. I wanted to change everything.'

'What happened to your brother? What was his first name?'

'Giuseppe. He went wrong in various ways. But he was a wonderful flyer. Last time I heard of him he'd been given some high-up job in Paris. Perhaps that'll make him settle down. I pray every night that it will. He's all I've got. I love him in spite of everything. You understand that?'

Bond stabbed out his cigarette in the ashtray. He called for the bill. He said, 'Yes, I understand that.'

16

SWIMMING THE GAUNTLET

THE DARK WATER below the police wharf sucked and kissed at the rusty iron stanchions. In the latticed shadows cast through the ironwork by the three-quarter moon, Constable Santos heaved the single aqualung cylinder up on to Bond's back and Bond secured the webbing at his waist so that it would not snarl the strap of Leiter's second Geiger counter, the underwater model. He fitted the rubber mouthpiece between his teeth and adjusted the valve release until the air supply was just right. He turned off the supply and took out the mouthpiece. The music of the steel band in the Junkanoo night-club tripped gaily out over the water. It sounded like a giant spider dancing on a tenor xylophone.

Santos was a huge coloured man, naked except for his swimming trunks, with pectoral muscles the size of dinner plates. Bond said, 'What should I expect to see at this time of night? Any big fish about?'

Santos grinned. 'Usual harbour stuff, sah. Some barracuda perhaps. Mebbe a shark. But they's lazy an overfed with the refuse and muck from de drains. Dey won't trouble you — less you bleedin' that is. They'll be night-crawlin' things on the bottom — lobster, crab, mebbe a small pus-feller or two. The bottom's mostly seagrass on bits o' iron from wrecks an plenty of bottle and suchlike. Mucky, if you get me, sah. But the water's clear and you'll be hokay with this moon and the lights from the *Disco* to guide you. Tek you bout twelve, fifteen minute, I'da say. Funny ting. I been lookin' for an hour an dere's no watchman on deck an no one in the wheelhouse. An the bit o' breeze should hide you bubbles. Coulda give you an oxygen rebreather, but ah doan like dem tings. Them dangerous.'

'All right, let's go then. See you in about half an hour.' Bond felt for the knife at his waist, shifted the webbing and put the mouthpiece between his teeth. He turned on the air and, his fins slapping on the muddy sand, walked down and into the water. There he bent down, spat into his mask to prevent it steaming up, washed it out and adjusted it. Then he walked slowly on, getting used to the breathing. By the end of the wharf he was up to his ears. He quietly submerged and launched himself forward into an easy leg crawl, his hands along his flanks.

The mud shelved steeply and Bond kept on going down, until, at about forty feet, he was only a few inches above the bottom. He glanced at the big luminous figures on the dial of his watch — 12.10. He untensed himself and put his legs into an easy, relaxed rhythm.

Through the roof of small waves the pale moonlight flickered on the grey bottom, and the refuse — motor tyres, cans, bottles — cast black shadows. A small octopus, feeling his shock-wave, turned from dark brown to pale grey and squeezed itself softly back into the mouth of the oil-drum that was its home. Sea flowers, the gelatinous polyps that grow out of the sand at night, whisked down their holes as Bond's black shadow touched them. Other tiny night things puffed thin jets of silt out of their small volcanoes in the mud as they felt the tremor of Bond's passage, and an occasional hermit crab snapped itself back into its borrowed shell. It was like travelling across a moon landscape, on and under which many mysterious creatures lived minute lives. Bond watched it all, carefully, as if he had been an underwater naturalist. He knew that was the way to keep nerves steady under the sea — to focus the whole attention on the people who lived there and not try and probe the sinister grey walls of mist for imaginary monsters.

The rhythm of his steady progress soon became automatic, and while Bond, keeping the moon at his right shoulder, held to his course, his mind reached back to Domino. So she was the sister of the man who probably hijacked the plane! Probably even Largo, if Largo was in fact involved in the plot, didn't know this. So what did the relationship amount to? Coincidence. It could be nothing else. Her whole manner was so entirely innocent. And yet it was one more thin straw to add to the meagre pile that seemed in some indeterminate way to be adding up to Largo's involvement. And Largo's reaction at the word 'spectre'. That could be put down to Italian superstition — or it could not. Bond had a deadly feeling that all these tiny scraps amounted to the tip of an iceberg — a few feet of ice pinnacle, with, below, a thousand tons of the stuff. Should he report? Or shouldn't he? Bond's mind boiled with indecision. How to put it? How to grade the intelligence so that it would reflect his doubts? How much to say and how much to leave out?

The extrasensory antennae of the human body, the senses left over from the jungle life of millions of years ago, sharpen unconsciously when man knows that he is on the edge of danger. Bond's mind was concentrating on something far away from his present risks, but beneath his conscious thoughts his senses were questing for enemies. Now suddenly the alarm was sounded by a hidden nerve — Danger! Danger! Danger!

Bond's body tensed. His hand went to his knife and his head swivelled sharply to the right — not to the left or behind him. His senses told him to look to the right.

A big barracuda, if it is twenty pounds or over, is the most fearsome fish in the sea. Clean and straight and malevolent, it is all hostile weapon from the long snarling mouth in the cruel jaw that can open like a rattlesnake's to an angle of ninety degrees, along the blue and silver steel of the body to the lazy power of the tail-fin that helps to make this fish one of the five fastest sprinters in the sea. This one, moving parallel with Bond, ten yards away just inside the wall of grey mist that was the edge of visibility, was showing its danger signals. The broad lateral stripes showed vividly — the angry hunting sign — the gold and black tiger's eye was on him, watchful, incurious, and the long mouth was open half an inch so that the moonlight glittered on the sharpest row of teeth in the ocean — teeth that don't bite at the flesh, teeth that tear out a chunk and swallow and then hit and scythe again.

Bond's stomach crawled with the ants of fear and his skin tightened at his groin. Cautiously he glanced at his watch. About three more minutes to go before he was due to come up with the *Disco*. He made a sudden turn and attacked fast towards the great fish, flashing his knife in fast offensive lunges. The giant barracuda gave a couple of lazy wags of its tail and, when Bond turned back on his course, it also turned and resumed its indolent, sneering cruise, weighing him up, choosing which bit — the shoulder, the buttock, the foot — to take first.

Bond tried to recall what he knew about big predator fish, what he had experienced with them before. The first rule was not to panic, to be unafraid. Fear communicates itself to fish as it does to dogs and horses. Establish a quiet pattern of behaviour and stick to it. Don't show confusion or act chaotically. In the sea, untidiness, ragged behaviour, mean that the possible victim is out of control, vulnerable. So keep to a rhythm. A thrashing fish is everyone's prey. A crab or a shell thrown upside down by a wave is offering its underside to a hundred enemies. A fish on its side is a dead fish. Bond trudged rhythmically on, exuding immunity.

Now the pale moonscape changed. A meadow of soft seagrass showed up ahead. In the deep, slow currents it waved languidly, like deep fur. The hypnotic motion made Bond feel slightly seasick. Dotted sparsely in the grass were the big black footballs of dead sponges growing out of the sand like giant puffballs — Nassau's only export until a fungus had got at them and had killed the sponge crop as surely as myxomatosis has killed rabbits. Bond's black shadow flickered across the breathing lawn like a clumsy bat. To the right of his shadow, the thin black lance cast by the barracuda moved with quiet precision.

A dense mass of silvery small fry showed up ahead, suspended in mid-stream as if they had been bottled in aspic. When the two parallel bodies approached, the mass divided sharply, leaving wide channels for the two enemies, and then closing behind them into the phalanx they adopted for an illusory protection. Through the cloud of fish, Bond watched the barracuda. It moved majestically on, ignoring the food around it as a fox creeping up on the chicken run will ignore the rabbits in the warren. Bond sealed himself in the armour of his rhythm, transmitting to the barracuda that he was a bigger, a more dangerous fish, that the barracuda must not be misled by the whiteness of the flesh.

Amongst the waving grass, the black barb of the anchor looked like another enemy. The trailing chain rose from the bottom and disappeared into the upper mists. Bond followed it up, forgetting the barracuda in his relief at hitting the target and in the excitement of what he might find.

Now he swam very slowly, watching the white explosion of the moon on the surface contract and define itself. Once he looked down. There was no sign of the barracuda. Perhaps the anchor and chain had seemed inimical. The long hull of the ship grew out of the upper mists and took shape, a great Zeppelin in the water. The folded mechanism of the hydrofoil looked ungainly, as if it did not belong. Bond clung for a moment to its starboard flange to get his bearings. Far down to his left, the big twin screws, bright in the moonlight, hung suspended, motionless but somehow charged with thrashing speed. Bond moved slowly along the hull towards them, staring upwards for what he sought. He drew in his breath. Yes, it was there, the ridge of a wide hatch below the waterline. Bond groped over it, measuring. About twelve feet square, divided down the centre. Bond paused for a moment, wondering what was inside the closed doors. He pressed the switch of the Geiger counter and held the machine against the steel plates. He watched the dial of the meter on his left wrist. It trembled to show the machine was alive, but it registered only the fraction Leiter had told him to expect from the hull. Bond switched the thing off. So much for that. Now for home.

The clang beside his car and the sharp impact against his left shoulder were simultaneous. Automatically, Bond sprang back from the hull. Below him the bright needle of the spear wavered slowly down into the depths. Bond whirled. The man, his black rubber suit glinting like armour in the moonlight, was pedalling furiously in the water while he thrust another spear down the barrel of the CO_2 gun. Bond hurled himself towards him, flailing at the water with his fins. The man pulled back the loading lever and levelled the gun. Bond knew he couldn't make it. He was six strokes away. He stopped suddenly, ducked his head, and jack-knifed down. He felt the small shock-wave of the silent explosion of gas and something hit his foot. Now! He soared up below the man and scythed upwards with his knife. The blade went in. He felt the black rubber against his hand. Then the butt of the gun hit him behind the ear and a white hand came down and scrabbled at his air-pipe. Bond slashed wildly with the knife, his hand moving with terrifying slowness through the water. The point ripped something. The hand let go of the mask, but now Bond couldn't see. Again the butt of the gun crashed down on his head. Now the water was full of black smoke, heavy, stringy stuff that clung to the glass of his mask.

Bond backed painfully, slowly away, clawing at the glass. At last it cleared. The black smoke was coming out of the man, out of his stomach. But the gun was coming up again slowly, agonizingly, as if it weighed a ton, and the bright sting of the spear showed at its mouth. Now the webbed feet were hardly stirring, but the man was sinking slowly down to Bond's level. Suspended straight in the water, he looked like one of those little celluloid figures in a Ptolemy jar that rise and fall gracefully with pressure on the rubber top to the jar. Bond couldn't get his limbs to obey. They felt like lead. He shook his head to clear it, but still his hands and flippers moved only half consciously, all speed gone. Now he could see the bared teeth round the other man's rubber mouthpiece. The gun was at his head, at his throat, at his heart. Bond's hands crept up his chest to protect him while his flippers moved sluggishly, like broken wings, below him.

And then, suddenly, the man was hurled towards Bond as if he had been kicked in the back. His arms spread in a curious gesture of embrace for Bond and the gun tumbled slowly away between them and disappeared. A puff of black blood spread out into the sea from behind the man's back and his hands wavered out and up in vague surrender while his head twisted on his shoulders to see what had done this to him.

And now, a few yards behind the man, shreds of black rubber hanging from its jaws, Bond saw the barracuda. It was lying broadside on, seven or eight feet of silver and blue torpedo, and round its jaws there was a thin mist of blood, the taste in the water that had triggered its attack.

Now the great tiger's eye looked coldly at Bond and then downwards at the slowly sinking man. It gave a horrible yawning gulp to rid itself of the shreds of rubber, turned lazily three-quarters on, quivered in all its length and dived like a bolt of white light. It hit the man on the right shoulder with wide open jaws, shook him once, furiously, like a dog with a rat, and then backed away. Bond felt the vomit rising in his gorge like molten lava. He swallowed it down and slowly, as if in a dream, began swimming with languid, sleepy strokes away from the scene.

Bond had not gone many yards when something hit the surface to his left and the moonlight glinted on a silvery kind of egg that turned lazily over and over as it went down. It meant nothing to Bond, but, two strokes later, he received a violent blow in the stomach that knocked him sideways. It also knocked sense into him and he began to move fast through the water, at the same time planing downwards towards the bottom. More buffets hit him in quick succession, but the grenades were bracketing the blood patch near the ship's hull and the shock-waves of the explosions became less.

The bottom showed up — the friendly waving fur, the great black toadstools of the dead sponges and the darting shoals of small fish fleeing with Bond from the explosions. Now Bond swam with all his strength. At any moment a boat would be got over the side and another diver would go down. With any luck he would find no traces of Bond's visit and conclude that the underwater sentry had been killed by shark or barracuda. It would be interesting to see what Largo would report to the harbour police. Difficult to explain the necessity for an armed underwater sentry for a pleasure yacht in a peaceful harbour!

Bond trudged on across the shifting seagrass. His head ached furiously. Gingerly he put up a hand and felt the two great bruises. The skin felt intact. But for the cushion of water, the two blows with the butt of the gun would have knocked him out. As it was, he still felt half stunned and when he came to the end of the seagrass and to the soft white moon landscape with its occasional little volcano puffs from the sea-worms he felt as if he was on the edge of delirium. Wild commotion at the edge of his field of vision shocked him out of the semi-trance. A giant fish, the barracuda, was passing him. It seemed to have gone mad. It was snaking wildly along, biting at its tail, its long body curling and snapping back in a jack-knife motion, its mouth opening wide and shutting again in spasms. Bond watched it hurtle away into the grey mist. He felt somehow sorry to see the wonderful king of the sea reduced to this hideous jiggling automaton. There was something obscene about it, like the blind weaving of a punchy boxer before he finally crashes to the canvas. One of the explosions must have crushed a nerve centre, wrecked some delicate balance mechanism in the fish's brain. It wouldn't last long. A greater predator than itself, a shark, would note the signs, the loss of symmetry that is suicide in the sea. He would follow for a while until the spasms slackened. Then the shark would make a short jabbing run. The barracuda would react sluggishly and that would be the end — in three great grunting bites, the head first and then the still jerking body. And the shark would cruise quietly on, its sickle mouth trailing morsels for the black and yellow pilot fish below his jaws and perhaps for the remora or two, the parasites that travel with the great host, that pick the shark's teeth when it is sleeping and the jaws are relaxed.

And now there were the grey-slimed motor tyres, the bottles, the cans and the scaffolding of the wharf. Bond slid over the shelving sand and knelt in the shallows, his head down, not capable of carrying the heavy aqualung up the beach, an exhausted animal ready to drop.

17

THE RED-EYED CATACOMB

BOND, PUTTING ON his clothes, dodged the comments of Constable Santos. It seemed there had been sort of underwater explosions, with eruptions on the surface, on the starboard side of the yacht. Several men had appeared on deck and there had been some kind of commotion. A boat had been lowered on the port side, out of sight of the shore. Bond said he knew nothing of these things. He had cracked his head against the side of the ship. Silly thing to do. He had seen what he had wanted to see and had then swum back. Entirely successful. The constable had been a great help. Thank you very much and good night. Bond would be seeing the Commissioner in the morning.

Bond walked with careful steadiness up the side street to where he had parked Leiter's Ford. He got to the hotel and telephoned Leiter's room and together they drove to police headquarters. Bond described what had happened and what he had discovered. Now he didn't care what the consequences might be. He was going to make a report. It was eight a.m. in London and there were under forty hours to go to zero hour. All these straws added up to half a haystack. His suspicions were boiling like a pressure cooker. He couldn't sit on the lid any longer.

Leiter said decisively, 'You do just that. And I'll file a copy to C.I.A. and endorse it. What's more I'm going to call up the *Manta* and tell her to get the hell over here.'

'You are?' Bond was amazed at this change of tune. 'What's got into you all of a sudden?'

'Well, I was sculling around the Casino taking a good look at anyone I thought might be a shareholder or a treasure hunter. They were mostly in groups, standing around trying to put up the front of having a good time — sunshine holiday and all that. They weren't succeeding. Largo was doing all the work, being gay and boyish. The others looked like private dicks or the rest of the Torrio gang just after the St Valentine Day massacre. Never seen such a bunch of thugs in my life — dressed up in tuxedos and smoking cigars and drinking champagne and all that — just a glass or two to show the Christmas spirit. Orders, I suppose. But all of them with that smell one gets to know in the Service, or in Pinkertons for the matter of that. You know, careful, cold-fish, thinking-of-something-else kinda look the pros have. Well, none of the faces meant anything to me until I came across a little guy with a furrowed brow and a big egg-head with pebble glasses who looked like a Mormon who's got into a whorehouse by mistake. He was peering about nervously and every time one of these other guys spoke to him he blushed and said what a wonderful place it was and he was having a swell time. I got close enough to hear him say the same thing to two different guys. Rest of the time he just mooned around, sort of helpless and almost sucking a corner of his handkerchief, if you get me. Well that face meant something to me. I knew I'd seen it before somewhere. You know how it is. So after puzzling for a bit I went to the reception and told one of the guys behind the desk in a cheery fashion that I thought I'd located an old classmate who'd migrated to Europe, but I couldn't for the life of me remember his name. Very embarrassing as he seemed to recognize me. Would the guy help? So he came along and I pointed this feller out and he went back to his desk and went through the membership cards and came up with the one I wanted. Seemed he was a man called Traut, Emil Traut. Swiss passport. One of Mr Largo's group from the yacht.' Leiter paused. 'Well I guess it was the Swiss passport that did it.' He turned to Bond. 'Remember a fellow called Kotze, East German physicist? Came over to the West about five years ago and sang all he knew to the Joint Scientific Intelligence boys? Then he disappeared, thanks to a fat payment for the info, and went to ground in Switzerland. Well, James. Take my word for it. That's the same guy. The file went through my hands when I was still with C.I.A. doing desk work in Washington. All came back to me. It was one hell of a scoop at the time. Only saw his mug on the file, but there's absolutely no doubt about it. That man's Kotze. And now what the hell is a top physicist doing on board the *Disco*? Fits doesn't it?'

They had come to police headquarters. Lights burned only on the ground floor. Bond waited until they had reported to the duty sergeant and had gone up to their room before he answered. He stood in the middle of the room and looked at Leiter. He said, 'That's the clincher, Felix. So now what do we do?'

'With what you got this evening, I'd pull the whole lot in on suspicion. No question at all.'

'Suspicion of what? Largo would reach for his lawyer and they'd be out in five minutes. Democratic processes of the law and so forth. And what single fact have we got that Largo couldn't dodge? All right, so Traut is Kotze. We're hunting for treasure, gentlemen, we need an expert mineralogist. This man offered his services. Said his name was Traut. No doubt he's still worried about the Russians getting after him. Next question? Yes, we've got an underwater compartment on the *Disco*. We're going to hunt treasure through it. Inspect it? Well, if you must. There you are, gentlemen — underwater gear, skids, perhaps even a small bathyscaphe. Underwater sentry? Of course. People have spent six months trying to find out what we're after, how we're going to get it. We're professionals, gentlemen. We like to keep our secrets. And anyway, what was this Mr Bond, this rich gentleman looking for a property in Nassau, doing underneath my ship in the middle of the night? Petacchi? Never heard of him. Don't care what Miss Vitali's family name was. Always known her as Vitali . . .' Bond made a throwaway gesture with one hand. 'See what I mean? This treasure-hunting cover is perfect. It explains everything. And what are we left with? Largo pulls himself up to his full height and says, "Thanks, gentlemen. So I may go now? And so I shall, within the hour. I shall find another base for my work and you will be hearing from my lawyers forthwith — wrongful detention and trespass. And good luck to your tourist trade, gentlemen." ' Bond smiled grimly. 'See what I mean?'

Leiter said impatiently, 'So what do we do? Limpet mine? Send her to the bottom — in error, so to speak?'

'No. We're going to wait.' At the expression on Leiter's face, Bond held up a hand. 'We're going to send our report, in careful, guarded terms so we don't get an airborne division landing on Windsor Field. And we're going to say the *Manta* is all we need. And so it is. With her, we can keep tabs on the *Disco* just as we please. And we'll stay under cover, keep a hidden watch on the yacht and see what happens. At present we're not suspected. Largo's plan, if there is one, that is, and don't forget this treasure-hunting business still covers everything perfectly well, is going along all right. All he's got to do now is collect the bombs and make for Target No. 1 ready for zero hour in around thirty hours' time. We can do absolutely nothing to him until he's got one or both of those bombs on board or we catch him at their hiding place. Now, that can't be far away. Nor can the Vindicator, if she's hereabouts. So tomorrow we take that amphibian they've got for us and hunt the area inside a radius of a hundred miles. We'll hunt the seas and not the land. She must be in shoal water somewhere and damned well hidden. With this calm weather, we should be able to locate her — if she's here. Now, come on! Let's get those reports off and get some sleep. And say we're out of communication for ten hours. And disconnect your telephone when you get back to your room. However careful we are, this signal is going to set the Potomac on fire as well as the Thames.'

Six hours later, in the crystal light of early morning, they were out at Windsor Field and the ground crew was hauling the little Grumman amphibian out of the hangar with a jeep. They had climbed on board and Leiter was gunning the engines when a uniformed motorcycle dispatch rider came driving uncertainly towards them across the tarmac.

Bond said, 'Get going! Quick! Here comes paper-work.'

Leiter released the brakes and taxi'd fast towards the single north–south runway. The radio crackled angrily. Leiter took a careful look over the sky. It was clear. He slowly pushed down on the joystick and the little plane snarled its way faster and faster down the concrete and, with a final bump, soared off over the low bush. The radio still crackled. Leiter reached up and switched it off.

Bond sat with the Admiralty chart on his lap. They were flying north. They had decided to start with the Grand Bahama group and have a first look at the possible area of Target No. 1. They flew at a thousand feet. Below them the Berry Islands were a necklace of brown spits set in cream and emerald and turquoise. 'See what I mean?' said Bond. 'You can see anything big through that water down to fifty feet. Anything as big as the Vindicator would have been spotted anywhere on any of the air routes. So I've marked off the areas where there's the minimum traffic. They'd have ditched somewhere well out of the way. Assuming, and it's the hell of an assumption, that, when the *Disco* made off to the south-east on the night of the third, it was a ruse, it'll be reasonable to hunt to the north and the west. She was away eight hours. Two of those would have been at anchor doing the salvage work. That leaves six hours' sailing at around thirty knots. Cut an hour off for laying the false trail, and that leaves five. I've marked off an area from the Grand Bahamas down to south of the Bimini Group. That fits — if anything fits.'

'Did you get on to the Commissioner?'

'Yes. He's going to have a couple of good men with day-and-night glasses keeping an eye on the *Disco*. If she moves from her Palmyra anchorage where she's due back at midday, and if we're not back in time, he'll have her shadowed by one of the Bahama Airways charter planes. I got him quite worried with just one or two bits of information. He wanted to go to the Governor with the story. I said not yet. He's a good man. Just doesn't want too much responsibility without someone else's okay. I used the P.M.'s name to keep him quiet until we get back. He'll play all right. When do you think the *Manta* could be here?'

'S'evening, I'd say.' Leiter's voice was uneasy. 'I must have been drunk last night to have sent for her. Christ, we're creating one hell of a flap, James. It doesn't look too good in the cold light of dawn. Anyway, what the hell? There's Grand Bahama coming up dead ahead. Want me to give the rocket base a buzz? Prohibited flying area, but we might as well go in up to our ears while we're about it. Just listen to the bawling out we'll be getting in just a minute or two.' He reached up and switched on the radio.

They flew eastwards along the fifty miles of beautiful coast towards what looked like a small city of aluminium hutments amongst which red and white and silver structures rose like small skyscrapers above the low roofs. 'That's it,' said Leiter. 'See the yellow warning balloons at the corners of the base? Warning to aircraft and fishermen. There's a flight test on this morning. Better get out to sea a bit and keep south. If it's a full test, they'll be firing towards Ascension Island — about five thousand miles east. Off the African coast. Don't want to get an

Atlas missile up our backsides. Look over there to the left — sticking up like a pencil beside that red and white gantry! Atlas or a Titan — intercontinental. Or might be a prototype Polaris. The other two gantries'll be for Matador and Snark and perhaps your Thunderbird. That big gun thing, like a howitzer, that's the camera tracker. The two saucer-shaped reflectors are the radar screen. Golly! One of them's turning away towards us! We're going to get hell in a minute. That strip of concrete down the middle of the island. That's the skid strip for bringing in missiles that are recallable. Can't see the central control for telemetering and guidance and destruction of the things if they go mad. That'll be underground — one of those squat blockhouse things. Some brass hat'll be sitting down there with his staff getting all set for the count-down or whatever's going to happen and telling someone to do something about that goddam little plane that's fouling up the works.'

Above their heads the radio crackled. A metallic voice said, 'N/AKOI, N/AKOI. You're in a prohibited area. Can you hear me? Change course southwards immediately. N/AKOI. This is Grand Bahama Rocket Base. Keep clear. Keep clear.'

Leiter said, 'Oh hell! No use interfering with world progress. Anyway we've seen all we want. No good getting on the Windsor Field report to add to our troubles.' He banked the little plane sharply. 'But you see what I mean? If that little heap of ironmongery isn't worth a quarter of a billion dollars my name's P. Rick. And it's just about a hundred miles from Nassau. Perfect for the *Disco*.'

The radio started again: 'N/AKOI, N/AKOI. You will be reported for entering a prohibited area and for failing to acknowledge. Keep flying south and watch out for sudden turbulence. Over.' The radio went silent.

Leiter said, 'That means they're going to fire a test. Keep an eye on them and let me know when. I'll cut down the revs. No harm in watching ten million dollars of the taxpayer's money being blown off. Look! The radar scanner's turned back to the east. They'll be sweating it out in that block-house all right. I've seen 'em at it. Lights'll be blinking all over the big board way down underground. The kibitzers'll be at their periscopes. Voices'll come down over the P.A. System. "Beacon contact . . . Warning balloons up . . . Telemeter contact . . . Tank pressure okay . . . Gyros okay . . . Rocket-tank pressure correct . . . Rocket clear . . . Recorders alive . . . Lights all green . . . Ten, nine, eight, seven, six . . . Fire!" '

Despite Leiter's graphic count-down, nothing happened. Then, through his glasses, Bond saw a wisp of steam coming from the base of the rocket. Then a great cloud of steam and smoke and a flash of bright light that turned red. Breathlessly, for there was something terrible in the sight, Bond gave the blow-by-blow to Leiter. 'It's edging up off the pad. There's a jet of flame. It seems to be sitting on it. Now it's going up like a lift. Now it's off! God, it's going fast! Now there's nothing but a spark of fire in the sky. Now it's gone. Whew!' Bond mopped his brow. 'Remember that Moonraker job I was on a few years back? Interesting to see what the people out front saw.'

'Yeah. You were lucky to get out of that deep fry.' Leiter brushed aside Bond's reminiscences. 'Now then, next stop those spits in the ocean north of Bimini and then a good run down the Bimini Group. Around seventy miles south-west. Keep an eye out. If we miss those dots, we'll end up in the grounds of the Fountain Blue in Miami.'

A quarter of an hour later, the tiny necklet of cays showed up. They were barely above the waterline. There was much shoal. It looked an ideal hiding place for the plane. They came down to a hundred feet and slowly cruised in a zig-zag down the group. The water was so clear that Bond could see big fish meandering around the dark clumps of coral and seaweed in the brilliant sand. A big diamond-shaped stingray cowered and buried itself in the sand as the black shadow of the plane pursued and shot over it. There was nothing else and no possibility of concealment. The green shoal waters were as clean and innocent as if they had been open desert. The plane flew on south to North Bimini. Here there were a few houses and some small fishing hotels. Expensive-looking deep-sea fishing craft were out, their tall rods streaming. Gay people in the well-decks waved to the little plane. A girl, sunbathing naked on the roof of a smart cabin cruiser, hastily snatched at a towel. 'Authentic blonde!' commented Leiter. They flew on south to the Cat Cays that trail away south from the Biminis. Here there was still an occasional fishing craft. Leiter groaned. 'What the hell's the good of this? These fishermen would have found it by now if it was here.' Bond told him to keep on south. Thirty miles further south there were little unnamed specks on the Admiralty chart. Soon the dark blue water began to shoal again to green. They passed over three sharks circling aimlessly. Then there was nothing — just dazzling sand under the glassy surface, and occasional patches of coral.

They went on carefully down to where the water turned again to blue. Leiter said dully, 'Well, that's that. Fifty miles on there's Andros. Too many people there. Someone would have heard the plane — if there was a plane.' He looked at his watch. '11.30. What next, Hawkshaw? I've only got fuel for another two hours' flying.'

Something was itching deep down in Bond's mind. Something, some small detail, had raised a tiny question-mark. What was it? Those sharks! In about forty feet of water! Circling on the surface! What were they doing there? Three of them. There must be something — something dead that had brought them to that particular patch of sand and coral. Bond said urgently, 'Just go back up once more, Felix. Over the shoals. There's something —'

The little plane made a tight turn. Felix cut down the revs and just kept flying speed about fifty feet above the surface. Bond opened the door and craned out, his glasses at short focus. Yes, there were the sharks, two on the surface with their dorsals out, and one deep down. It was nosing at something. It had its teeth into something and was pulling at it. Among the dark and pale patches, a thin straight line showed on the bottom. Bond shouted, 'Get back over again!' The plane zoomed round and back. Christ! Why did they have to go so fast? But now Bond had seen another straight line on the bottom, leading off at 90 degrees from the first. He flopped back into his seat and banged the door shut. He said quietly, 'Put her down over those sharks, Felix. I think this is it.'

Leiter took a quick glance at Bond's face. He said, 'Christ!' Then, 'Well, I hope I can make it. Damned difficult to get a true horizon. This water's like glass.' He pulled away, curved back and slowly put the nose down. There was a slight jerk and then the hiss of the water under the skids. Leiter cut his engines and the plane came to a quick stop, rocking in the water about ten yards from where Bond wanted. The two sharks on the surface paid no attention. They completed their circle and came slowly back. They passed so close to the plane that Bond could see the incurious, pink button eyes. He peered down through the small ripples cast by the two dorsal fins. Yes! Those 'rocks' on the bottom were bogus. They were painted patches. So were the areas of 'sand'. Now Bond could clearly see the straight edges of the giant tarpaulin. The third shark had nosed back a big section. Now it was shovelling with its flat head trying to get underneath.

Bond sat back. He turned to Leiter. He nodded. 'That's it, all right. Big camouflaged tarpaulin over her. Take a look.'

While Leiter leant across Bond and stared down, Bond's mind was racing furiously. Get the Police Commissioner on the police wavelength and report? Get signals sent off to London? No! If the radio operator on the *Disco* was doing his job, he would be keeping watch on the police frequency. So go on down and have a look. See if the bombs were still there. Bring up a piece of evidence. The sharks? Kill one and the others would go for the corpse.

Leiter sat back. His face was shining with excitement. 'Well, I'll be goddammed! Boy oh boy!' He clapped Bond on the back. 'We've found it! We've found the goddam plane. Whaddya know? Jesus Kerist!'

Bond had taken out the Walther PPK. He checked to see there was a round in the chamber, rested it on his left forearm and waited for the two sharks to come round again. The first was the bigger, a hammerhead, nearly twelve feet long. Its hideously distorted head moved slowly from side to side as it nuzzled through the water, watching what went on below, waiting for a sign of meat. Bond aimed for the base of the dorsal fin that cut through the water like a dark sail. It was fully erect, a sign of tension and awareness in the big fish. Just below it was the spine, unassailable except with a nickel-plated bullet. He pulled the trigger. There was a phut as the bullet hit the surface just behind the dorsal. The boom of the heavy gun rolled away over the sea. The shark paid no attention. Bond fired again. The water foamed as the fish reared itself above the surface, dived shallowly and came up thrashing sideways like a broken snake. It was a brief flurry. The bullet must have severed the spinal cord. Now the great brown shape began moving sluggishly in circles that grew ever wider. The hideous snout came briefly out of the water to show the sickle mouth gasping. For a moment it rolled over on its back, its stomach white to the sun. Then it righted itself and, dead probably, continued its mechanical, disjointed swim.

The following shark had watched all this. Now it approached cautiously. It made a short snapping run and swerved away. Feeling safe, it darted in again, seemed to nuzzle at the dying fish and then lifted its snout above the surface and came down with all its force, scything into the flank of the hammerhead. It got hold, but the flesh was tough. It shook its great brown head like a dog, worrying at the mouthful, and then tore itself away. A cloud of blood poured over the sea. Now the other shark appeared from below and both fish, in a frenzy, tore and tore again at the still moving hulk whose nervous system refused to die.

The dreadful feast moved away on the current and was soon only a distant splashing on the surface of the quiet sea.

Bond handed Leiter the gun. 'I'll get on down. May be rather a long job. They've got enough to keep them busy for half an hour, but if they come back, wing one of them. And if for any reason you want me back on the surface, fire straight down at the water and go on firing. The shock-wave should just about reach me.'

Bond began to struggle out of his clothes and, with Leiter's help, into his aqualung. It was a cramped, difficult business. It would be still worse getting back into the plane and it occurred to Bond that he would have to jettison the underwater gear. Leiter said angrily, 'I wish to God I could get down there with you. Trouble with this damned hook, it just won't swim like a hand. Have to think up some rubber webbing gadget. Never occurred to me before.'

Bond said, 'You'll have to keep steam up on this crate. We've already drifted a hundred yards. Get her back up, like a good chap. I don't know who I'm going to find sharing the wreck with me. It's been here a good five days and other visitors may have moved in first.'

Leiter pressed the starter and taxi'd back into position. He said, 'You know the design of the Vindicator? You know where to look for the bombs and these detonator things the pilot has charge of?'

'Yes. Full briefing in London. Well, so long. Tell Mother I died game!' Bond scrambled on to the edge of the cockpit and jumped.

He got his head under and swam leisurely down through the brilliant water. Now he could see that there were swarms of fish over the whole area below him — bill fish, small barracuda, jacks of various types — the carnivores. They parted grudgingly to make room for their big, pale competitor. Bond touched down and made for the edge of the tarpaulin that had been dislodged by the shark. He pulled out a couple of the long corkscrew skewers that secured it to the sand, switched on his waterproof torch and, his other hand on his knife, slipped under the edge.

He had been expecting it, but the foulness of the water made him retch. He clamped his lips more tightly round the mouthpiece and squirmed on to where the bulk of the plane raised the tarpaulin into a domed tent. He stood up. His torch glittered on the underside of a polished wing and then, below it, on to something that lay under a scrabbling mass of crabs, langoustes, sea caterpillars and starfish. This also Bond had been prepared for. He knelt down to his grisly work.

It didn't take long. He unclipped the gold identification disc and unlatched the gold wrist-watch from the horrible wrists and noted the gaping wound under the chin that could not have been caused by sea creatures. He turned his torch on the gold disc. It said 'Giuseppe Petacchi. No. 15932'. He strapped the two bits of evidence to his own wrists and went on towards the fuselage that loomed in the darkness like a huge silver submarine. He inspected the exterior, noted the rent where the hull had been broken on impact, and then climbed up through the open safety hatch into the interior.

Inside, Bond's torch shone everywhere into red eyes that glowed like rubies in the darkness and there was a soft movement and scuttling. He sprayed the light up and down the fuselage. Everywhere there were octopuses, small ones, but perhaps a hundred of them, weaving on the tips of their tentacles, sliding softly away into protecting shadows, changing their camouflage nervously from brown to a pale phosphorescence that gleamed palely in the patches of darkness. The whole fuselage seemed to be crawling with them, evilly, horribly, and as Bond shone his torch on the roof the sight was even worse. There, bumping softly in the slight current, hung the corpse of a crew member. In decomposition, it had risen up from the floor, and octopuses, hanging from it like bats, now let go their hold and shot, jet propelled, to and fro inside the plane — dreadful, glinting, red-eyed comets that slapped themselves into dark corners and stealthily squeezed themselves into cracks and under seats.

Bond closed his mind to the disgusting nightmare and, weaving his torch in front of him, proceeded with his search.

He found the red-striped cyanide canister and tucked it into his belt. He counted the corpses, noted the open hatch to the bomb bay and verified that the bombs had gone. He looked in the open container under the pilot's seat and searched in alternative places for the vital fuses for the bombs. But they also had gone. Finally, having a dozen times had to slash away groping tentacles from his naked legs, he felt his nerve was quickly seeping away. There was much he should have taken with him, the identification discs of the crew, the pulp of the log book that showed nothing but routine flight details and no hint of emergency, readings from the instrument panel, but he couldn't stand another second of the squirming, red-eyed catacomb. He slid out through the escape hatch and swam almost hysterically towards the thin line of light that was the edge of the tarpaulin. Desperately, he scrabbled his way under it, snagged the cylinder on his back in the folds and had to back under again to free himself. And then he was out in the beautiful crystal water and soaring up to the surface. At twenty feet the pain in his ears reminded him to stop and decompress. Impatiently, staring up at the sweet hull of the seaplane above him, he waited until the pain had subsided. Then he was up and clinging to a float and tearing at his equipment to get rid of it and its contamination. He let it all go and watched it tumbling slowly down towards the sand. He rinsed his mouth out with the sweetness of pure salt water and swam to within reach of Leiter's outstretched hand.

18

HOW TO EAT A GIRL

AS THEY APPROACHED Nassau on their way back, Bond asked Leiter to take a look at the *Disco* lying off Palmyra. She was there all right, just where she had been the day before. The only difference, which had little meaning, was that she had only her bow anchor out. There was no movement on board. Bond was thinking that she looked beautiful and quite harmless lying there reflecting her elegant lines in the mirror of the sea, when Leiter said excitedly, 'Say, James, take a look at the beach place. The boathouse alongside the creek. See those double tracks leading up out of the water? Up to the door of the boathouse. They look odd to me. They're deep. What could have made them?'

Bond focused his glasses. The tracks ran parallel. Something, something heavy, had been hauled between the boathouse and the sea. But it couldn't be, surely it couldn't! He said tensely, 'Let's get away quick, Felix.' Then, as they zoomed off overland, 'I'm damned if I can think of anything that could have made those. And dammit, if it was what it might have been, they'd have swept off those tracks pretty quick.'

Leiter said laconically, 'People make mistakes. We'll have to give that place the going-over. Ought to have done it before. Nice-looking dump. I think I'll take Mr Largo up on his invitation and get out there on behalf of my esteemed client, Mr Rockefeller Bond.'

It was one o'clock by the time they got back to Windsor Field. For half an hour the control tower had been searching for them on the radio. Now they had to face the commandant of the field and, providentially as it happened, the Governor's A.D.C., who gave the Governor's blanket authorization for the string of their misdemeanours and then handed Bond a thick envelope which contained signals for both of them.

The contents began with the expected rockets for breaking communication and demands for further news ('That they'll get!' commented Leiter as they raced towards Nassau in the comfortable back of the Governor's Humber Snipe saloon). E.T.A. for the *Manta* was five o'clock that evening. Inquiries through Interpol and the Italian police confirmed that Giuseppe Petacchi was in fact the brother of Dominetta Vitali, whose personal history as given to Bond stood up in all other respects. The same sources confirmed that Emilio Largo was a big-time adventurer and suspected crook though technically his dossier was clean. The source of his wealth was unknown but did not stem from funds held in Italy. The *Disco* had been paid for in Swiss francs. The constructors confirmed the existence of the underwater compartment. It contained an electric hoist and provision for launching small underwater craft and releasing skin-divers. In Largo's specifications, this modification to the hull had been given as a requirement for underwater research. Further inquiry into the 'shareholders' had yielded no further facts — with the significant exception that most of their backgrounds and professions dated back no further than six years. This suggested the possibility that their identities might be of recent fabrication and, at any rate in theory, this would equate with possible membership of SPECTRE, if such a body did in fact exist. Kotze had left Switzerland for an unknown destination four weeks previously. Latest photographs of the man were on the midday Pan American plane. Nevertheless the Thunderball war-room had to accept the solidity of Largo's cover unless further evidence came to hand, and the present intention was to continue the world-wide search while allotting priority to the Bahamas area. In view of this priority, and the extremely urgent time factor, Brigadier Fairchild, C.B., D.S.O., British Military Attaché in Washington, with Rear Admiral Carlson, U.S.N. Ret., until recently Secretary to the U.S. Chiefs of Staff Committee, would be arriving at 1900 E.S.T. by the President's Boeing 707, 'Columbine', to take joint command of further operations. The full co-operation of Messrs Bond and Leiter was requested and, until the arrival of the above-named officers, full reports every hour on the hour were to be radioed to London, copy to Washington, under joint signature.

Leiter and Bond looked at each other in silence. Finally Leiter said, 'James, I propose we disregard the last bit and take formal note of the remainder. We've already missed four hours and I don't propose we spend the rest of the day sweating it out in our radio room. There's just too much to do. Tell you what. I'll do the stint of telling them the latest and then I'll say we're going off the air in view of the new emergency. I then propose to go and look over Palmyra on your behalf, sticking to our cover story. And I propose to have a damned good look at the boathouse and see what those tracks mean. Right? Then, at five, we'll rendezvous with the *Manta* and prepare to intercept the *Disco* if and when she sails. As for the Big Brass in the President's Special, well they can just play pinocle in Government House until tomorrow morning. Tonight's the night and we just can't waste it on the "After you Alphonse" routine. Okay?'

Bond reflected. They were coming into the outskirts of Nassau, through the shanty-town slums tucked away behind the millionaire façade along the waterfront. He had disobeyed many orders in his life, but this was to disobey the Prime Minister of England and the President of the United States — a mighty left and right. But things were moving a damned sight too fast. M had given him this territory and, right or wrong, M would back him up, as he always backed up his staff, even if it meant M's own head on a charger. Bond said, 'I agree, Felix. With the *Manta* we can manage this on our own. The vital thing is to find out when those bombs go on board the *Disco*. I've got an idea for that. May work, may not. It means giving the Vitali girl a rough time, but I'll try and handle that side. Drop me at the hotel and I'll get cracking. Meet you here again around four thirty. I'll call up Harling and see if he's got anything new on the *Disco* and ask him to pass the word upstairs to you if anything's cooking. You've got all that straight about the plane? Okay. I'll hang on to Petacchi's identification disc for the time being. Be seeing you.'

Bond almost ran through the lobby of the hotel. When he picked up his key at the reception desk they gave him a telephone message. He read it going up in the lift. It was from Domino: 'Please telephone quickly.'

In his room, Bond first ordered a club sandwich and a double Bourbon on the rocks and then called the Police Commissioner. The *Disco* had moved to the oiling wharf at first light and had filled her tanks. Then she had moved back to her anchorage off Palmyra. Half an hour ago, at one thirty precisely, the seaplane had been lowered over the side and, with Largo and one other on board, had taken off eastwards. When the Commissioner had heard this on the walkie-talkie from his watchers he had got on to the control tower at Windsor Field and had asked for the plane to be radar-tracked. But she had flown low, at about 300 feet, and they had lost her among the islands about fifty miles to the south-east. Nothing else had come up except that the harbour authorities had been alerted to expect an American submarine, the *Manta*, the nuclear-powered one, at around five in the evening. That was all. What did Bond know?

Bond said carefully that it was too early to tell. It looked as if the operation was hotting up. Could the watchers be asked to rush the news back as soon as the seaplane was sighted coming back to the *Disco*? This was vital. Would the Commissioner please pass on his news to Felix Leiter who was on his way to the radio room at that moment? And could Bond be lent a car — anything — to drive himself? Yes, a Land-Rover would be fine. Anything with four wheels.

Then Bond got on to Domino out at Palmyra. She sounded eager for his voice. 'Where have you been all morning, James?' — it was the first time she had used his Christian name — 'I want you to come swimming this afternoon. I have been told to pack and come on board this evening. Emilio says they are going after the treasure tonight. Isn't it nice of him to take me? But it's a dead secret, so don't tell anyone, will you. But he is vague about when we will be back. He said something about Miami. I thought' — she hesitated — 'I thought you might have gone back to New York by the time we get back. I have seen so little of you. You left so suddenly last night. What was it?'

'I suddenly got a headache. Touch of the sun I suppose. It had been quite a day. I didn't want to go. And I'd love to come for a swim. Where?'

She gave him careful directions. It was a beach a mile further along the coast from Palmyra. There was a side road and a thatched hut. He couldn't miss it. The beach was sort of better than Palmyra's. The skin-diving was more fun. And of course there weren't so many people. It belonged to some Swedish millionaire who had gone away. When could he get there? Half an hour would be all right. They would have more time. On the reef that is.

Bond's drink came and the sandwich. He sat and consumed them, looking at the wall, feeling excited about the girl, but knowing what he was going to do to her life that afternoon. It was going to be a bad business — when it could have been so good. He remembered her as he had first seen her, the ridiculous straw hat tilted down over the nose, the pale blue ribbons flying as she sped up Bay Street. Oh well . . .

Bond rolled his swimming trunks into a towel, put on a dark blue sea-island cotton shirt over his slacks and slung Leiter's Geiger counter over his shoulder. He glanced at himself in the mirror. He looked like any other tourist with a camera. He felt in his trousers pocket to make sure he had the identification bracelet and went out of the room and down in the lift.

The Land-Rover had Dunlopillo cushions, but the ripple-edged tarmac and the pitted bends of Nassau's coastal road were tough on the springs and the quivering afternoon sun was a killer. By the time Bond found the sandy track leading off into the casuarinas and had parked the car on the edge of the beach, all he wanted to do was get into the sea and stay in it. The beach-hut was a Robinson Crusoe affair of plaited bamboo and screwpine with a palm thatch whose wide eaves threw black shadows. Inside were two changing rooms labelled 'HIS' and 'HERS'. HERS contained a small pile of soft clothes and the white doeskin sandals. Bond changed and walked out again into the sun. The small beach was a dazzling half-moon of white sand enclosed on both sides by rocky points. There was no sign of the girl. The beach shelved quickly through green to blue under the water. Bond took a few steps through the shallows and dived through the blood-warm upper water down into the cool depths. He kept down there as long as possible, feeling the wonderful cold caress on his skin and through his hair. Then he surfaced and crawled lazily out to sea, expecting to see the girl skin-diving round one of the headlands. But there was no sign of her, and after ten minutes Bond turned back to the shore, chose a patch of firm sand, and lay down on his stomach, his face cradled in his arms.

Minutes later, something made Bond open his eyes. Coming towards him across the middle of the quiet bay was a thin trail of bubbles. When it passed over the dark blue into the green, Bond could see the yellow single cylinder of the aqualung tank and the glint of a mask with a fan of dark hair streaming out behind. The girl beached herself in the shallows. She raised herself on one elbow and lifted the mask. She said severely, 'Don't lie there dreaming. Come and rescue me.'

Bond got to his feet and walked the few steps to where she lay. He said, 'You oughtn't to aqualung by yourself. What's happened? Has a shark been lunching off you?'

'Don't make silly jokes. I've got some sea-egg spines in my foot. You'll have to get them out somehow. First of all get this aqualung off me. It hurts too much to stand on my foot with all this weight.' She reached for the buckle at her stomach and released the catch. 'Now just lift it off.'

Bond did as he was told and carried the cylinder up into the shade of the trees. Now she was sitting in the shallow water inspecting the sole of her right foot. She said, 'There are only two of them. They're going to be difficult.'

Bond came and knelt beside her. The two black spots, close together, were almost under the curl of the middle toes. He got up and held out a hand. 'Come on. We'll get into the shade. This is going to take time. Don't put your foot down or you'll push them in further. I'll carry you.'

She laughed up at him. 'My hero! All right. But don't drop me.' She held up both arms. Bond reached down and put one arm under her knees and another under her armpits. Her arms closed round his neck. Bond picked her up easily. He stood for a moment in the lapping water and looked down into her upturned face. The bright eyes said yes. He bent his head and kissed her hard on the half-open, waiting mouth.

The soft lips held his and drew slowly away. She said rather breathlessly, 'You shouldn't take your reward in advance.'

'That was only on account.' Bond closed his hand firmly over her right breast and walked out of the water and up the beach into the shade of the casuarinas. He laid her gently down in the soft sand. She put her hands behind her head to keep the sand out of her straggling hair and lay waiting, her eyes half hidden behind the dark mesh of her eyelashes.

The mounded V of the bikini looked up at Bond and the proud breasts in the tight cups were two more eyes. Bond felt his control going. He said roughly, 'Turn over.'

She did as she was told. Bond knelt down and picked up her

right foot. It felt small and soft, like a captured bird, in his hand. He wiped away the specks of sand and uncurled the toes. The small pink pads were like the buds of some multiple flower. Holding them back, he bent and put his lips to where the broken ends of the black spines showed. He sucked hard for about a minute. A small piece of grit from one of the spines came into his mouth and he spat it out. He said, 'This is going to be a long business unless I hurt a bit. Otherwise it'll take all day and I can't waste too much time over just one foot. Ready?'

He saw the muscles of her behind clench to take the pain. She said dreamily, 'Yes.'

Bond sunk his teeth into the flesh round the spines, bit as softly as he could and sucked hard. The foot struggled to get away. Bond paused to spit out some fragments. The marks of his teeth showed white and there were pinpoints of blood at the two tiny holes. He licked them away. There was almost no black left under the skin. He said, 'This is the first time I've eaten a woman. They're rather good.'

She squirmed impatiently but said nothing.

Bond knew how much it would be hurting. He said, 'It's all right, Domino. You're doing fine. Last mouthful.' He gave the sole of her foot a reassuring kiss and then, as tenderly as he could, put his teeth and lips back to work.

A minute or two later and he spat out the last section of spine. He told her it was over and gently laid the foot down. He said, 'Now you mustn't get sand into it. Come on, I'll give you another lift into the hut and you can put your sandals on.'

She rolled over. Her black eyelashes were wet with the tears of small pain. She wiped a hand over them. She said, looking seriously up at him, 'Do you know, you're the first man who's ever made me cry.' She held up her arms and now there was complete surrender.

Bond bent and picked her up. This time he didn't kiss the waiting mouth. He carried her to the door of the hut. HIS or HERS? He carried her into HIS. He reached out a hand for his shirt and shorts and threw them down to make a scrap of a bed. He put her down softly so that she was standing on his shirt. She kept her arms round his neck while he undid the single button of the brassiere and then the tapes of the taut slip. He stepped out of his bathing trunks and kicked them away.

19

WHEN THE KISSING STOPPED

BOND LEANT ON one elbow and looked down at the beautiful drowned face. There was a dew of sweat below the eyes and at the temples. A pulse beat fast at the base of the neck. The lines of authority had been sponged away by the lovemaking and the face had a soft, sweet, bruised look. The wet eyelashes parted and the tawny eyes, big and faraway, looked up with remote curiosity into Bond's. They focused lazily and examined him as if they were seeing him for the first time.

Bond said, 'I'm sorry. I shouldn't have done that.'

The words amused her. The dimples at each side of the mouth deepened into clefts. She said, 'You talk like a girl who has had it for the first time. Now you are frightened that you will have a baby. You will have to tell your mother.'

Bond leant down and kissed her. He kissed the two corners of her mouth and then the parted lips. He said, 'Come and swim. Then I must talk to you.' He got to his feet and held out his hands. Reluctantly she took them. He pulled her up and against him. Her body flirted with his, knowing it was safe. She smiled impishly up at him and became more wanton. Bond crushed her fiercely to him, to stop her and because he knew they had only a few more minutes of happiness. He said, 'Stop it, Domino. And come on. We don't need any clothes. The sand won't hurt your foot. I was only pretending.'

She said, 'So was I when I came out of the sea. The spines didn't hurt all that much. And I could have cured them if I'd wanted to. Like the fishermen do. You know how?'

Bond laughed. 'Yes I do. Now, into the sea.' He kissed her once and stood back and looked at her body to remember how it had been. Then he turned abruptly and ran to the sea and dived deeply down.

When he got back to shore she was already out and dressing. Bond dried himself. He answered her laughing remarks through the partition with monosyllables. Finally she accepted the change in him. She said, 'What is the matter with you, James? Is anything wrong?'

'Yes, darling.' Pulling on his trousers Bond heard the rattle of the little gold chain against the coins in his pocket. He said, 'Come outside. I've got to talk to you.'

Sentimentally, Bond chose a patch of sand on the other side of the hut from where they had been before. She came out and stood in front of him. She examined his face carefully, trying to read it. Bond avoided her eyes. He sat with his arms round his knees and looked out to sea. She sat down beside him, but not close. She said, 'You are going to hurt me. Is it that you too are going away? Be quick. Do it cleanly and I will not cry.'

Bond said, 'I'm afraid it's worse than that, Domino. It's not about me. It's about your brother.'

Bond sensed the stiffening of her body. She said in a low, tense voice, 'Go on. Tell me.'

Bond took the bracelet out of his pocket and silently handed it to her.

She took it. She hardly gave it a glance. She turned a little away from Bond. 'So he is dead. What happened to him?'

'It is a bad story, and a very big one. It involves your friend Largo. It is a very great conspiracy. I am here to find out things for my government. I am really a kind of policeman. I am telling you this and I will tell you the rest because hundreds and perhaps thousands of people will die unless you help to prevent it. That is why I had to show you that bracelet and hurt you so that you would believe me. I am breaking my oath in doing this. Whatever happens, whatever you decide to do, I trust you not to tell what I am going to say.'

'So that is why you made love to me — to make me do what you want. And now you blackmail me with the death of my brother.' The words came out between her teeth. Now in a soft, deadly whisper, she said, 'I hate you, I hate you, I hate you.'

Bond said coldly, in a matter-of-fact voice, 'Your brother was killed by Largo, or on his orders. I came here to tell you that. But then,' he hesitated, 'you were there and I love you and want you. When what happened began to happen I should have had strength to stop it. I hadn't. I knew it was then or perhaps never.

Knowing what I knew, it was a dreadful thing to have done. But you looked so beautiful and happy. I wanted to put off hurting you. That is my only excuse.' Bond paused. 'Now listen to what I have to tell you. Try and forget about your hate for me. In a moment you will realize that we are nothing in all this. This is a thing by itself.' Bond didn't wait for her to comment. He began from the beginning and went slowly, minutely, through the whole case, omitting only the advent of the *Manta*, the one factor that could now be of help to Largo and perhaps later his plans. He ended, 'So you see, there is nothing we can do until those weapons are actually on board the *Disco*. Until that moment comes, Largo has a perfect alibi with his treasure-hunt story. There is nothing to link him with the crashed plane or with SPECTRE. If we interfere with him now, this moment, arrest the ship on some excuse, put a watch on her, prevent her sailing, there will only be a delay in the SPECTRE plan. Only Largo and his men know where the bombs are hidden. If the plane has gone for them, it will be keeping contact with the *Disco* by radio. If there's any hitch, the plane can leave the bombs at the hiding place or at another, dump them in shallow water anywhere, and return for them when the trouble has blown over. Even the *Disco* could be taken off the job and some other ship or plane used any time in the future. SPECTRE headquarters, wherever they are, will inform the Prime Minister that there has been a change of plan, or they can say nothing at all. Then, perhaps weeks from now, they will send another communication. And this time there will perhaps be only twenty-four hours' notice for the money to be dropped. The terms will be tougher. And we shall have to accept them. So long as those bombs are still lost to us, the threat is there. You see that?'

'Yes. So what is to be done?' The voice was harsh. The girl's eyes glittered fiercely as they looked at and through Bond towards some distant target — not, he thought, at Largo the great conspirator, but at Largo who had had her brother killed.

'We have got to know when those bombs are on board the *Disco*. That is all that matters. Then we can act with all our weight. And we have one great factor on our side. We are pretty sure that Largo feels secure. He still believes that the wonderful plan, and it is wonderful, is going exactly as it was meant to do. That is our strength and our only strength. You see that?'

'And how are you to know when the bombs come on board the yacht?'

'You must tell us.'

'Yes.' The monosyllable was dull, indifferent. 'But how am I to know? And how am I to tell you? This man is no fool. He is only foolish in wanting his mistress' — she spat the word out — 'when so much else is at stake.' She paused. 'These people have chosen badly. Largo cannot live without a woman within reach. They should have known that.'

'When did Largo tell you to come back on board?'

'Five. The boat is coming to fetch me at Palmyra.'

Bond looked at his watch. 'It is now four. I have this Geiger counter. It is simple to use. It will tell at once if the bombs are on board. I want you to take it with you. If it says there is a bomb on board, I want you to show a light at your porthole — switch the lights on in your cabin several times, anything like that. We have men watching the ship. They will be told to report. Then get rid of the Geiger counter. Drop it overboard.'

She said scornfully, 'That is a silly plan. It is the sort of melodramatic nonsense people write about in thrillers. In real life people don't go into their cabins and switch on their lights in daylight. No. If the bombs are there, I will come up on deck — show myself to your men. That is natural behaviour. If they are not there, I will stay in my cabin.'

'All right. Have it your own way. But will you do this?'

'Of course. If I can prevent myself killing Largo when I see him. But on condition that when you get him you will see that he is killed.' She was entirely serious. She looked at him with matter-of-fact eyes as if he was a travel agent and she was reserving a seat on a train.

'I doubt if that will happen. I should say that every man on board will get a life sentence in prison.'

She considered this. 'Yes. That will do. That is worse than being killed. Now show me how this machine works.' She got to her feet and took a couple of steps up the beach. She seemed to remember something. She looked down at the bracelet in her hand. She turned and walked down to the edge of the sea and stood for a moment looking out across the quiet water. She said some words that Bond couldn't hear. Then she leant back and with all her strength threw the gold chain far out over the shoal into the dark blue. The chain twinkled briefly in the strong sun and there was a small splash. She watched the ripples widen and, when the smashed mirror was whole again, turned and walked back up the sand, her small limp leaving footmarks of uneven depth.

Bond showed her the working of the machine. He eliminated the wrist-watch indicator and told her to depend entirely on the telltale clicking. 'Anywhere in the ship should be all right,' he explained. 'But better near the hold if you can get there. Say you want to take a photograph from the well-deck aft or something. This thing's made up to look like a Rolleiflex. It's got all the Rolleiflex lenses and gadgets on the front, lever to press and all. It just hasn't got a film. You could say that you'd decided to take some farewell pictures of Nassau and the yacht, couldn't you?'

'Yes.' The girl, who had been listening attentively, now seemed distracted. Tentatively she put out a hand and touched Bond's arm. She let the hand fall. She looked up at him and then swiftly away. She said shyly, 'What I said, what I said about hating you. That is not true. I didn't understand. How could I — all this terrible story? I still can't quite believe it, believe that Largo has anything to do with it. We had a sort of an affair in Capri. He is an attractive man. Everyone else wanted him. It was a challenge to take him from all these other smart women. Then he explained about the yacht and this wonderful trip looking for treasure. It was like a fairy tale. Of course I agreed to come. Who wouldn't have? In exchange, I was quite ready to do what I had to do.' She looked briefly at him and away. 'I am sorry. But that is how it is. When we got to Nassau and he kept me ashore, away from the yacht, I was surprised but I was not offended. The islands are beautiful. There was enough for me to do. But what you have told me explains many small things. I was never allowed in the radio room. The crew were silent and unfriendly — they treated me like someone who was not wanted on board, and they were on curious terms with Largo, more like equals than paid men. And they were tough men and better educated than sailors usually are. So it all fits. I can even remember that, for a whole week before last Thursday, Largo was terribly nervous and irritable. We were already getting tired of each other. I put it down to that. I was even making plans for flying home by myself. But he has been better the last few days and when he told me to be packed and ready to come on board this evening, I thought I might just as well do as he said. And of course I was very excited over this treasure hunt. I wanted to see what it was all about. But then,' she looked out to sea, 'there was you. And this afternoon, after what happened, I had decided to tell Largo I would not go. I would stay here and see where you went and go with you.' For the first time she looked him full in the face and held his eyes. 'Would you have let me do that?'

Bond reached out and put his hand against her cheek. 'Of course I would.'

'But what happens now? When shall I see you again?'

This was the question Bond had dreaded. By sending her back on board, and with the Geiger counter, he was putting her in double danger. She could be found out by Largo, in which case her death would be immediate. If it came to a chase, which seemed almost certain, the *Manta* would sink the *Disco* by gunfire or torpedo, probably without warning. Bond had added up these factors and had closed his mind to them. He kept it closed. He said, 'As soon as this is over. I shall look for you wherever you are. But now you are going to be in danger. You know this. Do you want to go on with it?'

She looked at her watch. She said, 'It is half past four. I must go. Do not come with me to the car. Kiss me once and stay here. Do not worry about what you want done. I will do it well. It is either that or a stiletto in the back for this man.' She held out her arms. 'Come.'

Minutes later Bond heard the engine of the MG come to life. He waited until the sound had receded in the distance down the Western Coast Road, then he went to the Land-Rover and climbed in and followed.

A mile down the coast, at the two white obelisks that marked the entrance to Palmyra, dust still hung in the driveway. Bond sneered at his impulse to drive in after her and stop her from going out to the yacht. What in hell was he thinking of? He drove on fast down the road to Old Fort Point, where the police watchers were housed in the garage of a deserted villa. They were there, one man reading a paperback in a canvas chair while the other sat before tripod binoculars that were trained on the *Disco* through a gap in the blinds of a side window. The khaki walkie-talkie set was beside them on the floor. Bond gave them the new briefing and got on the radio to the Police Commissioner and confirmed it to him. The Commissioner passed two messages to him from Leiter. One was to the effect that the visit to Palmyra had been negative except that a servant had said the girl's baggage had gone on board the *Disco* that afternoon. The boathouse was completely innocent. It contained a glass-bottomed boat and a pedallo. The pedallo would have made the tracks they had seen from the air. The second message said that the *Manta* was expected in twenty minutes. Would Bond meet Leiter at the Prince George Wharf, where she would dock.

The *Manta*, coming with infinite caution up-channel, had none of the greyhound elegance of the conventional submarine. She was blunt and thick and ugly. The bulbous metal cucumber, her rounded nose shrouded with tarpaulin to hide the secrets of her radar scanner from the Nassavians, held no suggestion of her speed, which Leiter said was around forty knots submerged. 'But they won't tell you that, James. That's Classified. I guess we're going to find that even the paper in the can is Classified when we go aboard. Watch out for these Navy guys. Nowadays they're so tight-lipped they think even a belch is a security risk.'

'What else do you know about her?'

'Well, we won't tell this to the captain, but of course in C.I.A. we had to be taught the basic things about these atom subs, so as we could brief agents on what to look for and recognize clues in their reports. She's one of the George Washington Class, about 4,000 tons, crew of around a hundred, cost about a hundred million dollars. Range, anything you want until the chow runs out or until the nuclear reactor needs topping up — say every 100,000 miles or so. If she has the same armament as the George Washington, she'll have sixteen vertical launching tubes, two banks of eight, for the Polaris solid fuel missile. These have a range of around 1,200 miles. The crews call the tubes "the Sherwood Forest" because they're painted green and the missile compartment looks like rows of great big tree trunks. These Polaris jobs are fired from way down below the surface. The sub stops and holds dead steady. They have the ship's exact position at all times through radio fixes and star sights through a tricky affair called a star-tracker periscope. All this dope is fed into the missiles automatically. Then the chief gunner presses a button and a missile shoots up through the water by compressed air. When it breaks surface the solid fuel rockets ignite and take the missile the rest of the way. Hell of a weapon really when you come to think of it. Imagine these damned things shooting up out of the sea anywhere in the world and blowing some capital city to smithereens. We've got six of them already and we're going to have more. Good deterrent when you come to think of it. You don't know where they are or when. Not like bomber bases and firing pads and so on you can track down and put out of action with your first rocket wave.'

Bond commented drily, 'They'll find some way of spotting them. And presumably an atomic depth charge set deep would send a shock-wave through hundreds of miles of water and blow anything to pieces over a huge area. But has she got anything smaller than these missiles? If we're going to do a job on the *Disco* what are we going to use?'

'She's got six torpedo tubes up front and I dare say she's got some smaller stuff — machine-guns and so forth. The trouble's going to be to get the commander to fire them. He's not going to like firing on an unarmed civilian yacht on the orders of a couple of plain-clothes guys, and one of them a Limey at that. Hope his orders from the Navy Department are as solid as mine and yours.'

The huge submarine bumped gently against the wharf. Lines were thrown and an aluminium gangplank was run ashore. There was a ragged cheer from the crowd of watchers being held back by a cordon of police. Leiter said, 'Well, here we go. And to one hell of a bad start. Not a hat between us to salute the quarter deck with. You curtsy, I'll bow.'

20

TIME FOR DECISION

THE INTERIOR OF the submarine was incredibly roomy, and it was stairs and not a ladder that led down into the interior. There was no clutter, and the sparkling paintwork was in two-tone green. Powerlines painted in vivid colours provided a cheerful contrast to the almost hospital décor. Preceded by the officer of the watch, a young man of about twenty-eight, they went down two decks. The air (70° with 46% humidity, explained the officer) was beautifully cool. At the bottom of the stairs he turned left and knocked on a door that said 'Commander P. Pedersen, U.S.N.'

The captain looked about forty. He had a square, rather Scandinavian face with a black crew-cut just going grey. He had shrewd, humorous eyes but a dangerous mouth and jaw. He was sitting behind a neatly stacked metal desk smoking a pipe. There was an empty coffee cup in front of him and a signal pad on which he had just been writing. He got up and shook hands, waved them to two chairs in front of his desk and said to the officer of the watch, 'Coffee, please, Stanton. And have this sent, would you?' He tore the top sheet off the signal pad and handed it across. 'Most Immediate.'

He sat down. 'Well, gentlemen. Welcome aboard. Commander Bond, it's a pleasure to have a member of the Royal Navy visit the ship. Ever been in subs before?'

'I have,' said Bond, 'but only as a supercargo. I was in intelligence — R.N.V.R. Special Branch. Strictly a chocolate sailor.'

The captain laughed. 'That's good! And you, Mr Leiter?'

'No, Captain. But I used to have one of my own. You operated it with a sort of rubber bulb and tube. Trouble was they'd never let me have enough depth of water in the bath to see what she could really do.'

'Sounds rather like the Navy Department. They'll never let me try this ship full out. Except once on trials. Every time you want to get going, the needle comes across a damn red line some interfering so-and-so has painted on the dial. Well, gentlemen,' the captain looked at Leiter, 'what's the score? Haven't had such a flood of Top Secret Most Immediates since Korea. I don't mind telling you, the last one was from the Chief of the Navy, Personal. Said I was to consider myself under your orders, or, on your death or incapacity, under Commander Bond's, until Admiral Carlson arrives at 1900 this evening. So what? What's cooking? All I know is that all signals have been prefixed Operation Thunderball. What is this operation?'

Bond had greatly taken to Commander Pedersen. He liked his ease and humour and, in general — the old Navy phrase came back to him — the cut of his jib. Now he watched the stolid good-humoured face as Leiter told his story down to the departure of Largo's amphibian at 1.30 and the instructions Bond had given to Domino Vitali.

In the background to Leiter's voice there was a medley of soft noises — the high, constant whine of a generator overlaid by the muted background of canned music — the Ink Spots singing 'I love coffee, I love tea'. Occasionally the P.A. System above the captain's desk crackled and sang with operational double-talk — 'Roberts to Chief of the Boat' — 'Chief Engineer wants Oppenshaw' — 'Team Blue to Compartment F' — and from somewhere came the suck and gurgle of a pumplike apparatus that sounded punctually every two minutes. It was like being inside the simple brain of a robot that worked by hydraulics and electrical impulses with a few promptings from its human masters.

After ten minutes, Commander Pedersen sat back. He reached for his pipe and began filling it absent-mindedly. He said, 'Well, that's one hell of a story.' He smiled. 'And strangely enough, even if I hadn't had these signals from the Navy Department, I'd believe it. Always did think something like this would happen one of these days. Hell! I have to carry these missiles around, and I'm in command of a nuclear ship. But that doesn't mean that I'm not terrified by the whole business. Got a wife and two children, and that doesn't help either. These atomic weapons are just too damned dangerous. Why, any one of these little sandy cays around here could hold the whole of the United States to ransom — just with one of my missiles trained on Miami. And here am I, fellow called Peter Pedersen, age thirty-eight, maybe sane or maybe not, toting around sixteen of the things — enough to damn near wipe out England. However,' he put his hands down on the desk in front of him, 'that's all by the way. Now we've got just one small piece of the problem on our hands — small, but as big as the world. So what are we to do? As I see it, the idea of you gentlemen is that this man Largo will be coming back any minute now in his plane after picking up the bombs from where he hid them. If he's got the bombs, and on what you've told me I'll go along with the probability that he has, this girl will give us the tip-off. Then we close in and arrest his ship or blow it out of the water. Right? But supposing he hasn't got the bombs on board, or for one reason or another we don't get the tip-off, what do we do then?'

Bond said quietly, 'We follow him, sit close on his tail, until the time limit, that's about twenty-four hours from now, is up. That's all we can do without causing one hell of a legal stink. When the time limit's up, we can hand the whole problem back to our governments and they can decide what to do with the *Disco* and the sunken plane and all the rest. By that time, some little man in a speedboat we've never heard of may have left one of the bombs off the coast of America, and Miami may have gone up in the air. Or there may be a big bang somewhere else in the world. There's been plenty of time to take those bombs off the plane and get them thousands of miles from here. Well, that'll be too bad and we'll have muffed it. But at this moment we're in the position of a detective watching a man he thinks is going to commit a murder. Doesn't even know for sure whether he's got a gun on him or not. There's nothing the detective can do but follow the man and wait until he actually pulls the gun out of his pocket and points it. Then, and only then, the detective can shoot the man or arrest him.' Bond turned to Leiter. 'Isn't that about it, Felix?'

'That's how it figures. And Captain, Commander Bond here and I are damn sure Largo's our man and that he'll be sailing for his target in no time at all. That's why we agreed to panic and ask you along. One gets you a hundred he'll be placing that bomb at night and tonight's the last night he's got. By the way, Captain, have you got steam up, or whatever the atom boys call it?'

'I have, and we can be under way in just about five minutes.'

The captain shook his head. 'But there's one bit of bad news for you, gentlemen. I just can't figure how we're going to keep track of the *Disco*.'

'How's that? You've got the speed, haven't you?' Leiter caught himself pointing his steel hook threateningly at the captain, and hastily brought it down again to his lap.

The captain smiled. 'Guess so. Guess we could give her a good race on a straight course, but you gentlemen don't seem to have figured on the navigational hazards in this part of the ocean.' He pointed at the British Admiralty chart on the wall. 'Take a look at that. Ever seen a chart with so many figures on it? Looks like a spilled ants' nest. Those are soundings, gentlemen, and I can tell you that unless the *Disco* sticks to one of the deep-water channels — Tongue of the Ocean, North-West Providence Channel, or the North-East — we've had it, as Commander Bond would say. All the rest of that area' — he waved a hand — 'may look the same blue colour on a map, but after your trip in that Grumman Goose you know darned well it isn't the same blue colour. Darned near the whole of that area is banks and shoal with only around three to ten fathoms over it. If I was quite crazy and looking for a nice cosy job ashore, I'd take the ship along surfaced in ten fathoms — if I could bribe the navigator and seal off the echo-sounder from crew members. But even if we got a long spell of ten fathoms on the chart, you got to remember that's an old chart, dates back to the days of sail, and these banks have been shifting for more than fifty years since it was drawn up. Then there's the tides that set directly on to and off the banks, and the coral nigger-heads that won't show up on the echo-sounder until you hear the echo of them smashing up the hull or the screw.' The captain turned back to his desk. 'No, gentlemen. This Italian vessel was darned well chosen. With that hydrofoil device of hers, she probably doesn't draw more than a fathom. If she chooses to keep to the shallows, we just haven't got a chance. And that's flat.' The captain looked from one to another of them. 'Want me to call up the Navy Department and have Fort Lauderdale take over with those fighter bombers you've got on call — get them to do a shadowing job?'

The two men looked at each other. Bond said, 'She won't be showing lights. They'll have the hell of a job picking her up at night. What do you say, Felix? Maybe we'd better call them out even if it's only to keep some sort of a watch off the American coast. Then, if the captain's willing, we'll take the North-West Channel — if the *Disco* sails, that is — and bank on the Bahamas Rocket Station being Target No. 1.'

Felix Leiter ran his left hand through the mop of straw-coloured hair. 'Goddammit,' he said angrily. 'Hell yes, I suppose so. We're looking fools enough already bringing the *Manta* on stage. What's a squadron of planes? Sure. We've just *got* to back our hunch that it's Largo and the *Disco*. Come on, let's get together with the captain and whip off a signal that doesn't look too damned silly — copy to C.I.A. and to your Chief. How do you want it to go?'

'Admiralty for M, prefixed Operation Thunderball.' Bond wiped a hand down over his face. 'God, this is going to put the cat among the pigeons.' He looked up at the big metal wall clock. 'Six. That'll be midnight in London. Popular time to get a signal like this.'

The P.A. System in the ceiling spoke more clearly. 'Watch Officer to Captain. Police officer with urgent message for Commander Bond.' The captain pressed a switch and spoke into a desk microphone. 'Bring him below. Prepare to cast off lines. All hands prepare for sailing.' The captain waited for the acknowledgment and released the switch. The captain smiled across at them. He said to Bond, 'What's the name of that girl? Domino? Well, Domino, say the good word.'

The door opened. A police corporal, his hat off, crashed to attention on the steel flooring and extended a stiff arm. Bond took the buff O.H.M.S. envelope and slit it open. He ran his eyes down the pencilled message signed by the Police Commissioner. Unemotionally he read out:

'PLANE RETURNED 1730 HOISTED INBOARD. DISCO SAILED AT 1755, FULL SPEED, COURSE NORTH WEST STOP GIRL DID NOT REPEAT NOT REAPPEAR ON DECK AFTER BOARDING.'

Bond borrowed a signal blank from the captain and wrote:

MANTA WILL ENDEAVOUR SHADOW VIA NORTH WEST

PROVIDENCE CHANNEL STOP FIGHTER BOMBER SQUADRON FROM FORT LAUDERDALE WILL BE ASKED THROUGH NAVY DEPARTMENT TO COOPERATE WITHIN RADIUS OF TWO HUNDRED MILES OFF FLORIDA COAST STOP MANTA WILL KEEP CONTACT THROUGH WINDSOR FIELD AIR CONTROL STOP NAVY DEPARTMENT AND ADMIRALTY BEING INFORMED STOP PLEASE INFORM GOVERNOR ALSO ADMIRAL CARLSON AND BRIGADIER FAIRCHILD ON ARRIVAL.

Bond signed the message and passed it to the captain, who also signed, as did Leiter. Bond put the message in an envelope and gave it to the corporal, who wheeled smartly and clanked out in his heavy boots.

When the door was shut, the captain pressed down the switch on the intercom. He gave orders to sail, surfaced, course due north, at ten knots. Then he switched off. In the short silence, there was a flurry of background noise, piping of bosuns' whistles, a thin mechanical whine, and the sound of running feet. The submarine trembled slightly. The captain said quietly, 'Well, gentlemen, that's that. I'd like to have the goose a bit less wild and a bit more solid. But I'll be glad to chase her for you. Now then, that signal.'

With only half his mind on the wording of the signal, Bond sat and worried about the significance of the Commissioner's message and about Domino. It looked bad. It looked as if either the plane had not brought back the two bombs, or one of them, in which case the mobilization of the *Manta* and of the fighter bombers was a pretty meaningless precaution, hardly justified by the evidence. It could easily be that the crashed Vindicator and the missing bombs were the work of some entirely different group and that, while they chased the *Disco*, the field was being left clear for SPECTRE. But Bond's instincts refused to allow him to accept this possibility. As cover, the whole *Disco*–Largo set-up was one hundred per cent watertight. It could not be faulted in any respect. That in itself was enough to arouse Bond's suspicions. A plot of this magnitude and audacity could only have been conceived under faultless cover and down to the smallest detail. Largo could have just set off on his treasure hunt, and everything, down to the last-minute plane recce of the treasure location, to see if there were any fishing boats about for instance, fitted in with that possibility. Or he could be sailing to lay the bomb, adjust the time fuse for perhaps a few hours after the deadline to allow time for its recovery or destruction if England and America at the last moment agreed to pay the ransom, and get far enough away from the danger area to avoid the explosion and establish an alibi. But where was the bomb? Had it arrived on board in the plane and had Domino for some reason been unable to go up on deck to make her signal? Or was it going to be picked up en route to the target area? The westerly course from Nassau, heading perhaps for the North-West Light, through the Berry Island Channel, fitted both possibilities. The sunken plane lay westwards, south of the Biminis, and so did Miami and other possible targets on the American coast. Or, after passing through the channel, about fifty miles west of Nassau, the *Disco* could veer sharply northwards and, after another fifty miles of sailing through shoal water that would discourage pursuit, get back into the North-West Providence Channel and make straight for the Grand Bahamas and the missile station.

Bond, fretted with indecision and the fear that he and Leiter were making majestic fools of themselves, forced himself to face one certainty — he and Leiter and the *Manta* were engaged on a crazy gamble. If the bomb was on board, if the *Disco* veered north for the Grand Bahamas and the missile station, then, by racing up the North-West Channel, the *Manta* might intercept her in time.

But if this gamble came off, with all its possibilities of error, why hadn't Domino made her signal? What had happened to her?

21

VERY SOFTLY, VERY SLOWLY

THE *DISCO*, A dark torpedo leaving a deep, briefly creaming wake, hurtled across the indigo mirror of the sea. In the big stateroom there was silence save for the dull boom of the engines and the soft tinkle of a glass on the sideboard. Although, as a precaution, the storm shutters were battened down over the portholes, the only light inside came from a single port navigation lantern hung from the roof. The dim red light only just illuminated the faces of the twenty men sitting round the long table, and the red-and-black-shadowed features, contorting with the slight sway of the top light, gave the scene the appearance of a conspiracy in hell.

At the top of the table Largo, his face, though the cabin was air-conditioned, shining with sweat, began to speak. His voice was tense and hoarse with strain. 'I have to report that we are in a state of emergency. Half an hour ago, No. 17 found Miss Vitali in the well-deck. She was standing fiddling with a camera. When No. 17 came upon her she lifted the camera and pretended to take a photograph of Palmyra, although the safety cap was over the lens. No. 17 was suspicious. He reported to me. I went below and took her to her cabin. She struggled with me. Her whole attitude aroused my suspicions. I was forced to subdue her by drastic measures. I took the camera and examined it.' Largo paused. He said quietly, 'The camera was a fake. It concealed a Geiger counter. The counter was, very naturally, registering over 500 milliroentgens. I brought her back to consciousness and questioned her. She refused to talk. In due course I shall force her to do so and then she will be eliminated. It was time to sail. I again rendered her unconscious and roped her securely to her bunk. I have now summoned this meeting to acquaint you of this occurrence, which I have already reported to No. 2.'

Largo was silent. A threatening, exasperated growl came

from round the table. No. 14, one of the Germans, said through his teeth, 'And what, Mister No. 1, did No. 2 have to say about this?'

'He said we were to carry on. He said the whole world is full of Geiger counters looking for us. The secret services of the whole world have been mobilized against us. Some busybody in Nassau, the police probably, was perhaps ordered to have a radiation search made of all ships in harbour. Perhaps Miss Vitali was bribed to bring the counter on board. But No. 2 said that once we have placed the weapon in the target area there will be nothing to fear. I have had the radio operator listening for unusual traffic between Nassau and the Coast. The density is quite normal. If we were suspected, Nassau would be deluged with wireless traffic from London and Washington. But all is quiet. So the operation will proceed as planned. When we are well away from the area, we will dispose of the lead casing of the weapon. The lead casing will contain Miss Vitali.'

No. 14 persisted: 'But you will first obtain the truth from this woman? It is not pleasant for our future plans to think that we may be under suspicion.'

'Interrogation will begin as soon as the meeting is over. If you want my opinion, those two men who came on board yesterday — this Bond and the man Larkin — may be involved. They may be secret agents. The so-called Larkin had a camera. I did not look at it closely, but it was similar to that in the possession of Miss Vitali. I blame myself for not having been more careful with these two men. But their story was convincing. On our return to Nassau tomorrow morning, we shall have to be circumspect. Miss Vitali will have fallen overboard. I will work out the details of the story. There will be an inquest. This will be irritating but nothing more. Our witness will be unshakeable. It will be wise to use the coins as additional alibi for our whereabouts tonight. No. 5, is the state of erosion of the coins satisfactory?'

No. 5, Kotze the physicist, said judiciously, 'It is no more than adequate. But they will pass examination, a cursory examination. They are authentic doubloons and Reals of the early seventeenth century. Sea water has no great effect on gold and silver. I have used a little acid to pit them. They will of course have to be handed to the coroner and declared as treasure trove. It would need a far greater expert than he or the court to pass judgment on them. There will be no compulsion to reveal the location of the treasure. We could perhaps give the depth of water — ten fathoms let us say, and an unspecified reef. I see no means by which our story could be upset. There is often very deep water outside reefs. Miss Vitali could have had trouble with her aqualung and could have been seen disappearing over the deep shelf where our echo-sounder gave the depth as a hundred fathoms. We did our best to dissuade her from taking part in the search. But she was an expert swimmer. The romance of the occasion was too much for her.' No. 5 opened his hands. 'There are often accidents of this nature. Many lives are lost in this way every year. A thorough search was instituted, but there were shark. The treasure hunt was broken off and we immediately returned to Nassau to report the tragedy.' No. 5 shook his head decisively. 'I see no reason to be dismayed by this occurrence. But I am in favour of a most rigorous interrogation.' No. 5 turned his head politely in Largo's direction. 'There are certain uses of electricity of which I have knowledge. The human body cannot resist them. If I can be of any service . . .?'

Largo's voice was equally polite. They might have been discussing remedies for a seasick passenger. 'Thank you. I have means of persuasion that I have found satisfactory in the past. But I shall certainly call upon you if the case is an obstinate one.' Largo looked down the table into the shadowed, ruby faces. 'And now we will quickly run through the final details.' He glanced down at his watch. 'It is midnight. There will be two hours' moonlight starting at three a.m. The first light of dawn will be shortly after five a.m. We thus have two hours for the operation. Our course will bring us in towards West End from the south. This is a normal entry to the islands, and even if our further progress towards the target area is noted by the missile station radar it will only be assumed that we are a yacht that has strayed slightly off course. We shall anchor at exactly three a.m. and the swimming party will leave for the half-mile swim to the laying point. The fifteen of you who will be taking part in this swim will, as arranged, swim in arrow formation, the chariot and the sled with the missile in the centre. Formation must be strictly kept to avoid straying. The blue torch on my back should be an adequate beacon, but if any man gets lost, he returns to the ship. Is that understood? The first duty of the escort will be to watch for shark and barracuda. I will again remind you that the range of your guns is not much more than twenty feet and that fish must be hit in or behind the head. Any man who is about to fire must warn his neighbour, who will then stand by to give additional fire if required. However, one hit should be sufficient to kill if the curare is, as we have been informed, not affected by the passage through sea water. Above all,' Largo put his hands decisively down on the table before him, 'do not forget to remove the small protective sheath from the barb before firing.' Largo raised his hands. 'You will forgive me for repeating these points. We have had many exercises in similar conditions and I have confidence that all will be well. But the underwater terrain will be unfamiliar and the effect of the dexedrine pills — they will be issued to the swimming party after this meeting — will be to sensitize the nervous system as well as provide the extra stamina and encouragement. So we must all be prepared for the unexpected and know how to handle it. Are there any further questions?'

During the planning stages, months before in Paris, Blofeld had warned Largo that if trouble was caused by any members of his team it was to be expected from the two Russians, the ex-members of SMERSH, No. 10 and No. 11. 'Conspiracy,' Blofeld had said, 'is their lifeblood. Hand in hand with conspiracy walks suspicion. These two men will always be wondering if they are not the object of some subsidiary plot — to give them the most dangerous work, to make them fall-guys for the police, to kill them and steal their share of the profits. They will be inclined to inform against their colleagues and always to have reservations about the plans that are agreed upon. For them, the obvious plan, the right way to do a thing, will have been chosen for some ulterior reason which is being kept hidden from them. They will need constant reassurance that nothing is being kept hidden from them, but, once they have accepted their orders, they will carry them out meticulously and without regard for their personal safety. Such men, apart from their special talents, are worth having. But you will please remember what I have said and, should there be trouble, should they try and sow mistrust within the team, you must act quickly and with utter ruthlessness. The maggots of mistrust and disloyalty must not be allowed to get a hold in your team. They are the enemies within that can destroy even the most meticulous planning.'

Now No. 10, a once-famous SMERSH terrorist called Strelik, began talking. He was sitting two places away from Largo, on his left. He did not address Largo, but the meeting. He said, 'Comrades, I am thinking of the interesting matters recounted by No. 1, and I am telling myself that everything has been excellently arranged. I am also thinking that this operation will be a very fine one and that it will certainly not be necessary to explode the second weapon on Target No. 2. I have some documentations on these islands and I am learning from the *Yachtsman's'* (No. 10 had trouble with the word) '*Guide to the Bahamas* that there is a big new hotel within a few miles of our target site, also a scattered township. I am therefore estimating that the explosion of Weapon No. 1 will destroy perhaps two thousand persons. Two thousand persons is not very many in my country and their death, compared with the devastation of this important missile station, would not, in the Soviet Union, be considered of great importance. I am thinking that it will be otherwise in the West and that the destruction of these people and the rescuing of the survivors will be considered a grave matter that will act decisively towards immediate agreement with our terms and the saving of Target No. 2 from destruction. This being so, Comrades,' the dull, flat voice gained a trace of animation, 'I am saying to myself that within as little as twenty-four hours our labours will have been completed and the great prize will be within our grasp. Now, Comrades,' the red and black shadows turned the taut little smile into a dark grimace, 'with so much money so near at hand, a most unworthy thought has come into my mind.' (Largo put his hand in his coat pocket and put up the safe on the little Colt 25.) 'And I would not be performing my duty to my Russian comrade, No. 11, nor to the other members of our team, if I did not share this thought with you, at the same time requesting forbearance for what may be unfounded suspicions.'

The meeting was very quiet, ominously so. These men had all been secret agents or conspirators. They recognized the smell of insurrection, the shadow of approaching disloyalty. What did No. 10 know? What was he going to divulge? Each man got ready to decide very quickly which way to jump when the cat was let out of the bag. Largo slipped the gun out of his pocket and held it along his thigh.

'There will come a moment,' continued No. 10, watching the faces of the men opposite for a quick gauge of their reactions, 'very shortly, when fifteen of us, leaving five members and six sub-agents on board this ship, will be out there,' he waved a hand at the cabin wall, 'in the darkness, at least half an hour's swim from this ship. At that moment, Comrades,' the voice became sly, 'what a thing it would be if those remaining on board were to sail the ship away and leave us in the water.' There was a shifting and muttering round the table. No. 10 held up a hand. 'Ridiculous I am thinking, and so no doubt are you, Comrades. But we are men of a feather. We recognize the unworthy urges that can come upon even the best of friends and comrades when fortunes are at stake. And, Comrades, with fifteen of us gone, how much more of a fortune would there be for those remaining, with their story for No. 2 of a great fight with sharks in which we all succumbed?'

Largo said softly, 'And what is it you propose, No. 10?'

For the first time, No. 10 looked to his right. He could not see the expression in Largo's eye. He spoke at the great red and black mass of his face. The tone of his voice was obstinate. He said, 'I am proposing that one member of each national group should stay on board to safeguard the interests of the other members of his national group. That would reduce the swimming party to ten. In this way those who are undertaking this dangerous work would go about it with more enthusiasm knowing that no such happening as I have mentioned could come about.'

Largo's voice was polite, unemotional. He said, 'I have one very short and simple answer to your suggestion, No. 10.' The light glittered redly on the metal thumb that protruded from the big hand. The three bullets pumped so quickly into the face of the Russian that the three explosions, the three bright flashes, were almost one. No. 10 put up two feeble hands, palms forward, as if to catch any further bullets, gave a jerk forward with his stomach at the edge of the table and then crashed heavily backwards, in a splinter of chair wood, on to the floor.

Largo put the muzzle of the gun up to his nose and delicately sniffed at it, moving it to and fro under the nostrils as if it was some delicious vial of perfume. In the silence, he looked slowly down one rank of faces and up the other. Finally he said softly, 'The meeting is now at an end. Will all members please return to their cabins and look for a last time to their equipment. Food will be ready from now on in the galley. One drink of alcohol will also be available for those who want it. I will detail two crew members to look after the late No. 10. Thank you.'

When Largo was alone he got to his feet, stretched, and gave a great cavernous yawn. Then he turned to the sideboard, opened a drawer and took out a box of Corona cigars. He chose one and, with a gesture of distaste, lit it. He then took the closed red rubber container that held the ice cubes and walked out of the door and along to the cabin of Domino Vitali.

He closed the door and locked it. Here also, a red riding light hung from the ceiling. Under it, on the double bunk, the girl lay offered like a starfish, her ankles and wrists strapped to the four corners of the ironwork below the mattress. Largo put the ice-box down on the chest of drawers and balanced the cigar carefully beside it so that the glowing tip would not spoil the varnish.

The girl watched him, her eyes glittering red points in the semi-darkness.

Largo said, 'My dear, I have had great enjoyment out of your body, much pleasure. In return, unless you tell me who gave you that machine to bring on board, I shall be forced to cause you great pain. It will be caused with these two simple instruments,' he held up the cigar and blew on the tip until it glowed brightly, 'this for heat, and these ice cubes for cold. Applied scientifically, as I shall apply them, they will have the inevitable effect of causing your voice, when it has stopped screaming, to speak, and speak the truth. Now then. Which is it to be?'

The girl's voice was deadly with hate. She said, 'You killed my brother and you will now kill me. Go on and enjoy yourself. You are already a piece of death yourself. When the rest of it comes, very soon, I pray God you will suffer a million times more than both of us.'

Largo's laugh was a short, harsh bark. He walked over to the edge of the bunk. He said, 'Very well, my dear. We must see what we can do with you, very softly and very, very slowly.'

He bent down and hooked his fingers in the neckline of her

shirt and the join of the brassiere. Very slowly, but with great force, he tore downwards, the whole length of her. Then he threw aside the torn halves of material and exposed the whole gleaming length of her body. He examined it carefully and reflectively and then went to the chest of drawers and took the cigar and the bowl of ice cubes and came back and made himself comfortable on the edge of the bunk.

Then he took a puff at the cigar, knocked the ash off on to the floor and leant forward.

22

THE SHADOWER

IN THE ATTACK centre of the *Manta* it was very quiet. Commander Pedersen, standing behind the man at the echo-sounder, occasionally made a comment over his shoulder to Bond and Leiter, who had been given canvas-backed chairs well away from the depth- and speed-gauges, which had been hooded so that they could only be read by the navigating team. These three men sat side by side on red leather, foam-cushioned, aluminium seats, handling the rudder and the forward and aft diving planes as if they were pilots in an airliner. Now the captain left the echo-sounder and came over to Bond and Leiter. He smiled cheerfully. 'Thirty fathoms and the nearest cay is a mile to westwards. Now we've got a clear course all the way to Grand Bahama. And we're making good speed. If we keep it up, we've got about four hours' sailing. Be off Grand Bahama about an hour before first light. How about some food and a bit of sleep? There won't be anything on the radar for an hour — these Berry Islands'll fill the screen until we're clear of them. Then'll come the big question. When we clear them, shall we see that one of the smallest of the cays has broken loose and is sailing fast northwards on a parallel course to ours? If we see that on the screen, it'll be the *Disco*. If she's there, we'll submerge. You'll hear the alarm bells. But you can just roll over and have a bit more sleep. Nothing can happen until it's certain that she's in the target area. Then we'll have to think again.' The captain made for the stairway. 'Mind if I lead the way? Watch your head on the pipes. This is the one part of the ship where there isn't much clearance.'

They followed him down and along a passage to the mess hall, a well-lighted dining-room finished in cream with pastel pink and green panels. They took their places at the head of one of the Formica-top tables away from the other officers and men, who looked curiously at the two civilians. The captain waved a hand at the walls of the room. 'Bit of a change from the old battleship grey. You'd be surprised how many eggheads are involved in the design of these ships. Have to be, if you want to keep your crew happy when the ship's submerged for a month or more at a time. The trick-cyclists said we couldn't have just one colour, must have contrast everywhere or the men's eyes get sort of depressed. This hall's used for movies, closed-circuit television, cribbage tournaments, bingo, God knows what — anything to keep the men off duty from getting bored. And you notice there's no smell of cooking or engine smells. Electrostatic precipitators all over the ship that filter them off.' A steward came with menus. 'Now then, let's get down to it. I'm having the baked Virginia ham with red-eye gravy, apple-pie with ice cream, and iced coffee. And steward, don't go too easy on that red-eye.' He turned to Bond. 'Getting out of harbour always gives me an appetite. You know, it isn't the sea the captain hates, it's the land.'

Bond ordered poached eggs with rye toast and coffee. He was grateful for the captain's cheerful talk, but he himself had no appetite. There was a gnawing tension inside him which would only be released when the *Disco* was picked up on the radar and there would be a prospect of action. And lurking behind his concern about the whole operation was worry about the girl. Had he been right to trust her with so much of the truth? Had she betrayed him? Had she been caught? Was she alive? He drank down a glass of iced water, and listened to the captain explaining how the ice cubes and the water were distilled from the sea.

Finally Bond became impatient with the cheerful, even tone of the conversation. He said, 'Forgive me, Captain, but could I interrupt for a moment and clear my mind about what we're going to do if we're right about the *Disco* and if we come up with her off the Grand Bahama? I can't quite figure what the next step ought to be. I've got my own ideas, but were you thinking we'd try and go alongside and board her, or just blow her out of the water?'

The captain's grey eyes were quizzical. He said, 'I was kind of leaving all that to you fellers. The Navy Department says that I'm under your orders. I'm just the chauffeur. Supposing you tell me what you have in mind and I'll be glad to go along with anything you suggest so long as it doesn't endanger my ship' — he smiled — 'too much, that is. In the last resort, if the Navy Department means what it says, and from your account of this operation it does, the safety of the ship will also have to go by the board. As I told you aloft in the attack centre, I got acknowledgment of our signal and full approval for our proposed course of action. That's all the clearance I need. Now then, you tell me.'

The food came. Bond pecked at his eggs and pushed them away. He lit a cigarette. He said, looking at Felix Leiter, 'Well, I don't know what you've worked out, Felix, but this is how I see the picture we may find around four o'clock in the morning, on the assumption, that is, that the *Disco* has been sailing north in shoal water under cover of the Berry Islands and that she'll then make for the Grand Bahama shore somewhere off the site of the missile station. Well now, on that assumption, I've had a good look at the charts and it seems to me that, if she's going to lay that bomb as close to the target as she can, she'll heave to and anchor about a mile offshore in about ten fathoms and get the bomb another half-mile or so closer to the target, lay it in twelve feet of water or so, switch on the time mechanism and get the hell away. That's how I'd go about it. She'd be away by first light and there's plenty of yacht traffic around West End from what I can gather from the pilot. She'd show up on the station radar of course, but she'd be just another yacht. Assuming the bomb's set for the twelve hours Largo's got before the time limit expires, he could be back in Nassau or twice as far away if he wanted in the time he's got. For my money, he'll go back to Nassau with his treasure-hunting story and wait for the next lot of orders from SPECTRE.' Bond paused. He avoided Leiter's eyes. 'That is, unless he's managed to get information out of the girl.'

Leiter said staunchly, 'Hell, I don't believe that girl would talk. She's a tough cookie. And supposing she did? He's only got to drop her overboard with some lead round her neck and say her aqualung failed on the treasure hunt, or some spiel of that sort. He'd go back to Nassau all right. That man's cover's as solid as J. P. Morgan and Company.'

The captain interrupted. 'Leaving all that aside, Commander Bond, and sticking to the operational angles, how do you suggest he's going to get that bomb out of the ship and right into the target area? I agree that according to the charts he can't get much closer in the yacht, and if he did he might be in trouble with the waterfront guard at the missile station. I see from my dope on the place that they've got some kind of a guard-boat for chasing away fishermen and suchlike when they're going to do a practice shoot.'

Bond said decisively, 'I'm sure that's the real purpose of the underwater compartment in the *Disco*. They've got one of those underwater sleds in there, and probably an electric torpedo to haul it. They'll load the bomb on the sled and take it in with a team of underwater swimmers, lay it and come back to the ship. Otherwise, why have all that underwater gear?'

The captain said slowly, 'You may be right, Commander. It makes sense. But so what do you want me to do about it?'

Bond looked the captain in the eye. 'There's only one moment to nail these people. If we show our hand too soon, the *Disco* can get the hell away — only a few hundred yards maybe, and dump the bombs in a hundred fathoms. The only time to get them, and the bomb, the first bomb anyway, is when that team has left the ship and is on its way to the laying point. We've got to get their underwater team with our underwater team. The second bomb, if it's aboard, doesn't matter. We can sink the ship with the second bomb inside her.'

The captain looked down at his plate. He arranged the knife and fork tidily together, straightened the dessert spoon and took the remains of his iced coffee and swirled the fragments of ice round so that they tinkled. He put the glass back on the table and looked up, first at Leiter then at Bond. He said thoughtfully, 'I guess what you say makes sense, Commander. We have plenty of oxygen rebreathers on board. We also have ten of the finest swimmers in the Nuclear Flotilla. But they'll only have knives to fight with. I'll have to ask for volunteers.' He paused. 'Who's going to lead them?'

Bond said, 'I'll do that. Skin-diving happens to be one of my hobbies. And I know what fish to look out for and which ones not to mind about. I'll brief your men about those things.'

Felix Leiter interrupted. He said obstinately, 'And don't think you're going to leave me behind eating Virginia ham. I put an extra foot-flipper on this,' he held up the shining hook, 'and I'll race you over half a mile any day, gammy leg and all. You'd be surprised the things one gets around to improvise when someone chews off one of your arms. Compensation it's called by the medics, in case you hadn't heard about it.'

The captain smiled. He got to his feet. 'Okay, okay. I'll leave you two heroes to fight it out while I have a word to the men over the speaker system. Then we'll have to get together with the charts and see that the gear's okay and suchlike. You fellers aren't going to get any sleep after all. I'll have a ration of battle pills issued to you. You're going to need them.' He raised a hand and went off down the mess hall.

Leiter turned to Bond. 'You goddam shyster. Thought you were going to leave your old pal behind, didn't you? God, the treachery of you Limeys! Perfidious Albion is right, all right.'

Bond laughed. 'How the hell was I to know you'd been in the hands of rehabilitators and therapists and so on? I never knew you took life so seriously. I suppose you've even found some way of petting with that damned meathook of yours.'

Leiter said darkly, 'You'd be surprised. Get a girl round the arm with this and you'd be amazed the effect it has on their good resolutions. Now then, let's get down to cases. What sort of formation are we going to swim in? Can we get some of those knives made into lances? How are we going to recognize our side from theirs underwater, and in semi-darkness at that? We've got to make this operation pretty solid. That Pedersen's a good guy. We don't want to get some of his men killed through some damn silly mistake of ours.'

The voice of the captain sounded over the communication system. 'Now hear this. This is your captain speaking. It is possible that we may encounter hazards in the course of this operation. I will tell you how this may come about. This ship has been chosen by the Navy Department for an exercise that is tantamount to an operation of war. I will tell you the story, which will remain classified top secret until further orders. This is what has happened . . .'

Bond, asleep in one of the duty officers' bunks, was awakened by the alarm bell. The iron voice of the P.A. System said: 'Diving stations. Diving stations,' and almost at once his bunk tilted slightly and the distant whine of the engines altered pitch. Bond smiled grimly to himself. He slipped off the bunk and went along and up to the attack centre. Felix Leiter was already there. The captain turned away from the plot. His face was tense. He said, 'It looks as if you were right, gentlemen. We've got her all right. About five miles ahead and two points to starboard. She's doing around thirty knots. No other ship could be holding that speed, or would be likely to. And she's showing no lights. Here, care to have a look through the scope? She's raising quite a wake and kicking up plenty of phosphorescence. No moon yet, but you'll see the white blur when your eyes get used to the dark.'

Bond bent to the rubber eye sockets. In a minute he had her, a white scut on the horizon of the soft, feathery swell. He stood back. 'What's her course?'

'Same as ours — western end of Grand Bahama. We'll go deeper now and put on a bit of speed. We've got her on the Sonar as well, so we shan't lose her. We'll get up parallel and close in a bit later. The met. report gives a light westerly breeze in the early hours. That'd be a help. Don't want it too calm when we unload the swimming party. The surface'll boil quite a bit as each man goes out. Here,' he turned to a powerful-looking man in white ducks, 'this is Petty Officer Fallon. He's in command of the swimming party, under your and Mr Leiter's orders of course. All the top swimmers volunteered. He's chosen nine of them. I've taken them off all duties. Maybe you gentlemen would like to get acquainted with your team. You'll want to discuss your routines. I guess discipline'll have to be pretty tight — recognition signals and so forth. Okay? The sergeant at arms is looking after the weapons.' He smiled. 'He's rustled up a dozen flick knives. Had some difficulty persuading the men to give them up, but he's done it. He's barbed them and sharpened them down almost to needles then fitted them into the tops of broom handles. Guess he'll make you sign an indent for the brooms or he'll have the supply officer on top of him when we get out of this. All right then. Be seeing you. Ask for anything you want.' He turned back to the plot.

Bond and Leiter followed Petty Officer Fallon along the lower deck to the engine room and then to the engine repair shop. On their way they passed through the reactor room. The reactor, the equivalent of a controlled atomic bomb, was an obscene knee-level bulge rising out of the thickly leaded deck. As they passed it, Leiter whispered to Bond, 'Liquid sodium Submarine Intermediate Reactor Mark B.' He grinned sourly and crossed himself.

Bond gave the thing a sideway kick with his shoe. 'Steam-age stuff. Our Navy's got the Mark C.'

The repair shop, a long low room equipped with various forms of precision machinery, presented a curious sight. At one end were grouped the nine swimmers clad only in bathing trunks, their fine bodies glowing with sunburn. At the other, two men in grey overalls, drab figures of the machine age, were working in semi-darkness with only pinpoints of bright light cast on the whirring lathes from which the knife blades threw small fountains of blue and orange sparks. Some of the swimmers already had their spears. After the introductions, Bond took one and examined it. It was a deadly weapon, the blade, sharpened to a stiletto and notched near the top into a barb, firmly wired into the top of a long stout stave. Bond thumbed the needle-sharp steel and touched the tip. Even a shark's skin would not stand up to that. But what would the enemy have? CO_2 guns for a certainty. Bond looked the smiling bronzed young men over. There were going to be casualties — perhaps many. Everything must be done to effect surprise. But those golden skins and his own and Leiter's paler skins would show at twenty feet in the moonlight — all right for the guns, but well out of range of the spears. Bond turned to Petty Officer Fallon: 'I suppose you don't have rubber suits on board?'

'Why sure, Commander. Have to, for escape in cold waters.' He smiled. 'We're not always sailing among the palm trees.'

'We'll all need them. And could you get white or yellow numbers, big ones, painted on their backs? Then we'll know more or less who's who.'

'Sure, sure.' He called to his men. 'Hey, Fonda and Johnson. Go along to the quartermaster and draw rubber suits for the whole team. Bracken, get a pail of rubber solution paint from Stores. Paint numbers on the backs of the suits. A foot deep. From one to twelve. Get going.'

Later, with the gleaming black suits hanging like giant batskins along the wall, Bond called the team together. 'Men, we're going to have one hell of an underwater battle. There'll be casualties. Anyone care to change his mind?' The faces grinned back at him. 'All right then. Now, we'll be swimming at around ten feet for a quarter, perhaps half a mile. It'll be pretty light. The moon'll be up and the bottom's white sand with some sea-grass. We'll take it easy and go in triangle formation with me, No. 1, leading, followed by Mr Leiter here as No. 2, and Petty Officer Fallon as No. 3. Then we broaden out behind like a wedge of geese. All you have to do is follow the number in front of you and no one'll get lost. Watch out for isolated nigger-heads. As far as I can gather from the chart there's no true reef, only broken clumps. It'll be getting on for early feeding time for the fish, so watch out for anything big. But leave it alone unless it gets too inquisitive. Then three of you take it on with the spears. But don't forget that it's most unlikely any fish will attack us. Close together we'll look like one hell of a big black fish to anyone else and I guess we'll be given a wide berth. Watch out for sea eggs on the coral and mind the tips of your spears. Hold them right up near the blade. Above all, keep quiet. We must try and get surprise on our side. The enemy's got CO_2 guns, range about twenty feet. But they're slow things to reload. If one's aimed at you, try and give a small target. Keep flat in the water. Don't put your feet down and give him a full-length target. As soon as he's fired, go for him like hell with your spear right out. One jab of those things in almost any part of the head or body and your man's had it. Wounded men will have to look after themselves. We can't spare stretcher bearers. If you're wounded, back out of the fight and get away to a coral clump and rest on it. Or make for the shore and shallow water. If you've got a spear in you, don't try and pull it out. Just hold it in the wound until someone gets to you. Petty Officer Fallon will have one of the ship's signal flares. He'll release that to the surface as soon as our attack begins and your captain will at once surface and put out an escape dinghy with an armed party and the ship's surgeon. Now then, any questions?'

'What do we do as soon as we get out of the sub, sir?'

'Try and not make any fuss on the surface. Get down quickly to ten feet and take your place in the formation. We're likely to get help from a light breeze, but we're bound to create turbulence on the surface. Keep it down as much as you can.'

'What about signals underwater, sir. Suppose a mask goes wrong or something.'

'Thumbs down for any kind of emergency. Arm held straight out for a big fish. Thumbs up means "I understand" or "Coming to help you". That's all you'll need.' Bond smiled. 'If the feet go up, that's the signal that you've had it.'

The men laughed various kinds of laugh.

There came the sudden voice of the P.A. System. 'Swimming party to the escape hatch. I repeat, swimming party to the escape hatch. Don equipment. Don equipment. Commander Bond to the attack centre, please.'

The whine of the engines died to a moan and then was silent. There was a slight bump as the *Manta* hit bottom.

23
NAKED WARFARE

BOND SHOT UPWARDS out of the escape hatch in a blast of compressed air. Far above him the surface of the sea was a glittering plate of quicksilver bubbling and swirling with the small waves that Bond was glad to see had materialized. The balloon of air rushed on past him and he watched it hit the silver ceiling like a small bomb. There was a sharp pain in his ears. To get decompression he fought with his fins and slowed down until he hung suspended ten feet below the surface. Below him the long black shape of the *Manta* looked sinister and dangerous. He thought of the electric light blazing inside her and a hundred men going about their business. It gave him a creepy feeling. Now there came a great explosion from the escape hatch as if the *Manta* was firing at Bond and the black projectile of Leiter shot up at him through the burst of silver air-bubbles. Bond moved out of his path and swam on up to the surface. Cautiously he looked above the small flurry of the waves. The *Disco*, still blacked out, lay stopped less than a mile away to his left. There were no signs of activity on board. A mile to the north lay the long dark outline of Grand Bahama edged with the white of sand and small waves. There were small patches of broken white on the coral and niggerheads in the intervening water. Above the island, on top of the tall rocket gantries that showed as indistinct black skeletons, the red aircraft warning lights winked on and off. Bond got his bearings and quietly jack-knifed his body down below the surface. He stopped at about ten feet and, keeping his body pointed like a compass needle along the course he would have to follow, lay, paddling softly with his fins to keep position, and waited for the rest of his team.

Ten minutes before, Commander Pedersen's stolid calm had given way to controlled excitement. 'By gum, it's working out like you said it would!' he had said wonderingly when Bond came into the attack centre. 'They hove to just about ten minutes ago, and since then the Sonar keeps on picking up odd noises, underwater noises, just what one would expect if they were getting things mobilized in that underwater compartment of theirs. Nothing else to go on, but it's quite enough. I guess you and the boys had better get going. As soon as you're out of the way, I'm going to float up a surface antenna and get a signal off to Navy Department, give them a Sitrep and have the missile station warned to stand by to evacuate if things go wrong. Then I'm going to come up to twenty feet or so and have two tubes loaded and keep a periscope watch. I'm issuing Petty Officer Fallon with a second flare. I've told him to keep out of trouble as much as he can and be ready to let off the second flare if it looks as if things are going really bad for our side. Unlikely, but I can't take chances with things as they are. If that second flare comes up, I'm going to close in. Knock a piece or two off the *Disco* with the 4-inch and then board her. Then I'm going to be rough as hell until that bomb's been recovered and rendered safe.' The captain shook his head doubtfully. He ran his hand over the black iron filings of his crew-cut. 'This is one hell of a situation, Commander. We'll just have to play it by ear.' He held out his hand. 'Well. You'd better get going. Good luck. I hope my boys'll be a credit to the ship.'

Bond felt a tap on his shoulder. It was Leiter. He grinned through his mask and jerked up a thumb. Bond took a quick look behind him. The men lay spread out in a rough wedge, their fins and hands working slowly as they marked time in the water. Bond nodded and got going, moving forward with a slow, even trudge, one hand at his side and the other holding his spear up the shaft against his chest. Behind him, the black wedge fanned out into formation and cruised forward like some giant delta-winged stingray on the prowl.

It was hot and sticky inside the black suit and the recirculating oxygen coming through the mouthpiece tasted of rubber, but Bond forgot the discomfort as he concentrated on keeping an even pace and a dead steady course on a prominent nigger-head with waves washing its head that he had chosen as a fix for his first contact with the shoal waters.

Far below, where the dancing moon shadows could not penetrate, the bottom was even white sand with an occasional dark patch that would be seagrass. All around there was nothing but the great pale luminous hall of the sea at night, a vast lonely mist through which, against his will and his intelligence, Bond expected at any moment the dark torpedo of a great fish to materialize, its eyes and senses questing towards the rippling shape of the black intruder. But there was nothing, and nothing came, and gradually the patches of seagrass became more distinct and ripples showed on the sandy bottom as it shelved slowly up from fifty to forty and then to thirty feet.

To reassure himself that all was well, Bond took a quick glance over his shoulder. Yes, they were all there, the oval panes of eleven gleaming masks with the fluttering fins kicking up behind them and the glint of the moonlight on the blades of the spears. Bond thought, By God, if only we can achieve surprise! What a terrifying ambush to meet coming at you through the shadows and shapes of the reef! His heart lifted momentarily at the thought, only to be checked by the deep gnawing of his hidden fears about the girl. Supposing she was part of the enemy team! Supposing he came face to face with her. Would he bring himself to do it — with the spear? But the whole idea was ridiculous. She was on board, safe. He would be seeing her again soon, as soon as this work was done.

A small coral clump showed up below and refocused his mind. Now he gazed watchfully ahead. There were more clumps, the ink splashes of sea eggs, crowds of small glittering reef fish, a small forest of sea fans that beckoned and waved with the ebb and flow like the hair of drowned women. Bond slowed and felt Leiter or Fallon bump into his fins. He made the slowing signal with his free hand. Now he crept carefully forward, looking for the silvery wash of the waves against the top of his navigation mark. Yes, it was there, away to the left. He was a good twenty feet off course. He swerved towards it, gave the halt signal and came slowly up under its protection. With infinite caution he raised his head through the sucking waves. He glanced first towards the *Disco*. Yes, she was still there, showing more plainly with the moon now full on her. No sign of life. Bond inched his gaze slowly across the intervening sea. Nothing. A flurry of wavelets down the mirrored pathway of the moon. Now Bond slid round to the other side of the coral head. Nothing but the broken waters of the shoal and, five or six hundred yards away, the clear coastline and the beach. Bond searched the clear channels for unusual turbulence in the water, for shapes, for anything moving. What was that? A hundred yards away, on the edge of a big patch, almost a lagoon, of clear water amongst the coral, a head, a pale head with the glitter of a mask across it, had broken the surface for an instant, taken a quick look round and immediately submerged.

Bond held his breath. He could feel his thrilled heart hammering against the inside of his rubber suit. Feeling stifled, he took the breathing tube from between his teeth and let his breath burst out of him. He quickly gulped in some mouthfuls of fresh air, got a good fix on the position, crammed the tube roughly between his lips and slid back and down.

Behind, the masks gazed blankly at him, waiting for a signal. Bond jerked up his thumb several times. Through the near masks he could see the answering flash of teeth. Bond shifted his grasp on the spear down to an attacking position and surged forward over the low coral.

Now it was only a question of speed and careful navigation among the occasional higher outcrops. Fish squirted out of his path and all the reef seemed to waken with the shock-wave of the twelve hastening bodies. Fifty yards on, Bond signalled to slow, to fan out in the attacking line. Then he crept on again, his eyes, aching and bloodshot with the strain, boring ahead through the jagged shapes amongst the pale mist. Yes! There was the glitter of white flesh, and there and there. Bond's arm made the hurling signal for the attack. He plunged forward, his spear held in front of him like a lance.

Bond's group came in from the flank. It was a mistake, as Bond quickly saw, for the SPECTRE team was still moving forward and at a speed that surprised Bond until he saw the small whirring propellers on the backs of the enemy. Largo's men were wearing compressed-air speed-packs, bulky cylinders strapped between the twin cylinders of their aqualungs, that operated small screws. Combined with the trudge of the fins, this gave them at least double normal swimming speed in open water, but here, amongst the broken coral, and slowed by the manœuvring of the sled preceded by the electric chariot, the team was perhaps only a knot faster than Bond's group, now thrashing their way forward to an interception point that was rapidly escaping them. And there were the hell of a lot of the enemy. Bond stopped counting after twelve. And most of them carried CO_2 guns with extra spears in quivers strapped to their legs. The odds were bad. If only he could get within spear range before the alarm was given!

Thirty yards, twenty. Bond glanced behind him. There were six of his men almost at arm's length, the rest straggled out in a crooked line. Still the masks of Largo's men pointed forward. Still they hadn't seen the black shapes making for them through the coral. But now, when Bond was level with Largo's rear-guard, the moon threw his shadow forward across a pale patch of sand and one man, then another, glanced quickly round. Bond got a foot against a lump of coral and, with this to give him impetus, flung himself forward. The man had no time to defend himself. Bond's spear caught him in the side and hurled him against the next man in line. Bond thrust and wrenched sickeningly. The man dropped his gun and bent double, clutching his side. Bond bored on into the mass of naked men now scattering in all directions, with their jet packs accelerated. Another man went down in front of him, clawing at his face. A chance thrust of Bond's had smashed the glass of his mask. He thrashed his way up towards the surface, kicking Bond in the face as he went. A spear ripped into the rubber protecting Bond's stomach and Bond felt pain and wetness that might be blood or sea water. He dodged another flash of metal and a gun butt hit him hard on the head, but with most of its force spent against the cushion of water. It knocked him silly and he clung for a moment to a niggerhead to get his bearings while the black tide of his men swept past him and individual fights filled the water with black puffs of blood.

The battleground had now shifted to a wide expanse of clear water fringed with broken coral. On the far side of this, Bond saw the grounded sled laden with something long and bulky with a rubber covering, the silver torpedo of the chariot, and a close group of men that included the unmistakable, oversize figure of Largo. Bond melted back among the coral clumps, got close down to the sand and began to swim cautiously round the flank of the big clear pool. Almost immediately he had to stop.

A squat figure was cowering in the shadows. His gun was raised and he was taking careful aim. It was at Leiter, in difficulties with one of Largo's men who had him by the throat while Leiter, the swim fin on his hook gone, clawed with the hook at the man's back. Bond gave two hard kicks of his flippers and hurled his spear from six feet. The light wood of the handle had no momentum, but the blade cut into the man's arm just as the bubbles of gas burst from the muzzle of the gun. His shot went wide, but he flashed round and thrust at Bond with the empty gun. Out of the corner of his eye Bond saw his spear floating slowly up towards the surface. He dived for the man's legs in a clumsy rugby tackle and clawed them off the ground. Then, as the gun muzzle hit him on the temple, he reached a desperate hand for the enemy's mask and ripped it off his face. That was enough. Bond swam aside and watched the man, blinded by the salt water, groping his way up towards the surface. Bond felt a nudge at his arm. It was Leiter, clutching at his oxygen tube. His face inside the mask was contorted. He made a feeble gesture upwards. Bond got the message. He seized Leiter round the waist and leaped for the surface fifteen feet up. As they broke through the silver ceiling, Leiter tore the broken tube from his mouth and gulped frantically for air. Bond held him through the paroxysm and then guided him to a clump of shallow coral and when Leiter pushed him angrily away and told him to get the hell back under and leave him alone, he put up a thumb and dived down again.

Now he kept well in the forest of coral and began again his stalk of Largo. Occasionally he caught glimpses of individual battles and once he passed under a man, one of his men from the *Manta*, staring down at him from the surface. But the face under the water, framed in its streaming hair, had no mask or oxygen tube, and the mouth gaped hideously in death. On the bottom, among the coral clumps, there were bits of wrack from the tide of battle — an oxygen pack, strips of black rubber, a complete aqualung and several spears from the CO_2 guns. Bond picked up two of them. Now he was on the edge of the open lagoon of battle water. The sled, with its obscene rubber sausage, was still there, guarded by two of Largo's men with their guns at the ready. But there was no sign of Largo. Bond peered into the misty wall through which the moonlight, paler now, filtered down on to the ripples in the sand, their pretty patterns scuffed and churned by the feet of the combatants. Where the sand had been disturbed, reef fish were swarming to pick up minute fragments of algae and other fodder, like seagulls and rooks when the plough has passed. There was nothing else to be seen and there was no way for Bond to guess how the battle, dispersed into a dozen separate running fights, was going. What was happening on the surface? When Bond had taken Leiter up, the sea had been lit by the red flare. How soon would the rescue dinghy from the *Manta* be on the scene? Ought he to stay where he was and watch over the bomb?

With frightening suddenness, the decision was made for him. Out of the mists to Bond's right the gleaming torpedo shape of the electric chariot shot into the arena. Largo sat astride it in the saddle. He was bent down behind the small perspex shield to get extra speed and his left hand held two of the *Manta* spears pointing forward while he controlled the single joystick with his right. As he appeared, the two guards dropped their guns on the sand and held up the coupling of the sled. Largo slowed down and drifted up to them. One man caught the rudder and wrestled to pull the chariot backwards towards the couplings. They were going to get out! Largo was going to take the bomb back out through the reef and drop it in deep water or bury it! The same thing would be done with the second bomb in the *Disco*. With the evidence gone, Largo would say that he had been ambushed by rival treasure hunters. How was he to know they came from a United States submarine? His men had fought back with their shark guns, but only because they had been attacked first. Once again the treasure hunt cover would hide everything!

The men were still wrestling with the coupling. Largo was looking back anxiously. Bond measured the distance and flung himself forward with a great kick against the coral.

Largo turned in time to fling up an arm and parry Bond's stab with his right-hand spear and Bond's stab with the left rattled harmlessly off the aqualung cylinders on Largo's back. Bond drove on head first, his hands outstretched for the air tube in Largo's mouth. Largo's hands flashed to protect himself, dropping his two spears and jerking back the joystick he had been holding in his right. The chariot surged forward away from the two guards and shot obliquely upwards towards the surface while the two bodies clung and struggled on its back.

It was impossible to fight scientifically. Both men tore vaguely at each other while their teeth clenched desperately on the rubber mouthpieces that were their lifelines, but Largo had a firm grip of the chariot between his knees while Bond had to use one hand to hang on to Largo's equipment to prevent himself being thrown. Again and again Largo's elbow crashed into Bond's face while Bond dodged from side to side to take the blows on the mouth and not on the precious glass of his mask. At the same time Bond hammered with his free hand at his only target, Largo's kidneys, beneath the brown square of flesh that was all he could reach.

The chariot broke surface fifty yards down the wide channel leading to the open sea and tore crazily on, its nose, tilted by Bond's weight over the tail, sticking at forty-five degrees out of the water. Now Bond was half in the wash and it would only be minutes before Largo managed to twist and get both hands to him. Bond made up his mind. He let go of Largo's aqualung and, clutching the stern of the torpedo between his legs, slid back until he felt the top of the rudder at his back. Now, if he could avoid the screw! He reached one hand down between his legs, got a firm grip of the rudder, and heaved himself backwards and off the machine. Now his face, inches away from the whirring propeller, was buffeted by the turbulence, but he dragged hard downwards and felt the stern coming with him. Soon the damned thing would be almost upright. Bond wrenched the blade of the rudder sideways in a right-angled turn and then, his arms almost torn out of their sockets by the strain, let go. Above and in front of him, as the torpedo veered right-handed, Largo's body, thrown by the sharp turn and the change of balance, crashed into the water, twisted quickly over and faced downwards, the mask searching for Bond.

Bond was beat, utterly defeated by exhaustion. Now there was nothing for him but to get away and somehow stay alive. The bomb was immobilized, the chariot gone, careering in circles over the sea. Largo was finished. Bond summoned the remains of his strength and sluggishly dived down towards his last hope, a refuge among the coral.

Almost lazily, Largo, his strength unimpaired, came down

after him, swimming in a giant, easy crawl. Bond swerved in among the coral heads. A white sand passage showed up and he followed it, then there was a fork. Bond, trusting to the small extra protection of his rubber suit, followed the narrower lane between the sharp clumps. But now a black shadow was above him, following him. Largo had not bothered to get into the channel. He was swimming above the coral, looking down, watching Bond, biding his time. Bond looked up. There was a gleam of teeth round the mouthpiece. Largo knew he had got him. Bond flexed his fingers to get more life into them. How could he hope to defeat those great hands, those hands that were machine-tools?

And now the narrow passage was widening. There was the glint of a sandy channel ahead. There was no room for Bond to turn round. He could only swim on into the open trap. Bond stopped and stood. It was the only thing to do. Largo had him like a rat in a trap. But at least Largo would have to come in and get him. Bond looked upwards. Yes, the great gleaming body, followed by its string of silver bubbles, was forging carefully on into the open water. Now, swiftly, like a pale seal, he dived down to the firm sand and stood facing Bond. Slowly he advanced between the walls of coral, the big hands held forward for the first hold. At ten paces he stopped. His eyes swivelled sideways to a coral clump. His right hand shot out at something and gave a quick yank. When the hand pulled back, it was writhing, writhing with eight more fingers. Largo held the baby octopus in front of him like a small, waving flower. His teeth drew away from the rubber mouthpiece and the clefts of a smile appeared in his cheeks. He put up one hand and significantly tapped his mask. Bond bent down and picked up a rock covered with seaweed. Largo was being melodramatic. A rock in Largo's mask would be more efficient than having an octopus slapped across his. Bond wasn't worried by the octopus. Only a day before he had been in company with a hundred of them. It was Largo's longer reach that worried him.

Largo took a pace forward and then another. Bond crouched, backing carefully, so as not to cut his rubber skin, into the narrow passage. Largo came on, slowly, deliberately. In two more paces he would attack.

Bond caught a glint of movement out in the open behind

Largo. Someone to the rescue? But the glint was white, not black. It was one of theirs!

Largo leaped forward.

Bond kicked off the coral and dived down for Largo's groin, the jagged rock in his hand. But Largo was ready. His knee came up hard against Bond's head and at the same time his right hand came swiftly down and clamped the small octopus across Bond's mask. Then from above, both his hands came down and got Bond by the neck, lifted him up like a child and held him at arm's length, pressing.

Bond could see nothing. Vaguely he felt the slimy tentacles groping over his face, getting a grip of the mouthpiece between his teeth, pulling. But the blood was roaring in his head and he knew he was gone.

Slowly he sank to his knees. But how, why was he sinking? What had happened to the hands at his throat? His eyes, squeezed tight in agony, opened and there was light. The octopus, now at his chest, let go and shot away among the coral. In front of him Largo, Largo with a spear sticking horribly through his neck, lay kicking feebly on the sand. Behind him and looking down at the body, stood a small, pale figure fitting another spear into an underwater gun. The long hair flowed round her head like a veil in the luminous sea.

Bond got slowly to his feet. He took a step forward. Suddenly he felt his knees beginning to give. A wave of blackness began to creep up over his vision. He leant against the coral, his mouth slackening round the oxygen tube. Water seeped into his mouth. No! he said to himself. No! Don't let that happen!

A hand took one of his. But Domino's eyes behind her mask were somewhere else. They were blank, lost. She was ill! What was the matter with her? Bond was suddenly awake again. His eyes took in the blood patches on her bathing dress, the angry red marks on her body between the scraps of bikini. They would both die, standing there, unless he did something about it. Slowly his leaden legs began to stir the black fins. They were moving up. It wasn't so difficult after all. And now, vaguely, her own fins were helping.

The two bodies reached the surface together and lay, face downwards, in the shallow troughs of the waves.

The oyster light of dawn slowly turned pink. It was going to be a beautiful day.

24

'TAKE IT EASY, MR BOND'

FELIX LEITER CAME into the white, antiseptic room and closed the door conspiratorially behind him. He came and stood beside the bed where Bond lay on the edge of drugged sleep. 'How's it going, feller?'

'Not bad. Just doped.'

'Doctor said I wasn't to see you. But I thought you might care to hear the score. Okay?'

'Sure.' Bond struggled to concentrate. He didn't really care. All he could think about was the girl.

'Well, I'll make it quick. Doctor's just doing his rounds and I'll get hell if he finds me here. They've recovered both bombs, and Kotze — the physicist chap — is singing like a bird. Seems SPECTRE's a bunch of really big-time hoodlums — ex-operators of SMERSH, the Mafia, the Gestapo — all the big outfits. Headquarters in Paris. Top man's called Blofeld, but the bastard got away — or anyway they haven't caught up with him yet, according to C.I.A. Probably Largo's radio silence warned him. Must be quite a Mister Genius. Kotze says SPECTRE's banked millions of dollars since they got going five or six years ago. This job was going to be the final haul. We were right about Miami. It *was* going to be Target No. 2. Same sort of operation. They were going to plant the second bomb in the yacht basin.'

Bond smiled weakly. 'So now everybody's happy.'

'Oh sure. Except me. Haven't been able to get away from my damned radio until now. Valves were almost blowing. And there's a pile of cipher stuff from M just longing for you to get around to it. Thank God the top brass from C.I.A. and a team from your outfit are flying in this evening to take charge. Then we can hand over and watch our two governments getting snarled up over the epilogue — what to tell the public, what to do with these SPECTRE guys, whether to make you a lord or a duke, how to persuade me to run for President — tricky little details like that. And then we'll damned well get away and have ourselves a ball some place. Maybe you'd care to take that girl along? Hell, she's the one that rates the medals! The guts! They cottoned on to her Geiger counter. God knows what that bastard Largo did to her. But she didn't sing — not a damned word! Then, when the team was under way, she somehow got herself out of the cabin porthole, with her gun and aqualung, and went to get him. Got him, and saved your life into the bargain! I swear I'll never call a girl a "frail" again — not an Italian girl anyway.' Leiter cocked an ear. He moved swiftly to the door. 'Hell, there's that damned medic gumshoeing down the corridor! Be seeing you, James.' He quickly turned the door handle, listened for a moment, and slipped out of the room.

Feebly, desperately, Bond called, 'Wait! Felix! Felix!' But the door had closed. Bond sank back and lay staring at the ceiling. Slowly anger boiled up inside him — and panic. Why in hell didn't someone tell him about the girl? What the hell did he care about all the rest? Was she all right? Where was she? Was she . . .

The door opened. Bond jerked himself upright. He shouted furiously at the white-coated figure. 'The girl. How is she? Quick! Tell me!'

Dr Stengel, the fashionable doctor of Nassau, was not only fashionable but a good doctor. He was one of the Jewish refugee doctors who, but for Hitler, would have been looking after some big hospital in a town the size of Düsseldorf. Instead, rich and grateful patients had built a modern clinic for him in Nassau where he treated the natives for shillings and the millionaires and their wives for ten guineas a visit. He was more used to handling overdoses of sleeping pills and the ailments of the rich and old than multiple abrasions, curare poisoning and odd wounds that looked more as if they belonged to the days of the pirates. But these were Government orders, and under the Official Secrets Act at that. Dr Stengel hadn't asked any questions about his patients, nor about the sixteen autopsies he had had to perform, six for Americans from the big submarine, and ten, including the corpse of the owner, from the fine yacht that had been in harbour for so long.

Now he said carefully, 'Miss Vitali will be all right. For the moment she is suffering from shock. She needs rest.'

'What else? What was the matter with her?'

'She had swum a long way. She was not in a condition to undertake such a physical strain.'

'Why not?'

The doctor moved towards the door. 'And now you too must rest. You have been through much. You will take one of those hypnotics once every six hours. Yes? And plenty of sleep. You will soon be on your feet again. But for some time you must take it easy, Mr Bond.'

Take it easy. You must take it easy, Mr Bond. Where had he heard those idiotic words before? Suddenly Bond was raging with fury. He lurched out of bed. In spite of the sudden giddiness, he staggered towards the doctor. He shook a fist in the urbane face — urbane because the doctor was used to the emotional storms of patients, and because he knew that in minutes the strong soporific would put Bond out for hours. 'Take it easy! God damn you! What do you know about taking it easy? Tell me what's the matter with that girl! Where is she? What's the number of her room?' Bond's hands fell limply to his sides. He said feebly, 'For God's sake tell me, Doctor. I, I need to know.'

Dr Stengel said patiently, kindly, 'Someone has ill-treated her. She is suffering from burns — many burns. She is still in great pain. But,' he waved a reassuring hand, 'inside she is well. She is in the next room, in No. 4. You may see her, but only for a minute. Then she will sleep. And so will you. Yes?' He held open the door.

'Thank you. Thank you, Doctor.' Bond walked out of the room with faltering steps. His blasted legs were beginning to give again. The doctor watched him go to the door of No. 4, watched him open it and close it again behind him with the exaggerated care of a drunken man. The doctor went off along the corridor thinking: it won't do him any harm and it may do her some good. It is what she needs — some tenderness.

Inside the small room, the jalousies threw bands of light and shadow over the bed. Bond staggered over to the bed and knelt down beside it. The small head on the pillow turned towards him. A hand came out and grasped his hair, pulling his head closer to her. Her voice said huskily, 'You are to stay here. Do you understand? You are not to go away.'

When Bond didn't answer, she feebly shook his head to and fro. 'Do you hear me, James? Do you understand?' She felt Bond's body slipping to the floor. When she let go his hair, he slumped down on the rug beside her bed. She carefully shifted her position and looked down at him. He was already asleep with his head cradled on the inside of his forearm.

The girl watched the dark, rather cruel face for a moment. Then she gave a small sigh, pulled the pillow to the edge of the bed so that it was just above him, laid her head down so that she could see him whenever she wanted to, and closed her eyes.

ON HER MAJESTY'S SECRET SERVICE

‘It was one of those Septembers when it seemed that the summer would never end . . .’

But it did end, and winter came in a lethal welter of mystery, bloodshed and multiple death amidst the snow.

This, the eleventh chapter in the biography of James Bond, is one of the longest. It is also the most enthralling.

Really the most? Really the most.

I

SEASCAPE WITH FIGURES

It was one of those Septembers when it seemed that the summer would never end.

The five-mile promenade of Royale-les-Eaux, backed by trim lawns emblazoned at intervals with tricolor beds of salvia, alyssum and lobelia, was bright with flags and, on the longest beach in the north of France, the gay bathing tents still marched prettily down to the tide-line in big, money-making battalions. Music, one of those lilting accordion waltzes, blared from the loudspeakers around the Olympic-size *piscine* and, from time to time, echoing above the music, a man's voice announced over the public address system that Philippe Bertrand, aged seven, was looking for his mother, that Yolande Lefèvre was waiting for her friends below the clock at the entrance, or that a Madame Dufours was demanded on the telephone. From the beach, particularly from the neighbourhood of the three playground enclosures — 'Joie de Vivre', 'Hélio' and 'Azur' — came a twitter of children's cries that waxed and waned with the thrill of their games and, farther out, on the firm sand left by the now distant sea, the shrill whistle of the physical-fitness instructor marshalled his teenagers through the last course of the day.

It was one of those beautiful, naive seaside panoramas for which the Brittany and Picardy beaches have provided the setting — and inspired their recorders, Boudin, Tissot, Monet — ever since the birth of *plages* and *bains de mer* more than a hundred years ago.

To James Bond, sitting in one of the concrete shelters with his face to the setting sun, there was something poignant, ephemeral about it all. It reminded him almost too vividly of childhood — of the velvet feel of the hot powder sand, and the painful grit of wet sand between young toes when the time came for him to put his shoes and socks on, of the precious little pile of sea-shells and interesting wrack on the sill of his bedroom window ('No, we'll have to leave that behind, darling. It'll dirty up your trunk!'), of the small crabs scuttling away from the nervous fingers groping beneath the seaweed in the rockpools, of the swimming and swimming and swimming through the dancing waves — always in those days, it seemed, lit with sunshine — and then the infuriating, inevitable 'time to come out'. It was all there, his own childhood, spread out before him to have another look at. What a long time ago they were, those spade-and-bucket days! How far he had come since the freckles and the Cadbury milk-chocolate Flakes and the fizzy lemonade! Impatiently Bond lit a cigarette, pulled his shoulders out of their slouch and slammed the mawkish memories back into their long-closed file. Today he was a grown-up, a man with years of dirty, dangerous memories — a spy. He was not sitting in this concrete hideout to sentimentalize about a pack of scrubby, smelly children on a beach scattered with bottle-tops and lolly-sticks and fringed by a sea thick with sun-oil and putrid with the main drains of Royale. He was here, he had chosen to be here, to spy. To spy on a woman.

The sun was getting lower. Already one could smell the September chill that all day had lain hidden beneath the heat. The cohorts of bathers were in quick retreat, striking their little camps and filtering up the steps and across the promenade into the shelter of the town where the lights were going up in the cafés. The announcer at the swimming-pool harried his customers: 'Allo! Allo! Fermeture en dix minutes! A dix-huit heures, fermeture de la piscine!' Silhouetted in the path of the setting sun, the two Bombard rescue-boats with flags bearing a blue cross on a yellow background were speeding northwards for their distant shelter up-river in the Vieux Port. The last of the gay, giraffe-like sand-yachts fled down the distant water-line towards its corral among the sand dunes, and the three *agents cyclistes* in charge of the car parks pedalled away through the melting ranks of cars towards the police station in the centre of the town. In a matter of minutes the vast expanse of sand — the tide, still receding, was already a mile out — would be left to the seagulls that would soon be flocking in their hordes to forage for the scraps of food left by the picnickers. Then the orange ball of the sun would hiss down into the sea and the beach would, for a while, be entirely deserted, until, under cover of darkness, the prowling lovers would come to writhe briefly, grittily in the dark corners between the bathing huts and the sea-wall.

On the beaten stretch of sand below where James Bond was sitting, two golden girls in exciting bikinis packed up the game of Jokari which they had been so provocatively playing, and raced each other up the steps towards Bond's shelter. They flaunted their bodies at him, paused and chattered to see if he would respond, and, when he didn't, linked arms and sauntered on towards the town, leaving Bond wondering why it was that French girls had more prominent navels than any others. Was it that French surgeons sought to add, even in this minute respect, to the future sex-appeal of girl babies?

And now, up and down the beach, the lifeguards gave a final blast on their horns to announce that they were going off duty, the music from the *piscine* stopped in mid-tune and the great expanse of sand was suddenly deserted.

But not quite! A hundred yards out, lying face downwards on a black and white striped bathing-wrap, on the private patch of firm sand where she had installed herself an hour before, the girl was still there, motionless, spreadeagled in direct line between James Bond and the setting sun that was now turning the left-behind pools and shallow rivulets into blood-red, meandering scrawls across the middle distance. Bond went on watching her — now, in the silence and emptiness, with an ounce more tension. He was waiting for her to do something — for something, he didn't know what, to happen. It would be more true to say that he was watching *over* her. He had an instinct that she was in some sort of danger. Or was it just that there was the smell of danger in the air? He didn't know. He only knew that he mustn't leave her alone, particularly now that everyone else had gone.

James Bond was mistaken. Not everyone else had gone. Behind him, at the Café de la Plage on the other side of the promenade, two men in raincoats and dark caps sat at a secluded table bordering the sidewalk. They had half-empty cups of coffee in front of them and they didn't talk. They sat and watched the blur on the frosted-glass partition of the shelter that was James Bond's head and shoulders. They also watched, but less intently, the distant white blur on the sand that was the girl. Their stillness, and their unseasonable clothes, would have made a disquieting impression on anyone who, in his turn, might have been watching them. But there was no such person, except their waiter who had simply put them in the category of 'bad news' and hoped they would soon be on their way.

When the lower rim of the orange sun touched the sea, it was almost as if a signal had sounded for the girl. She slowly got to her feet, ran both hands backwards through her hair and began to walk evenly, purposefully towards the sun and the far-away froth of the water-line over a mile away. It would be violet dusk by the time she reached the sea and one might have guessed that this was probably the last day of her holiday, her last bathe.

James Bond thought otherwise. He left his shelter, ran down the steps to the sand and began walking out after her at a fast pace. Behind him, across the promenade, the two men in rain-coats also seemed to think otherwise. One of them briskly threw down some coins and they both got up and, walking strictly in step, crossed the promenade to the sand and, with a kind of urgent military precision, marched rapidly side by side in Bond's tracks.

Now the strange pattern of figures on the vast expanse of empty, blood-streaked sand was eerily conspicuous. Yet it was surely not one to be interfered with! The pattern had a nasty, a secret smell. The white girl, the bare-headed young man, the two squat, marching pursuers — it had something of a kind of deadly Grandmother's Steps about it. In the café, the waiter collected the coins and looked after the distant figures, still outlined by the last quarter of the orange sun. It smelt like police business — or the other thing. He would keep it to himself but remember it. He might get his name in the papers.

James Bond was rapidly catching up with the girl. Now he knew that he would get to her just as she reached the water-line. He began to wonder what he would say to her, how he would put it. He couldn't say, 'I had a hunch you were going to commit suicide so I came after you to stop you.' 'I was going for a walk on the beach and I thought I recognized you. Will you have a drink after your swim?' would be childish. He finally decided to say, 'Oh, Tracy!' and then, when she turned round, 'I was worried about you.' Which would at least be inoffensive and, for the matter of that, true.

The sea was now gunmetal below a primrose horizon. A small, westerly offshore breeze, drawing the hot land-air out to sea, had risen and was piling up wavelets that scrolled in whitely as far as the eye could see. Flocks of herring gulls lazily rose and settled again at the girl's approach, and the air was full of their mewing and of the endless lap-lap of the small waves. The soft indigo dusk added a touch of melancholy to the empty solitude of sand and sea, now so far away from the comforting bright lights and holiday bustle of 'La Reine de la Côte Opale', as Royale-les-Eaux had splendidly christened herself. Bond looked forward to getting the girl back to those bright lights. He watched the lithe golden figure in the white one-piece bathing-suit and wondered how soon she would be able to hear his voice above the noise of the gulls and the sea. Her pace had slowed a fraction as she approached the water-line and her head, with its bell of heavy fair hair to the shoulders, was slightly bowed, in thought perhaps, or tiredness.

Bond quickened his step until he was only ten paces behind her. 'Hey! Tracy!'

The girl didn't start or turn quickly round. Her steps faltered and stopped, and then, as a small wave creamed in and died at her feet, she turned slowly and stood squarely facing him. Her eyes, puffed and wet with tears, looked past him. Then they met his. She said dully, 'What is it? What do you want?'

'I was worried about you. What are you doing out here? What's the matter?'

The girl looked past him again. Her clenched right hand went up to her mouth. She said something, something Bond couldn't understand, from behind it. Then a voice, from very close behind Bond, said softly, silkily, 'Don't move or you get it back of the knee.'

Bond swirled round into a crouch, his gun hand inside his coat. The steady silver eyes of the two automatics sneered at him.

Bond slowly straightened himself. He dropped his hand to his side and the held breath came out between his teeth in a quiet hiss. The two dead-pan, professional faces told him even more than the two silver eyes of the guns. They held no tension, no excitement. The thin half-smiles were relaxed, contented. The eyes were not even wary. They were almost bored. Bond had looked into such faces many times before. This was routine. These men were killers — pro-killers.

Bond had no idea who these men were, who they worked for, what this was all about. On the theory that worry is a dividend paid to disaster before it is due, he consciously relaxed his muscles and emptied his mind of questions. He stood and waited.

'Position your hands behind your neck.' The silky, patient voice was from the south, from the Mediterranean. It fitted with the men's faces — tough-skinned, widely pored, yellow-brown. Marseillais perhaps, or Italian. The Mafia? The faces belonged to good secret police or tough crooks. Bond's mind ticked and whirred, selecting cards like an IBM machine. What enemies had he got in those areas? Might it be Blofeld? Had the hare turned upon the hound?

When the odds are hopeless, when all seems to be lost, then is the time to be calm, to make a show of authority — at least of indifference. Bond smiled into the eyes of the man who had spoken. 'I don't think your mother would like to know what you are doing this evening. You are a Catholic? So I will do as you ask.' The man's eyes glittered. Touché! Bond clasped his hands behind his head.

The man stood aside so as to have a clear field of fire while his Number Two removed Bond's Walther PPK from the soft leather holster inside his trouser belt and ran expert hands down his sides, down his arms to the wrists and down the inside of his thighs. Then Number Two stood back, pocketed the Walther and again took out his own gun.

Bond glanced over his shoulder. The girl had said nothing, expressed neither surprise nor alarm. Now she was standing with her back to the group, looking out to sea, apparently relaxed, unconcerned. What in God's name was it all about? Had she been used as a bait? But for whom? And now what? Was he to be executed, his body left lying to be rolled back inshore by the tide? It seemed the only solution. If it was a question of some kind of a deal, the four of them could not just walk back across the mile of sand to the town and say polite goodbyes on the promenade steps. No. This was the terminal point. Or was it? From the north, through the deep indigo dusk, came the fast, rattling hum of an outboard and, as Bond watched, the cream of a thick bow-wave showed and then the blunt outline of one of the Bombard rescue-craft, the flat-bottomed inflatable rubber boats with a single Johnson engine in the flattened stern. So they had been spotted! By the coast-guards perhaps? And here was rescue! By God, he'd roast these two thugs when they got to the harbour police at the Vieux Port! But what story would he tell about the girl?

Bond turned back to face the men. At once he knew the worst. They had rolled their trousers up to the knees and were waiting, composedly, their shoes in one hand and their guns in the other. This was no rescue. It was just part of the ride. Oh well! Paying no attention to the men, Bond bent down, rolled up his trousers as they had done and, in the process of fumbling with his socks and shoes, palmed one of his heel knives and, half turning towards the boat that had now grounded in the shallows, transferred it to his right-hand trouser pocket.

No words were exchanged. The girl climbed aboard first, then Bond, and lastly the two men who helped the engine with a final shove on the stern. The boatman, who looked like any other French deep-sea fisherman, whirled the blunt nose of the Bombard round, changed gears to forward, and they were off northwards through the buffeting waves while the golden hair of the girl streamed back and softly whipped James Bond's cheek.

'Tracy. You're going to catch cold. Here. Take my coat.' Bond slipped his coat off. She held out a hand to help him put it on her. In the process her hand found his and pressed it. Now what the hell? Bond edged closer to her. He felt her body respond. Bond glanced at the two men. They sat hunched against the wind, their hands in their pockets, watchful, but somehow uninterested. Behind them the necklace of lights that was Royale receded swiftly until it was only a golden glow on the horizon. James Bond's right hand felt for the comforting knife in his pocket and ran his thumb across the razor-sharp blade.

While he wondered how and when he might have a chance to use it, the rest of his mind ran back over the previous twenty-four hours and panned them for the gold-dust of truth.

2

GRAN TURISMO

ALMOST EXACTLY TWENTY-FOUR hours before, James Bond had been nursing his car, the old Continental Bentley — the 'R' type chassis with the big 6 engine and a 13:40 back-axle ratio — that he had now been driving for three years, along that fast but dull stretch of N.1 between Abbeville and Montreuil that takes the English tourist back to his country via Silver City Airways from Le Touquet or by ferry from Boulogne or Calais. He was hurrying safely, at between eighty and ninety, driving by the automatic pilot that is built in to all rally-class drivers, and his mind was totally occupied with drafting his letter of resignation from the Secret Service.

The letter, addressed 'Personal for M', had got to the following stage:

> Sir,
>
> I have the honour to request that you will accept my resignation from the Service, effective forthwith.
>
> My reasons for this submission, which I put forward with much regret, are the following:
>
> (1) My duties in the Service, until some twelve months ago, have been connected with the Double-O Section and you, Sir, have been kind enough, from time to time, to express your satisfaction with my performance of those duties, which I, for my part, have enjoyed. To my chagrin, [Bond had been pleased with this fine word] however, on the successful completion of Operation 'Thunderball', I received personal instructions from you to concentrate all my efforts, without a terminal date, [another felicitous phrase!] on the pursuit of Ernst Stavro Blofeld and on his apprehension, together with any members of SPECTRE — otherwise 'The Special Executive for Counter-Intelligence, Revenge and Extortion' — if that organization had been

recreated since its destruction at the climax of Operation 'Thunderball'.

(2) I accepted the assignment with, if you will recall, reluctance. It seemed to me, and I so expressed myself at the time, that this was purely an investigatory matter which could well have been handled, using straightforward police methods, by other sections of the Service — local Stations, allied foreign secret services and Interpol. My objections were overruled, and for close on twelve months I have been engaged all over the world in routine detective work which, in the case of every scrap of rumour, every lead, has proved abortive. I have found no trace of this man nor of a revived SPECTRE, if such exists.

(3) My many appeals to be relieved of this wearisome and fruitless assignment, even when addressed to you personally, Sir, have been ignored or, on occasion, curtly dismissed, and my frequent animadversions [another good one!] to the effect that Blofeld is dead have been treated with a courtesy that I can only describe as scant. [Neat, that! Perhaps a bit too neat!]

(4) The above unhappy circumstances have recently achieved their climax in my undercover mission (Ref. Station R'S PX 437/007) to Palermo, in pursuit of a hare of quite outrageous falsity. This animal took the shape of one 'Blauenfelder', a perfectly respectable German citizen engaged in viniculture — specifically the grafting of Moselle grapes on to the Sicilian strains to enhance the sugar content of the latter which, for your passing information, [Steady on, old chap! Better redraft all this!] are inclined to sourness. My investigations into this individual brought me to the attention of the Mafia and my departure from Sicily was, to say the least, ignominious.

(5) Having regard, Sir, to the above and, specifically, to the continued misuse of the qualities, modest though they may be, that have previously fitted me for the more arduous, and, to me, more rewarding, duties associated with the work of the Double-O Section, I beg leave to submit my resignation from the Service.

I am, Sir,

Your Obedient Servant,

007

Of course, reflected Bond, as he nursed the long bonnet of his car through a built-up S-bend, he would have to rewrite a lot of it. Some of it was a bit pompous and there were one or two cracks that would have to be ironed out or toned down. But that was the gist of what he would dictate to his secretary when he got back to the office the day after tomorrow. And if she burst into tears, to hell with her! He meant it. By God he did. He was fed to the teeth with chasing the ghost of Blofeld. And the same went for SPECTRE. The thing had been smashed. Even a man of Blofeld's genius, in the impossible event that he still existed, could never get a machine of that calibre running again.

It was then, on a ten-mile straight cut through a forest, that it happened. Triple wind-horns screamed their banshee discord in his ear, and a low white two-seater, a Lancia Flaminia Zagato Spyder with its hood down, tore past him, cut in cheekily across his bonnet and pulled away, the sexy boom of its twin exhausts echoing back from the border of trees. And it was a girl driving, a girl with a shocking-pink scarf tied round her hair, leaving a brief pink tail that the wind blew horizontal behind her.

If there was one thing that set James Bond really moving in life, with the exception of gun-play, it was being passed at speed by a pretty girl; and it was his experience that girls who drove competitively like that were always pretty — and exciting. The shock of the wind-horn's scream had automatically cut out 'George', emptied Bond's head of all other thought, and brought his car back under manual control. Now, with a tight-lipped smile, he stamped his foot into the floorboard, held the wheel firmly at a quarter to three, and went after her.

100, 110, 115, and he still wasn't gaining. Bond reached forward to the dashboard and flicked up a red switch. The thin high whine of machinery on the brink of torment tore at his eardrums and the Bentley gave an almost perceptible kick forward. 120, 125. He was definitely gaining. 50 yards, 40, 30! Now he could just see her eyes in her rear mirror. But the good road was running out. One of those exclamation marks that the French use to denote danger flashed by on his right. And now, over a rise, there was a church spire, the clustered houses of a small village at the bottom of a steepish hill, the snake sign of another S-bend. Both cars slowed down — 90, 80, 70. Bond watched her tail-lights briefly blaze, saw her right hand reach down to the floor stick, almost simultaneously with his own, and change down. Then they were in the S-bend, on cobbles, and he had to brake as he enviously watched the way her de Dion axle married her rear wheels to the rough going, while his own live axle hopped and skittered as he wrenched at the wheel. And then it was the end of the village, and, with a brief wag of her tail as she came out of the S, she was off like a bat out of hell up the long straight rise and he had lost fifty yards.

And so the race went on, Bond gaining a little on the straights but losing it all to the famous Lancia road-holding through the villages — and, he had to admit, to her wonderful, nerveless driving. And now a big Michelin sign said 'Montreuil 5, Royale-les-Eaux 10, Le Touquet-Paris-Plage 15', and he wondered about her destination and debated with himself whether he shouldn't forget about Royale and the night he had promised himself at its famous casino and just follow where she went, wherever it was, and find out who this devil of a girl was.

The decision was taken out of his hands. Montreuil is a dangerous town with cobbled, twisting streets and much farm traffic. Bond was fifty yards behind her at the outskirts, but, with his big car, he couldn't follow her fast slalom through the hazards and, by the time he was out of the town and over the Étaples-Paris level-crossing, she had vanished. The left-hand turn for Royale came up. Was there a little dust hanging in the bend? Bond took the turn, somehow knowing that he was going to see her again.

He leaned forward and flicked down the red switch. The moan of the blower died away and there was silence in the car as he motored along, easing his tense muscles. He wondered if the supercharger had damaged the engine. Against the solemn warnings of Rolls-Royce, he had had fitted, by his pet expert at the Headquarters' motor pool, an Arnott supercharger controlled by a magnetic clutch. Rolls-Royce had said the crankshaft bearings wouldn't take the extra load and, when he confessed to them what he had done, they regretfully but firmly withdrew their guarantees and washed their hands of their bastardized child. This was the first time he had notched 125 and the rev. counter had hovered dangerously over the red line at 4,500. But the temperature and oil were O.K. and there were no expensive noises. And, by God, it had been fun!

James Bond idled through the pretty approaches to Royale, through the young beeches and the heavy-scented pines, looking forward to the evening and remembering his other annual pilgrimages to this place and, particularly, the great battle across the baize he had had with Le Chiffre so many years ago. He had come a long way since then, dodged many bullets and much death and loved many girls, but there had been a drama and a poignancy about that particular adventure that every year drew him back to Royale and its casino and to the small granite cross in the little churchyard that simply said 'Vesper Lynd. R.I.P.'

And now what was the place holding for him on this beautiful September evening? A big win? A painful loss? A beautiful girl — that beautiful girl?

To think first of the game. This was the weekend of the 'clôture annuelle'. Tonight, this very Saturday night, the Casino Royale was holding its last night of the season. It was always a big event and there would be pilgrims even from Belgium and Holland, as well as the rich regulars from Paris and Lille. In addition, the 'Syndicat d'Initiative et des Bains de Mer de Royale' traditionally threw open its doors to all its local contractors and suppliers, and there was free champagne and a great groaning buffet to reward the town people for their work during the season. It was a tremendous carouse that rarely finished before breakfast time. The tables would be packed and there would be a very high game indeed.

Bond had one million francs of private capital — Old Francs, of course — about seven hundred pounds' worth. He always reckoned his private funds in Old Francs. It made him feel so rich. On the other hand, he made out his official expenses in New Francs because that made them look smaller — but probably not to the Chief Accountant at Headquarters! One million francs! For that evening he was a millionaire! Might he so remain by tomorrow morning!

And now he was coming into the Promenade des Anglais and there was the bastard Empire frontage of the Hotel Splendide. And there, by God, on the gravel sweep alongside its steps, stood the little white Lancia and, at this moment, a *bagagiste*, in a striped waistcoat and green apron, was carrying two Vuitton suitcases up the steps to the entrance!

So!

James Bond slid his car into the million-pound line of cars in the car park, told the same *bagagiste*, who was now taking rich, small stuff out of the Lancia, to bring up his bags, and went in to the reception desk. The manager impressively took over from the clerk and greeted Bond with golden-toothed effusion, while making a mental note to earn a good mark with the Chef de Police by reporting Bond's arrival, so that the Chef could, in his turn, make a good mark with the Deuxième and the SDT by putting the news on the teleprinter to Paris.

Bond said, 'By the way, Monsieur Maurice. Who is the lady who has just driven up in the white Lancia? She is staying here?'

'Yes, indeed, Mon Commandant.' Bond received an extra two teeth in the enthusiastic smile. 'The lady is a good friend of the house. The father is a very big industrial from the South. She is La Comtesse Teresa di Vicenzo. Monsieur must surely have read of her in the papers. Madame la Comtesse is a lady — how shall I put it?' — the smile became secret, between men — 'a lady, shall we say, who lives life to the full.'

'Ah, yes. Thank you. And how has the season been?'

The small talk continued as the manager personally took Bond up in the lift and showed him into one of the handsome grey and white Directoire rooms with the deep rose coverlet on the bed that Bond remembered so well. Then, with a final exchange of courtesies, James Bond was alone.

Bond was faintly disappointed. She sounded a bit grand for him, and he didn't happen to like girls, film stars for instance, who were in any way public property. He liked private girls, girls he could discover himself and make his own. Perhaps, he admitted, there was inverted snobbery in this. Perhaps, even less worthily, it was that the famous ones were less easy to get.

His two battered suitcases came and he unpacked leisurely and then ordered from Room Service a bottle of the Taittinger Blanc de Blancs that he had made his traditional drink at Royale. When the bottle, in its frosted silver bucket, came, he drank a quarter of it rather fast and then went into the bathroom and had an ice-cold shower and washed his hair with Pinaud Elixir, that prince among shampoos, to get the dust of the roads out of it. Then he slipped on his dark-blue tropical worsted trousers, white sea-island cotton shirt, socks and black casual shoes (he abhorred shoe-laces), and went and sat by the window and looked out across the promenade to the sea and wondered where he would have dinner and what he would choose to eat.

James Bond was not a gourmet. In England he lived on grilled soles, œufs cocotte and cold roast beef with potato salad. But when travelling abroad, generally by himself, meals were a welcome break in the day, something to look forward to, something to break the tension of fast driving, with its risks taken or avoided, the narrow squeaks, the permanent background of concern for the fitness of his machine. In fact, at this moment, after covering the long stretch from the Italian frontier at Ventimiglia in a comfortable three days (God knew there was no reason to hurry back to Headquarters!), he was fed to the teeth with the sucker-traps for gourmandizing tourists. The 'Hostelleries', the 'Vieilles Auberges', the 'Relais Fleuris' — he had had the lot. He had had their 'Bonnes Tables', and their 'Fines Bouteilles'. He had had their 'Spécialités du Chef' — generally a rich sauce of cream and wine and a few button mushrooms concealing poor-quality meat or fish. He had had the whole lip-smacking ritual of winemanship and foodmanship and, incidentally, he had had quite enough of the Bisodol that went with it!

The French belly-religion had delivered its final kick at him the night before. Wishing to avoid Orléans, he had stopped south of this uninspiring city and had chosen a mock-Breton auberge on the south bank of the Loire, despite its profusion of window-boxes and sham beams, ignoring the china cat pursuing the china bird across its gabled roof, because it was right on the edge of the Loire — perhaps Bond's favourite river in the world. He had stoically accepted the hammered copper warming pans, brass cooking utensils and other antique bogosities that cluttered the walls of the entrance hall, had left his bag in his room and had gone for an agreeable walk along the softly running, swallow-skimmed river. The dining-room, in which he was one of a small handful of tourists, had sounded the alarm. Above a fire-place of electric logs and over-polished fire-irons there had hung a coloured plaster escutcheon bearing the dread device: ICY DOULCE FRANCE. All the plates, of some hideous local ware, bore the jingle, irritatingly inscrutable, 'Jamais en Vain, Toujours en Vin', and the surly waiter, stale with 'fin de saison', had served him with the fly-walk of the Pâté Maison (sent back for a new slice) and a Poularde à la crème that was the only genuine antique in the place. Bond had moodily washed down this sleazy provender with a bottle of instant Pouilly-Fuissé and was finally insulted the next morning by a bill for the meal in excess of five pounds.

It was to efface all these dyspeptic memories that Bond now sat at his window, sipped his Taittinger and weighed up the pros and cons of the local eating places and wondered what dishes it would be best to gamble on. He finally chose one of his favourite restaurants in France, a modest establishment, unpromisingly placed exactly opposite the railway station of Étaples, rang up his old friend Monsieur Bécaud for a table and, two hours later, was motoring back to the Casino with Turbot poché, sauce mousseline, and half the best roast partridge he had eaten in his life, under his belt.

Greatly encouraged, and further stimulated by half a bottle of Mouton Rothschild '53 and a glass of ten-year-old Calvados with his three cups of coffee, he went cheerfully up the thronged steps of the Casino with the absolute certitude that this was going to be a night to remember.

3

THE GAMBIT OF SHAME

(THE BOMBARD HAD now beaten round the dolefully clanging bell-buoy and was hammering slowly up the River Royale against the current. The gay lights of the little marina, haven of cross-Channel yachtsmen, showed way up on the right bank, and it crossed Bond's mind to wait until they were slightly above it and then plunge his knife into the side and bottom of the rubber Bombard and swim for it. But he already heard in his mind the boom of the guns and heard the zwip and splash of the bullets round his head until, probably, there came the bright burst of light and the final flash of knowledge that he had at last had it. And anyway, how well could the girl swim, and in this current? Bond was now very cold. He leant closer against her and went back to remembering the night before and combing his memories for clues.)

After the long walk across the Salle d'Entrée, past the *vitrines* of Van Cleef, Lanvin, Hermès and the rest, there came the brief pause for identification at the long desk backed by the tiers of filing cabinets, the payment for the Carte d'Entrée pour les Salles de Jeux, the quick, comptometer survey of the physiognomiste at the entrance, the bow and flourish of the garishly uniformed huissier at the door, and James Bond was inside the belly of the handsome, scented machine.

He paused for a moment by the caisse, his nostrils flaring at the smell of the crowded, electric, elegant scene, then he walked slowly across to the top chemin de fer table beside the entrance to the luxuriously appointed bar, and caught the eye of Monsieur Pol, the Chef de Jeu of the high game. Monsieur Pol spoke to a huissier and Bond was shown to Number Seven, reserved by a counter from the huissier's pocket. The huissier gave a quick brush to the baize inside the line — that famous line that had been the bone of contention in the Tranby Croft case involving King Edward VII — polished an ashtray and pulled out the chair for Bond. Bond sat down. The shoe was at the other end of the table, at Number Three. Cheerful and relaxed, Bond examined the faces of the other players while the Changeur changed his notes for a hundred thousand into ten blood-red counters of ten thousand each. Bond stacked them in a neat pile in front of him and watched the play which, he saw from the notice hanging between the green-shaded lights over the table, was for a minimum of one hundred New Francs, or ten thousand of the old. But he noted that the game was being opened by each banker for up to five hundred New Francs — serious money — say forty pounds as a starter.

The players were the usual international mixture — three Lille textile tycoons in over-padded dinner-jackets, a couple of heavy women in diamonds who might be Belgian, a rather Agatha Christie-style little Englishwoman who played quietly and successfully and might be a villa owner, two middle-aged Americans in dark suits who appeared cheerful and slightly drunk, probably down from Paris, and Bond. Watchers and casual punters were two-deep round the table. No girl!

The game was cold. The shoe went slowly round the table, each banker in turn going down on that dread third coup which, for some reason, is the sound barrier at chemin de fer which must be broken if you are to have a run. Each time, when it came to Bond's turn, he debated whether to bow to the pattern and pass his bank after the second coup. Each time, for nearly an hour of play, he obstinately told himself that the pattern would break, and why not with him? That the cards have no memory and that it was time for them to run. And each time, as did the other players, he went down on the third coup. The shoe came to an end. Bond left his money on the table and wandered off among the other tables, visiting the roulette, the trente et quarante and the baccarat table, to see if he could find the girl. When she had passed him that evening in the Lancia, he had only caught a glimpse of fair hair and of a pure, rather authoritative profile. But he knew that he would recognize her at once, if only by the cord of animal magnetism that had bound them together during the race. But there was no sign of her.

Bond went back to the table. The croupier was marshalling the six packs into the oblong block that would soon be slipped into the waiting shoe. Since Bond was beside him, the croupier offered him the neutral, plain red card to cut the pack with. Bond rubbed the card between his fingers and, with amused deliberation, slipped it as nearly half-way down the block of cards as he could estimate. The croupier smiled at him and at his deliberation, went through the legerdemain that would in due course bring the red stop card into the tongue of the shoe and stop the game just seven cards before the end of the shoe, packed the long block of cards into the shoe, slid in the metal tongue that held them prisoner and announced, loud and clear: 'Messieurs [the 'mesdames' are traditionally not mentioned; since Victorian days it has been assumed that ladies do not gamble], les jeux sont faits. Numéro six à la main.' The Chef de Jeu, on his throne behind the croupier, took up the cry, the huissiers shepherded distant stragglers back to their places, and the game began again.

James Bond confidently bancoed the Lille tycoon on his left, won, made up the cagnotte with a few small counters, and doubled the stake to two thousand New Francs — two hundred thousand of the old.

He won that, and the next. Now for the hurdle of the third coup and he was off to the races! He won it with a natural nine! Eight hundred thousand in the bank (as Bond reckoned it)! Again he won, with difficulty this time — his six against a five. Then he decided to play it safe and pile up some capital. Of the one million six, he asked for the six hundred to be put 'en garage', removed from the stake, leaving a bank of one million. Again he won. Now he put a million 'en garage'. Once more a bank of a million, and now he would have a fat cushion of one million six coming to him anyway! But it was getting difficult to make up his stake. The table was becoming wary of this dark Englishman who played so quietly, wary of the half-smile of certitude on his rather cruel mouth. Who was he? Where did he come from? What did he do? There was a murmur of excited speculation round the table. So far a run of six. Would the Englishman pocket his small fortune and pass the bank? Or would he continue to run it? Surely the cards must change! But James Bond's mind was made up. The cards have no memory in defeat. They also have no memory in victory. He ran the bank three more times, adding each time a million to his 'garage', and then the little old English lady, who had so far left the running to the others, stepped in and bancoed him at the tenth turn, and Bond smiled across at her, knowing that she was going to win. And she did, ignominiously, with a one against Bond's 'bûche' — three kings, making zero.

There was a sigh of relief round the table. The spell had been broken! And a whisper of envy as the heavy, mother-of-pearl plaques piled nearly a foot high, four million, six hundred thousand francs' worth, well over three thousand pounds, were shunted across to Bond with the flat of the croupier's spatula. Bond tossed a plaque for a hundred New Francs to the croupier, received the traditional 'Merci, monsieur! Pour le personnel!' and the game went on.

James Bond lit a cigarette and paid little attention as the shoe went shunting round the table away from him. He had made a packet, dammit! A bloody packet! Now he must be careful. Sit on it. But not too careful, not sit on all of it! This was a glorious evening. It was barely past midnight. He didn't want to go home yet. So be it! He would run his bank when it came to him, but do no bancoing of the others — absolutely none. The cards had got hot. His run had shown that. There would be other runs now, and he could easily burn his fingers chasing them.

Bond was right. When the shoe got to Number Five, to one of the Lille tycoons two places to the left of Bond, an ill-mannered, loud-mouthed player who smoked a cigar out of an amber-and-gold holder and who tore at the cards with heavily manicured, spatulate fingers and slapped them down like a German tarot player, he quickly got through the third coup and was off. Bond, in accordance with his plan, left him severely alone and now, at the sixth coup, the bank stood at twenty thousand New Francs — two million of the old, and the table had got wary again. Everyone was sitting on his money.

The croupier and the Chef de Jeu made their loud calls, 'Un banco de vingt mille! Faites vos jeux, messieurs. Il reste à compléter! Un banco de vingt mille!'

And then there she was! She had come from nowhere and was standing beside the croupier, and Bond had no time to take in more than golden arms, a beautiful golden face with brilliant blue eyes and shocking-pink lips, some kind of a plain white dress, a bell of golden hair down to her shoulders, and then it came. 'Banco!'

Everyone looked at her and there was a moment's silence. And then 'Le banco est fait' from the croupier, and the monster from Lille (as Bond now saw him) was tearing the cards out of the shoe, and hers were on their way over to her on the croupier's spatula.

She bent down and there was a moment of discreet cleavage in the white V of her neckline.

'Une carte.'

Bond's heart sank. She certainly hadn't anything better than a five. The monster turned his up. Seven. And now he scrabbled out a card for her and flicked it contemptuously across. A simpering queen!

The croupier delicately faced her other two cards with the tip of his spatula. A four! She had lost!

Bond groaned inwardly and looked across to see how she had taken it.

What he saw was not reassuring. The girl was whispering urgently to the Chef de Jeu. He was shaking his head, sweat was beading on his cheeks. In the silence that had fallen round the table, the silence that licks its lips at the strong smell of scandal, which was now electric in the air, Bond heard the Chef de Jeu say firmly, 'Mais c'est impossible. Je regrette, madame. Il faut vous arranger à la caisse.'

And now that most awful of all whispers in a casino was running among the watchers and the players like a slithering reptile: 'Le coup du déshonneur! C'est le coup du déshonneur! Quelle honte! Quelle honte!'

Oh, my God! thought Bond. She's done it! She hasn't got the money! And for some reason she can't get any credit at the caisse!

The monster from Lille was making the most of the situation. He knew that the Casino would pay in the case of a default. He sat back with lowered eyes, puffing at his cigar, the injured party.

But Bond knew of the stigma the girl would carry for the rest of her life. The Casinos of France are a strong trade union. They have to be. Tomorrow the telegrams would go out: 'Madame la Comtesse Teresa di Vicenzo, passport number X, is to be put on the black list.' That would be the end of her casino life in France, in Italy, probably also in Germany, Egypt and, today, England. It was like being declared a bad risk at Lloyd's or with the City security firm of Dun and Bradstreet. In American gambling circles, she might even have been liquidated. In Europe, for her, the fate would be almost as severe. In the circles in which, presumably, she moved, she would be bad news, unclean. The 'coup du déshonneur' simply wasn't done. It was social ostracism.

Not caring about the social ostracism, thinking only about the wonderful girl who had outdriven him, shown him her tail, between Abbeville and Montreuil, James Bond leant slightly forward. He tossed two of the precious pearly plaques into the centre of the table. He said, with a slightly bored, slightly puzzled intonation, 'Forgive me. Madame has forgotten that we agreed to play in partnership this evening.' And, not looking at the girl, but speaking with authority to the Chef de Jeu, 'I beg your pardon. My mind was elsewhere. Let the game continue.'

The tension round the table relaxed. Or rather it changed to another target, away from the girl. Was it true what this Englishman had said? But it must be! One does not pay two million francs for a girl. But previously there there had been no relationship between them — so far as one could see. They had been at opposite sides of the table. No signs of complicity had been exchanged. And the girl? She had shown no emotion. She had looked at the man, once, with directness. Then she had quietly moved away from the table, towards the bar. There was certainly something odd here — something one did not understand. But the game was proceeding. The Chef de Jeu had surreptitiously wiped a handkerchief across his face. The croupier had raised his head, which, previously, had seemed to be bowed under some kind of emotional guillotine. And now the old pattern had re-established itself. 'La partie continue. Un banco de quarante mille!'

James Bond glanced down at the still formidable pile of counters between his curved, relaxed arms. It would be nice to get that two million francs back. It might be hours before a banco of equal size offered the chance. After all, he was playing with the Casino's money! His profits represented 'found' money and, if he lost, he could still go away with a small profit — enough and to spare to pay for his night at Royale. And he had taken a dislike to the monster from Lille. It would be amusing to reverse the old fable — first to rescue the girl, then to slay the monster. And it was time for the man's run of luck to end. After all, the cards have no memory!

James Bond had not enough funds to take the whole banco, only half of it, what is known as 'avec la table', meaning that the other players could make up the remaining half if they wanted to. Bond, forgetting the conservative strategy he had sworn himself to only half an hour before, leant slightly forward and said, 'Avec la table,' and pushed twenty thousand New Francs over the line.

Money followed his on to the table. Was this not the Englishman with the green fingers? And Bond was pleased to note that the little old Agatha Christie Englishwoman supported him with ten thousand. That was a good omen! He looked at the banker, the man from Lille. His cigar had gone out in its holder and his lips, where they gripped the holder, were white. He was sweating profusely. He was debating whether to pass the hand and take his fat profits or have one more go. The sharp, pig-like eyes darted round the table, estimating if his four million was covered.

The croupier wanted to hurry the play. He said firmly, 'C'est plus que fait, monsieur.'

The man from Lille made up his mind. He gave the shoe a fat slap, wiped his hand on the baize and forced out a card. Then one for himself, another for Bond, the fourth for him. Bond did not reach across Number Six for the cards. He waited for them to be nudged towards him by the croupier. He raised them just off the table, slid them far enough apart between his hands to see the count, edged them together again and laid them softly face down again on the table. He had a five! That dubious jade on which one can either draw or not! The chances of improving your hand towards or away from a nine are equal. He said 'Non,' quietly, and looked across at the two anonymous pink backs of the cards in front of the banker. The man tore them up, disgustedly tossed them out on to the table. Two knaves. A 'bûche'! Zero!

Now there were only four cards that could beat Bond and only one, the five, that could equal him. Bond's heart thumped. The man scrabbled at the shoe, snatched out the card, faced it. A nine, the nine of diamonds! The curse of Scotland! The best!

It was a mere formality to turn over and reveal Bond's miserable five. But there was a groan round the table. 'Il fallait tirer,' said someone. But if he had, Bond would have drawn the nine and disimproved down to a four. It all depended on what the next card, its pink tongue now hiding its secret in the mouth of the shoe, might have been. Bond didn't wait to see. He smiled a thin, rueful smile round the table to apologize to his fellow losers, shovelled the rest of his chips into his coat pocket, tipped the huissier who had been so busy emptying his ashtray over the hours of play, and slipped away from the table towards the bar, while the croupier triumphantly announced, 'Un banco de quatre-vingt mille francs! Faites vos jeux, messieurs! Un banco de quatre-vingt mille Nouveaux Francs.' To hell with it! thought Bond. Half an hour before he had had a small fortune in his pocket. Now, through a mixture of romantic quixotry and sheer folly he had lost it all. Well, he shrugged, he had asked for a night to remember. That was the first half of it. What would be the second?

The girl was sitting by herself, with half a bottle of Bollinger in front of her, staring moodily at nothing. She barely looked up when Bond slipped into the chair next to hers and said, 'Well, I'm afraid our syndicate lost again. I tried to get it back. I went "avec". I should have left that brute alone. I stood on a five and he had a "bûche" and then drew a nine.'

She said dully, 'You should have drawn on the five. I always do.' She reflected. 'But then you would have had a four. What was the next card?'

'I didn't wait to see. I came to look for you.'

She gave him a sideways, appraising glance. 'Why did you rescue me when I made the "coup du déshonneur"?'

Bond shrugged. 'Beautiful girl in distress. Besides, we made friends between Abbeville and Montreuil this evening. You drive like an angel.' He smiled. 'But I don't think you'd have passed me if I'd been paying attention. I was doing about ninety and not bothering to keep an eye on the mirror. And I was thinking of other things.'

The gambit succeeded. Vivacity came into her face and voice. 'Oh, yes. I'd have beaten you anyway. I'd have passed you in the villages. Besides' — there was an edge of bitterness in her voice — 'I would always be able to beat you. You want to stay alive.'

Oh, lord! thought Bond. One of those! A girl with a wing, perhaps two wings, down. He chose to let the remark lie. The half-bottle of Krug he had ordered came. After the huissier had half filled the glass, Bond topped it to the brim. He held it towards her without exaggeration. 'My name is Bond, James Bond. Please stay alive, at any rate for tonight.' He drank the glass down at one long gulp and filled it again.

She looked at him gravely, considering him. Then she also drank. She said, 'My name is Tracy. That is short for all the names you were told at the reception in the hotel. Teresa was a saint. I am not a saint. The manager is perhaps a romantic. He told me of your inquiries. So shall we go now? I am not interested in conversation. And you have earned your reward.'

She rose abruptly. So did Bond, confused. 'No. I will go alone. You can come later. The number is 45. There, if you wish, you can make the most expensive piece of love of your life. It will have cost you four million francs. I hope it will be worth it.'

4

ALL CATS ARE GREY

SHE WAS WAITING in the big double bed, a single sheet pulled up to her chin. The fair hair was spread out like golden wings under the single reading light that was the only light in the room, and the blue eyes blazed with a fervour that, in other girls, in other beds, James Bond would have interpreted. But this one was in the grip of stresses he could not even guess at. He locked the door behind him and came over and sat on the edge of her bed and put one hand firmly on the little hill that was her left breast. 'Now listen, Tracy,' he began, meaning to ask at least one or two questions, find out something about this wonderful girl who did hysterical things like gambling without the money to meet her debts, driving like a potential suicide, hinting that she had had enough of life.

But the girl reached up a swift hand that smelt of Guerlain's 'Ode' and put it across his lips. 'I said "no conversation". Take off those clothes. Make love to me. You are handsome and strong. I want to remember what it can be like. Do anything you like. And tell me what you like and what you would like from me. Be rough with me. Treat me like the lowest whore in creation. Forget everything else. No questions. Take me.'

An hour later, James Bond slipped out of bed without waking her, dressed by the light of the promenade lights filtering between the curtains, and went back to his room.

He showered and got in between the cool, rough French sheets of his own bed and switched off his thinking about her. All he remembered, before sleep took him, was that she had said when it was all over, 'That was heaven, James. Will you please come back when you wake up. I must have it once more.' Then she had turned over on her side away from him and, without answering his last endearments, had gone to sleep — but not before he had heard that she was crying.

What the hell? All cats are grey in the dark.

True or false?

Bond slept.

At eight o'clock he woke her and it was the same glorious thing again. But this time he thought that she held him to her more tenderly, kissed him not only with passion but with affection. But, after, when they should have been making plans about the day, about where to have lunch, when to bathe, she was at first evasive and then, when he pressed her, childishly abusive.

'Get to hell away from me! Do you hear? You've had what you wanted. Now get out!'

'Wasn't it what you wanted too?'

'No. You're a lousy goddam lover. Get out!'

Bond recognized the edge of hysteria, at least of desperation. He dressed slowly, waiting for the tears to come, for the sheet that now covered her totally to shake with sobs. But the tears didn't come. That was bad! In some way this girl had come to the end of her tether, of too many tethers. Bond felt a wave of affection for her, a sweeping urge to protect her, to solve her problems, make her happy. With his hand on the door-knob he said softly, 'Tracy. Let me help you. You've got some troubles. That's not the end of the world. So have I. So has everyone else.'

The dull clichés fell into the silent, sun-barred room, like clinker in a grate.

'Go to hell!'

In the instant of opening and closing the door, Bond debated whether to bang it shut, to shake her out of her mood, or to close it softly. He closed it softly. Harshness would do no good with this girl. She had had it, somehow, somewhere — too much of it. He went off down the corridor, feeling, for the first time in his life, totally inadequate.

(The Bombard thrashed on up river. It had passed the marina and, with the narrowing banks, the current was stronger. The two thugs in the stern still kept their quiet eyes on Bond. In the bows, the girl still held her proud profile into the wind like the figure-head on a sailing ship. In Bond, the only warmth was in his contact with her back and his hand on the haft of his knife. Yet, in a curious way, he felt closer to her, far closer, than in the transports of the night before. Somehow he felt that she was as much a prisoner as he was. How? Why? Way ahead the lights of the Vieux Port, once close to the sea, but now left behind by some quirk of the Channel currents that had built up the approaches to the river, shone sparsely. Before many years they would go out and a new harbour, nearer the mouth of the river, would be built for the deep-sea trawlers that served Royale with their soles and lobsters and crabs and prawns. On this side of the lights were occasional gaunt jetties built out into the river by private yacht-owners. Behind them were villas that would have names like 'Rosalie', 'Toi et Moi', 'Nid Azur' and 'Nouvelle Vague'. James Bond nursed the knife and smelt the 'Ode' that came to him above the stink of mud and seaweed from the river banks. His teeth had never chattered before. Now they chattered. He stopped them and went back to his memories.)

Normally, breakfast was an important part of Bond's day, but today he had barely noticed what he was eating, hurried through the meal and sat gazing out of his window and across the promenade, chain-smoking and wondering about the girl. He knew nothing positive about her, not even her nationality. The Mediterranean was in her name, yet she was surely neither Italian nor Spanish. Her English was faultless and her clothes and the way she wore them were the products of expensive surroundings — perhaps a Swiss finishing school. She didn't smoke, seemed to drink only sparingly, and there was no sign of drug-taking. There had not even been sleeping pills beside the bed or in her bathroom. She could only be about twenty-five, yet she made love with the fervour and expertness of a girl who, in the American phrase, had 'gone the route'. She hadn't laughed once, had hardly smiled. She seemed in the grip of some deep melancholy, some form of spiritual accidie that made life, on her own admission, no longer worth living. And yet there were none of those signs that one associates with the hysteria of female neurotics — the unkempt hair and sloppy make-up, the atmosphere of disarray and chaos they create around them. On the contrary, she seemed to possess an ice-cold will, authority over herself and an exact idea of what she wanted and where she was going. And where was that? In Bond's book she had desperate intentions, most likely suicide, and last night had been the last fling.

He looked down at the little white car that was now not far from his in the parking lot. Somehow he must stick close to her, watch over her, at least until he was satisfied that his deadly conclusions were wrong. As a first step, he rang down to the concierge and ordered a drive-yourself Simca Aronde. Yes, it should be delivered at once and left in the parking lot. He would bring his international driving licence and green insurance card down to the concierge who would kindly complete the formalities.

Bond shaved and dressed and took the papers down and returned to his room. He stayed there, watching the entrance and the little white car until 4.30 in the afternoon. Then, at last, she appeared, in the black and white striped bathing-wrap, and Bond ran down the corridor to the lift. It was not difficult to follow her as she drove along the promenade and left her car in one of the parking lots, and it was also no problem for the little anonymous 2CV Citroën that followed Bond.

And then had been set up the train of the watchers and the watched which was now drawing to its mysterious climax as the little Bombard thrashed its way up the River Royale under the stars.

What to make of it all? Had she been a witting or unwitting bait? Was this a kidnapping? If so, of one or of both? Was it blackmail? The revenge of a husband or another lover? Or was it to be murder?

Bond was still raking his mind for clues when the helmsman turned the Bombard in a wide curve across the current towards a battered, skeletal jetty that projected from the muddy bank into the stream. He pulled up under its lee, a powerful flashlight shone down on them out of the darkness, a rope clattered down and the boat was hauled to the foot of muddy wooden steps. One of the thugs climbed out first, followed by the girl, the white bottom of her bathing dress lascivious below Bond's coat, then Bond, then the second thug. Then the Bombard backed quickly away and continued up river, presumably, thought Bond, to its legitimate mooring in the Vieux Port.

There were two more men, of much the same build as the others, on the jetty. No words were spoken as, surrounded, the girl and Bond were escorted up the small dust road that led away from the jetty through the sand dunes. A hundred yards from the river, tucked away in a gully between tall dunes, there was a glimmer of light. When Bond got nearer he saw that it came from one of those giant corrugated aluminium transport-trucks that, behind an articulated driver's cabin, roar down the arterial routes of France belching diesel smoke and hissing angrily with their hydraulic brakes as they snake through the towns and villages. This one was a glinting, polished affair. It looked new, but might be just well cared for. As they approached, the man with the flashlight gave some signal, and an oblong of yellow light promptly blazed as the caravan-like door in the rear was thrown open. Bond fingered his knife. Were the odds in any way within reason? They were not. Before he climbed up the steps into the interior, he glanced down at the number-plate. The commercial licence said, 'Marseille-Rhône. M. Draco. Appareils Électriques. 397694.' So! One more riddle!

Inside it was, thank God, warm. A passageway led between stacked rows of cartons marked with the famous names of television manufacturers. Dummies? There were also folded chairs and the signs of a disturbed game of cards. This was presumably used as the guard-room. Then, on both sides, the doors of cabins. Tracy was waiting at one of the doors. She held out his coat to him, said an expressionless 'Thank you' and closed the door after Bond had caught a brief glimpse of a luxurious interior. Bond took his time putting on his coat. The single man with the gun who was following him said impatiently, 'Allez!' Bond wondered whether to jump him. But, behind, the other three men stood watching. Bond contented himself with a mild 'Merde à vous!' and went ahead to the aluminium door that presumably sealed off the third and forward compartment in this strange vehicle. Behind this door lay the answer. It was probably one man — the leader. This might be the only chance. Bond's right hand was already grasping the hilt of his knife in his trouser pocket. Now he put out his left hand and, in one swirl of motion, leaped through, kicked the door shut behind him and crouched, the knife held for throwing.

Behind him he felt the guard throw himself at the door, but Bond had his back to it and it held. The man, ten feet away behind the desk, within easy range for the knife, called out something, an order, a cheerful, gay order in some language Bond had never heard. The pressure on the door ceased. The man smiled a wide, a charming smile that cracked his creased walnut of a face in two. He got to his feet and slowly raised his hands. 'I surrender. And I am now a much bigger target. But do not kill me, I beg of you. At least not until we have had a stiff whisky and soda and a talk. Then I will give you the choice again. O.K.?'

Bond rose to his full height. He smiled back. He couldn't help it. The man had such a delightful face, so lit with humour and mischief and magnetism that, at least in the man's present role, Bond could no more have killed him than he could have killed, well, Tracy.

There was a calendar hanging on the wall beside the man. Bond wanted to let off steam against something, anything. He said, 'September the sixteenth,' and jerked his right hand forward in the underhand throw. The knife flashed across the room, missed the man by about a yard, and stuck, quivering, half-way down the page of the calendar.

The man turned and looked inquisitively at the calendar. He laughed out loud. 'Actually the fifteenth. But quite respectable. I must set you against my men one of these days. And I might even bet on you. It would teach them a lesson.'

He came out from behind his desk, a smallish, middle-aged man with a brown, crinkled face. He was dressed in the sort of comfortable dark-blue suit Bond himself wore. The chest and the arms bulged with muscle. Bond noticed the fullness of the cut of the coat under the armpits. Built for guns? The man held out a hand. It was warm and firm and dry. 'Marc-Ange Draco is my name. You have heard of it?'

'No.'

'Aha! But I have heard of yours. It is Commander James Bond. You have a decoration called the C.M.G. You are a member, an important member, of Her Majesty's Secret Service. You have been taken off your usual duties and you are on temporary assignment abroad.' The impish face creased with delight. 'Yes?'

James Bond, to cover his confusion, walked across to the calendar, verified that he had in fact pierced the fifteenth, pulled out the knife and slipped it back in his trouser pocket. He turned and said, 'What makes you think so?'

The man didn't answer. He said, 'Come. Come and sit down.

I have much to talk to you about. But first the whisky and soda. Yes?' He indicated a comfortable armchair across the desk from his own, put in front of it a large silver box containing various kinds of cigarettes, and went to a metal filing cabinet against the wall and opened it. It contained no files. It was a complete and compact bar. With efficient, housekeeperly movements he took out a bottle of Pinchbottle Haig, another of I.W. Harper's Bourbon, two pint glasses that looked like Waterford, a bucket of ice cubes, a siphon of soda and a flagon of iced water. One by one he placed these on the desk between his chair and Bond's. Then, while Bond poured himself a stiff Bourbon and water with plenty of ice, he went and sat down across the desk from Bond, reached for the Haig and said, looking Bond very directly in the eye, 'I learned who you are from a good friend in the Deuxième in Paris. He is paid to give me such information when I want it. I learned it very early this morning. I am in the opposite camp to yourself — not directly opposite. Let us say at a tangent on the field.' He paused. He lifted his glass. He said with much seriousness, 'I am now going to establish confidence with you. By the only means. I am going once again to place my life in your hands.'

He drank. So did Bond. In the filing cabinet, in its icebox, the hum of the generator broke in on what Bond suddenly knew was going to be an important moment of truth. He didn't know what the truth was going to be. He didn't think it was going to be bad. But he had an instinct that, somehow, perhaps because he had conceived respect and affection for this man, it was going to mean deep involvement for himself.

The generator stopped.

The eyes in the walnut face held his.

'I am the head of the Union Corse.'

5

THE CAPU

THE UNION CORSE! Now at least some of the mystery was explained. Bond looked across the desk into the brown eyes that were now shrewdly watching his reactions while his mind flicked through the file that bore the innocent title, 'The Union Corse', more deadly and perhaps even older than the Unione Siciliano, the Mafia. He knew that it controlled most organized crime throughout metropolitan France and her colonies — protection rackets, smuggling, prostitution and the suppression of rival gangs. Only a few months ago a certain Rossi had been shot dead in a bar in Nice. A year before that, a Jean Giudicelli had been liquidated after several previous attempts had failed. Both these men had been known pretenders to the throne of Capu — the ebullient, cheerful man who now sat so peacefully across the table from Bond. Then there was this mysterious business of Rommel's treasure, supposed to be hidden beneath the sea somewhere off Bastia. In 1948 a Czech diver called Fleigh, who had been in the Abwehr, and had got on the track of it, was warned off by the Union and then vanished off the face of the earth. Quite recently the body of a young French diver, André Mattei, was found riddled with bullets by the roadside near Bastia. He had foolishly boasted in the local bars that he knew the whereabouts of the treasure and had come to dive for it. Did Marc-Ange know the secret of this treasure? Had he been responsible for the killing of these two divers? The little village of Calenzana in the Balagne boasted of having produced more gangsters than any other village in Corsica and of being in consequence one of the most prosperous. The local mayor had held office for fifty-six years — the longest reigning mayor in France. Marc-Ange would surely be a son of that little community, know the secrets of that famous mayor, know, for instance, of that big American gangster who had just returned to discreet retirement in the village after a highly profitable career in the States.

It would be fun to drop some of these names casually in this quiet little room — fun to tell Marc-Ange that Bond knew of the old abandoned jetty called the Port of Crovani near the village of Galeria, and of the ancient silver mine called Argentella in the hills behind, whose maze of underground tunnels accommodates one of the great world junctions in the heroin traffic. Yes, it would be fun to frighten his captor in exchange for the fright he had given Bond. But better keep this ammunition in reserve until more had been revealed! For the time being it was interesting to note that this was Marc-Ange Draco's travelling headquarters. His contact in the Deuxième Bureau would be an essential tip-off man. Bond and the girl had been 'sent for' for some purpose that was still to be announced. The 'borrowing' of the Bombard rescue-boat would have been a simple matter of finance in the right quarter, perhaps accompanied by a 'pot de vin' for the coastguards to look the other way. The guards were Corsicans. On reflection, that was anyway what they looked like. The whole operation was simple for an organization as powerful as the Union — as simple in France as it would have been for the Mafia in most of Italy. And now for more veils to be lifted! James Bond sipped his drink and watched the other man's face with respect. This was one of the great professionals of the world!

[How typical of Corsica, Bond thought, that their top bandit should bear the name of an angel! He remembered that two other famous Corsican gangsters had been called 'Gracieux' and 'Toussaint' — 'All-Saints'.] Marc-Ange spoke. He spoke excellent but occasionally rather clumsy English, as if he had been well taught but had little occasion to use the language. He said, 'My dear Commander, everything I am going to discuss with you will please remain behind your Herkos Odonton. You know the expression? No?' The wide smile lit up his face. 'Then, if I may say so, your education was incomplete. It is from the classical Greek. It means literally "the hedge of the teeth". It was the Greek equivalent of your "top secret". Is that agreed?'

Bond shrugged. 'If you tell me secrets that affect my profession, I'm afraid I shall have to pass them on.'

'That I fully comprehend. What I wish to discuss is a personal matter. It concerns my daughter, Teresa.'

Good God! The plot was indeed thickening! Bond concealed

his surprise. He said, 'Then I agree.' He smiled. ' "Herkos Odonton" it is.'

'Thank you. You are a man to trust. You would have to be, in your profession, but I see it also in your face. Now then.' He lit a Caporal and sat back in his chair. He gazed at a point on the aluminium wall above Bond's head, only occasionally looking into Bond's eyes when he wished to emphasize a point. 'I was married once only, to an English girl, an English governess. She was a romantic. She had come to Corsica to look for bandits —' he smiled — 'rather like some English women adventure into the desert to look for sheiks. She explained to me later that she must have been possessed by a subconscious desire to be raped. Well —' this time he didn't smile — 'she found me in the mountains and she was raped — by me. The police were after me at the time, they have been for most of my life, and the girl was a grave encumbrance. But for some reason she refused to leave me. There was a wildness in her, a love of the unconventional, and, for God knows what reason, she liked the months of being chased from cave to cave, of getting food by robbery at night. She even learned to skin and cook a moufflon, those are our mountain sheep, and even eat the animal, which is tough as shoe leather and about as palatable. And in those crazy months, I came to love this girl and I smuggled her away from the island to Marseilles and married her.' He paused and looked at Bond. 'The result, my dear Commander, was Teresa, my only child.'

So, thought Bond. That explained the curious mixture the girl was — the kind of wild 'lady' that was so puzzling in her. What a complex of bloods and temperaments! Corsican English. No wonder he hadn't been able to define her nationality.

'My wife died ten years ago —' Marc-Ange held up his hand, not wanting sympathy — 'and I had the girl's education finished in Switzerland. I was already rich and at that time I was elected Capu, that is chief, of the Union, and became infinitely richer — by means, my dear Commander, which you can guess but need not inquire into. The girl was — how do you say? — that charming expression, "the apple of my eye", and I gave her all she wanted. But she was a wild one, a wild bird, without a proper home, or, since I was always on the move, without proper supervision. Through her school in Switzerland, she entered the fast international set that one reads of in the newspapers — the South American millionaires, the Indian princelings, the Paris English and Americans, the playboys of Cannes and Gstaad. She was always getting in and out of scrapes and scandals, and when I remonstrated with her, cut off her allowance, she would commit some even grosser folly — to spite me, I suppose.' He paused and looked at Bond and now there was a terrible misery in the happy face. 'And yet all the while, behind her bravado, the mother's side of her blood was making her hate herself, despise herself more and more, and as I now see it, the worm of self-destruction had somehow got a hold inside her and, behind the wild, playgirl façade, was eating away what I can only describe as her soul.' He looked at Bond. 'You know that this can happen, my friend — to men and to women. They burn the heart out of themselves by living too greedily, and suddenly they examine their lives and see that they are worthless. They have had everything, eaten all the sweets of life at one great banquet, and there is nothing left. She made what I now see was a desperate attempt to get back on the rails, so to speak. She went off, without telling me, and married, perhaps with the idea of settling down. But the man, a worthless Italian called Vicenzo, Count Giulio di Vicenzo, took as much of her money as he could lay his hands on and deserted her, leaving her with a girl child. I purchased a divorce and bought a small château for my daughter in the Dordogne and installed her there, and for once, with the baby and a pretty garden to look after, she seemed almost at peace. And then, my friend, six months ago, the baby died — died of that most terrible of all children's ailments, spinal meningitis.'

There was silence in the little metal room. Bond thought of the girl a few yards away down the corridor. Yes. He had been near the truth. He had seen some of this tragic story in the calm desperation of the girl. She had indeed come to the end of the road!

Marc-Ange got slowly up from his chair and came round and poured out more whisky for himself and for Bond. He said, 'Forgive me. I am a poor host. But the telling of this story, which I have always kept locked up inside me, to another man, has been a great relief.' He put a hand on Bond's shoulder. 'You understand that?'

'Yes. I understand that. But she is a fine girl. She still has nearly all her life to live. Have you thought of psycho-analysis? Of her church? Is she a Catholic?'

'No. Her mother would not have it. She is Presbyterian. But wait while I finish the story.' He went back to his chair and sat down heavily. 'After the tragedy, she disappeared. She took her jewels and went off in that little car of hers, and I heard occasional news of her, selling the jewels and living furiously all over Europe, with her old set. Naturally I followed her, had her watched when I could, but she avoided all my attempts to meet her and talk to her. Then I heard from one of my agents that she had reserved a room here, at the Splendide, for last night, and I hurried down from Paris —' he waved a hand — 'in this, because I had a presentiment of tragedy. You see, this was where we had spent the summers in her childhood and she had always loved it. She is a wonderful swimmer and she was almost literally in love with the sea. And, when I got the news, I suddenly had a dreadful memory, the memory of a day when she had been naughty and had been locked in her room all afternoon instead of going bathing. That night she had said to her mother, quite calmly, "You made me very unhappy keeping me away from the sea. One day, if I get really unhappy I shall swim out into the sea, down the path of the moon or the sun, and go on swimming until I sink. So there!" Her mother told me the story and we laughed over it together, at the childish tantrum. But now I suddenly remembered again the occasion and it seemed to me that the childish fantasy might well have stayed with her, locked away deep down, and that now, wanting to put an end to herself, she had resurrected it and was going to act on it. And so, my dear friend, I had her closely watched from the moment she arrived. Your gentlemanly conduct in the Casino, for which —' he looked across at Bond — 'I now deeply thank you, was reported to me, as of course were your later movements together.' He held up his hand as Bond shifted with embarrassment. 'There is nothing to be ashamed of, to apologize for, in what you did last night. A man is a man and, who knows? — but I shall come to that later. What you did, the way you behaved in general, may have been the beginning of some kind of therapy.'

Bond remembered how, in the Bombard, she had yielded when he leaned against her. It had been a tiny reaction, but it had held more affection, more warmth, than all the physical ecstasies of the night. Now, suddenly, he had an inkling of why he might be here, where the root of the mystery lay, and he gave an involuntary shudder, as if someone had walked over his grave.

Marc-Ange continued. 'So I put in my inquiry to my friend from the Deuxième, at six o'clock this morning. At eight o'clock he went to his office and to the central files and by nine o'clock he had reported to me fully about you — by radio. I have a high-powered station in this vehicle.' He smiled. 'And that is another of my secrets that I deliver into your hands. The report, if I may say so, was entirely to your credit, both as an officer in your Service, and, more important, as a man — a man, that is, in the terms that I understand the word. So I reflected. I reflected all through this morning. And, in the end, I gave orders that you were both to be brought to me here.' He made a throw-away gesture with his right hand. 'I need not tell you the details of my instructions. You yourself saw them in operation. You have been inconvenienced. I apologize. You have perhaps thought yourself in danger. Forgive me. I only trust that my men behaved with correctness, with finesse.'

Bond smiled. 'I am very glad to have met you. If the introduction had to be effected at the point of two automatics, that will only make it all the more memorable. The whole affair was certainly executed with neatness and expedition.'

Marc-Ange's expression was rueful. 'Now you are being sarcastic. But believe me, my friend, drastic measures were necessary. I knew they were.' He reached to the top drawer of his desk, took out a sheet of writing-paper and passed it over to Bond. 'And now, if you read that, you will agree with me. That letter was handed in to the concierge of the Splendide at 4.30 this afternoon for posting to me in Marseilles, when Teresa went out and you followed her. You suspected something? You also feared for her? Read it, please.'

Bond took the letter. He said, 'Yes. I was worried about her. She is a girl worth worrying about.' He held up the letter. It contained only a few words, written clearly, with decision.

Dear Papa,

I am sorry, but I have had enough. It is only sad because tonight I met a man who might have changed my mind. He is an Englishman called James Bond. Please find him and pay him 20,000 New Francs which I owe him. And thank him from me.

This is nobody's fault but my own.

Goodbye and forgive me.

TRACY

Bond didn't look at the man who had received this letter. He slid it back to him across the desk. He took a deep drink of the whisky and reached for the bottle. He said, 'Yes, I see.'

'She likes to call herself Tracy. She thinks Teresa sounds too grand.'

'Yes.'

'Commander Bond.' There was now a terrible urgency in the man's voice — urgency, authority and appeal. 'My friend, you have heard the whole story and now you have seen the evidence. Will you help me? Will you help me save this girl? It is my only chance, that you will give her hope. That you will give her a reason to live. Will you?'

Bond kept his eyes on the desk in front of him. He dared not look up and see the expression on this man's face. So he had been right, right to fear that he was going to become involved in all this private trouble! He cursed under his breath. The idea appalled him. He was no Good Samaritan. He was no doctor for wounded birds. What she needed, he said fiercely to himself, was the psychiatrist's couch. All right, so she had taken a passing fancy to him and he to her. Now he was going to be asked, he knew it, to pick her up and carry her perhaps for the rest of his life, haunted by the knowledge, the unspoken blackmail, that, if he dropped her, it would almost certainly be to kill her. He said glumly, 'I do not see that I can help. What is it you have in mind?' He picked up his glass and looked into it. He drank, to give him courage to look across the desk into Marc-Ange's face.

The man's soft brown eyes glittered with tension. The creased dark skin round the mouth had sunk into deeper folds. He said, holding Bond's eyes, 'I wish you to pay court to my daughter and marry her. On the day of the marriage, I will give you a personal dowry of one million pounds in gold.'

James Bond exploded angrily. 'What you ask is utterly impossible. The girl is sick. What she needs is a psychiatrist. Not me. And I do not want to marry, not anyone. Nor do I want a million pounds. I have enough money for my needs. I have my profession.' (Is that true? What about that letter of resignation? Bond ignored the private voice.) 'You must understand all this.' Suddenly he could not bear the hurt in the man's face. He said, softly, 'She is a wonderful girl. I will do all I can for her. But only when she is well again. Then I would certainly like to see her again — very much. But, if she thinks so well of me, if you do, then she must first get well of her own accord. That is the only way. Any doctor would tell you so. She must go to some clinic, the best there is, in Switzerland probably, and bury her past. She must want to live again. Then, only then, would there be any point in our meeting again.' He pleaded with Marc-Ange. 'You do understand, don't you, Marc-Ange? I am a ruthless man. I admit it. And I have not got the patience to act as anyone's nurse, man or woman. Your idea of a cure might only drive her into deeper despair. You must see that I cannot take the responsibility, however much I am attracted by your daughter.' Bond ended lamely, 'Which I am.'

The man said resignedly, 'I understand you, my friend. And I will not importune you with further arguments. I will try and act in the way you suggest. But will you please do one further favour for me? It is now nine o'clock. Will you please take her out to dinner tonight? Talk to her as you please, but show her that she is wanted, that you have affection for her. Her car is here and her clothes. I have had them brought. If only you can persuade her that you would like to see her again, I think I may be able to do the rest. Will you do this for me?'

Bond thought, God, what an evening! But he smiled with all the warmth he could summon. 'But of course. I would love to do that. But I am booked on the first morning flight from Le Touquet tomorrow morning. Will you be responsible for her from then?'

'Certainly, my friend. Of course I will do that.' Marc-Ange brusquely wiped a hand across his eyes. 'Forgive me. But you have given me hope at the end of a long night.' He straightened his shoulders and suddenly leaned across the desk and put his hands decisively down. 'I will not thank you. I cannot, but tell me, my dear friend, is there anything in this world that I can do for you, now at this moment? I have great resources, great knowledge, great power. They are all yours. Is there nothing I can do for you?'

Bond had a flash of inspiration. He smiled broadly. 'There is a piece of information I want. There is a man called Blofeld, Ernst Stavro Blofeld. You will have heard of him. I wish to know if he is alive and where he is to be found.'

Marc-Ange's face underwent a remarkable change. Now the bandit, cold, cruel, avenging, looked out through the eyes that had suddenly gone as hard as brown opals. 'Aha!' he said thoughtfully. 'The Blofeld. Yes, he is certainly alive. Only recently he suborned three of my men, bribed them away from the Union. He has done this to me before. Three of the members of the old SPECTRE were taken from the Union. Come, let us find out what we can.'

There was a single black telephone on the desk. He picked up the receiver and at once Bond heard the soft crackle of the operator responding. '*Dammi u commandu.*' Marc-Ange put the receiver back. 'I have asked for my local headquarters in Ajaccio. We will have them in five minutes. But I must speak fast. The police may know my frequency, though I change it every week. But the Corsican dialect helps.' The telephone burred. When Marc-Ange picked up the receiver, Bond could hear the zing and crackle he knew so well. Marc-Ange spoke, in a voice of rasping authority. '*Ecco u Capu. Avette nuttizie di Blofeld, Ernst Stavro? Duve sta?*' A voice crackled thinly. '*Site sigura? Ma no ezzatu indirizzu?*' More crackle. '*Buon. Sara tutto.*'

Marc-Ange put back the receiver. He spread his hands apologetically. 'All we know is that he is in Switzerland. We have no exact address for him. Will that help? Surely your men there can find him — if the Swiss Sécurité will help. But they are difficult brutes when it comes to the privacy of a resident, particularly if he is rich.'

Bond's pulse had quickened with triumph. Got you, you bastard! He said enthusiastically, 'That's wonderful, Marc-Ange. The rest shouldn't be difficult. We have good friends in Switzerland.'

Marc-Ange smiled happily at Bond's reaction. He said seriously, 'But if things go wrong for you, on this case or in any other way, you will come at once to me. Yes?' He pulled open a drawer and handed a sheet of notepaper over to Bond. 'This is my open address. Telephone or cable to me, but put your request or your news in terms that would be used in connection with electrical appliances. A consignment of radios is faulty. You will meet my representative at such and such a place, on such and such a date. Yes? You understand these tricks, and anyway —' he smiled slyly — 'I believe you are connected with an international export firm. "Universal Export", isn't it?'

Bond smiled. How did the old devil know these things? Should he warn Security? No. This man had become a friend. And anyway, all this was Herkos Odonton!

Marc-Ange said diffidently, 'And now may I bring in Teresa? She does not know what we have been discussing. Let us say it is about one of the South of France jewel robberies. You represent the insurance company. I have been making a private deal with you. You can manage that? Good.' He got up and came over to Bond and put his hand on Bond's shoulder. 'And thank you. Thank you for everything.' Then he went out of the door.

Oh my God! thought Bond. Now for my side of the bargain.

6

BOND OF BOND STREET?

IT WAS TWO months later, in London, and James Bond was driving lazily up from his Chelsea flat to his headquarters.

It was nine-thirty in the morning of yet another beautiful day of this beautiful year, but, in Hyde Park, the fragrance of burning leaves meant that winter was only just round the corner. Bond had nothing on his mind except the frustration of waiting for Station Z somehow to penetrate the reserves of the Swiss Sécurité and come up with the exact address of Blofeld. But their 'friends' in Zürich were continuing to prove obtuse, or, more probably, obstinate. There was no trace of any man, either tourist or resident, called Blofeld in the whole of Switzerland. Nor was there any evidence of the existence of a reborn SPECTRE on Swiss soil. Yes, they fully realized that Blofeld was still urgently 'wanted' by the governments of the NATO alliance. They had carefully filed all the circulars devoted to the apprehension of this man, and for the past year he had been constantly reconfirmed on their 'watch' lists at all frontier posts. They were very sorry, but unless the SIS could come up with further information or evidence about this man, they must assume that the SIS was acting on mistaken evidence. Station Z had asked for an examination of the secret lists at the banks, a search through those anonymous 'numbered' accounts which conceal the owners of most of the fugitive money in the world. This request had been peremptorily refused. Blofeld was certainly a very great criminal, but the Sécurité must point out that such information could only be legally obtained if the criminal in question was guilty of some crime committed on Federal soil and indictable under the Federal Code. It was true that this Blofeld had held up Britain and America to ransom by his illegal possession of atomic weapons. But this could not be considered a crime under the laws of Switzerland, and particularly not having regard to Article 47B of the banking laws. So that was that!

The Holy Franc, and the funds which backed it, wherever they came from, must remain untouchable. *Wir bitten höflichst um Entschuldigung!*

Bond wondered if he should get in touch with Marc-Ange. So far, in his report, he had revealed only a lead into the Union Corse, whom he gave, corporately, as the source of his information. But he shied away from this course of action, which would surely have, as one consequence, the reopening with Marc-Ange of the case of Tracy. And that corner of his life, of his heart, he wanted to leave undisturbed for the time being. Their last evening together had passed quietly, almost as if they had been old friends, old lovers. Bond had said that Universal Export was sending him abroad for some time. They would certainly meet when he returned to Europe. The girl had accepted this arrangement. She herself had decided to go away for a rest. She had been doing too much. She had been on the verge of a nervous breakdown. She would wait for him. Perhaps they could go skiing together around Christmas time? Bond had been enthusiastic. That night, after a wonderful dinner at Bond's little restaurant, they had made love, happily, and this time without desperation, without tears. Bond was satisfied that the cure had really begun. He felt deeply protective towards her. But he knew that their relationship, and her equanimity, rested on a knife-edge which must not be disturbed.

It was at this moment in his reflections that the Syncraphone in his trouser pocket began to bleep. Bond accelerated out of the park and drew up beside the public telephone booth at Marble Arch. The Syncraphone had recently been introduced and was carried by all officers attached to Headquarters. It was a light plastic radio receiver about the size of a pocket watch. When an officer was somewhere in London, within a range of ten miles of Headquarters, he could be bleeped on the receiver. When this happened, it was his duty to go at once to the nearest telephone and contact his office. He was urgently needed.

Bond rang his exchange on the only outside number he was allowed to use, said '007 reporting,' and was at once put through to his secretary. She was a new one. Loelia Ponsonby had at last left to marry a dull, but worthy and rich member of the Baltic Exchange, and confined her contacts with her old job to rather yearning Christmas and birthday cards to the members of the Double-O Section. But the new one, Mary Goodnight, an ex-Wren with blue-black hair, blue eyes and 37-22-35, was a honey and there was a private five-pound sweep in the Section as to who would get her first. Bond had been lying equal favourite with the ex-Royal Marine Commando who was 006 but, since Tracy, had dropped out of the field and now regarded himself as a rank outsider, though he still, rather bitchily, flirted with her. Now he said to her, 'Good morning, Goodnight. What can I do for you? Is it war or peace?'

She giggled unprofessionally. 'It sounds fairly peaceful, as peaceful as a hurry message from upstairs can be. You're to go at once to the College of Arms and ask for Griffon Or.'

'Or what?'

'Just Or. Oh, and he's Pursuivant as well, whatever that means. He's one of the Heralds. Apparently they've got some kind of a line on "Bedlam".'

'Bedlam' was the code name for the pursuit of Blofeld. Bond said respectfully, 'Have they indeed? Then I'd better get cracking. Goodbye, Goodnight.' He heard her giggle before he put the receiver down.

Now what the hell? Bond got back into his car, that had mercifully not yet attracted the police or the traffic wardens, and motored fast across London. This was a queer one. How the hell did the College of Arms, of which he knew very little except that they hunted up people's family trees, allotted coats of arms, and organized various royal ceremonies, get into the act?

The College of Arms is in Queen Victoria Street on the fringe of the City. It is a pleasant little Queen Anne backwater in ancient red brick with white sashed windows and a convenient cobbled courtyard, where Bond parked his car. There are horseshoe-shaped stone stairs leading up to an impressive entrance, over which, that day, there hung a banner showing a splendid heraldic beast, half animal and half bird, in gold against a pale blue background. Griffon, thought Bond. Made of Or. He went through the door into a large gloomy hall whose dark panelling was lined with the musty portraits of proud-looking gentlemen in ruffs and lace, and from whose cornice hung the banners of the Commonwealth. The porter, a kindly, soft-spoken man in a cherry-coloured uniform with brass buttons, asked Bond what he could do for him. Bond asked for the Griffon Or and confirmed that he had an appointment.

'Ah yes, sir,' said the porter mysteriously. 'Griffon Or is in waiting this week. That is why his banner is flying outside. This way please, sir.'

Bond followed the porter along a passage hung with gleaming coats of arms in carved wood, up a dank, cobwebby staircase and round a corner to a heavy door over which was written in gold 'Griffon Or Pursuivant' under a representation of the said golden griffon. The porter knocked, opened the door and announced Bond, and left him facing, across an unkempt study littered with books, papers and important-looking inscribed parchments, the top of a bald, round pink head fringed with grizzled curls. The room smelt like the crypt of a church. Bond walked down the narrow lane of carpet left between the piles of litter and stood beside the single chair that faced the man behind the books on the desk. He cleared his throat. The man looked up and the Pickwickian, pince-nez'd face broke into an absent smile. He got to his feet and made a little bow. 'Bond,' he said in a voice that creaked like the lid of an old chest. 'Commander James Bond. Now then, Bond, Bond, Bond. I think I've got you here.' He had kept his finger at the open page of a vast tome. He now sat down and Bond followed suit. 'Yes, yes, yes. Very interesting indeed. Very. But I fear I have to disappoint you, my dear sir. The title is extinct. Actually it's a baronetcy. Most desirable. But no doubt we can establish a relationship through a collateral branch. Now then —' he put his pince-nez very close to the page — 'we have some ten different families of Bonds. The important one ended with Sir Thomas Bond, a most distinguished gentleman. He resided in Peckham. He had, alas, no issue —' the pince-nez gleamed encouragingly at Bond — 'no legitimate issue that is. Of course in those days, ahem, morals were inclined to be laxer. Now if we could establish some connection with Peckham . . .'

'I have no connection with Peckham. Now, I . . .'

Griffon Or held up his hand. He said severely, 'Where did your parents come from, if I may ask? That, my dear fellow, is the first step in the chain. Then we can go back from there — Somerset House, parish records, old tombstones. No doubt, with a good old English name like yours, we will get somewhere in the end.'

'My father was a Scot and my mother was Swiss. But the point is . . .'

'Quite, quite. You are wondering about the cost of the research. That, my dear fellow, we can leave until later. But, now tell me. From whereabouts in Scotland did your father come? That is important. The Scottish records are of course less fully documented than those from the South. In those days I am forced to admit that our cousins across the border were little more than savages.' Griffon Or bobbed his head politely. He gave a fleeting and, to Bond's eye, rather false smile. 'Very pleasant savages, of course, very brave and all that. But, alas, very weak at keeping up their records. More useful with the sword than with the pen, if I may say so. But perhaps your grandparents and their forebears came from the South?'

'My father came from the Highlands, from near Glencoe. But look here . . .'

But Griffon Or was not to be diverted from the scent. He pulled another thick book towards him. His finger ran down the page of small print. 'Hum. Hum. Hum. Yes, yes. Not very encouraging, I fear. *Burke's General Armory* gives more than ten different families bearing your name. But, alas, nothing in Scotland. Not that that means there is no Scottish branch. Now, perhaps you have other relatives living. So often in these matters there is some distant cousin . . .' Griffon Or reached into the pocket of the purple-flowered silk waistcoat that buttoned almost up to his neat bow tie, fished out a small silver snuff-box, offered it to Bond and then himself took two tremendous sniffs. He exploded twice into an ornate bandana handkerchief.

Bond took his opportunity. He leaned forward and said distinctly and forcibly, 'I didn't come here to talk about myself. It's about Blofeld.'

'What's that?' Griffon Or looked at him in astonishment. 'You are not interested in your line of descent?' He held up an admonishing finger. 'Do you realize, my dear fellow, that if we are successful, you may be able to claim direct —' he hesitated — 'or at any rate collateral descent from an ancient baronetcy founded —' he went back to his first volume and peered at it — 'in the year 1658! Does it not excite you that a possible ancestor of yours was responsible for the name of one of the most famous streets in the world — I refer of course to Bond Street? That was the Sir Thomas Bond, Baronet of Peckham in the County of Surrey, who, as you are no doubt aware, was Comptroller of the household of the Queen Mother, Henrietta Maria. The street was built in 1686 and its associations with famous British folk are, of course, well known. The first Duke of St Albans, son of Nell Gwynn, lived there, as did Laurence Sterne. Boswell's famous dinner party took place there, with Johnson, Reynolds, Goldsmith and Garrick being present. Dean Swift and Canning were residents at different times, and it is intriguing to recall that while Lord Nelson lived at number 141, Lady Hamilton lived at number 145. And this, my dear sir, is the great thoroughfare of which you bear the name! Do you still wish to establish no claim to this vastly distinguished connection? No?' The bushy eyebrows, raised in astonishment, were now lowered in further admonishment. 'This is the very warp and woof of history, my dear Commander Bond.' He reached for another volume that lay open on his desk and that he had obviously prepared for Bond's delectation. 'The coat of arms, for instance. Surely that must concern you, be at least of profound interest to your family, to your own children? Yes, here we are. "Argent on a chevron sable three bezants".' He held up the book so that Bond could see. 'A bezant is a golden ball, as I am sure you know. Three balls.'

Bond commented drily, 'That is certainly a valuable bonus —' the irony was lost on Griffon Or — 'but I'm afraid I am still not interested. And I have no relatives and no children. Now about this man . . .'

Griffon Or broke in excitedly, 'And this charming motto of the line, "The World is not Enough". You do not wish to have the right to it?'

'It is an excellent motto which I shall certainly adopt,' said Bond curtly. He looked pointedly at his watch. 'Now; I'm afraid we really must get down to business. I have to report back to my Ministry.'

Griffon Or Pursuivant looked genuinely affronted. 'And here is a name going back at least to Norman le Bond in 1180! A fine old English name, though one perhaps originally of lowly origin. The *Dictionary of British Surnames* suggests that the meaning is clearly "husbandman, peasant, churl".' Was there an edge of malice in the Griffon's watery eye? He added with resignation, 'But, if you are not interested in your ancestry, in the womb of your family, then, my dear sir, in what can I be of service?'

At last! James Bond let out a sigh of relief. He said patiently, 'I came here to inquire about a certain Blofeld, Ernst Stavro Blofeld. It seems that your organization has some information about this man.'

Griffon Or's eyes were suddenly suspicious. 'But you represented yourself as a Commander James Bond. And now the name is Blofeld. How does this come about?'

Bond said icily, 'I am from the Ministry of Defence. Somewhere in this building is information about a man called Blofeld. Where can I find it?'

Griffon Or ran a puzzled hand round his halo of curls. 'Blofeld, is it? Well, well.' He looked accusingly at Bond. 'Forgive me, but you certainly have wasted plenty of my, of the College's, time, Commander Bond. It is a mystery to me why you did not mention this man's name before. Now let me see, Blofeld, Blofeld. Seem to recall that it came up at one of our Chapter meetings the other day. Now who had the case? Ah, yes.' He reached for a telephone among the nest of books and papers. 'Give me Sable Basilisk.'

7

THE HAIRY HEEL OF ACHILLES

JAMES BOND'S HEART was still in his boots as he was conducted again through the musty corridors. Sable Basilisk indeed! What kind of a besotted old fogy would this be?

There came another heavy door with the name in gold and this time with a nightmare black monster, with a vicious beak, above it. But now Bond was shown into a light, clean, pleasantly furnished room with attractive prints on the walls and meticulous order among its books. There was a faint smell of Turkish tobacco. A young man, a few years younger than Bond, got up and came across the room to meet him. He was rapier-slim, with a fine, thin, studious face that was saved from seriousness by wry lines at the edges of the mouth and an ironical glint in the level eyes.

'Commander Bond?' The handshake was brief and firm. 'I'd been expecting you. How did you get into the claws of our dear Griffon? He's a bit of an enthusiast, I'm afraid. We all are here, of course. But he's getting on. Nice chap, but he's a bit dedicated, if you know what I mean.'

It was indeed like a college, this place, reflected Bond. Much of the atmosphere one associates with the Senior Common Room at a university. No doubt Griffon Or mentally put down Sable Basilisk as a young dilettante who was too big for his boots. He said, 'He seemed very anxious to establish a connection between me and Bond Street. It took some time to persuade him that I'm perfectly content to be an ordinary Bond, which, by the way, he, rather churlishly I thought, said meant "a churl".'

Sable Basilisk laughed. He sat down behind his desk, pulled a file towards him, and gestured Bond to a chair beside him. 'Well, then. Let's get down to business. First of all —' he looked Bond very straight in the eye — 'I gather, I guess that is, that this is an Intelligence matter of some kind. I did my national service with Intelligence in BAOR, so please don't worry about security. Secondly, we have in this building probably as many secrets as a government department — and nastier ones at that. One of our jobs is to suggest titles to people who've been ennobled in the Honours Lists. Sometimes we're asked to establish ownership to a title that has become lost or defunct. Snobbery and vanity positively sprawl through our files. Before my time, a certain gentleman who had come up from nowhere, made millions in some light industry or another, and had been given a peerage "for political and public services" — i.e., charities and the party funds — suggested that he should take the title of Lord Bentley Royal, after the village in Essex. We explained that the word Royal could not be used except by the reigning family, but, rather naughtily I fear, we said that "Lord Bentley Common" was vacant.' He smiled. 'See what I mean? If that got about, this man would become the laughing-stock of the country. Then sometimes we have to chase up lost fortunes. So-and-so thinks he's the rightful Duke of Blank and ought to have his money. His name happens to be Blank and his ancestors migrated to America or Australia or somewhere. So avarice and greed come to join snobbery and vanity in these rooms. Of course,' he added, putting the record straight, 'that's only the submerged tenth of our job. The rest is mostly official stuff for governments and embassies — problems of precedence and protocol, the Garter ceremonies and others. We've been doing it for around five hundred years so I suppose it's got its place in the scheme of things.'

'Of course it has,' said Bond staunchly. 'And certainly, so far as security is concerned, I'm sure we can be open with each other. Now this man Blofeld. Truth of the matter is he's probably the biggest crook in the world. Remember that Thunderball affair about a year ago? Only some of it leaked into the papers, but I can tell you that this Blofeld was at the bottom of it all. Now, how did you come to hear of him? Every detail, please. Everything about him is important.'

Sable Basilisk turned back to the first letter on the file. 'Yes,' he said thoughtfully, 'I thought this might be the same chap when I got a lot of urgent calls from the Foreign Office and the Ministry of Defence yesterday. Hadn't occurred to me before, I'm afraid, that this is a case where our secrets have to come second, or I'd have done something about it earlier. Now then, in June last, the tenth, we got this confidential letter from a firm of respectable Zürich solicitors, dated the day before. I'll read it out:

> 'Honoured Sirs,
>
> 'We have a valued client by the name of Ernst Stavro Blofeld. This gentleman styles himself Monsieur le Comte Balthazar de Bleuville in the belief that he is the rightful heir to this title which we understand to be extinct. His belief is based on stories he heard from his parents in childhood to the effect that his family fled France at the time of the Revolution, settled in Germany under the adopted name of Blofeld, assumed in order to evade the Revolutionary authorities and safeguard their fortune which they had sequestered in Augsburg, and subsequently, in the 1850s, migrated to Poland.
>
> 'Our client is now anxious to have these facts established in order legally to obtain right to the de Bleuville title supported by an Acte de Notoriété which would in due course receive the stamp of approval of the Ministère de la Justice in Paris.
>
> 'In the meantime, our client proposes to continue to adopt, albeit provisionally, the title of Comte de Bleuville together with the family arms which he informs us are "Argent four fusils in fesse gules" and the de Bleuville motto which, in English, is "For Hearth and Home".'

'That's a good one!' interjected Bond. Sable Basilisk smiled and continued:

> 'We understand that you, honoured sirs, are the only body in the world who is capable of undertaking this research work and we have been instructed to get in touch with you *under the strictest conditions of confidence*, which, in view of the social aspects involved, we think we have the right to request.
>
> 'The financial standing of our client is impeccable and expense is no object in this matter. As a preliminary honorarium and upon acceptance of this commission, we pro-

pose a payment of one thousand pounds sterling to your account in such bank as you may designate.

'Awaiting the favour of an early reply, we remain, honoured sirs etc. etc., Gebrüder Gumpold-Moosbrugger, Advokaten, 16 bis, Bahnhofstrasse, Zürich.'

Sable Basilisk looked up. James Bond's eyes were glittering with excitement. Sable Basilisk smiled. 'We were even more interested than you seem to be. You see, to let you in on a secret, our salaries are extremely modest. So we all have private means which we supplement from fees received for special work like this. These fees rarely go above fifty guineas for a piece of pretty tough research and all the leg work at Somerset House and in parish records and graveyards that is usually involved in tracking a man's ancestry. So this looked like a real challenge for the College, and as I was "in waiting" the day the letter came in, sort of "officer of the watch", the job fell into my lap.'

Bond said urgently, 'So what happened? Have you kept the contact?'

'Oh yes, but rather tenuously, I'm afraid. Of course I wrote at once accepting the commission and agreeing to the vow of secrecy which —' he smiled — 'you now force me to break presumably by invoking the Official Secrets Act. That is so, isn't it? I am acting under force majeure?'

'You are indeed,' said Bond emphatically.

Sable Basilisk made a careful note on the top paper in the file and continued. 'Of course the first thing I had to ask for was the man's birth certificate and, after a delay, I was told that it had been lost and that I was on no account to worry about it. The Count had in fact been born in Gdynia of a Polish father and a Greek mother — I have the names here — on May 28th, 1908. Could I not pursue my researches backwards from the de Bleuville end? I replied temporizing, but by this time I had indeed established from our library that there had been a family of de Bleuvilles, at least as lately as the seventeenth century, at a place called Blonville-sur-Mer, Calvados, and that their arms and motto were as claimed by Blofeld.' Sable Basilisk paused. 'This of course he must have known for himself. There would have been no purpose in inventing a family of de Bleuvilles and trying to stuff them down our throats. I told the lawyers of my discovery and, in my summer holidays — the North of France is more or less my private heraldic beat, so to speak, and very rich it is too in connections with England — I motored down there and sniffed around. But meanwhile I had, as a matter of routine, written to our Ambassador in Warsaw and asked him to contact our Consul in Gdynia and request him to employ a lawyer to make the simple researches with the Registrar and the various churches where Blofeld might have been baptized. The reply, early in September, was, but is no longer, surprising. The pages containing the record of Blofeld's birth had been neatly cut out. I kept this information to myself, that is to say I did not pass it on to the Swiss lawyers because I had been expressly instructed to make no inquiries in Poland. Meanwhile I had carried out similar inquiries through a lawyer in Augsburg. There, there was indeed a record of Blofelds, but of a profusion of them, for it is a fairly common German name, and in any case nothing to link any of them with the de Bleuvilles from Calvados. So I was stumped, but no more than I have been before, and I wrote a neutral report to the Swiss lawyers and said that I was continuing my researches. And there —' Sable Basilisk slapped the file shut — 'until my telephone began ringing yesterday, presumably because someone in the Northern Department of the Foreign Office was checking the file copies from Warsaw and the name Blofeld rang a bell, and you appeared looking very impatient from the cave of my friend the Griffon, the case rests.'

Bond scratched his head thoughtfully. 'But the ball's still in play?'

'Oh yes, definitely.'

'Can you keep it in play? I take it you haven't got Blofeld's present address?' Sable Basilisk shook his head. 'Then would there be any conceivable excuse for an envoy from you?' Bond smiled. 'Me, for example, to be sent out from the College to have an interview with Blofeld — some tricky point that cannot be cleared up by correspondence, something that needs a personal inquiry from Blofeld?'

'Well, yes, there is in a way.' Sable Basilisk looked rather dubious. 'You see, in some families there is a strong physical characteristic that goes on inevitably from generation to generation. The Habsburg lip is a case in point. So is the tendency to haemophilia amongst descendants of the Bourbons. The hawk nose of the Medici is another. A certain royal family have minute, vestigial tails. The original maharajahs of Mysore were born with six fingers on each hand. I could go on indefinitely, but those are the most famous cases. Now, when I was scratching around in the crypt of the chapel at Blonville, having a look at the old Bleuville tombs, my flashlight, moving over the stone faces, picked out a curious fact that I tucked away in my mind but that your question has brought to the surface. None of the de Bleuvilles, as far as I could tell, and certainly not through a hundred and fifty years, had lobes to their ears.'

'Ah,' said Bond, running over in his mind the Identicast picture of Blofeld and the complete, printed physiognometry of the man in Records. 'So he shouldn't by rights have lobes to his ears. Or at any rate it would be a strong piece of evidence for his case if he hadn't?'

'That's right.'

'Well, he *has* got lobes,' said Bond, annoyed. 'Rather pronounced lobes as a matter of fact. Where does that get us?'

'To begin with, added to what I know anyway, that makes him probably not a de Bleuville. But after all —' Sable Basilisk looked sly — 'there's no reason why he should know what physical characteristic we're looking for in this interview.'

'You think we could set one up?'

'Don't see why not. But —' Sable Basilisk was apologetic — 'would you mind if I got clearance from Garter King of Arms? He's my boss, so to speak, under the Duke of Norfolk that is, the Earl Marshal, and I can't remember that we've ever been mixed up in this sort of cloak-and-dagger stuff before. Actually —' Sable Basilisk waved a deprecating hand — 'we are, we have to be, damned meticulous. You do see that, don't you?'

'Naturally. And I'm sure there'd be no objection. But, even if Blofeld agreed to see me, how in hell could I play the part? This stuff is all double Dutch to me.' He smiled. 'I don't know the difference between a gule and a bezant and I've never been able to make out what a baronet is. What's my story to Blofeld? Who am I exactly?'

Sable Basilisk was getting enthusiastic. He said cheerfully, 'Oh that'll be all right. I'll coach you in all the dope about the de Bleuvilles. You can easily mug up a few popular books on heraldry. It's not difficult to be impressive on the subject. Very few people know anything about it.'

'Maybe. But this Blofeld is a pretty smart animal. He'll want the hell of a lot of credentials before he sees anyone but his lawyer and his banker. Who exactly am I?'

'You think Blofeld's smart because you've seen the smart side of him,' said Sable Basilisk sapiently. 'I've seen hundreds of smart people from the City, industry, politics — famous people I've been quite frightened to meet when they walked into this room. But when it comes to snobbery, to buying respectability so to speak, whether it's the title they're going to choose or just a coat of arms to hang over their fire-places in Surbiton, they dwindle and dwindle in front of you —' he made a downward motion over his desk with his hand — 'until they're no bigger than nomunculi. And the women are even worse. The idea of suddenly becoming a "lady" in their small community is so intoxicating that the way they bare their souls is positively obscene. It's as if —' Sable Basilisk furrowed his high, pale brow, seeking for a simile — 'these fundamentally good citizens, these Smiths and Browns and Joneses and —' he smiled across the desk — 'Bonds, regarded the process of ennoblement as a sort of laying-on of hands, a way of ridding themselves of all the drabness of their lives, of all their, so to speak, essential meagreness, their basic inferiority. Don't worry about Blofeld. He has already swallowed the bait. He may be a tremendous gangster, and he must be from what I remember of the case. He may be tough and ruthless in his corner of human behaviour. But if he is trying to prove that he is the Comte de Bleuville, you can be sure of various things. He wants to change his name. That is obvious. He wants to become a new, a respectable personality. That is obvious too. But above all he wants to become a Count.' Sable Basilisk brought his hand flat down on his desk for emphasis. 'That, Mr Bond, is tremendously significant. He is a rich and successful man in his line of business — no matter what it is. He no longer admires the material things, riches and power. He is now 54, as I reckon it. He wants a new skin. I can assure you, Mr Bond, that he will receive you, if we play our cards right that is, as if he were consulting his doctor about —' Sable Basilisk's aristocratic face took on an expression of distaste — 'as if he were consulting his doctor after contracting

V.D.' Sable Basilisk's eyes were now compelling. He sat back in his chair and lit his first cigarette. The smell of Turkish tobacco drifted across to Bond. 'That's it,' he said with certitude. 'This man knows he is unclean, a social pariah. Which of course he is. Now he has thought up this way of buying himself a new identity. If you ask me, we must help the hair to grow and flourish on his heel of Achilles until it is so luxuriant that he trips on it.'

8

FANCY COVER

'AND WHO THE hell are *you* supposed to be?'

M more or less repeated Bond's question when, that evening, he looked up from the last page of the report that Bond had spent the afternoon dictating to Mary Goodnight. M's face was just outside the pool of yellow light cast by the green-shaded reading lamp on his desk, but Bond knew that the lined sailor's face was reflecting, in varying degrees, scepticism, irritation and impatience. The 'hell' told him so. M rarely swore and when he did it was nearly always at stupidity. M obviously regarded Bond's plan as stupid, and now, away from the dedicated, minutely focused world of the Heralds, Bond wasn't sure that M wasn't right.

'I'm to be an emissary from the College of Arms, sir. This Basilisk chap recommended that I should have some kind of a title, the sort of rather highfalutin one that would impress a man with this kind of bee in his bonnet. And Blofeld's obviously got this bee or he wouldn't have revealed his existence, even to such a presumably secure and — er — sort of remote corner of the world as the College of Arms. I've put down there the arguments of this chap and they make a lot of sense to me. Snobbery's a real Achilles heel with people. Blofeld's obviously got the bug badly. I think we can get to him through it.'

'Well, I think it's all a pack of nonsense,' said M testily. (Not many years before, M had been awarded the K.C.M.G. for his services, and Miss Moneypenny, his desirable secretary, had revealed in a moment of candour to Bond that M had not replied to a single one of the notes and letters of congratulation. After a while he had refused even to read them and had told Miss Moneypenny not to show him any more but to throw them in the wastepaper basket.) 'All right then, what's this ridiculous title to be? And what happens next?'

If Bond had been able to blush, he would have blushed. He

said, 'Er — well, sir, it seems there's a chap called Sir Hilary Bray. Friend of Sable Basilisk's. About my age and not unlike me to look at. His family came from some place in Normandy. Family tree as long as your arm. William the Conqueror and all that. And a coat of arms that looks like a mixture between a jigsaw puzzle and Piccadilly Circus at night. Well, Sable Basilisk says he can fix it with him. This man's got a good war record and sounds a reliable sort of chap. He lives in some remote glen in the Highlands, watching birds and climbing the hills with bare feet. Never sees a soul. No reason why anyone in Switzerland should have heard of him.' Bond's voice became defensive, stubborn. 'Well, sir, the idea is that I should be him. Rather fancy cover, but I think it makes sense.'

'Sir Hilary Bray, eh?' M tried to conceal his scorn. 'And then what do you do? Run around the Alps waving this famous banner of his?'

Bond said patiently, obstinately, refusing to be browbeaten. 'First I'll get Passport Control to fix up a good passport. Then I mug up Bray's family tree until I'm word-perfect on the thing. Then I swot away at the rudiments of this heraldry business. Then, if Blofeld takes the bait, I go out to Switzerland with all the right books and suggest that I work out his de Bleuville pedigree with him.'

'Then what?'

'Then I try and winkle him out of Switzerland, get him over the frontier to somewhere where we can do a kidnap job on him, rather like the Israelis did with Eichmann. But I haven't worked out all the details yet, sir. Had to get your approval and then Sable Basilisk has got to make up a damned attractive fly and throw it over these Zürich solicitors.'

'Why not try putting pressure on the Zürich solicitors and winkle Blofeld's address out of them? Then we might think of doing some kind of a commando job.'

'You know the Swiss, sir. God knows what kind of a retainer these lawyers have from Blofeld. But it's bound to be millionaire size. We might eventually get the address, but they'd be bound to tip off Blofeld if only to lay their hands on their fees before he vamoosed. Money's the religion of Switzerland.'

'I don't need a lecture on the qualities of the Swiss, thank you, 007. At least they keep their trains clean and cope with the beatnik problem [two very rampant bees in M's bonnet!], but I daresay there's some truth in what you say. Oh, well.' M wearily pushed the file over to Bond. 'Take it away. It's a messy-looking bird's-nest of a plan. But I suppose it had better go ahead.' M shook his head sceptically. 'Sir Hilary Bray! Oh, well, tell the Chief of Staff I approve. But reluctantly. Tell him you can have the facilities. Keep me informed.' M reached for the Cabinet telephone. His voice was deeply disgruntled. 'Suppose I'll have to tell the P.M. we've got a line on the chap. The kind of tangle it is, I'll keep to myself. That's all, 007.'

'Thank you, sir. Good night.' As Bond went across to the door he heard M say into the green receiver, 'M speaking. I want the Prime Minister personally, please.' He might have been asking for the mortuary. Bond went out and softly closed the door behind him.

So, as November blustered its way into December, James Bond went unwillingly back to school, swotting up heraldry at his desk instead of top-secret reports, picking up scraps of medieval French and English, steeping himself in fusty lore and myth, picking the brains of Sable Basilisk and occasionally learning interesting facts, such as that the founders of Gamages came from the de Gamaches in Normandy and that Walt Disney was remotely descended from the D'Isignys of the same part of France. But these were nuggets in a wasteland of archaisms, and when, one day, Mary Goodnight, in reply to some sally of his, addressed him as 'Sir Hilary' he nearly bit her head off.

Meanwhile the highly delicate correspondence between Sable Basilisk and the Gebrüder Moosbrugger proceeded haltingly and at a snail's pace. They, or rather Blofeld behind them, posed countless irritating but, Sable Basilisk admitted, erudite queries each one of which had to be countered with this or that degree of heraldic obfuscation. Then there were minute questions about this emissary, Sir Hilary Bray. Photographs were asked for, and, suitably doctored, were provided. His whole career since his schooldays had to be detailed and was sent down from Scotland with a highly amused covering note from the real man. To test the market, more funds were asked for by Sable Basilisk and, with encouraging promptitude, were forthcoming in the shape of a further thousand pounds. When the cheque arrived on December 15th Sable Basilisk telephoned Bond delightedly. 'We've got him,' he said. 'He's hooked!' And, sure enough, the next day came a letter from Zürich to say that their client agreed to a meeting with Sir Hilary. Would Sir Hilary please arrive at Zürich Central Airport by Swissair flight Number 105, due at Zürich at 1300 hours on December 21st. On Bond's prompting, Sable Basilisk wrote back that the date was not convenient to Sir Hilary owing to a prior engagement with the Canadian High Commissioner regarding a detail in the Arms of the Hudson's Bay Company. Sir Hilary could, however, manage the 22nd. By return came a cable agreeing and, to Bond, confirming that the fish had not only swallowed the hook but the line and sinker as well.

The last few days were spent in a flurry of meetings, with the Chief of Staff presiding, at Headquarters. The main decisions were that Bond should go to the meeting with Blofeld absolutely 'clean'. He would carry no weapons, no secret gear of any kind, and he would not be watched or followed by the Service in any way. He would communicate only with Sable Basilisk, getting across such information as he could by using heraldic double talk (Sable Basilisk had been cleared by M.I.5 immediately after Bond's first meeting with him), and Sable Basilisk, who vaguely thought that Bond was employed by the Ministry of Defence, would be given a cut-out at the Ministry who would be his go-between with the Service. This was all assuming that Bond managed to stay close to Blofeld for at least a matter of days. And that was to be his basic stratagem. It was essential to find out as much as possible about Blofeld, his activities and his associates, in order to proceed with planning the next step, his abduction from Switzerland. Physical action might not be necessary. Bond might be able to trick the man into a visit to Germany, as a result of a report which Sable Basilisk had prepared of certain Blofeld family documents at the Augsburg Zentral Archiv, which would need Blofeld's personal identification. Security precautions would include keeping Station Z completely in the dark about Bond's mission to Switzerland and a closure of the 'Bedlam' file at Headquarters which would be announced in the routine 'Orders of the Day'. Instead, a new codeword for the operation, known only to an essential handful of senior officers, would be issued. It would be 'Corona'.

Finally, the personal dangers to Bond himself were discussed. There was total respect for Blofeld at Headquarters. Nobody questioned his abilities or his ruthlessness. If Bond's true identity somehow became known to Blofeld, Bond would of course instantly be liquidated. A more dangerous and likely event would be that, once Blofeld had probed Bond's heraldic gen to its rather shallow bottom and it had been proved that he was or was not the Comte de Bleuville, Sir Hilary Bray, his usefulness expended, might 'meet with an accident'. Bond would just have to face up to these hazards and watch out particularly for the latter. He, and Sable Basilisk behind him, would have to keep some tricks up their sleeves, tricks that would somehow make Sir Hilary Bray's continued existence important to Blofeld. In conclusion, the Chief of Staff said he considered the whole operation 'a lot of bezants' and that 'Bezants' would have been a better codeword than 'Corona'. However, he wished Bond the best of luck and said, cold-heartedly, that he would instruct the Technical Section to proceed forthwith with the devising of a consignment of explosive snowballs for Bond's protection.

It was on this cheery note that Bond, on the evening of December 21st, returned to his office for a last run-through of his documentation with Mary Goodnight.

He sat sideways to his desk, looking out over the triste winter twilight of Regent's Park under snow, while she sat opposite him and ran through the items: '*Burke's Extinct and Dormant Baronetage*, property of the College of Heralds. Stamped "Not to be removed from the Library". The printed *Visitations in the College of Arms*, stamped ditto. *Genealogist's Guide*, by G. W. Marshall, with Hatchard's receipted bill to Sable Basilisk inserted. *Burke's General Armory*, stamped "Property of the London Library", wrapped and franked December 10th. Passport in the name of Sir Hilary Bray, containing various recently dated frontier stamps in and out of France, Germany and the Low Countries, fairly well used and dog-eared. One large file of correspondence with Augsburg and Zürich on College of Arms writing-paper and the writing-paper of the addressees. And that's the lot. You've fixed your laundry tags and so on?'

'Yes,' said Bond dully. 'I've fixed all that. And I've got two new suits with cuffs and double vents at the back and four buttons down the front. Also a gold watch and chain with the Bray seal. Quite the little baronet.' Bond turned and looked across the desk at Mary Goodnight. 'What do you think of this caper, Mary? Think it'll come off?'

'Well, it should do,' she said staunchly. 'With all the trouble that's been taken. But —' she hesitated — 'I don't like you taking this man on without a gun.' She waved a hand at the pile on the floor. 'And all these stupid books about heraldry! It's just not *you*. You will take care, won't you?'

'Oh, I'll do that all right,' said Bond reassuringly. 'Now, be a good girl and get a radio taxi to the Universal Export entrance. And put all that junk inside it, would you? I'll be down in a minute. I'll be at the flat all this evening —' he smiled sourly — 'packing my silk shirts with the crests on them.' He got up. 'So long, Mary. Or rather good night, Goodnight. And keep out of trouble till I get back.'

She said, 'You do that yourself.' She bent and picked up the books and papers from the floor and, keeping her face hidden from Bond, went to the door and kicked it shut behind her with her heel. A moment or two later she opened the door again. Her eyes were bright. 'I'm sorry, James. Good luck! And Happy Christmas!' She closed the door softly behind her.

Bond looked at the blank face of the Office of Works cream door. What a dear girl Mary was! But now there was Tracy. He would be near her in Switzerland. It was time to make contact again. He had been missing her, wondering about her. There had been three non-committal but cheerful postcards from the Clinique de l'Aube at Davos. Bond had made inquiries and had ascertained that this was run by a Professor Auguste Kommer, President of the Société Psychiatrique et Psychologique Suisse. Over the telephone, Sir James Molony, the nerve specialist by appointment to the Service, had told Bond that Kommer was one of the top men in the world at his job. Bond had written affectionately and encouragingly to Tracy and had had the letters posted from America. He had said he would be home soon and would be in touch with her. Would he? And what would he do then? Bond had a luxurious moment feeling sorry for himself, for the miscellaneous burdens he was carrying alone. He then crushed out his cigarette and, banging doors behind him, got the hell out of his office and down in the lift to the discreet side entrance that said 'Universal Export'.

The taxi was waiting. It was seven o'clock. As the taxi got under way, Bond made his plan for the evening. He would first do an extremely careful packing job of his single suitcase, the one that had no tricks to it, have two double vodkas and tonics with a dash of Angostura, eat a large dish of May's speciality — scrambled eggs fines herbes — have two more vodkas and tonics, and then, slightly drunk, go to bed with half a grain of seconal.

Encouraged by the prospect of this cosy self-anaesthesia, Bond brusquely kicked his problems under the carpet of his consciousness.

9

IRMA LA NOT SO DOUCE

THE NEXT DAY, at London Airport, James Bond, bowler hat, rolled umbrella, neatly folded *Times* and all, felt faintly ridiculous. He felt totally so when he was treated with the deference due to his title and shown into the V.I.P. lounge before take-off. At the ticket desk, when he had been addressed as Sir Hilary, he had looked behind him to see who the girl was talking to. He really must pull himself together and damn well *be* Sir Hilary Bray!

Bond had a double brandy and ginger ale and stood aloof from the handful of other privileged passengers in the gracious lounge, trying to *feel* like a baronet. Then he remembered the real Sir Hilary Bray, perhaps now gralloching a hind with his bare hands somewhere up in the Glens. There was nothing of the baronet about him! He really must get rid of the inverted snobbery that, with its opposite, is ingrained in so many of the English! He must stop acting a part, being a stage nobleman! He would just be himself and, if he gave the appearance of being rather a rough-hewn baronet, the easy-going kind, well, that at least was like the real one up in Scotland. Bond threw down the *Times* that he had been carrying as an extra badge of Top Peopleship, picked up the *Daily Express*, and asked for another brandy and ginger ale.

Then, with its twin jets whispering far back of the first-class cabin, the Swissair Caravelle was airborne and Bond's mind was reaching forward to the rendezvous that had been so briefly detailed by the Zürich solicitors. Sir Hilary would be met at the airport by one of the Comte de Bleuville's secretaries. He would be seeing the Count that day or the next. Bond had a moment of panic. How should he address the man when he met him? Count? Monsieur le Comte? No, he would call him nothing — perhaps an occasional patronizing 'my dear sir' in context. What would Blofeld look like? Would he have changed his appearance much? Probably, or the fox wouldn't have kept ahead of the hounds so efficiently. Bond's excitement mounted as he consumed a delicious lunch served by a delicious stewardess, and the winter-brown chequerboard of France fled backwards distantly below. Now there was scattered snow and barren trees as they crossed the tiny hillocks of the Vosges, then permanent snow and ice-floes on the Rhine, a short stop at Basle, and then the black criss-cross of Zürich Airport and 'fasten your lap-straps' in three languages, and they were planing down, a slight bump, the roar of jet deflection, and then they were taxiing up to the apron in front of the imposing, very European-looking buildings decked with the gay flags of the nations.

At the Swissair desk inside the door, a woman was standing beside the reception counter. As soon as Bond appeared in the entrance she came forward. 'Sair Hilary Bray?'

'Yes.'

'I am Fräulein Irma Bunt. Personal secretary to the Count. Good afternoon. I hope you had a happy flight.'

She looked like a very sunburned female wardress. She had a square, brutal face with hard yellow eyes. Her smile was an oblong hole without humour or welcome, and there were sunburn blisters at the left corner of her mouth which she licked from time to time with the tip of a pale tongue. Wisps of brownish grey hair, with a tight, neat bun at the back, showed from under a skiing hat with a yellow talc visor that had straps which met under her chin. Her strong, short body was dressed in unbecomingly tight vorlage trousers topped by a grey wind-jacket ornamented over the left breast with a large red G topped by a coronet. Irma la not so Douce, thought Bond. He said, 'Yes. It was very pleasant.'

'You have your baggage check? Will you follow me, please? And first your passport. This way.'

Bond followed her through the passport control and out into the customs hall. There were a few standers-by. Bond noticed her head nod casually. A man with a briefcase under his arm, hanging about, moved away. Bond studiously examined his baggage check. Beyond the scrap of cardboard, he noticed the man slip into one of the row of telephone booths in the main hall outside the customs area.

'You speak German?' The tongue flicked out and licked the blisters.

'No, I'm afraid not.'

'French perhaps?'

'A little. Enough for my work.'

'Ah, yes. That is important, yes?'

Bond's suitcase was unloaded off the trolley on to the barrier. The woman flashed some kind of a pass at the customs officer. It was very quickly done, but Bond caught a glimpse of her photograph and the heading 'Bundespolizei'. So! Blofeld had got the fix in!

The officer said deferentially, 'Bitte sehr,' and chalked his symbol in the colour of the day, yellow, on Bond's suitcase. A porter took it and they walked across to the entrance. When they came out on the steps, an anonymous black Mercedes 300 SE saloon pulled smartly out of the parking area and slid to a stop beside them. Next to the chauffeur sat the man who had gone to the telephone. Bond's suitcase was put in the boot and they moved off fast in the direction of Zürich. A few hundred yards down the wide road, the man beside the driver, who, Bond noticed, had been surreptitiously watching in the twin driving-mirror, said softly, 'Is' gut,' and the car turned right-handed up a side road which was marked 'Eingang Verboten! Mit Ausnahme von Eigentümer und Personell von Privat-flugzeugen'.

Bond was amused as he ticked off the little precautions. It was obvious that he was still very much on probation.

The car came up with the hangars to the left of the main building, drove slowly between them and pulled up beside a bright orange Alouette helicopter, adapted by Sud Aviation for mountain rescue work. But this one had the red G with the coronet on its fuselage. So! He was going to be taken for a flight rather than a ride!

'You have travelled in one of these machines before? No? It is very pleasant. One obtains a fine view of the Alps.' Fräulein Bunt's eyes were blank with disinterest. They climbed up the aluminium ladder. 'Mind your head, please!' Bond's suitcase was handed up by the chauffeur.

It was a six-seater, luxurious in red leather. Above and in front of them under his Perspex canopy the pilot lifted a thumb.

The ground staff pulled away the chocks and the big blades began to move. As they accelerated, the men on the ground drew away, shielding their faces against the whirling snow. There was a slight jolt and then they were climbing fast, and the crackle of radio from the control tower went silent.

Irma Bunt was across the passage-way from Bond. The extra man was in the rear, hidden behind the *Züricher Zeitung*. Bond leaned sideways and said loudly, against the rattle of the machine, 'Where are we heading for?'

She pretended not to hear. Bond repeated his question, shouting it.

'Into the Alps. Into the high Alps,' shouted the woman. She waved towards the window. 'It is very beautiful. You like the mountains, isn't it?'

'I love them,' shouted Bond. 'Just like Scotland.' He leaned back in his seat, lit a cigarette and looked out of the window. Yes, there was the Zürichersee to port. Their course was more or less east-south-east. They were flying at about 2,000 feet. And now there was the Wallensee. Bond, apparently uninterested, took the *Daily Express* out of his briefcase and turned to the sports pages. He read the paper from last page to first, meticulously, every now and then casting a bored glance out of the window. The big range to port would be the Rhätikon Alps. That would be the railway junction of Landquart below them. They held their course up the valley of the Pratigau. Would they keep on at Klosters or veer to starboard? Starboard it was. So! Up the Davos Valley! In a few minutes he would be flying over Tracy! A casual glance. Yes, there was Davos under its thin canopy of evening mist and smoke, while, above her, he was still in bright sunshine. At least she seemed to have had plenty of snow. Bond remembered the tremendous run down the Parsenn. Those had been the days! And now back on the old course again and giant peaks to right and left. This must be the Engadine. The Silvretta Group away to starboard, to port Piz Languard and, ahead, the Bernina range diving down, like a vast ski-jump, into Italy. That forest of lights away to starboard must be St Moritz! Now where? Bond buried himself in his paper. A slight veer to port. More lights. Pontresina? And now the radio began to crackle and the 'Seat belts' sign went up. Bond thought it time to express open interest. He gazed out.

Below, the ground was mostly in darkness, but ahead the giant peaks were still golden in the dying sun. They were making straight for one of them, for a small plateau near its summit. There was a group of buildings from which golden wires swooped down into the darkness of the valley. A cable car, spangled in the sun, was creeping down. Now it had been swallowed up in the murk. The helicopter was still charging the side of the peak that towered above them. Now it was only a hundred feet up above the slope, coming in to the plateau and the buildings. The pilot's arms moved on his joystick. The machine pitched a little and slowed. The rotor arms swung languidly and then accelerated as the machine hovered and settled. There came a slight bump as the inflated rubber 'floats' met the snow, a dying whirr from the rotor and they were there.

Where? Bond knew. They were in the Languard range, somewhere above Pontresina in the Engadine, and their altitude would be about 10,000 feet. He buttoned up his raincoat and prepared for the rasping dagger of the cold air on his lungs when the door was opened.

Irma Bunt gave her box-like smile. 'We have arrived,' she said unnecessarily.

The door, with a clatter of falling ice particles, was wrenched open. The last rays of the sun shone into the cabin. They caught the woman's yellow sun visor and shone through, turning her face Chinese. The eyes gave out a false blaze, like the glass eyes of a toy animal, under the light. 'Mind your head.' She bent low, her tight, squat behind inviting an enormous kick, and went down the ladder.

James Bond followed her, holding his breath against the searing impact of the arctic, oxygenless air. There were one or two men standing around dressed like ski guides. They looked at Bond with curiosity, but there was no greeting. Bond went on across the hard-trodden snow in the wake of the woman, the extra man following with his suitcase. He heard the engine stutter and roar, and a blizzard of snow particles stung the right side of his face. Then the iron grasshopper rose into the air and rattled off into the dusk.

It was perhaps fifty yards from where the helicopter had landed to the group of buildings. Bond dawdled, getting preliminary bearings. Ahead was a long, low building, now ablaze with lights. To the right, and perhaps another fifty yards away, were the outlines of the typical modern cable railhead, a box-like structure, with a thick flat roof canted upwards from close to the ground. As Bond examined it, its lights went out. Presumably the last car had reached the valley and the line was closed for the night. To the right of this was a large, bogus-chalet-type structure with a vast veranda, sparsely lit, that would be for the mass tourist trade — again a typical piece of high-Alpine architecture. Down to the left, beneath the slope of the plateau, lights shone from a fourth building that, except for its flat roof, was out of sight.

Bond was now only a few yards from the building that was obviously his destination. An oblong of yellow opened invitingly as the woman went in and held the door for him. The light illuminated a big sign with the red G surmounted by the coronet. It said GLORIA KLUB. 3605 METRES. PRIVAT! NUR FÜR MITGLIEDER. Below in smaller letters it said 'Alpenberghaus und Restaurant Piz Gloria', and the drooping index finger of the traditional hand pointed to the right, towards the building near the cable-head.

So! Piz Gloria! Bond walked into the inviting yellow oblong. The door, released by the woman, closed with a pneumatic hiss.

Inside it was deliciously warm, almost hot. They were in a small reception room, and a youngish man with a very pale crew-cut and shrewd eyes got to his feet from behind a desk and made a slight bob in their direction. 'Sir Hilary is in Number Two.'

'Weiss schon,' said the woman curtly and, only just more politely, to Bond, 'Follow me, please.' She went through a facing door and down a thickly piled, red-carpeted passage. The left-hand wall was only occasionally broken by windows interspersed with fine skiing and mountain photographs. On the right were at first the doors of the club rooms, marked Bar, Restaurant, and Toiletten. Then came what were obviously the doors of bedrooms. Bond was shown into Number Two. It was an extremely comfortable, chintzy room in the American motel style with a bathroom leading off. The broad picture window was now curtained, but Bond knew that it must offer a tremendous view over the valley to the Suvretta Group above St Moritz. Bond threw his briefcase on the double bed and gratefully disposed of his bowler hat and umbrella. The extra man appeared with his suitcase, placed it on the luggage stand without looking at Bond and withdrew, closing the door behind him. The woman stayed where she was. 'This is to your satisfaction?' The yellow eyes were indifferent to his enthusiastic reply. She had more to say. 'That is good. Now perhaps I should explain some things, convey to you some laws of the club, isn't it?'

Bond lit a cigarette. 'That would certainly be helpful.' He put a politely interested expression on his face. 'Where are we, for instance?'

'In the Alps. In the high Alps,' said the woman vaguely. 'This alp, Piz Gloria, is the property of the Count. Together with the Gemeinde, the local authorities, he constructed the Seilbahn. You have seen the cables, yes? This is the first year it is opened. It is very popular and brings in much money. There are some fine ski runs. The Gloria Abfahrt is already famous. There is also a bob-sleigh run that is much greater than the Cresta at St Moritz. You have heard of that? You ski perhaps? Or make the bob-sleigh?'

The yellow eyes were watchful. Bond thought he would continue to answer no to all questions. Instinct told him to. He said apologetically, 'I'm afraid not. Never got around to it, you know. Too much bound up with my books, perhaps.' He smiled ruefully, self-critically.

'Schade! That is a pity.' But the eyes registered satisfaction. 'These installations bring good income for the Count. That is important. It helps to support his life's work, the Institut.'

Bond raised his eyebrows a polite fraction.

'The Institut für physiologische Forschung. It is for scientific research. The Count is a leader in the field of allergies — you understand? This is like the hay fever, the unableness to eat shellfish, yes?'

'Oh really? Can't say I suffer from any myself.'

'No? The laboratories are in a separate building. There the Count also lives. In this building, where we are, live the patients. He asks that you will not disturb them with too many questions. These treatments are very delicate. You understand?'

'Yes, of course. And when may I see the Count? I'm afraid I am a very busy man, Fräulein Bunt. There are matters awaiting my attention in London.' Bond spoke impressively. 'The new African States. Much work has to be done on their flags, the design of their currency, their stamps, their medals. We are very short-handed at the College. I hope the Count understands that his personal problem, interesting and important though it is, must take second place to the problems of Government.'

Bond had got through. Now she was all eagerness, reassurance. 'But of course, my dear Sair Hilary. The Count asks to be excused tonight, but he would much like to receive you at eleven o'clock tomorrow morning. That is suitable?'

'Certainly, certainly. That will give me time to marshal my documents, my books. Perhaps —' Bond waved to the small writing desk near the window — 'I could have an extra table to lay these things out. I'm afraid —' Bond smiled deprecatingly — 'we bookworms need a lot of space.'

'Of course, Sair Hilary. It will be done at once.' She moved to the door and pressed a bell-button. She gestured downwards, now definitely embarrassed. 'You will have noticed that there is no door handle on this side?' (Bond had done so. He said he hadn't.) 'You will ring when you wish to leave the room. Yes? It is on account of the patients. It is necessary that they have quiet. It is difficult to prevent them visiting each other for the sake of gossiping. It is for their good. You understand? Bedtime is at ten o'clock. But there is a night staff in case you should need any service. And the doors are of course not locked. You may re-enter your room at any time. Yes? We meet for cocktails in the bar at six. It is — how do you say? — the rest-pause of the day.' The box-like smile made its brief appearance. 'My girls are much looking forward to meeting you.'

The door opened. It was one of the men dressed as guides, a swarthy, bull-necked man with brown Mediterranean eyes. One of Marc-Ange's Corsican defectors? In rapid, bad French, the woman said that another table was desired. This was to be furnished during dinner. The man said 'Entendu.' She held the door before he could close it and he went off down the passage to the right. Guards' quarters at the end of the passage? Bond's mind went on clicking up the clues.

'Then that is all for the present, Sair Hilary? The post leaves at midday. We have radio telephone communications if you wish to use them. May I convey any message to the Count?'

'Please say that I look forward greatly to meeting him tomorrow. Until six o'clock then.' Bond suddenly wanted to be alone with his thoughts. He gestured towards his suitcase. 'I must get myself unpacked.'

'Of course, of course, Sair Hilary. Forgive me for detaining you.' And, on this gracious note, Irma Bunt closed the door, with its decisive click, behind her.

Bond stood still in the middle of the room. He let out his breath with a quiet hiss. What the hell of a kettle of fish! He would have liked to kick one of the dainty bits of furniture very hard indeed. But he had noticed that, of the four electric light prisms in the ceiling, one was a blank protruding eyeball. Closed-circuit television? If so, what would be its range? Not much more than a wide circle covering the centre of the room. Microphones? Probably the whole expanse of ceiling was one. That was the war-time gimmick. He must, he simply must assume that he was under constant supervision.

James Bond, his thoughts racing, proceeded to unpack, take a shower and make himself presentable for 'my girls'.

10

TEN GORGEOUS GIRLS

IT WAS ONE of those leather-padded bars, bogus-masculine, and still, because of its newness, smelling like the inside of a new motor-car. It was made to look like a Tyrolean Stube by a big stone fire-place with a roaring log fire and cartwheel chandeliers with red-stemmed electric 'candles'. There were many wrought-iron gimmicks — wall-light brackets, ashtrays, table lamps — and the bar itself was 'gay' with small flags and miniature liqueur bottles. Attractive zither music tripped out from a hidden loudspeaker. It was not, Bond decided, a place to get seriously drunk in.

When he closed the leather-padded, brass-studded door behind him, there was a moment's hush, then a mounting of decibels to hide the covert glances, the swift summing-up. Bond got a fleeting impression of one of the most beautiful groups of girls he had ever seen, when Irma Bunt, hideous in some kind of home-made, homespun 'après-ski', in which orange and black predominated, waddled out from among the galaxy and took him in charge. 'Sair Hilary.' She grasped his hand with a dry, monkey grip. 'How delightful, isn't it? Come please, and meet my girls.'

It was tremendously hot in the room and Bond felt the sweat bead on his forehead as he was led from table to table and shook this cool, this warm, this languid hand. Names like Ruby, Violet, Pearl, Anne, Elizabeth, Beryl, sounded in his ears, but all he saw was a sea of beautiful, sunburned faces and a succession of splendid, sweatered young bosoms. It was like being at home to the Tiller or the Bluebell Girls. At last he got to the seat that had been kept for him, between Irma Bunt and a gorgeous, bosomy blonde with large blue eyes. He sat down, overcome. The barman hovered. Bond pulled himself together. 'Whisky and soda, please,' he said, and heard his voice from far away. He took some time lighting a cigarette while sham, stage conversation broke out among the four tables in the semicircular embrasure that must, during the day, be the great lookout point. Ten girls and Irma. All English. No surnames. No other man. Girls in their twenties. Working girls probably. Sort of air-hostess type. Excited at having a man amongst them — a personable man and a baronet to boot — if that was what one did to a baronet. Pleased with his private joke, Bond turned to the blonde. 'I'm terribly sorry, but I didn't catch your name.'

'I'm Ruby.' The voice was friendly but refined. 'It must be quite an ordeal being the only chap — amongst all us girls, I mean.'

'Well, it was rather a surprise. But a very pleasant one. It's going to be difficult getting all your names right.' He lowered his voice conspiratorially. 'Be an angel and run through the field, so to speak.'

Bond's drink came and he was glad to find it strong. He took a long but discreet pull at it. He had noticed that the girls were drinking Colas and squashes with a sprinkling of feminine cocktails — Orange Blossoms, Daiquiris. Ruby was one of the ones with a Daiquiri. It was apparently O.K. to drink, but he would be careful to show a gentlemanly moderation.

Ruby seemed pleased to be able to break the ice. 'Well, I'll start on your right. That's Miss Bunt, the sort of matron, so to speak. You've met her. Then, in the violet camelot sweater, well, that's Violet of course. Then at the next table. The one in the green and gold Pucci shirt is Anne and next to her in green is Pearl. She's my sort of best friend here.' And so it went on, from one glorious golden girl to the next. Bond heard scraps of their conversation. 'Fritz says I'm not getting enough Vorlage. My skis keep on running away from me.' 'It's the same with me —' a giggle — 'my sit-upon's black and blue.' 'The Count says I'm getting on very well. Won't it be awful when we have to go?' 'I wonder how Polly's doing? She's been out a month now.' 'I think Skol's the only stuff for sunburn. All those oils and creams are nothing but frying fat.' And so on — mostly the chatter you would expect from a group of cheerful, healthy girls learning to ski, except for the occasional rather awed reference to the Count and the covert glances at Irma Bunt and Bond to make sure that they were behaving properly, not making too much noise.

While Ruby continued her discreet roll-call, Bond tried to fix the names to the faces and otherwise add to his comprehension of this lovely but bizarre group locked up on top of a very high alp indeed. The girls all seemed to share a certain basic, girl-guidish simplicity of manners and language, the sort of girls who, in an English pub, you would find sitting demurely with a boy friend sipping a Babycham, puffing rather clumsily at a cigarette and occasionally saying 'pardon'. Good girls, girls who, if you made a pass at them, would say, 'Please don't spoil it all', 'Men only want one thing' or, huffily, 'Please take your hand away'. And there were traces of many accents, accents from all over Britain — the broad vowels of Lancashire, the lilt of Wales, the burr of Scotland, the adenoids of refined Cockney.

Yours truly foxed, concluded Bond as Ruby finished with 'And that's Beryl in the pearls and twin-set. Now do you think you've got us all straight?'

Bond looked into the round blue eyes that now held a spark of animation. 'Frankly no. And I feel like one of those comic film stars who get snarled up in a girls' school. You know. Sort of St Trinian's.'

She giggled. (Bond was to discover that she was a chronic giggler. She was too 'dainty' to open her lovely lips and laugh. He was also to find that she couldn't sneeze like a human, but let out a muffled, demure squeak into her scrap of lace handkerchief, and that she took very small mouthfuls at meals and barely masticated with the tips of her teeth before swallowing with hardly a ripple of her throat. She had been 'well brought up'.) 'Oh, but we're not at all like St Trinian's. Those awful girls! How could you ever say such a thing!'

'Just a thought,' said Bond airily. 'Now then, how about another drink?'

'Oh, thenks awfully.'

Bond turned to Fräulein Bunt. 'And you, Miss Bunt?'

'Thank you, Sair Hilary. An apple-juice, if you please.'

Violet, the fourth at their table, said demurely that she wouldn't have another Coke. 'They give me wind,' she explained.

'Oh Violet!' Ruby's sense of the proprieties was outraged. 'How can you say such a thing!'

'Well, anyway, they do,' said Violet obstinately. 'They make me hiccup. No harm in saying that, is there?'

Good old Manchester, thought Bond. He got up and went to the bar, wondering how he was going to plough on through this and other evenings. He ordered the drinks and had a brainwave. He would break the ice! By hook or by crook he would become the life and soul of the party! He asked for a tumbler and that its rim should be dipped in water. Then he picked up a paper cocktail napkin and went back to the table. He sat down. 'Now,' he said as eyes goggled at him, 'if we were paying for our drinks, I'll show you how we'd decide who should pay. I learned this in the Army.' He placed the tumbler in the middle of the table, opened the paper napkin and spread the centre tightly over the top so that it clung to the moist edge of the glass. He took his small change out of his pocket, selected a five-centime piece and dropped it gently on to the centre of the stretched tissue. 'Now then,' he announced, remembering that the last time he had played this game had been in the dirtiest bar in Singapore. 'Who else smokes? We need three others with lighted cigarettes.' Violet was the only one at their table. Irma clapped her hands with authority. 'Elizabeth, Beryl, come over here. And come and watch, girls, Sair Hilary is making the joke game.' The girls clustered round, chattering happily at the diversion. 'What's he doing?' 'What's going to happen?' 'How do you play?'

'Now then,' said Bond, feeling like the games director on a cruise ship, 'this is for who pays for the drinks. One by one, you take a puff at your cigarette, knock off the ash, like this, and touch the top of the paper with the lighted end — just enough to burn a tiny hole, like this.' The paper sparkled briefly. 'Now Violet, then Elizabeth, then Beryl. The point is, the paper gets like a sort of cobweb with the coin just supported in the middle. The person who burns the last hole and makes the coin drop has to pay for the drinks. See? Now then, Violet.'

There were squeaks of excitement. 'What a lovely game!' 'Oh Beryl, look out!' Lovely heads craned over Bond. Lovely hair brushed his cheek. Quickly the three girls got the trick of very delicately touching a space that would not collapse the cobweb until Bond, who considered himself an expert at the game, decided to be chivalrous and purposely burned a vital strand. With the chink of the coin falling into the glass there was a burst of excited laughter and applause.

'See, you see, girls.' It was as if Irma Bunt had invented the game. 'Sair Hilary pays, isn't it? A most delightful pastime. And now —' she looked at her mannish wristwatch — 'we must finish our drinks. It is five minutes to supper time.'

There were cries of 'Oh, one more game, Miss Bunt!' But Bond politely rose with his whisky in his hand. 'We will play again tomorrow. I hope it's not going to start you all off smoking. I'm sure it was invented by the tobacco companies!'

There was laughter. But the girls stood admiringly round Bond. What a sport he was! And they had all expected a stuffed shirt! Bond felt justifiably proud of himself. The ice had been broken. He had got them all minutely on his side. Now they were all chums together. From now on he would be able to get to talk to them without frightening them. Feeling reasonably pleased with his gambit, he followed the tight pants of Irma Bunt into the dining-room next door.

It was seven-thirty. Bond suddenly felt exhausted, exhausted with the prospect of boredom, exhausted with playing the most difficult role of his career, exhausted with the enigma of Blofeld and the Piz Gloria. What in hell was the bastard up to? He sat down on the right of Irma Bunt in the same placing as for drinks, with Ruby on his right and Violet, dark, demure, self-effacing, opposite him, and glumly opened his napkin. Blofeld had certainly spent money on his eyrie. Their three tables, in a remote corner by the long, curved, curtained window, occupied only a fraction of the space in the big, low, luxuriously appointed, mock-German baroque room, ornate with candelabra suspended from the stomachs of flying cherubs, festooned with heavy gilt plaster-work, solemnized by the dark portraits of anonymous noblemen. Blofeld must be pretty certain he was here to stay. What was the investment? Certainly not less than a million sterling, even assuming a fat mortgage from Swiss banks on the cost of the cable railway. To lease an alp, put up a cable railway on mortgage, with the engineers and the local district council participating — that, Bond knew, was one of the latest havens for fugitive funds. If you were successful, if you and the council could bribe or bully the local farmers to allow right-of-way through their pastures, cut swaths through the tree-line for the cable pylons and the ski-runs, the rest was publicity and amenities for the public to eat their sandwiches. Add to that the snob-appeal of a posh, heavily restricted club such as Bond imagined this, during the daytime, to be, the coroneted G, and the mystique of a research institute run by a Count, and you were off to the races. Skiing today, Bond had read, was the most widely practised sport in the world. It sounded unlikely, but then one reckoned the others largely by spectators. Skiers were participants, and bigger spenders on equipment than in other sports. Clothes, boots, skis, bindings and now the whole 'après-ski' routine which took care of the day from four o'clock, when the sun went, onwards, were a tremendous industry. If you could lay your hands on a good alp, which Blofeld had somehow managed to do, you really had it good. Mortgages paid off — snow was the joker, but in the Engadine, at this height, you would be all right for that — in three or four years, and then jam for ever! One certainly had to hand it to him!

It was time to make the going again! Resignedly, Bond turned to Fräulein Bunt. 'Fräulein Bunt. Please explain to me. What is the difference between a piz and an alp and a berg?'

The yellow eyes gleamed with academic enthusiasm. 'Ah, Sair Hilary, but that is an interesting question. It had not occurred to me before. Now let me see.' She gazed into the middle distance. 'A piz, that is only a local name in this department of Switzerland for a peak. An alp, that one would think would be smaller than a berg — a hill, perhaps, or an upland pasture, as compared with a mountain. But that is not so. These —' she waved her hand — 'are all alps and yet they are great mountains. It is the same in Austria, certainly in the Tyrol. But in Germany, in Bavaria for instance, which is my homeland, there it is all bergs. No Sair Hilary —' the box-like smile was switched on and off — 'I cannot help you. But why do you ask?'

'In my profession,' said Bond prosily, 'the exact meaning of words is vital. Now, before we met for cocktails, it amused me to look up your surname, Bunt, in my books of reference. What I found, Fräulein, was most interesting. Bunt, it seems, is German for "gay", "happy". In England, the name has almost certainly been corrupted into Bounty, perhaps even into Brontë, because the grandfather of the famous literary family by that name had in fact changed his name from the less aristocratic name of Brunty. Now this is most interesting.' (Bond knew that it wasn't, that this was all hocus-pocus, but he thought it would do no harm to stretch his heraldic muscles.) 'Can you remember if your ancestors had any connection with England? There is the Dukedom of Brontë, you see, which Nelson assumed. It would be interesting to establish a connection.'

The penny dropped! A duchess! Irma Bunt, hooked, went off into a dreary chronicle of her forebears, including, proudly, distant relationship with a Graf von Bunt. Bond listened politely, prodding her back to the immediate past. She gave the name of her father and mother. Bond filed them away. He now had enough to find out in due course exactly who Irma Bunt was. What a splendid trap snobbery was! How right Sable Basilisk had been! There is a snob in all of us and only through snobbery could Bond have discovered who the parents of this woman were.

Bond finally calmed down the woman's momentary fever, and the head waiter, who had been politely hovering, presented giant menus covered in violet ink. There was everything from caviar down to Double Mokka au whisky irlandais. There were also many 'spécialités Gloria' — Poulet Gloria, Homard Gloria, Tournedos Gloria and so on. Bond, despite his forswearing of spécialités, decided to give the chicken a chance. He said so and was surprised by the enthusiasm with which Ruby greeted his choice. 'Oh, how right you are, Sir Hilary! I adore chicken too. I absolutely dote on it. Can I have that too, please, Miss Bunt?'

There was such surprising fervour in her voice that Bond watched Irma Bunt's face. What was that matronly gleam in her eye as she gave her approval? It was more than approval for a good appetite among her charges. There was enthusiasm, even triumph there. Odd! And it happened again when Violet stipulated plenty of potatoes with her tournedos. 'I simply love potatoes,' she explained to Bond, her eyes shining. 'Don't you?'

'They're fine,' agreed Bond, 'when you're taking plenty of exercise, that is.'

'Oh, they're just darling,' enthused Violet. 'Aren't they, Miss Bunt?'

'Very good indeed, my dear. Very good for you too. And Fritz, I will just have the mixed salad with some cottage cheese.' She gave the caricature of a simper. 'Alas — ' she spoke to Bond — 'I have to watch my figure. These young things take plenty of exercise, while I must stay in my office and do the paper-work, isn't it?'

At the next table Bond heard the girl with the Scottish burr, her voice full of saliva, ask that her Aberdeen Angus steak should be cooked very rare indeed. 'Guid and bluidy,' she emphasized.

What was this? wondered Bond. A gathering of beautiful ogresses? Or was this a day off from some rigorous diet? He felt completely clueless, out of his depth. Well, he would just go on digging. He turned to Ruby. 'You see what I mean about surnames. Fräulein Bunt may even have distant claim to an English title. Now what's yours, for instance? I'll see what I can make of it.'

Fräulein Bunt broke in sharply. 'No surnames here, Sair Hilary. It is a rule of the house. We use only first names for the girls. It is part of the Count's treatment. It is bound up with a change, a transference of identity, to help the cure. You understand?'

'No, I'm afraid that's way out of my depth,' said Bond cheerfully.

'No doubt the Count will explain some of these matters to you tomorrow. He has special theories. One day the world will be startled when he reveals his methods.'

'I'm, sure,' said Bond politely. 'Well now —' He searched for a subject that would leave his mind free to roam on its own. 'Tell me about your skiing. How are you getting on? Don't do it myself, I'm afraid. Perhaps I shall pick up some tips watching your classes.'

It was an adequate ball which went bouncing on between Ruby and Violet, and Bond kept it in play while their food came and proved delicious. Poulet Gloria was spatchcocked, with a mustard and cream sauce. The girls fell silent over their dishes, consuming them with polite but concentrated greed. There was a similar pause in the chatter at the other tables. Bond made conversation about the décor of the room and this gave him a chance to have a good look at the waiters. There were twelve of them in sight. It was not difficult to sum them up as three Corsicans, three Germans, three vaguely Balkan faces, Turks, Bulgars or Yugoslavs, and three obvious Slavs. There would probably be three Frenchmen in the kitchen. Was this the old pattern of SPECTRE? The well-tried communist-cell pattern of three men from each of the great gangster and secret-service organizations in Europe? Were the three Slavs ex-SMERSH men? The whole lot of them looked tough enough, had that quiet smell of the pro. The man at the airport was one of them. Bond recognized others as the reception steward and the man who had come to his room about the table. He heard the girls calling them Fritz, Joseph, Ivan, Achmed. And some of them were ski-guides during the day. Well, it was a nice little set-up if Bond was right.

Bond excused himself after dinner on the grounds of work. He went to his room and laid out his books and papers on the desk and on the extra table that had been provided. He bent over them studiously while his mind reviewed the day.

At ten o'clock he heard the good-nights of the girls down the corridor and the click of the doors shutting. He undressed, turned the thermostat on the wall down from eighty-five to sixty, switched off the light and lay on his back for a while staring up into the darkness. Then he gave an authentic sigh of exhaustion for the microphones, if any, and turned over on his side and went to sleep.

Later, much later, he was awakened by a very soft murmuring that seemed to come from somewhere under the floor, but very, very far away. He identified it as a minute, spidery whispering that went on and on. But he could not make out any words and he finally put it down to the central-heating pipes, turned over and went to sleep again.

11

DEATH FOR BREAKFAST

JAMES BOND AWOKE to a scream. It was a terrible, masculine scream out of hell. It fractionally held its first high, piercing note and then rapidly diminished as if the man had jumped off a cliff. It came from the right, from somewhere near the cable station perhaps. Even in Bond's room, muffled by the double windows, it was terrifying enough. Outside it must have been shattering.

Bond jumped up and pulled back the curtains, not knowing what scene of panic, of running men, would meet his eyes. But the only man in sight was one of the guides, walking slowly, stolidly up the beaten snow-path from the cable station to the club. The spacious wooden veranda that stretched from the wall of the club out over the slope of the mountain was empty, but tables had been laid for breakfast and the upholstered chaises-longue for the sunbathers had already been drawn up in their meticulous, colourful rows. The sun was blazing down out of a crystal sky. Bond looked at his watch. It was eight o'clock. Work began early in this place! People died early. For that had undoubtedly been the death-scream. He turned back into his room and rang the bell.

It was one of the three men Bond had suspected of being Russians. Bond became the officer and gentleman. 'What is your name?'

'Peter, sir.'

'Piotr?' Bond longed to say. 'And how are all my old friends from SMERSH?' He didn't. He said, 'What was that scream?'

'Pliss?' The granite-grey eyes were careful.

'A man screamed just now. From over by the cable station. What was it?'

'It seems there has been an accident, sir. You wish for breakfast?' He produced a large menu from under his arm and held it out clumsily.

'What sort of an accident?'

'It seems that one of the guides has fallen.'

How could this man have known that, only minutes after the scream? 'Is he badly hurt?'

'Is possible, sir.' The eyes, surely trained in investigation, held Bond's blandly. 'You wish for breakfast?' The menu was once again nudged forward.

Bond said, with sufficient concern, 'Well, I hope the poor chap's all right.' He took the menu and ordered. 'Let me know if you hear what happened.'

'There will no doubt be an announcement if the matter is serious. Thank you, sir.' The man withdrew.

It was the scream that triggered Bond into deciding that, above all things, he must keep fit. He suddenly felt that, despite all the mystery and its demand for solution, there would come a moment when he would need all his muscle. Reluctantly he proceeded to a quarter of an hour of knee-bends and press-ups and deep-breathing chest-expansions — exercises of the skiing muscles. He guessed that he might have to get away from this place. But quick!

He took a shower and shaved. Breakfast was brought by Peter. 'Any more news about this poor guide?'

'I have heard no more, sir. It concerns the outdoor staff. I work inside the club.'

Bond decided to play it down. 'He must have slipped and broken an ankle. Poor chap! Thank you, Peter.'

'Thank you, sir.' Did the granite eyes contain a sneer?

James Bond put his breakfast on the desk and, with some difficulty, managed to prise open the double window. He removed the small bolster that lay along the sill between the panes to keep out draughts, and blew away the accumulated dust and small fly-corpses. The cold, savourless air of high altitudes rushed into the room and Bond went to the thermostat and put it up to 90 as a counter-attack. While, his head below the level of the sill, he ate a spare continental breakfast, he heard the chatter of the girls assembling outside on the terrace. The voices were high with excitement and debate. Bond could hear every word.

'I really don't think Sarah should have told on him.'

'But he came in in the dark and started mucking her about.'

'You mean actually *interfering* with her?'

'So she says. If I'd been her, I'd have done the same. And he's such a beast of a man.'

'*Was*, you mean. Which one was it, anyway?'

'One of the Yugos. Bertil.'

'Oh, I know. Yes, he was pretty horrible. He had such dreadful teeth.'

'You oughtn't to say such things of the dead.'

'How do you know he's dead? What happened to him, anyway?'

'He was one of the two you see spraying the start of the bob-run. You see them with hoses every morning. It's to get it good and icy so they'll go faster. Fritz told me he somehow slipped, lost his balance or something. And that was that. He just went off down the run like a sort of human bob-sleigh.'

'Elizabeth! How can you be so heartless about it!'

'Well, that's what happened. You asked.'

'But couldn't he save himself?'

'Don't be idiotic. It's sheet ice, a mile of it. And the bobs get up to sixty miles an hour. He hadn't got a prayer.'

'But didn't he fly off at one of the bends?'

'Fritz said he went all the way to the bottom. Crashed into the timing hut. But Fritz says he must have been dead in the first hundred yards or so.'

'Oh, here's Franz. Franz, can I have scrambled eggs and coffee? And tell them to make the scrambled eggs runny like I always have them.'

'Yes, miss. And you, miss?' The waiter took the orders and Bond heard his boots creak off across the boards.

The sententious girl was being sententious again. 'Well, all I can say is it must have been some kind of punishment for what he tried to do to Sarah. You always get paid off for doing wrong.'

'Don't be ridiculous. God would never punish you as severely as that.' The conversation followed this new hare off into a maze of infantile morality and the Scriptures.

Bond lit a cigarette and sat back, gazing thoughtfully at the sky. No, the girl was right. God wouldn't mete out such a punishment. But Blofeld would. Had there been one of those Blofeld meetings at which, before the full body of men, the crime and the verdict had been announced? Had this Bertil been taken out and dropped on to the bob-run? Or had his companion been quietly dealt the card of death, told to give the sinner the trip or the light push that was probably all that had been needed? More likely. The quality of the scream had been of sudden, fully realized terror as the man fell, scrabbled at the ice with his fingernails and boots, and then, as he gathered speed down the polished blue gully, the blinding horror of the truth. And what a death! Bond had once gone down the Cresta, from 'Top', to prove to himself that he dared. Helmeted, masked against the blast of air, padded with leather and foam rubber, that had still been sixty seconds of naked fear. Even now he could remember how his limbs had shaken when he rose stiffly from the flimsy little skeleton bob at the end of the run-out. And that had been a bare three-quarters of a mile. This man, or the flayed remains of him, had done over a mile. Had he gone down head or feet first? Had his body started tumbling? Had he tried, while consciousness remained, to brake himself over the edge of one of the early, scientifically banked bends with the unspiked toe of this boot or that . . . ? No. After the first few yards, he would already have been going too fast for any rational thought or action. God, what a death! A typical Blofeld death, a typical SPECTRE revenge for the supreme crime of disobedience. That was the way to keep discipline in the ranks! So, concluded Bond as he cleared the tray away and got down to his books, SPECTRE walks again! But down what road this time?

At ten minutes to eleven, Irma Bunt came for him. After an exchange of affabilities, Bond gathered up an armful of books and papers and followed her round the back of the club building and along a narrow, well-trodden path past a sign that said PRIVAT. EINTRITT VERBOTEN.

The rest of the building, whose outlines Bond had seen the night before, came into view. It was an undistinguished but powerfully built one-storey affair made of local granite blocks, with a flat cement roof from which, at the far end, protruded a small, professional-looking radio mast which, Bond assumed, had given the pilot his landing instructions on the previous night and which would also serve as the ears and mouth of

Blofeld. The building was on the very edge of the plateau and below the final peak of Piz Gloria, but out of avalanche danger. Beneath it the mountain sloped sharply away until it disappeared over a cliff. Far below again was the tree-line and the Bernina valley leading up to Pontresina, the glint of a railway track and the tiny caterpillar of a long goods train of the Rhätische Bahn, on its way, presumably, over the Bernina Pass into Italy.

The door to the building gave the usual pneumatic hiss, and the central corridor was more or less a duplicate of the one at the club, but here there were doors on both sides and no pictures. It was dead quiet and there was no hint of what went on behind the doors. Bond put the question.

'Laboratories,' said Irma Bunt vaguely. 'All laboratories. And of course the lecture-room. Then the Count's private quarters. He lives with his work, Sair Hilary.'

'Good show.'

They came to the end of the corridor. Irma Bunt knocked on the facing door.

'Herein!'

James Bond was tremendously excited as he stepped over the threshold and heard the door sigh shut behind him. He knew what not to expect, the original Blofeld, last year's model — about twenty stone, tall, pale, bland face with black crew-cut, black eyes with the whites showing all round, like Mussolini's, ugly thin mouth, long pointed hands and feet — but he had no idea what alterations had been contrived on the envelope that contained the man.

But Monsieur le Comte de Bleuville, who now rose from the chaise-longue on the small private veranda and came in out of the sun into the penumbra of the study, his hands outstretched in welcome, was surely not even a distant relative of the man on the files!

Bond's heart sank. This man was tallish, yes, and, all right, his hands and naked feet were long and thin. But there the resemblance ended. The Count had longish, carefully tended, almost dandified hair that was a fine silvery white. His ears, that should have been close to his head, stuck out slightly and, where they should have had heavy lobes, had none. The body that should have weighed twenty stone, now naked save for a black woollen slip, was not more than twelve stone, and there were no signs of the sagging flesh that comes from middle-aged weight-reduction. The mouth was full and friendly, with a pleasant, up-turned, but perhaps rather unwavering smile. The forehead was serrated with wrinkles above a nose that, while the files said it should be short and squat, was aquiline and, round the right nostril, eaten away, poor chap, by what looked like the badge of tertiary syphilis. The eyes? Well, there might be something there if one could see them, but they were only rather frightening dark-green pools. The Count wore, presumably against the truly dangerous sun at these altitudes, dark-green tinted contact lenses.

Bond unloaded his books on to a conveniently empty table and took the warm, dry hand.

'My dear Sir Hilary. This is indeed a pleasure.' Blofeld's voice had been said to be sombre and even. This voice was light and full of animation.

Bond said to himself, furiously, by God this has *got* to be Blofeld! He said, 'I'm so sorry I couldn't come on the 21st. There's a lot going on at the moment.'

'Ah yes. So Fräulein Bunt told me. These new African States. They must indeed present a problem. Now, shall we settle down here —' he waved towards his desk — 'or shall we go outside? You see —' he gestured at his brown body — 'I am a heliotrope, a sun-worshipper. So much so that I have had to have these lenses devised for me. Otherwise, the ultra-violet rays, at this altitude . . .' He left the phrase unfinished.

'I haven't seen that kind of lens before. After all, I can leave the books here and fetch them if we need them for reference. I have the case pretty clear in my mind. And —' Bond smiled chummily — 'it would be nice to go back to the fogs with something of a sunburn.'

Bond had equipped himself at Lillywhites with clothing he thought would be both appropriate and sensible. He had avoided the modern elasticized vorlage trousers and had chosen the more comfortable but old-fashioned type of ski-trouser in a smooth cloth. Above these he wore an aged black windcheater that he used for golf, over his usual white sea-island cotton shirt. He had wisely reinforced this outfit with long and ugly cotton and wool pants and vests. He had conspicuously brand-new ski-boots with powerful ankle-straps. He said, 'Then I'd better take off my sweater.' He did so and followed the Count out on to the veranda.

The Count lay back again in his upholstered aluminium chaise-longue. Bond drew up a light chair made of similar materials. He placed it also facing the sun, but at an angle so that he could watch the Count's face.

'And now,' said the Comte de Bleuville, 'what have you got to tell me that necessitated this personal visit?' He turned his fixed smile on Bond. The dark-green glass eyes were unfathomable. 'Not of course that the visit is not most welcome, most welcome. Now then, Sir Hilary.'

Bond had been well trained in two responses to this obvious first question. The first was for the event that the Count had lobes to his ears. The second, if he had not. He now, in measured, serious tones, launched himself into Number Two.

'My dear Count —' the form of address seemed dictated by the silvery hair, by the charm of the Count's manners — 'there are occasions in the work of the College when research and paper-work are simply not enough. We have, as you know, come to a difficult passage in our work on your case. I refer of course to the hiatus between the disappearance of the de Bleuville line around the time of the French Revolution and the emergence of the Blofeld family, or families, in the neighbourhood of Augsburg. And —' Bond paused impressively — 'in the latter context I may later have a proposal that I hope will find favour with you. But what I am coming to is this. You have already expended serious funds on our work, and it would not have been fair to suggest that the researches should go forward unless there was a substantial ray of hope in the sky. The possibility of such a ray existed, but it was of such a nature that it definitely demanded a physical confrontation.'

'Is that so? And for what purpose, may I inquire?'

James Bond recited Sable Basilisk's examples of the Habsburg lip, the royal tail and the others. He then leaned forward in his chair for emphasis. 'And such a physical peculiarity exists in connection with the de Bleuvilles. You did not know this?'

'I was not aware of it. No. What is it?'

'I have good news for you, Count.' Bond smiled his congratulations. 'All the de Bleuville effigies or portraits that we have been able to trace have been distinctive in one vital respect, in one inherited characteristic. It appears that the family had no lobes to their ears!'

The Count's hands went up to his ears and felt them. Was he acting?

'I see,' he said slowly. 'Yes, I see.' He reflected. 'And you had to see this for yourself? My word, or a photograph, would not have been sufficient?'

Bond looked embarrassed. 'I am sorry, Count. But that was the ruling of Garter King of Arms. I am only a junior free-lance research worker for one of the Pursuivants. He in turn takes his orders in these matters from above. I hope you will appreciate that the College has to be extremely strict in cases concerned with a most ancient and honourable title such as the one in question.'

The dark pools aimed themselves at Bond like the muzzles of guns. 'Now that you have seen what you came to see, you regard the title as still in question?'

This was the worst hurdle. 'What I have seen certainly allows me to recommend that the work should continue, Count. And I would say that our chances of success have greatly multiplied. I have brought out the materials for a first sketch of the Line of Descent, and that, in a matter of days, I could lay before you. But alas, as I have said, there are still many gaps, and it is most important for me to satisfy Sable Basilisk particularly about the stages of your family's migration from Augsburg to Gdynia. It would be of the greatest help if I might question you closely about your parentage in the male line. Even details about your father and grandfather would be of the greatest assistance. And then, of course, it would be of the utmost importance if you could spare a day to accompany me to Augsburg to see if the handwriting of these Blofeld families in the Archives, their Christian names and other family details, awaken any memories or connections in your mind. The rest would then remain with us at the College. I could spare no more than a week on this work. But I am at your disposal if you wish it.'

The Count got to his feet. Bond followed suit. He walked casually over to the railing and admired the view. Would this bedraggled fly be taken? Bond now desperately hoped so. During the interview he had come to one certain conclusion. There was not a single one of the peculiarities in the Count's appearance that could not have been achieved by good acting and by the most refined facial and stomach surgery applied to the original Blofeld. Only the eyes could not have been tampered with. And the eyes were obscured.

'You think that with patient work, even with the inclusion of a few question marks where the connecting links are obscure, I would achieve an Acte de Notoriété that would satisfy the Minister of Justice in Paris?'

'Most certainly,' lied Bond. 'With the authority of the College in support.'

The fixed smile widened minutely. 'That would give me much satisfaction, Sir Hilary. I *am* the Comte de Bleuville. I am certain of it in my heart, in my veins.' There was real fervour in the voice. 'But I am determined that my title shall be officially recognized. You will be most welcome to remain as my guest and I shall be constantly at your disposal to help with your researches.'

Bond said politely, but with a hint of weariness, of resignation, 'All right, Count. And thank you. I will go and make a start straight away.'

12

TWO NEAR MISSES

BOND WAS SHOWN out of the building by a man in a white coat with the conventional white gauze of the laboratory worker over the lower half of his face. Bond attempted no conversation. He was now well inside the fortress, but he would have to continue to walk on tiptoe and be damned careful where he put his feet!

He returned to his room and got out one of the giant sheets of squared paper with which he had been furnished. He sat down at his table and wrote firmly at the top centre of the paper 'Guillaume de Bleuville, 1207–1243'. Now there were five hundred years of de Bleuvilles, with their wives and children, to be copied down from his books and notes. That would fill up an impressive number of pages with impeccable fact. He could certainly spread that chore over three days, interspersed with more tricky work — gassing with Blofeld about the Blofeld end of the story. Fortunately there were some English Blofields he could throw in as make-weight. And some Bluefields and Blumfields. He could start some pretty hares running in those directions! And, in between these idiotic activities, he would ferret and ferret away at the mystery of what in hell the new Blofeld, the new SPECTRE, were up to!

One thing was certain, they had already been through his belongings. Before going for his interview, Bond had gone into the bathroom, away from that seemingly watchful hole in the ceiling, and had painfully pulled out half a dozen of his hairs. These, while he had selected the books he needed to take with him, he had dispersed inconspicuously among his other papers and in his passport. The hairs were all gone. Someone had been through all his books. He got up and went to the chest of drawers, ostensibly for a handkerchief. Yes, the careful patterns in which he had laid out his things had all been minutely disturbed. Unemotionally he went back to his work, thanking heaven he had travelled as 'clean' as a whistle! But by God he'd have to keep his cover solid! He didn't at all like the thought of that one-way trip down the bob-run!

Bond got as far as 1350 and then the noise from the veranda became too distracting. Anyway, he had done a respectable stint, almost to the bottom of the giant page. He would go out and do a little very discreet exploring. He wanted to get his bearings, or rather confirm them, and this would be a perfectly reasonable activity for a newcomer. He had left his door into the passage ajar. He went out and along to the reception lounge, where the man in the plum coat was busy entering the names of the morning's visitors in a book. Bond's greeting was politely answered. There was a ski-room and workshop to the left of the exit. Bond wandered in. One of the Balkan types was at the work-bench, screwing a new binding on to a ski. He looked up and went on with his work while Bond gazed with seeming curiosity at the ranks of skis standing along the wall. Things had changed since his day. The bindings were quite different and designed, it seemed, to keep the heel dead flat on the ski. And there were new safety releases. Many of the skis were of metal and the ski-sticks were fibre-glass lances that looked to Bond extremely dangerous in the event of a bad fall. Bond wandered over to the work-bench and feigned interest in what the man was doing. In fact he had seen something that excited him very much — an untidy pile of lengths of thin plastic strip for the boot to rest on in the binding, so that, on the shiny surface, snow would not ball under the sole. Bond leaned over the work-bench, resting on his right elbow, and commented on the precision of the man's work. The man grunted and concentrated all the more closely to avoid further conversation. Bond's left hand slid under his leaning arm, secured one of the strips and slid it up his sleeve. He made a further inane comment, which was not answered, and strolled out of the ski-room.

(When the man in the workshop heard the front door hiss shut, he turned to the pile of plastic strips and counted them carefully twice. Then he went out to the man in the plum-coloured coat and spoke to him in German. The man nodded and picked up the telephone receiver and dialled O. The workman went stolidly back to his ski-room.)

As Bond strolled along the path that led to the cable station, he transferred the plastic strip from his sleeve to his trouser pocket, feeling pleased with himself. He had at least provided himself with one tool — the traditional burglar's tool for opening the Yale-type locks that secured the doors.

Away from the club house, to which only a thin trickle of smart-looking people were making their way, he got into the usual mountain-top crowd — people swarming out of the cable-head, skiers wobbling or schussing down the easy nursery slopes on the plateau, little groups marshalled under individual teachers and guides from the valley. The terrace of the public restaurant was already crowded with the under-privileged who hadn't got the money or the connections to join the club. He walked below it on the well-trampled snow and stood amongst the skiers at the top of the first plunging schuss of the Gloria run. A large notice-board, crowned with the G and the coronet, announced GLORIA ABFAHRT! Then below, ROT — FREIE FAHRT. GELB — FREIE FAHRT. SCHWARZ — GESPERRT, meaning that the red and yellow runs were open but the black closed, presumably because of avalanche danger. Below this again was a painted metal map of the three runs. Bond had a good look at it, reflecting that it might be wise to commit to memory the red, which was presumably the easiest and most popular. There were red, yellow and black marker flags on the map, and Bond could see the actual flags fluttering way down the mountain until the runs, studded with tiny moving figures, disappeared to the left, round the shoulder of the mountain and under the cable railway. The red seemed to continue to zigzag under the cable and between the few high pylons until it met the tree-line. Then there was a short stretch of wood-running until the final easy schuss across the undulating lower meadows to the bottom cable-head, beyond which lay the main railway line and then the Pontresina–Samaden road. Bond tried to get it all fixed in his mind. Then he watched some of the starts. These varied between the arrow-like dive of the Kannonen, the stars, who took the terrific schuss dead straight in a low crouch with their sticks jauntily tucked under their armpits, the average amateur who braked perhaps three or four times on his way down, and the terrified novice who, with stuck-out behind, stemmed his way down, his skis angled and edged like a snow-plough, with occasional straight runs diagonally across the polished slope — dashing little sprints that usually ended in a mild crash as he ran off the flattened surface into the thick powder snow that edged the wide, beaten piste.

The scene was the same as a thousand others Bond had witnessed when, as a teenager, he learned his skiing in the old Hannes Schneider School at St Anton in the Arlberg. He had got pretty good and had won his golden K, but the style in those days was rudimentary compared with what he was now witnessing from the occasional expert who zoomed down and away from beside him. Today the metal skis seemed to run faster and truer than the old steel-edged hickory. There was less shoulder-work and the art of Wedeln, a gentle waggling of the hips, was a revelation. Would it be as effective in deep new snow as it was on the well-beaten piste? Bond was doubtful, but he was envious of it. It was so much more graceful than the old Arlberg crouch. Bond wondered how he would fare on this terrific run. He would certainly not dare to take the first schuss straight. He would brake at least twice, perhaps there and there. And his legs would be trembling before he had been going for five minutes. His knees and ankles and wrists would be giving out. He *must* get on with his exercises!

Bond, excited, left the scene and followed arrows that pointed to the GLORIA EXPRESS BOB-RUN. It lay on the other side of the cable station. There was a small wooden hut, the starter's hut, with telephone-wires connected to the station, and, beneath the cable station, a little 'garage' that housed the bob-sleighs and one-man skeleton-bobs. A chain, with a notice on it saying ABFAHRTEN TÄGLICH 0900–1100, was stretched across the wide mouth of the gulch of blue ice that curved away to the left and then disappeared over the shoulder. Here again was a metal map showing the zigzag course of the run down into the valley. In deference to the English traditions at the sport, outstanding curves and hazards were marked with names such as 'Dead Man's Leap', 'Whizz-Bang Straight', 'Battling S', 'Hell's Delight', 'The Boneshaker', and the finishing straight down 'Paradise Alley'. Bond visualized the scene that morning, heard again that heart-rending scream. Yes, that death certainly had the old Blofeld touch!

'Sair Hilary! Sair Hilary!'

Startled out of his thoughts, Bond turned. Fräulein Irma Bunt, her short arms akimbo, was standing on the path to the club.

'Lunch-time! Lunch!'

'Coming,' Bond called back, and strolled up the slope towards her. He noted that, even in that hundred yards, his breathing was shallow and his limbs were heavy. This blasted height! He really must get into training!

He came up with her. She looked surly. He said that he was sorry, he had not noticed the time. She said nothing. The yellow eyes surveyed him with active dislike before she turned her back and led the way along the path.

Bond looked back over the morning. What had he done? Had he made a mistake? Well, he just might have. Better re-insure! As they came through the entrance into the reception lounge, Bond said casually, 'Oh, by the way, Fräulein Bunt, I was in the ski-room just now.'

She halted. Bond noticed that the head of the receptionist bent a fraction lower over his visitors' book.

'Yes?'

Bond took the length of plastic out of his pocket. 'I found just what I wanted.' He stitched a smile of innocent pleasure on his face. 'Like an idiot I forgot to bring a ruler with me. And there were these things on the work-bench. Just right. So I borrowed one. I hope that was all right. Of course I'll leave it behind when I go. But for these family trees, you know — ' Bond sketched a series of descending straight lines in the air — 'one has to get them on the right levels. I hope you don't mind.' He smiled charmingly. 'I was going to confess the next time I saw you.'

Irma Bunt veiled her eyes. 'It is of no consequence. In future, anything you need you will perhaps ring for, isn't it? The Count wishes you to have every facility. Now —' she gestured — 'if you will perhaps go out on the terrace. You will be shown to our table. I will be with you in a moment.'

Bond went through the restaurant door. Several of the interior tables were occupied by those who had had enough sun. He went across the room and out through the now open french windows. The man Fritz, who appeared to be the maître d'hôtel, came towards him through the crowded tables. His eyes too were cold with hostility. He held up a menu. 'Please to follow me.'

Bond followed him to the table up against the railing. Ruby and Violet were already there. Bond felt almost light-hearted with relief at having clean hands again. By God, he must pay attention, take care! This time he had got away with it. And he still had the strip of plastic! Had he sounded innocent enough, stupid enough? He sat down and ordered a double medium dry vodka Martini, on the rocks, with lemon peel, and edged his foot up against Ruby's.

She didn't withdraw hers. She smiled. Violet smiled. They all started talking at once. It was suddenly a beautiful day.

Fräulein Bunt appeared and took her place. She was gracious again. 'I am so pleased to hear that you will be staying with us for a whole week, Sair Hilary. You enjoyed your interview with the Count? Is he not an interesting man?'

'Very interesting. Unfortunately our talk was too short and we discussed only my own subject. I was longing to ask him about his research work. I hope he didn't think me very rude.'

Irma Bunt's face closed perceptibly. 'I am sure not. The Count does not often like to discuss his work. In these specialized scientific fields, you understand, there is much jealousy and, I am sorry to say, much intellectual thieving.' The box-like smile. 'I do not of course refer to yourself, my dear Sair Hilary, but to scientists less scrupulous than the Count, to spies from the chemical companies. That is why we keep ourselves very much to ourselves in our little Eagle's Nest up here. We have total privacy. Even the police in the valley are most co-operative in safeguarding us from intruders. They appreciate what the Count is doing.'

'The study of allergies?'

'Just so.' The maître d'hôtel was standing by her side. His feet came together with a perceptible click. Menus were handed round and Bond's drink came. He took a long pull at it and ordered Oeufs Gloria and a green salad. Chicken again for Ruby, cold cuts 'with stacks of potatoes' for Violet. Irma Bunt ordered her usual cottage cheese and salad.

'Don't you girls eat anything but chicken and potatoes? Is this something to do with your allergies?'

Ruby began, 'Well, yes, in a way. Somehow I've come to simply love . . .'

Irma Bunt broke in sharply. 'Now then, Ruby. No discussion of treatments, you remember? Not even with our good friend Sair Hilary.' She waved a hand towards the crowded tables around them. 'A most interesting crowd, do you not find, Sair Hilary? Everybody who is anybody. We have quite taken the international set away from Gstaad and St Moritz. That is your Duke of Marlborough over there with such a gay party of young things. And near by that is Mr Whitney and Lady Daphne Straight. Is she not chic? They are both wonderful skiers. And that beautiful girl with the long fair hair at the big table, that is Ursula Andress, the film star. What a wonderful tan she has! And Sir George Dunbar, he always has the most enchanting companions.' The box-like smile. 'Why, we only need the Aga Khan and perhaps your Duke of Kent and we would have everybody, but everybody. Is it not sensational for the first season?'

Bond said it was. The lunch came. Bond's eggs were delicious — chopped hard-boiled eggs, with a cream and cheese sauce laced with English mustard (English mustard seemed to be the clue to the Gloria specialities) gratinés in a copper dish. Bond commented on the excellence of the cooking.

'Thank you,' said Irma Bunt. 'We have three expert Frenchmen in the kitchen. Men are very good at cooking, is it not?'

Bond felt rather than saw a man approaching their table. He came up to Bond. He was a military-looking man, of about Bond's age, and he had a puzzled expression on his face. He bowed slightly to the ladies and said to Bond, 'Excuse me, but I saw your name in the visitors' book. It is Hilary Bray, isn't it?'

Bond's heart sank. This situation had always been a possibility and he had prepared a fumbling counter to it. But this was the worst possible moment with that damned woman watching and listening!

Bond said, 'Yes, it is,' with heartiness.

'*Sir* Hilary Bray?' The pleasant face was even more puzzled.

Bond got to his feet and stood with his back to his table, to Irma Bunt. 'That's right.' He took out his handkerchief and blew his nose to obscure the next question, which might be fatal.

'In the Lovat Scouts during the war?'

'Ah,' said Bond. He looked worried, lowered his voice appropriately. 'You're thinking of my first cousin. From Ben Trilleachan. Died six months ago, poor chap. I inherited the title.'

'Oh, lord!' The man's puzzlement cleared. Grief took its place. 'Sorry to hear that. Great pal of mine in the war. Funny! I didn't see anything about it in *The Times*. Always read the "Births, Marriages and Deaths". What was it?'

Bond felt the sweat running down under his arms. 'Fell off one of those bloody mountains of his. Broke his neck.'

'My God! Poor chap! But he was always fooling around the tops by himself. I must write to Jenny at once.' He held out his hand. 'Well, sorry to have butted in. Thought this was a funny place to find old Hilary. Well, so long, and sorry again.' He moved off between the tables. Out of the corner of his eye, Bond saw him rejoin a very English-looking table of men and, obviously, wives to whom he began talking animatedly.

Bond sat down, reached for his drink and drained it and went back to his eggs. The woman's eyes were on him. He felt the sweat running down his face. He took out his handkerchief and mopped at it. 'Gosh, it's hot out here in the sun! That was some pal of my first cousin's. My cousin had the same name. Collateral branch. Died not long ago, poor chap.' He frowned sadly. 'Didn't know this man from Adam. Nice-looking fellow.' Bond looked bravely across the table. 'Do you know any of his party, Fräulein Bunt?'

Without looking at the party, Fräulein Bunt said shortly, 'No, I do not know everyone who comes here.' The yellow eyes were still inquisitive, holding his. 'But it was a curious coincidence. Were you very alike, you and your cousin?'

'Oh, absolutely,' said Bond, gushing. 'Spit image. Often used to get taken for each other.' He looked across at the English group. Thank God they were picking up their things and going. They didn't look particularly smart or prosperous. Probably staying at Pontresina or under the ex-officers' scheme at St Moritz. Typical English skiing party. With any luck they were just doing the big runs in the neighbourhood one by one. Bond reviewed the way the conversation had gone while coffee came and he made cheerful small talk with Ruby, whose foot was again clamped against his, about her skiing progress that morning.

Well, he decided, the woman couldn't have heard much of it

with all the clatter and chatter from the surrounding tables. But it had been a narrow squeak, a damned narrow squeak. The second of the day!

So much for walking on tiptoe inside the enemy lines!

Not good enough! Definitely not good enough!

13
PRINCESS RUBY?

MY DEAR SABLE BASILISK,

I arrived safely — by helicopter, if you please! — at this beautiful place called Piz Gloria, 10,000 feet up somewhere in the Engadine. Most comfortable with an excellent male staff of several nationalities and a most efficient secretary to the Count named Fräulein Irma Bunt who tells me that she comes from Munich.

I had a most profitable interview with the Count this morning as a result of which he wishes me to stay on for a week to complete the first draft of his genealogical tree. I do hope you can spare me for so long. I warned the Count that we had much work to do on the new Commonwealth States. He himself, though busily engaged on what sounds like very public-spirited research work on allergies and their cause (he has ten English girls here as his patients), has agreed to see me daily in the hope that together we may be able to bridge the gap between the migration of the de Bleuvilles from France and their subsequent transference, as Blofelds, from Augsburg to Gdynia. I have suggested to him that we conclude the work with a quick visit to Augsburg for the purposes you and I discussed, but he has not yet given me his decision.

Please tell my cousin Jenny Bray that she may be hearing from a friend of her late husband who apparently served with him in the Lovat Scouts. He came up to me at lunch today and took me for the other Hilary! Quite a coincidence!

Working conditions are excellent. We have complete privacy here, secure from the madding world of skiers, and very sensibly the girls are confined to their rooms after ten at night to put them out of the temptation of roaming and gossiping. They seem a very nice lot, from all over the United Kingdom, but rather on the dumb side!

Now for my most interesting item. The Count has *not* got lobes to his ears! Isn't that good news! He also is of a most distinguished appearance and bearing with a fine head of silvery hair and a charming smile. His slim figure also indicates noble extraction. Unfortunately he has to wear dark-green contact lenses because of weak eyes and the strength of the sunshine at this height, and his aquiline nose is blemished by a deformed nostril which I would have thought could easily have been put right by facial surgery. He speaks impeccable English with a gay lilt to his voice and I am sure that we will get on very well.

Now to get down to business. It would be most helpful if you would get in touch with the old printers of the Almanach de Gotha and see if they can help us over our gaps in the lineage. They may have some traces. Cable anything helpful. With the new evidence of the ear-lobes I am quite confident that the connection exists.

That's all for now.

Yours ever,
HILARY BRAY

P.S. Don't tell my mother, or she will be worried for my safety among the eternal snows! But we had a nasty accident here this morning. One of the staff, a Yugoslav it seems, slipped on the bob-run and went the whole way to the bottom! Terrible business. He's apparently being buried in Pontresina tomorrow. Do you think we ought to send some kind of a wreath? H.B.

Bond read the letter several times. Yes, that would give the officers in charge of Operation Corona plenty to bite on. Particularly the hint that they should get the dead man's name from the registrar in Pontresina. And he had covered up a bit on the Bray mix-up when the letter, as Bond was sure it would be, was steamed open and photostated before dispatch. They might of course just destroy it. To prevent this, the bit of bogosity about the Almanach de Gotha would be a clincher. This source of heraldic knowledge hadn't been mentioned before. It would surely excite the interest of Blofeld.

Bond rang the bell, handed out the letter for dispatch, and got back to his work, which consisted initially of going into the bathroom with the strip of plastic and his scissors in his pocket and snipping two inch-wide strips off the end. These would be enough for the purposes he and, he hoped, Ruby would put them to. Then, using the first joint of his thumb as a rough guide, he marked off the remaining eighteen inches into inch measures, to support his lie about the ruler, and went back to his desk and to the next hundred years of the de Bleuvilles.

At about five o'clock the light got so bad that Bond got up from his table and stretched, preparatory to going over to the light-switch near the door. He took a last look out of the window before he closed it. The veranda was completely deserted and the foam rubber cushions for the reclining-chairs had already been taken in. From the direction of the cable-head there still came the whine of machinery that had been part of the background noises to the day. Yesterday the railway had closed at about five, and it must be time for the last pair of gondolas to complete their two-way journey and settle in their respective stations for the night. Bond closed the double windows, walked across to the thermostat and put it down to seventy. He was just about to reach for the light-switch when there came a very soft tapping at the door.

Bond kept his voice low. 'Come in!'

The door opened and quickly closed to within an inch of the lock. It was Ruby. She put her fingers to her lips and gestured towards the bathroom. Bond, highly intrigued, followed her in and shut the door. Then he turned on the light. She was blushing. She whispered imploringly, 'Oh, please forgive me, Sir Hilary. But I did so want to talk to you for a second.'

'That's fine, Ruby. But why the bathroom?'

'Oh, didn't you know? No, I suppose you wouldn't. It's supposed to be a secret, but of course I can tell you. You won't let on, will you?'

'No, of course not.'

'Well, all the rooms have microphones in them. I don't know where. But sometimes we girls have got together in each other's rooms, just for a gossip, you know, and Miss Bunt has always known. We think they've got some sort of television too.' She giggled. 'We always undress in the bathroom. It's just a sort of feeling. As if one was being watched the whole time. I suppose it's something to do with the treatment.'

'Yes, I expect so.'

'The point is, Sir Hilary, I was tremendously excited by what you were saying at lunch today, about Miss Bunt perhaps being a duchess. I mean, is that really possible?'

'Oh yes,' said Bond airily.

'I was so disappointed at not being able to tell you my surname. You see, you see —' her eyes were wide with excitement — 'it's Windsor!'

'Gosh,' said Bond, 'that's interesting!'

'I knew you'd say that. You see, there's always been talk in my family that we're distantly connected with the Royal Family!'

'I can quite understand that.' Bond's voice was thoughtful, judicious. 'I'd like to be able to do some work on that. What were your parents' names? I must have them first.'

'George Albert Windsor and Mary Potts. Does that mean anything?'

'Well, of course, the Albert's significant.' Bond felt a cur. 'You see, there was the Prince Consort to Queen Victoria. He was Albert.'

'Oh golly!' Ruby's knuckles went up to her mouth.

'But of course all this needs a lot of working on. Where do you come from in England? Where were you born?'

'In Lancashire. Morecambe Bay, where the shrimps come from. But a lot of poultry too. You know.'

'So that's why you love chicken so much.'

'Oh, no.' She seemed surprised by the remark. 'That's just the point. You see, I was allergic to chickens. I simply couldn't bear them — all those feathers, the stupid pecking, the mess and the smell. I loathed them. Even eating chicken brought me out in a sort of rash. It was awful, and of course my parents were mad at me, they being poultry farmers in quite a big way and me being supposed to help clean out the batteries — you know, those modern mass-produced chicken places. And then one day I saw this advertisement in the paper, in the *Poultry Farmer's Gazette*. It said that anyone suffering from chicken allergy — then followed a long Latin name — could apply for a course of re . . . of re . . . for a cure in a Swiss institute doing research work on the thing. All found and ten pounds a week pocket-money. Rather like those people who go and act as rabbits in that place that's trying to find a cure for colds.'

'I know,' said Bond encouragingly.

'So I applied and my fare was paid down to London and I met Miss Bunt and she put me through some sort of exam.' She giggled. 'Heaven only knows how I passed it, as I failed my G.C.E. twice. But she said I was just what the Institute wanted and I came out here about two months ago. It's not bad. They're terribly strict. But the Count has absolutely cured my trouble. I simply love chickens now.' Her eyes became suddenly rapt. 'I think they're just the most beautiful, wonderful birds in the world.'

'Well, that's a jolly good show,' said Bond, totally mystified. 'Now about your name. I'll get to work on it right away. But how are we going to talk? You all seem to be pretty carefully organized. How can I see you by yourself? The only place is my room or yours.'

'You mean *at night*?' The big blue eyes were wide with fright, excitement, maidenly appraisal.

'Yes, it's the only way.' Bond took a bold step towards her and kissed her full on the mouth. He put his arms round her clumsily. 'And you know I think you're terribly attractive.'

'Oh, Sir Hilary!'

But she didn't recoil. She just stood there like a great lovely doll, passive, slightly calculating, wanting to be a princess. 'But how would you get out of here? They're terribly strict. A guard goes up and down the passage every so often. Of course —' the eyes were calculating — 'it's true that I'm next door to you, in Number Three actually. If only we had some way of getting out.'

Bond took one of the inch strips of plastic out of his pocket and showed it to her. 'I knew you were somewhere close to me. Instinct, I suppose. [Cad!] I learned a thing or two in the Army. You can get out of these sort of doors by slipping this in the door crack in front of the lock and pushing. It slips the latch. Here, take this, I've got another. But hide it away. And promise not to tell anyone.'

'Ooh! You are a one! But of course I promise. But do you think there's any hope — about the Windsors, I mean?' Now she put her arms round his neck, round the witch-doctor's neck, and the big blue orbs gazed appealingly into his.

'You definitely mustn't rely on it,' said Bond firmly, trying to get back an ounce of his self-respect. 'But I'll have a quick look now in my books. Not much time before drinks. Anyway, we'll see.' He gave her another long and, he admitted to himself, extremely splendid kiss, to which she responded with an animalism that slightly salved his conscience. 'Now then, baby.' His right hand ran down her back to the curve of her behind, to which he gave an encouraging and hastening pat. 'We've got to get you out of here.'

His bedroom was dark. They listened at the door like two children playing hide-and-seek. The building was in silence. He inched open the door. He gave the behind an extra pat and she was gone.

Bond paused for a moment. Then he switched on the light. The innocent room smiled at him. Bond went to his table and reached for the *Dictionary of British Surnames*. Windsor, Windsor, Windsor. Here we are! Now then! As he bent over the small print, an important reflection seared his spy's mind like a shooting star. All right. So sexual perversions, and sex itself, were a main security risk. So was greed for money. But what about status? What about that most insidious of vices, snobbery?

Six o'clock came. Bond had a nagging headache, brought on by hours of poring over small-print reference books and aggravated by the lack of oxygen at the high altitude. He needed a drink, three drinks. He had a quick shower and smartened himself up, rang his bell for the 'warder' and went along to the bar. Only a few of the girls were already there. Violet sat alone at the bar and Bond joined her. She seemed pleased to see him. She was drinking a Daiquiri. Bond ordered another and, for himself, a double Bourbon on the rocks. He took a deep pull at it and put the squat glass down. 'By God, I needed that! I've been working like a slave all day while you've been waltzing about the ski-slopes in the sun!'

'Have I indeed!' A slight Irish brogue came out with the indignation. 'Two lectures this morning, frightfully boring, and I had to catch up with my reading most of this afternoon. I'm way behind with it.'

'What sort of reading?'

'Oh, sort of agricultural stuff.' The dark eyes watched him carefully. 'We're not supposed to talk about our cures, you know.'

'Oh, well,' said Bond cheerfully, 'then let's talk about something else. Where do you come from?'

'Ireland. The South. Near Shannon.'

Bond had a shot in the dark. 'All that potato country.'

'Yes, that's right. I used to hate them. Nothing but potatoes to eat and potato crops to talk about. Now I'm longing to get back. Funny, isn't it?'

'Your family'll be pleased.'

'You can say that again! And my boy friend! He's on the wholesale side. I said I wouldn't marry anyone who had anything to do with the damned, dirty, ugly things. He's going to get a shock all right . . .'

'How's that?'

'All I've learned about how to improve the crop. The latest scientific ways, chemicals and so on.' She put her hand up to her mouth. She glanced swiftly round the room, at the bartender. To see if anyone had heard this innocent stuff? She put on a hostess smile. 'Now you tell me what you've been working on, Sir Hilary.'

'Oh, just some heraldic stuff for the Count. Like I was talking about at lunch. I'm afraid you'd find it frightfully dry stuff.'

'Oh no, I wouldn't. I was terribly interested in what you were saying to Miss Bunt. You see —' she lowered her voice and spoke into her raised glass — 'I'm an O'Neill. They used to be almost kings of Ireland. Do you think . . .' She had seen something over his shoulder. She went on smoothly, 'And I simply can't get my shoulders round enough. And when I try to I simply overbalance.'

''Fraid I don't know anything about skiing,' said Bond loudly.

Irma Bunt appeared in the mirror over the bar. 'Ah, Sair Hilary.' She inspected his face. 'But yes, you are already getting a little of the sunburn, isn't it? Come! Let us go and sit down. I see poor Miss Ruby over there all by herself.'

They followed her meekly. Bond was amused by the little undercurrent of rule-breaking that went on among the girls — the typical resistance pattern to strict discipline and the governessy ways of this hideous matron. He must be careful how he handled it, useful though it was proving. It wouldn't do to get these girls too much 'on his side'. But, if only because the Count didn't want him to know them, he must somehow ferret away at their surnames and addresses. Ferret! That was the word! Ruby would be his ferret. Bond sat down beside her, the back of his hand casually brushing against her shoulder.

More drinks were ordered. The Bourbon was beginning to uncoil Bond's tensions. His headache, instead of occupying his whole head, had localized itself behind the right temple. He said, gaily, 'Shall we play the game again?'

There was a chorus of approval. The glass and paper napkins were brought from the bar and now more of the girls joined in. Bond handed round cigarettes and the girls puffed vigorously, occasionally choking over the smoke. Even Irma Bunt seemed infected by the laughter and squeals of excitement as the cobweb of paper became more and more tenuous. 'Careful! Gently, Elizabeth! Ayee! But now you have done it! And there was still this little corner that was safe!'

Bond was next to her. Now he sat back and suggested that the girls should have a game among themselves. He turned to Fräulein Bunt. 'By the way, if I can find the time, it crossed my mind that it might be fun to go down in the cable car and pay a visit to the valley. I gathered from talk among the crowds today that St Moritz is the other side of the valley. I've never been there. I'd love to see it.'

'Alas, my dear Sair Hilary, but that is against the rules of the house. Guests here, and the staff too, have no access to the Seilbahn. That is only for the tourists. Here we keep ourselves to ourselves. We are — how shall I say? — a little dedicated community. We observe the rules almost of a monastery. It is better so, isn't it? Thus we can pursue our researches in peace.'

'Oh, I quite see that.' Bond's smile was understanding, friendly. 'But I hardly count myself as a patient here, really. Couldn't an exception be made in my case?'

'I think that would be a mistake, Sair Hilary. And surely you will need all the time you have to complete your duties for the Count. No —' it was an order — 'I am afraid, with many apologies, that what you ask is out of the question.' She glanced at her watch and clapped her hands. 'And now, girls,' she called, 'it is time for the supper. Come along! Come along!'

It had only been a try-on, to see what form the negative answer would take. But, as Bond followed her into the dining-room, it was quite an effort to restrain his right shoe from giving Irma Bunt a really tremendous kick in her tight, bulging behind.

14

SWEET DREAMS — SWEET NIGHTMARE!

IT WAS ELEVEN o'clock and the place was as quiet as the grave. Bond, with due respect for the eye in the ceiling, went through the motions of going to the bathroom and then climbing into bed and switching off his light. He gave it ten minutes, then got quietly out of bed and pulled on his trousers and shirt. Working by touch, he slipped the end of the inch of plastic into the door crack, found the lock and pressed gently. The edge of the plastic caught the curve of the lock and slid it back. Bond now only had to push gently and the door was open. He listened, his ears pricked like an animal's. Then he carefully put his head out. The empty corridor yawned at him. Bond slipped out of the door, closed it softly, took the few steps along to Number Three and gently turned the handle. It was dark inside but there was a stirring in the bed. Now to avoid the click of the shutting door! Bond took his bit of plastic and got it against the lock, holding it in the mortice. Then he inched the door shut, at the same time gently withdrawing the plastic. The lock slid noiselessly into place.

There came a whisper from the bed. 'Is that you?'

'Yes, darling.' Bond slid out of his clothes and, assuming the same geography as in his own room, walked gingerly over to the bed and sat down on its edge.

A hand came out of the darkness and touched him. 'Ooh, you've got nothing on!'

Bond caught the hand and reached along it. 'Nor have you,' he whispered. 'That's how it should be.'

Gingerly he lay down on the bed and put his head beside hers on the pillow. He noticed with a pang of pleasure that she had left room for him. He kissed her, at first softly and then with fierceness. Her body stirred. Her mouth yielded to his and when his left hand began its exploration she put her arms round him.

'I'm catching cold.' Bond followed the lie by pulling the single sheet away from under him and then covering them both with it. The warmth and softness of her splendid body were now all his. Bond lay against her. He drew the fingernails of his left hand softly down her flat stomach. The velvety skin fluttered. She gave a small groan and reached down for his hand and held it. 'You do love me a little bit?'

That awful question! Bond whispered, 'I think you're the most adorable, beautiful girl. I wish I'd met you before.'

The stale, insincere words seemed to be enough. She removed her restraining hand.

Her hair smelt of new-mown summer grass, her mouth of Pepsodent and her body of Mennen's Baby Powder. A small night wind rose up outside and moaned round the building, giving an extra sweetness, an extra warmth, even a certain friendship to what was no more than an act of physical passion. There was real pleasure in what they did to each other, and in the end, when it was over and they lay quietly in each other's arms, Bond knew, and knew that the girl knew, that they had done nothing wrong, done no harm to each other.

After a while Bond whispered into her hair, 'Ruby!'

'Mmmm.'

'About your name. About the Windsors. I'm afraid there's not much hope.'

'Oh, well, I never really believed. You know these old family stories.'

'Anyway, I haven't got enough books here. When I get back I'll dig into it properly. Promise. It'll be a question of starting with your family and going back — church and town records and so forth. I'll have it done properly and send it to you. Great slab of parchment with a lot of snazzy print. Heavy black italics with coloured letters to start each line. Although it mayn't get you anywhere, it might be nice to have.'

'You mean like old documents in museums?'

'That's right.'

'That'd be nice.'

There was silence in the little room. Her breathing became regular. Bond thought: how extraordinary! Here on top of this mountain, a death's run away from the nearest hamlet in the valley, in this little room were peace, silence, warmth, happiness

— many of the ingredients of love. It was like making love in a balloon. Which nineteenth-century rake had it been who had recorded a bet in a London club that he would make love to a woman in a balloon?

Bond was on the edge of sleep. He let himself slide down the soft, easy slope. Here it was wonderful. It would be just as easy for him to get back to his room in the early hours. He softly eased his right arm from under the sleeping girl, took a lazy glance at his left wrist. The big luminous numerals said midnight.

Bond had hardly turned over on his right side, up against the soft flanks of the sleeping girl, when, from underneath the pillow, under the floor, deep in the bowels of the building, there came the peremptory ringing of a deep-toned, melodious electric bell. The girl stirred. She said sleepily, 'Oh, damn!'

'What is it?'

'Oh, it's only the treatment. I suppose it's midnight?'

'Yes.'

'Don't pay any attention. It's only for me. Just go to sleep.'

Bond kissed her between the shoulder-blades but said nothing.

Now the bell had stopped. In its place there started up a droning whine, rather like the noise of a very fast electric fan, with, behind it, the steady, unvarying tick-pause-tock, tick-pause-tock of some kind of metronome. The combination of the two sounds was wonderfully soothing. It compelled attention, but only just on the fringe of consciousness — like the night-noises of childhood, the slow tick of the nursery clock combined with the sound of the sea or the wind outside. And now a voice, the Count's voice, came over the distant wire or tape that Bond assumed was the mechanical source of all this. The voice was pitched in a low, singsong murmur, caressing yet authoritative, and every word was distinct. 'You are going to sleep.' The voice fell on the word 'sleep'. 'You are tired and your limbs feel like lead.' Again the falling cadence on the last word. 'Your arms feel as heavy as lead. Your breathing is quite even. Your breathing is as regular as a child's. Your eyes are closed and the eyelids are heavy as lead. You are becoming tireder and tireder. Your whole body is becoming tired and heavy as lead. You are warm and comfortable. You are slipping, slipping, slipping down into sleep. Your bed is as soft and downy as a nest. You are as soft and sleepy as a chicken in a nest. A dear little chicken, fluffy and cuddly.' There came the sound of a sweet cooing and clucking, the gentle brushing together of wings, the dozy murmuring of mother hens with their chicks. It went on for perhaps a full minute. Then the voice came back. 'The little darlings are going to sleep. They are like you, comfortable and sleepy in their nests. You love them dearly, dearly, dearly. You love all chickens. You would like to make pets of them all. You would like them to grow up beautiful and strong. You would like no harm to come to them. Soon you will be going back to your darling chickens. Soon you will be able to look after them again. Soon you will be able to help all the chickens of England. You will be able to improve the breed of chickens all over England. This will make you very, very happy. You will be doing so much good that it will make you very, very happy. But you will keep quiet about it. You will say nothing of your methods. They will be your own secret, your very own secret. People will try and find out your secret. But you will say nothing because they might try and take your secret away from you. And then you would not be able to make your darling chickens happy and healthy and strong. Thousands, millions of chickens made happier because of you. So you will say nothing and keep your secret. You will say nothing, nothing at all. You will remember what I say. You will remember what I say.' The murmuring voice was getting farther and farther away. The sweet cooing and clucking of chickens softly obscured the vanishing voice, then that too died away and there was only the electric whine and the tick-pause-tock of the metronome.

Ruby was deeply asleep. Bond reached out for her wrist and felt the pulse. It was plumb on beat with the metronome. And now that, and the whine of the machine, receded softly until all was dead silence again save for the soft moan of the night wind outside.

Bond let out a deep sigh. So now he had heard it all! He suddenly wanted to get back to his room and think. He slipped out from under the sheet, got to his clothes and put them on. He manipulated the lock without trouble. There was no movement, no sound, in the passage. He slipped back into Number Two and eased the door shut. Then he went into his bathroom, closed the door, switched on the light and sat down on the lavatory and put his head in his hands.

Deep hypnosis! That was what he had heard. The Hidden Persuader! The repetitive, singsong message injected into the brain while it was on the twilight edge of consciousness. Now, in Ruby's subconscious, the message would work on all by itself through the night, leaving her, after weeks of repetition, with an in-built mechanism of obedience to the voice that would be as deep, as compelling, as hunger.

But what in hell was the message all about? Surely it was a most harmless, even a praiseworthy message to instil in the simple mind of this country girl. She had been cured of her allergy and she would return home fully capable of helping with the family poultry business — more than that, enthusiastic, dedicated. Had the leopard changed his spots? Had the old lag become, in the corny, hackneyed tradition, a do-gooder? Bond simply couldn't believe it. What about all those high-powered security arrangements? What about the multi-racial staff that positively stank of SPECTRE? And what about the bob-run murder? Accident? So soon after the man's attempted rape of this Sarah girl? An impossible coincidence! Malignity must somewhere lie behind the benign, clinical front of this maddeningly innocent research outfit! But where? How in hell could he find out?

Bond, exhausted, got up and turned off the light in the bathroom and quietly got himself into bed. The mind whirred on for a sterile half-hour in the overheated brain and then, mercifully, he went to sleep.

When, at nine o'clock, he awoke and threw open his windows, the sky was overcast with the heavy blank grey that meant snow. Over by the Berghaus, the Schneefinken and Schneevögel, the snow-finches and Alpine choughs, that lived on the crumbs and left-overs of the picnickers, were fluttering and swooping close round the building — a sure storm-warning. The wind had got up and was blowing in sharp, threatening gusts, and no whine of machinery came from the cable railway. The light aluminium gondolas would have too bad a time in winds of this strength, particularly over the last great swoop of cable that brought them a good quarter of a mile over the exposed shoulder beneath the plateau.

Bond shut the windows and rang for his breakfast. When it came there was a note from Fräulein Bunt on the tray. 'The Count will be pleased to receive you at eleven o'clock. I.B.'

Bond ate his breakfast and got down to his third page of de Bleuvilles. He had quite a chunk of work to show up, but this was easy stuff. The prospect of successfully bamboozling his way along the Blofeld part of the trail was not so encouraging. He would start boldly at the Gdynia end and work back — get the old rascal to talk about his youth and his parents. Old rascal? Well, dammit, whatever he had become since Operation Thunderball, there weren't two Ernst Stavro Blofelds in the world!

They met in the Count's study. 'Good morning, Sir Hilary. I hope you slept well? We are going to have snow.' The Count waved towards the window. 'It will be a good day for work. No distractions.'

Bond smiled a man-to-man smile. 'I certainly find those girls pretty distracting. But most charming. What's the matter with them, by the way? They all look healthy enough.'

The Count was off-hand. 'They suffer from allergies, Sir Hilary. Crippling allergies. In thc agricultural field. They are country girls and their disabilities affect the possibility of their employment. I have devised a cure for such symptoms. I am glad to say that the signs are propitious. We are making much progress together.' The telephone by his side buzzed. 'Excuse me.' The Count picked up the receiver and listened. 'Ja. Machen Sie die Verbindung.' He paused. Bond politely studied the papers he had brought along. 'Zdies de Bleuville . . . Da . . . Da . . . Kharascho!' He put the receiver back. 'Forgive me. That was one of my research workers. He has been purchasing some materials for the laboratories. The cable railway is closed, but they are making a special trip up for him. Brave man. He will probably be very sick, poor fellow.' The green contact lenses hid any sympathy he may have felt. The fixed smile showed none. 'And now, my dear Sir Hilary, let us get on with our work.'

Bond laid out his big sheets on the desk and proudly ran his finger down through the generations. There was excitement and satisfaction in the Count's comments and questions. 'But this is tremendous, really tremendous, my dear fellow. And you say there is mention of a broken spear or a broken sword in the arms? Now when was that granted?'

Bond rattled off a lot of stuff about the Norman Conquest. The broken sword had probably been awarded as a result of some battle. More research in London would be needed to pin the occasion down. Finally Bond rolled up the sheets and got out his notebook. 'And now we must start working back from the other end, Count.' Bond became inquisitorial, authoritative. 'We have your birth date in Gdynia, May 28th, 1908. Yes?'

'Correct.'

'Your parents' names?'

'Ernst George Blofeld and Maria Stavro Michelopoulos.'

'Also born in Gdynia?'

'Yes.'

'Now your grandparents?'

'Ernst Stefan Blofeld and Elizabeth Lubomirskaya.'

'Hm, so the Ernst is something of a family Christian name?'

'It would seem so. My great-grandfather, he was also Ernst.'

'That is most important. You see, Count, among the Blofelds of Augsburg there are no less than two Ernsts!'

The Count's hands had been lying on the green blotting-pad on his desk, relaxed. Now, impulsively, they joined together and briefly writhed, showing white knuckles.

My God, you've got it bad! thought Bond.

'And that is important?'

'Very. Christian names run through families. We regard them as most significant clues. Now, can you remember any farther back? You have done well. We have covered three generations. With the dates I shall later ask you for, we have already got back to around 1850. Only another fifty years to go and we shall have arrived at Augsburg.'

'No.' It was almost a cry of pain. 'My great-great-grandfather. Of him I know nothing.' The hands writhed on the blotting-paper. 'Perhaps, perhaps. If it is a question of money. People, witnesses could be found.' The hands parted, held themselves out expansively. 'My dear Sir Hilary, you and I are men of the world. We understand each other. Extracts from archives, registry offices, the churches — these things, do they have to be completely authentic?'

Got you, you old fox! Bond said affably, with a hint of conspiracy, 'I don't quite understand what you mean, Count.'

The hands were now flat on the desk again, happy hands.

Blofeld had recognized one of his kind. 'You are a hard-working man, Sir Hilary. You live modestly in this remote region of Scotland. Life could perhaps be made easier for you. There are perhaps material benefits you desire — motor-cars, a yacht, a pension. You have only to say the word, name a figure.' The dark-green orbs bored into Bond's modestly evasive eyes, holding them. 'Just a little co-operation. A visit here and there in Poland and Germany and France. Of course your expenses would be heavy. Let us say five hundred pounds a week. The technical matters, the documents and so forth. Those I can arrange. It would only require your supporting evidence. Yes? The Ministry of Justice in Paris, for them the word of the College of Arms is the word of God. Is that not so?'

It was too good to be true! But how to play it? Diffidently, Bond said, 'What you are suggesting, Count, is — er — not without interest. Of course —' Bond's smile was sufficiently expansive, sufficiently bland — 'if the documents were convincing, so to speak solid, very solid, then it would be quite reasonable for me to authenticate them.' Bond put spaniel into his eyes, asking to be patted, to bc told that everything would be all right, that he would be completely protected. 'You see what I mean?'

The Count began, with force, sincerity, 'You need have absolutely no . . .' when there was the noise of an approaching hubbub down the passage. The door burst open. A man, propelled from behind, lurched into the room and fell, writhing, to the floor.

Two of the guards came stiffly to attention behind him. They looked first at the Count and then, sideways, towards Bond, surprised to see him there.

The Count said sharply, 'Was ist denn los?'

Bond knew the answer and, momentarily, he died. Behind the snow and the blood on the face of the man on the floor, Bond recognized the face of a man he knew.

The blond hair, the nose broken boxing for the Navy, belonged to a friend of his in the Service. It was, unmistakably, Number 2 from Station Z in Zürich!

15

THE HEAT INCREASES

YES, IT WAS Shaun Campbell all right! Christ Almighty, what a mess! Station Z had especially been told nothing about Bond's mission. Campbell must have been following a lead of his own, probably trailing this Russian who had been 'buying supplies'. Typical of the sort of balls-up that over-security can produce!

The leading guard was talking in rapid, faulty German with a Slav accent. 'He was found in the open ski compartment at the back of the gondola. Much frozen, but he put up a strong resistance. He had to be subdued. He was no doubt following Captain Boris.' The man caught himself up. 'I mean, your guest from the valley, Herr Graf. He says he is an English tourist from Zürich. That he had got no money for the fare. He wanted to pay a visit up here. He was searched. He carried five hundred Swiss francs. No identity papers.' The man shrugged. 'He says his name is Campbell.'

At the sound of his name, the man on the ground stirred. He lifted his head and looked wildly round the room. He had been badly battered about the face and head with a pistol or a cosh. His control was shot to pieces. When his eyes lit on the familiar face of Bond, he looked astonished, then, as if a lifebuoy had been thrown to him, he said hoarsely, 'Thank God, James. Tell 'em it's me! Tell 'em I'm from Universal Export. In Zürich. You know! For God's sake, James! Tell 'em I'm O.K.' His head fell forward on the carpet.

The Count's head slowly turned towards Bond. The opaque green eyes caught the pale light from the window and glinted whitely. The tight, face-lifted smile was grotesquely horrible. 'You know this man, Sir Hilary?'

Bond shook his head sorrowfully. He knew he was pronouncing the death sentence on Campbell. 'Never seen him before in my life. Poor chap. He sounds a bit daft to me. Concussed, probably. Why not ship him down to a hospital in the valley? He looks in a pretty bad way.'

'And Universal Export?' The voice was silky. 'I seem to have heard that name before.'

'Well, *I* haven't,' said Bond indifferently. 'Never heard of it.' He reached in his pocket for his cigarettes, lit one with a dead steady hand.

The Count turned back to the guards. He said softly, 'Zur Befragungszelle.' He nodded his dismissal. The two guards bent down and hauled Campbell up by his armpits. The hanging head raised itself, gave one last terrible look of appeal at Bond. Then the man who was Bond's colleague was hustled out of the room and the door was closed softly behind his dragging feet.

To the interrogation cell! That could mean only one thing, under modern methods, total confession! How long would Campbell hold out for? How many hours had Bond got left?

'I have told them to take him to the sick-room. He will be well looked after.' The Count looked from the papers on his desk to Bond. 'I am afraid this unhappy intrusion has interfered with my train of thought, Sir Hilary. So perhaps you will forgive me for this morning?'

'Of course, of course. And, regarding your proposition, that we should work a little more closely together on your interests, I can assure you, Count, that I find it most interesting.' Bond smiled conspiratorially. 'I'm sure we could come to some satisfactory arrangement.'

'Yes? That is good.' The Count linked his hands behind his head and gazed for a moment at the ceiling and then, reflectively, back at Bond. He said casually, 'I suppose you would not be connected in any way with the British Secret Service, Sir Hilary?'

Bond laughed out loud. The laugh was a reflex, forced out of him by tension. 'Good God, no! Didn't even know we had one. Didn't all that sort of thing go out with the end of the war?' Bond chuckled to himself, fatuously amused. 'Can't quite see myself running about behind a false moustache. Not my line of country at all. Can't bear moustaches.'

The Count's unwavering smile did not seem to share Bond's amusement. He said coldly, 'Then please forget my question, Sir Hilary. The intrusion by this man has made me over-suspicious.

I value my privacy up here, Sir Hilary. Scientific research can only be pursued in an atmosphere of peace.'

'I couldn't agree more.' Bond was effusive. He got to his feet and gathered up his papers from the desk. 'And now I must get on with my own research work. Just getting into the fourteenth century. I think I shall have some interesting data to show you tomorrow, Count.'

The Count got politely to his feet and Bond went out of the door and along the passage.

He loitered, listening for any sound. There was none, but half-way down the corridor one of the doors was ajar. A crack of blood-red light showed. Bond thought, I've probably had it anyway. In for a penny, in for a pound! He pushed the door open and stuck his head into the room. It was a long, low laboratory with a plastic-covered work-bench extending its whole length beneath the windows, which were shuttered. Dark-red light, as in a film-developing chamber, came from neon strips above the cornice. The bench was littered with retorts and test-tubes, and there were line upon line of test-tubes and phials containing a cloudy liquid in racks against the far wall. Three men in white, with gauze pads over the bottoms of their faces and white surgical caps over their hair, were at work, absorbed. Bond took in the scene, a scene from a theatrical hell, withdrew his head and walked on down the corridor and out into what was now a driving snow-storm. He pulled the top of his sweater over his head and forced his way along the path to the blessed warmth of the club house. Then he walked quickly to his room, closed the door, and went into the bathroom and sat down on his usual throne of reflection and wondered what in God's name to do.

Could he have saved Campbell? Well, he could have had a desperate shot at it. 'Oh, yes. I know this man. Perfectly respectable chap. We used to work for the same export firm, Universal, in London. You look in pretty bad shape, old boy. What the devil happened?' But it was just as well he hadn't tried. As cover, solid cover, Universal was 'brûlé' with the pros. It had been in use too long. All the secret services in the world had penetrated it by now. Obviously Blofeld knew all about it. Any effort to save Campbell would simply have tied Bond in with him. There had been no alternative except to throw him to the wolves. If Campbell had a chance to get his wits back before they really started on him, he would know that Bond was there for some purpose, that his disavowal by Bond was desperately important to Bond, to the Service. How long would he have the strength to cover for Bond, retrieve his recognition of Bond? At most a few hours. But how many hours? That was the vital question. That and how long the storm would last. Bond couldn't possibly get away in this stuff. If it stopped, there might be a chance, a damned slim one, but better than the alternatives, of which, if and when Campbell talked, there was only one — death, probably a screaming death.

Bond surveyed his weapons. They were only his hands and feet, his Gillette razor and his wristwatch, a heavy Rolex Oyster Perpetual on an expanding metal bracelet. Used properly, these could be turned into most effective knuckledusters. Bond got up, took the blade out of his Gillette and dropped the razor into his trouser pocket. He slipped the shaft between the first and second fingers of his left hand so that the blade-carrier rested flat along his knuckles. Yes, that was the way! Now was there anything, any evidence he should try and take with him? Yes, he must try and get more, if not all, of the girls' names and, if possible, addresses. For some reason he knew they were vital. For that he would have to use Ruby. His head full of plans for getting the information out of her, Bond went out of the bathroom and sat down at his desk and got on with a fresh page of de Bleuvilles. At least he must continue to show willing, if only to the recording eye in the ceiling.

It was about twelve-thirty when Bond heard his door-knob being softly turned. Ruby slipped in and, her finger to her lips, disappeared into his bathroom. Bond casually threw down his pen, got up and stretched and strolled over and went in after her.

Ruby's blue eyes were wide and frightened. 'You're in trouble,' she whispered urgently. 'What *have* you been doing?'

'Nothing,' said Bond innocently. 'What's up?'

'We've all been told that we mustn't talk to you unless Miss Bunt is there.' Her knuckles went distractedly up to her teeth. 'Do you think they know about *us*?'

'Couldn't possibly,' said Bond, radiating confidence. 'I think I know what it is.' (With so much obfuscation in the air, what did an extra, a reassuring, lie matter?) 'This morning the Count told me I was an upsetting influence here, that I was what he called "disruptive", interfering with your treatments. He asked me to keep myself more to myself. Honestly —' (how often that word came into a lie!) — 'I'm sure that's all it is. Rather a pity really. Apart from you — I mean you're sort of special — I think all you girls are terribly sweet. I'd like to have helped you all.'

'How do you mean? Helped us?'

'Well, this business of surnames. I talked to Violet last night. She seemed awfully interested. I'm sure it would have amused all the others to have theirs done. Everyone's interested in where they came from. Rather like palmistry in a way.' Bond wondered how the College of Arms would have liked *that* one! He shrugged. 'Anyway, I've decided to get the hell away from here. I can't bear being shepherded and ordered about like this. Who the hell do they think I am? But I'll tell you what I'll do. If you can give me the names of the girls, as many as you know, I'll do a piece on each of them and post them when you all get back to England. How much longer have you got, by the way?'

'We're not told exactly, but the rumour is about another week. There's another batch of girls due about then. When we're slow at our work or get behindhand with our reading, Miss Bunt says she hopes the next lot won't be so stupid. The old bitch! But Sir Hilary —' the blue eyes filled with concern — 'how *are* you going to get away? You know we're practically prisoners up here.'

Bond was off-hand. 'Oh, I'll manage somehow. They can't hold *me* here against my will. But what about the names, Ruby? Don't you think it would give the girls a treat?'

'Oh, they'd love it. Of course I know all of them. We've found plenty of ways of exchanging secrets. But you won't be able to remember. Have you got anything to write down on?'

Bond tore off some strips of lavatory paper and took out a pencil. 'Fire away!'

She laughed. 'Well, you know me and Violet, then there's Elizabeth Mackinnon. She's from Aberdeen. Beryl Morgan from somewhere in Herefordshire. Pearl Tampion, Devonshire — by the way, all those simply loathed every kind of cattle.

Now they live on steaks! Would you believe it? I must say the Count's a wonderful man.'

'Yes, indeed.'

'Then there's Anne Charter from Canterbury and Caresse Ventnor from the National Stud, wherever that is — fancy her working there and she came up in a rash all over whenever she went near a horse! Now all she does is dream of pony clubs and read every word she can get hold of about Pat Smythe! And Denise Robertson . . .'

The list went on until Bond had got the whole ten. He said, 'What about that Polly somebody who left in November?'

'Polly Tasker. She was from East Anglia. Don't remember where, but I can find out the address when I get back to England. Sir Hilary —' she put her arm round his neck — 'I *am* going to see you again, aren't I?'

Bond held her tight and kissed her. 'Of course, Ruby. You can always get me at the College of Arms in Queen Victoria Street. Just send me a postcard when you get back. But for God's sake cut out the "Sir". You're my girl friend. Remember?'

'Oh, yes, I will — er — Hilary,' she said fervently. 'And you will be careful, getting away I mean. You're sure it's all right? Is there anything I can do to help?'

'No, darling. Just don't breathe a word of all this. It's a secret between us. Right?'

'Of course, darling.' She glanced at her watch. 'Oh lord! I must simply fly. Only ten minutes to lunch-time. Now, can you do your trick with the door? There shouldn't be anyone about. It's their lunch-time from twelve till one.'

Bond, out of any possible line of vision from the eye in the ceiling, did his trick with the door and she was gone with a last whispered goodbye.

Bond eased the door shut. He let out a deep sigh and went over to the window and peered out through the snow-heaped panes. It was thick as Hades outside and the fine powder snow on the veranda was whirling up in little ghosts as the wind tore at the building. Pray God it would let up by night-time! Now, what did he need in the way of equipment? Goggles and gloves were two items he might harvest over lunch. Bond went into the bathroom again and rubbed soap into his eyes. It stung like hell, but the blue-grey eyes emerged from the treatment realistically bloodshot. Satisfied, Bond rang for the 'warden' and went thoughtfully off to the restaurant.

Silence fell as he went through the swing doors, followed by a polite, brittle chatter. Eyes followed him discreetly as he crossed the room and the replies to his good-mornings were muted. Bond took his usual seat between Ruby and Fräulein Bunt. Apparently oblivious to her frosty greeting, he snapped his fingers for a waiter and ordered his double vodka dry Martini. He turned to Fräulein Bunt and smiled into the suspicious yellow eyes. 'Would you be very kind?'

'Yes, Sair Hilary. What is it?'

Bond gestured at his still watering eyes. 'I've got the Count's trouble. Sort of conjunctivitis, I suppose. The tremendous glare up here. Better today of course, but there's still a lot of reflection from the snow. And all this paper-work. Could you get me a pair of snow-goggles? I'll only need to borrow them for a day or two. Just till my eyes get used to the light. Don't usually have this sort of trouble.'

'Yes. That can be done. I will see that they are put in your room.' She summoned the head waiter and gave him the order in German. The man, looking at Bond with overt dislike, said, 'Sofort, gnädiges Fräulein,' and clicked his heels.

'And one more thing, if you will,' said Bond politely. 'A small flask of schnapps.' He turned to Fräulein Bunt. 'I find I am not sleeping well up here. Perhaps a nightcap would help. I always have one at home — generally whisky. But here I would prefer schnapps. When in Gloria, do as the Glorians do. Ha ha!'

Fräulein Bunt looked at him stonily. She said to the waiter curtly, 'In Ordnung!' The man took Bond's order of Pâté Maison followed by Oeufs Gloria and the cheese tray (Bond thought he had better get some stuffing into him!), clicked his heels and went away. Was he one of those who had been at work in the interrogation room? Bond silently ground his teeth. By God, if it came to hitting any of these guards tonight, he was going to hit them damned hard, with everything he'd got! He felt Fräulein Bunt's eyes inquisitively on him. He untensed himself and began to make amiable conversation about the storm. How long would it last? What was the barometer doing?

Violet, guardedly but helpfully, said the guides thought it would clear up during the afternoon. The barometer was rising.

She looked nervously at Fräulein Bunt to see if she had said too much to the pariah, and then, not reassured, went back to her two vast baked potatoes with poached eggs in them.

Bond's drink came. He swallowed it in two gulps and ordered another. He felt like making any gesture that would startle and outrage. He said, combatively, to Fräulein Bunt, 'And how is that poor chap who came up in the cable car this morning? He looked in terrible shape. I do hope he's up and about again.'

'He makes progress.'

'Oh! Who was that?' asked Ruby eagerly.

'It was an intruder.' Fräulein Bunt's eyes were hard with warning. 'It is not a subject for conversation.'

'Oh, but why not?' asked Bond innocently. 'After all, you can't get much excitement up here Anything out of the ordinary should be a bit of a relief.'

She said nothing. Bond raised his eyebrows politely and then accepted the snub with a good grace. He asked if any newspapers came up. Or was there a radio bulletin like on board ship? Did they get any news from the outside world?

'No.'

Bond gave up the struggle and got on with his lunch. Ruby's foot crept up against his in sympathy with the man sent to Coventry. Bond gave it a gentle kick of warning and withdrew his. The girls at the other tables began to leave. Bond toyed with his cheese and coffee until Fräulein Bunt got to her feet and said, 'Come, girls.' Bond rose and sat down again. Now, except for the waiters clearing up, he was alone in the restaurant. That was what he wanted. He got up and strolled to the door. Outside, on pegs against the wall, the girls' outdoor coats and skiing gloves hung in an orderly row. The corridor was empty. Bond swept the largest pair of leather gauntlets he could see off the peg where they hung by their joining cord and stuffed them inside his sweater. Then he sauntered along to the reception room. It was empty. The door to the ski-room was open and the surly man was at his work-bench. Bond went in and made one-sided conversation about the weather. Then, under cover of desultory talk about whether the metal skis were not more dangerous than the old wooden ones, he wandered, his hands innocently in his pockets, round the numbered racks in which the skis stood against the wall. They were mostly the girls' skis.

No good! The bindings would be too small for his boots. But, by the door, in unnumbered slots, stood the guides' skis. Bond's eyes narrowed to slits as he scanned them, measuring, estimating. Yes, the pair of metal Heads with the red Vs painted on the black curved tips was the best bet. They were of the stiffer, Master's, category, designed for racing. Bond remembered reading somewhere that the Standard model was inclined to 'float' at speed. His choice had the Attenhofer Flex forward release with the Marker lateral release. Two transverse leather thongs wound round the ankle and buckled over the instep would, if he fell, which he was certain to do, ensure against losing a ski.

Bond made a quick guess at how much the bindings would need adjustment to fit his boots and went off down the corridor to his room.

16

DOWNHILL ONLY

NOW IT WAS just a question of sitting out the hours. When would they have finished with Campbell? Quick, rough torture is rarely effective against a professional, apart from the likelihood of the man rapidly losing consciousness, becoming so punch-drunk that he is incoherent. The pro, if he is a tough man spiritually, can keep the 'game' alive for hours by minor admissions, by telling long, rambling tales and sticking to them. Such tales need verification. Blofeld would undoubtedly have his man in Zürich, would be able to contact him on his radio, get him to check this or that date or address, but that also would require time. Then, if it was proved that Campbell had told lies, they would have to begin again. So far as Bond and his identity were concerned, it all depended on Campbell's reading of why Bond was up at the Gloria Club. He must guess, because of Bond's curt disavowal of him, that it was something clandestine, something important. Would he have the wits to cover up Bond, the guts, against the electrical and mechanical devices they would surely use against him? He could say that, when he came to and saw Bond, in his semi-conscious state he had for a moment thought Bond was his brother, James Campbell. Some story like that. If he had the wits! If he had the guts! Had Campbell got a death pill, perhaps one of the buttons on his ski-jacket or trousers? Bond sharply put the thought away. He had been on the edge of wishing that Campbell had!

Well, he would be wise to assume that it was only a matter of hours and then they would come for him. They wouldn't do it until after lights-out. To do it before would cause too much talk among the girls. No, they would fetch him at night and the next day it would be put about that he had left by the first cable car down to the valley. Meanwhile he would be buried deep in a snow overcoat, or more likely deposited in a high crevasse in the near-by Piz Languard glacier, to come out at the bottom, fifty years later, out of his deep freeze, with multiple contusions but no identification marks — a nameless victim of 'les neiges éternelles'!

Yes, he must plan for that. Bond got up from the desk where he had been automatically scribbling down lists of fifteenth-century de Bleuvilles and opened the window. The snow had stopped and there was broken blue in the sky. It would be perfect powder snow, perhaps a foot of it, on the Gloria Run. Now to make everything ready!

There are hundreds of secret inks, but there was only one available to Bond, the oldest one in the world, his own urine. He went into the bathroom (what must the televising eye think of his digestive tracts?) with his pen, a clean nib, and his passport. Then he sat down and proceeded to transcribe, from the flimsy pieces of paper in his pocket on to a blank page of his passport, the names and approximate locations by county of the girls. The page showed nothing. Held in front of a flame, the writing would come up brown. He slipped the passport into his hip-pocket. Next he took the gloves from under his sweater, tried them on and found them an adequate but tight fit, took the top off the lavatory cistern and laid the gloves along the arm of the stop-cock.

What else? It was going to be fiendishly cold at the start, but his body would soon be drenched in sweat. He would just have to make do with the ski-clothes he possessed, the gloves, the goggles that had been placed on his table, and the flat glass flask of schnapps that he would carry in one of his side pockets and not, in case of a fall, in his hip-pocket. Extra covering for his face? Bond thought of using one of his warm vests and cutting eyeholes in it. But it would surely slip and perhaps blind him. He had some dark-red silk bandana handkerchiefs. He would tie one tight over his face below the goggles and discard it if it interfered with his breathing. So! That was the lot! There was nothing else he could do or insure against. The rest was up to the Fates. Bond relaxed his thoughts and went out and back to his desk. He sat down and bent to his paper-work and tried not to listen to the hastening tick of the Rolex on his wrist, tried to fix in his mind the rough geography of the Gloria Run he had inadequately learned from the metal map. It was too late now to go and have another look at it. He must stay put and continue to play the toothless tiger!

Dinner was as ghastly as lunch. Bond concentrated on getting plenty of whisky and food under his belt. He made urbane conversation and pretended he didn't notice the chill in the air. Then he gave Ruby's foot one warm press under the table, excused himself on the grounds of work, and strode with dignity out of the room.

He had changed for dinner and he was relieved to find his ski-clothes in the half-tidy heap in which he had left them. He went, with utter normalcy, about his work — sharpened pencils, laid out his books, bent to the squared paper: 'Simon de Bleuville, 1510–1570. Alphonse de Bleuville, 1546–1580, married 1571 Mariette d'Escourt, and had issue, Jean, Françoise, Pierre'. Thank God he would soon be released from all this blether!

9.15, 9.30, 9.45, 10! Bond felt the excitement ball up inside him like cat's fur. He found that his hands were wet. He wiped them down the sides of his trousers. He got up and stretched. He went into the bathroom and made appropriate noises, retrieved the gloves and laid them on the bathroom floor just inside the door. Then, naked, he came back into the room and got into bed and switched off the light. He regularized his breathing and, in ten minutes, began to snore softly. He gave it another ten, then slid out of bed and, with infinite precaution, dressed himself in his ski-clothes. He softly retrieved his gloves from the bathroom, put on the goggles so that they rested in his hair above the forehead, tied the dark-red handkerchief tightly across his nose, schnapps into pocket, passport into hip-pocket and, finally, Gillette through the fingers of the left hand and the Rolex transferred to his right, the bracelet clasped in the palm of his hand and round the fingers so that the face of the watch lay across his middle knuckles.

James Bond paused and ran over his equipment. The ski-gloves, their cord drawn through his sweater and down the sleeves, hung from his wrists. They would be a hindrance until he was outside. Nothing to be done about that. The rest was all right. He was set! He bent to the door, manipulated the lock with the plastic and, praying that the television eye had been closed down and would not see the light shining in from the passage, listened briefly and slipped out.

There was, as usual, light from the reception room to his left. Bond crept along, inched round the door jamb. Yes! The guard was there, bent over something that looked like a time sheet. The neck was offered. Bond dropped the Gillette in his pocket and stiffened the fingers of his left hand into the old Commando cutting edge. He took the two steps into the room and crashed the hand down on the back of the offered neck. The man's face hit the table top with a thud, bounced up and half turned towards Bond. Bond's right flashed out and the face of the Rolex disintegrated against the man's jaw. The body slid sluggishly off its chair on to the carpet and lay still, its legs untidy as if in sleep. The eyes fluttered and stared, unseeing, upwards. Bond went round the desk and bent down. There was no heartbeat. Bond straightened himself. It was the man he had seen coming back alone from the bob-run on his first morning, when Bertil had met with his accident. So! Rough justice!

The telephone on the desk buzzed like a trapped wasp. Bond looked at it. He picked up the receiver and spoke through the handkerchief across his mouth. 'Ja?'

'Alles in Ordnung?'

'Ja.'

'Also hör zu! Wir kommen für den Engländer in zehn Minuten. Verstanden?'

'Is' recht.'

'Also, aufpassen. Ja?'

'Zu Befehl!'

At the other end the receiver went down. The sweat was beading on Bond's face. Thank God he had answered! So they were coming for him in ten minutes! There was a bunch of keys on the desk. Bond snatched them up and ran to the front door. After three misfits, he had the right one. He tried the door. It was now only held by its air-pressure device. Bond leaped for the ski-room. Unlocked! He went in and, by the light from the reception room, found his skis. There were sticks beside them. Carefully he lifted everything out of its wooden slot and strode to the main door and opened it. He laid the skis and sticks softly down in the snow, turned back to the door, locked it from the outside and threw the keys far away into the snow.

The three-quarter moon burned down with an almost dazzling fire and the snow crystals scintillated back at it like a carpet of diamond dust. Now minutes would have to be wasted getting the bindings absolutely right. James Bond kicked one boot into the groove of the Marker toe-hold and knelt down, feeling for the steel cable that went behind his heel. It was too short. Coolly, unhurriedly, he adjusted the regulating screw on the forward latch and tried again. This time it was all right. He pressed down on the safety latch and felt it lock his boot into the toe-hold. Next, the safety thong round the top of his boot that would keep the ski prisoner if the latch sprung, which it would do with a fall. His fingers were beginning to freeze. The tip of the thong refused to find its buckle! A full minute wasted! Got it! And now the same job on the other ski. At last Bond stood up, slipped the gloves over his aching fingers, picked up the lance-like sticks and pushed himself off along the faint ridge that showed the outlines of yesterday's well-trodden path. It felt all right! He pulled the goggles down over his eyes and now the vast snowscape was a silvery green as if he was swimming under sunny water. The skis hissed smoothly through the powder snow. Bond tried to get up more speed down the gentle slope by langlaufing, the sliding, forward stride of the first Norwegian skiers. But it didn't work. The heels of his boots felt nailed to the skis. He punted himself forward as fast as he could with his sticks. God, what a trail he must be leaving — like a tram-line! As soon as they got the front door open, they would be after him. Their fastest guide would certainly catch him easily unless he got a good start! Every minute, every second was a bonus. He passed between the black outlines of the cable-head and the Berghaus. There was the starting point of the Gloria Run, the metal notices beside it hatted with snow! Bond didn't pause. He went straight for it and over the edge.

The first vertical drop had a spine-chilling bliss to it. Bond got down into his old Arlberg crouch, his hands forward of his boots, and just let himself go. His skis were an ugly six inches apart. The Kannonen he had watched had gone down with their boots locked together, as if on a single ski. But this was no time for style, even if he had been capable of it! Above all he must stay upright!

Bond's speed was now frightening. But the deep cushion of

cold, light powder snow gave him the confidence to try a parallel swing. Minimum of shoulder turn needed at this speed — weight on to the left ski — and he came round and held it as the right-hand edges of his skis bit against the slope, throwing up a shower of moonlit snow crystals. Danger was momentarily forgotten in the joy of speed, technique, and mastery of the snow. Bond straightened up and almost dived into his next turn, this time to the left, leaving a broad S on the virgin mountain behind him. Now he could afford to schuss the rest down to the hard left-hand turn round the shoulder. He pointed his skis down and felt real rapture as, like a black bullet on the giant slope, he zoomed down the 45-degree drop. Now for the left-hand corner. There was the group of three flags, black, red and yellow, hanging limply, their colours confused by the moonlight! He would have to stop there and take a recce over the next lap. There was a slight upward slope short of the big turn. Bond took it at speed, felt his skis leave the ground at the crest of it, jabbed into the snow with his left stick as an extra lever and threw his skis and his right shoulder and hips round to the left. He landed in a spray of snow, at a dead halt. He was delighted with himself! A Sprung-Christiana is a showy and not an easy turn at speed. He wished his old teacher, Fuchs, had been there to see that one!

He was now on the shoulder of the mountain. High overhead the silver strands of the cable railway plunged downwards in one great swoop towards the distant black line of the trees, where the moonlight glinted on a spidery pylon. Bond remembered that there now followed a series of great zigs and zags more or less beneath the cables. With the piste unobscured, it would have been easy, but the new snow made every descent look desirable. Bond jerked up his goggles to see if he could spot a flag. Yes, there was one away down to the left. He would do some S turns down the next slope and then make for it.

As he pulled down his goggles and gripped his sticks, two things happened. First there came a deep boom from high up the mountain, and a speck of flame, that wobbled in its flight, soared into the sky above him. There was a pause at the top of its parabola, a sharp crack and a blazing magnesium flare on a parachute began its wandering descent, wiping out the black shadows in the hollows, turning everything into a hideous daylight. Another and another sprayed out across the sky, lighting every cranny over the mountain side.

And, at the same time, the cables high above Bond's head began to sing! They were sending the cable car down after him!

Bond cursed into the sodden folds of his silk handkerchief and got going. The next thing would be a man after him — probably a man with a gun!

He took the second lap more carefully than the first, got across to the second flag, turned at it and made back across the plunging slope for the series of linked S's under the cables. How fast did these bloody gondolas go? Ten, fifteen, twenty miles an hour? This was the latest type. It would be the fastest. Hadn't he read somewhere that the one between Arosa and the Weisshorn did 25? Even as he got into his first S, the tune of the singing cable above him momentarily changed and then went back to its usual whine. That was the gondola passing the first pylon! Bond's knees, the Achilles heel of all skiers, were beginning to ache. He cut his S's narrower, snaking down faster, but now feeling the rutted tracks of the piste under his skis at every turn. Was that a flag away over to the left? The magnesium flares were swaying lower, almost directly over him. Yes. It looked all right. Two more S turns and he would do a traverse schuss to it!

Something landed with a tremendous crack amidst a fountain of snow to his right! Another to his left! They had a grenade-thrower up front in the cable car! A bracket! Would the next one be dead on? Almost before the thought flashed through his mind, there came a tremendous explosion just ahead of him and he was hurled forward and sideways in a catherine wheel of sticks and skis.

Bond got gingerly to his feet, gasping and spitting snow. One of his bindings had opened. His trembling fingers found the forward latch and banged it tight again. Another sharp crack, but wide by twenty yards. He must get away from the line of fire from the blasted railway! Feverishly he thought, the left-hand flag! I must do the traverse now. He took a vague bearing across the precipitous slope and flung himself down it.

17

BLOODY SNOW

IT WAS TRICKY, undulating ground. The magnesium flares had sailed lower and there were ugly patches of black shadow, any of which might have been a small ravine. Bond had to check at all of them and each time the sharp Christie reminded him of his legs and ankles. But he got across without a fall and pulled up at the flag, panting. He looked back. The gondola had stopped. They had telephone communication with the top and bottom stations, but why had it stopped? As if in answer, blue flames fluttered gaily from the forward cabin. But Bond heard no bullets. The gondola would be swaying on its cable. But then, high up above him, from somewhere near the first flags on the shoulder, came more rapid fire, from two points, and the snow kicked up daintily around him. So the guides had finally got after him! His fall would have cost him minutes. How much lead had he got? Certainly less than ten minutes. A bullet whanged into one of his skis and sang off down the mountain. Bond took a last gulp of breath and got going again, still left-handed, away from the cable railway, towards the next flag, a distant dot on the edge of the shadow thrown by the great Matterhorn-shaped peak of Piz Gloria, which knifed up into the spangled sky in dreadful majesty.

It looked as if the run was going to take him dangerously close to the skirts of the peak. Something was nagging at his mind, a tiny memory. What was it? It was something unpleasant. Yes, by God! The last flag! It had been black. He was on the Black Run, the one closed because of avalanche danger! God! Well, he'd had it now. No time to try and get back on the Red Run. And anyway the Red had a long stretch close to the cables. He'd just have to chance it. And what a time to chance it, just after a heavy fall of new snow, and with all these detonations to loosen up the stuff! When there was danger of an avalanche, guides forbade even speech! Well, to hell with it! Bond zoomed on across the great unmarked slope, got to the next flag, spotted the next, away down the mountain side towards the tree-line. Too steep to schuss! He would just have to do it in S's.

And then the bastards chose to fire off three more flares followed by a stream of miscellaneous rockets that burst prettily among the stars. Of course! Bright idea! This was for the sake of watchers in the valley who might be inquisitive about the mysterious explosions high up the mountain. They were having a party up there, celebrating something. What fun these rich folk had, to be sure! And then Bond remembered. But of course! It was Christmas Eve! God rest ye merry gentlemen, let nothing ye dismay! Bond's skis hissed an accompaniment as he zigzagged fast down the beautiful snow slope. White Christmas! Well, he'd certainly got himself that!

But then, from high up above him, he heard that most dreaded of all sounds in the high Alps, that rending, booming crack! The Last Trump! Avalanche!

The ground shook violently under Bond's skis and the swelling rumble came down to him like the noise of express trains roaring through a hundred tunnels. God Almighty, now he really had had it! What was the rule? Point the skis straight downhill! Try and race it! Bond pointed his skis down towards the tree line, got down in his ugly crouch and shot, his skis screaming, into white space.

Keep forward, you bastard! Get your hands way in front of you! The wind of his speed was building up into a great wall in front of him, trying to knock him off balance. Behind him the giant roar of the mountain seemed to be gaining. Other, smaller cracks sounded high up among the crags. The whole bloody mountain was on the move! If he beat the gigantic mass of hurtling snow to the tree line, what comfort would he find there? Certainly no protection until he was deep in the wood. The avalanche would snap perhaps the first hundred yards of firs down like match-sticks. Bond used his brain and veered slightly left-handed. The opening, the glade cut for the Black Run, would surely be somewhere below the last flag he had been aiming for. If it wasn't, he was a dead duck!

Now the wild schuss was coming to an end. The trees were rushing towards him. Was there a break in the bloody black line of them? Yes! But more to the left. Bond veered, dropping his speed, gratefully, but with his ears strained to gauge the range of the thunder behind and above him. It couldn't be far from him. The shudder in the ground had greatly increased and a lot of the stuff would also find the hole through the trees, funnel itself in and pursue him even down there! Yes! There was the flag! Bond hurtled into a right-hand Christie just as, to his left, he heard the first trees come crashing down with the noise of a hundred monster crackers being pulled — Christmas crackers! Bond flung himself straight down the wide white glade between the trees. But he could hear that he was losing! The crashing of the trees was coming closer. The first froth of the white tide couldn't be far behind his heels! What did one do when the avalanche hit? There was only one rule. Get your hands to your boots and grip your ankles. Then, if you were buried, there was some hope of undoing your skis, being able, perhaps, to burrow your way to the surface — if you knew in your tomb where the surface lay! If you couldn't go down like a ball, you would end up immovable, a buried tangle of sticks and skis at all angles. Thank God the opening at the end of the glade, the shimmer of the last, easily sloping fields before the finish, was showing up! The crackling roar behind him was getting louder! How high would the wall of snow be? Fifty feet? A hundred? Bond reached the end of the glade and hurled himself into a right-hand Christie. It was his last hope, to get below the wide belt of trees and pray that the avalanche wouldn't mow down the lot of them. To stay in the path of the roaring monster at his heels would be suicide!

The Christie came off, but Bond's right ski snarled a root or a sapling and he felt himself flying through space. He landed with a crash and lay gasping, all the wind knocked out of him. Now he was done for! Not even enough strength to get his hands to his ankles! A tremendous buffet of wind hit him and a small snow-storm covered him. The ground shook wildly and a deep crashing roar filled his ears. And then it had passed him and given way to a slow, heavy rumble. Bond brushed the snow out of his eyes and got unsteadily to his feet, both skis loose, his goggles gone. Only a cricket pitch away, a great torrent of snow, perhaps twenty feet high, was majestically pouring out of the wood and down into the meadows. Its much higher, tumbling snout, tossing huge crags of broken snow around it, was already a hundred yards ahead and still going fast. But, where Bond stood, it was now silent and peaceful except for the machine-gun-fire crackling of the trees as they went down in the wood that had finally protected him. The crackling was getting nearer! No time to hang about! But Bond took off one sodden glove and dug into his trouser pocket. If ever he needed a drink it was now! He tilted the little flask down his throat, emptied it and threw the bottle away. Happy Christmas! he said to himself, and bent to his bindings.

He got to his feet and, rather light-headed but with the wonderful glow of the Enzian in his stomach, started on the last mile of finishing schuss across the meadows to the right, away from the still hurtling river of snow. Blast! There was a fence across the bottom of the meadows! He would have to take the normal outlet for the runs beside the cable station. It looked all right. There was no sign of the gondola, but he could now hear the song of the cables. Had the downcoming car reversed back up to Piz Gloria, assuming him to have been killed by the avalanche? There was a large black saloon car in the forecourt to the cable station, and lights on in the station, but otherwise no sign of life. Well, it was his only way to get off the run and on to the road that was his objective. Bond schussed easily downwards, resting his limbs, getting his breath back.

The sharp crack of a heavy-calibre pistol and the phut as the bullet hit the snow beside him pulled him together. He jinked sideways and glanced quickly up to the right, where the shot had come from. The gun blazed again. A man on skis was coming fast after him. One of the guides! Of course! He would have taken the Red Run. Had the other followed Bond on the Black? Bond hoped so, gave a deep sigh of anger and put on all the speed he could, crouching low and jinking occasionally to spoil the man's aim. The single shots kept on coming. It was going to be a narrow shave who got to the end of the run first!

Bond studied the finishing point that was now coming at him fast. There was a wide break in the fence to let the skiers through, a large parking place in front of the cable station and then the low embankment that protected the main line of the Rhätische Bahn up to Pontresina and the Bernina Pass. On the other side of the rails the railway embankment dropped into the road from Pontresina to Samaden, the junction for St Moritz, perhaps two miles down the valley.

Another shot kicked up the snow in front of him. That was six that had gone. With any luck the man's pistol was empty. But that wouldn't help much. There was no stuffing left in Bond for a fight.

Now a great blaze of light showed coming up the railway line, and, before it was hidden by the cable station, Bond identified an express and could just hear the thudding of its electro-diesels. By God, it would just about be passing the cable station as he wanted to get across the track! Could he make it — take a run at the low embankment and clear it and the lines before the train got there? It was his only hope! Bond dug in with his sticks to get on extra speed. Hell! A man had got out of the black car and was crouching, aiming at him. Bond jinked and jinked again as fire bloomed from the man's hand. But now Bond was on top of him. He thrust hard with the rapier point of a ski-stick and felt it go through clothing. The man gave a scream and went down. The guide, now only yards behind, yelled something. The great yellow eye of the diesel glared down the tracks, and Bond caught a sideways glimpse of a huge red snow-fan below the headlight that was fountaining the new snow to right and left of the engine in two white wings. Now! He flashed across the parking place, heading straight at the mound of the embankment and, as he hit, dug both his sticks in to get his skis off the ground, and hurled himself forward into the air. There was a brief glimpse of steel rails below, a tremendous thudding in his ears and a ferocious blast, only yards away, from the train's siren. Then he crashed on to the icy road, tried to stop, failed and fetched up in an almighty skid against the hard snow wall on the other side. As he did so, there came a terrible scream from behind him, a loud splintering of wood and the screech of the train's brakes being applied.

At the same time, the spray from the snow-fan, that had now reached Bond, turned pink!

Bond wiped some of it off his face and looked at it. His stomach turned. God! The man had tried to follow him, had been too late or had missed his jump, and had been caught by the murderous blades of the snow-fan! Mincemeat! Bond dug a handful of snow off the bank and wiped it over his face and hair. He rubbed more of it down his sweater. He suddenly realized that people were pulling down the windows in the brilliantly lit train above him. Others had got down on the line. Bond pulled himself together and punted off down the black ice of the road. Shouts followed him — the angry bawls of Swiss citizens. Bond edged his skis a little against the camber of the road and kept going. Ahead of him, down the black gulch of the road, in his mind's eye, the huge red propeller whirred, sucking him into its steel whirlpool. Bond, close to delirium, slithered on towards its bloody, beckoning vortex.

Bond, a grey-faced, lunging automaton, somehow stayed upright on the two miles of treacherous Langlauf down the gentle slope to Samaden. Once a passing car, its snow-chains clattering, forced him into the bank. He leaned against the comforting soft snow for a moment, the breath sobbing in his throat. Then he drove himself on again. He had got so far, done so well! Only a few more hundred yards to the lights of the darling, straggling little paradise of people and shelter! The slender campanile of the village church was floodlit and there was a great warm lake of light on the left of the twinkling group of houses. The strains of a waltz came over the still, frozen air. The skating-rink! A Christmas Eve skaters' ball. That was the place for him! Crowds! Gaiety! Confusion! Somewhere to lose himself from the double hunt that would now be on — by SPECTRE and the Swiss police, the cops and the robbers hand in hand!

Bond's skis hit a pile of horse's dung from some merrymaker's sleigh. He lurched drunkenly into the snow wall of the road and righted himself, cursing feebly. Come on! Pull yourself together! Look respectable! Well, you needn't look *too* respectable. After all, it's Christmas Eve. Here were the first houses. The noise of accordion music, deliciously nostalgic, came from a Gasthaus with a beautiful iron sign over its door. Now there was a twisty, uphill bit — the road to St Moritz. Bond shuffled up it, placing his sticks carefully. He ran a hand through his matted hair and pulled the sweat-soaked handkerchief down to his neck, tucking the ends into his shirt collar. The music lilted down towards him from the great pool of light over the skating-rink. Bond pulled himself a little more upright. There were a lot of cars drawn up, skis stuck in mounds of snow, luges and toboggans, festoons of paper streamers, a big notice in three languages across the entrance: 'Grand Christmas Eve Ball! Fancy Dress! Entrance 2 Francs! Bring all your friends! Hooray!'

Bond dug in his sticks and bent down to unlatch his skis. He fell over sideways. If only he could just lie there, go to sleep on the hard, trodden snow that felt like swansdown! He gave a small groan and heaved himself gingerly into a crouch. The bindings were frozen solid, caked, like his boots, with ice. He got one of his sticks and hacked feebly at the metal and tried again. At last the latches sprang and the thongs were off. Where to put the bloody things, hide their brilliant red markings? He lugged them down the trodden path towards the entrance, gay with fairy lights, shoved the skis and the sticks under a big saloon car, and staggered on. The man at the ticket-table was as drunk as Bond seemed. He looked up blearily: 'Zwo Franken. Two francs. Deux francs.' The routine incantation was slurred into one portmanteau word. Bond held on to the table, put down the coins and got his ticket. The man's eyes focused. 'The fancy dress, the travesti, it is obligatoire.' He reached into a box by his side and threw a black and white domino-mask on the table. 'One franc.' He gave a lop-sided smile. 'Now you are the gangster, the spy. Yes?'

'Yeah, that's right.' Bond paid and put on the mask. He reluctantly let go of the table and wove through the entrance. There were raised tiers of wooden benches round the big square rink. Thank God for a chance to sit down! There was an empty seat on the aisle in the bottom row at rink level. Bond stumbled down the wooden steps and fell into it. He righted himself, said 'Sorry,' and put his head in his hands. The girl beside him, part of a group of harlequins, Wild Westerners and pirates, drew her spangled skirt away, whispered something to her neighbour. Bond didn't care. They wouldn't throw him out on a night like this. Through the loudspeakers the violins sobbed into 'The Skaters' Waltz'. Above them the voice of the M.C. called, 'Last dance, ladies and gentlemen. And then all out on to the rink and join hands for the grand finale. Only ten minutes to go to midnight! Last dance, ladies and gentlemen. Last dance!' There was a rattle of applause. People laughed excitedly.

God in Heaven! thought Bond feebly. Now this! Won't anybody leave me alone? He fell asleep.

Hours later he felt his shoulder being shaken. 'On to the rink, sir. Please. All on to the rink for the grand finale. Only a minute to go.' A man in purple and gold uniform was standing beside him, looking down impatiently.

'Go away,' said Bond dully. Then some inner voice told him not to make a scene, not to be conspicuous. He struggled to his feet, made the few steps to the rink, somehow stood upright. His head lowered, like a wounded bull, he looked to left and right, saw a gap in the human chain round the rink and slid gingerly towards it. A hand was held out to him and he grasped it thankfully. On the other side someone else was trying to get hold of his free hand. And then there came a diversion. From right across the rink, a girl in a short black skating-skirt topped by a shocking-pink fur lined parka, sped like an arrow across the ice and came to a crash-stop in front of Bond. Bond felt the ice particles hit his legs. He looked up. It was a face he recognized — those brilliant blue eyes, the look of authority now subdued beneath golden sunburn and a brilliant smile of excitement. Who in hell?

The girl slipped in beside him, seized his right hand in her left, joined up on her right. 'James —' it was a thrilling whisper — 'oh, James. It's me! Tracy! What's the matter with you? Where have you come from?'

'Tracy,' said Bond dully. 'Tracy. Hold on to me. I'm in bad shape. Tell you later.'

Then Auld Lang Syne began and everyone swung linked hands in unison to the music.

18

FORK LEFT FOR HELL!

BOND HAD NO idea how he managed to stay upright, but at last it was over and everyone cheered and broke up into pairs and groups.

Tracy got her arm under his. Bond pulled himself together. He said hoarsely, 'Mix with the crowd, Tracy. Got to get away from here. People after me.' A sudden hope came to him. 'Got your car?'

'Yes, darling. Everything'll be all right. Just hang on to me. Are people waiting for you outside?'

'Could be. Watch out for a big black Mercedes. There may be shooting. Better stay away from me. I can make it. Where's the car?'

'Down the road to the right. But don't be silly. Here, I've got an idea. You get into this parka.' She ran the zip down and stripped it off. 'It'll be a tight fit. Here, put your arm into this sleeve.'

'But you'll get cold.'

'Do as I tell you. I've got a sweater and plenty on underneath. Now the other arm. That's right.' She pulled up the zip. 'Darling James, you look sweet.'

The fur of the parka smelt of Guerlain's 'Ode'. It took Bond back to Royale. What a girl! The thought of her, of having an ally, of not being on his own, of being away from that bloody mountain, revived Bond. He held her hand and followed her through the crowd that was now streaming towards the exit. This was going to be a bad moment! Whether or not that cable car had come on down the mountain, by now Blofeld would have had time to get one down full of SPECTRE men. Bond had been seen from the train, would be known to have made for Samaden. By now they would have covered the railway station. They would expect him to try and hide in a crowd. Perhaps the drunken man at the entrance had remembered him. If that saloon moved off and revealed the red-arrowed skis, it would be a cert. Bond let go the girl's hand and slipped the shattered Rolex back over the knuckles of his right hand. He had gathered enough strength, mostly from the girl, to have one more bash at them!

She looked at him. 'What are you doing?'

He took her hand again. 'Nothing.'

They were getting near the exit. Bond peered through the slits in his mask. Yes, by God! Two of the thugs were standing beside the ticket man watching the throng with deadly concentration. On the far side of the road stood the black Mercedes, petrol vapour curling up from its exhaust. No escape. There was only bluff. Bond put his arm round Tracy's neck and whispered, 'Kiss me all the way past the ticket-table. They're there, but I think we can make it.'

She flung an arm over his shoulder and drew him to her. 'How did you know that that's what I've been waiting for?' Her lips crushed down sideways on his and, in a tide of laughing, singing people, they were through and on the street.

They turned, still linked, down the road. Yes! There was the darling little white car!

And then the horn on the Mercedes began sounding urgently. Bond's gait, or perhaps his old-fashioned ski-trousers, had given him away to the man in the car!

'Quick, darling!' said Bond urgently.

The girl threw herself in under the wheel, pressed the starter and the car was moving as Bond scrambled in through the opposite door. Bond looked back. Through the rear window he could see the two men standing in the road. They would not shoot with so many witnesses about. Now they ran to the Mercedes. Thank God it was pointing up the hill towards St Moritz! And then Tracy had done a controlled skid round the S bend in the village and they were on the main road that Bond had staggered down half an hour before.

It would be five minutes at least before the Mercedes could turn and get after them. The girl was going like hell, but there was traffic on the road — tinkling sleighs full of fur-wrapped merrymakers on their way back to Pontresina, an occasional car, its snow-chains rattling. She drove on her brakes and her horn, the same triple wind-horn that sounded the high discord

Bond remembered so well. Bond said, 'You're an angel, Tracy. But take it easy. We don't want to end up in the ditch.'

The girl glanced sideways at him and laughed with pleasure. 'That sounds as if you were feeling better. But I cannot see you. Now you can take off that silly mask and my parka. In a minute the heat will come on and you will be roasted. And I would like to see you as I remember you. But you are pleased with me?'

Life was beginning to come back into Bond. It was so wonderful to be in this little car with this marvellous girl. The memory of the dreadful mountain, of all that he had been through, was receding. Now there was hope again, after so much dread and despair. He could feel the tensions uncoiling in his stomach. He said, 'I'll tell you if I'm pleased when we get to Zürich. Can you make it? It's a hell of a way to spend Christmas.' He wound down the window and threw the domino-mask out, stripped off the parka and draped it over her shoulders. The big sign for the main road down into the valley came up. He said, 'Left here, Tracy. Filisur and then Coire.'

She took the turning, in Bond's estimation, dangerously fast. She went into a skid that Bond swore was going to be uncontrolled. But, even on the black ice of the road, she got out of it and motored blithely on. Bond said, 'For God's sake, Tracy! How in hell did you manage that? You haven't even got chains on.'

She laughed, pleased at the awe in his voice. 'Dunlop Rally studs on all the tyres. They're only supposed to be for Rally drivers, but I managed to wangle a set out of them. Don't worry. Just sit back and enjoy the drive.'

There was something entirely new in the girl's voice, a lilt and happiness that had certainly not been there at Royale. Bond turned and looked at her carefully for the first time. Yes, she was somehow a new woman, radiating health and a kind of inner glow. The tumbled fair hair glittered with vitality and the half-open, beautiful lips seemed always to be on the verge of a smile.

'Satisfied?'

'You look absolutely wonderful. But now for God's sake tell me how you happened to be at Samaden. It was a bloody miracle. It saved my life.'

'All right. But then you tell. I've never seen a man look so dead on his feet. I couldn't believe my eyes. I thought you must be plastered.' She gave him a quick glance. 'You still look pretty bad. Here —' she leant forward to the dashboard — 'I'll switch on the blower. Get you properly warmed up.' She paused. 'Well, my bit of the story's quite simple really. Papa rang me up one day from Marseilles to find out how I was. He asked if I had seen you and seemed very annoyed when he heard I hadn't. He practically ordered me to go and find you.' She glanced at him. 'He's quite taken to you, you know. Anyway he said he had found out the address of a certain man you were looking for. He said he was sure that by now you would have found out that address too. He said that, knowing you, I would find you somewhere close to this address. It was the Piz Gloria Club. He told me if I found you to tell you to watch your step, to look after yourself.' She laughed. 'How right he was! Well, so I left Davos, which had really put me on my feet again, like you said it would, and I came up to Samaden the day before yesterday. The Seilbahn wasn't running yesterday, so I was going to come up today to look for you. It was all as simple as that. Now you tell.'

They had been keeping up a good speed down the sloping, winding road into the valley. Bond turned to look through the rear window. He swore under his breath. Perhaps a mile behind, twin lights were coming after them. The girl said, 'I know. I've been watching in the mirror. I'm afraid they're gaining a little. Must be a good driver who knows the road. Probably got snow-chains. But I think I can hold them. Now go on. What have you been up to?'

Bond gave her a garbled version. There was a big gangster up the mountain, living under a false name. He was wanted by the police in England. Bond was vaguely connected with the police, with the Ministry of Defence. (She snorted, 'Don't try and fool me. I know you're in the Secret Service. Papa told me so.' Bond said curtly, 'Well, Papa's talking through his hat.' She laughed knowingly.) Anyway, Bond continued, he had been sent out to make sure this was the man they wanted. He had found out that he was. But the man had become suspicious of Bond and Bond had had to get out quickly. He gave her a graphic account of the moonlit nightmare of the mountain, of the avalanche, of the man who had been killed by the train, of how he had got to

Samaden, dead beat, and had tried to hide in the crowd on the skating-rink. 'And then,' he ended lamely, 'you turned up like a beautiful angel on skates, and here we are.'

She thought the story over for a minute. Then she said calmly, 'And now, my darling James, just tell me how many of them you killed. And tell me the truth.'

'Why?'

'I'm just curious.'

'You promise to keep this between you and me?'

She said enigmatically, 'Of course. Everything's between you and me from now on.'

'Well, there was the main guard at the so-called Club. That had to be done or I'd be dead myself by now. Then I suppose one got caught by the avalanche. Then, at the bottom, one of them shot at me and I had to spear him with my ski-stick — self-defence. I don't know how badly he's hurt. And then there was the man killed by the train. He'd fired six shots at me. And anyway it was his own fault. Let's say three and a half got themselves killed one way or another.'

'How many are left?'

'What are you getting at?'

'I just want to know. Trust me.'

'Well, I think there were about fifteen up there all told. So that leaves eleven and a half — plus the big man.'

'And there are three in the car behind? Would they kill us if they caught us?'

'I'm afraid so. I haven't got any weapons. I'm sorry, Tracy, but I'm afraid you wouldn't have much chance either, being a witness and a sort of accomplice of mine. These people think I'm pretty bad news for them.'

'And you are?'

'Yes. From now on, I'm the worst.'

'Well, I've got pretty bad news for you. They're gaining on us and I've only got a couple of gallons left in the tank. We'll have to stop in Filisur. There won't be a garage open and it'll mean waking someone up. Can't hope to do it under ten minutes and they'll have us. You'll have to think up something clever.'

There was a ravine and an S turn over a bridge. They were coming out of the first curve over the bridge. Lights blazed at them from across the ravine. There was half a mile between the two cars, but the range across the ravine was perhaps only three hundred yards. Bond wasn't surprised to see the familiar blue flames flutter from the front of the car. Chips of granite from the overhang splattered down on the bonnet of the car. Then they were into the second half of the S bend and out of sight of their pursuers.

Now came a stretch of reconstruction work where there had been a landslide. There were big warning notices: 'Achtung! Baustelle! Vorsichtig Fahren!' The broken road hugged the mountain side on the right. On the left was rickety fencing and then a precipice falling hundreds of feet down into a gorge with an ice-floed river. In the middle of the bad stretch, a huge red wooden arrow pointed right to a narrow track across a temporary bridge. Bond suddenly shouted 'Stop!'

Tracy pulled up, her front wheels on the bridge. Bond tore open the door. 'Get on! Wait for me round the next corner. It's the only chance.'

Good girl! She got going without a word. Bond ran back the few yards to the big red arrow. It was held in the forks of two upright poles. Bond wrenched it off, swung it round so that it pointed to the left, towards the flimsy fence that closed off the yards of old road leading to the collapsed bridge. Bond tore at the fence, pulling the stakes out, flattening it. Glare showed round the corner behind him. He leaped across the temporary road into the shadow of the mountain, flattened himself against it, waited, holding his breath.

The Mercedes was coming faster than it should over the bumpy track, its chains clattering inside the mudguards. It made straight for the black opening to which the arrow now pointed. Bond caught a glimpse of white, strained faces and then the desperate scream of brakes as the driver saw the abyss in front of him. The car seemed almost to stop, but its front wheels must have been over the edge. It balanced for a moment on its iron belly and then slowly, slowly toppled and there was a first appalling crash as it hit the rubble beneath the old bridge. Then another crash and another. Bond ran forward past the lying arrow and looked down. Now the car was flying upside-down through the air. It hit again and a fountain of sparks flashed from a rock ledge. Then, somersaulting, and with its lights somehow still blazing, it smashed on down into the gorge. It hit a last outcrop that knocked it sideways and, spinning laterally, but now with its lights out and only the glint of the moon on metal, it took the last great plunge into the iced-up river. A deep rumble echoed up from the gorge and there was the patter of rocks and stones following the wreckage. And then all was peaceful, moonlit silence.

Bond let out his breath in a quiet hiss between his clenched teeth. Then, mechanically, he straightened things out again, put up the remains of the fence, lifted the arrow and put it back facing to the right. Then he wiped his sweating hands down the side of his trousers and walked unsteadily down the road and round the next corner.

The little white car was there, pulled in to the side, with its lights out. Bond got in and slumped into his seat. Tracy said nothing but got the car going. The lights of Filisur appeared, warm and yellow in the valley below. She reached out a hand and held his tightly. 'You've had enough for one day. Go to sleep. I'll get you to Zürich. Please do what I say.'

Bond said nothing. He pressed her hand weakly, leaned his head against the door jamb and was instantly asleep.

He was out for the count.

19

LOVE FOR BREAKFAST

IN THE GREY dawn, Zürich Airport was depressing and almost deserted, but, blessedly, there was a Swissair Caravelle, delayed by fog at London Airport, waiting to take off for London. Bond parked Tracy in the restaurant and, regretfully forsaking the smell of coffee and fried eggs, went and bought himself a ticket, had his passport stamped by a sleepy official (he had half expected to be stopped, but wasn't), and went to a telephone booth and shut himself in. He looked up Universal Export in the telephone book, and read underneath, as he had hoped, 'Hauptvertreter Alexander Muir. Privat Wohnung' and the number. Bond glanced through the glass window at the clock in the departure hall. Six o'clock. Well, Muir would just have to take it.

He rang the number and, after minutes, a sleepy voice said, 'Ja! Hier Muir.'

Bond said, 'Sorry, 410, but this is 007. I'm calling from the airport. This is bloody urgent so I'll have to take a chance on your line being bugged. Got a paper and pencil?'

The voice at the other end had grown brisker. 'Hang on, 007. Yes, got it. Go ahead.'

'First of all I've got some bad news. Your Number Two has had it. Almost for sure. Can't give you any details over this line, but I'm off to London in about an hour — Swissair Flight 110 — and I'll signal the dope back straight away. Could you put that on the teleprinter? Right. Now I'm guessing that in the next day or so a party of ten girls, British, will be coming in here by helicopter from the Engadine. Yellow Sud Aviation Alouette. I'll be teleprinting their names back from London some time today. My bet is they'll be flying to England, probably on different flights and perhaps to Prestwick and Gatwick as well as London Airport, if you've any planes using those airports. Anyway, I guess they'll be dispersed. Now, I think it may be very important to tell London their flight numbers and

E.T.A. Rather a big job, but I'll get you authority in a few hours to use men from Berne and Geneva to lend a hand. Got it? Right. Now I'm pretty certain you're blown. Remember the old Operation Bedlam that's just been cancelled? Well, it's him and he's got radio and he'll probably have guessed I'd be contacting you this morning. Just take a look out of the window and see if there's any sign of watchers. He's certainly got his men in Zürich.'

'Christ, what a shambles!' The voice at the other end was tight with tension. 'Hang on.' There was a pause. Bond could visualize Muir, whom he didn't know except as a number, going over to the window, carefully drawing aside the curtain. Muir came back on the wire. 'Looks damn like it. There's a black Porsche across the road. Two men in it. I'll get my friends in the Sécurité to chase them away.'

Bond said, 'Be careful how you go about it. My guess is that our man has got a pretty good fix in with the police. Anyway, put all this on the telex to M personally, would you? Ciphered of course. And tell him if I get back in one piece I must see him today, with 501 [the Chief Scientific Officer to the Service] and if possible with someone in the same line of business from the Ministry of Agriculture and Fisheries. Sounds daft, but there it is. It's going to upset their paper hats and Christmas pudding, but I can't help that. Can you manage all that? Good lad. Any questions?'

'Sure I oughtn't to come out to the airport and get some more about my Number Two? He was tailing one of Redland's men. Chap's been buying some pretty odd stuff from the local rep. of Badische Anilin. Number Two thought it seemed damned fishy. Didn't tell me what the stuff was. Just thought he'd better see where it was being delivered to.'

'I thought it must be some kind of a spiel like that. No. You stay away from me. I'm hot as a pistol, going to be hotter later in the day when they find a certain Mercedes at the bottom of a precipice. I'll get off the line now. Sorry to have wrecked your Christmas. 'Bye.'

Bond put down the receiver and went up to the restaurant. Tracy had been watching the door. Her face lit up when she saw him. He sat down very close to her and took her hand, a typical airport farewell couple. He ordered plenty of scrambled eggs and coffee. 'It's all right, Tracy. I've fixed everything at my end. But now about you. That car of yours is going to be bad news. There'll be people who'll have seen you drive away with the Mercedes on your tail. There always are, even at midnight on Christmas Eve. And the big man on top of the mountain has got his men down here too. You'd better finish your breakfast and get the hell on over the frontier. Which is the nearest?'

'Schaffhausen or Konstanz, I suppose, but —' she pleaded — 'James, do I have to leave you now? It's been so long waiting for you. And I *have* done well, haven't I? Why do you want to punish me?' Tears, that would never have been there in the Royale days, sparkled in her eyes. She wiped them angrily away with the back of her hand.

Bond suddenly thought, Hell! I'll never find another girl like this one. She's got everything I've ever looked for in a woman. She's beautiful, in bed and out. She's adventurous, brave, resourceful. She's exciting always. She seems to love me. She'd let me go on with my life. She's a lone girl, not cluttered up with friends, relations, belongings. Above all, she needs me. It'll be someone for me to look after. I'm fed up with all these untidy, casual affairs that leave me with a bad conscience. I wouldn't mind having children. I've got no social background into which she would or wouldn't fit. We're two of a pair, really. Why not make it for always?

Bond found his voice saying those words that he had never said in his life before, never expected to say.

'Tracy. I love you. Will you marry me?'

She turned very pale. She looked at him wonderingly. Her lips trembled. 'You mean that?'

'Yes, I mean it. With all my heart.'

She took her hand away from his and put her face in her hands. When she removed them she was smiling. 'I'm sorry, James. It's so much what I've been dreaming of. It came as a shock. But yes. Yes, of course I'll marry you. And I won't be silly about it. I won't make a scene. Just kiss me once and I'll be going.' She looked seriously at him, at every detail of his face. Then she leaned forward and they kissed.

She got up briskly. 'I suppose I've got to get used to doing what you say. I'll drive to Munich. To the Vier Jahreszeiten. It's my favourite hotel in the world. I'll wait for you there. They know me. They'll take me in without any luggage. Everything's at Samaden. I'll just have to send out for a toothbrush and stay in bed for two days until I can go out and get some things. You'll telephone me? Talk to me? When can we get married? I must tell Papa. He'll be terribly excited.'

'Let's get married in Munich. At the Consulate. I've got a kind of diplomatic immunity. I can get the papers through quickly. Then we can be married again in an English church, or Scottish rather. That's where I come from. I'll call you up tonight and tomorrow. I'll get to you just as soon as I can. I've got to finish this business first.'

'You promise you won't get hurt?'

Bond smiled. 'I wouldn't think of it. For once I'll run away if someone starts any shooting.'

'All right then.' She looked at him carefully again. 'It's time you took off that red handkerchief. I suppose you realize it's bitten to ribbons. Give it to me. I'll mend it.'

Bond undid the red bandana from round his neck. It was a dark, sweat-soaked rag. And she was right. Two corners of it were in shreds. He must have got them between his teeth and chewed on them when the going was bad down the mountain. He couldn't remember having done so. He gave it to her.

She took it and, without looking back, walked straight out of the restaurant and down the stairs towards the exit.

Bond sat down. His breakfast came and he began eating mechanically. What had he done? What in hell had he done? But the only answer was a feeling of tremendous warmth and relief and excitement. James and Tracy Bond! Commander and Mrs Bond! How utterly, utterly extraordinary!

The voice of the Tannoy said, 'Attention, please. Passengers on Swissair Flight Number 110 for London, please assemble at gate Number 2. Swissair Flight Number 110 for London. Passengers to gate Number 2, please.'

Bond stubbed out his cigarette, gave a quick glance round their trysting-place to fix its banality in his mind, and walked to the door, leaving the fragments of his old life torn up amidst the debris of an airport breakfast.

20

M EN PANTOUFLES

BOND SLEPT IN the plane and was visited by a terrible nightmare. It was the hallway of a very grand town-house, an embassy perhaps, and a wide staircase led up under a spangled chandelier to where the butler was standing at the door of the drawing-room, from which came the murmur of a large crowd of guests. Tracy, in oyster satin, was on his arm. She was loaded with jewels and her golden hair had been piled up grandly into one of those fancy arrangements you see in smart hairdressers' advertisements. On top of the pile was a diamond tiara that glittered gorgeously. Bond was dressed in tails (where in hell had he got *those* from?), and the wing collar stuck into his neck below the chin. He was wearing his medals, and his order as C.M.G., on its blue and scarlet ribbon, hung below his white tie. Tracy was chattering, gaily, excitedly, looking forward to the grand evening. Bond was cursing the prospect before him and wishing he was playing a tough game of bridge for high stakes at Blades. They got to the top of the stairs and Bond gave his name.

'Commander and Mrs James Bond!' It was the stentorian bellow of a toast-master. Bond got the impression that a sudden hush fell over the elegant crowd in the gilt and white drawing-room.

He followed Tracy through the double doors. There was a gush of French from Tracy as she exchanged those empty 'Mayfair' kisses, that end up wide of the kissers' ears, with her hostess. Tracy drew Bond forward. 'And this is James. Doesn't he look sweet with that beautiful medal round his neck? Just like the old De Reszke cigarette advertisements!'

'Fasten your seat belts, please, and extinguish your cigarettes.'

Bond awoke, sweating. God Almighty! What had he done? But no! It wouldn't be like that! Definitely not. He would still have his tough, exciting life, but now there would be Tracy to come home to. Would there be room in his flat in Chelsea? Perhaps he could rent the floor above. And what about May, his Scottish treasure? That would be tricky. He must somehow persuade her to stay.

The Caravelle hit the runway and there came the roar of jet deflection, and then they were trundling over the tarmac in a light drizzle. Bond suddenly realized that he had no luggage, that he could go straight to Passport Control and then out and back to his flat to change out of these ridiculous skiing clothes that stank of sweat. Would there be a car from the pool for him? There was, with Miss Mary Goodnight sitting beside the driver.

'My God, Mary, this is a hell of a way to spend your Christmas! This is far beyond the line of duty. Anyway, get in the back and tell me why you're not stirring the plum pudding or going to church or something.'

She climbed into the back seat and he followed. She said, 'You don't seem to know much about Christmas. You make plum puddings at least two months before and let them sort of settle and mature. And church isn't till eleven.' She glanced at him. 'Actually I came to see how you were. I gather you've been in trouble again. You certainly look pretty ghastly. Don't you own a comb? And you haven't shaved. You look like a pirate. And —' she wrinkled her nose — 'when did you last have a bath? I wonder they let you out of the airport. You ought to be in quarantine.'

Bond laughed. 'Winter sports are very strenuous — all that snowballing and tobogganing. Matter of fact, I was at a Christmas Eve fancy-dress party last night. Kept me up till all hours.'

'In those great clod-hopping boots? I don't believe you.'

'Well, sucks to you! It was on a skating-rink. But seriously, Mary, tell me the score. Why this V.I.P. treatment?'

'M. You're to check with H.Q. first and then go down to lunch with him at Quarterdeck. Then, after lunch, he's having these men you wanted brought down for a conference. Everything top priority. So I thought I'd better stand by too. As you're wrecking so many other people's Christmases, I thought I might as well throw mine on the slag-heap with the others. Actually, if you want to know, I was only having lunch with an aunt. And I loathe turkey and plum pudding. Anyway, I just didn't want to miss the fun and when the Duty Officer got on to me about an hour ago and told me there was a major flap, I asked him to tell the car to pick me up on the way to the airport.'

Bond said seriously, 'Well, you're a damned good girl. As a matter of fact it's going to be the hell of a rush getting down the bare bones of a report. And I've got something for the lab to do. Will there be someone there?'

'Of course there will. You know M insists on a skeleton staff in every Section, Christmas Day or not. But seriously, James. Have you been in trouble? You really do look awful.'

'Oh, somewhat. You'll get the photo as I dictate.' The car drew up outside Bond's flat. 'Now be an angel and stir up May while I clean myself up and get out of these bloody clothes. Get her to brew me plenty of black coffee and to pour two jiggers of our best brandy into the pot. You ask May for what you like. She might even have some plum pudding. Now then, it's nine-thirty. Be a good girl and call the Duty Officer and say O.K. to M's orders and that we'll be along by ten-thirty. And get him to ask the lab to stand by in half an hour.' Bond took his passport out of his hip-pocket. 'Then give this to the driver and ask him to get the hell over and give it to the Duty Officer personally. Tell the D.O. —' Bond turned down the corner of a page — 'to tell the lab that the ink used is — er — home-made. All it needs is exposure to heat. They'll understand. Got that? Good girl. Now come on and we'll get May going.' Bond went up the steps and rang two shorts and a long on the bell.

When Bond got to his desk a few minutes after ten-thirty, feeling back to nine-tenths human, he found a folder on his desk with the red star in the top right corner that meant Top Secret. It contained his passport and a dozen copies of blown-up photostats of its page 21. The list of girls' names was faint but legible. There was also a note marked 'personal'. Bond opened it. He laughed. It just said, 'The ink showed traces of an excess of uric acid. This is often due to a super-abundancy of alcohol in the blood-stream. You have been warned!' There was no signature. So the Christmas spirit had permeated even into the solemn crevices of one of the most secret Sections in the building! Bond crumpled the paper and then, thinking of Mary Goodnight's susceptibilities, more prudently burned it with his lighter.

She came in and sat down with her shorthand book. Bond said, 'Now this is only a first draft, Mary, and it's got to be fast. So don't mind about mistakes. M'll understand. We've got about an hour and a half if I'm to get down to Windsor by lunch-time. Think you can manage it? All right then, here goes. "Top Secret. Personal to M. As instructed, on December 22nd I arrived at Zürich Central Airport at 1330 by Swissair to make first contact in connection with Operation Corona . . ." '

Bond turned sideways to his secretary and, as he talked, looked out across the bare trees in Regent's Park, remembering every minute of the last three days — the sharp, empty smell of the air and the snow, the dark-green pools of Blofeld's eyes, the crunch as the edge of his left hand, still bruised, thudded down across the offered neck of the guard. And then all the rest until Tracy, whom, without mention of romance, he left in his report on her way to the Vier Jahreszeiten in Munich. Then the report was finished and the muted clack of Mary's typewriter came from behind the closed door. He would ring Tracy up that night when he got back to his flat. He could already hear her laughing voice at the other end of the wire. The nightmare in the plane was forgotten. Now there was only the happy, secret looking-forward to the days to come. Bond lost himself in his plans — how to get the days off, how to get the necessary papers, where to have the service in Scotland. Then he pulled himself together, picked up the photostat containing the girls' names and went up to the Communications Centre to get on the teleprinter to Station Z.

M would have preferred to live by the sea, near Plymouth perhaps or Bristol — anywhere where he could see the stuff whenever he wanted to and could listen to it at night. As it was, and since he had to be within easy call of London, he had chosen the next best thing to water, trees, and had found a small Regency manor-house on the edge of Windsor Forest. This was on Crown Lands, and Bond had always suspected that an ounce of 'Grace and Favour' had found its way into M's lease. The head of the Secret Service earned £5,000 a year, with the use of an ancient Rolls-Royce and driver thrown in. M's naval pay (as a Vice-Admiral on the retired list) would add perhaps another £1,500. After taxes, he would have about £4,000 to spend. His

London life would probably take at least half of that. Only if his rent and rates came to no more than £500 would he be able to keep a house in the country, and a beautiful small Regency house at that.

These thoughts ran again through Bond's mind as he swung the clapper of the brass ship's-bell of some former H.M.S. *Repulse*, the last of whose line, a battle-cruiser, had been M's final sea-going appointment. Hammond, M's Chief Petty Officer in that ship, who had followed M into retirement, greeted Bond as an old friend, and he was shown into M's study.

M had one of the stock bachelor's hobbies. He painted in water-colour. He painted only the wild orchids of England, in the meticulous but uninspired fashion of the naturalists of the nineteenth century. He was now at his painting-table up against the window, his broad back hunched over his drawing-board, with, in front of him, an extremely dim little flower in a toothglass full of water. When Bond came in and closed the door, M gave the flower one last piercingly inquisitive glance. He got to his feet with obvious reluctance. But he gave Bond one of his rare smiles and said, 'Afternoon, James.' (He had the sailor's meticulous observance of the exact midday.) 'Happy Christmas and all that. Take a chair.' M himself went behind his desk and sat down. He was about to come on duty. Bond automatically took his traditional place across the desk from his Chief.

M began to fill a pipe. 'What the devil's the name of that fat American detective who's always fiddling about with orchids, those obscene hybrids from Venezuela and so forth? Then he comes sweating out of his orchid house, eats a gigantic meal of some foreign muck and solves the murder. What's he called?'

'Nero Wolfe, sir. They're written by a chap called Rex Stout. I like them.'

'They're readable,' condescended M. 'But I was thinking of the orchid stuff in them. How in hell can a man like those disgusting flowers? Why, they're damned near animals, and their colours, all those pinks and mauves and the blotchy yellow tongues, are positively hideous! Now that —' M waved at the meagre little bloom in the toothglass — 'that's the real thing. That's an Autumn Lady's Tresses — *spiranthes spiralis*, not that I care particularly. Flowers in England as late as October and should be under the ground by now. But I got this forced-late specimen from a man I know — assistant to a chap called Summerhayes who's the orchid king at Kew. My friend's experimenting with cultures of a fungus which oddly enough is a parasite on a lot of orchids, but, at the same time, gets eaten by the orchids and acts as its staple diet. Mycorhiza it's called.' M gave another of his rare smiles. 'But you needn't write it down. Just wanted to take a leaf out of this fellow Nero Wolfe's book. However —' M brushed the topic aside — 'can't expect you to get excited about these things. Now then.' He settled back. 'What the devil have you been up to?' The grey eyes regarded Bond keenly. 'Looks as if you haven't been getting much sleep. Pretty gay these winter sport places, they tell me.'

Bond smiled. He reached into his inside pocket and took out the pinned sheets of paper. 'This one provided plenty of miscellaneous entertainment, sir. Perhaps you'd like to have a look at my report first. 'Fraid it's only a draft. There wasn't much time. But I can fill in anything that isn't clear.'

M reached across for the papers, adjusted his spectacles, and began reading.

Soft rain scratched at the windows. A big log fell in the grate. The silence was soft and comfortable. Bond looked round the walls at M's treasured collection of naval prints. Everywhere there were mountainous seas, crashing cannon, bellying sails, tattered battle pennants — the fury of ancient engagements, the memories of ancient enemies, the French, the Dutch, the Spaniards, even the Americans. All gone, all friends now with one another. Not a sign of the enemies of today. Who was backing Blofeld, for instance, in the inscrutable conspiracy in which he was now certainly engaged? The Russians? The Chinese? Or was it an independent job, as Thunderball had been? And what was the conspiracy? What was the job for the protection of which six or seven of Blofeld's men had died within less than a week? Would M read anything into the evidence? Would the experts who were coming that afternoon? Bond lifted his left wrist. Remembered that he no longer had a watch. *That* he would certainly be allowed on expenses. He would get another one as soon as the shops opened after Boxing Day. Another Rolex? Probably. They were on the heavy side, but they worked. And at least you could see the time in the dark with those big phosphorous numerals. Somewhere in the hall, a clock struck the half-hour. 1.30. Twelve hours before, he must have just set up the trap that killed the three men in the Mercedes. Self-defence, but the hell of a way to celebrate Christmas!

M threw the papers down on his desk. His pipe had gone out and he now slowly lit it again. He tossed the spent match accurately over his shoulder into the fire. He put his hands flat on the desk and said — and there was an unusual kindness in his voice — 'Well, you were pretty lucky to get out of that one, James. Didn't know you could ski.'

'I only just managed to stay upright, sir. Wouldn't like to try it again.'

'No. And I see you say you can't come to any conclusions about what Blofeld is up to?'

'That's right, sir. Haven't got a clue.'

'Well, nor have I. I just don't understand any part of it. Perhaps the professors'll help us out this afternoon. But you're obviously right that it's SPECTRE all over again. By the way, your tip about Pontresina was a good one. He was a Bulgar. Can't remember his name, but Interpol turned him up for us. Plastic explosives expert. Worked for K.G.B in Turkey. If it's true that the U.2 that fellow Powers was piloting was brought down by delayed charges and not by rockets, it may be this man was implicated. He was on the list of suspects. Then he turned freelance. Went into business on his own. That's probably when SPECTRE picked him up. We were doubtful about your identification of Blofeld. The Pontresina lead helped a lot. You're absolutely sure of him, are you? He certainly seems to have done a good job on his face and stomach. Better set him up on the Identicast when you get back this evening. We'll have a look at him and get the views of the medical gentry.'

'I think it must be him, sir. I was really getting the authentic smell of him on the last day — yesterday, that is. It seems a long time ago already.'

'You were lucky to run into this girl. Who is she? Some old flame of yours?' M's mouth turned down at the corners.

'More or less, sir. She came into my report on the first news we got that Blofeld was in Switzerland. Daughter of this man Draco, head of the Union Corse. Her mother was an English governess.'

'Hm. Interesting breeding. Now then. Time for lunch. I told

Hammond we weren't to be disturbed.' M got up and pressed the bell by the fire-place. ''Fraid we've got to go through the turkey and plum pudding routine. Mrs Hammond's been brooding over her pots and pans for weeks. Damned sentimental rubbish.'

Hammond appeared at the door, and Bond followed M through and into the small dining-room beyond the hall whose walls glittered with M's other hobby, the evolution of the naval cutlass. They sat down. M said, with mock ferocity, to Hammond, 'All right, Chief Petty Officer Hammond. Do your worst.' And then, with real vehemence, 'What in hell are those things doing here?' He pointed at the centre of the table.

'Crackers, sir,' said Hammond stolidly. 'Mrs Hammond thought that seeing as you have company . . .'

'Throw them out. Give 'em to the schoolchildren. I'll go so far with Mrs Hammond, but I'm damned if I'm going to have my dining-room turned into a nursery.'

Hammond smiled. He said, 'Aye, aye, sir,' gathered up the shimmering crackers and departed.

Bond was aching for a drink. He got a small glass of very old Marsala and most of a bottle of very bad Algerian wine.

M treated his two glasses as if they had been Château Lafitte. 'Good old "Infuriator". Staple drink for the fleet in the Mediterranean. Got real guts to it. I remember an old shipmate of mine, McLachlan, my Chief Gunnery Officer at the time, betting he could get down six bottles of the stuff. Damn fool. Measured his length on the wardroom floor after only three. Drink up, James! Drink up!'

At last the plum pudding arrived, flaming traditionally. Mrs Hammond had implanted several cheap silver gew-gaws in it and M nearly broke a tooth on the miniature horseshoe. Bond got the bachelor's button. He thought of Tracy. It should have been the ring!

21

THE MAN FROM AG. AND FISH.

THEY HAD COFFEE in M's study and smoked the thin black cheroots of which M allowed himself two a day. Bond burnt his tongue on his. M continued with his stories about the Navy which Bond could listen to all day — stories of battles, tornadoes, bizarre happenings, narrow shaves, courts martial, eccentric officers, neatly worded signals, as when Admiral Somerville, commanding the battleship *Queen Elizabeth*, had passed the liner *Queen Elizabeth* in mid-Atlantic and had signalled the one word 'SNAP'! Perhaps it was all just the stuff of boys' adventure books, but it was all true and it was about a great navy that was no more and a great breed of officers and seamen that would never be seen again.

It was three o'clock. A car's wheels scrunched on the gravel outside. Dusk was already creeping into the room. M got up and switched on the lights and Bond arranged two more chairs up against the desk. M said, 'That'll be 501. You'll have come across him. Head of the Scientific Research Section. And a man called Franklin from the Ministry of Agriculture. 501 says he's the top on his subject — Pest Control. Don't know why Ag. and Fish. chose to send him in particular, but the Minister told me they've got a bit of trouble on their hands, wouldn't tell even me what it is, and they think you may have run into something pretty big. We'll let them have a look at your report and see what they make of it. All right?'

'Yes, sir.'

The door opened and the two men came in.

Number 501 of the Secret Service, whose name Bond remembered was Leathers, was a big-boned, rangy man with the stoop and thick spectacles of the stage scientist. He had a pleasant, vague smile and no deference, but only politeness, towards M. He was appropriately dressed in shaggy tweeds and his knitted woollen tie didn't cover his collar stud. The other man was small and brisk and keen-looking, with darting, amused eyes. As became a senior representative of a Ministry who had received his orders from his Minister in person and who knew nothing of Secret Services, he had put on a neat dark-blue pinstripe and a stiff white collar. His black shoes gleamed efficiently. So did the leather of his fat briefcase. His greeting was reserved, neutral. He wasn't quite sure where he was or what this was all about. He was going to smell his way carefully in this business, be wary of what he said and how far he committed his Ministry. Of such, Bond reflected, is 'Government'.

When the appropriate greetings and apologies for disturbed Christmases had been made, and they were in their chairs, M said, 'Mr Franklin, if you'll forgive my saying so, everything you are going to see and hear in this room is subject to the Official Secrets Act. You will no doubt be in possession of many secret matters affecting your own Ministry. I would be grateful if you would respect those of the Ministry of Defence. May I ask you to discuss what you are about to hear only with your Minister personally?'

Mr Franklin made a little bow of acquiescence. 'My Minister has already instructed me accordingly. My particular duties in the Ministry have accustomed me to handling Top Secret matters. You need have no reservations in what you tell me. Now then —' the amused eyes rested on each of the other three in turn — 'perhaps you can tell me what this is all about. I know practically nothing except that a man on top of an alp is making efforts to improve our agriculture and livestock. Very decent of him. So why are we treating him as if he had stolen atomic secrets?'

'He did once, as a matter of fact,' said M drily. 'I think the best course would be for you and Mr Leathers to read the report of my representative here. It contains code numbers and other obscure references which need not concern you. The story tells itself without them.' M handed Bond's report to 501. 'Most of this will be new to you also. Perhaps you would like to read a page at a time and then pass them on to Mr Franklin.'

A long silence fell in the room. Bond looked at his fingernails and listened to the rain on the window panes and the soft noises of the fire. M sat hunched up, apparently in a doze. Across the table the sheets of paper rustled slowly. Bond lit a cigarette. The rasp of his Ronson caused M's eyes to open lazily and then close again. 501 passed across the last page and sat back. Franklin finished his reading, shuffled the pages together and stacked them neatly in front of him. He looked at Bond and smiled. 'You're lucky to be here.'

Bond smiled back but said nothing.

M turned to 501. 'Well?'

501 took off his thick spectacles and polished them on a none too clean handkerchief. 'I don't get the object of the exercise, sir. It seems perfectly above-board — praiseworthy, in fact, if we didn't know what we do know about Blofeld. Technically, what he has done is this. He has obtained ten, or rather eleven, counting the one that's left the place, suitable subjects for deep hypnosis. These are all simple girls from the country. It is significant that the one called Ruby had failed her G.C.E. twice. They seem to suffer, and there's no reason to believe that they don't, from certain fairly common forms of allergy. We don't know the origins of their allergies and these are immaterial. They are probably psychosomatic — the adverse reaction to birds is a very common one, as is the one brought on by cattle. The reactions to crops and plants are less common. Blofeld appears to be attempting cures of these allergies by hypnosis, and not only cures, but a pronounced affinity with the cause of the allergy in place of the previous repulsion. In the case of Ruby, for instance, she is told, in the words of the report, to "love" chickens, to wish to "improve their breed" and so forth. The mechanical means of the cure are, in practice, simple. In the twilight stage, on the edge of sleep — the sharp ringing of the bell would waken those who were already asleep — the use of the metronome exactly on the pulse-beat, and the distant whirring noise, are both common hypnotic aids. The singsong, authoritative murmur is the usual voice of the hypnotist. We have no knowledge of what lectures these girls attended or what reading they did, but we can assume that these were merely additional means to influence the mind in the path desired by Blofeld. Now, there is plenty of medical evidence for the efficacy of hypnosis. There are well-authenticated cases of the successful treatment by these means of such stubborn disabilities as warts, certain types of asthma, bed-wetting, stammering, and even alcoholism, drug-taking and homosexual tendencies.

Although the British Medical Association frowns officially on the practitioners of hypnosis, you would be surprised, sir, to know how many doctors themselves, as a last resort, particularly in cases of alcoholism, have private treatment from qualified hypnotists. But this is by the way. All I can contribute to this discussion is that Blofeld's ideas are not new and that they can be completely efficacious.'

M nodded. 'Thank you, Mr Leathers. Now would you like to be unscientific and hazard any wild guesses that would contribute in any way to what you have told us?' M smiled briefly. 'You will not be quoted, I can assure you.'

501 ran a worried hand through his hair. 'Well, sir, it may be nonsense, but a train of thought came to me as I read the report. This is a very expensive set-up of Blofeld's. Whether his intentions are benign or malignant, and I must say that I think we can accept them as being malignant, who is paying for all this? How did he fall upon this particular field of research and find the finance for it? Well, sir, this may sound fanciful, looking for burglars under the bed, so to speak, but the leaders in this field, ever since Pavlov and his salivating dogs, have been the Russians. If you recall, sir, at the time of the first human orbiting of the earth by the Russians, I put in a report on the physiology of the astronaut Yuri Gagarin. I drew attention to the simple nature of this man, his equable temperament when faced with his hysterical welcome in London. This equability never failed him and, if you will remember, we kept him under discreet observation throughout his visit and on his subsequent tours abroad, at the request of the Atomic Energy authorities. That bland, smiling face, sir, those wide-apart, innocent eyes, the extreme psychological simplicity of the man, all added up, as I said in my report, to the perfect subject for hypnosis, and I hazarded the guess that, in the extremely complicated movements required of him in his space capsule, Gagarin was operating throughout in a state of deep hypnosis. All right, sir —' 501 made a throw-away gesture of his hand — 'my conclusions were officially regarded as fanciful. But, since you ask, I now repeat them, and I throw out the suggestion that the Power behind Blofeld in all this may well be the Russians.' He turned to Bond. 'Was there any sign of Russian inspiration or guidance at this Gloria place? Any Russians anywhere in the offing?'

'Well, there was this man, Captain Boris. I never saw him, but he was certainly a Russian. Otherwise nothing I can think of except the three SPECTRE men who I'd guess were ex-SMERSH. But they seemed definitely staff men, what the Americans would call "mechanics".'

501 shrugged. He said to M, 'Well, I'm afraid that's all I can contribute, sir. But, if you come to the conclusion that this is dirty business, for my money, this Captain Boris was either the paymaster or supervisor of the scheme and Blofeld the independent operator. It would fit in with the free-lance character of the old SPECTRE — an independent gang working for whoever was willing to pay them.'

'Perhaps you've got something there, Mr Leathers,' said M reflectively. 'But what the devil's the object of the exercise?' He turned to Franklin. 'Well now, Mr Franklin, what do *you* think of all this?'

The man from Ag. and Fish. had lit a small, highly polished pipe. He kept it between his teeth and reached down for his briefcase and took out some papers. From among them he extracted a black and white outline map of Britain and Eire and smoothed it down across the desk. The map was dotted with symbols, forests of them here, blank spaces there. He said, 'This is a map showing the total agricultural and livestock resources of Britain and Eire, leaving out grassland and timber. Now, at my first sight of the report, I admit I was completely confused. As Mr Leathers said, these experiments seem perfectly harmless — more than that, to use his word, praiseworthy. But —' Franklin smiled — 'you gentlemen are concerned with searching for the dark side of the moon. I adjusted my mind accordingly. The result was that I am filled with a very deep and terrible suspicion. Perhaps these black thoughts have entered my mind by a process of osmosis with the present company's way of looking at the world —' he looked deprecatingly at M — 'but I also have one piece of evidence which may be decisive. Excuse me, but there was one sheet of paper missing from the report — the list of the girls and their addresses. Is that available?'

Bond took the photostat out of his inside pocket. 'Sorry. I didn't want to clutter up the report too much.' He slipped it across the table to Franklin.

Franklin ran his eyes down it. Then he said, and there was awe in his voice, 'I've got it! I do believe I've got it!' He sat back heavily in his chair as if he couldn't believe what he had seen.

The three men watched him tensely, believing him, because of what was written on his face — waiting for it.

Franklin took a red pencil out of his breast pocket and leaned over the map. Glancing from time to time at the list, he made a series of red circles at seemingly unrelated points across Britain and Eire, but Bond noticed that they covered the areas where the forests of symbols were at their densest. As he made the circles he commented, 'Aberdeen — Aberdeen Angus, Devon — Red Poll, Lancashire — poultry, Kent — fruit, Shannon — potatoes,' until ten red circles stood out on the map. Finally he poised his pencil over East Anglia and made a big cross. He looked up, said 'Turkeys,' and threw his pencil down.

In the silence that followed, M said, rather testily, 'Well, Mr Franklin, what have you in mind?'

The man from Ag. and Fish. had no intention of being pushed about by someone, however grand and hush-hush, from another Ministry. He bent and dug again into his briefcase. He came up with several papers. He selected one, a newspaper cutting. He said, 'I don't expect you gentlemen have time to read much of the agricultural news in the paper, but this is from the *Daily Telegraph* of early December. I won't read it all. It's from their agricultural correspondent, good man by the name of Thomas. These are the headlines: "CONCERN OVER TURKEYS. FLOCKS RAVAGED BY FOWL PEST". Then it goes on: "Supplies of turkeys to the Christmas market may be hit by recent fowl pest outbreaks which have resulted in large numbers of bird being slaughtered . . ." and further down, "Figures available show that 218,000 birds have been slaughtered . . . last year, total supplies for the Christmas market were estimated at between 3,700,000 and 4,000,000 birds, so much will depend now on the extent of further fowl pest outbreaks." '

Mr Franklin put the cutting down. He said seriously, 'That news was only the tip of the iceberg. We managed to keep later details out of the press. But I can tell you this, gentlemen. Within the past four weeks or so we have slaughtered three million turkeys. And that's only the beginning of it. Fowl pest is running wild in East Anglia and there are signs of it in Suffolk and

Hampshire, where a lot of turkey-raising goes on. What you ate at lunch today was almost certainly a foreign bird. We allowed the import of two million from America to cover this position up.'

M said sourly, 'Well, so far as I'm concerned, I don't care if I never eat another turkey again. However, I see you've had quite a problem on your hands. But to get back to our case. Where do we go from turkeys?'

Franklin was not amused. He said, 'We have one clue. All the birds that died first were exhibited at the National Poultry Show at Olympia early this month. Olympia had been cleared and cleaned out for the next exhibition before we had reached that conclusion, and we could find no trace on the premises of the virus — fowl pest is a virus, by the way, highly infectious, with a mortality of one hundred per cent. Now then —' he held up a stout white pamphlet with the insignia of the United States on it — 'how much do you gentlemen know about Biological Warfare?'

Leathers said, 'We were indirectly concerned in the fringes of the subject during the war. But in the end neither side used it. Around 1944 the Americans had a plan for destroying the whole of the Japanese rice crop by the use of aerial sprays. But, as I recall, Roosevelt vetoed the idea.'

'Right,' said Franklin. 'Dead right. But the subject is still very much alive. And very much so in my Ministry. We happen to be the most highly agriculturalized country in the world. We had to make ourselves so during the war to keep ourselves from starvation. So, in theory, we would be an ideal target for an attack of this kind.' He slowly brought his hands down on the table for emphasis. 'I don't think it would be too much to say, gentlemen, that if such an attack could be launched, and it can only be countered by slaughtering the poultry and animals and burning the crops, we would be a bankrupt country within a matter of months. We would literally be down on our knees, begging for bread!'

'Never thought of that,' said M reflectively, 'but it seems to make sense.'

'Now this,' continued Franklin, holding up the pamphlet, 'is the latest thinking on the subject by our friends in America. It also covers Chemical and Radiological Warfare, but we're not concerned with those — CW, BW and RW they call them. It's a United States Senate paper, Number 58991, dated August 29th, 1960, prepared by "The Subcommittee on Disarmament of the Committee on Foreign Relations". My Ministry goes along with the general findings on BW, with the reservation that America is a vast country and we are a very small and tightly packed one. BW would hit us a thousand times harder than it would hit the States. May I read you a few extracts?'

M positively loathed the problems of other Ministries. In the end, on the Intelligence side, they all ended up on his plate. Bond, amused, watched him summon an expression of polite interest. 'Go ahead, Mr Franklin.'

22

SOMETHING CALLED 'BW'

FRANKLIN BEGAN READING in an even, expository tone of voice, frequently stopping to explain a point or when he skipped irrelevant passages.

'This section,' he said, 'is headed "Biological Warfare Weapons and Defense". This is how it goes on:

' "Biological Warfare,' he read, 'is often referred to as bacteriological, bacterial, or germ warfare but it is preferred over those terms because it includes all micro-organisms, insects and other pests, and toxic products of plant and animal life. The Army lists five groups of BW agents, including certain chemical compounds used to inhibit or destroy plant growth:

> Micro-organisms (bacteria, viruses, rickettsiae, fungi, protozoa.)
> Toxins (microbial, animal, plant.)
> Vectors of disease (arthropods (insects and acarids), birds and animals.)
> Pests (of animals and crops.)
> Chemical anti-crop compounds (plant-growth inhibitors, herbicides, defoliants.)

' "Biological Warfare agents, like Chemical Warfare agents, vary in lethality, making it possible to select an agent best suited to accomplish the objective desired, whether it be temporary incapacity with little after-effects or serious illness and many deaths. There are some important differences between BW and CW other than their scientific classifications. BW agents have an incubation period of days, sometimes weeks —' (Franklin looked up. 'See what I mean about Olympia?') — 'which produces a lag in their action while CW weapons usually bring reactions within a few seconds to a few hours. CW agents are easier to detect than BW agents, and identification of the latter could often be too late to permit effective countermeasures.' (Franklin again looked significantly at his audience) ' . . . BW agents theoretically are more dangerous, weight for weight, than CW agents, though this advantage may be cancelled because of loss of virulence by BW agents under exposure." '

Franklin paused. His finger went down the page. 'Then it goes on to talk about anti-personnel BW agents like anthrax, typhus, smallpox, botulism and so on. Yes —' his finger stopped — 'here we are. "Anti-animal BW agents which might be used to incapacitate or destroy domestic animals are

> Bacteria: Anthrax, three closely related species of brucella, and glanders.
> Viruses: Foot-and-mouth disease, rinderpest, Rift Valley fever, vesicular stomatitis, vesicular exanthema, hog cholera, African swine fever, fowl plague, Newcastle disease, and equine encephalomyelitis." '

Franklin looked up apologetically. 'Sorry about all this jawbreaking stuff, but there's not much more of it. Then it goes on to "Anti-crop BW agents", which they say would be used as economic weapons, as I personally think is the case with the Blofeld scheme, and they mention a whole list including potato blight, cereal stem disease, crown rust of oats, curly top disease of sugar beets, block rot of crucifers and potato ring rot, and insects such as the Colorado beetle and something called "the Giant African Land-snail", which I somehow don't think we need worry about. Then they talk about "chemical anti-crop agents", but I don't think we need worry about those either as they'd have to be sprayed from an aeroplane, though, for what it's worth, they're damned lethal. Now, this is more to the point.' Franklin's finger halted on the page. ' "The nature of BW agents makes them very adaptable for covert or undercover operations. The fact that these agents are so concentrated, cannot be detected by physical senses, and have a delayed casualty effect, would enable an operator quietly to introduce effective amounts into building ventilation systems, food and water supplies, and other places where they would be spread rapidly through contact with a heavily concentrated population." '

Franklin paused. 'And that means us. You see what I mean about livestock shows and so on? After the show, the virus gets carried off all over the country by the exhibits.' He went back to his pamphlet. 'And here it goes on, "A significant factor is that the possible area of effective coverage is generally greater with BW than with CW agents. Tests have been made which show that coverage measured in the thousands of square miles is quite feasible with biological agents." ' Franklin tapped the paper in front of him. 'How about that, gentlemen? We talk about the new poison gases, the nerve gases the Germans invented in the war. We march and counter-march about radiation and the atom bomb. "Thousands of square miles" it says here. A Committee of the United States Senate says it. How many thousands of square miles are there in the United Kingdom and Eire, gentlemen?' The eyes, urgent and holding humour no longer, looked almost scornfully into the faces of these three top officers of the Secret Service. 'I'll tell you. There are only something over one hundred thousand square miles of this little atoll of ours, including the little atoll of all Ireland.' His eyes retained their fire. 'And let me just give you a last quote and then perhaps —' the eyes regained some of their humour — 'you'll realize why I'm getting so steamed up on this Day of Goodwill to all Men. Look here, what it says under "Defensive Measures". It says, "Defense against BW warfare is greatly complicated by the difficulties involved in detection of BW agents, a situation which is almost unique as to these weapons." ' (Franklin looked up and now he smiled. 'Bad English. Perhaps we might improve on "as to".') ' "They cannot be detected by sight, smell, or any other physical sense. So far no means have been devised for their quick detection and identification." '

Franklin threw the pamphlet on to the desk. Suddenly he gave a big, embracing smile. He reached for his little polished pipe and began filling it. 'All right, gentlemen. The prosecution rests.'

Franklin had had his day, a Christmas he would never forget.

M said, 'Thank you, Mr Franklin. Am I right in thinking that you conclude that this man Blofeld is mounting Biological Warfare against this country?'

'Yes.' Franklin was definite. 'I am.'

'And how do you work that out? It seems to me he's doing

exactly the opposite — or rather it would if I didn't know something about the man. Anyway, what are your deductions?'

Franklin reached over and pointed to the red cross he had made over East Anglia. 'That was my first clue. The girl, Polly Tasker, who left this Gloria place over a month ago, came from somewhere round here where you'll see from the symbols that there's the greatest concentration of turkey farmers. She suffered from an allergy against turkeys. She came back inspired to improve the breed. Within a week of her return, we have the biggest outbreak of fowl pest affecting turkeys in the history of England.'

Leathers suddenly slapped his thigh. 'By God, I think you've got it, Franklin! Go on!'

'Now —' Franklin turned to Bond — 'when this officer took a look into the laboratory up there he saw rack upon rack of test-tubes containing what he describes as "a cloudy liquid". How would it be if those were viruses, fowl pest, anthrax, God knows what all? The report mentions that the laboratory was lit with a dim red light. That would be correct. Virus cultures suffer from exposure to bright light. And how would it be if before this Polly girl left she was given an aerosol spray of the right stuff and told that this was some kind of turkey elixir — a tonic to make them grow fatter and healthier. Remember that stuff about "improving the breed" in the hypnosis talk? And suppose she was told to go to Olympia for the show, perhaps even take a job for the meeting as a cleaner or something, and just casually spray this aerosol here and there among the prize birds. It wouldn't be bigger than one of those shaving-soap bombs. That'd be quite enough. She'd been told to keep it secret, that it was patent stuff. Perhaps even that she'd be given shares in the company if the tonic proved the success this man Blofeld claimed it would. It'd be quite easy to do. She'd just wander round the cages — perhaps she was even given a special purse to carry the thing in — lean up against the wire and psst! the job would be done. Easy as falling off a log. All right, if you'll go along with me so far, she was probably told to do the job on one of the last two days of the show, so that the effects wouldn't be seen too soon. Then, at the end of the show, all the prize birds are dispersed back to their owners all over England. And that's that! And —' he paused — 'mark you, that *was* that.

Three million birds dead and still dying all over the place, and a great chunk of foreign currency coughed up by the Treasury to replace them.'

Leathers, his face red with excitement, butted in. He swept his hand over the map. 'And the other girls! All from the danger spots. All from the areas of greatest concentration. Local shows taking place all the time — cattle, poultry, even potatoes — Colorado beetle for that crop, I suppose, swine fever for the pigs. Golly!' There was reverence in Leathers's voice. 'And it's so damned simple! All you'd need would be to keep the viruses at the right temperature for a while. They'd be instructed in that, the little darlings. And all the time they'd be sure they were being saints! Marvellous. I really must hand it to the man.'

M's face was thunderous with the fury of his indecision. He turned to Bond. He barked, 'What do you think?'

'I'm afraid it fits, sir. The whole way along the line. We know the man. It fits him too. Right up his street. And it doesn't even matter who's paying him. He can pay himself, make a fortune. All he has to do is go a bear of sterling or Gilt-Edged. If Mr Franklin's right, and that Senate paper's pretty solid backing for him, our currency'll literally go through the floor — and the country with it.'

M got to his feet. He said, 'All right, gentlemen. Mr Franklin, will you tell your Minister what you've heard? It'll be up to him to tell the P.M. and the Cabinet as he thinks fit. I'll get on with the preventive measures, first of all through Sir Ronald Vallance of the C.I.D. We must pick up this Polly woman and get the others as they come into the country. They'll be gently treated. It's not their fault. Then we'll have to think what to do with Mister Blofeld.' He turned to Bond. 'Stay behind, would you?'

Goodbyes were said and M rang for Hammond to see the other two out. He then rang again. 'Tea, please, Hammond.' He turned to Bond. 'Or rather have a whisky and soda?'

'Whisky, please, sir,' said Bond with infinite relief.

'Rot-gut,' commented M. He walked over to the window and looked out at the darkness and rain.

Bond drew Franklin's map towards him and studied it. He reflected that he was learning quite a lot on this case — about other people's business, other people's secrets, from the innards of the College of Arms to the innards of Ag. and Fish. Odd how this gigantic, many-branched tree had grown from one tiny seed in September — a girl calling banco in a casino and not having the money to pay. And what about Bond's letter of resignation? That looked pretty silly now. He was up to his ears, as deeply as ever in his life before, in his old profession. And now a big mopping-up job would have to be done. And he would have to do it, or at any rate lead it, organize it. And Bond knew exactly what he was going to put to M when the tea and whisky came. Only *he* could do the cleaning up. It was written in his stars!

Hammond came in with the tray and withdrew. M came back to his desk, gruffly told Bond to pour himself a whisky, and himself took a vast cup, as big as a baby's chamber-pot, of black tea without sugar or milk, and put it in front of him.

At length he said moodily, 'This is a dirty business, James. But I'm afraid it makes sense. Better do something about it, I suppose.' He reached for the red telephone with scrambler attachment that stood beside the black one on his desk and picked up the receiver. It was a direct line to that very private switchboard in Whitehall to which perhaps fifty people in all Britain have access. 'Put me on to Sir Ronald Vallance, would you? Home number, I suppose.' He reached out and took a deep gulp at his cup of tea and put the cup back on its saucer. Then, 'That you, Vallance? M here. Sorry to disturb your afternoon nap.' There was an audible explosion at the other end of the line! M smiled. 'Reading a report on teenage prostitution? I'm ashamed of you. On Christmas Day too. Well, scramble, would you?' M pressed down the large black button on the side of the cradle. 'Right? Now I'm afraid this is top priority. Remember Blofeld and the Thunderball case? Well, he's up to his tricks again. Too long to explain now. You'll get my side of the report in the morning. And Ag. and Fish. are mixed up in it. Yes, of all people. Man called Franklin is your contact. One of their top pest-control men. Only him and his Minister. So would your chaps report to him, copy to me? I'm only dealing with the foreign side. Your friend 007's got the ball. Yes, same chap. He can fill you in with any extra detail you may need on the foreign angles. Now, the point is this. Even though it's Christmas and all that, could your chaps try at once and lay their hands on a certain girl, Polly Tasker, aged about 25, who lives in East Anglia? Yes, I know it's a hell of a big area, but she'll probably come from a respectable lower-middle-class family connected with turkey farming. Certainly find the family in the telephone book. Can't give you any description, but she's just been spending several weeks in Switzerland. Got back the last week in November. Don't be ridiculous! Of course you can manage it. And when you find her, take her into custody for importing fowl pest into the country. Yes, that's right.' M spelt it out. 'The stuff that's been killing all our turkeys.' M muttered 'Thank God!' away from the receiver. 'No, I didn't say anything. Now, be kind to the girl. She didn't know what she was doing. And tell the parents it'll be all right. If you need a formal charge, you'll have to get one out of Franklin. Then tell Franklin when you've got her and he'll come down and ask her one or two simple questions. When he's got the answers, you can let her go. Right? But we've *got* to find that girl. You'll see why all right when you've read the report. Now then, next assignment. There are ten girls of much the same type as this Polly Tasker who'll probably be flying from Zürich to England and Eire any day from tomorrow on. Each one has got to be held by the Customs at the port or airport of entry. 007 has a list of their names and fairly good descriptions. My people in Zürich may or may not be able to give us warning of their arrival. Is that all right? Yes, 007 will bring the list to Scotland Yard this evening. No, I can't tell you what it's all about. Too long a story. But have you ever heard of Biological Warfare? That's right. Anthrax and so on. Well, this is it. Yes. Blofeld again. I know. That's what I'm just going to talk to 007 about. Well now, Vallance, have you got all that? Fine.' M listened. He smiled grimly. 'And a Happy Christmas to *you*.'

He put the receiver back and the scrambler button automatically clicked to OFF. He looked across at Bond. He said, with a hint of weariness, 'Well, that's taken care of this end. Vallance said it was about time we had this fellow Blofeld in the bag. I agree. And that's *our* job. And I don't for a moment think we're going to get any help from the Swiss. Even if we were to, they'd trample all over the case with their big boots for weeks before we saw any action. By that time the man would be in Peking or somewhere, cooking up something else.' M looked straight at Bond. 'Any ideas?'

It had come, as Bond knew it would. He took a deep pull at his whisky and put the glass carefully down. He began talking, urgently, persuasively. As he expounded his plan, M's face sank deeper and deeper in gloom, and, when Bond concluded with 'And that's the only way I can see, sir. All I need is two weeks' leave of absence. I could put in a letter of resignation if it would help,' M turned in his chair and gazed deep into the dying flames of the log fire.

Bond sat quietly, waiting for the verdict. He hoped it would be yes, but he also hoped it would be no. That damned mountain! He never wanted to see the bloody thing again!

M turned back. The grey eyes were fierce. 'All right, 007. Go ahead. I can't go to the P.M. about it. He'd refuse. But for God's sake bring it off. I don't mind being sacked, but we don't want to get the Government mixed up in another U.2 fiasco. Right?'

'I understand, sir. And I can have the two weeks' leave?'

'Yes.'

23

GAULOISES AND GARLIC

WITH THE WALTHER PPK in its leather holster warm against his stomach and his own name in his passport, James Bond looked out of the window at the English Channel sliding away beneath the belly of the Caravelle and felt more like his old, his pre-Sir-Hilary-Bray, self.

He glanced at the new Rolex on his wrist — the shops were still shut and he had had to blarney it out of Q Branch — and guessed they would be on time, 6 p.m. at Marseilles. It had been the hell of a rush to get off. He had worked until late in the night at H.Q. and all that morning, setting up the Identicast of Blofeld, checking details with Ronnie Vallance, fixing up the private, the Munich side of his life, chattering on the teleprinter to Station Z, even remembering to tell Mary Goodnight to get on to Sable Basilisk after the holiday and ask him to please do some kind of a job on the surnames of the ten girls and please to have the family tree of Ruby Windsor embellished with gold capitals.

At midnight he had called Tracy in Munich and heard her darling, excited voice. 'I've got the toothbrush, James,' she had said, 'and a pile of books. Tomorrow I'm going to go up the Zugspitze and sit in the sun so as to look pretty for you. Guess what I had for dinner tonight in my room! Krebsschwänze mit Dilltunke. That's crayfish tails with rice and a cream and dill sauce. And Rehrücken mit Sahne. That's saddle of roebuck with a smitane sauce. I bet it was better than what you had.'

'I had two ham sandwiches with stacks of mustard and half a pint of Harper's Bourbon on the rocks. The Bourbon was better than the ham. Now listen, Tracy, and stop blowing down the telephone.'

'I was only sighing with love.'

'Well, you must have got a Force Five sigh. Now listen. I'm posting my birth certificate to you tomorrow with a covering letter to the British Consul saying I want to get married to you as soon as possible. Look, you're going up to Force Ten! For God's sake pay attention. It'll take a few days, I'm afraid. They have to post the banns or something. He'll tell you all about it. Now, you must quickly get your birth certificate and give it to him, too. Oh, you have, have you?' Bond laughed. 'So much the better. Then we're all set. I've got three days or so of work to do and I'm going down to see your father tomorrow and ask for your hand, both of them, and the feet and all the rest, in marriage. No, you're to stay where you are. This is men's talk. Will he be awake? I'm going to ring him up now. Good. Well, now you go off to sleep or you'll be too tired to say "Yes" when the time comes.'

They had not wanted to let go of each other's voices, but finally the last good-night, the last kiss, had been exchanged, and Bond called the Marseilles number of Appareils Électriques Draco, and Marc-Ange's voice, almost as excited as Tracy's, was on the line. Bond dampened down the raptures about the 'fiançailles' and said, 'Now listen, Marc-Ange. I want you to give me a wedding present.'

'Anything, my dear James. Anything I possess.' He laughed. 'And perhaps certain things of which I could take possession. What is it you would like?'

'I'll tell you tomorrow evening. I'm booked on the afternoon Air France to Marseilles. Will you have someone meet me? And it's business, I'm afraid. So could you have your other directors present for a little meeting? We shall need all our brains. It is about our sales organization in Switzerland. Something drastic needs to be done about it.'

'Aha!' There was full understanding in the voice. 'Yes, it is indeed a bad spot on our sales map. I will certainly have my colleagues available. And I assure you, my dear James, that anything that can be done will be done. And of course you will be met. I shall perhaps not be there in person — it is very cold out these winter evenings. But I shall see that you are properly looked after. Good night, my dear fellow. Good night.'

The line had gone dead. The old fox! Had he thought Bond might commit an indiscretion, or had he got fitted to his telephone a 'bug-meter', the delicate instrument that measures the resonance on the line and warns of listening-in?

The winter sun spread a last orange glow over the thick overcast 10,000 feet below the softly whistling plane and switched itself off for the night.

Bond dozed, reflecting that he must somehow, and pretty soon, find a way of catching up on his sleep.

There was a stage-type Marseilles taxi-driver to meet Bond — the archetype of all Mariuses, with the face of a pirate and the razor-sharp badinage of the lower French music-halls. He was apparently known and enjoyed by everyone at the airport, and Bond was whisked through the formalities in a barrage of wise-cracks about 'le milord anglais', which made Marius, for his name turned out in fact to be Marius, the centre of attraction and Bond merely his butt, the dim-witted English tourist. But, once in the taxi, Marius made curt, friendly apologies over his shoulder. 'I ask your pardon for my bad manners.' His French had suddenly purified itself of all patois. It also smelt like acetylene gas. 'I was told to extract you from the airport with the least possible limelight directed upon you. I know all those "flics" and douaniers. They all know me. If I had not been myself, the cabdriver they know as Marius, if I had shown deference, eyes, inquisitive eyes, would have been upon you, mon Commandant. I did what I thought best. You forgive me?'

'Of course I do, Marius. But you shouldn't have been so funny. You nearly made me laugh. That would have been fatal.'

'You understand our talk here?'

'Enough of it.'

'So!' There was a pause. Then Marius said, 'Alas, since Waterloo, one can never underestimate the English.'

Bond said, seriously, 'The same date applied to the French. It was a near thing.' This was getting too gallant. Bond said, 'Now tell me, is the bouillabaisse chez Guido always as good?'

'It is passable,' said Marius. 'But this is a dish that is dead, gone. There is no more true bouillabaisse, because there is no more fish in the Mediterranean. For the bouillabaisse, you must have the rascasse, the tender flesh of the scorpion fish. Today they just use hunks of morue. The saffron and the garlic, they are always the same. But you could eat pieces of a woman soaked in those and it would be good. Go to any of the little places down by the harbour. Eat the plat du jour and drink the vin du Cassis that they give you. It will fill your stomach as well as it fills the fishermen's. The toilette will be filthy. What does that matter? You are a man. You can walk up the Canebière and do it at the Noailles for nothing after lunch.'

They were now weaving expertly through the traffic down the famous Canebière and Marius needed all his breath to insult the other drivers. Bond could smell the sea. The accordions were playing in the cafés. He remembered old times in this most criminal and tough of all French towns. He reflected that it was rather fun, this time, being on the side of the devil.

At the bottom of the Canebière, where it crosses the Rue de Rome, Marius turned right and then left into the Rue St Ferréol, only a long stone's throw from the Quai des Belges and the Vieux Port. The lights from the harbour's entrance briefly winked at them and then the taxi drew up at a hideous, but very new apartment house with a broad vitrine on the ground floor, which announced in furious neon 'Appareils Électriques Draco'. The well-lit interior of the store contained what you would expect — television sets, radios, gramophones, electric irons, fans and so forth. Marius very quickly carried Bond's suitcase across the pavement and through the swing doors beside the vitrine. The close-carpeted hallway was more luxurious than Bond had expected. A man came out of the porter's lodge beside the lift and wordlessly took the suitcase. Marius turned to Bond, gave him a smile and a wink and a bone-crushing handshake, said curtly, 'A la prochaine,' and hurried out. The porter stood beside the open door of the lift. Bond noticed the bulge under his right arm and, out of curiosity, brushed against the man as he entered the lift. Yes, and something big too, a real stopper. The man gave Bond a bored look, as much as to say, 'Clever? Eh?' and pressed the top button. The porter's twin, or very nearly his twin — dark, chunky, brown-eyed, fit — was waiting at the top floor. He took Bond's suitcase and led the way down a corridor, close-carpeted and with wall brackets in good taste. He opened a door. It was an extremely comfortable bedroom with a bathroom leading off. Bond imagined that the big picture window, now curtained, would have a superb view of the harbour. The man put down his suitcase and said, 'Monsieur Draco est immédiatement à votre disposition.'

Bond thought it time to make some show of independence. He said firmly, 'Un moment, je vous en prie,' and went into the bathroom and cleaned himself up — amused to notice that the soap was that most English of soaps, Pears Transparent, and that there was a bottle of Mr Trumper's 'Eucris' beside the very masculine brush and comb by Kent. Marc-Ange was indeed making his English guest feel at home!

Bond took his time, then went out and followed the man to the end door. The man opened it without knocking and closed it behind Bond. Marc-Ange, his creased walnut face split by his great golden-toothed smile, got up from his desk (Bond was getting tired of desks!), trotted across the broad room, threw his arms round Bond's neck and kissed him squarely on both cheeks. Bond suppressed his recoil and gave a reassuring pat to Marc-Ange's broad back. Marc-Ange stood away and laughed. 'All right! I swear never to do it again. It is once and for ever. Yes? But it had to come out — from the Latin temperament, isn't it? You forgive me? Good. Then come and take a drink —' he waved at a loaded sideboard — 'and sit down and tell me what I can do for you. I swear not to talk about Teresa until you have finished with your business. But tell me —' the brown eyes pleaded — 'it is all right between you? You have not changed your mind?'

Bond smiled. 'Of course not, Marc-Ange. And everything is arranged. We will be married within the week. At the Consulate in Munich. I have two weeks' leave. I thought we might spend the honeymoon in Kitzbühel. I love that place. So does she. You will come to the wedding?'

'Come to the wedding!' Marc-Ange exploded. 'You will have a time keeping me away from Kitzbühel. Now then —' he waved at the sideboard — 'take your drink while I compose myself. I must stop being happy and be clever instead. My two best men, my organizers if you like, are waiting. I wanted to have you for a moment to myself.'

Bond poured himself a stiff Jack Daniel's sourmash Bourbon on the rocks and added some water. He walked over to the desk and took the right-hand of the three chairs that had been arranged in a semicircle facing the 'Capu'. 'I wanted that too, Marc-Ange. Because there are some things I must tell you which affect my country. I have been granted leave to tell them to you, but they must remain, as you put it, behind the Herkos Odonton — behind the hedge of your teeth. Is that all right?'

Marc-Ange lifted his right hand and crossed his heart, slowly, deliberately, with his forefinger. His face was now deadly serious, almost cruelly implacable. He leaned forward and rested his forearms on the desk. 'Continue.'

Bond told him the whole story, not even omitting his passage with Ruby. He had developed much love, and total respect, for this man. He couldn't say why. It was partly animal magnetism and partly that Marc-Ange had so opened his heart to Bond, so completely trusted him with his own innermost secrets.

Marc-Ange's face remained impassive throughout. Only his quick, animal eyes flickered continually across Bond's face. When Bond had finished, Marc-Ange sat back. He reached for a blue packet of Gauloises, fixed one in the corner of his mouth and talked through the blue clouds of smoke that puffed continuously out through his lips, as if somewhere inside him there was a small steam-engine. 'Yes, it is indeed a dirty business. It must be finished with, destroyed, and the man too. My dear James —' the voice was sombre — 'I am a criminal, a great criminal. I run houses, chains of prostitutes, I smuggle, I sell protection, whenever I can, I steal from the very rich. I break many laws and I have often had to kill in the process. Perhaps one day, perhaps very soon, I shall reform. But it is difficult to step down from being Capu of the Union. Without the protection of my men, my life would not be worth much. However, we shall see. But this Blofeld, he is too bad, too disgusting. You have come to ask the Union to make war on him, to destroy him. You need not answer. I know it is so. This is something that cannot be done officially. Your Chief is correct. You would get nowhere with the Swiss. You wish me and my men to do the job.' He smiled suddenly. 'That is the wedding present you talked of. Yes?'

'That's right, Marc-Ange. But I'll do my bit. I'll be there too. I want this man for myself.'

Marc-Ange looked at him thoughtfully. 'That I do not like. And you know why I do not like it.' He said mildly, 'You are a bloody fool, James. You are already lucky to be alive.' He shrugged. 'But I am wasting my breath. You started on a long road after this man. And you want to come to the end of it. Is that right?'

'That's right. I don't want someone else to shoot my fox.'

'O.K., O.K. We bring in the others, yes? They will not need to know the reason why. My orders are my orders. But we all need to know *how* we are to bring this about. I have some ideas. I think it can be done and swiftly done. But it must also be well done, cleanly done. There must be no untidiness about this thing.'

Marc-Ange picked up his telephone and spoke into it. A minute later the door opened and two men came in and, with hardly a glance at Bond, took the other two chairs.

Marc-Ange nodded at the one next to Bond, a great ox of a man with the splayed ears and broken nose of a boxer or wrestler. 'This is Ché-Ché — Ché-Ché le Persuadeur. And —' Marc-Ange smiled grimly — 'he is very adept at persuading.'

Bond got a glimpse of two hard yellow-brown eyes that looked at him quickly, reluctantly, and then went back to the Capu. 'Plaisir.'

'And this is Toussaint, otherwise known as "Le Pouff". He is our expert with le plastique. We shall need plenty of plastique.'

'We shall indeed,' said Bond, 'with pretty quick time-pencils.'

Toussaint leaned forward to show himself. He was thin and grey-skinned, with an almost fine Phoenician profile pitted with smallpox. Bond guessed that he was on heroin, but not as a mainliner. He gave Bond a brief, conspiratorial smile. 'Plaisir.' He sat back.

'And this —' Marc-Ange gestured at Bond — 'is my friend. My absolute friend. He is simply "Le Commandant". And now to business.' He had been speaking in French, but he now broke into rapid Corsican which, apart from a few Italian and French roots, was incomprehensible to Bond. At one period he drew a large-scale map of Switzerland out of a drawer of his desk, spread it out, searched with his finger and pointed to a spot in the centre of the Engadine. The two men craned forward, examined the map carefully and then sat back. Ché-Ché said something which contained the word Strasbourg and Marc-Ange nodded enthusiastically. He turned to Bond and handed him a large sheet of paper and a pencil. 'Be a good chap and get to work on this, would you? A map of the Gloria buildings, with approximate sizes and distances from each other. Later we will do a complete maquette in plasticine so that there is no confusion. Every man will have his job to do —' he smiled — 'like the commandos in the war. Yes?'

Bond bent to his task while the others talked. The telephone rang. Marc-Ange picked it up. He jotted down a few words and rang off. He turned to Bond, his eyes momentarily suspicious. It is a telegram for me from London signed Universal. It says, "The birds have assembled in the town and all fly tomorrow." What is this, my friend?'

Bond kicked himself for his forgetfulness. 'I'm sorry, Marc-Ange. I meant to tell you you might get a signal like that. It means that the girls are in Zürich and are flying to England tomorrow. It is very good news. It was important to have them out of the way.'

'Ah, good! Very good indeed! That is fine news. And you were quite right not to have the telegram addressed to you. You are not supposed to be here or to know me at all. It is better so.' He fired some more Corsican at the two men. They nodded their understanding.

After that, the meeting soon broke up. Marc-Ange examined Bond's handiwork and passed it over to Toussaint. The man glanced at the sketch and folded it as if it were a valuable share-certificate. With short bows in Bond's direction, the two men left the room.

Marc-Ange sat back with a sigh of satisfaction. 'It goes well,' he said. 'The whole team will receive good danger money. And they love a good rough fight. And they are pleased that I am coming to lead them.' He laughed slyly. 'They are less certain of you, my dear James. They say you will get in the way. I had to tell them that you could outshoot and outfight the lot of them. When I say something like that, they have to believe me. I have never let them down yet. I hope I am right?'

'Please don't try me,' said Bond. 'I've never taken on a Corsican and I don't want to start now.'

Marc-Ange was delighted. 'You might win with guns. But not in close combat. They are pigs, my men. Great pigs. The greatest. I am taking five of the best. With you and me that is seven. How many did you say there are on the mountain?'

'About eight. And the big one.'

'Ah yes, the big one,' said Marc-Ange reflectively. 'That is one that must not get away.' He got up. 'And now, my friend, I have ordered dinner, a good dinner, to be served us up here. And then we will go to bed stinking of garlic and, perhaps, just a little bit drunk. Yes?'

From his heart Bond said, 'I can't think of anything better.'

24

BLOOD-LIFT

THE NEXT DAY, after lunch, Bond made his way by plane and train to the Hotel Maison Rouge at Strasbourg, his breath bearing him close company like some noisome captive pet.

He was totally exhilarated by his hours with Marc-Ange in Marseilles and by the prospects before him — the job that was to be done and, at the end of it, Tracy.

The morning had been an endless series of conferences round the model of Piz Gloria and its buildings that had been put up in the night. New faces came, received their orders in a torrent of dialect, and disappeared — rough, murderous faces, bandits' faces, but all bearing one common expression, devotion to their Capu. Bond was vastly impressed by the authority and incisiveness of Marc-Ange as he dealt with each problem, each contingency, from the obtaining of a helicopter down to the pensions that would be paid to the families of the dead. Marc-Ange hadn't liked the helicopter business. He had explained to Bond, 'You see, my friend, there is only one source for this machine, the O.A.S., the French secret army of the right wing. It happens that they are under an obligation to me, a heavy one, and that is the way I would have it. I do not like being mixed up in politics. I like the country where I operate to be orderly, peaceful. I do not like revolutions. They make chaos everywhere. Today, I never know when an operation of my own is not going to be interfered with by some damned emergency concerning Algerian terrorists, the rounding up of some nest of these blasted O.A.S. And road blocks! House to house searches! They are the bane of my existence. My men can hardly move without falling over a nest of flics or S.D.T. spies — that, as I'm sure you know, is the latest of the French Secret Services. They are getting as bad as the Russians with their constant changes of initials. It is the Section Défense Territoire. It comes under the Ministry of the Interior and I am finding it most troublesome and difficult to penetrate. Not like the good old Deuxième. It makes life for the peace-loving very difficult. But I naturally have my men in the O.A.S. and I happen to know that the O.A.S. has a military helicopter, stolen from the French Army, hidden away at a château on the Rhine not far from Strasbourg. The château belongs to some crazy fascist count. He is one of those Frenchmen who cannot live without conspiring against something. So now he has put all his money and property behind this General Salan. His château is remote. He poses as an inventor. His farm people are not surprised that there is some kind of flying machine kept in an isolated barn with mechanics to tend it — O.A.S. mechanics, bien entendu. And now, early this morning, I have spoken on my radio to the right man and I have the machine on loan for twenty-four hours with the best pilot in their secret air force. He is already on his way to the place to make his preparations, fuel and so on. But it is unfortunate. Before, these people were in my debt. Now I am in theirs.' He shrugged. 'What matter? I will soon have them under my thumb again. Half the police and Customs officers in France are Corsicans. It is an important laissez-passer for the Union Corse. You understand?'

At the Maison Rouge, a fine room had been booked for Bond. He was greeted with exaggerated courtesy tinged with reserve. Where didn't the freemasonry of the Union operate? Bond, obedient to the traditions of the town, made a simple dinner off the finest foie gras, pink and succulent, and half a bottle of champagne, and retired gratefully to bed. He spent the next morning in his room, changed into his ski-clothes and sent out for a pair of snow-goggles and thin leather gloves, sufficient to give some protection to his hands but close-fitting enough for the handling of his gun. He took the magazine out of his gun, pumped out the single round in the chamber and practised shooting himself in the wardrobe mirror with the gloves on until he was satisfied. Then he reloaded and got the fitting of the stitched pigskin holster comfortable inside the waist-band of his trousers. He had his bill sent up and paid it, and ordered his suitcase to be forwarded on to Tracy at the Vier Jahreszeiten. Then he sent for the day's papers and sat in front of the window, watching the traffic in the street and forgetting what he read.

When, at exactly midday, the telephone rang, he went straight down and out to the grey Peugeot 403 he had been told to expect. The driver was Ché-Ché. He acknowledged Bond's greeting curtly and, in silence, they drove for an hour across the uninteresting countryside, finally turning left off a secondary road into a muddy lane that meandered through thick forest. In due course there was the ill-kept stone wall of a large property and then a vast broken-down iron gateway leading into a park. On the unweeded driveway were the recent tracks of vehicles. They followed these past the dilapidated façade of a once-imposing château, on through the forest to where the trees gave way to fields. On the edge of the trees was a large barn in good repair. They stopped outside and Ché-Ché sounded three shorts on his horn. A small door in the wide double doors of the barn opened and Marc-Ange came out. He greeted Bond cheerfully. 'Come along in, my friend. You are just in time for some good Strasbourg sausage and a passable Riquewihr. Rather thin and bitter. I would have christened it "Château Pis-de-Chat", but it serves to quench the thirst.'

Inside it was almost like a film set. Lights blazed down on the ungainly shape of the Army helicopter and from somewhere came the cough of a small generator. The place seemed to be full of people. Bond recognized the faces of the Union men. The others were, he assumed, the local mechanics. Two men on ladders were busily engaged painting red crosses on white backgrounds on the black-painted fuselage of the machine, and the paint of the recognition letters, FL-BGS, presumably civilian and false, still glittered wetly. Bond was introduced to the pilot, a bright-eyed, fair-haired young man in overalls called Georges. 'You will be sitting beside him,' explained Marc-Ange. 'He is a good navigator, but he doesn't know the last stretch up the valley and he has never heard of Piz Gloria. You had better go over the maps with him after some food. The general route is Basle–Zürich.' He laughed cheerfully. He said in French, 'We are going to have some interesting conversation with the Swiss Air Defences, isn't it, Georges?'

Georges didn't smile. He said briefly, 'I think we can fool them,' and went about his business.

Bond accepted a foot of garlic sausage, a hunk of bread and a bottle of the 'Pis-de-Chat', and sat on an upturned packing-case while Marc-Ange went back to supervising the loading of the 'stores' — Schmeisser sub-machine guns and six-inch-square packets in red oilcloth.

In due course, Marc-Ange lined up his team, including Bond, and carried out a quick inspection of side-arms, which, in the case of the Union men, included well-used flick-knives. The men, as well as Marc-Ange, were clothed in brand-new ski-clothes of grey cloth. Marc-Ange handed to all of them armlets in black cloth bearing the neatly stitched words 'Bundesalpenpolizei'. When Marc-Ange gave Bond his, he commented, 'There is no such force as the "Federal Police of the Alps". But I doubt if our SPECTRE friends will know that. At least the armbands will make an important first impression.'

Marc-Ange looked at his watch. He turned and called out in French, 'Two forty-five. All ready? Then let us roll!'

The farm tractor attached to thc wheel-base of the helicopter started up, the gates of the barn were thrown wide and the great metal insect moved slowly out on to the grassland under the pale winter sun. The tractor was uncoupled and the pilot, followed by Bond, climbed up the little aluminium ladder and then into the raised cockpit and strapped themselves in. The others followed into the ten-seat cabin, the ladder was pulled up and the door banged and locked. On the ground, the mechanics lifted their thumbs and the pilot bent to his controls. He pressed the starter and, after a first indecisive cough, the engine fired healthily and the great blades began to turn.

The pilot glanced back at the whirring tail-rotor. He waited while the needle on the rotor speed-indicator crept up to 200, then he released the wheel-brakes and pulled up slowly on the pitch-lever. The helicopter trembled, unwilling to leave the earth, but then came a slight jerk and they were up and climbing rapidly above the trees. The pilot retracted his wheels above the inflated snow-floats, gave the machine left rudder, pushed forward the joystick, and they were off.

Almost at once they were over the Rhine and Basle lay ahead under a thick canopy of chimney-smoke. They reached two thousand feet and the pilot held it, skirting the town to the north. Now there came a crackle of static over Bond's earphones and Swiss Air Control, in thick Schwyzerdütch, asked them politely to identify themselves. The pilot made no reply and the question was repeated with more urgency. The pilot said in French, 'I don't understand you.' There was a pause, then a French voice again queried them. The pilot said, 'Repeat yourself more clearly.' The voice did so. The pilot said, 'Helicopter of the Red Cross flying blood plasma to Italy.' The radio went dead. Bond could imagine the scene in the control room somewhere down below — the arguing voices, the doubtful faces. Another voice, with more authority to it, spoke in French. 'What is your destination?' 'Wait,' said the pilot. 'I have it here. A moment please.' After minutes he said, 'Swiss Air Control?' 'Yes, yes.' 'FL-BGS reporting. My destination is Ospedale Santa Monica at Bellinzona.' The radio again went dead, only to come to life five minutes later. 'FL-BGS, FL-BGS.' 'Yes,' said the pilot. 'We have no record of your identification symbol. Please explain.' 'Your registration manual must be out of date. The aircraft was commissioned only one month ago.' Another long pause. Now Zürich lay ahead and the silver boomerang of the Zürichersee. Now Zürich Airport came on the air. They must have been listening to Swiss Air Control. 'FL-BGS, FL-BGS.' 'Yes, yes. What is it now?' 'You have infringed the Civil Airlines Channel. Land and report to Flying Control. I repeat. Land and report.' The pilot became indignant. 'What do you mean "land and report"? Have you no comprehension of human suffering? This is a mercy flight carrying blood plasma of a rare category. It is to save the life of an illustrious Italian scientist at Bellinzona. Have you no hearts down there? You tell me to "land and report" when a life is at stake? Do you wish to be responsible for murder?' This Gallic outburst gave them peace until they had passed the Zürichersee. Bond chuckled. He gave a thumbs-up sign to the pilot. But then Federal Air Control at Berne came on the air and a deep, resonant voice said, 'FL-BGS, FL-BGS. Who gave you clearance? I repeat. Who gave you clearance for your flight?' 'You did.' Bond smiled into his mouthpiece. The Big Lie! There was nothing like it. Now the Alps were ahead of them — those blasted Alps, looking beautiful and dangerous in the evening sun. Soon they would be in the shelter of the valleys, off the radar screens. But records had been hastily checked in Berne and the sombre voice came over to them again. The voice must have realized that the long debate would have been heard at every airport and by most pilots flying over Switzerland that evening. It was extremely polite, but firm. 'FL-BGS, we have no record at Federal Air Control of your proposed flight. I regret but you are transgressing Swiss air space. Unless you can give further authority for your flight, kindly return to Zürich and report to Flying Control.'

The helicopter rocked. There was a flash of silver and a Dassault Mirage with Swiss markings flashed by not a hundred yards away, turned, leaving a trail of black vapour from the slow-burning of its fuel at this low altitude, and headed straight back at them, swerving off to port only at the last moment. The helicopter gave another lurch. The pilot spoke angrily into his mouthpiece. 'Federal Air Control. This is FL-BGS. For further information contact International Red Cross at Geneva. I am just a pilot. I am not a "rond de cuir", a chairborne flyer. If you have lost the papers, that is not my fault. I repeat, check with Geneva. And, in the meantime, kindly call off the whole of the Swiss Air Force which is at present trying to make my passengers air-sick.' The voice came back, but now more faintly, because of the mountains. 'Who are your passengers?' The pilot played his trump card. 'Representatives of the world's press. They have been listening to all this nonsense coming from the home of the famous International Red Cross. I wish you happy reading of your newspapers at breakfast time tomorrow, gentlemen. And now, a little peace, yes? And please record in your log-books that I am not, repeat, not, the Soviet Air Force invading Switzerland.'

There was silence. The Dassault Mirage had disappeared. They were climbing up the valley and were already past Davos. The gold-tipped needles of the glittering mountains seemed to be closing in on them from right and left. Ahead were the great peaks. Bond looked at his watch. Barely another ten minutes to go.

He turned and glanced down the hatch. The faces of Marc-Ange and of the others looked up at him, tense and livid under the setting sun that poured in through the windows, their eyes glinting redly.

Bond held up his thumb encouragingly. He spread out his ten fingers in their thin leather gloves.

Marc-Ange nodded. There was a shifting of the bodies in their seats. Bond turned back and gazed ahead, looking for the soaring peak that he loathed and feared.

25

HELL'S DELIGHT, ETC.

YES! THERE WAS the bloody place! Now only the peak was golden. The plateau and the buildings were in indigo shadow, soon to be lit by the full moon.

Bond pointed. The helicopter wasn't liking the altitude. At 10,000 feet its rotors were finding it hard to get a grip of the thin air and the pilot was struggling to keep it at maximum revs. As he turned to port, in towards the face of the mountain, his radio crackled sharply and a harsh voice said, in German and then in French, 'Landing forbidden. This is private property. I repeat, landing forbidden!' The pilot reached up to the cockpit roof and switched off the radio. He had studied his landing-point on the plateau on the mock-up. He got to it, hovered and gently came down. The helicopter bounced once on its rubber floats and settled. Already there was a group of men waiting for them. Eight men. Bond recognized some of them. They all had their hands in their pockets or in their wind-jackets. The engine coughed to a stop and the rotors swung round briefly in neutral and halted. Bond heard the bang of the door being opened behind him and the rattle of the men piling down the ladder. The two groups lined up facing each other. Marc-Ange said, with authority, 'This is the Federal Police Alpine Patrol. There was trouble up here on Christmas Eve. We have come to investigate.'

Fritz, the 'head waiter', said angrily, 'The local police have already been here. They have made their report. All is in order. Please leave at once. What is the Federal Police Alpine Patrol? I have never heard of it.'

The pilot nudged Bond and pointed over to the left, to the building that housed the Count and the laboratories. A man, clumsy in bob-sleigh helmet and padding, was running down the path towards the cable station. He would be out of sight of the men on the ground. Bond said 'Blast!' and scrambled out of his seat and into the cabin. He leaned out of the door and shouted, 'The Big One. He's getting away!'

As Bond jumped, one of the SPECTRE men shouted, 'Der Engländer. Der Spion!' And then, as Bond started running away to the right, weaving and dodging, all hell broke loose. There came the boom of heavy automatics as the SPECTRE team got off their first rounds, and bullets, tracer, flashed past Bond with the noise of humming-birds' wings. Then came the answering roar of the Schmeissers and Bond was left alone.

Now he was round the corner of the club, and, a hundred yards down the slope, the man in the crash helmet had torn open the door of the 'garage' for the bob-sleighs in the foundations of the cable station. He emerged carrying a one-man skeleton bob. Holding it in front of him as a shield, he fired a burst from a heavy automatic at Bond and again the humming-birds whirred past. Bond knelt and, steadying his gun with two hands, fired three rounds with his Walther, but the man was now running the few yards to the glistening ice-mouth of the Gloria Express bob-run. Bond got a glimpse of the profile under the moon. Yes, it was Blofeld all right! Even as Bond ran on down the slope, the man had flung himself down on his skeleton and had disappeared as if swallowed up by the glistening landscape. Bond got to the 'garage'. Damn, they were all six-men or two-men models! No, there was one skeleton at the back! Bond hauled it out. No time to see if the runners were straight, the steering-arm shifting easily! He ran to the start and hurled himself under the protecting chain in a mad forward dive that landed him half on and half off his skeleton. He straightened himself and shifted his body well forward on the flimsy little aluminium platform and gripped the steering-arm, keeping his elbows well in to his sides. He was already going like hell down the dark-blue gutter! He tried braking with the toes of both his boots. Damned little difference! What came first on the blasted run? There was this lateral straight across the shoulder of the mountain, then a big banked curve. He was into it now! Bond kept his right shoulder down and inched right on the steering-arm. Even so, he went perilously near the top edge of the bank before he dived down into the dark gully again. What came next on that metal map? Why in hell hadn't he studied it more carefully? He got his answer! It looked like a straight, but the shadows camouflaged a sharp dip. Bond left the ground and flew. The crash of his landing almost knocked the wind out of his body. He frantically dug his toes into the ice, managed to get down from perhaps fifty m.p.h. to forty. Well, well! So that was 'Dead Man's Leap'. What in hell was the next bit of murder? 'Whizz-Bang Straight'! And by God it was! — 200 yards when he must have been doing around seventy. He remembered that on the finishing straight of the Cresta the stars got up to over eighty. No doubt something like that was still to come! But now, flashing towards him, in silver and black, came an S-bend — 'Battling S'. The toes of Bond's boots slid maddeningly on the black ice. Under his nose he could see the parallel tracks of Blofeld's runners and, between them, the grooves of his toe-spikes. The old fox! As soon as he heard the helicopter, he must have got himself fixed for his only escape route. But at this speed Bond must surely be catching up with him! For God's sake look out! Here comes the S! There was nothing he could do about it. He swayed his body as best he could, felt the searing crash of one elbow against one wall, was hurled across into the opposite one and was then spewed out into the straight again. God Almighty, but it hurt! He could feel the cold wind on both elbows. The cloth had gone! Then so had the skin! Bond clenched his teeth. And he was only half-way down, if that! But then, ahead, flashing through a patch of moonlight, was the other body, Blofeld! Bond took a chance, heaved himself up on one hand and reached down for his gun. The wind tried to tear him off the bob, but he had the gun. He opened his mouth wide and gripped the gun between his teeth, flexed the ice-caked leather on his right hand. Then he got the gun in his right hand, lifted his toes off the ice and went like hell. But now the man had disappeared into the shadows and a giant bank reared up ahead. This would be 'Hell's Delight'! Oh well, if he could make this, there would be another straight and he could begin shooting. Bond dug his toes in, got a glimpse of an ice-wall ahead and to the left, and in a flash was climbing it, straight up! God, in a split second he would be over the edge! Bond hammered in his right boot and lurched his body to the right, tearing at the steering-arm. Reluctantly the sliver of aluminium answered and Bond, inches from the top of the wall, found himself swooping down into blackness and then out again on to a moonlit straight. Only fifty yards ahead was the flying figure, with chips of ice fountaining up from the braking spikes on his boots. Bond held his breath and got off two shots. He thought they were good ones, but now the man had gone into shadow again. But Bond was gaining, gaining. His lips drew back from his teeth in an almost animal snarl. You bastard! You're a dead duck! You can't stop or fire back. I'm coming after you like lightning! Soon I shall only be ten, five yards behind you. Then you'll have had it!

But the shadows concealed another hazard, long transverse waves in the ice — 'The Boneshaker'! Bond crashed from one to the next, felt his boots being almost torn from his feet as he tried to brake, nearly lost his gun, felt his stomach flatten against his spine with each shattering impact, felt his rib cage almost cracking. But then it was over and Bond sucked in air through his clenched teeth. Now for a length of straight! But what was that ahead on the track? It was something black, something the size of a big lemon that was bouncing along gaily like a child's rubber ball. Had Blofeld, now only about thirty yards ahead, dropped something, a bit of his equipment? *Had he?* The realization came to Bond in a surge of terror that almost made him vomit. He ground his toes into the ice. No effect! He was gaining on the gaily bouncing thing. Flashing down on it. On the grenade!

Bond, sick in the stomach, lifted his toes and let himself go. What setting had Blofeld put on it? How long had he held it with the pin out? The only hope was to pray to God and race it!

The next thing Bond knew was that the whole track had blown up in his face and that he and his skeleton bob were flying through the air. He landed in soft snow, with the skeleton on top of him, and passed out like a light.

Later, Bond was to estimate that he lay there only a matter of minutes. It was a tremendous explosion from the mountain above him that brought him staggering to his feet, up to his belly in snow. He looked vaguely up to where it had come from. It must have been the club building going up, because now there was the glare of flames and a tower of smoke that rose towards the moon. There came the echoing crack of another explosion and Blofeld's block disintegrated, great chunks of it crashing down the mountain side, turning themselves into giant snowballs that bounded off down towards the tree-line. By God, they'll start another avalanche! thought Bond vaguely. Then he realized that it didn't matter this time, he was away to the right, almost underneath the cable railway. And now the station went up and Bond stared fascinated as the great wires, their tension released, came hissing and snaking down the mountain towards him. There was nothing he could do about it but stand and watch. If they cut him down, they cut him down. But they lashed past in the snow, wrapped themselves briefly round the tall pylon above the tree-line, tore it away in a metallic crackling, and disappeared over the edge of the shoulder.

Bond laughed weakly with pleasure and began feeling himself for damage. His torn elbows he already knew about, but his forehead hurt like hell. He felt it gingerly, then scooped up a handful of snow and held it against the wound. The blood showed black in the moonlight. He ached all over, but there didn't seem to be anything broken. He bent dazedly to the twisted remains of the skeleton. The steering-arm had gone, had probably saved his head, and both runners were bent. There were a lot of rattles from the rivets, but perhaps the damned thing would run. It had bloody well got to! There was no other way for Bond to get down the mountain! His gun? Gone to hell, of course. Wearily Bond heaved himself over the wall of the track and slid carefully down, clutching the remains of his skeleton. As soon as he got to the bottom of the gutter, everything began to slip downwards, but he managed to haul himself on to the bob and get shakily going. In fact, the bent runners were a blessing and the bob scraped slowly down, leaving great furrows in the ice. There were more turns, more hazards, but, at a bare ten miles an hour, they were child's play and soon Bond was through the tree-line and into 'Paradise Alley', the finishing straight, where he slowly came to a halt. He left the skeleton where it stopped and scrambled over the low ice-wall. Here the snow was beaten hard by spectators' feet and he stumbled slowly along, nursing his aches and occasionally dabbing at his head with handfuls of snow. What would he find at the bottom, by the cable station? If it was Blofeld, Bond would be a dead duck! But there were no lights on in the station into which the cables now trailed limply along the ground. By

God, that had been an expensive bang! But what of Marc-Ange and his merry men, and the helicopter?

As if to answer him, he heard the clatter of its engine high up in the mountains and in a moment the ungainly black shape crossed the moon and disappeared down the valley. Bond smiled to himself. They were going to have a tough time arguing themselves across Swiss air space this time! But Marc-Ange had thought out an alternative route over Germany. That would also not be fun. They would have to argue the toss with NATO! Well, if a Marseillais couldn't blarney his way across two hundred miles, nobody could!

And now, up the road from Samaden that Bond knew so well, came the iron hee-haw warning of the local fire-engine. The blinking red light on its cabin roof was perhaps a mile away. Bond, carefully approaching the corner of the darkened cable station, prepared his story. He crept up to the wall of the building and looked round. Nobody! No trace except fresh tyremarks outside the entrance door. Blofeld must have telephoned his man down here before he started and used him and his car for the getaway. Which way had he gone? Bond walked out on to the road. The tracks turned left. Blofeld would be at the Bernina Pass or over it by now, on his way down into Italy and away. It might still have been possible to have him held at the frontier by alerting the fire-brigade, whose lights now held Bond in their beam. No! That would be idiotic. How had Bond got this knowledge unless he himself had been up at Piz Gloria that night? No, he must just play the part of the stupidest tourist in the Engadine!

The shining red vehicle pulled up in front of the cable station and the warning klaxons ran down with an iron groan. Men jumped to the ground. Some went into the station while others stood gazing up at the Piz Gloria, where a dull red glow still showed. A man in a peaked cap, presumably the captain of the team, came up to Bond and saluted. He fired off a torrent of Schwyzerdütch. Bond shook his head. The man tried French. Bond again showed incomprehension. Another man with fragmentary English was called over. 'What is it that is happening?' he asked.

Bond shook his head dazedly. 'I don't know. I was walking down from Pontresina to Samaden. I came on a day excursion from Zürich and missed my bus. I was going to take a train from Samaden. Then I saw these explosions up the mountain —' he waved vaguely — 'and I walked up there past the station to see better, and the next thing I knew was a bang on the head and being dragged along the path.' He indicated his bleeding head and the raw elbows that protruded from his torn sleeves. 'It must have been the broken cable. It must have hit me and dragged me with it. Have you got a Red Cross outfit with you?'

'Yes, yes.' The man called over to the group, and one of his colleagues wearing a Red Cross brassard on his arm fetched his black box from the vehicle and came over. He clucked his tongue over Bond's injuries and, while his interrogator told Bond's story to the captain, bade Bond follow him into the toilette in the station. There, by the light of a torch, he washed Bond's wounds, applied quantities of iodine that stung like hell and then strapped wide strips of Elastoplast over the damage. Bond looked at his face in the mirror. He laughed. Hell of a bridegroom he was going to make! The Red Cross man cluck-clucked in sympathy, produced a flask of brandy out of his box and offered it to Bond. Bond gratefully took a long swig. The interpreter came in. 'There is nothing we can do here. It will need a helicopter from the mountain rescue team. We must go back to Samaden and report. You wish to come?'

'I certainly do,' said Bond enthusiastically, and, with many politenesses and no question of why he should attempt the icy walk to Samaden in the dark instead of taking a taxi, he was borne comfortably to Samaden and dropped off, with the warmest gestures of goodwill and sympathy, at the railway station.

By a rattling Personenzug to Coire and then by express to Zürich, Bond got to the door of the flat of Head of Station Z in the Bahnhofstrasse at two in the morning. He had had some sleep in the train but he was almost out on his feet, and his whole body felt as if it had been beaten with wooden truncheons. He leaned wearily against the bell ticketed 'Muir' until a tousled man in pyjamas came and opened the door and held it on the chain. 'Um Gottes Willen! Was ist denn los?' he inquired angrily. The English accent came through. Bond said, 'It's me that's "los". It's 007 again, I'm afraid.'

'Good God, man, come in, come in!' Muir opened the door and looked quickly up and down the empty street. 'Anyone after you?'

'Shouldn't think so,' said Bond thickly, coming gratefully into the warmth of the entrance hall. Head of Z closed the door and locked it. He turned and looked at Bond. 'Christ, old boy, what in hell's been happening to you? You look as if you'd been through a mangle. Here, come in and have a drink.' He led the way into a comfortable sitting-room. He gestured at the sideboard. 'Help yourself. I'll just tell Phyllis not to worry — unless you'd like her to have a look at the damage. She's quite a hand at that sort of thing.'

'No, it's all right, thanks. A drink'll fix me. Nice and warm in here. I never want to see a patch of snow again as long as I live.'

Muir went out and Bond heard a quick confabulation across the passage. Muir came back. 'Phyllis is fixing the spare room. She'll put some fresh dressings and stuff out in the bathroom. Now then —' he poured himself a thin whisky and soda to keep Bond company and sat down opposite him — 'tell me what you can.'

Bond said, 'I'm terribly sorry, but I can't tell you much. The same business as the other day. Next chapter. I promise you'd do better to know nothing about it. I wouldn't have come here only I've got to get a signal off to M, personal, Triple X cipher to be deciphered by recipient only. Would you be a good chap and put it on the printer?'

'Of course.' Muir looked at his watch. 'Two-thirty a.m. Hell of a time to wake the old man up. But that's your business. Here, come into the cockpit, so to speak.' He walked across to the book-lined wall, took out a book and fiddled. There was a click and a small door swung open. 'Mind your head,' said Muir. 'Old disused lavatory. Just the right size. Gets a bit stuffy when there's a lot of traffic coming or going, but that can't be helped. We can afford to leave the door open.' He bent down to a safe on the floor, worked the combination and brought out what looked like a portable typewriter. He set it on the shelf next to the bulky teleprinter, sat down and clacked off the prefix and routing instructions, winding a small handle at the side of the machine at the end of each word. 'O.K. Fire away!'

Bond leaned up against the wall. He had toyed with various

formulas on his journey down to Samaden. It had to be something that would get through accurately to M and yet keep Muir in the dark, keep his hands clean. Bond said, 'All right. Make it this, would you? REDOUBT PROPERLY FIXED STOP DETAILS LACKING AS EYE WENT SOLO AFTER THE OWNER WHO GREATLY REGRET GOT AWAY AND PROBABLY ITALICIZED BY NOW STOP FORWARDING FULL REPORT FROM STATION M THEN GRATEFULLY ACCEPTING TEN DAYS LEAVE SIGNED 007.'

Muir repeated the signal and then began putting it, in the five-figure groups that had come off the Triple X machine, on to the teleprinter.

Bond watched the message go, the end of another chapter of his duties, as Marc-Ange had put it, 'On Her Majesty's Secret Service'. What would Her Majesty think of this string of crimes committed in her name? God, it was stuffy in the little room! Bond felt the cold sweat break out on his forehead. He put his hand up to his face, muttered something indistinctly about 'that bloody mountain' and gracefully crumpled to the floor.

26

HAPPINESS WITHOUT A SHADOW?

TRACY GAZED AT him wide-eyed when she met him outside Passport Control at Munich Airport, but she waited until they were inside the little Lancia before she burst into tears. 'What have they been doing to you?' she said through her sobs. 'What have they been doing to you now?'

Bond took her in his arms. 'It's all right, Tracy. I promise you. These are only cuts and bruises, like a bad ski-fall. Now don't be a goose. They could happen to anyone.' He smoothed back her hair and took out his handkerchief and dabbed at her eyes.

She took the handkerchief from him and laughed through her tears. 'Now you've ruined my eye-black. And I put it on so carefully for you.' She took out her pocket mirror and carefully wiped away the smudges. She said, 'It's so silly. But I knew you were up to no good. As soon as you said you were going off for a few days to clean up something instead of coming to me, I knew you were going to get into more trouble. And now Marc-Ange has telephoned and asked me if I've seen you. He was very mysterious and sounded worried. And when I said I hadn't he just rang off. And now there's this story in the papers about Piz Gloria. And you were so guarded on the telephone this morning. And from Zürich. I knew it all tied up.' She put back her mirror and pressed the self-starter. 'All right. I won't ask questions. And I'm sorry I cried.' She added fiercely, 'But you *are* such an idiot! You don't seem to think it matters to *anyone*. The way you go on playing Red Indians. It's so — so selfish.'

Bond reached out and pressed her hand on the wheel. He hated 'scenes'. But it was true what she said. He hadn't thought of her, only of the job. It never crossed his mind that anybody really cared about him. A shake of the head from his friends when he went, a few careful lines in the obituary columns of *The Times*, a momentary pang in a few girls' hearts. But now, in three days' time, he would no longer be alone. He would be a half of two people. There wouldn't only be May and Mary Goodnight who would tut-tut over him when he came back from some job as a hospital case. Now, if he got himself killed, there would be Tracy who would at any rate partially die with him.

The little car wove expertly through the traffic. Bond said, 'I'm sorry, Tracy. It was something that had to be done. You know how it is. I just couldn't back out of it. I really wouldn't have been happy here, like I am now, if I'd shirked it. You do see that, don't you?'

She reached out and touched his cheek. 'I wouldn't love you if you weren't a pirate. I expect it's in the blood. I'll get used to it. Don't change. I don't want to draw your teeth like women do with their men. I want to live with *you*, not with somebody else. But don't mind if I howl like a dog every now and then. Or rather like a bitch. It's only love.' She gave him a fleeting smile. '*Die Welt*, with the story in it, is behind the seat on the floor.'

Bond laughed at her mind-reading. 'Damn you, Tracy.' He reached for the paper. He had been aching to see what it said, how much had come out.

There it was, down the central gutter between the first lead, inevitably on Berlin, and the second, equally inevitably, on the miracle of the latest German export figures. All it said, 'from our correspondent', date-lined St Moritz, was 'MYSTERIOUS EXPLOSIONS ON PIZ GLORIA. Cable Railway to Millionaires' Resort Destroyed.' And then a few lines repeating the content of the headings and saying that the police would investigate by helicopter at first light in the morning. The next headline caught Bond's eye: 'IN ENGLAND, POLIO SCARE'. And then, date-lined the day before from London, a brief Reuter dispatch: 'The nine girls held at various British airports on suspicion of having had contact with a possible polio carrier at Zürich Airport, also an English girl, are still being held in quarantine. A Ministry of Health representative said that this was purely a routine precaution. A tenth girl, the origin of the scare, a Miss Violet O'Neill, is under observation at Shannon Hospital. She is a native of Eire.'

Bond smiled to himself. When they were pushed, the British could do this sort of thing supremely well. How much co-ordination had this brief report required? To begin with, M. Then the C.I.D., M.I.5, Ag. and Fish., H.M. Customs, Passport Control, the Ministry of Health and the Government of Eire. All had contributed, and with tremendous speed and efficiency. And the end product, put out to the world, had been through the Press Association to Reuter. Bond tossed the paper over his shoulder and watched the Kaiser Yellow buildings of what had once been one of the most beautiful towns in Europe, now slowly being rebuilt in the same old Kaiser Yellow, file by in their post-war drabness. So the case was closed, the assignment over!

But still The Big One had got away!

They got to the hotel at about three o'clock. There was a message for Tracy to call Marc-Ange at the Maison Rouge at Strasbourg. They went up to her room and got through. Tracy said, 'Here he is, Papa, and almost in one piece.' She handed the receiver to Bond.

Marc-Ange said, 'Did you get him?'

'No, damn it. He's in Italy now. At least I think he is. That was the way he went. How did you get on? It looked fine from down below.'

'Satisfactory. All accounted for.'

'Gone?'

'Yes. Gone for good. There was no trace of your man from Zürich. I lost two. Our friend had left a surprise in his filing cabinet. That accounted for Ché-Ché. Another one wasn't quick enough. That is all. The trip back was entertaining. I will give you the details tomorrow. I shall travel tonight in my sleeping-car. You know?'

'Yes. By the way, what about the girl friend, Irma?'

'There was no sign of her. Just as well. It would have been difficult to send her away like the others.'

'Yes. Well, thanks, Marc-Ange. And the news from England is also good. See you tomorrow.'

Bond put down the receiver. Tracy had discreetly retired to the bathroom and locked the door. She now called, 'Can I come out?'

'Two minutes, darling.' Bond got on to Station M. His call was expected. He arranged to visit the Head of Station, a man he knew slightly called Lieutenant-Commander Savage, in an hour's time. He released Tracy and they made plans for the evening, then he went along to his room.

His suitcase had been unpacked and there was a bowl of crocuses beside his bed. Bond smiled, picked up the bowl and placed it firmly on the window-sill. Then he had a quick shower, complicated by having to keep his dressings dry, changed out of his stinking ski-clothes into the warmer of the two dark-blue suits he had brought with him, sat down at the writing-desk and jotted down the headings of what he would have to put on the teleprinter to M. Then he put on his dark-blue raincoat and went down into the street and along to the Odeons Platz.

(If he had not been thinking of other things, he might have noticed the woman on the other side of the street, a squat, toad-like figure in a frowsty dark-green Loden cloak, who gave a start of surprise when she saw him sauntering along, hustled across the street through the traffic, and got on his tail. She was expert at what she was doing, and, when he went into the new-ish apartment house on the Odeons Platz, she didn't go near the door to verify the address, but waited on the far side of the square until he came out. Then she tailed him back to the Vier Jahreszeiten, took a taxi back to her flat and put in a long-distance call to the Metropole Hotel on Lake Como.)

Bond went up to his room. On the writing-desk an impressive array of dressings and medicaments had been laid out. He got on to Tracy and said, 'What the hell is this? Have you got a pass-key or something?'

She laughed. 'The maid on this floor has become a friend. She understands people who are in love. Which is more than you do. What do you mean by moving those flowers?'

'They're lovely. I thought they looked prettier by the window and they will get some sun there. Now I'll make a deal. If you'll come along and change my dressings, I'll take you down and buy you a drink. Just one. And three for me. That's the right ratio between men and women. All right?'

'Wilco.' Her receiver went down.

It hurt like hell and Bond couldn't prevent the tears of pain from squeezing out of his eyes. She kissed them away. She looked pale at what she had seen. 'You're sure you oughtn't to see a doctor?'

'I'm just seeing one. You did it beautifully. What worries me is how we're going to make love. In the proper fashion, elbows are rather important for the man.'

'Then we'll do it in an improper fashion. But not tonight, or tomorrow. Only when we're married. Till then I am going to pretend I'm a virgin.' She looked at him seriously. 'I wish I was, James. I am in a way, you know. People can make love without loving.'

'Drinks,' said Bond firmly. 'We've got all the time in the world to talk about love.'

'You *are* a pig,' she said indignantly. 'We've got so much to talk about and all you think about is drink.'

Bond laughed. He put an arm gingerly round her neck and kissed her long and passionately. He broke away. 'There, that's just the beginning of my conversation. We'll go on with the duller bits in the bar. Then we'll have a wonderful dinner in Walterspiel's and talk about rings and whether we'll sleep in twin beds or one, and whether I've got enough sheets and pillows for two, and other exciting things to do with being married.'

And it was in that way that the evening passed and Bond's head reeled with all the practical feminine problems she raised, in high seriousness, but he was surprised to find that all this nest-building gave him a curious pleasure, a feeling that he had at last come to rest and that life would now be fuller, have more meaning, for having someone to share it with. Togetherness! What a curiously valid cliché it was!

The next day was occupied with hilarious meals with Marc-Ange, whose giant trailer had come during the night to take up most of the parking space behind the hotel, and with searching the antique shops for an engagement and a wedding ring. The latter was easy, the traditional plain gold band, but Tracy couldn't make up her mind about the engagement ring and finally dispatched Bond to find something he liked himself while she had her last fitting for her 'going-away' dress. Bond hired a taxi, and he and the taxi-man, who had been a Luftwaffe pilot during the war and was proud of it, tore round the town together until, at an antique shop near the Nymphenburg Palace, Bond found what he wanted — a baroque ring in white gold with two diamond hands clasped. It was graceful and simple and the taxi-man was also in favour, so the deal was done and the two men went off to celebrate at the Franziskaner Keller, where they ate mounds of Weisswurst and drank four steins of beer each and swore they wouldn't ever fight each other again. Then, happy with his last bachelor party, Bond returned tipsily to the hotel, avoided being embraced by the taxi-man and went straight up to Tracy's room and put the ring on her finger.

She burst into tears, sobbing that it was the most beautiful ring in the world, but when he took her in his arms she began to giggle. 'Oh, James, you are bad. You stink like a pig of beer and sausages. Where *have* you been?'

When Bond told her, she laughed at the picture he painted of his last fling and then paraded happily up and down the room, making exaggeratedly gracious gestures with her hand to show off the ring and for the diamonds to catch the light. Then the telephone rang and it was Marc-Ange saying that he wanted to talk to Bond in the bar, and would Tracy kindly keep out of the way for half an hour?

Bond went down and, after careful consideration, decided that schnapps would go with his beer and ordered a double Steinhäger. Marc-Ange's face was serious. 'Now listen, James. We have not had a proper talk. It is very wrong. I am about to become your father-in-law and I insist. Many months ago, I made you a serious offer. You declined it. But now you have accepted it. What is the name of your bank?'

Bond said angrily, 'Shut up, Marc-Ange. If you think I'll accept a million pounds from you or from anyone else you're mistaken. I don't want my life to be ruined. Too much money is the worst curse you can lay on anyone's head. I have enough. Tracy has enough. It will be fun saving up to buy something we want but can't quite afford. That is the only kind of money to have — not quite enough.'

Marc-Ange said furiously, 'You have been drinking. You are drunk. You don't understand what you are saying. What I am giving you is only a fifth of my fortune. You understand? It means nothing to me. Tracy is used to having whatever she wants. I wish it to remain so. She is my only child. You cannot possibly keep her on a civil servant's pay. You have got to accept!'

'If you give me any money, I swear I will pass it on to charity.

You want to give your money away to a dogs' home? All right. Go ahead!'

'But James —' Marc-Ange was now pleading — 'what will you accept from me? Then a trust fund for any children you may have. Yes?'

'Even worse. If we have children, I will not have this noose hung round their heads. I didn't have any money and I haven't needed it. I've loved winning money gambling because that is found money, money that comes out of the air like a great surprise. If I'd inherited money, I'd have gone the way of all those playboy friends of Tracy's you complained about so much. No, Marc-Ange.' Bond drained his Steinhäger decisively. 'It's no good.'

Marc-Ange looked as if he would burst into tears. Bond relented. He said, 'It's very kind of you, Marc-Ange, and I appreciate it from the heart. I'll tell you what. If I swear to come to you if either of us ever needs help, will that do? There may be illnesses and things. Perhaps it would be nice if we had a cottage in the country somewhere. We may need help if we have children. Now. How about that? Is it a bargain?'

Marc-Ange turned doubtful, dog's eyes on Bond. 'You promise? You would not cheat me of helping you, adding to your happiness when you allow me to?'

Bond reached over and took Marc-Ange's right hand and pressed it. 'My word on it. Now come on, pull yourself together. Here comes Tracy. She'll think we've been having a fight.'

'So we have,' said Marc-Ange gloomily. 'And it is the first fight I have ever lost.'

27

ALL THE TIME IN THE WORLD

'I DO.'

James Bond said the words at ten-thirty in the morning of a crystal-clear New Year's Day in the British Consul General's drawing-room.

And he meant them.

The Consul General had proved himself, as British Consuls so often do, to be a man of efficiency and a man with a heart. It was a holiday for him and, as he confessed, he should have been recovering from a New Year's Eve hangover. And he had shaved many days off the formal period of notice, but that, he explained, he had occasionally, and improperly, risked in his career if there were exceptional circumstances such as the imminent death of either party. 'You both look healthy enough,' he had said when they first visited him together, 'but that's a nasty cut on your head, Commander Bond, and the Countess is perhaps looking a little pale. And I have taken the precaution of obtaining special dispensation from the Foreign Secretary, which I may say, to my surprise, was immediately forthcoming. So let's make it New Year's Day. And come to my home. My wife is hopelessly sentimental about these occasional jobs I have to do, and I know she'd love to meet you both.'

The papers were signed, and Head of Station M, who had agreed to act as Bond's best man and who was secretly longing to write a sensational note to the head of his London Section about all this, produced a handful of confetti and threw most of it over Marc-Ange, who had turned up in a 'cylindre' and a full suit of very French tails with, surprisingly, two rows of medals of which the last, to Bond's astonishment, was the King's Medal for foreign resistance-fighters.

'I will tell you all about it one day, my dear James,' he had said in answer to Bond's admiring inquiry. 'It was tremendous fun. I had myself what the Americans call "a ball". And —' his voice sank to a whisper and he put one finger along his brown, sensitive nose — 'I confess that I profited by the occasion to lay my hands on the secret funds of a certain section of the Abwehr. But Herkos Odonton, my dear James! Herkos Odonton! Medals are so often just the badges of good luck. If I am a hero, it is for things for which no medals are awarded. And —' he drew lines with his fingers across his chest — 'there is hardly room on the breast of this "frac", which, by the way, is by courtesy of the excellent Galeries Barbès in Marseilles, for all that I am due under that heading.'

The farewells were said and Bond submitted himself, he swore for the last time, to Marc-Ange's embraces and they went down the steps to the waiting Lancia. Someone, Bond suspected the Consul's wife, had tied white ribbons from the corners of the windscreen to the grill of the radiator, and there was a small group of bystanders, passers-by, who had stopped, as they do all over the world, to see who it was, what they looked like.

The Consul General shook Bond by the hand. 'I'm afraid we haven't managed to keep this as private as you'd have liked. A woman reporter came on from the *Münchener Illustrierte* this morning. Wouldn't say who she was. Gossip-writer, I suppose. I had to give her the bare facts. She particularly wanted to know the time of the ceremony, if you can call it that, so that they could send a cameraman along. At least you've been spared that. All still tight, I suppose. Well, so long and the best of luck.'

Tracy, who had elected to 'go away' in a dark-grey Tyroler outfit with the traditional dark-green trimmings and stag's-horn buttons, threw her saucy mountaineer's hat with its gay chamois-beard cockade into the back seat, climbed in and pressed the starter. The engine purred and then roared softly as she went through the gears down the empty street. They both waved one hand out of a window and Bond, looking back, saw Marc-Ange's 'cylindre' whirling up into the air. There was a small flutter of answering hands from the pavement and then they were round the corner and away.

When they found the Autobahn exit for Salzburg and Kufstein, Bond said, 'Be an angel and pull in to the side, Tracy. I've got two things to do.'

She pulled in on to the grass verge. The brown grass of winter showed through the thin snow. Bond reached for her and took her in his arms. He kissed her tenderly. 'That's the first thing, and I just wanted to say that I'll look after you, Tracy. Will you mind being looked after?'

She held him away from her and looked at him. She smiled. Her eyes were introspective. 'That's what it means being Mr and Mrs, doesn't it? They don't say Mrs and Mr. But *you* need looking after too. Let's just look after each other.'

'All right. But I'd rather have my job than yours. Now. I simply must get out and take down those ribbons. I can't stand looking like a coronation. D'you mind?'

She laughed. 'You like being anonymous. I want everyone to cheer as we go by. I know you're going to have this car sprayed grey or black as soon as you get a chance. That's all right. But nothing's going to stop me wearing you like a flag from now on. Will you sometimes feel like wearing me like a flag?'

'On all holidays and feast days.' Bond got out and removed the ribbons. He looked up at the cloudless sky. The sun felt warm on his face. He said, 'Do you think we'd be too cold if we took the roof down?'

'No, let's. We can only see half the world with it up. And it's a lovely drive from here to Kitzbühel. We can always put it up again if we want to.'

Bond unscrewed the two butterfly nuts and folded the canvas top back behind the seats. He had a look up and down the Autobahn. There was plenty of traffic. At the big Shell station on the roundabout they had just passed, his eye was caught by a bright-red open Maserati being tanked up. Fast job. And a typical sporty couple, a man and a woman in the driving-seat — white dust-coats and linen helmets buttoned under the chin. Big dark-green talc goggles that obscured most of the rest of the faces. Usual German speedsters' uniform. Too far away to see if they were good-looking enough for the car, but the silhouette of the woman wasn't promising. Bond got in beside Tracy and they set off again down the beautifully landscaped road.

They didn't talk much. Tracy kept at about eighty and there was wind-roar. That was the trouble about open cars. Bond glanced at his watch. 11.45. They would get to Kufstein at about one. There was a splendid Gasthaus up the winding streets towards the great castle. Here was a tiny lane of pleasure, full of the heart-plucking whine of zither music and the gentle melancholy of Tyrolean yodellers. It was here that the German tourist traditionally stopped after his day's outing into cheap Austria, just outside the German frontier, for a last giant meal of Austrian food and wine. Bond put his mouth up close to Tracy's ear and told her about it and about the other attraction at Kufstein — the most imaginative war memorial, for the 1914–18 war, ever devised. Punctually at midday every day, the windows of the castle are thrown open and a voluntary is played on the great organ inside. It can be heard for kilometres down the valley between the giant mountain ranges for which Kufstein provides the gateway. 'But we shall miss it. It's coming up for twelve now.'

'Never mind,' said Tracy, 'I'll make do with the zithers while you guzzle your beer and schnapps.' She turned into the right-hand fork leading to the underpass for Kufstein, and they were at once through Rosenheim and the great white peaks were immediately ahead.

The traffic was much sparser now and there were kilometres where theirs was the only car on the road that arrowed away between white meadows and larch copses, towards the glittering barrier where blood had been shed between warring armies for centuries. Bond glanced behind him. Miles away down the great highway was a speck of red. The Maserati? They certainly hadn't got much competitive spirit if they couldn't catch the Lancia at eighty! No good having a car like that if you didn't drive it so as to lose all other traffic in your mirror. Perhaps he was doing them an injustice. Perhaps they too only wanted to motor quietly along and enjoy the day.

Ten minutes later, Tracy said, 'There's a red car coming up fast behind. Do you want me to lose him?'

'No,' said Bond. 'Let him go. We've got all the time in the world.'

Now he could hear the rasping whine of the eight cylinders. He leaned over to the left and jerked a laconic thumb forwards, waving the Maserati past.

The whine changed to a shattering roar. The windscreen of the Lancia disappeared as if hit by a monster fist. Bond caught a glimpse of a taut, snarling mouth under a syphilitic nose, the flash-eliminator of some automatic gun being withdrawn, and then the red car was past and the Lancia was going like hell off the verge across a stretch of snow and smashing a path through a young copse. Then Bond's head crashed into the windscreen frame and he was out.

When he came to, a man in the khaki uniform of the Autobahn Patrol was shaking him. The young face was stark with horror. 'Was ist denn geschehen? Was ist denn geschehen?'

Bond turned towards Tracy. She was lying forward with her face buried in the ruins of the steering-wheel. Her pink handkerchief had come off and the bell of golden hair hung down and hid her face. Bond put his arm round her shoulders, across which the dark patches had begun to flower.

He pressed her against him. He looked up at the young man and smiled his reassurance.

'It's all right,' he said in a clear voice as if explaining something to a child. 'It's quite all right. She's having a rest. We'll be going on soon. There's no hurry. You see —' Bond's head sank down against hers and he whispered into her hair — 'you see, we've got all the time in the world.'

The young patrolman took a last scared look at the motionless couple, hurried over to his motorcycle, picked up the hand-microphone and began talking urgently to the rescue headquarters.

YOU ONLY LIVE TWICE

When Ernst Stavro Blofeld blasted into eternity the girl whom James Bond had married only hours before, the heart, the zest for life, went out of Bond. Incredibly, from being a top agent of the Secret Service, he had gone to pieces, was even on the verge of becoming a security risk. M. is persuaded to give him one last chance — an impossible mission far removed from his usual duties — and Bond leaves for Japan. There, coming under the orders of the formidable 'Tiger' Tanaka, Head of the Japanese Secret Service, the *Kōan-Chōsa-Kyōku*, he is indeed subjected to the shock treatment his condition demanded.

Shock treatment? The reader will also be subjected to it in full measure in this, perhaps the most bizarre and doom-fraught of all James Bond's adventures.

You only live twice:
Once when you are born,
And once when you look death in the face.

After BASHŌ
Japanese poet,
1643–94

Part One — 'IT IS BETTER TO TRAVEL HOPEFULLY . . .

Part Two — . . . THAN TO ARRIVE'

To
Richard Hughes
and
Torao Saito

But
for
whom
etc. . . .

Part One

‘IT IS BETTER TO TRAVEL HOPEFULLY . . .

I

SCISSORS CUT PAPER

THE GEISHA CALLED 'Trembling Leaf', on her knees beside James Bond, leant forward from the waist and kissed him chastely on the right cheek.

'That's a cheat,' said Bond severely. 'You agreed that if I won it would be a real kiss on the mouth. At the very least,' he added.

'Grey Pearl', the Madame, who had black lacquered teeth, a bizarre affectation, and was so thickly made up that she looked like a character out of a No play, translated. There was much giggling and cries of encouragement. Trembling Leaf covered her face with her pretty hands as if she were being required to perform some ultimate obscenity. But then the fingers divided and the pert brown eyes examined Bond's mouth, as if taking aim, and her body lanced forward. This time the kiss was full on the lips and it lingered fractionally. In invitation? In promise? Bond remembered that he had been promised a 'pillow geisha'. Technically, this would be a geisha of low caste. She would not be proficient in the traditional arts of her calling — she would not be able to tell humorous stories, sing, paint or compose verses about her patron. But, unlike her cultured sisters, she might agree to perform more robust services — discreetly, of course, in conditions of the utmost privacy and at a high price. But, to the boorish, brutalized tastes of a *gaijin*, a foreigner, this made more sense than having a *tanka* of thirty-one syllables, which in any case he couldn't understand, equate, in exquisite ideograms, his charms with budding chrysanthemums on the slopes of Mount Fuji.

The applause which greeted this unbridled exhibition of lasciviousness died quickly and respectfully. The powerful, chunky man in the black *yukata*, sitting directly across the low red lacquer table from Bond, had taken the Dunhill filter holder from between his golden teeth and had laid it beside his ash-tray.

'Bondo-san,' said Tiger Tanaka, Head of the Japanese Secret Service, 'I will now challenge you to this ridiculous game, and I promise you in advance that you will not win.' The big, creased brown face that Bond had come to know so well in the past month split expansively. The wide smile closed the almond eyes to slits — slits that glittered. Bond knew that smile. It wasn't a smile. It was a mask with a golden hole in it.

Bond laughed. 'All right, Tiger. But first, more *saké*! And not in these ridiculous thimbles. I've drunk five flasks of the stuff and its effect is about the same as one double Martini. I shall need another double Martini if I am to go on demonstrating the superiority of Western instinct over the wiles of the Orient. Is there such a thing as a lowly glass tumbler discarded in some corner behind the cabinets of Ming?'

'Bondo-san. Ming is Chinese. Your knowledge of porcelain is as meagre as your drinking habits are gross. Moreover, it is unwise to underestimate *saké*. We have a saying, "It is the man who drinks the first flask of *saké*; then the second flask drinks the first; then it is the *saké* that drinks the man." ' Tiger Tanaka turned to Grey Pearl and there followed a laughing conversation which Bond interpreted as jokes at the expense of this uncouth Westerner and his monstrous appetites. At a word from the Madame, Trembling Leaf bowed low and scurried out of the room. Tiger turned to Bond. 'You have gained much face, Bondo-san. It is only the *sumo* wrestlers who drink *saké* in these quantities without showing it. She says you are undoubtedly an eight-flask man.' Tiger's face became sly. 'But she also suggests that you will not make much of a companion for Trembling Leaf at the end of the evening.'

'Tell her that I am more interested in her own more mature charms. She will certainly possess talents in the art of love-making which will overcome any temporary lassitude on my part.'

This leaden gallantry got what it deserved. There came a spirited crackle of Japanese from Grey Pearl. Tiger translated. 'Bondo-san, this is a woman of some wit. She has made a joke. She says she is already respectably married to one *bonsan* and there is no room on her *futon* for another. *Bonsan* means a priest, a greybeard. *Futon*, as you know, is a bed. She has made a joke on your name.'

The geisha party had been going on for two hours, and Bond's jaws were aching with the unending smiles and polite repartee. Far from being entertained by the geisha, or bewitched by the inscrutable discords issuing from the catskin-covered box of the three-stringed *samisen*, Bond had found himself having to try desperately to make the party go. He also knew that Tiger Tanaka had been observing his efforts with a sadistic pleasure. Dikko Henderson had warned him that geisha parties were more or less the equivalent, for a foreigner, of trying to entertain a lot of unknown children in a nursery with a strict governess, the Madame, looking on. But Dikko had also warned him that he was being done a great honour by Tiger Tanaka, that the party would cost Tiger a small fortune, whether from secret funds or from his own pocket, and that Bond had better put a good face on the whole thing since this looked like being a breakthrough in Bond's mission. But it could equally well be disaster.

So now Bond smiled and clapped his hands in admiration. He said to Tiger, 'Tell the old bitch she's a clever old bitch,' accepted the brimming tumbler of hot *saké* from the apparently adoring hands of Trembling Leaf, and downed it in two tremendous gulps. He repeated the performance so that more *saké* had to be fetched from the kitchen, then he placed his fist decisively on the red lacquer table and said with mock belligerence, 'All right, Tiger! Go to it!'

It was the old game of Scissors cut Paper, Paper wraps Stone, Stone blunts Scissors, that is played by children all over the world. The fist is the Stone, two outstretched fingers are the Scissors, and a flat hand is the Paper. The closed fist is hammered twice in the air simultaneously by the two opponents and, at the third downward stroke, the chosen emblem is revealed. The game consists of guessing which emblem the opponent will choose, and of you yourself choosing one that will defeat him. Best of three goes or more. It is a game of bluff.

Tiger Tanaka rested his fist on the table opposite Bond. The two men looked carefully into each other's eyes. There was dead silence in the box-like little lath-and-paper room, and the soft gurgling of the tiny brook in the ornamental square of garden outside the opened partition could be heard clearly for the first time that evening. Perhaps it was this silence, after all the talk and giggling, or perhaps it was the deep seriousness and purpose that was suddenly evident in Tiger Tanaka's formidable, cruel, *samurai* face, but Bond's skin momentarily crawled. For some reason this had become more than a children's game. Tiger had promised he would beat Bond. To fail would be to lose much face. How much? Enough to breach a friendship that had become oddly real between the two of them over the past weeks? This was one of the most powerful men in Japan. To be defeated by a miserable *gaijin* in front of the two women might be a matter of great moment to this man. The defeat might leak out through the women. In the West, such a trifle would be farcically insignificant, like a Cabinet Minister losing a game of backgammon at Blades. But in the East? In a very short while, Dikko Henderson had taught Bond total respect for Oriental conventions, however old-fashioned or seemingly trivial, but Bond was still at sea in their gradations. This was a case in point. Should Bond try and win at this baby game of bluff and double-bluff, or should he try to lose? But to try and lose involved the same cleverness at correctly guessing the other man's symbols in advance. It was just as difficult to lose on purpose as to win. And anyway, did it really matter? Unfortunately, on the curious assignment in which James Bond was involved, he had a nasty feeling that even this idiotic little gambit had significance towards success or failure.

As if with second sight, Tiger Tanaka spelled the problem out. He gave a harsh, taut laugh that was more of a shout than an expression of humour or pleasure. 'Bondo-san, with us, and certainly at a party at which I am the host and you are the honoured guest, it would be good manners for me to let you win this game that we are to play together. It would be more. It would be required behaviour. So I must ask your forgiveness in advance for defeating you.'

Bond smiled cheerfully. 'My dear Tiger, there is no point in playing a game unless you try to win. It would be a very great insult to me if you endeavoured to play to lose. But if I may say so, your remarks are highly provocative. They are like the taunts of the *sumo* wrestlers before the bout. If I was not myself so certain of winning, I would point out that you spoke in English. Please tell our dainty and distinguished audience that I propose to rub your honourable nose in the dirt at this despicable game and thus display not only the superiority of Great

Britain, and particularly Scotland, over Japan, but also the superiority of our Queen over your Emperor.' Bond, encouraged perhaps by the crafty ambush of the *saké*, had committed himself. This kind of joking about their different cultures had become a habit between himself and Tiger, who, with a first in P.P.E. at Trinity before the war, prided himself in the *demokorasu* of his outlook and the liberality and breadth of his understanding of the West. But Bond, having spoken, caught the sudden glitter in the dark eyes, and he thought of Dikko Henderson's cautionary, 'Now listen, you stupid limey bastard. You're doing all right. But don't press your luck. T.T.'s a civilized kind of a chap — as Japs go, that is. But don't overdo it. Take a look at that mug. There's Manchu there, and Tartar. And don't forget the soanso was a Black Belt at judo before he ever went up to your bloody Oxford. And don't forget he was spying for Japan when he called himself assistant naval attaché in their London Embassy before the war and you stupid bastards thought he was okay because he'd got a degree at Oxford. And don't forget his war record. Don't forget he ended up as personal aide to Admiral Ohnishi and was training as a *kamikaze* when the Americans made loud noises over Nagasaki and Hiroshima and the Rising Sun suddenly took a backward somersault into the sea. And, if you forget all that, just ask yourself why it's T.T. rather than any other of the ninety million Japanese who happens to hold down the job as head of the *Kōan-Chōsa-Kyōku*. Okay, James? Got the photo?'

Since Bond had arrived in Japan he had assiduously practised sitting in the lotus position. Dikko Henderson had advised it. 'If you make the grade with these people,' he had said, 'or even if you don't, you'll be spending a lot of time sitting on your ass on the ground. There's only one way to do it without cracking your joints; that's in the Indian position, squatting with your legs crossed and the sides of your feet hurting like hell on the floor. It takes a bit of practice, but it won't kill you and you'll end up gaining plenty of face.' Bond had more or less mastered the art, but now, after two hours, his knee-joints were on fire and he felt that if he didn't alter his posture he would end up bandy-legged for life. He said to Tiger, 'Playing against a master such as yourself, I must first adopt a relaxed position so that my brain may be totally concentrated.' He got painfully to his feet, stretched and sat down again — this time with one leg extended under the low table and with his left elbow resting on the bent knee of the other. It was a blessed relief. He lifted his tumbler and, obediently, Trembling Leaf filled it from a fresh flagon. Bond downed the *saké*, handed the tumbler to the girl and suddenly crashed his right fist down on the lacquer table so that the little boxes of sweetmeats rattled and the porcelain tinkled. He looked belligerently across at Tiger Tanaka. 'Right!'

Tiger bowed. Bond bowed back. The girl leant forward expectantly.

Tiger's eyes bored into Bond's, trying to read his plan. Bond had decided to have no plan, display no pattern. He would play completely at random, showing the symbol that his fist decided to make at the psychological moment after the two hammer-blows.

Tiger said, 'Three games of three?'

'Right.'

The two fists rose slowly from the table top, quickly hammered twice in unison and shot forward. Tiger had kept his fist balled in the Stone. Bond's palm was open in the Paper that wrapped the Stone. One up to Bond. Again the ritual and the moment of truth. Tiger had kept to the Stone. Bond's first and second fingers were open in the Scissors, blunted by Tiger's Stone. One all.

Tiger paused and placed his fist against his forehead. He closed his eyes in thought. He said, 'Yes. I've got you, Bondo-san. You can't escape.'

'Good show,' said Bond, trying to clear his mind of the suspicion that Tiger would keep to the Stone, or alternatively, that Tiger would expect him to play it that way, expect Bond to play the Paper and himself riposte with the Scissors to cut the Paper. And so on and so forth. The three emblems whirled round in Bond's mind like the symbols on a fruit machine.

The two fists were raised — one, two, forward!

Tiger had kept to his Stone. Bond had wrapped it up with the Paper. First game to Bond.

The second game lasted longer. They both kept on showing the same symbol, which meant a replay. It was as if the two players were getting the measure of each other's psychology. But that could not be so, since Bond had no psychological intent. He continued to play at random. It was just luck. Tiger won the game. One all.

Last game! The two contestants looked at each other. Bond's smile was bland, rather mocking. A glint of red shone in the depths of Tiger's dark eyes. Bond saw it and said to himself, 'I would be wise to lose. Or would I?' He won the game in two straight goes, blunting Tiger's Scissors with his Stone, wrapping Tiger's Stone with his Paper.

Tiger bowed low. Bond bowed even lower. He sought for a throwaway remark. He said, 'I must get this game adopted in time for your Olympics. I would certainly be chosen to play for my country.'

Tiger Tanaka laughed with controlled politeness. 'You play with much insight. What was the secret of your method?'

Bond had had no method. He quickly invented the one that would be most polite to Tiger. 'You are a man of rock and steel, Tiger. I guessed that the paper symbol would be the one you would use the least. I played accordingly.'

This bit of mumbo-jumbo got by. Tiger bowed. Bond bowed and drank more *saké*, toasting Tiger. Released from the tension, the geisha applauded and the Madame instructed Trembling Leaf to give Bond another kiss. She did so. How soft the skins of Japanese women were! And their touch was almost weightless! James Bond was plotting the rest of his night when Tiger said, 'Bondo-san, I have matters to discuss with you. Will you do me the honour of coming to my house for a nightcap?'

Bond immediately put away his lascivious thoughts. According to Dikko, to be invited to a Japanese private house was a most unusual sign of favour. So, for some reason, he had done right to win this childish game. This might mean great things. Bond bowed. 'Nothing would give me more pleasure, Tiger.'

An hour later they were sitting in blessed chairs with a drink-tray between them. The lights of Yokohama glowed a deep orange along the horizon, and a slight smell of the harbour and the sea came in through the wide-open partition leading on to the garden. Tiger's house was designed, enchantingly, as is even the meanest Japanese salary-man's house, to establish the thinnest possible dividing line between the inhabitant and nature. The three other partitions in the square room were also fully slid back, revealing a bedroom, a small study and a passage.

Tiger had opened the partitions when they entered the room. He had commented, 'In the West, when you have secrets to discuss, you shut all the doors and windows. In Japan, we throw everything open to make sure that no one can listen at the thin walls. And what I have now to discuss with you is a matter of the very highest secrecy. The *saké* is warm enough? You have the cigarettes you prefer? Then listen to what I have to say to you and swear on your honour to divulge it to no one.' Tiger Tanaka gave his great golden shout of mirthless laughter. 'If you were to break your promise, I would have no alternative but to remove you from the earth.'

2

CURTAINS FOR BOND?

EXACTLY ONE MONTH before, it had been the eve of the annual closing of Blades. On the next day, September 1st, those members who were still unfashionably in London would have to pig it for a month at Whites or Boodle's. Whites they considered noisy and 'smart', Boodle's too full of superannuated country squires who would be talking of nothing but the opening of the partridge season. For Blades, it was one month in the wilderness. But there it was. The staff, one supposed, had to have their holiday. More important, there was some painting to be done and there was dry-rot in the roof.

M., sitting in the bow window looking out over St James's Street, couldn't care less. He had two weeks' trout fishing on the Test to look forward to and, for the other two weeks, he would have sandwiches and coffee at his desk. He rarely used Blades, and then only to entertain important guests. He was not a 'clubable' man and if he had had the choice he would have stuck to The Senior, that greatest of all Services' clubs in the world. But too many people knew him there, and there was too much 'shop' talked. And there were too many former shipmates who *would* come up and ask him what he had been doing with himself since he retired. And the lie, 'Got a job with some people called Universal Export,' bored him, and, though verifiable, had its risks.

Porterfield hovered with the cigars. He bent and offered the wide case to M.'s guest. Sir James Molony raised a quizzical eyebrow. 'I see the Havanas are still coming in.' His hand hesitated. He picked out a Romeo y Julieta, pinched it gently and ran it under his nose. He turned to M. 'What's Universal Export sending Castro in return? Blue Streak?'

M. was not amused. Porterfield observed that he wasn't. As Chief Petty Officer, he had served under M. in one of his last commands. He said quickly, but not too quickly, 'As a matter of fact, Sir James, the best of the Jamaicans are quite up to the Havanas these days. They've got the outer leaf just right at last.' He closed the glass lid of the case and moved away.

Sir James Molony picked up the piercer the head waiter had left on the table and punctured the tip of his cigar with precision. He lit a Swan Vesta and waved its flame to and fro across the tip and sucked gently until he had got the cigar going to his satisfaction. Then he took a sip, first at his brandy and then at his coffee, and sat back. He observed the corrugated brow of his host with affection and irony. He said, 'All right, my friend. Now tell me. What's the problem?'

M.'s mind was elsewhere. He seemed to be having difficulty getting his pipe going. He said vaguely, between puffs, 'What problem?'

Sir James Molony was the greatest neurologist in England. The year before, he had been awarded a Nobel Prize for his now famous *Some Psychosomatic Side-effects of Organic Inferiority*. He was also nerve specialist by appointment to the Secret Service and, though he was rarely called in, and then only in extremis, the problems he was required to solve intrigued him greatly because they were both human and vital to the State. And, since the war, the second qualification was a rare one.

M. turned sideways to his guest and watched the traffic up St James's.

Sir James Molony said, 'My friend, like everybody else, you have certain patterns of behaviour. One of them consists of occasionally asking me to lunch at Blades, stuffing me like a Strasbourg goose, and then letting me in on some ghastly secret and asking me to help you with it. The last time, as I recall, you wanted to find out if I could extract certain information from a foreign diplomat by getting him under deep hypnosis without his knowledge. You said it was a last resort. I said I couldn't help you. Two weeks later, I read in the paper that this same diplomat had come to a fatal end by experimenting with the force of gravity from a tenth-floor window. The coroner gave an open verdict of the "Fell Or Was Pushed" variety. What song am I to sing for my supper this time?' Sir James Molony relented. He said with sympathy, 'Come on, M.! Get it off your chest!'

M. looked him coldly in the eye. 'It's 007. I'm getting more and more worried about him.'

'You've read my two reports on his condition. Anything new?'

'No. Just the same. He's going slowly to pieces. Late at the office. Skimps his work. Makes mistakes. He's drinking too much and losing a lot of money at one of these new gambling clubs. It all adds up to the fact that one of my best men is on the edge of becoming a security risk. Absolutely incredible considering his record.'

Sir James Molony shook his head with conviction. 'It's not in the least incredible. You either don't read my reports or you don't pay enough attention to them. I have said all along that the man is suffering from shock.' Sir James Molony leant forward and pointed his cigar at M.'s chest. 'You're a hard man, M. In your job you have to be. But there are some problems, the human ones for instance, that you can't always solve with a rope's end. This is a case in point. Here's this agent of yours, just as tough and brave as I expect you were at his age. He's a bachelor and a confirmed womanizer. Then he suddenly falls in love, partly, I suspect, because this woman was a bird with a wing down and needed his help. It's surprising what soft centres these so-called tough men always have. So he marries her and within a few hours she's shot dead by this super-gangster chap. What was his name?'

'Blofeld,' said M. 'Ernst Stavro Blofeld.'

'All right. And your man got away with nothing worse than a crack on the head. But then he started going to pieces and your M.O. thought he might have suffered some brain injury and sent him along to me. Nothing wrong with him at all. Nothing physical that is — just shock. He admitted to me that all his zest had gone. That he wasn't interested in his job any more, or even in his life. I hear this sort of talk from patients every day. It's a form of psycho-neurosis, and it can grow slowly or suddenly. In your man's case, it was brought on out of the blue by an intolerable life-situation — or one that he found intolerable because he had never encountered it before — the loss of a loved one, aggravated in his case by the fact that he blamed himself for her death. Now, my friend, neither you nor I have had to carry such a burden, so we don't know how we would react under it. But I can tell you that it's a hell of a burden to lug around. And your man's caving in under it. I thought, and I said so in my report, that his job, its dangers and emergencies and so forth, would shake him out of it. I've found that one must try and teach people that there's no top limit to disaster — that, so long as breath remains in your body, you've got to accept the miseries of life. They will often seem infinite, insupportable. They are part of the human condition. Have you tried him on any tough assignments in the last few months?'

'Two,' said M. drearily. 'He bungled them both. On one he nearly got himself killed, and on the other he made a mistake that was dangerous for others. That's another thing that worries me. He didn't make mistakes before. Now suddenly he's become accident-prone.'

'Another symptom of his neurosis. So what are you going to do about it?'

'Fire him,' said M. brutally. 'Just as if he'd been shot to pieces or got some incurable disease. I've got no room in his Section for a lame-brain, whatever his past record or whatever excuses you psychologists can find for him. Pension, of course. Honourable discharge and all that. Try and find him a job. One of these new security organizations for the banks might take him.' M. looked defensively into the clear blue comprehending eyes of the famous neurologist. He said, seeking support for his decision, 'You do see my point, Sir James? I'm tightly staffed at Headquarters, and in the field, for that matter. There's just no place where I can tuck away 007 so that he won't cause harm.'

'You'll be losing one of your best men.'

'Used to be. Isn't any longer.'

Sir James Molony sat back. He looked out of the window and puffed thoughtfully at his cigar. He liked this man Bond. He had had him as his patient perhaps a dozen times before. He had seen how the spirit, the reserves in the man, could pull him out of badly damaged conditions that would have broken the normal human being. He knew how a desperate situation would bring out those reserves again, how the will to live would spring up again in a real emergency. He remembered how countless neurotic patients had disappeared for ever from his consulting rooms when the last war had broken out. The big worry had driven out the smaller ones, the greater fear the lesser. He made up his mind. He turned back to M. 'Give him one more chance, M. If it'll help, I'll take the responsibility.'

'What sort of chance are you thinking of?'

'Well now, I don't know much about your line of business, M. And I don't want to. Got enough secrets in my own job to look after. But haven't you got something really sticky, some apparently hopeless assignment you can give this man? I don't mean necessarily dangerous, like assassination or stealing Russian ciphers or whatever. But something that's desperately important but apparently impossible. By all means give him a kick in the pants at the same time if you want to, but what he needs most of all is a supreme call on his talents, something that'll really make him sweat so that he's simply forced to forget his personal troubles. He's a patriotic sort of a chap. Give him something that really matters to his country. It would be easy enough if a war broke out. Nothing like death or glory to take a man out of himself. But can't you dream up something that simply stinks of urgency? If you can, give him the job. It might get him right back on the rails. Anyway, give him the chance. Yes?'

The urgent thrill of the red telephone, that had been silent for so many weeks, shot Mary Goodnight out of her seat at the typewriter as if it had been fitted with a cartridge ejector. She dashed through into the next room, waited a second to get her breath back and picked up the receiver as if it had been a rattlesnake.

'Yes, sir.'

'No, sir. It's his secretary speaking.' She looked down at her watch, knowing the worst.

'It's most unusual, sir. I don't expect he'll be more than a few minutes. Shall I ask him to call you, sir?'

'Yes, sir.' She put the receiver back on its cradle. She noticed that her hand was trembling. Damn the man! Where the hell was he? She said aloud, 'Oh James, please hurry.' She walked disconsolately back and sat down again at her empty typewriter. She gazed at the grey keys with unseeing eyes and broadcast with all her telepathic strength, 'James! James! M. wants you! M. wants you! M. wants you!' Her heart dropped a beat. The Syncraphone. Perhaps just this once he hadn't forgotten it.

She hurried back into his room and tore open the right-hand drawer. No! There it was, the little plastic receiver on which he could have been bleeped by the switchboard. The gadget that it was mandatory for all senior Headquarters staff to carry when they left the building. But for weeks he had been forgetting to carry it, or worse, not caring if he did or didn't. She took it out and slammed it down in the centre of his blotter. 'Oh, damn you! Damn you! Damn you!' she said out loud, and walked back into her room with dragging feet.

The state of your health, the state of the weather, the wonders of nature — these are things that rarely occupy the average man's mind until he reaches the middle thirties. It is only on the threshold of middle-age that you don't take them all for granted, just part of an unremarkable background to more urgent, more interesting things.

Until this year, James Bond had been more or less oblivious to all of them. Apart from occasional hangovers, and the mending of physical damage that was merely, for him, the extension of a child falling down and cutting its knee, he had taken good health for granted. The weather? Just a question of whether or not he had to carry a raincoat or put the hood up on his Bentley Convertible. As for birds, bees and flowers, the wonders of nature, it only mattered whether or not they bit or stung, whether they smelled good or bad. But today, on the last day of August, just eight months, as he had reminded himself that morning, since Tracy had died, he sat in Queen Mary's Rose Garden in Regent's Park, and his mind was totally occupied with just these things.

First his health. He felt like hell and knew that he also looked it. For months, without telling anyone, he had tramped Harley Street, Wigmore Street and Wimpole Street looking for any kind of doctor who would make him feel better. He had appealed to specialists, G.P.s, quacks — even to a hypnotist. He had told them, 'I feel like hell. I sleep badly. I eat practically nothing. I drink too much and my work has gone to blazes. I'm shot to pieces. Make me better.' And each man had taken his blood pressure, a specimen of his urine, listened to his heart and chest, asked him questions he had answered truthfully, and had told him there was nothing basically wrong with him. Then he had paid his five guineas and gone off to John Bell and Croyden to have the new lot of prescriptions — for tranquillizers, sleeping pills, energizers — made up. And now he had just come from breaking off relations with the last resort — the hypnotist, whose basic message had been that he must go out and regain his manhood by having a woman. As if he hadn't tried that! The ones who had told him to take it easy up the stairs. The ones who had asked him to take them to Paris. The ones who had inquired indifferently, 'Feeling better now, dearie?' The hypnotist hadn't been a bad chap. Rather a bore about how he could take away warts and how he was persecuted by the B.M.A., but Bond had finally had enough of sitting in a chair and listening to the quietly droning voice while, as instructed, he relaxed and gazed at a naked electric light bulb. And now he had thrown up the fifty-guinea course after only half the treatment and had come to sit in this secluded garden before going back to his office ten minutes away across the park.

He looked at his watch. Just after three o'clock, and he was due back at two thirty. What the hell! God, it was hot. He wiped a hand across his forehead and then down the side of his trousers. He used not to sweat like this. The weather must be changing. Atomic bomb, whatever the scientists might say to the contrary. It would be good to be down somewhere in the South of France. Somewhere to bathe whenever he wanted. But he had had his leave for the year. That ghastly month they had given him after Tracy. Then he had gone to Jamaica. And what hell that had been. No! Bathing wasn't the answer. It was all right here, really. Lovely roses to look at. They smelled good and it was pleasant looking at them and listening to the faraway traffic. Nice hum of bees. The way they went around the flowers, doing their work for their queen. Must read that book about them by the Belgian chap, Metternich or something. Same man who wrote about the ants. Extraordinary purpose in life. They didn't have troubles. Just lived and died. Did what they were supposed to do and then dropped dead. Why didn't one see a lot of bees' corpses around? Ants' corpses? Thousands, millions of them must die every day. Perhaps the others ate them. Oh, well! Better go back to the office and get hell from Mary. She was a darling. She was right to nag at him as she did. She was his conscience. But she didn't realize the troubles he had. What troubles? Oh well. Don't let's go into that! James Bond got to his feet and went over and read the lead labels of the roses he had been gazing at. They told him that the bright vermilion ones were 'Super Star' and the white ones 'Iceberg'.

Then, with a jumble of his health, the heat, and the corpses of bees revolving lazily round his mind, James Bond strolled off in the direction of the tall grey building whose upper storeys showed themselves above the trees.

It was three thirty. Only two more hours to go before his next drink!

The lift man, resting the stump of his right arm on the operating handle, said, 'Your secretary's in a bit of a flap, sir. Been asking everywhere for you.'

'Thank you, Sergeant.'

He got the same message when he stepped out at the fifth floor and showed his pass to the security guard at the desk. He walked unhurriedly along the quiet corridor to the group of end rooms whose outer door bore the Double-O sign. He went through and along to the door marked 007. He closed it behind him. Mary Goodnight looked up at him and said calmly, 'M. wants you. He rang down half an hour ago.'

'Who's M.?'

Mary Goodnight jumped to her feet, her eyes flashing. 'Oh for God's sake, James, snap out of it! Here, your tie's crooked.' She came up to him and he docilely allowed her to pull it straight. 'And your hair's all over the place. Here, use my comb.' Bond took the comb and ran it absentmindedly through his hair. He said, 'You're a good girl, Goodnight.' He fingered his chin. 'Suppose you haven't got your razor handy? Must look my best on the scaffold.'

'Please, James.' Her eyes were bright. 'Go and get on to him. He hasn't talked to you for weeks. Perhaps it's something important. Something exciting.' She tried desperately to put encouragement into her voice.

'It's always exciting starting a new life. Anyway, who's afraid of the Big Bad M.? Will you come and lend a hand on my chicken farm?'

She turned away and put her hands up to her face. He patted

her casually on the shoulder and walked through into his office and went over and picked up the red telephone. '007 here, sir.'

'I'm sorry, sir. Had to go to the dentist.'

'I know, sir. I'm sorry. I left it in my desk.'

'Yes, sir.'

He put the receiver down slowly. He looked round his office as if saying goodbye to it, walked out and along the corridor and went up in the lift with the resignation of a man under sentence.

Miss Moneypenny looked up at him with ill-concealed hostility. 'You can go in.'

Bond squared his shoulders and looked at the padded door behind which he had so often heard his fate pronounced. Almost as if it were going to give him an electric shock, he tentatively reached out for the door handle and walked through and closed the door behind him.

3

THE IMPOSSIBLE MISSION

M., HIS SHOULDERS hunched inside the square-cut blue suit, was standing by the big window looking out across the park. Without looking round he said, 'Sit down.' No name, no number!

Bond took his usual place across the desk from M.'s tall-armed chair. He noticed that there was no file on the expanse of red leather in front of the chair. And the In and Out baskets were both empty. Suddenly he felt really bad about everything — about letting M. down, letting the Service down, letting himself down. This empty desk, the empty chair, were the final accusation. We have nothing for you, they seemed to say. You're no use to us any more. Sorry. It's been nice knowing you, but there it is.

M. came over and sat heavily down in the chair and looked across at Bond. There was nothing to read in the lined sailor's face. It was as impassive as the polished blue leather of the empty chair-back had been.

M. said, 'You know why I've sent for you?'

'I can guess, sir. You can have my resignation.'

M. said angrily, 'What in hell are you talking about? It's not your fault that the Double-O Section's been idle for so long. It's the way things go. You've had flat periods before now — months with nothing in your line.'

'But I made a mess of the last two jobs. And I know my Medical's been pretty poor these last few months.'

'Nonsense. There's nothing the matter with you. You've been through a bad time. You've had good reason to be a bit under the weather. As for the last two assignments, anyone can make mistakes. But I can't have idle hands around the place, so I'm taking you out of the Double-O Section.'

Bond's heart had temporarily risen. Now it plummeted again. The old man was being kind, trying to let him down lightly. He said, 'Then, if it's all the same to you, sir, I'd still like to put in my resignation. I've held the Double-O number for too long. I'm not interested in staff work, I'm afraid, sir. And no good at it either.'

M. did something Bond had never seen him do before. He lifted his right fist and brought it crashing down on the desk. 'Who the devil do you think you're talking to? Who the devil d'you think's running this show? God in Heaven! I send for you to give you promotion and the most important job of your career and you talk to me about resignation! Pig-headed young fool!'

Bond was dumbfounded. A great surge of excitement ran through him. What in hell was all this about? He said, 'I'm terribly sorry, sir. I thought I'd been letting the side down lately.'

'I'll soon tell you when you're letting the side down.' M. thumped the desk for a second time, but less hard. 'Now listen to me, I'm giving you acting promotion to the Diplomatic Section. Four figure number and a thousand a year extra pay. You won't know much about the Section, but I can tell you there are only two other men in it. You can keep your present office and your secretary, if you like. In fact I would prefer it. I don't want your change of duty to get about. Understand?'

'Yes, sir.'

'In any case, you'll be leaving for Japan inside a week. The Chief of Staff is handling the arrangements personally. Not even my secretary knows about it. As you can see,' M. waved his hand, 'there's not even a file on the case. That's how important it is.'

'But why have you chosen me, sir?' Bond's heart was thumping. This was the most extraordinary change in his fortunes that had ever come about! Ten minutes before he had been on the rubbish heap, his career, his life in ruins, and now here he was being set up on a pinnacle! What the hell was it all about?

'For the simple reason that the job's impossible. No, I won't go as far as that. Let's say totally improbable of success. You've shown in the past that you have an aptitude for difficult assignments. The only difference here is that there won't be any strong-arm stuff,' M. gave a frosty smile, 'none of the gun-play you pride yourself on so much. It'll just be a question of your wits and nothing else. But if you bring it off, which I very much doubt, you will just about double our intelligence about the Soviet Union.'

'Can you tell me some more about it, sir?'

'Have to, as there's nothing written down. Lower echelon stuff, about the Japanese Secret Service and so forth, you can get from Section J. The Chief of Staff will tell Colonel Hamilton to answer your questions freely, though you will tell him nothing about the purpose of your mission. Understood?'

'Yes, sir.'

'Well now. You know a bit about cryptography?'

'The bare bones, sir. I've preferred to keep clear of the subject. Better that way in case the Opposition ever got hold of me.'

'Quite right. Well now, the Japanese are past masters at it. They've got the right mentality for finicky problems in letters and numbers. Since the war, under C.I.A. guidance, they've built incredible cracking machines — far ahead of I.B.M. and so forth. And for the last year they've been reading the cream of the Soviet traffic from Vladivostok and Oriental Russia — diplomatic, naval, air-force, the lot.'

'That's terrific, sir.'

'Terrific for the C.I.A.'

'Aren't they passing it on to us, sir? I thought we were hand in glove with C.I.A. all along the line.'

'Not in the Pacific. They regard that as their private preserve. When Allen Dulles was in charge, we used at least to get digests of any stuff that concerned us, but this new man McCone has cracked down on all that. He's a good man, all right, and we get along well personally, but he's told me candidly that he's acting under orders — National Defence Council. They're worried about our security. Can't blame them. I'm equally worried about theirs. Two of their top cryptographers defected a couple of years ago and they must have blown a lot of the stuff we give the Americans. Trouble with this so-called democracy of ours is that the Press get hold of these cases and write them up too big. *Pravda* doesn't burst into tears when one of their men come over to us. *Izvestia* doesn't ask for a public inquiry. Somebody in K.G.B. gets hell, I suppose. But at least they're allowed to get on with their job instead of having retired members of the Supreme Soviet pawing through their files and telling them how to run a secret service.'

Bond knew that M. had tendered his resignation after the Prenderghast case. This had involved a Head of Station with homosexual tendencies who had recently, amidst worldwide publicity, been given thirty years for treason. Bond himself had had to give evidence in that particular case, and he knew that the Questions in the House, the case at the Old Bailey, and the hearings before the Farrer Tribunal on the Intelligence Services that had followed, had held up all work at Headquarters for at least a month and brought about the suicide of a totally innocent Head of Section who had taken the whole affair as a direct reflection on his own probity. To get M. back on the track, Bond said, 'About this stuff the Japanese are getting. Where do I come in, sir?'

M. put both hands flat on the table. It was the old gesture when he came to the 64-dollar question, and Bond's heart lifted even further at the sight of it. 'There's a man in Tokyo called Tiger Tanaka. Head of their Secret Service. Can't remember what they call it. Some unpronounceable Japanese rubbish. He's quite a man. First at Oxford. Came back here and spied for them before the war. Joined the Kempeitai, their wartime Gestapo, trained as a *kami-kaze* and would be dead by now but for the surrender. Well, he's the chap who has control of the stuff we want, I want, the Chiefs of Staff want. You're to go out there and get it off him. How, I don't know. That's up to you. But you can see why I say you're unlikely to succeed. He's in fief' — Bond was amused by the old Scottish expression — 'to the C.I.A. He probably doesn't think much of us.' M.'s mouth bent down at the corners. 'People don't these days. They may be right or wrong. I'm not a politician. He doesn't know much about the Service except what he's penetrated or heard from the C.I.A. And that won't be greatly to our advantage, I'd say. We haven't had a Station in Japan since 1950. No traffic. It all went to the Americans. You'll be working under the Australians. They tell me their man's good. Section J says so too. Anyway, that's the way it is. If anyone can bring it off, you can. Care to have a try, James?'

M.'s face was suddenly friendly. It wasn't friendly often. James Bond felt a quick warmth of affection for this man who had ordered his destiny for so long, but whom he knew so little. His instinct told him that there were things hidden behind this assignment, motives which he didn't understand. Was this a rescue job on him? Was M. giving him his last chance? But it sounded solid enough. The reasons for it stood up. Hopeless? Impossible? Perhaps. Why hadn't M. chosen a Jap speaker? Bond had never been east of Hongkong. But then Orientalists had their own particular drawbacks — too much tied up with tea ceremonies and flower arrangements and Zen and so forth. No. It sounded a true bill. He said, 'Yes, sir. I'd like to have a try.'

M. gave an abrupt nod. 'Good.' He leant forward and pressed a button on the intercom. 'Chief of Staff? What number have you allotted to 007? Right. He's coming to see you straight away.'

M. leant back. He gave one of his rare smiles. 'You're stuck with your old digit. All right, four sevens. Go along and get briefed.'

Bond said, 'Right, sir. And, er, thank you.' He got up and walked over to the door and let himself out. He walked straight over to Miss Moneypenny and bent down and kissed her on the cheek. She turned pink and put a hand up to where he had kissed her. Bond said, 'Be an angel, Penny, and ring down to Mary and tell her she's got to get out of whatever she's doing tonight. I'm taking her out to dinner. Scotts. Tell her we'll have our first roast grouse of the year and pink champagne. Celebration.'

'What of?' Miss Moneypenny's eyes were suddenly wide and excited.

'Oh I don't know. The Queen's birthday or something. Right?' James Bond crossed the room and went into the Chief of Staff's office.

Miss Moneypenny picked up the inter-office telephone and passed on the message in a thrilled voice. She said, 'I do think he's all right again, Mary. It's all there again like it used to be. Heaven knows what M.'s been saying to him. He had lunch with Sir James Molony today. Don't tell James that. But it may have something to do with it. He's with the Chief of Staff now. And Bill said he wasn't to be disturbed. Sounds like some kind of a job. Bill was very mysterious.'

Bill Tanner, late Colonel Tanner of the Sappers and Bond's best friend in the Service, looked up from his heavily laden desk. He grinned with pleasure at what he saw. He said, 'Take a pew, James. So you've bought it? Thought you might. But it's a stinker all right. Think you can bring it off?'

'Not an earthly, I'd guess,' said Bond cheerfully. 'This man Tanaka sounds a tough nut, and I'm no great hand at diplomacy. But why did M. pick on me, Bill? I thought I was in the dog house because of messing up those last two jobs. I was all set to go into chicken farming. Now, be a good chap and tell me what's the real score.'

Bill Tanner had been ready for that one. He said easily, 'Balls, James. You've been running through a bad patch. We all hit 'em sometimes. M. just thought you'd be the best man for the job. You know he's got an entirely misplaced opinion of your abilities. Anyway, it'll be a change from your usual rough-housing. Time you moved up out of that damned Double-O Section of yours. Don't you ever think about promotion?'

'Absolutely not,' said Bond with fervour. 'As soon as I get back from this caper, I'll ask for my old number back again. But tell me, how am I supposed to set about this business? What's this Australian cover consist of? Have I got anything to offer this wily Oriental in exchange for his jewels? How's the stuff to be transmitted back here if I do get my hands on it? Must be the hell of a lot of traffic.'

'He can have the entire product of Station H. He can send one of his own staffers down to Hongkong to sit in with us if he likes. He'll probably be pretty well off on China already, but he won't have anything as high grade as our Macao link, the "Blue Route". Hamilton will tell you all about that. In Tokyo, the man you'll be working with is an Aussie called Henderson — Richard Lovelace Henderson. Fancy name, but Section J and all the old Jap hands say he's a good man. You'll have an Australian passport and we'll fix for you to go out as his number two. That'll give you diplomatic status and a certain amount of face, which counts for damn near everything out there according to Hamilton. If you get the stuff, Henderson will push it back to us through Melbourne. We'll give him a communications staff to handle it. Next question.'

'What are the C.I.A. going to say about all this? After all, it's bare-faced poaching.'

'They don't own Japan. Anyway, they're not to know. That's

up to this fellow Tanaka. He'll have to fix the machinery for getting it into the Australian Embassy. That's his worry. But the whole thing's on pretty thin ice. The main problem is to make sure he doesn't go straight along to the C.I.A. and tell 'em of your approach. If you get blown, we'll just have to get the Australians to hold the baby. They've done it before when we've been bowled out edging our way into the Pacific. We're good friends with their Service. First-rate bunch of chaps. And, anyway, the C.I.A.'s hands aren't as clean as all that. We've got a whole file of cases where they've crossed wires with us round the world. Often dangerously. We can throw that book at McCone if this business blows up in our faces. But part of your job is to see that it doesn't.'

'Seems to me I'm getting all balled up in high politics. Not my line of country at all. But is this stuff really as vital as M. says?'

'Absolutely. If you get hold of it, your grateful country will probably buy you that chicken farm you're always talking about.'

'So be it. Now, if you'll give Hamilton a buzz I'll go and start learning all about the mysterious East.'

'*Kangei!* Welcome aboard,' said the pretty kimonoed and obied stewardess of Japan Air Lines as, a week later, James Bond settled into the comfortable window seat of the four-jet, turbofan Douglas DC 8 at London Airport and listened to the torrent of soft Japanese coming from the tannoy that would be saying all those things about life jackets and the flying time to Orly. The sick-bags 'in case of motion disturbance' were embellished with pretty bamboo emblems and, according to the exquisitely bound travel folder, the random scribbles on the luggage rack above his head were 'the traditional and auspicious tortoiseshell motif'. The stewardess bowed and handed him a dainty fan, a small hot towel in a wicker basket and a sumptuous menu that included a note to the effect that an assortment of cigarettes, perfumes and pearls were available for sale. Then they were off with 50,000 pounds of thrust on the first leg of the four that would take the good aircraft Yoshino over the North Pole to Tokyo.

Bond gazed at the picture of three oranges (no! After an hour he decided they were persimmons) in a blue bowl that faced him and, when the aircraft flattened out at 30,000 feet, ordered the first of the chain of brandies and ginger ales that was to sustain him over the Channel, a leg of the North Sea, the Kattegat, the Arctic Ocean, the Beaufort Sea, the Bering Sea and the North Pacific Ocean and decided that, whatever happened on this impossible assignment, he would put up no resistance to his old skin being sloughed off him on the other side of the world. By the time he was admiring the huge stuffed polar bear at Anchorage, in Alaska, the embrace of J.A.L.'s soft wings had persuaded him that he didn't even mind if the colour of the new skin was to be yellow.

4

DIKKO ON THE GINZA

THE HUGE RIGHT FIST crashed into the left palm with the noise of a .45 pistol shot. The great square face of the Australian turned almost purple and the veins stood out on the grizzled temples. With controlled violence, but almost under his breath, he intoned savagely:

'I bludge,
Thou bludgest,
He bludges,
We bludge,
You bludge,
They all bludge.'

He reached under the low table and then seemed to think better of it and moved his hand to the glass of *saké*, picked it up and poured it down his throat without a swallow.

Bond said mildly, 'Take it easy, Dikko. What's bitten you? And what does this vulgar-sounding colonial expression mean?'

Richard Lovelace Henderson, of Her Majesty's Australian Diplomatic Corps, looked belligerently round the small crowded bar in a by-street of the Ginza and said out of the corner of his large and usually cheerful mouth that was now turned down in bitterness and anger, 'You stupid pommy bastard, we've been miked! That bludger Tanaka's miked us! Here, under the table! See the little wire down the leg? And see that wingy over at the bar? Chap with one arm looking bloody respectable in his blue suit and black tie? That's one of Tiger's men. I can smell 'em by now. They've been trailing me off and on for ten years. Tiger dresses 'em all like little C.I.A. gentlemen. You watch out for any Jap who's drinking Western and wearing that rig. All Tiger's men.' He grumbled, 'Damn good mind to go over and call the bastard.'

Bond said, 'Well, if we're being miked, all this'll make sweet reading for Mr Tanaka tomorrow morning.'

'What the hell,' said Dikko Henderson resignedly. 'The old bastard knows what I think of him. Now he'll just have it in writing. Teach him to stop leaning on me. And my friends,' he added, with a blistering glance at Bond. 'It's really you he wants to size up. And I don't mind if he hears me saying so. Bludger? Well, hear me now, Tiger! This is the great Australian insult. You can use it anyways.' He raised his voice. 'But in general it means a worthless pervert, ponce, scoundrel, liar, traitor and rogue — with no redeeming feature. And I hope your stewed seaweed sticks in your gullet at breakfast tomorrow when you know what I think of you.'

Bond laughed. The torrent of powerful swear-words had started its ceaseless flow the day before at the airport — Haneda, 'the field of wings'. It had taken Bond nearly an hour to extract his single suitcase from the customs area, and he had emerged fuming into the central hall only to be jostled and pushed aside by an excited crowd of young Japanese bearing paper banners that said 'International Laundry Convention'. Bond was exhausted from his flight. He let out one single four-letter expletive.

Behind him a big voice repeated the same word and added some more. 'That's my boy! That's the right way to greet the East! You'll be needing all those words and more before you're through with the area.'

Bond had turned. The huge man in the rumpled grey suit thrust out a hand as big as a small ham. 'Glad to meet you. I'm Henderson. As you were the only pommy on the plane, I guess you're Bond. Here. Give me that bag. Got a car outside and the sooner we get away from this blankety blank madhouse the better.'

Henderson looked like a middle-aged prize fighter who has retired and taken to the bottle. His thin suit bulged with muscle round the arms and shoulders and with fat round the waist. He had a craggy, sympathetic face, rather stony blue eyes, and a badly broken nose. He was sweating freely (Bond was to find that he was always sweating), and as he barged his way through the crowd, using Bond's suitcase as a battering ram, he extracted a rumpled square of terry cloth from his trouser-pocket and wiped it round his neck and face. The crowd parted unresentfully to let the giant through, and Bond followed in his wake to a smart Toyopet saloon waiting in a no-parking area. The chauffeur got out and bowed. Henderson fired a torrent of instructions at him in fluent Japanese and followed Bond into the back seat, settling himself with a grunt. 'Taking you to your hotel first — the Okura, latest of the Western ones. American tourist got murdered at the Royal Oriental the other day and we don't want to lose you all that soon. Then we'll do a bit of serious drinking. Had some dinner?'

'About six of them, as far as I can remember. J.A.L. certainly takes good care of your stomach.'

'Why did you choose the willow-pattern route? How was the old ruptured duck?'

'They told me the bird was a crane. Very dainty. But efficient. Thought I might as well practise being inscrutable before plunging into all this.' Bond waved at the cluttered shambles of the Tokyo suburbs through which they were tearing at what seemed to Bond a suicidal speed. 'Doesn't look the most attractive city in the world. And why are we driving on the left?'

'God knows,' said Henderson moodily. 'The bloody Japs do everything the wrong way round. Read the old instruction books wrong, I daresay. Light switches go up instead of down. Taps turn to the left. Door handles likewise. Why, they even race their horses clockwise instead of anti-clockwise like civilized people. As for Tokyo, it's bloody awful. It's either too hot or too cold or pouring with rain. And there's an earthquake about every day. But don't worry about them. They just make you feel slightly drunk. The typhoons are worse. If one starts to blow, go into the stoutest bar you can see and get drunk. But the first ten years are the worst. It's got its points when you know your way around. Bloody expensive if you live Western, but I stick to the back alleys and do all right. Really quite exhilarating. Got to know the lingo though, and when to bow and take off your shoes and so on. You'll have to get the basic routines straight pretty quickly if you're going to make any headway with the people you've come to see. Underneath the stiff collars and striped pants in the government departments, there's still plenty of the old *samurai* tucked away. I laugh at them for it, and they laugh back because they've got to know my line of patter. But that doesn't mean I don't bow from the waist when I know it's expected of me and when I want something. You'll get the hang of it all right.' Henderson fired some Japanese at the driver who had been glancing frequently in his driving mirror. The driver laughed and replied cheerfully. 'Thought so,' said Henderson. 'We've got ourselves a tail. Typical of old Tiger. I told him you were staying at the Okura, but he wants to make sure for himself. Don't worry. It's just part of his crafty ways. If you find one of his men breathing down your neck in bed tonight, or a girl if you're lucky, just talk to them politely and they'll bow and hiss themselves out.'

But a solitary sleep had followed the serious drinking in the Bamboo Bar of the Okura, and the next day had been spent doing the sights and getting some cards printed that described Bond as Second Secretary in the Cultural Department of the Australian Embassy. 'They know that's our intelligence side,' said Henderson, 'and they know I'm the head of it and you're my temporary assistant, so why not spell it out for them?' And that evening they had gone for more serious drinking to Henderson's favourite bar, Melody's, off the Ginza, where everybody called Henderson 'Dikko' or 'Dikko-san', and where they were ushered respectfully to the quiet corner table that appeared to be his *Stammtisch*.

And now Henderson reached under the table and, with a powerful wrench, pulled out the wires and left them hanging. 'I'll give that black bastard Melody hell for this when I get around to it,' he said belligerently. 'And to think of all I've done for the dingo bastard! Used to be a favourite pub of the English Colony and the Press Club layabouts. Had a good restaurant attached to it. That's gone now. The Eyetie cook trod on the cat and spilled the soup and he picked up the cat and threw it into the cooking stove. Of course that got around pretty quick, and all the animal-lovers and sanctimonious bastards got together and tried to have Melody's licence taken away. I managed to put in squeeze in the right quarter and saved him, but everyone quit his restaurant and he had to close it. I'm the only regular who's stuck to him. And now he goes and does this to me! Oh well, he'll have had the squeeze put on *him*, I suppose. Anyway, that's the end of the tape so far as T.T.'s concerned. I'll give him hell too. He ought to have learned by now that me and my friends don't want to assassinate the Emperor or blow up the Diet or something.' Dikko glared around him as if he proposed to do both those things. 'Now then, James, to business. I've fixed up for you to meet Tiger tomorrow morning at eleven. I'll pick you up and take you there. "The Bureau of All-Asian Folkways". I won't describe it to you. It'd spoil it. Now, I don't really know what you're here for. Spate of top secret cables from Melbourne. To be deciphered by yours truly in person. Thanks very much! And my Ambassador, Jim Saunderson, good bloke, says he doesn't want to know anything about it. Thinks it'd be even better if he didn't meet you at all. Okay with you? No offence, but he's a wise guy and likes to keep his hands clean. And I don't want to know anything about your job either. That way, you're the only one who gets the powdered bamboo in his coffee. But I gather you want to get some high-powered gen out of Tiger without the C.I.A. knowing anything about it. Right? Well that's going to be a dicey business. Tiger's a career man with a career mind. Although, on the surface, he's a hundred per cent *demokorasu*, he's a deep one — very deep indeed. The American occupation and the American influence here look like a very solid basis for a total American–Japanese alliance. But once a Jap, always a Jap. It's the same with all the other great nations — Chinese, Russian, German, English. It's their bones that matter, not their lying faces. And all those races have got tremendous bones. Compared with the bones, the smiles or scowls don't mean a thing. And time means nothing for them either. Ten years is the blink of a star for the big ones. Get me? So Tiger, and his superiors, who, I suppose, are the Diet and, in the end, the Emperor, will look at your proposition principally from two angles. Is it immediately desirable, today? Or is it a long-term investment? Something that may pay off for the country in ten, twenty years. And, if I were you, I'd stick to that spiel — the long-term talk. These people, people like Tiger, who's an absolutely top man in Japan, don't think in terms of days or months or years. They think in terms of centuries. Quite right, when you come to think of it.'

Dikko Henderson made a wide gesture with his left hand. Bond decided that Dikko was getting cheerfully tight. He had found a Palomar pony to run with. They must be rare enough in Tokyo. They were both past the eighth flask of *saké*, but Dikko had also laid a foundation of Suntory whisky in the Okura while he'd been waiting for Bond to write out an innocuous cable to Melbourne with the prefix 'Informationwise', which meant that it was for Mary Goodnight, to announce his arrival and give his current address. But it was all right with Bond that Dikko should be getting plastered. He would talk better and looser and, in the end, wiser that way. And Bond wanted to pick his brains.

Bond said, 'But what sort of a chap is this Tanaka? Is he your enemy or your friend?'

'Both. More of a friend probably. At least I'd guess so. I amuse him. His C.I.A. pals don't. He loosens up with me. We've got things in common. We share a pleasure in the delights of *samsara* — wine and women. He's a great cocksman. I also have ambitions in that direction. I've managed to keep him out of two marriages. Trouble with Tiger is he always wants to marry 'em. He's paying cock-tax, that's alimony in the Australian vernacular, to three already. So he's acquired an ON with regard to me. That's an obligation — almost as important in the Japanese way of life as "face". When you have an ON, you're not very happy until you've discharged it honourably, if you'll pardon the bad pun. And if a man makes you a present of a salmon, you mustn't repay him with a shrimp. It's got to be with an equally large salmon — larger if possible, so that then you've jumped the man, and now he has an ON with regard to you, and you're quids in morally, socially and spiritually — and the last one's the most important. Well now. Tiger's ON towards me is a very powerful one, very difficult to discharge. He's paid little slices of it off with various intelligence dope. He's paid off another big slice by accepting your presence here and giving you an interview so soon after your arrival. If you'd been an ordinary supplicant, it might have taken you weeks. He'd have given you a fat dose of *shikiri-naoshi* — that's making you wait, giving you the great stone face. The *sumo* wrestlers use it in the ring to make an opponent look and feel small in front of the audience. Got it? So you start with that in your favour. He would be predisposed to do what you want because that would remove all his ON towards me and, by his accounting, stick a whole packet of ON on my back towards him. But it's not so simple as that. All Japanese have permanent ON towards their superiors, the Emperor, their ancestors and the Japanese gods. This they can only discharge by doing "the right thing". Not easy, you'll say. Because how can you know what the higher echelon thinks is the right thing? Well, you get out of that by doing what the bottom of the ladder thinks right — i.e. your immediate superiors. That passes the buck, psychologically, on to the Emperor, and he's got to make his peace with ancestors and gods. But that's all right with him, because he embodies all the echelons above him, so he can get on with dissecting fish, which is his hobby, with a clear conscience. Got it? It's not really as mysterious as it sounds. Much the same routine as operates in big corporations, like I.C.I. or Shell, or in the Services, except with them the ladder stops at the Board of Directors or the Chiefs of Staff. It's easier that way. You don't have to involve the Almighty and your great-grandfather in a decision to cut the price of aspirin by a penny a bottle.'

'It doesn't sound very *demokorasu* to me.'

'Of course it isn't, you dumb bastard. For God's sake, get it into your head that the Japanese are a separate human species. They've only been operating as a civilized people, in the debased sense we talk about it in the West, for fifty, at the most a hundred years. Scratch a Russian and you'll find a Tartar. Scratch a Japanese and you'll find a *samurai* — or what he thinks is a *samurai*. Most of this *samurai* stuff is a myth, like the Wild West bunk the Americans are brought up on, or your knights in shining armour at King Arthur's court. Just because people play baseball and wear bowler hats doesn't mean they're quote civilized unquote. Just to show you I'm getting rather tight — not drunk, mark you — I'd add that the U.N. are going to reap the father and mother of a whirlwind by quote liberating unquote the colonial peoples. Give 'em a thousand years, yes. But give 'em ten, no. You're only taking away their blow-pipes and giving them machine guns. Just you wait for the first one to start crying to high heaven for nuclear fission. Because they must have quote parity unquote with the lousy colonial powers. I'll give you ten years for that to happen, my friend. And when it does, I'll dig myself a deep hole in the ground and sit in it.'

Bond laughed. 'That also doesn't sound very *demokorasu*.'

' "I fornicate upon thy *demokorasu*" as brother Hemingway

would have said. I stand for government by an elite.' Dikko Henderson downed his ninth pint of *saké*. 'And voting graded by each individual's rating in that elite. And one tenth of a vote for my government if you don't agree with me!'

'For God's sake, Dikko! How in hell did we get on to politics? Let's go and get some food. I'll agree there's a certain aboriginal common sense in what you say . . . '

'Don't talk to me about the aborigines! What in hell do you think you know about the aborigines? Do you know that in my country there's move afoot, not afoot, at full gallop, to give the aborigines the vote? You pommy poofter. You give me any more of that liberal crap and I'll have your balls for a bow tie.'

Bond said mildly, 'What's a poofter?'

'What you'd call a pansy. No,' Dikko Henderson got to his feet and fired a string of what sounded like lucid Japanese at the man behind the bar, 'before I condemn you utterly, we'll go and eat eels — place where you can get a serious bottle of plonk to match. Then we'll go to "The House of Total Delight". After that, I will give you my honest verdict, honestly come by.'

Bond said, 'You're a no-good kangaroo bum, Dikko. But I like eels. As long as they're not jellied. I'll pay for them and for the later relaxation. You pay for the rice wine and the plonk, whatever that is. Take it easy. The wingy at the bar has an appraising look.'

'I come to appraise Mr Richard Lovelace Henderson, not to bury him.' Dikko Henderson produced a wad of thousand-yen notes and began counting them out for the waiter. 'Not yet, that is.' He walked, with careful majesty, up to the bar and addressed himself to the large Negro in a plum-coloured coat behind it. 'Melody, be ashamed of yourself!' Then he led the way, with massive dignity, out of the bar.

5

MAGIC 44

DIKKO HENDERSON CAME to fetch Bond at ten o'clock next morning. He was considerably overhung. The hard blue eyes were veined with blood and he made straight for the Bamboo Bar and ordered himself a double brandy and ginger ale. Bond said mildly, 'You shouldn't have poured all that *saké* on top of the Suntory. I can't believe Japanese whisky makes a good foundation for anything.'

'You've got something there, sport. I've got myself a proper *futsukayoi* — honourable hangover. Mouth like a vulture's crutch. Soon as we got home from that lousy cat house, I had to go for the big spit. But you're wrong about Suntory. It's a good enough brew. Stick to the cheapest, the White Label at around fifteen bob a bottle. There are two smarter brands, but the cheap one's the best. Went up to the distillery some whiles ago and met one of the family. Told me an interesting thing about whisky. He said you can only make good whisky where you can take good photographs. Ever heard that one? Said it was something to do with the effect of clear light on the alcohol. But did I talk a lot of crap last night? Or did you? Seem to recollect that one of us did.'

'You only gave me hell about the state of the world and called me a poofter. But you were quite friendly about it. No offence given or taken.'

'Oh, Christ!' Dikko Henderson gloomily pushed a hand through his tough, grizzled hair. 'But I didn't hit anyone?'

'Only that girl you slapped so hard on the bottom that she fell down.'

'Oh that!' said Dikko Henderson with relief. 'That was just a love-pat. What's a girl's bottom for, anyway? And so far as I recall they all screamed with laughter. Including her. Right? How did you make out with yours by the way? She looked pretty enthusiastic.'

'She was.'

'Good show.' He swallowed the remains of his drink and got to his feet. 'Come on, bud. Let's go. Wouldn't do to keep Tiger waiting. I once did and he wouldn't speak to me for a week.'

It was a typical Tokyo day in late summer — hot, sticky and grey — the air full of fine dust from the endless demolition and reconstruction work. They drove for half an hour towards Yokohama and pulled up outside a dull grey building which announced itself in large letters to be 'The Bureau of All-Asian Folkways'. There was a busy traffic of Japanese scurrying in and out through the bogusly important-looking entrance, but no one glanced at Dikko and Bond, and they were not asked their business as Dikko led the way through an entrance hall where there were books and postcards on sale as if the place were some kind of museum. Dikko made for a doorway marked 'Co-ordination Department' and there was a long corridor with open rooms on both sides. The rooms were full of studious-looking young men at desks. There were large wall maps with coloured pins dotted across them, and endless shelves of books. A door marked 'International Relations' gave on to another corridor, this time lined with closed doors which had people's names on them in English and Japanese. A sharp right turn took them through the 'Visual Presentation Bureau' with more closed doors, and on to 'Documentation', a large hall-shaped library with more people bent over desks. Here, for the first time, they were scrutinized by a man at a desk near the entrance. He rose to his feet and bowed wordlessly. As they walked on Dikko said quietly, 'This is where the cover tapers off. Up till now, all those people really were researching Asian Folkways. But these here are part of Tiger's outside staff, doing more or less classified work. Sort of archivists. This is where we'd be politely turned back if we'd lost our way.' Behind a final wall of bookshelves that stretched out into the room a small door was concealed. It was marked 'Proposed Extension to Documentation Department. Danger! Construction work in progress.' From behind it came the sound of drills, a circular saw cutting through wood and other building noises. Dikko walked through the door into a totally empty room with a highly polished wood floor. There was no sign of construction work. Dikko laughed at Bond's surprise. He gestured towards a large metal box fitted to the back of the door through which they had come. 'Tape recorder,' he said. 'Clever gimmick. Sounds just like the real thing. And this' — he pointed to the stretch of bare floor ahead — 'is what the Japanese call a "nightingale floor". Relic of the old days when people wanted to be warned of intruders. Serves the same purpose here. Imagine trying to get across here without being heard.' They set off, and immediately the cunningly sprung boards gave out penetrating squeaks and groans. In a small facing door, a spy-hole slid open and one large eye surveyed them. The door opened to reveal a stocky man in plain clothes who had been sitting at a small deal table reading a book. It was a tiny box-like room that seemed to have no other exit. The man bowed. Dikko said some phrases containing the words 'Tanaka-san'. The man bowed again. Dikko turned to Bond. 'You're on your own now. Be in it, champ! Tiger'll send you back to your hotel. See you.'

Bond said, 'Tell mother I died game,' and walked into the little box and the door was closed behind him. There was a row of buttons by the desk and the guard pressed one of them. There came a barely perceptible whine and Bond got the impression of descent. So the room was a lift. What a box of tricks the formidable Tiger had erected as a screen for himself! The authentic Eastern nest of boxes. What next?

The descent continued for some time. When it stopped, the guard opened the door and Bond stepped out and stood stock still. He was standing on the platform of an underground station! There it all was: the red and green signals over the two yawning tunnels, the conventional white tiles on the walls and the curved roof — even an empty cigarette kiosk let into the wall beside him! A man had come out of this. He now said in good English, 'Please to follow me, Commander,' and led the way through an arch marked 'Exit'. But here all the floor space of the hall that would one day lead to the moving stairways was occupied by trim prefabricated offices on both sides of a wide corridor. Bond was led into the first of these which revealed itself as a waiting-room and outer office. A male secretary rose from his typewriter, bowed and went through a communicating door. He immediately reappeared, bowed again and held the door open. 'Please to come this way, Commander.'

Bond went through and the door was softly closed behind

him. The big square figure that Dikko had described to him came forward across the handsome red carpet and held out a hand that was hard and dry. 'My dear Commander. Good morning. It is a great pleasure to meet you.' The wide, gold-toothed smile signalled welcome. The eyes glittered between long dark lashes that were almost feminine. 'Come and sit down. How do you like my offices? Rather different from your own Chief's, no doubt. But the new underground will take another ten years to complete and there is little office space in Tokyo. It crossed my mind to make use of this disused station. It is quiet. It is private. It is also cool. I shall be sorry when the trains are required to run and we shall have to move out.'

Bond took the proffered chair across the empty desk from Tanaka. 'It's a brilliant idea. And I enjoyed the Folkways above our heads. Are there really so many people in the world interested in Folkways?'

Tiger Tanaka shrugged. 'What does it matter? The literature is given away free. I have never asked the Director who reads it. Americans, I expect, and Germans. Perhaps some Swiss. The serious-minded can always be found for such stuff. It is an expensive conceit, of course. But fortunately the expense is not carried by the Ministry of Internal Affairs with whom I am concerned. Down here, we have to count our pennies. I suppose it is the same with your own budget.'

Bond assumed that this man would know the published facts of the Secret Service Vote. He said, 'Under ten million pounds a year doesn't go far when there is the whole world to cover.'

The teeth glistened under the neon strip lighting. 'At least for the last ten years you have saved money by closing down your activities in this part of the world.'

'Yes. We rely on the C.I.A. to do our work here for us. They are most efficient and helpful.'

'As much so under McCone as under Dulles?'

The old fox! 'Nearly so. Nowadays they are even more inclined to regard the Pacific as their own back garden.'

'From which you wish to borrow the mowing machine. Without them knowing.' Tiger's smile was even more tigerish.

Bond had to laugh. The wily devil had certainly been putting two and two together. When Bond laughed, Tiger also laughed, but carefully. Bond said, 'We had a man called Captain Cook and various others who discovered much of this garden. Australia and New Zealand are two very great countries. You must admit that our interest in this half of the world is perfectly legitimate.'

'My dear Commander. You were lucky that we struck at Pearl Harbour rather than at Australia. Can you doubt that we would have occupied that country and New Zealand if we had done otherwise? These are big and important land spaces, insufficiently developed. You could not have defended them. The Americans would not have. If our policy had been different, we would now own half the British Commonwealth. Personally, I have never understood the strategy behind Pearl Harbour. Did we wish to conquer America? The supply lines were too long. But Australia and New Zealand were ripe for the plucking.' He pushed forward a large box of cigarettes. 'Do you smoke? These are Shinsei. It is an acceptable brand.'

James Bond was running out of his Morland specials. He would soon have to start on the local stuff. He also had to collect his thoughts. This was rather like being involved in a Summit meeting between the United Kingdom and Japan. He felt way out of his depth. He took a cigarette and lit it. It burned rapidly with something of the effect of a slow-burning firework. It had a vague taste of American blends, but it was good and sharp on the palate and lungs like 90 proof spirits. He let the smoke out in a quiet hiss and smiled. 'Mr Tanaka, these are matters for political historians. I am concerned with much lower matters. And matters concerning the future rather than the past.'

'I quite understand, Commander.' Tiger Tanaka was obviously displeased that his game of generalities had been dodged by Bond. 'But we have a saying, "Speak of next year and the devil laughs". The future is inscrutable. But tell me, what are your impressions of Japan? You have been enjoying yourself?'

'I imagine that one always enjoys oneself with Dikko Henderson.'

'Yes, he is a man who lives as if he were going to die tomorrow. This is a correct way to live. He is a good friend of mine. I greatly enjoy his company. We have certain tastes in common.'

Bond said ironically, 'Folkways?'

'Exactly.'

'He has a great affection for you. I do not know him well, but I suspect that he is a lonely man. It is an unfortunate combination to be both lonely and intelligent. Wouldn't it be a good thing for him to marry a Japanese girl and settle down? Couldn't you find him one?' Bond was pleased that the conversation had descended to personalities. He sensed that he was on the right track. At least on a better track than this talk about power politics. But there would come a bad moment when he would have to get down to business. He didn't care for the prospect.

As if he had sensed this, Tiger Tanaka said, 'I have arranged for our friend to meet many Japanese girls. The result in every case has been negative, or, at the best, fleeting. But tell me, Commander. We have not met here to discuss Mr Henderson's private life. In what respect can I be of service to you? Is it the lawn mower?'

Bond smiled. 'It is. The manufacturers' trade mark for this particular implement is MAGIC 44.'

'Ah yes. A most valuable implement of many uses. I can understand that your country would wish to have the services of this implement. A case in point is an example of its capabilities which came into my hands only this morning.' Tiger Tanaka opened a drawer in his desk and extracted a file. It was a pale green file stamped in a square box with the word GOKUHI in black Japanese and Roman characters. Bond assumed this to be the equivalent of Top Secret. He put this to Mr Tanaka who confirmed it. Mr Tanaka opened the file and extracted two sheets of yellow paper. Bond could see that one was covered with Japanese ideograms and that the other had perhaps fifty lines of typewriting. Mr Tanaka slipped the typewritten one across the desk. He said, 'May I beg you on oath not to reveal to anyone what you are about to read?'

'If you insist, Mr Tanaka.'

'I am afraid I must, Commander.'

'So be it.' Bond drew the sheet of paper towards him. The text was in English. This is what it said:

TO ALL STATIONS OF GRADE TWO AND ABOVE. TO BE DECIPHERED BY ADDRESSEE PERSONALLY AND THEN DESTROYED. WHEN DESTRUCTION HAS BEEN EFFECTED

CONFIRM BY THE CODE WORD QUOTE SATURN UNQUOTE. TEXT BEGINS: IN AMPLIFICATION OF NUMBER ONES PUBLISHED SPEECH TO THE SUPREME SOVIET ON SEPTEMBER FIRST THIS CONFIRMS THAT WE ARE IN POSSESSION OF THE TWO HUNDRED MEGATON WEAPON AND THAT A TEST FIRING WILL TAKE PLACE ON SEPTEMBER TWENTIETH AT HIGH ALTITUDE IN THE NOVAYA ZEMLYA AREA STOP CONSIDERABLE FALLOUT CAN BE EXPECTED AND PUBLIC OUTCRY CAN BE ANTICIPATED IN THE ARCTIC, NORTH PACIFIC AND ALASKAN AREAS STOP THIS SHOULD BE COUNTERED AND WILL BE COUNTERED FROM MOSCOW BY REFERENCE TO THE MORE RECENT TESTS BY AMERICA AND TO NUMBER ONES REPEATED DEMANDS FOR AN END TO TESTS OF NUCLEAR FISSION WEAPONS OF OFFENCE WHICH HAVE SUCCESSIVELY BEEN REBUFFED STOP FOR INFORMATION THE DELIVERY OF ONE SUCH WEAPON BY ICBM ON LONDON WOULD DESTROY ALL LIFE AND PROPERTY SOUTH OF A LINE DRAWN BETWEEN NEWCASTLE AND CARLISLE STOP IT FOLLOWS THAT A SECOND MISSILE DROPPED IN THE NEIGHBOURHOOD OF ABERDEEN WOULD INEVITABLY RESULT IN THE TOTAL DESTRUCTION OF BRITAIN AND ALL IRELAND STOP THIS FACT WILL SHORTLY BE EMPLOYED BY NUMBER ONE AS THE TEETH IN A DIPLOMATIC DEMARCHE DESIGNED TO ACHIEVE THE REMOVAL OF ALL AMERICAN BASES AND OFFENSIVE WEAPONS FROM BRITAIN AND THE NUCLEAR DISARMAMENT OF BRITAIN ITSELF STOP THIS WILL TEST TO THE UTTERMOST AND PROBABLY DESTROY THE ANGLO HYPHEN AMERICAN ALLIANCE SINCE IT CAN BE ASSUMED THAT AMERICA WILL NOT RISK A NUCLEAR WAR INVOLVING HER TERRITORY FOR THE SAKE OF RESCUING A NOW MORE OR LESS VALUELESS ALLY DASH AN ALLY NOW OPENLY REGARDED IN WASHINGTON AS OF LITTLE MORE ACCOUNT THAN BELGIUM OR ITALY STOP IF THIS DIPLOMATIC DEMARCHE COMMA WHICH MUST OF COURSE BE CATEGORIZED AS CARRYING SOME DEGREE OF RISK COMMA IS SUCCESSFUL IT FOLLOWS THAT SIMILAR DEMARCHES WILL BE UNDERTAKEN IN EUROPE AND LATER IN THE PACIFIC AREA COMMA INDIVIDUAL COUNTRIES BEING SINGLED

OUT ONE BY ONE FOR TERRORIZATION AND DEMORALIZATION STOP THE FINAL FRUITS OF THIS GRAND STRATAGEM IF SUCCESSFUL WILL GUARANTEE THE SECURITY OF THE USSR FOR THE FORESEEABLE FUTURE AND ULTIMATELY RESULT IN PEACEFUL COEXISTENCE WITH AMERICA STOP PEACEFUL INTENT OF THE USSR WILL THEREFORE BE EMPHASIZED THROUGHOUT BY NUMBER ONE AND BY ALL GOVERNMENT AGENCIES STOP THIS LINE OF REASONING YOU WILL ALSO FOLLOW SHOULD YOUR STATION BE AT ANY TIME INVOLVED OR AFFECTED STOP INFORMATIVELY ALL SOVIET CITIZENS WORKING IN BRITAIN WILL BE WITHDRAWN FROM THAT COUNTRY ONE WEEK BEFORE THE INITIAL DEMARCHE STOP NO EXPLANATION WILL BE GIVEN BUT A CONSIDERABLE AND DESIRABLE HEIGHTENING OF TENSION WILL THUS BE ACHIEVED STOP THE SAME PROCEDURE WHICH CAN BE CATEGORIZED AS A SOFTENING UP OF THE TARGET COUNTRY WILL BE FOLLOWED IN THE SECONDARY DEMARCHES REFERRED TO ABOVE STOP FOR THE TIME BEING YOU SHOULD TAKE NO PRECAUTIONARY STEPS ON YOUR STATION EXCEPT TO PREPARE YOUR MIND IN TOTAL SECRECY FOR THE EVENTUALITY THAT YOUR STATION MAY BECOME INVOLVED AT SOME LATER DATE AND THAT EVACUATION OF YOUR STAFF AND THE BURNING OF ARCHIVES WILL BECOME MANDATORY ON RECEIPT OF THE CODE WORD QUOTE LIGHTNING UNQUOTE ADDRESSED TO YOU PERSONALLY OVER CIRCUIT FORTY HYPHEN FOUR STOP END OF TEXT SIGNED CENTRAL.

James Bond pushed the document away from him as if he feared contamination from it. He let out his breath in a quiet hiss. He reached for the box of Shinsei and lit one, drawing the harsh smoke deep down into his lungs. He raised his eyes to Mr Tanaka's, which were regarding him with polite interest. 'I suppose Number One is Khrushchev?'

'That is correct, and the meaning of stations grade two and above is consulates general and embassies. It is interesting material, is it not?'

'It is a mistake that you are keeping this material from us. We have a treaty of friendship and a trade treaty with you. Do you not regard the withholding of this vital information as a dishonourable act?'

'Honour is a very serious word in Japan, Commander. Would it not be even more dishonourable to break our word to our good American friends? They have several times assured me and my government that any information of vital importance to our other friends and allies will be passed on to them in such a way as not to divulge the source. I have no evidence that they are not pursuing this routine.'

'You know as well as I do, Mr Tanaka, that rewriting and doctoring to conceal the source reduces this type of material to a grade no higher than secret reports from countless other "delicate and reliable" sources. The nature of this particular source, the fact that one is reading the very words of the enemy, is at least fifty per cent of the value of the information this message contains. No doubt Washington will pass on a garbled version of this message to London. I hope they already have. But you realize that it might be in their interests to keep quiet about this terrible threat that hangs over England? At the same time, it is in England's interest to use every hour in devising some counter to this plan. One small step, which at once comes to mind, is preparations for the internment of all Soviet citizens in Britain at the first sign of the evacuation measures mentioned in the message.'

'I appreciate your point of view, Commander. There is of course, in this instance, an alternative route for this information to reach your government.' Mr Tanaka's face crinkled wickedly.

Bond leant urgently over the desk. 'But I gave my word of honour!'

Mr Tanaka's face underwent a curious change. All the upward lines turned downwards. The dark eyes lost their glitter and assumed an inward look. In a curious way, the whole face slumped into melancholy. He said, 'Commander, I was very happy in England. Your people were very good to me. I repaid them in an unworthy fashion.' (Ah! thought Bond. The ON.) 'I plead youth and the heat of a war that I thought would bring much glory to my country. I was mistaken. We were defeated. The expiation of that dishonour is a large matter, a matter for the youth of this country. I am not a politician and I do not know what course that expiation will take. At present we are going through the usual transition period of the vanquished. But I, Tanaka, have my own private accounting to balance. I am in great debt to your country. This morning I have betrayed a State secret to you. I was encouraged in my action by my friendship for Dikko. I was also encouraged by the sincerity of your bearing and the honesty of your approach to the duty that has been laid upon you. I fully realize the importance of this piece of paper to Britain. You remember its contents?'

'Exactly, I think.'

'And you are on your honour not to communicate it elsewhere.'

'Yes.'

Tiger Tanaka got to his feet and held out his hand. 'Goodbye for the time being, Commander. I hope that we shall be seeing more of each other.' The powerful face lit up again. Now there was no pretence in the great golden smile. 'Honour is a pattern of behaviour, Commander. The bamboo must bend to the breeze. But equally the cedar must bend to the typhoon. The meaning of this is that sometimes duty is more compelling than any words. A car is waiting to take you back to your hotel. Please give my deep respects to Dikko and tell him he owes me one thousand yen for repairs to electronic equipment that is the property of the State.'

James Bond took the hard dry paw. He said from his heart, 'Thank you, Mr Tanaka.' He walked out of the little secret room with one thought uppermost in his mind. How fast were Dikko's communications to Melbourne? How fast from Melbourne to London?

6

TIGER, TIGER!

AND NOW IT was a month later and Mr Tanaka had become 'Tiger' and Commander Bond had become 'Bondo-san'. Tiger had explained his name for James Bond. 'James,' he had said. 'That is a difficult word in Japanese. And it does not convey sufficient respect. Bond-san is too much like the Japanese word *bonsan*, which means a priest, a greybeard. The hard consonants at the end of "Bond" are also not easy for the Japanese, and when these occur in a foreign word we add an O. So you are Bondo-san. That is acceptable?'

'Does Bondo mean a pig or anything like that in Japanese?'

'No. It has no meaning.'

'Forgive my asking. The Japanese seem to enjoy many private jokes at the expense of the *gaijin*. I referred the other day to a friend of mine called "Monkey" McCall whom we used to call "Munko". You told me that this was an unmentionable word in your language. So I thought "Bondo" might be equally unmentionable.'

'Have no fear. It is totally respectable.'

The weeks had passed without any significant progress in Bond's mission except in the direction of what seemed to be a genuine friendship between Bond, Tiger and Dikko. Outside working hours the three men became well-nigh inseparable, but Bond sensed that on their excursions into the countryside and during their roistering in the evenings he was being constantly, but with great discretion, sized up. Dikko had confirmed Bond's impression. 'I think you're making progress, champ. Tiger would regard it as dishonourable to lead you up the garden path and then pull the rug out from under you with a flat refusal. Something's definitely cooking in the background, but what it is I haven't the faintest idea. I guess the ball's with Tiger's superiors, but with Tiger on your side. And, in the vernacular, Tiger's got what's called "a broad face". That means he has great powers as a fixer. And this ON he's got in respect of Britain is a huge factor in your favour. What he gave you on your first meeting was an unheard-of *presento*, as we call it here. But watch out! You're piling up a great heap of ON in respect of Tiger. And if it comes to striking a bargain, I hope you've got a pretty massive *presento* up your sleeve so that the ON on both sides is more or less evenly balanced. None of this salmon and shrimp business! Have got? Can do?'

'I'm not so sure,' said Bond doubtfully. The Macao 'Blue Route' material had already dwindled in his mind to the size of a minnow in comparison with the salmon that was Tiger's to give or withhold. The impact of the single slice he had handed Bond had already been formidable. The test of the 200-megaton bomb had duly taken place and had been greeted by the public uproar anticipated by Moscow. But counter-action by the West had been swift. On the excuse of protecting Soviet personnel in England from demonstrations of public animosity, they had been confined within a radius of twenty miles of their homes, and 'for their protection' police were thick round the Soviet Embassy, the consulates and their various trading offices. There had, of course, been reprisals on British diplomats and journalists in Russia, but these were to have been expected. Then President Kennedy had come out with the strongest speech of his career, and had committed total reprisals from the United States in the event of a single nuclear device being exploded by the Soviet Union in any country in the world outside Soviet territory. This thundering pronouncement, which had produced a growl of dismay from the American man-in-the-street, was greeted from Moscow by the feeble riposte that they would take similar action in answer to any Western nuclear device exploded on the territory of the U.S.S.R. or her allies.

A few days later Bond had been summoned again to Tiger's underground hideout. 'You will not of course repeat this,' Tiger had said with his wicked smile. 'But action in respect of the matter of which you are privately aware has been indefinitely postponed by the Central Authority.'

'Thank you for this private information,' Bond had said. 'But you do realize how your kindness of three weeks ago has greatly alleviated the international tension, particularly in relation to my country. My country would be immensely grateful if they knew of your personal generosity to me. Have I grounds for hoping for your further indulgence?' Bond had got used to the formalities of Oriental circumlocution, although he had not yet attained the refinements of Dikko's speech with Tiger, which included at least one four-letter word in each flowery sentence and which caused Tiger much amusement.

'Bondo-san, this implement which you wish to rent from us, in the most improbable event that it is made available, will command a very high price. As a fair trader, what has your country to offer in exchange for the full use of MAGIC 44?'

'We have a most important intelligence network in China known as the Macao "Blue Route". The fruits of this source would be placed entirely at your disposal.'

Melancholy settled over Tiger's massive face, but deep down in the Tartar eyes there was a wicked gleam. 'I am very much afraid that I have bad news for you, Bondo-san. "Blue Route" has been penetrated by my organization almost since its inception. We already receive the entire fruits of that source. I could show you the files if you wish. We have simply renamed it "Route Orange", and I admit that the material is very acceptable. But we already have it. What other goods had you in mind for exchange?'

Bond had to laugh. The pride of Section J — and of M., for that matter! The work, the expense, the danger of running the 'Blue Route'. And at least fifty per cent in aid of Japan! By God, his eyes were being opened on this trip. This news would put a fine cat among the pigeons at H.Q. He said blandly, 'We have many other commodities. Now that you have demonstrated the undoubted value of your implement, may I suggest that you name your price?'

'You believe that you have something on your shelves that is of comparable value? Perhaps material from a similar, though no doubt inferior, source that would be of equal importance in the defence of *our* country?'

'Undoubtedly,' said Bond staunchly. 'But, my dear Tiger, would it not be a good idea, once your mind is made up, for you to pay a visit to London and inspect the shelves for yourself? I am sure my Chief would be honoured to receive you.'

'You do not possess full powers of negotiation?'

'That would be impossible, my dear Tiger. Our security is

such that even I have not full knowledge of all our merchandise. So far as I personally am concerned, I am only in a position to pass on to my Chief the substance of what you say or to render you any other personal services you might ask of me.'

For a moment, Tiger Tanaka looked thoughtful. He seemed to be turning Bond's last words over in his mind. Then he closed the interview with the invitation to the geisha restaurant, and Bond went off with mixed feelings to report to Melbourne and London what he had gleaned.

In the room where he now sat after the geisha party, and where Tiger had just cheerfully threatened him with death, tigers' heads snarled at him from the walls and gnashed at him from the floor. His ash-tray was enclosed in a stuffed tiger's paw and the chair in which he was sitting was upholstered in tiger's skin. Mr Tanaka had been born in the year of the Tiger, whereas Bond, as Tiger had taken much pleasure in telling him, had been born in the year of the Rat.

Bond took a deep drink of *saké* and said, 'My dear Tiger, I would hate to put you to the inconvenience of having to remove me from the face of the earth. You mean that this time the cedar may not bow before the typhoon? So be it. This time you have my very topmost word of honour.'

Tiger pulled up a chair and faced Bond across the low drink table. He poured himself a liberal tot of Suntory and splashed in the soda. The sound of night traffic from the main Tokyo–Yokohama road came in from some way beyond the surrounding houses, only a few of which now showed doll's-house squares of yellow light. It was the end of September, but warm. It was ten minutes to midnight. Tiger began talking in a soft voice. 'In that case, my dear Bondo-san, and since I know you to be a man of honour, except, of course, in matters affecting your country, which this does not, I will tell you quite an interesting story. This is how it is.' He got out of his chair and sat down on the *tatami* and arranged himself in the lotus position. He was obviously more comfortable in this posture. He said, in an expository tone of voice, 'Ever since the beginning of the era of Meiji, who you will know was the Emperor who fathered the modernization and Westernization of Japan from the beginning of his reign nearly a hundred years ago, there have from time to time been foreigners who have come to this country and settled here. They have for the most part been cranks and scholars, and the European-born American Lafcadio Hearn, who became a Japanese citizen, is a very typical example. In general, they have been tolerated, usually with some amusement. So, perhaps, would be a Japanese who bought a castle in the Highlands of Scotland, and who learned and spoke Gaelic with his neighbours and expressed unusual and often impertinent interest in Scottish folkways. If he went about his researches politely and peaceably, he would be dubbed an amiable eccentric. And so it has been with the Westerners who have settled and spent their lives in Japan, though occasionally, in time of war, as would no doubt be the case with our mythical Japanese in Scotland, they have been regarded as spies and suffered internment and hardship. Now, since the occupation, there have been many such settlers, the great majority of whom, as you can imagine, have been American. The Oriental way of life is particularly attractive to the American who wishes to escape from a culture which, I am sure you will agree, has become, to say the least of it, more and more unattractive except to the lower grades of the human species to whom bad but plentiful food, shiny toys such as the automobile and the television, and the "quick buck", often dishonestly earned, or earned in exchange for minimal labour or skills, are the *summum bonum*, if you will allow the sentimental echo from my Cambridge education.'

'I will,' said Bond. 'But is this not a picture of the life that is being officially encouraged in your own country?'

Tiger Tanaka's face darkened perceptibly. 'For the time being,' he said with distaste, 'we are being subjected to what I can best describe as the "Scuola di Coca-Cola". Baseball, amusement arcades, hot dogs, hideously large bosoms, neon lighting — these are part of our payment for defeat in battle. They are the tepid tea of the way of life we know under the name of *demokorasu*. They are a frenzied denial of the official scapegoats for our defeat — a denial of the spirit of the *samurai* as expressed in the *kami-kaze*, a denial of our ancestors, a denial of our gods. They are a despicable way of life' — Tiger almost spat the words — 'but fortunately they are also expendable and temporary. They have as much importance in the history of Japan as the life of a dragonfly.' He paused. 'But to return to my story. Our American residents are of a sympathetic type — on a low level of course. They enjoy the subservience, which I may say is only superficial, of our women. They enjoy the remaining strict patterns of our life — the symmetry, compared with the chaos that reigns in America. They enjoy our simplicity, with its underlying hint of deep meaning, as expressed for instance in the tea ceremony, flower arrangements, No plays — none of which of course they understand. They also enjoy, because they have no ancestors and probably no family life worth speaking of, our veneration of the old and our worship of the past. For, in their impermanent world, they recognize these as permanent things just as, in their ignorant and childish way, they admire the fictions of the Wild West and other American myths that have become known to them, not through their education, of which they have none, but through television.'

'This is tough stuff, Tiger. I've got a lot of American friends who don't equate with what you're saying. Presumably you're talking of the lower-level G.I.s — second-generation Americans who are basically Irish or Germans or Czechs or Poles who probably ought to bc working in the fields or coalmines of their countries of origin instead of swaggering around a conquered country under the blessed coverlet of the Stars and Stripes with too much money to spend. I daresay they occasionally marry a Japanese girl and settle down here. But surely they pull up stumps pretty quickly. Our Tommies have done the same thing in Germany. But that's quite a different thing from the Lafcadio Hearns of the world.'

Tiger Tanaka bowed almost to the ground. 'Forgive me, Bondo-san. Of course you are right, and I have been diverted from my story down most unworthy paths. I did not ask you here to pour out my innermost repugnance at the occupation of my country. This of course is repugnance against the fact of defeat. I apologize. And of course you are correct. There are many cultured Americans who have taken up residence in this country and who are most valued citizens. You are right to correct me, for I have friends of this nature, in the arts, the sciences, in literature, and they are indeed valued members of the community. I was, let us say, letting off steam. You understand?'

'Of course, Tiger. My country has not been occupied for

many centuries. The imposition of a new culture on an old one is something we have not suffered. I cannot imagine my reactions in the same circumstances. Much the same as yours, I expect. Please go on with your story.' Bond reached for the *saké* flask. It stood in a jar of warm water being heated over a slow flame from a charcoal burner. He filled his glass and drank. Tiger Tanaka rocked two or three times on his buttocks and the sides of his feet. He resumed.

'As I have said, there are a number of foreigners who have taken up residence in Japan and, for the most part, they are inoffensive eccentrics. But there is one such person who entered the country in January of this year who has revealed himself to be an eccentric of the most devilish nature. This man is a monster. You may laugh, Bondo-san, but this man is no less than a fiend in human form.'

'I have met many bad men in my time, Tiger, and generally they have been slightly mad. Is that the case in this instance?'

'Very much the reverse. The calculated ingenuity of this man, his understanding of the psychology of my people, show him to be a man of quite outstanding genius. In the opinion of our highest scholars and savants he is a scientific research worker and collector probably unique in the history of the world.'

'What does he collect?'

'He collects death.'

7
THE DEATH COLLECTOR

JAMES BOND SMILED at this dramatic utterance. 'A collector of death? You mean he kills people?'

'No, Bondo-san. It is not as simple as that. He persuades, or rather entices people to kill themselves.' Tiger paused, the wide expanse of his brow furrowed. 'No, that also is not being just. Let us just say that he provides an easy and attractive opportunity — a resort — for people to do away with themselves. His present tally, in just under six months, is something over five hundred Japanese.'

'Why don't you arrest him, hang him?'

'Bondo-san, it is not as easy as that. I had better begin at the beginning. In January of this year, there entered the country, quite legally, a gentleman by the name of Doctor Guntram Shatterhand. He was accompanied by Frau Emmy Shatterhand, born de Bedon. They had Swiss passports and the doctor described himself as a horticulturalist and botanist specializing in sub-tropical species. He carried high references from the Jardin des Plantes in Paris, Kew Gardens, and other authorities, but these were couched in rather nebulous terms. He quickly got in touch with the equivalent authorities in Japan and with experts in the Ministry of Agriculture, and these gentlemen were astonished and delighted to learn that Doctor Shatterhand was prepared to spend no less than one million pounds on establishing an exotic garden or park in this country which he would stock with a priceless collection of rare plants and shrubs from all over the world. These he would import at his own expense in a sufficient state of maturity to allow his park to be planted with the minimum of delay — an extremely expensive procedure if you know anything about horticulture.'

'I know nothing about it. Like the Texan millionaires who import fully grown palms and tropical shrubs from Florida?'

'Exactly. Well, the park was not to be open to the public, but would be freely available for study and research work by authorized Japanese experts. All right. A wonderful offer that was enthusiastically accepted by the government, who, in return, granted the good doctor a ten-year residence permit — a very rare privilege. Meanwhile, as a matter of routine, the Immigration authorities made inquiries about the doctor through my department. Since I have no representative in Switzerland, I referred the matter to our friends of the C.I.A., and in due course he was given complete clearance. It appeared that he was of Swedish origin and was not widely known in Switzerland, where he only possessed the minimum requirement for residential status in the shape of two rooms in an apartment block in Lausanne. But his financial standing with the Union de Banques Suisses was Grade One, which I understand requires you to be a millionaire many times over. Since money is almost the unique status symbol in Switzerland, his clearance by the Swiss was impeccable, though no information could be obtained about his standing as a botanist. Kew and the Jardin des Plantes, on inquiry, referred to him as an enthusiastic amateur who had made valuable contributions to these institutions in the form of tropical and sub-tropical species collected for him by expeditions which he had financed. So! An interesting and financially sound citizen whose harmless pursuits would be of some benefit to Japan. Yes?'

'Sounds like it.'

'After travelling round the country in great style, the doctor took a fancy to a semi-ruined castle in Kyūshū, our southern island. The castle was in an extremely remote corner of the coast not far from Fukuoka, the principal prefecture of the island, and in ancient times it had been one of a line of castles facing the Tsushima Straits, the scene of the famous defeat of the Russian navy. These castles were originally designed to repel attacks from the Korean mainland. Most of them had fallen into disrepair, but the one chosen by the doctor was a giant edifice that had been occupied until the last war by a rich and eccentric family of textile millionaires, and its monumental surrounding wall was just what the doctor required for the privacy of his undertaking. An army of builders and decorators moved in. Meanwhile, the plants ordered by the doctor began arriving from all over the world and, with a blanket customs clearance from the Ministry of Agriculture, they were planted in appropriate soils and settings. Here I should mention that an additional reason for the doctor's choice of site was that the property, which extends for some five hundred acres, is highly volcanic and furnished with many geysers and fumaroles, which are common in Japan. These would provide, all the year round, the temperature needed for the successful propagation of these tropical shrubs, trees and plants from the equatorial zones. The doctor and his wife, who is by the way extremely ugly, moved into the castle with all speed and set about recruiting staff in the neighbourhood who would look after the establishment and its grounds.' Here Tiger assumed his sorrowful face. 'And it was at this time that I should not have dismissed as fanciful certain reports that reached me from the Chief of Police at Fukuoka. These were to the effect that the doctor was recruiting his staff uniquely from former members of the Black Dragon Society.'

'And what might that be?'

'Have been,' Tiger corrected him. 'The Society was officially disbanded before the war. But in its heyday it was the most feared and powerful secret society in Japan. It consisted originally of the dregs of the *sōshi* — the unemployed *samurai* who were left high and dry after the Meiji Restoration of about a hundred years ago — but it later recruited terrorists, gangsters, Fascist politicos, cashiered officers from the navy and army, secret agents, soldiers of fortune and other riff-raff, but also big men in industry and finance, and even the occasional Cabinet Minister who found Black Dragon support of much practical value when dirty work had to be done. And the odd thing is, though it does not seem so odd to me today, that the doctor should have chosen his site, leaving out its practical amenities, in just that corner of Japan that used to be the headquarters of the Black Dragons and has always been a hotbed of extremists. Toyama Mitsuru, the former head of the Black Dragons, came from Fukuoka; so did the anarchist Hirota, and Nakano, leader of the former Tohokai, or Fascist group, in the Diet. It has always been a nest of scoundrels, this district, and it remains so today. These extreme sects never die out completely, as you have recently, my dear Bondo-san, found in the resurgence of the Black Shirts in England, and this Doctor Shatterhand found no difficulty in collecting some twenty extremely tough and dangerous characters around him, all most correctly clothed as servants and gardeners and, no doubt, perfectly good at their ostensible jobs. On one occasion the Prefect of Police thought it his duty to make a courtesy call and give his distinguished inhabitant a word of caution. But the doctor dismissed the matter on the grounds that competent guards would be necessary to maintain his privacy and keep trespassers away from his valuable collection of plants. This seemed reasonable enough, and anyway the doctor appeared to be under high patronage in Tokyo. The Prefect bowed himself out, much impressed with the lavish display of wealth in evidence in the heart of his poor province.'

Tiger Tanaka paused and poured more *saké* for Bond and more Suntory for himself. Bond took the opportunity to ask just how dangerous this Black Dragon Society had really been. Was it the equivalent of the Chinese *tongs*?

'Much more powerful. You have heard of the Ching-Pang and Hung-Pang *tongs* that were so much feared in China in the days of the Kuomintang? No? Well the Black Dragons were a hundred times worse. To have them on your heels was certain death. They were totally ruthless, and not out of any particular political conviction. They operated strictly for cash.'

'Well, under this doctor from Switzerland, have they done any harm yet?'

'Oh no. They are nothing more than he says — personal staff, at the worst, if you like, a bodyguard. No. The trouble is quite different, much more complex. You see, this man Shatterhand has created what I can only describe as a garden of death.'

Bond raised his eyebrows. Really, for the head of a national secret service, Tiger's metaphors were almost ridiculously dramatic.

Tiger exploded his golden smile. 'Bondo-san, I can see from your face that you think I am either drunk or mad. Now listen. This Doctor Shatterhand has filled this famous park of his uniquely with poisonous vegetation, the lakes and streams with poisonous fish, and he has infested the place with snakes, scorpions and poisonous spiders. He and this hideous wife of his are not harmed by these things, because whenever they leave the castle he wears full suits of armour of the seventeenth century, and she wears some other kind of protective clothing. His workers are not harmed because they wear rubber boots up to the knee, and *maskos*, that is, antiseptic gauze masks such as many people in Japan wear over the mouth and nose to avoid infection or the spreading of infection.'

'What a daft set-up.'

Tiger reached into the folds of the *yukata* he had changed into when they entered the house. He brought out several sheets of paper pinned together. He handed them over to Bond and said, 'Be patient. Do not judge what you do not understand. I know nothing of these poisonous plants. Nor, I expect, do you. Here is a list of those that have so far been planted by this doctor, together with comments by our Ministry of Agriculture. Read it. Take your time. You will be interested to learn what charming vegetation grows on the surface of the globe.'

Bond took the papers. The first page was a general note on vegetable poisons. There followed an annotated list. The papers bore the seal of the Ministry of Agriculture. This is what he read:

The poisons listed fall into six main categories:

1. *Deliriant.* Symptoms: spectral illusions, delirium; dilated pupils; thirst and dryness; incoordination; then paralysis and spasms.

2. *Inebriant.* Symptoms: excitement of cerebral functions and of circulation; loss of co-ordination and muscular movements; double vision; then sleep and deep coma.

3. *Convulsivant.* Symptoms: intermittent spasms, from head downwards. Death from exhaustion, usually within three hours, or rapid recovery.

4. *Depressant.* Symptoms: vertigo, vomiting, abdominal pain, confused vision, convulsions, paralysis, fainting, sometimes asphyxia.

5. *Asthenic.* Symptoms: numbness, tingling mouth, abdominal pain, vertigo, vomiting, purging, delirium, paralysis, fainting.

6. *Irritant.* Symptoms: burning pain in throat and stomach, thirst, nausea, vomiting. Death by shock, convulsions or exhaustion; or starvation by injury to throat or stomach.

SPECIMENS LISTED BY CUSTOMS AND EXCISE DEPARTMENT AS IMPORTED BY DOCTOR GUNTRAM SHATTERHAND

Jamaica dogwood, fish-poison tree (*Piscidia erythrina*): Tree, 30 ft. White and blood-coloured flowers. Inebriant. Toxic principle: piscidine. W. Indies.

Nux-vomica tree, poison-nut, crow-fig, kachita (*Strychnos nux-vomica*): Tree, 40 ft. Smooth bark, attractive fruits, which have bitter taste. Greenish-white flowers. Seeds most poisonous part. Convulsivant. Toxic principle: strychnine, brucine. S. India, Java.

Guiana poison-tree (*Strychnos toxifera*): curare arrow poison taken from bark. Creeper. Death within one hour from respiratory paralysis. Toxic principles: curare, strychnine, brucine. Guiana.

St Ignatius's bean (*Strychnos ignatii*): small tree, seeds yield brucine. Convulsivant. Philippines.

False Upas-tree (*Strychnos tieuté*): large climbing shrub. Strychnine or brucine from leaf, seed, stem or root-bark. Java.

East Indian snakewood (*Strychnos colubrina*): climbing tree. Yields strychnine, brucine. Convulsivant. Java, Timor.

Ipecacuanha (*Psychotria ipecacuanha*): shrubby plant. Depressant. Toxic principle: emetine, from root. Brazil.

White-woolly Kombe bean, Gaboon arrow poison (*Stropanthus hispidus*): woody climber, 6 ft. Toxic principle: strophanthin, incine. Asthenic. W. Africa.

Ordeal-tree, poison tanghin (*Tanghinia venenifera* or *cerbera tanghin*): small evergreen tree, 20 ft. Fruit purplish, tinged with green. Toxic principle: tanghinine, cerberin. Asthenic. Madagascar.

Upas-tree, Malay arrow-poison tree (*Antiaris toxicaria*): jungle tree — 100 ft. before branches start. Wood light, white, hard, milk-bearing. Toxic principle: antiarin, from milky sap. Asthenic. Java, Borneo, Sumatra, Philippines.

Poison ivy, trailing poison oak (*Rhus toxicodendron*): climbing shrub. Greenish-yellow flowers. Stem contains milky juice — irritant. Toxic principle: toxicodendrol. U.S.A.

Yellow oleander, campanilla, be-still tree (*Thevetia peruviana*): small tree. All parts can be fatally toxic, particularly fruit. Pulse slows, vomiting, shock. Hawaii.

Castor bean plant (*Ricinus communis*): seeds are source of castor oil, also contain toxic principle, ricin. Harmless if eaten. If it enters the circulation through scratch or abrasion is fatal within 7–10 days. One-hundredth of a milligram can kill a 200 lb. man. Loss of appetite, emesis, purgation, delirium, collapse and death. Hawaii, S. America.

Common oleander (*Nerium indicum*): evergreen shrub. The roots, bark, juice, flowers and leaves all fatally toxic. Acts chiefly on the heart. Used in India as leprosy treatment, abortifacient, means of suicide. India, Hawaii. One death was due to the victim's having eaten meat cooked over an open fire, spitted on a stick of oleander wood.

Rosary pea, crab's eye, Jequiritz bean (*Abrus precatorius*): climbing shrub. Small shiny red seeds weigh average 1.75 grains, used by Indian goldsmiths as weights. Seeds are ground down into a paste with a little cold water, made into small pointed cylinders. If these are inserted beneath skin of human or animal death occurs within four hours. India, Hawaii.

Jimson weed (*Datura stramonium*): variety of thorn apple plant, found in N. Africa, India. Also: *Ololiuqui (D. meteloides)* from Mexico, and *D. tatula* from Central and South America. All three are hallucinatory. *D. stramonium*'s apples are smoked by Arabs and Swahilis, leaves eaten by E. African Negroes, seeds added to hashish and leaves to hemp by Bengalese Indians. *D. tatula* was used as a truth-drug by Zapotec Indians in courts of law. Addiction to toloachi, a drink made from *D. tatula*, causes chronic imbecility.

Gloriosa superba: spectacularly beautiful climbing lily. Roots, stalks, leaves contain an acrid narcotic, superbine, as well as colchicine and choline. Three grains of colchicine are fatal. Hawaii.

Sand-box tree (*Hura crepitans*): whole tree contains an active emetocathartic, used as a fish poison in Brazil. Also contains crepitin, same group of poisons as ricin. Harmless if swallowed, must be taken into circulation through wound to be fatal. Death comes in 7–10 days. C. and S. America.

Pride-of-India, Chinaberry tree, China tree (*Melia azedarach*): small tree. Beautiful dark green leaves, lavender blossoms. Fruit contains toxic narcotic which attacks entire central nervous system. Hawaii, C. and S. America.

Physic nut (*Jatropha curcas*): bushy tree. Raw seeds violently purgative, often fatal due to exhaustion. Caribbean.

Mexican tuber, camotillo: wild potato, grows generally. According to Indian tradition, it is plucked during the waning of the moon; it is alleged to begin deadly action the same number of days after consumption as it was stored after being dug up. Toxic principle: solanine. Central and S. America.

Divine mushroom (*Amanita mexicana*): closely related to European Fly Agaric. Black mushroom, eaten fresh or steeped in warm milk laced with agave spirits. Causes hypersensitivity of the skin surface, ultra-acute hearing and sight, then hallucinations for several hours, followed by deep melancholia. Active principle unknown. Central and S. America.

Bond finished his reading. He handed the papers back. He said, 'Doctor Shatterhand's garden is indeed a lovesome thing, God wot.'

'And you have of course heard of the South American piranha fish? They can strip a whole horse to the bones in less than an hour. The scientific name is Serrasalmus. The sub-species Nattereri is the most voracious. Our good doctor has preferred these fish to our native goldfish for his lakes. You see what I mean?'

'No,' said Bond, 'frankly I don't. What's the object of the good doctor's exercise?'

8

SLAY IT WITH FLOWERS

IT WAS THREE O'CLOCK in the morning. The noise of the traffic to Yokohama had died. James Bond didn't feel tired. He was now totally absorbed in this extraordinary story of the Swiss doctor, who, as Tiger had originally said, 'collected death'. Tiger wasn't telling him this bizarre case history for his entertainment. There was going to come a moment of climax. What would that climax be?

Tiger wiped his hand over his face. He said, 'Did you read a story in the evening edition of the *Asahi* today? It concerned a suicide.'

'No.'

'This was a young student aged eighteen who had failed his examination for the university for the second time. He lived in the suburbs of Tokyo. There was construction work on a new *departmento*, a department store, going on near where he lived. He went out of his room on to the site. A pile-driver was at work, sinking the foundations. Suddenly this youth broke through the surrounding workmen and, as the pile came crashing down, laid his head on the block beneath it.'

'What a ghastly business! Why?'

'He had brought dishonour on his parents, his ancestors. This was his way of expiation. Suicide is a most unfortunate aspect of the Japanese way of life.' Tiger paused. 'Or perhaps a most noble one. It depends how you look at it. That boy, and his family, will have gained great face in his neighbourhood.'

'You can't gain face from strawberry jam.'

'Think again, Bondo-san. Your posthumous V.C.s, for instance?'

'They're not awarded for committing suicide after failing in an examination.'

'We are not so *demokorasu* as you are.' There was irony in Tiger's voice. 'Dishonour must be expunged — according to those of us who remain what you would describe as old-fashioned. There is no apology more sincere than the offering up of your own life. It is literally all you have to give.'

'But even if this boy failed for the university, he could have gone for a lower standard of examination, for a lower grade of college. As you know, we say "Blast!" or perhaps a stronger word if we fail an examination in Britain. But we readjust our sights, or our parents do it for us, and have another bash. We don't kill ourselves. It wouldn't occur to us. It would be dishonourable rather than honourable. It would be cowardly — a refusal to stand up to reverses, to life. And it would give great pain to our parents, and certainly no satisfaction to our ancestors.'

'With us it is different. And despite *demokorasu*, the parents of this youth will be rejoicing this evening and their neighbours will be rejoicing with them. Honour is more important to us than life — more proud, more beautiful.'

Bond shrugged. 'Well, I just think that if the boy had the guts to do this thing, it was the waste of a perfectly good Japanese life. In fact, of course, this suicide business in Japan is nothing more than a form of hysteria — an expression of the streak of violence that seems to run all through the history of Japan. If you hold your own life so cheaply, it follows that you will hold others' lives even more cheaply. The other day, I saw a traffic accident at one of the main crossings. I don't know the name of it. It was a multiple affair, and there were bodies all over the place. The police came, but instead of concentrating on getting the wounded to hospital, insisted that they should lie where they were so that they could draw chalk lines round them and photograph them — presumably for use when the case came to court.'

'That is common practice,' said Tiger indifferently. 'We are much overpopulated. Abortion is legal. It is helping to solve one of our problems if a few extra people die in an automobile accident. But there is something in what you said earlier. Our word for suicide is *jisatsu*, literally "self-murder", and although it is a violent solution to a personal problem, it carries no stigma as it would in your country. In fact, one of our most famous folk-tales, known to all children, is of the forty-seven *ronin*, or bodyguards. Through their negligence, their lord, Asano, was assassinated. They swore to avenge him and they did so. But then they came together at a place called Ako and all committed *seppuku* to expiate their negligence. This is what you know as *hara-kiri*, which is a vulgar term meaning "belly-cutting". Today, at the time of the festival at the Ako shrine, special trains have to be laid on to accommodate the respectful pilgrims.'

'Well, if you bring your children up on that sort of stuff, you can't expect them not to venerate the act of suicide.'

'Just so,' said Tiger proudly. '25,000 Japanese commit suicide every year. Only the bureaucrats regard that as a shameful statistic. And the more spectacular the suicide, the more warmly it is approved. Not long ago, a young student achieved great renown by trying to saw his own head off. Lovers link hands and throw themselves over the very high Kegon Falls at Nikko. The Mihara volcano on the island of Oshima is another favourite locale. People run down the roasting slope of the crater and hurl themselves, their shoes on fire, into the bubbling cauldron in its centre. To combat this popular pastime, the interfering authorities have now opened, at great expense, a "Suicide Prevention Office" on the peak. But always the wheels of the good old-fashioned railway train provide the most convenient guillotine. They have the merit of being self-operating. All you need to do is make a four-foot jump.'

'You're a bloodthirsty old bastard, Tiger. But what's all this lecture about anyway? What's it got to do with friend Shatterhand and his pretty garden?'

'Everything, Bondo-san. Everything. You see, much against the good doctor's wishes of course, his poison garden has become the most desirable site for suicides in the whole of Japan. It has everything — a ride on our famous "Romance" express to Kyoto; a boat trip across our beautiful Inland Sea that is so full of Japanese history; a local train from the terminal harbour at Beppu to Fukuoka and a walk or taxi drive along a beautiful coast to the awe-inspiring ramparts of this mysterious Castle of Death. Climb these, or smuggle yourself in on a provision cart, and then a last delicious, ruminative walk, perhaps hand-in-hand with your lover, through the beautiful groves. And finally the great gamble, the game of *pachinko* the Japanese love so much. Which ball will have your number on it? Will your death be easy or painful? Will a Russell's Viper strike at your legs as you walk the silent, well-raked paths? Will some kindly, deadly dew fall upon you during the night as you rest under this or that gorgeous tree? Or will hunger or curiosity lead you to munch a handful of those red berries or pick one of those orange fruit? Of course, if you want to make it quick, there is always a bubbling, sulphurous fumarole at hand. In any one of those, the thousand degrees Centigrade will allow you just enough time for one scream. The place is nothing more than a *departmento* of death, its shelves laden with delicious packages of self-destruction, all given away for nothing. Can you not imagine that old and young flock there as if to a shrine? The police have erected a barricade across the road. Genuine visitors, botanists and so on, have to show a pass. But the suicides fight their way to the shrine across the fields and marshes, scrabble at the great walls, break their nails to gain entrance. The good doctor is of course much dismayed. He has erected stern notices of warning, with skulls and crossbones upon them. They act only as advertisements! He has even gone to the expense of flying one of those high helium balloons from the roof of his castle. The hanging streamers threaten trespassers with prosecution. But, alas for the doctor's precautions, the high balloon serves only to beckon. Here is death! it proclaims. Come and get it!'

'You're daft, Tiger. Why don't you arrest him? Burn the place down?'

'Arrest him for what? For presenting Japan with this unique collection of rare plants? Burn down a million-pound establishment belonging to a respected *gaijin* resident? The man has done nothing wrong. If anyone is to blame, it is the Japanese people. It is true that he could exercise more careful surveillance, have his grounds more regularly patrolled. And it is certainly odd that when he has the ambulance called, the victims are always totally dead and are usually in the form of a bag of calcined bones fished out of one of the fumaroles. From the list I have shown you, one would have expected some to be only crippled, or blinded. The Herr Doktor expresses himself as much puzzled. He suggests that, in the cases of blindness or amnesia, the victims presumably fall into one of the fumaroles by mistake. Maybe. But, as I have said, his tally so far is over five hundred and, with the stream of publicity, more and more people will be attracted to the Castle of Death. We have got to put a stop to it.'

'What steps have been taken so far?'

'Commissions of investigation have visited the doctor. They have been most courteously treated. The doctor has begged that something shall be done to protect him from these trespassers. He complains that they interfere with his work, break off precious boughs and pick valuable plants. He shows himself as entirely co-operative with any measures that can be suggested short of abandoning this project, which is so dear to his heart and so much appreciated by the Japanese specialists in botany and so forth. He has made a further most generous offer. He is constructing a research department — to be manned by workers of his own choice, mark you — to extract the poisons from his shrubs and plants and give the essences free to an appropriate medical research centre. You will have noted that many of these poisons are valuable medicines in a diluted form.'

'But how has all this come on your plate?' Bond was now getting drowsy. It was four o'clock and the horizon of jagged grey, porcelain-shingled roof-tops was lightening. He poured down the last of the *saké*. It had the flat taste of too much. It was time he was in bed. But Tiger was obviously obsessed with this lunatic business, and subtle, authentic glimpses of Japan were coming through the ridiculous, nightmare story with its undertones of Poe, Le Fanu, Bram Stoker, Ambrose Bierce.

Tiger seemed unaffected by the lateness of the hour. The *samurai* face was perhaps etched in more sinister, more brutal lines. The hint of Tartar, tamed and civilized, lurked with less concealment, like a caged animal, in the dark pools of his eyes. But the occasional rocking motion of the buttocks and sides of the feet was the only sign that he was interested, even excited. He said, 'One month ago, Bondo-san, I sent one of my best men into this place to try and discover what it was all about. I was so instructed by my Minister, the Minister of the Interior. He in turn was under orders from the Prime Minister. The matter was becoming one of public debate. I chose a good man. He was instructed to get into the place, observe, and report. One week later, Bondo-san, he was recovered from the sea on a beach near this Castle of Death. He was blinded and in delirium. All the lower half of his body was terribly burned. He could only babble a *haiku* about dragonflies. I later discovered that, as a youth, he had indulged in the pastime of our youngsters. He had tied a female dragonfly on a thread and let it go. This acts as a lure for the male dragonfly and you can quickly catch many males in this way. They attach themselves to the female and will not let go. The *haiku* — that is a verse of seventeen syllables — he kept on reciting until his death, which came soon, was "Desolation! Pink dragonflies flitting above the graves." '

James Bond felt he was living inside a dream: the little room, partitioned in imitation rice-paper and cedar plywood, the open vista of a small, inscrutable garden in which water tinkled, the distant redness of an imminent dawn, the long background of *saké* and cigarettes, the quiet voice of the story-teller telling a fairy tale, as it might be told in a tent under the stars. And yet this was something that had happened the other day, close by — was happening now, something that Tiger had brought him here to tell. Why? Because he was lonely? Because there was no one else he could trust? Bond pulled himself out of his somnolent slouch. He said, 'I'm sorry, Tiger. What did you do next?'

Tiger Tanaka seemed to sit slightly more upright on his black-edged rectangle of golden *tatami*. He looked very directly at James Bond and said, 'What was there to do? I did nothing except apologize to my superiors. I waited for an honourable solution to present itself. I waited for you to come.'

'Me!'

'You were sent. It might have been another.'

James Bond yawned. He couldn't help it. He could see no end to the evening. Tiger had got some Japanese bee in his Japanese bonnet. How in hell could Bond stop it buzzing? He said, 'Tiger. It's time for bed. Let's talk about the rest of this tomorrow. Of course I'll give you any advice I can. I can see it's a difficult problem. But those are just the ones to sleep on.' He made to rise from his chair.

Tiger said, and it was an order, 'Sit down, Bondo-san. If you have any regard for your country, you leave tomorrow.' He consulted his watch. 'By the twelve-twenty from Tokyo main station. Your ultimate destination is Fukuoka on the southern island of Kyūshū. You will not be going back to your hotel. You will not be seeing Dikko. From now on you are under my personal orders.' The voice went very quiet and velvety. 'Is that understood?'

Bond sat up as if he had been stung. 'What in God's name are you talking about, Tiger?'

Tiger Tanaka said, 'In my office the other day you made a significant statement. You said words to the effect that in exchange for MAGIC 44 you were empowered to carry out any personal services that I might require of you.'

'I didn't say that I was empowered. I meant that I would do anything for you on my personal responsibility.'

'That is quite good enough. I took you at your word and I requested an audience of the Prime Minister. He instructed me to proceed, but to regard the matter as a State secret known only to him and to me — and of course to you.'

'Come on, Tiger,' said Bond impatiently. 'Cut the cackle. What is it you want me to do?'

But Tiger was not to be hurried. He said, 'Bondo-san, I will now be blunt with you, and you will not be offended, because we are friends. Yes? Now it is a sad fact that I, and many of us in positions of authority in Japan, have formed an unsatisfactory opinion about the British people since the war. You have not only lost a great Empire, you have seemed almost anxious to throw it away with both hands. All right,' he held up a hand, 'we will not go deeply into the reasons for this policy, but when you apparently sought to arrest this slide into impotence at Suez, you succeeded only in stage-managing one of the most pitiful bungles in the history of the world, if not the worst. Further, your governments have shown themselves successively incapable of ruling and have handed over effective control of the country to the trade unions, who appear to be dedicated to the principle of doing less and less work for more money. This feather-bedding, this shirking of an honest day's work, is sapping at ever-increasing speed the moral fibre of the British, a quality the world once so much admired. In its place we now see a vacuous, aimless horde of seekers-after-pleasure — gambling at the pools and bingo, whining at the weather and the declining fortunes of the country, and wallowing nostalgically in gossip about the doings of the Royal Family and of your so-called aristocracy in the pages of the most debased newspapers in the world.'

James Bond roared with laughter. 'You've got a bloody cheek, Tiger! You ought to write that out and sign it "Octogenarian" and send it in to *The Times*. You just come over and take a look at the place. It's not doing all that badly.'

'Bondo-san, you have pleaded guilty out of your own mouth. "Not doing too badly," indeed! That is the crybaby excuse of a boy who gets a thoroughly bad end-of-term report. In fact you are doing very badly indeed in the opinion of your few remaining friends. And now you come to me and ask for some very important intelligence material to bolster up the pitiful ruins of a once great Power. Why should we give it to you? What good will it do us? What good will it do you, Bondo-san? It is like giving smelling salts to a punch-drunk heavyweight just before the inevitable knock-out.'

Bond said angrily, 'Balls to you, Tiger! And balls again! Just because you're a pack of militant potential murderers here, longing to get rid of your American masters and play at being *samurai* again, snarling behind your subservient smiles, you only judge people by your own jungle standards. Let me tell you this, my fine friend. England may have been bled pretty thin by a couple of World Wars, our Welfare State politics may have made us expect too much for free, and the liberation of our Colonies may have gone too fast, but we still climb Everest and beat plenty of the world at plenty of sports and win Nobel Prizes. Our politicians may be a feather-pated bunch, but I expect yours are too. All politicians are. But there's nothing wrong with the British people — although there are only fifty million of them.'

Tiger Tanaka smiled happily. 'Well spoken, Bondo-san. I thought your famous English stoicism might break down if I hit hard enough. I just wanted to see. And, for your information, those are very similar to the words I addressed to my Prime Minister. And do you know what he said? He said, all right, Mr Tanaka. Put this Commander Bond to the test. If he succeeds, I will agree that there is still an elite in Britain and that this valuable material would be safe in their hands. If he fails, you will politely turn down the request.'

Bond shrugged impatiently. He was still smarting under Tiger's onslaught, and the half-truths which he knew lay behind his words. 'All right, Tiger. What is this ridiculous test? Some typical bit of *samurai* nonsense, I suppose.'

'More or less,' agreed Tiger Tanaka, with equanimity. 'You are to enter this Castle of Death and slay the Dragon within.'

9

INSTANT JAPAN

THE BLACK TOPOYET hurtled through the deserted streets which were shiny with the dew of what would be a beautiful day.

Tiger had dressed in casual clothes as if for a country outing. He had a small overnight bag on the seat beside him. They were on the way to a bathhouse which Tiger said was of a very special, a very pleasurable nature. It was also, Tiger said, very discreet, and the opportunity would be taken to make a start in transforming Bond's appearance into something more closely resembling a Japanese.

Tiger had overridden all Bond's objections. On all the evidence, this doctor was a purveyor of death. Because he was mad? Because it amused him? Tiger neither knew nor cared. For obvious reasons of policy, his assassination, which had been officially agreed to, could not be carried out by a Japanese. Bond's appearance on the scene was therefore very timely. He had had much practice in such clandestine operations and, if he was subsequently arrested by the Japanese police, an adequate cover story involving foreign intelligence services could be cooked up. He would be tried, sentenced, and then quietly smuggled out of the country. If he failed, then presumably the doctor or his guards would kill him. That would be too bad. Bond argued that he had personally nothing against this Swiss botanist. Tiger replied that any good man's hand would be against a man who had already killed five hundred of his fellow creatures. Was that not so? And, in any case, Bond was being hired to do this act in exchange for MAGIC 44. Did that not quieten his conscience? Bond agreed reluctantly that it did. As a last resort, Bond said that the operation was in any case impossible. A foreigner in Japan could be spotted five miles away. Tiger replied that this matter had been provided for and the first step was a visit to this most discreet bathhouse.

Here Bond would receive his first treatment and then get some sleep before catching the train on which Tiger would be accompanying him. And Tiger, with a devilish grin, had assured him that at any rate part of his treatment would be most pleasurable and relaxing.

The exterior of the bathhouse looked like a Japanese inn — some carefully placed stepping-stones meandering briefly between dwarf pines, a wide-open, yellow-lighted doorway with a vista of polished wood floors behind, three bowing, smiling women in traditional dress, as bright as birds although it was nearly five in the morning, and the inevitable row of spotless but undersized slippers. After much bowing and counter-bowing and a few phrases from Tiger, Bond took off his shoes and, in his socks (explanation by Tiger; polite giggles behind raised hands), did as Tiger told him and followed one of the women along a gleaming corridor and through an open partition that revealed a miniature combination of a bedroom and a Turkish bath. A young girl, wearing nothing but tight, brief white shorts and an exiguous white brassière, bowed low, said, 'Excuse, please,' and began to unbutton Bond's trousers. Bond held the pretty hand where it was. He turned to the older woman who was about to close the partition and said, 'Tanaka-san,' in a voice that pleaded and ordered. Tiger was fetched. He was wearing nothing but his underpants. He said, 'What is it now?'

Bond said, 'Now listen, Tiger, I'm sure this pretty girl and I will get along very well indeed. But just tell me what the menu is. Am I going to eat her or is she going to eat me?'

Tiger said patiently, 'You really must learn to obey orders without asking questions, Bondo-san. That is the essence of our relationship during the next few days. You see that box? When she has undressed you, she will put you in the box which has a charcoal fire under it. You will sweat. After perhaps ten minutes she will help you out of the box and wash you from head to foot. She will even tenderly clean out your ears with a special ivory instrument. She will then pour a very tenacious dark dye with which she has been supplied into that tiled bath in the floor and you will get in. You will relax and bathe your face and hair. She will then dry you and cut your hair in the Japanese style. She will then give you a massage on that couch and, according to your indications, she will make this massage as delightful, as prolonged as you wish. You will then go to sleep. When you are awakened with eggs and bacon and coffee you will kiss the girl good morning and shave, or the other way round, and that will be that.' Tiger curtly asked the girl a question. She brushed back her bang of black hair coquettishly and replied. 'The girl says she is eighteen and that her name is Mariko Ichiban. Mariko means "Truth" and Ichiban means "Number One". The girls in these establishments are numbered. And now, please don't disturb me any more. I am about to enjoy myself in a similar fashion, but without the walnut stain. And please, in future, have faith. You are about to undergo a period of entirely new sensations. They may be strange and surprising. They will not be painful — while you are under my authority, that is. Savour them. Enjoy them as if each one was your last. All right? Then good night, my dear Bondo-san. The night will be short, alas, but if you embrace it fully, it will be totally delightful up to the last squirm of ecstasy. And,' Tiger gave a malicious wave of the hand as he went out and closed the partition, 'you will arise from it what is known as "a new man".'

James Bond got at any rate part of the message. As Mariko's busy fingers proceeded to remove his trousers and then his shirt, he lifted her chin and kissed her full on the soft, yielding, bud-like mouth.

Later, sitting sweating and reflecting in the comfortable wooden box, very tired, slightly, but cheerfully, drunk, he remembered his dismal thoughts in Queen Mary's Rose Garden. He also remembered his interview with M., and M. saying that he could leave the hardware behind on this purely diplomatic assignment; and the lines of irony round Bond's mouth deepened.

Mariko was looking into the wall mirror and fiddling with her hair and eyebrows. Bond said, 'Mariko. Out!'

Mariko smiled and bowed. She unhurriedly removed her brassière and came towards the wooden box.

Bond reflected. What was it that Tiger had said about becoming a new man? and he reached for Mariko's helping hands and watched her breasts tauten as she pulled him out and towards her.

It was indeed a new man who followed Tiger through the

thronged halls of Tokyo main station. Bond's face and hands were of a light brown tint, his black hair, brightly oiled, was cut and neatly combed in a short fringe that reached halfway down his forehead, and the outer corners of his eyebrows had been carefully shaved so that they now slanted upwards. He was dressed, like so many of the other travellers, in a white cotton shirt buttoned at the wrists and a cheap, knitted silk, black tie exactly centred with a rolled gold pin. His ready-made black trousers, held up by a cheap black plastic belt, were rather loose in the fork, because Japanese behinds are inclined to hang low, but the black plastic sandals and dark blue nylon socks were exactly the right size. A much-used overnight bag of Japan Air Lines was slung over his shoulder, and this contained a change of shirt, singlet, pants and socks, Shinsei cigarettes, and some cheap Japanese toilet articles. In his pockets were a comb, a cheap used wallet containing some five thousand yen in small denomination notes, and a stout pocket knife which, by Japanese law, had a blade not more than two inches long. There was no handkerchief, only a packet of tissues. (Later, Tiger explained. 'Bondo-san, this Western habit of blowing the nose and carefully wrapping up the result in silk or fine linen and harbouring it in your pocket as if it were something precious! Would you do the same thing with the other excretions of your body? Exactly! So, if in Japan you wish to blow your nose, perform the act decorously and dispose at once, tidily, of the result.')

Despite his height, Bond merged quite adequately into the bustling, shoving crowds of passengers. His 'disguise' had mysteriously appeared in his room at the bathhouse and Mariko had greatly enjoyed dressing him up. 'Now Japanese gentreman,' she had said approvingly as, with a last lingering kiss, she had gone to answer Tiger's rap on the partition. Bond's own clothes and possessions had already been taken away.

'They and your things from the hotel will be transferred to Dikko's apartment,' Tiger had said. 'Later today, Dikko will inform your Chief that you have left Tokyo with me for a visit to the MAGIC establishment, which is, in fact, a day's journey from Tokyo, and that you will be away for several days. Dikko believes that this is so. My own department merely know that I shall be absent on a mission to Fukuoka. They do not know that you are accompanying me. And now we will take the express to Gamagori on the south coast and the evening hydrofoil across Ise Bay to the fishing port of Toba. There we will spend the night. This is to be a slow journey to Fukuoka for the purpose of training and educating you. It is necessary that I make you familiar with Japanese customs and folkways so that you make as few mistakes as possible — when the time comes.'

The gleaming orange and silver express slid to a stop beside them. Tiger barged his way on board. Bond waited politely for two or three women to precede him. When he sat down beside Tiger, Tiger hissed angrily, 'First lesson, Bondo-san! Do not make way for women. Push them, trample them down. Women have no priority in this country. You may be polite to very old men, but to no one else. Is that understood?'

'Yes, master,' said Bond sarcastically.

'And do not make Western-style jokes while you are my pupil. We are engaged on a serious mission.'

'Oh, all right, Tiger,' said Bond resignedly. 'But damn it all . . .'

Tiger held up a hand. 'And that is another thing. No swearing, please. There are no swear-words in the Japanese language and the usage of bad language does not exist.'

'But good heavens, Tiger! No self-respecting man could get through the day without his battery of four-letter words to cope with the roughage of life and let off steam. If you're late for a vital appointment with your superiors, and you find that you've left all your papers at home, surely you say, well, Freddie Uncle Charlie Katie, if I may put it so as not to offend.'

'No,' said Tiger. 'I would say "*Shimata*", which means "I have made a mistake".'

'Nothing worse?'

'There is nothing worse to say.'

'Well, supposing it was your driver's fault that the papers had been forgotten. Wouldn't you curse him backwards and sideways?'

'If I wanted to get myself a new driver, I might conceivably call him "*bakyaro*" which means a "bloody fool", or even "*konchikisho*" which means "you animal". But these are deadly insults and he would be within his rights to strike me. He would certainly get out of the car and walk away.'

'And those are the worst words in the Japanese language!

What about your taboos? The Emperor, your ancestors, all these gods? Don't you ever wish them in hell, or worse?'

'No. That would have no meaning.'

'Well then, dirty words. Sex words?'

'There are two — "*chimbō*" which is masculine and "*mōnkō*" which is feminine. These are nothing but coarse anatomical descriptions. They have no meaning as swear-words. There are no such things in our language.'

'Well I'm . . . I mean, well I'm astonished! A violent people without a violent language! I must write a learned paper on this. No wonder you have nothing left but to commit suicide when you fail an exam, or cut your girl friend's head off when she annoys you.'

Tiger laughed. 'We generally push them under trams or trains.'

'Well, for my money, you'd do much better to say "You —",' Bond fired off the hackneyed string, 'and get it off your chest that way.'

'That is enough, Bondo-san,' said Tiger patiently. 'The subject is now closed. But you will kindly refrain both from using these words or looking them. Be calm, stoical, impassive. Do not show anger. Smile at misfortune. If you sprain your ankle, laugh.'

'Tiger, you're a cruel taskmaster.'

Tiger grinned with satisfaction. 'Bond-san, you don't know the half of it. But now let us go and get something to eat and drink in the buffet car. All that Suntory you forced on me last night is crying out for the skin of the dog that bit me.'

'The hair,' corrected Bond.

'One hair would not be enough, Bondo-san. I need the whole skin.'

James Bond wrestled with his chopsticks and slivers of raw octopus and a mound of rice ('You must get accustomed to the specialities of the country, Bondo-san') and watched the jagged coastline, interspersed with glittering paddy fields, flash by. He was lost in thought when he felt a hard jostle from behind. He had been constantly jostled as he sat up at the counter — the Japanese are great jostlers — but he now turned and caught a glimpse of the stocky back of a man disappearing into the next compartment. There were white strings round his ears which showed that he was wearing a *masko*, and he wore an ugly black leather hat. When they went back to their seat Bond found that his pocket had been picked. His wallet was gone. Tiger was astonished. 'That is very unusual in Japan,' he said defensively. 'But no matter. I will get you another at Toba. It would be a mistake to call the conductor. We do not wish to draw attention to ourselves. The police would be sent for at the next station and there would be much interrogation and filling out of forms. And there is no way of finding the thief. The man will have pocketed his *masko* and hat and will be unrecognizable. I regret the incident, Bondo-san. I hope you will forget it.'

'Of course. It's nothing.'

They left the train at Gamagori, a pretty seaside village with a humped island in the bay that Tiger said housed an important shrine, and the 50-knot ride in the hydrofoil to Toba, an hour away across the bay, was exhilarating. As they disembarked, Bond caught a glimpse of a stocky silhouette in the crowd. Could it be the thief on the train? But the man wore heavy horn-rimmed spectacles, and there were many other stocky men in the crowd. Bond dismissed the thought and followed Tiger along the narrow streets, gaily hung with paper banners and lanterns, to the usual discreet frontage and dwarf pines that he had become accustomed to. They were expected and were greeted with deference. Bond had had about enough of the day. There weren't many bows and smiles left in him, and he was glad when he was at last left alone in his maddeningly dainty room with the usual dainty pot of tea, dainty cup and dainty sweetmeat wrapped in rice-paper. He sat at the open partition that gave on to a handkerchief of garden and then the sea wall and gazed gloomily across the water at a giant statue of a man in a bowler hat and morning coat that Tiger had told him was Mr Mikimoto, founder of the cultured pearl industry, who had been born at Toba and had there, as a poor fisherman, invented the trick of inserting grains of sand under the mantle of a live oyster to form the kernel of a pearl. Bond thought, To hell with Tiger and his crazy plan. What in God's name have I got myself into? He was still sitting there cursing his lot when Tiger came in and brusquely ordered him to don one of the *yukatas* that hung with the bedding in the single cupboard in the paper wall.

'You really must concentrate, Bondo-san,' said Tiger mildly.

'But you are making progress. As a reward I have ordered *saké* to be brought in large quantities and then a dinner of the speciality of this place, lobster.'

Bond's spirits rose minutely. He undressed to his pants, donned the dark brown *yukata* ('Stop!' from Tiger. 'Wrap it round to the right! Only a corpse wraps it round to the left.') and adopted the lotus position across the low table from Tiger. He had to admit that the kimono was airy and comfortable. He bowed low. 'That sounds a most sincere programme. Now then, Tiger. Tell me about the time you were training as a *kami-kaze*. Every detail. What was it all about?'

The *saké* came. The pretty waitress knelt on the *tatami* and served them both. Tiger had been thoughtful. He had ordered tumblers. Bond swallowed his at one gulp. Tiger said, 'The grossness of your drinking habits fits well with your future identity.'

'And what is that to be?'

'A coalminer from Fukuoka. There are many tall men in that profession. Your hands are not rough enough, but you pushed a truck underground. Your nails will be filled with coal dust when the time comes. You were too stupid to wield a pick. You are deaf and dumb. Here.' Tiger slipped across a scrubby card, creased and dog-eared. There were some Japanese characters on it. 'That is "*Tsumbo de oshi*" — deaf and dumb. Your disability will inspire pity and some distaste. If someone talks to you, show that and they will desist. They may also give you a few pieces of small coin. Accept them and bow deeply.'

'Thanks very much. And I suppose I have to account for these tips to your secret fund?'

'That will not be necessary.' Tiger was wooden-faced. 'Our expenses on this mission are a direct charge on the Prime Minister's purse.'

Bond bowed. 'I am honoured.' He straightened himself. 'And now, you old bastard. More *saké* and tell me about the *kami-kaze*. In due course I am prepared to become a deaf and dumb miner from Fukuoka. In public I am prepared to hiss and bow with the best of them. But, by God, when we're alone, the password is Freddie Uncle Charlie Katie or I'll be putting my head under a pile-driver before you get me on to the first tee. Is that agreed?'

Tiger bowed low. '*Shimata!* I am in error. I have been pressing you hard. It is my duty to entertain a friend as well as instruct a pupil. Lift your glass, Bondo-san. Until you do so the girl will not pour. Right. Now you ask me about the *kami-kaze*.' Tiger rocked backwards and forwards and his dark, assassin's eyes became introspective. He didn't look up at Bond. He said, 'It was nearly twenty years ago. Things were looking bad for my country. I had been doing intelligence work in Berlin and Rome. I had been far from the air raids and even further from the front line, and every night when I listened to the radio from my homeland and heard the bad news of the slow but sure approach of the American forces, island by island, airstrip by airstrip, I paid no attention to the false news of the Nazis, but thought only that my country was in danger and that I was needed to to defend it.' Tiger paused. 'And the wine turned sour in my mouth and the girls turned cold in my bed. I listened to the accounts of this brilliant invention, the corps of *kami-kaze*. That is the "Divine Wind" that saved my country from invasion by Kublai Khan in the thirteenth century by destroying his fleet. I said to myself that that was the way to die — no medals, total death, suicide if you like, but at enormous cost to the enemy. It seemed to me the most heroic form of personal combat that had ever been invented. I was nearly forty. I had lived fully. It seemed to me that I could take the place of a younger man. The technique was simple. Anyone can learn to pilot a plane. The escorts of fighter planes led in to the attack. It was then just a question of aiming yourself at the largest ship, preferably an aircraft carrier that was bringing planes to the islands to attack the homeland. You got the ship lined up below you and you went for the flight deck and the lift which is the heart of a carrier. Pay no attention to the bridge or the water line. They are heavily armoured. Go for the vulnerable machinery of the flight deck. You understand?'

Tiger was completely sent. He was back there again fighting the war. Bond knew the symptoms. He often visited this haunted forest of memory himself. He lifted his glass. The kneeling girl bowed and poured. Bond said, 'Yes. Go on, Tiger.'

'I forced the Kempeitai to accept my resignation and I returned to Japan and more or less bribed my way into a *kami-kaze* training squadron. They were very difficult to get into. All the youth of the nation seemed to want to serve the Emperor in this way. At this time we were running out of aircraft and we were forced to use the more difficult *baku* — that was a small plane made mostly of wood with a thousand pounds of explosive in the nose, a kind of flying bomb. It had no engine, but was released from below the belly of a fighter bomber. The pilot had a single joystick for controlling direction.' Tiger looked up. 'I can tell you, Bondo-san, that it was a terrible and beautiful thing to see an attack wave going off. These young men in their pure white shifts, and with the ancient white scarf that was the badge of the *samurai* bound round their heads, running joyfully for their planes as if they were running to embrace a loved one. The roar of the engines of the mother planes, and then the take-off into the dawn or into the setting sun towards some distant target that had been reported by spies or intercepted on the radio. It was as if they were flying to their ancestors in heaven, as indeed they were, for of course none ever came back or were captured.'

'But what did it all achieve? Of course it frightened the American fleet all right, and the British. But you lost thousands of your best young men. Was it worth it?'

'Is it worth writing one of the most glorious pages in your country's history? Do you know that the *kami-kaze* is the only unit in the history of air warfare whose claims were less than the truth? The unit claimed as sunk or damaged 276 naval craft from aircraft carriers downwards. Those actually sunk or damaged were 322.'

'You were lucky the surrender came before you were sent on a mission.'

'Perhaps. And yet, Bondo-san, it is one of my most cherished dreams today to come diving out of the sun into a hail of anti-aircraft fire, see the tiny, terrified figures running for shelter from the flight deck of a wildly swerving carrier and know that you are about to kill a hundred or more of the enemy and destroy a million pounds' worth of his fighting machine, all by yourself.'

'And I suppose Admiral Ohnishi, who invented the whole idea, committed suicide when the surrender came?'

'Naturally. And in a most honourable fashion. When you commit *seppuku* you invite two of your best friends to be present to finish you off if you fail. The admiral executed the cross-cut from left to right of the belly, and then the upward cut to the breast-bone, most admirably. But it did not kill him. Yet he refused the coup de grâce. He sat there contemplating his insides for a whole day before he finally died. A most sincere gesture of apology to the Emperor.' Tiger waved a hand airily. 'However, I must not spoil your dinner. I can see that some of our honourable customs offend your soft Western susceptibilities. Here comes the lobster. Are they not splendid animals?'

Lacquer boxes of rice, raw quails' eggs in sauce and bowls of sliced seaweed were placed in front of them both. Then they were each given a fine oval dish bearing a large lobster whose head and tail had been left as a dainty ornament to the sliced pink flesh in the centre. Bond set to with his chopsticks. He was surprised to find that the flesh was raw. He was even more surprised when the head of his lobster began moving off his dish and, with questing antennae and scrabbling feet, tottered off across the table. 'Good God, Tiger!' Bond said, aghast. 'The damn thing's alive!'

Tiger hissed impatiently. 'Really, Bondo-san. I am much disappointed in you. You fail test after test. I sincerely hope you will show improvement during the rest of our journey. Now eat up and stop being squeamish. This is a very great Japanese delicacy.'

James Bond bowed ironically. '*Shimata!*' he said. 'I have made a mistake. It crossed my mind that honourable Japanese lobster might not like being eaten alive. Thank you for correcting the unworthy thought.'

'You will soon become accustomed to the Japanese way of life,' said Tiger graciously.

'It's their way of death that's got me a little bit puzzled,' said Bond amiably, and he handed his glass to the kneeling waitress for more *saké* to give him strength to try the seaweed.

10

ADVANCED STUDIES

TIGER AND BOND stood in the shade of the avenue of giant cryptomerias and observed the pilgrims, slung with cameras, who were visiting the famous Outer Shrine of Ise, the greatest temple to the creed of Shintoism. Tiger said, 'All right. You have observed these people and their actions. They have been saying prayers to the sun goddess. Go and say a prayer without drawing attention to yourself.'

Bond walked over the raked path and through the great wooden archway and joined the throng in front of the shrine. Two priests, bizarre in their red kimonos and black helmets, were watching. Bond bowed towards the shrine, tossed a coin on to the wire-netting designed to catch the offerings, clapped his hands loudly, bent his head in an attitude of prayer, clapped his hands again, bowed and walked out.

'You did well,' said Tiger. 'One of the priests barely glanced at you. The public paid no attention. You should perhaps have clapped your hands more loudly. It is to draw the attention of the goddess and your ancestors to your presence at the shrine. Then they will pay more attention to your prayer. What prayer did you in fact make?'

'I'm afraid I didn't make any, Tiger. I was concentrating on remembering the right sequence of motions.'

'The goddess will have noted that, Bondo-san. She will help you to concentrate still more in the future. Now we will go back to the car and proceed to witness another interesting ceremony in which you will take part.'

Bond groaned. In the parking place beyond the vast *torii* that guarded the entrance, char-à-bancs were disgorging hordes of students while the conductresses shouted '*Awri, awri, awri*' and blew whistles to help the drivers of other char-à-bancs to back in. The giggling girls were severely dressed in dark blue with black cotton stockings. The youths wore the handsome, high-collared black uniform of Japanese students. Tiger led the way through the middle of the crowd. When they emerged Tiger looked pleased. 'Did you notice anything, Bondo-san?'

'Only a lot of pretty girls. Rather too young for me.'

'Wrong. Yesterday many of them would have stared and giggled behind their hands and said "*gaijin!*". Today you were not recognized as a foreigner. Your appearance is one thing, but your comportment has also improved. You exude more self-confidence. You are more at home.' Tiger gave his golden sunburst of a smile. 'The Tanaka system. It is not so foolish as you think.'

Wadakin, on the road across the mountains to the ancient capital of Kyoto, was a little upland hamlet without distinction. Tiger gave decisive orders to the driver of the hired car and they arrived at a tall, barn-like building in a back street. There was a strong smell of cattle and manure. The chief herdsman, as he turned out to be, greeted them. He had the apple cheeks and wise kindly eyes of his counterparts in Scotland and the Tyrol. Tiger had a long conversation with him. The man looked at Bond and his eyes twinkled. He bowed perfunctorily and led the way inside. It was cool out of the sun. There were rows of stalls in which vastly fat brown cows lay chewing the cud. A gay small dog was licking the muzzle of one of them and being occasionally given a lick in return. The herdsman lifted a barrier and said something to one of the cows which got unsteadily up on to legs that had become spindly through lack of exercise. It ambled unsteadily out into the sunshine and looked warily at Tiger and Bond. The herdsman hauled out a crate of beer bottles. He opened one and handed it to Bond. Tiger said peremptorily, 'Give it to the cow to drink.'

Bond took the bottle and walked boldly up to the cow who raised her head and opened her slavering jaws. Bond thrust the bottle between them and poured. The cow almost ate the bottle in its delight and ran its harsh tongue gratefully over Bond's hand. Bond stood his ground. He was getting used to Tiger's ploys by now, and he was determined to show at any rate an approximation of the *kami-kaze* spirit whatever test Tiger put him to.

The herdsman now handed Bond a bottle of what appeared to be water. Tiger said, 'This is *shochu*. It is a very raw gin. Fill your mouth with it and spray it over the back of the cow and then massage it into the cow's flesh.'

Bond guessed that Tiger hoped he would swallow some of the gin and choke. He closed his throat but lustily filled his mouth with the stuff, compressed his lips and blew hard so that the vapour from the stuff would not go up his nostrils. He wiped his hands across his lips that were already stinging with the harsh spirit and scrubbed energetically at the rough pelt. The cow bent her head in ecstasy . . . Bond stood back. 'Now what?' he said belligerently. 'What's the cow going to do for me?'

Tiger laughed and translated for the herdsman, who also laughed and looked at Bond with some respect. Money changed hands, and with much happy talk between Tiger and the herdsman and final bows they got back into the car and drove into the village, where they were welcomed into a shuttered and discreet restaurant, polished, spotless and blessedly deserted. Tiger ordered and they sat in wonderful Western chairs at a real table while the usual dimpling waitresses brought *saké*. Bond swallowed down his first flask at one long gulp to wash away the rasp of the gin. He said to Tiger, 'And now, what was that all about?'

Tiger looked pleased with himself. 'You are about to eat what it was all about — the finest, most succulent beef in the world. Kobe beef, but of a grade you wouldn't find in the most expensive restaurant in Tokyo. This herd is owned by a friend of mine. The herdsman was a good man, was he not? He feeds each of his cows four pints of beer a day and massages them with *shochu* as you did. They also receive a rich meal of oaten porridge. You like beef?'

'No,' said Bond stolidly. 'As a matter of fact, I don't.'

'That is unfortunate,' said Tiger, not looking as if it were. 'For what you are about to eat is the finest steak that will be eaten today anywhere outside the Argentine. And you have earned it. The herdsman was greatly impressed by your sincere performance with his cow.'

'And what does that prove?' said Bond sourly. 'And what honourable experience is awaiting me this afternoon?'

The steak came. It was accompanied by various succulent side-dishes, including a saucer of blood, which Bond refused.

But the meat could be cut with a fork, and was indeed without equal in Bond's experience. Tiger, munching with gusto, answered Bond's question. 'I am taking you to one of the secret training establishments of my Service,' he said. 'It is not far from here, in the mountains, in an old fortified castle. It goes under the name of the "Central Mountaineering School". It arouses no comment in the neighbourhood, which is just as well, since it is here that my agents are trained in one of the arts most dreaded in Japan — *ninjutsu*, which is, literally, the art of stealth or invisibility. All the men you will see have already graduated in at least ten of the eighteen martial arts of *bushido*, or "ways of the warrior", and they are now learning to be *ninja*, or "stealers-in", which has for centuries been part of the basic training of spies and assassins and saboteurs. You will see men walk across the surface of water, walk up walls and across ceilings, and you will be shown equipment which makes it possible for them to remain submerged under water for a full day. And many other tricks besides. For of course, apart from physical dexterity, the *ninja* were never the superhumans they were built up to be in the popular imagination. But, nevertheless, the secrets of *ninjutsu* are still closely guarded today and are the property of two main schools, the Iga and the Togakure, from which my instructors are drawn. I think you will be interested and perhaps learn something yourself at this place. I have never approved of agents carrying guns and other obvious weapons. In China, Korea and Oriental Russia, which are, so to speak, my main beats, the possession of any offensive weapon on arrest would be an obvious confession of guilt. My men are expected to be able to kill without weapons. All they may carry is a staff and a length of thin chain which can be easily explained away. You understand?'

'Yes, that makes sense. We have a similar commando training school for unarmed combat attached to Headquarters. But, of course, your judo and karate are special skills requiring years of practice. How high did you get in judo, Tiger?'

Tiger picked his teeth reminiscently. 'No higher than a Black Belt of the Seventh Dan. I never graduated to a Red Belt, which is from the Eighth to the Eleventh Dan. To do so would have meant abandoning all other forms of activity. And with what object? To be promoted to the Twelfth and final Dan on my death? In exchange for spending the whole of my life tumbling about in the Kodokan Academy in Tokyo? No thank you. That is the ambition of a lunatic.' He smiled. 'No *saké*! No beautiful girls! Worse still, probably no opportunity in a whole lifetime to exercise my art in anger, to tackle a robber or murderer with a gun, and get the better of him. In the higher realms of judo, you are nothing but a mixture between a monk and a ballet dancer. Not for me!'

Back on the open, dusty road some instinct made Bond glance through the rear window between the dainty lace blinds that are both the hall-mark of a truly sincere hired car and a dangerous impediment to the driver's vision. Far behind, there was a solitary motor-cyclist. Later, when they turned up a minor road into the mountains, he was still there. Bond mentioned the fact. Tiger shrugged. 'He is perhaps a speed cop. If he is anyone else, he has chosen a bad time and place.'

The castle was the usual horned-roof affair of Japanese prints. It stood in a cleft between the mountains that must have once been an important pass, for ancient cannon pointed out from the summit of giant, slightly sloping walls of black granite blocks. They were stopped at the gate to a wooden causeway across a brimming moat and again at the castle entrance. Tiger showed his pass, and there was much hissing and deep bowing from the plain-clothes guards and a bell clanged in the topmost tier of the soaring edifice, which, as Bond could see from the inner courtyard, was badly in need of a coat of paint. As the car came to a stop young men in shorts and gym shoes came running from various doors in the castle and formed up behind three older men. They bowed almost to the ground as Tiger descended regally from the car. Tiger and Bond also bowed. Brief greetings were exchanged with the older men and Tiger then proceeded to fire off a torrent of staccato Japanese which was punctuated by respectful '*Hai*'s' from the middle-aged man who was obviously the commandant of the team. With a final '*Hai*, Tanaka-san' this official turned to the twenty-odd students whose ages seemed to be somewhere between twenty-five and thirty-five. He called numbers and six men fell out of the ranks. They were given orders and ran off into the castle. Tiger commented to Bond. 'They will put on camouflage clothes and go off into the mountains through which we have come. If anyone is lurking about they will bring him to us. And now we will see a little demonstration of an attack on the castle.' Tiger fired off some more orders, the men dispersed at the double and Bond followed Tiger out on to the causeway accompanied by the chief instructor with whom Tiger had a long and animated discussion. Perhaps a quarter of an hour later, there came a whistle from above them on the ramparts and at once ten men broke cover from the forest to their left. They were dressed from head to foot in some black material, and only their eyes showed through slits in the black hoods. They ran down to the edge of the moat, donned oval battens of what must have been some light wood such as balsa, and skimmed across the water with a kind of skiing motion until they reached the bottom of the giant black wall. There they discarded their battens, took lengths of rope and a handful of small iron pitons out of pockets in their black robes and proceeded to almost run up the walls like fast black spiders.

Tiger turned to Bond. 'You understand that it is night-time. In a few days, you will have to be doing something similar. Note that the lengths of rope terminate in an iron hook which they throw up and catch in crevices between the stone blocks.' The instructor said something to Tiger and pointed. Tiger nodded. He said to Bond, 'The man at the end is the weakest of the team. The instructor thinks he will soon fall.'

The line of climbing men was now almost at the summit of the two-hundred-foot wall, and sure enough, with only yards to go, the end man lost his foothold and, with arms and legs flailing, and with a scream of terror, fell back down the sheer black face. His body hit once and then crashed into the calm waters of the moat. The instructor muttered something, stripped off his shirt, clambered on to the rail of the causeway and dived the hundred feet down into the water. It was a perfect dive, and he swam in a swift crawl towards the body that lay ominously face downwards in the moat. Tiger turned to Bond. 'It is of no account. He was going to fail the man anyway. And now come into the courtyard. The invaders have scaled the wall and they will now use *bojutsu* on the defenders, that is fighting with the stave.'

Bond took a last glance at the instructor, who was now towing the corpse, which it certainly was, to the shore by its black hood. Bond wondered if any of the students was going to fail his test at *bojutsu*. Failure was certainly total in Tiger's training camp!

Back in the courtyard, individual couples, dancing and dodging, were fighting furious single combats with thick staves about two yards long. They swung and parried with two hands on the stave, lunged at the belly, using the stave as a lance, or did complicated in-fighting with face almost pressed against face. Bond was astonished to see tremendous thrusts and whacks into the groin leaving the victim unmoved when he, Bond, would have been writhing in agony. He asked Tiger about this. Tiger, his eyes bright with the lust of battle, answered briefly that he would explain this later. Meanwhile, the invaders were slowly being overcome by the defence. Black figures toppled unconscious or lay groaning with hands clutched to head or stomach or shin. Then there came a shrill blast on the whistle from one of the instructors and it was all over. The defenders had won. A doctor appeared and attended the fallen, and those who were on their feet bowed deeply to one another and then in the direction of Tiger. Tiger made a brief and fierce speech which he later told Bond was of congratulation on the sincerity of the display, and Bond was then led into the castle to drink tea and view the museum of *ninja* armament. This included spiked steel wheels, the size of a silver dollar, which could be whirled on the finger and thrown, chains with spiked weights at each end, used like the South American bolas for catching cattle, sharp nails twisted into knots for defeating barefoot pursuers (Bond remembered similar devices spread on the roads by the Resistance to puncture the tyres of German staff cars), hollowed bamboo for breathing under water (Bond had used the same device during an adventure on a Caribbean island), varieties of brass knuckles, gloves whose palms were studded with very sharp, slightly hooked nails for 'walking' up walls and across ceilings, and a host of similar rather primitive gadgets of offence and defence. Bond made appropriate noises of approval and amazement and reflected on the comparable Russian invention used with much success in West Germany, a cyanide gas pistol that left no trace and a sure diagnosis of heart failure. Tiger's much vaunted *ninjutsu* just wasn't in the same league!

Out in the courtyard again, the leader of the camouflaged troop reported the discovery of motor-cycle tyre tracks that stopped and turned back a mile from the castle. That had been the only trace of a tail. Then came, to Bond, the blessed bows and farewells and they were on their way again, bound for Kyoto.

'Well, Bondo-san. What did you think of my training school?'

'I thought it was very sincere. I can imagine that the skills that are learned would be most valuable, but I would have thought that the black dress for night work and the various gadgets would have been as incriminating, if you were caught, as a pistol. But they certainly went up that wall damned quick, and that *bojutsu* business would be very effective against the usual night-prowler with a bicycle chain or a flick-knife. I must get Swaine and Adeney to make me a two-yard-long walking stick.'

Tiger sucked his teeth impatiently. 'You speak like a man who only knows of the sort of fighting that goes on in a cheap Western. You would not get very far with your methods if you were trying to penetrate North Korea dressed as a simple peasant with his staff.'

James Bond was rather exhausted by the day. He was also sorry for the student who had died showing off for his and Tiger's delectation. He said shortly, 'None of your *ninjas* would last very long in East Berlin,' and relapsed into a surly silence.

11

ANATOMY CLASS

TO BOND'S UNSPEAKABLE relief, they put up that night at the smartest hotel in Kyoto, the Miyako. The comfortable bed, air-conditioning and Western-style lavatory on which one could actually sit were out of this world. Better still, Tiger said that unfortunately he had to dine with the Chief of Police of the prefecture and Bond ordered a pint of Jack Daniels and a double portion of eggs Benedict to be brought up to his room. Then, from a belated sense of duty, he watched *The Seven Detectives*, a famous Japanese television series, failed to spot the villain, and went to bed and slept for twelve hours.

The next morning, hungover and conscience-stricken, he obediently fell in with Tiger's plans that they should visit the oldest whore-house in Japan before a quick drive to Osaka for the day's journey across the Inland Sea to the southern island of Kyūshū. 'Bit early for visiting a whore-house,' had been his only comment.

Tiger laughed. 'It is a matter of deep regret to me that your baser instincts should always be in the ascendancy, Bondo-san. Prostitution is now illegal in Japan. What we are about to visit is a national monument.'

'Oh, good show!'

There was a deal of bowing and hissing at the whore-house, a spacious establishment in the now defunct red lamp street of the ancient capital, and they were presented with handsomely bound descriptive booklets by the earnest curator. They wandered over polished floors from chamber to chamber, and gravely inspected the sword cuts in the wooden supports that had been inflicted, according to Tiger, by *samurai* infuriated by lust and impatience. Bond inquired how many actual bedrooms there had been. It seemed to him that the whole place was taken up by a vast kitchen and many dining-rooms.

'Four rooms,' answered the curator.

'That's no way to run a whore-house,' commented Bond. 'You need quick through-put, like a casino.'

'Bondo-san,' complained Tiger. 'Please try and put out of your mind comparisons between our way of life and yours. In former times, this was a place of rest and recreation. Food was served and there was music and story-telling. People would write *tankas*. Take that inscription on the wall. It says "Everything is new tomorrow." Some man with a profound mind will have written that.'

'Then he threw his pen away and reached for his sword and shouted, "When is room No. 4 going to be empty?" National monument indeed! It's like in the new African States where they pretend the cannibal stewpot in the chief's hut was for cooking yams for the hungry children. Everyone tries to forget his rowdy past instead of being proud of it. Like we are of Bloody Morgan, or Nell Gwynne, for instance. The great murderer and the great whore are part of our history. You shouldn't try and pretend that your oldest whore-house is a sort of Stratford-on-Avon.'

Tiger uttered an explosive laugh. 'Bondo-san, your comments on our Japanese way of life become more and more outrageous. Come, it is time to cleanse your mind in the salubrious breezes of the Inland Sea.'

The *Murasaki Maru* was a very modern 3000-ton ship with all the luxuries of an ocean liner. Crowds waved her goodbye as if the ship was setting off across the Atlantic instead of doing a day trip down the equivalent of a long lake. There was much throwing of paper streamers by groups bearing placards to show whom they represented — business outings, schools, clubs — part of the vast travelling population of Japan, for ever on the move, making an outing, visiting relatives or shrines, or just seeing the sights of the country. The ship throbbed grandly through the endless horned islands. Tiger said that there were fine whirlpools 'like great lavatory pans, specially designed for suicides' between some of these. Meanwhile, Tiger and Bond sat in the first-class dining-room and consumed 'Hamlets' — ham omelettes — and *saké*. Tiger was in a lecturing mood. He was determined to correct Bond's boorish ignorance of Japanese culture. 'Bondo-san, I wonder if I will ever get you to appreciate the nuances of the Japanese *tanka*, or of the *haiku*, which are the classical forms of Japanese verse. Have you ever heard of Bashō, for instance?'

'No,' said Bond with polite interest. 'Who's he?'

'Just so,' said Tiger bitterly. 'And yet you would think me grossly uneducated if I had never heard of Shakespeare, Homer, Dante, Cervantes, Goethe. And yet Bashō, who lived in the seventeenth century, is the equal of any of them.'

'What did he write?'

'He was an itinerant poet. He was particularly at home with the *haiku*, the verse of seventeen syllables.' Tiger assumed a contemplative expression. He intoned:

'In the bitter radish
that bites into me, I feel
the autumn wind.

'Does that not say anything to you? Or this:

'The butterfly is perfuming
its wings, in the scent
of the orchid.

'You do not grasp the beauty of that image?'

'Rather elusive compared to Shakespeare.'

'In the fisherman's hut
mingled with dried shrimps
crickets are chirping.'

Tiger looked at him hopefully.

'Can't get the hang of that one,' said Bond apologetically.

'You do not catch the still-life quality of these verses? The flash of insight into humanity, into nature? Now, do me a favour, Bondo-san. Write a *haiku* for me yourself. I am sure you could get the hang of it. After all you must have had *some* education?'

Bond laughed. 'Mostly in Latin and Greek. All about Caesar and Balbus and so on. Absolutely no help in ordering a cup of coffee in Rome or Athens after I'd left school. And things like trigonometry, which I've totally forgotten. But give me a pen and a piece of paper and I'll have a bash, if you'll forgive the bad joke.' Tiger handed them over and Bond put his head in his hands. Finally, after much crossing out and rewriting he said, 'Tiger, how's this? It makes just as much sense as old Bashō and it's much more pithy.' He read out:

> 'You only live twice:
> Once when you are born
> And once when you look death in the face.'

Tiger clapped his hands softly. He said with real delight, 'But that is excellent, Bondo-san. Most sincere.' He took the pen and paper and jotted some ideograms up the page. He shook his head. 'No, it won't do in Japanese. You have the wrong number of syllables. But it is a most honourable attempt.' He looked keenly at Bond. 'You were perhaps thinking of your mission?'

'Perhaps,' said Bond with indifference.

'It is weighing on your mind?'

'The practical difficulties are bound to do so. I have swallowed the moral principles involved. Things being as they are, I have to accept that the end justifies the means.'

'Then you are not concerned with your own safety?'

'Not particularly. I've had worse jobs to do.'

'I must congratulate you on your stoicism. You do not appear to value your life as highly as most Westerners.' Tiger looked at him kindly. 'Is there perhaps a reason for that?'

Bond was offhand. 'Not that I can think of. But for God's sake chuck it, Tiger! None of your Japanese brain-washing! More *saké*, and answer my question of yesterday. Why weren't those men disabled by those terrific slashes to the groin? That might be of some practical value to me instead of all this waffle about poetry.'

Tiger ordered the *saké*. He laughed. 'Unfortunately you are too old to benefit. I would need to have caught you at the age of about fourteen. You see, it is this way. You know the *sumo* wrestlers? It is they who invented the trick many centuries ago. It is vital for them to be immune from damage to those parts of the body. Now, you know that, in men, the testicles, which until puberty have been held inside the body, are released by a particular muscle and descend between the legs?'

'Yes.'

'Well the *sumo* wrestler will have been selected for his profession by the time of puberty. Perhaps because of his weight and strength, or perhaps because he comes of a *sumo* family. Well, by assiduously massaging those parts, he is able, after much practice, to cause the testicles to re-enter the body up the inguinal canal down which they originally descended.'

'My God, you Japanese!' said Bond with admiration. 'You really are up to all the tricks. You mean he gets them right out of the way behind the bones of the pelvis or what not?'

'Your knowledge of anatomy is as vague as your appreciation for poetry, but that is more or less so, yes. Then, before a fight, he will bind up that part of the body most thoroughly to contain these vulnerable organs in their hiding-place. Afterwards, in the bath, he will release them to hang normally. I have seen them do it. It is a great pity that it is now too late for you to practise this art. It might have given you more confidence on your mission. It is my experience that agents fear most for that part of the body when there is fighting to be done or when they risk capture. These organs, as you know, are most susceptible to torture for the extraction of information.'

'Don't I know it!' said Bond from the heart. 'Some of our chaps wear a box when they think they're in for a rough house. I don't care for them. Too uncomfortable.'

'What is a box?'

'It is what our cricketers wear to protect those parts when they go out to bat. It is a light padded shield of aluminium.'

'I regret that we have nothing of that nature. We do not play cricket in Japan. Only baseball.'

'Lucky for you you weren't occupied by the British,' commented Bond. 'Cricket is a much more difficult and skilful game.'

'The Americans say otherwise.'

'Naturally. They want to sell you baseball equipment.'

They arrived at Beppu in the southern island of Kyūshū as the sun was setting. Tiger said that this was just the time to see the famous geysers and fumaroles of the little spa. In any case, there would be no time in the morning as they would have to start early for Fukuoka, their final destination. Bond shivered slightly at the name. The moment was rapidly approaching when the *saké* and sightseeing would have to stop.

Above the town of Beppu, they visited in turn the ten spectacular 'hells' as they are officially designated. The stink of sulphur was disgusting, and each bubbling, burping nest of volcanic fumaroles was more horrific than the last. The steaming mud and belching geysers were of different colours — red, blue and orange — and everywhere there were warning notices and skulls and crossbones to keep visitors at a safe distance. The tenth 'hell' announced in English and Japanese that there would be an eruption punctually every twenty minutes. They joined a small group of spectators under the arc lights that pinpointed a small quiescent crater in a rocky area bespattered with mud. Sure enough, in five minutes, there came a rumbling from underground and a jet of steaming grey mud shot twenty feet up into the air and splashed down inside the enclosure. As Bond was turning away, he noticed a large red-painted wheel, heavily padlocked and surrounded by wire-netting in a small separate enclosure. There were warning notices above it and a particularly menacing skull and crossbones. Bond asked Tiger what it was.

'It says that this wheel controls the pulse of the geyser. It says that if this wheel were screwed down it could result in the destruction of the entire establishment. It gives the explosive force of the volcano, if the exhaust valve of the geyser were to be closed, as the equivalent of a thousand pounds of T.N.T. It is, of course, all a bit of nonsense to attract the tourists. But now, back to the town, Bondo-san! Since it is our last day together,' he added hastily, 'on this particular voyage, I have arranged a special treat. I ordered it by radio from the ship. A *fugu* feast!'

Bond cursed silently. The memory of his eggs Benedict the night before was intolerably sweet. What new monstrosity was this? he asked.

'*Fugu* is the Japanese blow-fish. In the water, it looks like a brown owl, but when captured it blows itself up into a ball covered with wounding spines. We sometimes dry the skins and put candles inside and use them as lanterns. But the flesh is particularly delicious. It is the staple food of the *sumo* wrestlers because it is supposed to be very strength-giving. The fish is also very popular with suicides and murderers because its liver and sex glands contain a poison which brings death instantaneously.'

'That's just what I would have chosen for dinner. How thoughtful of you, Tiger.'

'Have no fear, Bondo-san. Because of the dangerous properties of the fish, every *fugu* restaurant has to be manned by experts and be registered with the State.'

They left their bags at a Japanese inn where Tiger had reserved rooms, enjoyed the *o-furo*, honourable bath, together in the blue-tiled miniature swimming pool whose water was very hot and smelled of sulphur, and then, totally relaxed, went off down the street leading to the sea.

(Bond had become enamoured of the civilized, vaguely Roman, bathing habits of the Japanese. Was it because of these, because they washed *outside* the bath instead of wallowing in their own effluvia, that they all smelled so clean? Tiger said bluntly that, at the very best, Westerners smelled of sweet pork.)

The restaurant had a giant blow-fish hanging as a sign above the door, and inside, to Bond's relief, there were Western-style chairs and tables at which a smattering of people were eating with the intense concentration of the Japanese. They were expected and their table had been prepared. Bond said, 'Now then, Tiger, I'm not going to commit honourable suicide without at least five bottles of *saké* inside me.' The flasks were brought, all five of them, to the accompaniment of much tittering by the waitresses. Bond downed the lot, tumbler by tumbler, and expressed himself satisfied. 'Now you can bring on this blasted blow-fish,' he said belligerently, 'and if it kills me it will be doing a good turn to our friend the doctor in his castle.'

A very beautiful white porcelain dish as big as a bicycle wheel was brought forward with much ceremony. On it were arranged, in the pattern of a huge flower, petal upon petal of a very thinly sliced and rather transparent white fish. Bond followed Tiger's example and set to with his chopsticks. He was proud of the fact that he had reached Black Belt standard with these instruments — the ability to eat an underdone fried egg with them.

The fish tasted of nothing, not even of fish. But it was very pleasant on the palate and Bond was effusive in his compliments because Tiger, smacking his lips over each morsel, obviously expected it of him. There followed various side-dishes containing other parts of the fish, and more *saké*, but this time containing raw *fugu* fins.

Bond sat back and lit a cigarette. He said, 'Well, Tiger. This is nearly the end of my education. Tomorrow you say I am to leave the nest. How many marks out of a hundred?'

Tiger looked at him quizzically. 'You have done well, Bondo-san. Apart from your inclination to make Western jokes about Eastern customs. Fortunately I am a man of infinite patience, and I must admit that your company has given me much pleasure and a certain amount of amusement. I will award you seventy-five marks out of a possible hundred.'

As they rose to go, a man brushed past Bond to get to the exit. He was a stocky man with a white *masko* over his mouth and he wore an ugly leather hat. The man on the train!

Well, well! thought Bond. If he shows up on the last lap to Fukuoka, I'll get him. If not I'll reluctantly put it down to 'Funny Coincidence Department'. But it looks like nought out of a hundred to Tiger for powers of observation.

Part Two

. . . THAN TO ARRIVE'

12

APPOINTMENT IN SAMARA

At six in the morning, a car from the Prefect of Police in Fukuoka came for them. There were two police corporals in the front seat. They went off northwards on the coast road at a good pace. After a while, Bond said, 'Tiger, we're being followed. I don't care what you say. The man who stole my wallet was in the *fugu* restaurant last night, and he's now a mile behind on a motor-cycle — or I'll eat my hat. Be a good chap and tell the driver to dodge up a side-road and then go after him and get him. I've got a sharp nose for these things and I ask you to do what I say.'

Tiger grunted. He looked back and then issued rapid instructions to the driver. The driver said, '*Hai!*' briskly, and the corporal at his side unbuttoned the holster of his M-14 automatic. Tiger flexed his powerful fingers.

They came to a track on the left which went into the scrub. The driver did a good racing change and pulled in out of sight of the road. He cut his engine. They listened. The roar of a motor-cycle approached and receded. The driver reversed sharply on to the road and tore off in pursuit. Tiger issued more sharp instructions. He said to Bond, 'I have told him to try warning the man with his siren and if he doesn't stop to ride him into the ditch.'

'Well, I'm glad you're giving him a chance,' said Bond, beginning to have qualms. 'I may be wrong and he may only be a Fuller brush man in a hurry.'

They were doing eighty along the winding road. They soon came up with the man's dust and then there was the machine itself. The man was hunched over the handlebars, going like hell.

The driver said something. Tiger translated. 'He says it's a 500 cc. Honda. On that, he could easily get away from us. But even Japanese crooks are men of discipline. He will prefer to obey the siren.'

The siren wailed and then screamed. The white mask gleamed as the man glanced over his shoulder. He braked slowly to a stop. His right hand went inside his jacket. Bond had his hand on the door-latch. He said, 'Watch out, Tiger, he's got a gun!' and, as they pulled up alongside, he hurled himself out of the door and crashed into the man, knocking him and his machine to the ground. The corporal beside the driver took a flying leap and the two bodies rolled into the ditch. Almost immediately the corporal got to his feet. He had a bloodstained knife in his hand. He threw it aside and tore at the man's coat and shirt. He looked up and shook his head. Tiger shouted something and the corporal began slapping the man's face as hard as he could from side to side. The *masko* was knocked off and Bond recognized the snarling rictus of death. He said, sickened, 'Stop him, Tiger! The man's dead.'

Tiger walked down into the ditch. He picked up the man's knife and bent down and slit the right sleeve of the corpse up to the shoulder. He looked and then called Bond down. He pointed to a black ideogram tattoed in the crook of the man's arm. He said, 'You were right, Bondo-san. He is a Black Dragon.' He stood up and, his face contorted, spat out: '*Shimata!*'

The two policemen were standing by looking politely baffled. Tiger gave them orders. They searched the man's clothing and extracted various commonplace objects including Bond's wallet, with the five thousand yen still intact, and a cheap diary. They handed everything to Tiger and then hauled the corpse out of the ditch and stuffed it roughly into the boot of the car. Then they hid the motor-cycle in some bushes and everyone dusted themselves and got back into the car.

After a few moments, Tiger said thoughtfully, 'It is incredible! These people must have a permanent tail on me in Tokyo.' He riffled through the diary. 'Yes, all my movements for the past week and all the stopping-places on our journey. You are simply described as a *gaijin*. But he could have telephoned a description. This is indeed an unfortunate business, Bondo-san. I apologize most deeply. You may already be incriminated. I will naturally absolve you from your mission. It is entirely my fault for being careless. I have not been taking these people seriously enough. I must talk with Tokyo as soon as we get to Fukuoka. But at least you have seen an example of the measures Doctor

Shatterhand takes for his protection. There is certainly more to this man than meets the eye. At some time in his life he must have been an experienced intelligence agent. To have discovered my identity, for instance, which is a State secret. To have recognized me as his chief enemy. To have taken the appropriate counter-measures to ensure his privacy. This is either a great madman or a great criminal. You agree, Bondo-san?'

'Looks mighty like it. I'm really getting quite keen to have a sight of the fellow. And don't worry about the mission. This was probably just the jolt I needed to get the wind under my tail.'

The headquarters of the local department of the Sosaka, the C.I.D., for the southern island of Kyūshū, was just off the main street of Fukuoka. It was a stern-looking building in yellow lavatory brick in a style derived from the German. Tiger confirmed that it had been the headquarters of the Kempeitai, the Japanese Gestapo, before and during the war. Tiger was received with pomp. The office of the Chief of the C.I.D. was small and cluttered. Superintendent Ando himself looked to Bond like any other Japanese salary-man, but he had a military bearing and the eyes behind the rimless spectacles were quick and hard. Bond sat patiently smoking while much conversation went on. A blown-up aerial mosaic of the Castle of Death and the surrounding country was produced from a filing cabinet and laid out on the desk. Superintendent Ando weighed down the corners with ash-trays and other hardware and Tiger called him over with a respect, Bond noticed, that was not lost on the Superintendent. It crossed Bond's mind that he had heaped much ON on Tiger, or alternatively that Tiger had lost much face vis-à-vis Bond by the business of the Black Dragon agent. Tiger said, 'Please to examine this photograph, Bondo-san. The Superintendent says that a clandestine approach from the landward side is now very difficult. The suicides pay local peasants to lead them through these marshlands,' he pointed, 'and there are recognized breaches in the walls surrounding the property which are constantly changed and kept open for the suicides. Every time the Superintendent posts a guard at one of them, another is made known to the peasants by the castle guards. He says he is at his wits' end. Twenty bodies have been fetched to the mortuary in the past week. The Superintendent wishes to hand in his resignation.'

'Naturally,' said Bond. 'And then perhaps honourable *fugu* poisoning. Let's have a look.'

At first glance, Bond's heart quailed. He might just as well try and storm Windsor Castle single-handed! The estate covered the whole expanse of a small promontory that jutted out into the sea from a rocky coast, and the two-hundred-foot cliff round the promontory had been revetted with giant stone blocks down to the breaking waves to form an unbroken wall that sloped slightly up to gun-ports and the irregularly sited, tiled watch-towers. From the top of this wall there appeared to be a ten-foot drop into the park, heavily treed and shrubbed between winding streams and a broad lake with a small island in its centre. Steam appeared to be rising from the lake and there were occasional wisps of it among the shrubbery. At the back of the property stood the castle, protected from the low-lying countryside by a comparatively modest wall. It would be over this wall that the suicides gained access. The castle itself was a giant five-storeyed affair in the Japanese tradition, with swooping, winged roofs of glazed tile. Dolphin-shaped finials decorated the topmost storey, and there was a profusion of other decorative devices, small balconies, isolated turrets and gazebos so that the whole black-painted edifice, edged here and there with what Tiger said was gold paint, gave the impression of a brilliant attempt to make a stage setting for Dracula. Bond picked up a large magnifying glass and ran over the whole property inch by inch, but there was nothing more to be gleaned except the presence of an occasional diminutive figure at work in the park or raking the gravel round the castle.

Bond laid down the glass. He said gloomily, 'That's not a castle! That's a fortress! How am I supposed to get into the bloody place?'

'The Superintendent asks if you are a good swimmer. I have had a complete outfit sent down from my *ninjutsu* establishment. The seaward wall would present no problems.'

'I can swim well enough, but how do I get to the base of the wall? Where do I start from?'

'The Superintendent says there is an Ama island called Kuro only half a mile out to sea.'

'What's an Ama island?'

'They exist at different places round Japan. I believe there are some fifty such settlements. The Ama are a tribe whose girls dive for the *awabi* shells — that is our local abalone. A clam. It is a great delicacy. They sometimes dive for pearl oysters. They dive naked. Some of them are very beautiful. But they keep themselves very much to themselves and visitors to their islands are completely discouraged. They have their own primitive culture and customs. I suppose you could compare them to sea-gypsies. They rarely marry outside the tribe, and it is that which has made them a race apart.'

'Sounds intriguing, but how am I going to make a base on this Kuro Island? I may have to wait days for the weather to be right.'

Tiger spoke rapidly to the Superintendent and there was a lengthy reply. '*Ah, so desu ka!*' said Tiger with interest and enthusiasm. He turned to Bond. 'It seems that the Superintendent is distantly related to a family on Kuro. It is a most interesting family. There is a father and a mother and one daughter. She is called Kissy Suzuki. I have heard of her. When she was seventeen, she became famous in Japan by being chosen to go to Hollywood to make a film. They wanted a Japanese diving girl of great beauty and someone had heard of her. She made the film, but hated Hollywood and longed only to return to her Ama life. She could have made a fortune, but she retired to this obscure island. There was a great to-do in the press at the time, and it was judged that she had behaved most honourably. They christened her "The Japanese Garbo". But Kissy will now be twenty-three and everyone has forgotten about her. The Superintendent says that he could arrange for you to stay with this family. They seem to have some obligation towards him. He says it is a simple house, but comfortable because of the money this girl earned in Hollywood. The other houses on the island are nothing but fishermen's shacks.'

'But won't the rest of the community resent me being there?'

'No. The people of the island belong to the Shinto religion. The Superintendent will speak to the Shinto priest and everything will be okay.'

'All right, so I stay on this island and then one night I swim across to the wall. How do I get up it?'

'You will have the *ninja* outfit. It is here. You have seen how it is used. You will use it. It is very simple.'

'As I saw from the man who fell into the moat. Then what do I do?'

'You hide up in the grounds and wait for an opportunity to kill him. How you do that is up to you. As I told you, he goes about in armour. A man in armour is very vulnerable. You only have to knock him off his feet. Then you will throttle him with the *ninja* chain you will be wearing round your waist. If his wife is with him, you will throttle her too. She is certainly involved in all this business, and anyway she is too ugly to live. Then you escape over the wall and swim back to Kuro. There you will be picked up by the police launch which will visit the place at once. The news of the death will quickly get round.'

Bond said doubtfully, 'Well, it all sounds very simple. But what about these guards? The place is crawling with them.'

'You must just keep out of their way. As you can see, the park is full of hiding-places.'

'Thanks very much. In one of those poison bushes or up one of those trees. I don't want to blind myself or go mad.'

'The *ninja* clothing will give you complete protection. You will have a black suit for night and a camouflage one for the day. You will wear the swimming goggles to protect your eyes. All this equipment you will tow over in a plastic bag which will be provided.'

'My dear Tiger, you've thought of everything. But I'd much rather have just one little gun.'

'That would be crazy, Bondo-san. You know perfectly well that silence will be essential. And with a silencer, which would be very heavy to swim with, the speed of the bullet would be so much reduced that you might not pierce the armour. No, my friend. Use *ninjutsu*. It is the only way.'

'Oh all right,' said Bond resignedly. 'Now let's have a look at a photograph of this chap. Has the Superintendent got one?'

It had been taken from a long way away with a telephoto lens. It showed a giant figure in full medieval chain armour with the jagged, winged helmet of ancient Japanese warriors. Bond studied the photograph carefully, noting the vulnerable spots at neck and joints. A metal shield protected the man's groin. A wide-bladed *samurai* sword hung from his waist, but there was no sign of any other weapon. Bond said thoughtfully, 'He doesn't look as daft as he ought to. Probably because of the

Dracula setting. Have you got one of his face? Perhaps he looks a bit madder in the raw.'

The Superintendent went to the bottom of his file and extracted what looked like a blown-up copy of Doctor Guntram Shatterhand's passport photograph and handed it over.

Bond took it nonchalantly. Then his whole body stiffened. He said to himself, God Almighty! God Almighty! Yes. There was no doubt, no doubt at all! He had grown a drooping black moustache. He had had the syphilitic nose repaired. There was a gold-capped tooth among the upper frontals, but there could be no doubt. Bond looked up. He said, 'Have you got one of the woman?'

Startled by the look of controlled venom on Bond's face, and by the pallor that showed through the walnut dye, the Superintendent bowed energetically and scrabbled through his file.

Yes, there she was, the bitch — the flat, ugly wardress face, the dull eyes, the scraped-back bun of hair.

Bond held the pictures, not looking at them, thinking. Ernst Stavro Blofeld. Irma Bunt. So this was where they had come to hide! And the long, strong gut of fate had lassoed him to them! They of all people! He of all people! A taxi-ride down the coast in this remote corner of Japan. Could they smell him coming? Had the dead spy got hold of his name and told them? Unlikely. The power and prestige of Tiger would have protected him. Privacy, discretion, are the heartbeat of Japanese inns. But would they know that an enemy was on his way? That fate had arranged this appointment in Samara? Bond looked up from the pictures. He was in cold control of himself. This was now a private matter. It had nothing to do with Tiger or Japan. It had nothing to do with MAGIC 44. It was ancient feud. He said casually, 'Tiger, could the Superintendent inquire what his detectives have made of that Black Dragon agent? And of his belongings? I am particularly interested to know whether he may have telephoned or telegraphed my description or my purpose in coming down here.'

There was a long and electric silence in the room. Tiger examined Bond's face with piercing interest before he passed the inquiry on to the Superintendent. The Superintendent picked up the receiver of an old-fashioned telephone on a double hook. He spoke into it, then, a Japanese habit, blew sharply into the mouthpiece to clear the line, and spoke again at length. He said, '*Ah, so desu ka!*' many times. Then he put down the receiver. When he had finished talking, Tiger turned to Bond. Again with the same piercing appraisal of Bond's face, he said, 'The man came from these parts. He has a police record. Fortunately, he was poorly educated and is known as nothing more than a stupid thug. On the first page of the diary he wrote down his assignment, which was only to follow me to my destination and then report to his master. It seems unlikely that he was provided with funds for expensive communications. But what is it, Bondo-san? Is it that you know these people?'

James Bond laughed. It was a laugh that grated. Even to Bond, it sounded harsh and false in the small room. He had immediately made up his mind to keep his knowledge to himself. To reveal the true identity of Doctor Shatterhand would be to put the whole case back into official channels. The Japanese Secret Service and the C.I.A. would swarm down to Fukuoka. Blofeld and Irma Bunt would be arrested. James Bond's personal prey would be snatched from him. There would be no revenge! Bond said, 'Good lord, no! But I am something of a physiognomist. When I saw this man's face, it was as if someone had walked over my grave. I have a feeling that, whether I succeed or not, the outcome of this mission is going to be decisive for one or the other of us. It will not be a drawn game. But now I have a number of further questions with which I must worry you and the Superintendent. They are small matters of detail, but I want to get everything right before I start.'

Tiger looked relieved. The raw animalism in Bond's face had been so different from the stoical, ironical face of the Bondo-san for whom he had come to have so much affection. He gave his great golden smile and said, 'But of course, my friend. And I am pleased with your worries and with the trouble you are taking to make sure of everything in advance. You will forgive me if I quote you one last Japanese proverb. It says, "A reasonable number of fleas is good for a dog. Otherwise the dog forgets he is a dog." '

'Good old Bashō!' said Bond.

13

KISSY SUZUKI

JAMES BOND WENT THROUGH the rest of the morning like an automaton. While he tried on his *ninja* equipment and watched each item being carefully packed into a floatable plastic container, his mind was totally occupied with the image of his enemy — this man Blofeld, the great gangster who had founded SPECTRE, the Special Executive for Counter-Intelligence, Terrorism, Revenge and Extortion, the man who was wanted by the police of all the NATO countries, the man who had murdered Tracy, Bond's wife for less than a day, a bare nine months ago. And, in those nine months, this evil genius had invented a new method of collecting death, as Tiger had put it. This cover as the Swiss Doctor Shatterhand, as a rich botanist, must have been one of the many he had wisely built up over the years. It would have been easy. A few gifts of rare plants to famous botanical gardens, the financing of a handful of expeditions, and all the while in the back of his mind the plan one day to retire and 'cultiver son jardin'. And what a garden! A garden that would be like a deadly fly-trap for human beings, a killing bottle for those who wanted to die. And of course Japan, with the highest suicide statistics in the world, a country with an unquenchable thirst for the bizarre, the cruel and the terrible, would provide the perfect last refuge for him. Blofeld must have gone off his head, but with a monstrous, calculating madness — the madness of the genius he undoubtedly was. And the whole demoniac concept was on Blofeld's usual grand scale — the scale of a Caligula, of a Nero, of a Hitler, of any other great enemy of mankind. The speed of execution was breathtaking, the expenditure fabulous, the planning, down to the use of the Black Dragon Society, meticulous, and the cover as impeccable as the Piz Gloria Clinic which, less than a year before, Bond had helped to destroy utterly. And now the two enemies were lined up again, but this time David was spurred on to kill his

Goliath not by duty but by blood feud! And with what weapons? Nothing but his bare hands, a two-inch pocket knife and a thin chain of steel. Well, similar weapons had served him before. Surprise would be the determining factor. Bond added a pair of black flippers to his equipment, a small supply of pemmican-like meat, benzedrine tablets, a plastic flask of water. Then he was ready.

They motored down the main street to where the police launch was waiting at the jetty and set off at a good twenty knots across the beautiful bay and round the headland into the Sea of Genkai. Tiger produced sandwiches and a flask of *saké* for each of them, and they ate their luncheon as the jagged green coast with its sandy beaches passed slowly by to port. Tiger pointed out a distant dot on the horizon. 'Kuro Island,' he said. 'Cheer up, Bondo-san! You seem preoccupied. Think of all those beautiful naked women you will soon be swimming with! And this Japanese Greta Garbo with whom you will be passing the nights!'

'And the sharks who will already be gathering at the news of my swim to the castle!'

'If they do not eat the Amas, why should they eat a bit of tough Englishman? Look at the two fish eagles circling! That is an excellent augury. One alone would have been less propitious. Four would have been disastrous, for with us four is the same as your thirteen — the worst number of all. But, Bondo-san, does it not amuse you to think of that foolish dragon dozing all unsuspecting in his castle while St George comes silently riding towards his lair across the waves? It would make the subject for a most entertaining Japanese print.'

'You've got a funny sense of humour, Tiger.'

'It is merely different from yours. Most of our funny stories involve death or disaster. I am not a "picture-daddy" — a professional story-teller — but I will tell you my favourite. It concerns the young girl who comes to the toll bridge. She tosses one sen, a very small piece of money, to the watchman, and walks on. The watchman calls after her, "Hey! You know that the toll for crossing the bridge is two sen." The girl answers, "But I do not intend to cross the bridge. I intend only to go halfway and then throw myself into the river." ' Tiger laughed uproariously.

Bond smiled politely. 'I must save that one up for London. They'll split their sides over it.'

The small speck on the horizon grew larger and soon revealed itself as a horned island about five miles in circumference with steep cliffs and a small harbour facing north. On the mainland, Doctor Shatterhand's small peninsula reached out into the sea, and the fortress-like black wall soared up out of the breaking waves. Above it were the tops of trees, and, behind them, in the distance, the winged roof of the topmost storey of the castle broke the skyline. The formidable silhouette reminded Bond vaguely of photographs of Alcatraz taken from sea-level. He shivered slightly at the thought of the night's swim across the half-mile channel and of the black spider that would then scale those soaring fortifications. Ah well! He turned his attention back to Kuro Island.

It appeared to be made of black volcanic rock, but there was much green vegetation right up to the summit of a small peak on which there was some kind of a stone beacon. When they rounded the headland that formed one arm of the bay, a crowded little village and a jetty appeared. Out to sea, thirty or more rowing boats were scattered and there was the occasional glint of pink flesh in the sunlight. Naked children were playing among the big smooth black boulders that tumbled like bathing hippos along the shoreline, and there were green nets hung up to dry. It was a pretty scene, with the delicate remoteness, the fairyland quality, of small fishing communities all the world over. Bond took an immediate liking to the place, as if he was arriving at a destination that had been waiting for him and that would be friendly and welcoming.

A group of village elders, grave, gnarled old men with the serious expressions of simple people on important occasions, led by the Shinto priest, was on the jetty to welcome them. The priest was in ceremonial robes, a dark red, three-quarter-length kimono with vast hanging sleeves, a turquoise skirt in broad pleats and the traditional shining black hat in the shape of a blunt cone. He was a man of simple dignity and considerable presence, middle-aged, with a round face and round spectacles and a pursed, judging mouth. His shrewd eyes took them in one by one as they came ashore, but they rested longest on Bond. Superintendent Ando was greeted with friendship as well as respect. This was part of his parish, and he was the ultimate source of all fishing permits, reflected Bond ungraciously, but he had to admit that the deference of the bows was not exaggerated and that he was lucky in his ambassador. They proceeded up the cobbled path of the main street to the priest's house, a modest, weather-beaten affair of stone and carpentered driftwood. They entered and sat on the spotless polished wood floor in an arc in front of the priest, and the Superintendent made a long speech punctuated by serious '*Hai*'s' and '*Ah, so desu ka*'s' from the priest, who occasionally let his wise eyes rest thoughtfully on Bond. He made a short speech in return, to which the Superintendent and Tiger listened with deference. Tiger replied, and the business of the meeting was over save for the inevitable tea.

Bond asked Tiger how his presence and mission had been explained. Tiger said that it would have been of no use lying to the priest who was a shrewd man, so he had been told most of the truth. The priest had expressed regret that such extreme measures were contemplated, but he agreed that the castle across the sea was a most evil place and its owner a man in league with the devil. In the circumstances, he would give the project his blessing and James Bond would be allowed to stay on the island for the minimum time necessary to accomplish his mission.

The priest would invite the Suzuki family to accord him an honourable welcome. Bond would be explained away to the elders as a famous *gaijin* anthropologist who had come to study the Ama way of life. Bond should therefore study it, but the priest requested that Bond should behave in a sincere manner. 'Which means,' explained Tiger with a malicious grin, 'that you are not to go to bed with the girls.'

In the evening they walked back to the jetty. The sea was a dark slate colour and mirror-calm. The little boats, bedecked with coloured flags which meant that it had been an exceptional day's fishing, were winging their way back. The entire population of Kuro, perhaps two hundred souls, was lined up along the shore to greet the heroines of the day, the older people holding carefully folded shawls and blankets to warm up the girls on their way to their homes where, according to Tiger, they would be given hot basin-baths to get back their circulation and remove all traces of salt. It was now five o'clock. They would be asleep by eight, said Tiger, and out again with the dawn. Tiger was sympathetic. 'You will have to adjust your hours, Bondo-san. And your way of life. The Ama live very frugally, very cheaply, for their earnings are small — no more than the price of sparrows' tears, as we say. And for heaven's sake be very polite to the parents, particularly the father. As for Kissy . . .' He left the sentence hanging in the air.

Eager hands reached for each boat and, with happy shouts, pulled it up on the black pebbles. Big wooden tubs were lifted out and rushed up the beach to a kind of rickety market where, according to Tiger, the *awabi* were graded and priced. Meanwhile, the chattering, smiling girls waded in through the shallows and cast modestly appraising glances at the three mainland strangers on the jetty.

To Bond, they all seemed beautiful and gay in the soft evening light — the proud, rather coarse-nippled breasts, the gleaming, muscled buttocks, cleft by the black cord that held in place the frontal triangle of black cotton, the powerful thong round the waist with its string of oval lead weights, through which was stuck an angular steel pick, the white rag round the tumbled hair and, below, the laughing dark eyes and lips that were happy with the luck of the day. At that moment, it all seemed to Bond as the world, as life, should be, and he felt ashamed of his city-slicker appearance, let alone the black designs it concealed.

One girl, rather taller than the rest, seemed to pay no attention to the men on the jetty or to the police launch riding beside it. She was the centre of a crowd of laughing girls as she waded with a rather long, perhaps studied, stride over the shiny black pebbles and up the beach. She flung back a remark at her companions and they giggled, putting their hands up to their mouths. Then a wizened old woman held out a coarse brown blanket to her and she wrapped it round herself and the group dispersed.

The couple, the old woman and the young one, walked up the beach to the market. The young one talked excitedly. The old one paid attention and nodded. The priest was waiting for them. They bowed very low. He talked to them and they listened with humility, casting occasional glances towards the group on the jetty. The tall girl drew her blanket more closely round her. James Bond had guessed it already. Now he knew. This was Kissy Suzuki.

The three people, the splendidly attired priest, the walnut-faced old fisherwoman and the tall naked girl wrapped in her drab blanket came along the jetty, the girl hanging back. In a curious way they were a homogeneous trio, and the priest might have been the father. The women stopped and the priest came forward. He bowed to Bond and addressed him. Tiger translated: 'He says that the father and mother of Kissy Suzuki would be honoured to receive you in their humble abode for whose poverty they apologize. They regret that they are not accustomed to Western ways, but their daughter is proficient in English as a result of her work in America and will endeavour to convey your wishes to them. The priest asks if you can row a boat. The father, who previously rowed for his daughter, is stricken with rheumatism. It would be of great assistance to the family if you would deign to take his place.'

Bond bowed. He said, 'Please convey to his reverence that I am most grateful for his intercession on my behalf. I would be most honoured to have a place to lay my head in the home of Suzuki-san. My needs are very modest and I greatly enjoy the Japanese way of life. I would be most pleased to row the family boat or help the household in any other way.' He added, sotto voce, 'Tiger, I may need these people's help when the time comes. Particularly the girl's. How much can I tell her?'

Tiger said softly, 'Use your discretion. The priest knows, therefore the girl can know. She will not spread it abroad. And now come forward and let the priest introduce you. Don't forget that your name here is Taro, which means "first son", Todoroki, which means "thunder". The priest is not interested in your real name. I have said that this is an approximation of your English name. It doesn't matter. Nobody will care. But you must try to assume some semblance of a Japanese personality for when you get to the other side. This name is on your identity card and on your miner's union card from the coalmines of Fukuoka. You need not bother with these things here for you are among friends. On the other side, if you are caught, you will show the card that says you are deaf and dumb. All right?'

Tiger talked to the priest and Bond was led forward to the two women. He bowed low to the mother, but he remembered not to bow too low as she was only a woman, and then he turned to the girl.

She laughed gaily. She didn't titter or giggle, she actually laughed. She said, 'You don't have to bow to me and I shall never bow to you.' She held out her hand. 'How do you do. My name is Kissy Suzuki.'

The hand was ice-cold. Bond said, 'My name is Taro Todoroki and I am sorry to have kept you here so long. You are cold and you ought to go and have your hot bath. It is very kind of your family to accept me as your guest, but I do not want to be an imposition. Are you sure it's all right?'

'Whatever the *kannushi-san*, the priest, says is all right. And I have been cold before. When you have finished with your distinguished friends, my mother and I will be happy to lead you to our house. I hope you are good at peeling potatoes.'

Bond was delighted. Thank God for a straightforward girl at last! No more bowing and hissing! He said, 'I took a degree in it. And I am strong and willing and I don't snore. What time do we take out the boat?'

'About five thirty. When the sun comes up. Perhaps you will bring me good luck. The *awabi* shells are not easy to find. We had a lucky day today and I earned about thirty dollars, but it is not always so.'

'I don't reckon in dollars. Let's say ten pounds.'

'Aren't Englishmen the same as Americans? Isn't the money the same?'

'Very alike, but totally different.'

'Is that so?'

'You mean "*Ah, so desu ka?*" '

The girl laughed. 'You have been well trained by the important man from Tokyo. Perhaps you will now say goodbye to him and we can go home. It is at the other end of the village.'

The priest, the Superintendent and Tiger had been talking together, ostensibly paying no attention to Bond and the girl. The mother had been standing humbly, but with shrewd eyes, watching every expression on the two faces. Bond now bowed again to her and went back to the group of men.

Farewells were brief. Dusk was creeping up over the sea and the orange ball of the sun had already lost its brilliance in the evening haze. The engine of the police boat had been started up and its exhaust bubbled softly. Bond thanked the Superintendent and was wished good fortune in his honourable endeavours. Tiger looked serious. He took Bond's hand in both of his, an unusual gesture for a Japanese. He said, 'Bondo-san, I am certain you will succeed, so I will not wish you luck. Nor will I say "*sayōnara*", farewell. I will simply say a quiet "*banzai!*" to you and give you this little *presento* in case the gods frown upon your venture and, through no fault of yours, things go wrong, very wrong.' He took out a little box and gave it to Bond.

The box rattled. Bond opened it. Inside was one long brownish pill. Bond laughed. He gave it back to Tiger and said, 'No thanks, Tiger. As Bashō said, or almost said, "You only live twice." If my second life comes up, I would rather look it in the face and not turn my back on it. But thanks, and thanks for everything. Those live lobsters were really delicious. I shall now look forward to eating plenty of seaweed while I'm here. So long! See you in about a week.'

Tiger got down into the boat and the engine revved up. As the boat took the swell at the entrance to the harbour, Tiger raised a hand and brought it swiftly down with a chopping motion and then the boat was round the sea wall and out of sight.

Bond turned away. The priest had gone. Kissy Suzuki said impatiently, 'Come along, Todoroki-san. The *kannushi-san* says I am to treat you as a comrade, as an equal. But give me one of those two little bags to carry. For the sake of the villagers who will be watching inquisitively, we will wear the Oriental face in public.'

And the tall man with the dark face, cropped hair and slanting eyebrows, the tall girl, and the old woman walked off along the shore with their angular Japanese shadows preceding them across the smooth black boulders.

14

ONE GOLDEN DAY

DAWN WAS A beautiful haze of gold and blue. Bond went outside and ate his bean curd and rice and drank his tea sitting on the spotless doorstep of the little cut-stone and timbered house, while indoors the family chattered like happy sparrows as the women went about their housework.

Bond had been allotted the room of honour, the small sitting-room with its *tatami* mats, scraps of furniture, house shrine and a cricket in a small cage 'to keep you company', as Kissy had explained. Here his *futon* had been spread on the ground and he had for the first time and with fair success tried sleeping with his head on the traditional wooden pillow. The evening before, the father, an emaciated greybeard with knotted joints and bright, squirrel eyes, had laughed with and at him as Kissy translated Bond's account of some of his adventures with Tiger, and there was from the first a complete absence of tension or self-consciousness. The priest had said that Bond should be treated as a member of the family and, although his appearance and some of his manners were strange, Kissy had apparently announced her qualified approval of him and the parents followed her lead. At nine o'clock, under the three-quarter moon, the father had beckoned to Bond and had hobbled out with him to the back of the house. He showed him the little shack with the hole in the ground and the neatly quartered pages of the *Asahi Shimbun* on a nail, and the last of Bond's private fears about life on the island was removed. His flickering candle showed the place to be as spotless as the house, and at least adequately salubrious. After the soft movements in the other two rooms had ceased, Bond had slept happily and like the dead.

Kissy came out of the house. She was wearing a kind of white cotton nightdress and a white cotton kerchief bound up the thick black waves of her hair. She wore her equipment, the weights and the heavy flat angular pick, over the white dress and only her arms and feet were bare. Bond may have shown his disappointment. She laughed, teasing him. 'This is ceremonial dress for diving in the presence of important strangers. The *kannushi-san* instructed me to wear it in your company. As a mark of respect, of course.'

'Kissy, I believe that is a fib. The truth of the matter is that you consider that your nakedness might arouse dishonourable thoughts in my impious Western mind. That is a most unworthy suspicion. However, I accept the delicacy of your respect for my susceptibilities. And now let's cut the cackle and get going. We'll beat the *awabi* record today. What should we aim at?'

'Fifty would be good. A hundred would be wonderful. But above all, you must row well and not let me drown. And you must be kind to David.'

'Who's David?' asked Bond, suddenly jealous at the thought that he would not be having this girl to himself.

'Wait and see.' She went back indoors and brought out the balsa-wood tub and a great coil of fine quarter-inch rope. She handed the rope to Bond and hoisted the tub on her hip, leading the way along a small path away from the village. The path descended slowly to a small cove in which one rowing boat, covered with dried reeds to protect it from the sun, was drawn high up on the flat black pebbles. Bond stripped off the reeds and laid them aside and hauled the simple, locally made craft down to the sea. It was constructed of some heavy wood and lay low but stable in the deeply shelving, totally transparent water. He loaded in the rope and the wooden tub. Kissy had gone to the other side of the little bay and had undone a string from one of the rocks. She began winding it in slowly and at the same time uttering a low, cooing whistle. To Bond's astonishment, there was a flurry in the water of the bay and a big black cormorant shot like a bullet through the shallows and waddled up the beach to Kissy's feet, craning its neck up and down and hissing, apparently in anger. But Kissy bent down and stroked the creature on its plumed head and down the outstretched neck, at the same time talking to it gaily. She came towards the boat, winding up the long line, and the cormorant followed clumsily. It paid no attention to Bond, but jumped untidily over the side of the boat and scrambled on to the small thwart in the bows where it squatted majestically and proceeded to preen itself, running its long bill down and through its breast feathers and occasionally opening its wings to the full extent of their five-foot span and flapping them with gentle grace. Then, with a final shimmy through all its length, it settled down and gazed out to sea with its neck coiled backwards as if to strike and its turquoise eyes questing the horizon imperiously.

Kissy climbed into the boat and settled herself with her knees hunched decorously between Bond's outstretched legs, and Bond slid the heavy, narrow-bladed oars into their wooden rowlocks and began rowing at a powerful, even pace, more or less, under Kissy's direction, due north.

He had noticed that Kissy's line to the cormorant ended with a thin brass ring, perhaps two inches in diameter, round the base of the bird's neck. This would be one of the famous fishing cormorants of Japan. Bond asked her about it.

Kissy said, 'I found him as a baby three years ago. He had oil on his wings and I cleaned him and cared for him and had him ringed. The ring has had to be made larger as he grew up. Now, you see, he can swallow small fish, but the big ones he brings to the surface in his beak. He hands them over quite willingly and occasionally he gets a piece of a big one as a reward. He swims a lot by my side and keeps me company. It can be very lonely down there, particularly when the sea is dark. You will have to hold the end of the line and look after him when he comes to the surface. Today he will be hungry. He has not been out for three days because my father could not row the boat. I have been going out with friends. So it is lucky for him that you came to the island.'

'So this is David?'

'Yes. I named him after the only man I liked in Hollywood, an Englishman as it happens. He was called David Niven. He is a famous actor and producer. You have heard of him?'

'Of course. I shall enjoy tossing him a scrap or two of fish in exchange for the pleasure he has given me in his other incarnation.'

The sweat began to pour down Bond's face and chest into his bathing pants. Kissy undid the kerchief round her hair and leant forward and mopped at him gently. Bond smiled into her almond eyes and had his first close-up of her snub nose and petalled mouth. She wore no make-up and did not need to, for she had that rosy-tinted skin on a golden background — the colours of a golden peach — that is quite common in Japan. Her hair, released from the kerchief, was black with dark brown high-lights. It was heavily waved, but with a soft fringe that ended an inch or so above the straight, fine eyebrows that showed no signs of having been plucked. Her teeth were even and showed no more prominently between the lips than with a European girl, so that she avoided the toothiness that is a weak point in the Japanese face. Her arms and legs were longer and less masculine than is usual with Japanese girls and, the day before, Bond had seen that her breasts and buttocks were firm and proud and that her stomach was almost flat — a beautiful figure, equal to that of any of the star chorus girls he had seen in the cabarets of Tokyo. But her hands and feet were rough and scarred with work, and her finger-nails and toe-nails, although they were cut very short, were broken. Bond found this rather endearing. Ama means 'sea-girl' or 'sea-man', and Kissy wore the marks of competing with the creatures of the ocean with obvious indifference, and her skin, which might have suffered from constant contact with salt water, in fact glowed with a golden sheen of health and vitality. But it was the charm and directness of her eyes and smile as well as her complete naturalness — for instance, when she mopped at Bond's face and chest — that endeared her so utterly to Bond. At that moment, he thought there would be nothing more wonderful than to spend the rest of his life rowing her out towards the horizon during the day and coming back with her to the small, clean house in the dusk.

He shrugged the whimsy aside. Only another two days to the full moon and he would have to get back to reality, to the dark, dirty life he had chosen for himself. He put the prospect out of his mind. Today and the next day would be stolen days, days with only Kissy and the boat and the bird and the sea. He must just see to it that they were happy days and lucky ones for her and her harvest of sea-shells.

Kissy said, 'Not much longer. And you have rowed well.' She gestured to the right, to where the rest of the Ama fleet was spread out over the ocean. 'With us, it is first come first served with the sites we choose. Today we can get out as far as a shoal most of us know of, and we shall have it to ourselves. There the seaweed is thick on the rocks and that is what the *awabi* feed on. It is deep, about forty feet, but I can stay down for almost a minute, long enough to pick up two, three *awabi* if I can find them. That is just a matter of luck in feeling about with the hands among the seaweed, for you rarely see the shells. You only feel them and dislodge them with this.' She tapped her angular pick. 'After a while I shall have to rest. Then perhaps you would like to go down. Yes? They tell me you are a good swimmer and I have brought a pair of my father's goggles. These bulbs at the sides,' she showed him, 'have to be squeezed to equalize the pressure between the glasses and the eyes. You will perhaps not be able to stay down long to begin with. But you will learn quickly. How long will you be staying on Kuro?'

'Only two or three days, I'm afraid.'

'Oh, but that is sad. What will David and I do for a boatman then?'

'Perhaps your father will get better.'

'That is so. I must take him to a cure place at one of the volcanoes on the mainland. Otherwise it will mean marrying one of the men on Kuro. That is not easy. The choice is not wide and, because I have a little money from my film work, and a little is a lot on Kuro, the man might want to marry me for the wrong reasons. That would be sad, and how is one to know?'

'Perhaps you will go back into films?'

Her expression became fierce. 'Never. I hated it. They were all disgusting to me in Hollywood. They thought that because I am a Japanese I am some sort of an animal and that my body is for everyone. Nobody treated me honourably except this Niven.' She shook her head to get rid of the memories. 'No. I will stay on Kuro for ever. The gods will solve my problems,' she smiled, 'like they have today.' She scanned the sea ahead. 'Another hundred yards.' She got up and, balancing perfectly despite the swell, tied the end of the long rope round her waist and adjusted the goggles above her forehead. 'Now remember, keep the rope taut and when you feel one tug, pull me up quickly. It will be hard work for you, but I will massage your back when we get home this evening. I am very good at it. I have had enough practice with my father. Now!'

Bond shipped the oars gratefully. Behind him, David began shifting on his feet, craning his long neck and hissing impatiently. Kissy tied a short line to the wooden tub and put it over the side. She followed, slipping decorously into the water and clasping her white dress between her knees so that it did not flower out around her. At once David dived and disappeared without a ripple. The line, tied to Bond's thwart, began paying out fast. He picked up the coil of Kissy's rope and stood up, his joints cracking. Kissy pulled down her goggles and put her head under water. In a moment she came up. She smiled. 'Yes, it looks fine down there.' She rested in the water and began making a soft cooing whistle through pursed lips — to fill her lungs to the uttermost, Bond assumed. Then, with a brief wave of the hand, she put down her head and arched her hips so that Bond had a brief sight of the black string cleaving her behind under the thin material. Suddenly, like a fleeting white wraith, she was gone, straight down, her feet twinkling behind her in a fast crawl to help the pull of the weights.

Bond paid out fast, keeping an anxious eye on his watch. David appeared below him, bearing a half-pound silvery fish cross-wise in his beak. Damn the bird! This was no time to get mixed up with retrieving fish from the extremely sharp-looking beak. But, with a contemptuous glance, the cormorant tossed the fish into the floating tub and disappeared like a black bullet.

Fifty seconds! Bond started nervously when the tug came. He pulled in fast. The white wraith appeared far below in the crystal water and, as she came up, Bond saw that her hands were tight against her sides to streamline her body. She broke surface beside the boat and held out two fat *awabi* to show him and then dropped them into the tub. She held on to the side of the boat to regain her breath and Bond gazed down at the wonderful breasts, taut beneath their thin covering. She smiled briefly up at him, began her cooing whistle, and then came the exciting arch of the back and she was gone again.

An hour went by. Bond got used to the routine and had time to watch the nearest of the fleet of other boats. They covered perhaps a mile of sea, and, from across the silent water, there came the recurrent eerie whistle — a soft, seabird sound — of the diving girls. The nearest boat rocked in the slow swell perhaps a hundred yards away, and Bond watched the young man at the rope and caught an occasional glimpse of a beautiful golden body, shiny as a seal, and heard the excited chattering of their voices. He hoped he would not disgrace himself when it came to his turn to dive. *Saké* and cigarettes! Not a good mixture to train on!

The pile of *awabi* was slowly growing in the tub and, amongst them, perhaps a dozen leaping fish. Occasionally Bond bent down and retrieved one from David. Once he dropped a slippery fish and the bird had to dive for it again. This time he received an even haughtier look of scorn from the turquoise eyes.

Then Kissy came up, her stint done, and climbed, not so decorously this time, into the boat, and tore off her kerchief and goggles and sat panting quietly in the stern. Finally she looked up and laughed happily. 'That is twenty-one. Very good. Now take my weights and pick and see for yourself what it is like down there. But I will pull you up anyway in thirty seconds. Give me your watch. And please do not lose my *tegane*, my pick, or our day's fishing will be over.'

Bond's first dive was a clumsy affair. He went down too slowly and barely had time to survey the grassy plain, scattered with black rocks and clumps of *Posidonia*, the common seaweed of all the oceans, when he felt himself being hauled up. He had to admit to himself that his lungs were in terrible shape, but he had spied one promising rock thick with weed and on his next dive he got straight to it and clung, searching among the roots with his right hand. He felt the smooth oval of a shell, but before he could get the pick to it he was being pulled up again. But he got the shell on his third try, and Kissy laughed with pleasure as he dropped it into the tub. He managed to keep the diving up for about half an hour, but then his lungs began to ache and his body to feel the cold of the October sea and he came up for the last time simultaneously with David, who shot past him like a beautiful gleaming black fish with green highlights and, as a mark of approval, pecked gently at his hair as Bond deposited his fifth shell in the tub.

Kissy was pleased with him. She had a rough brown kimono in the boat and she rubbed him down with it as he sat with bowed head and heaving chest. Then, while he rested, she hauled the wooden tub inboard and emptied its contents into the bottom of the boat. She produced a knife and cut one of the fish down the middle and fed the two halves to David who was riding expectantly beside the boat. He swallowed the pieces in two great gulps and set to preening his feathers contentedly.

Later they stopped for a lunch of rice with a few small bits of fish in it and dried seaweed which tasted of salty spinach. And then, after a short rest in the bottom of the boat, the work went on until four o'clock, when a small chill breeze came from nowhere and got between them and the warmth of the sun and it was time to make the long row home. Kissy climbed for the last time into the boat and gave several soft tugs at David's line. He surfaced some distance from the boat and, as if this was a well-worn routine, rose into the air and circled round them again and again before making a low dive and skiing in to the side of the boat on his webbed feet. He flapped his way over the side and went to his perch, where he stood with wings magnificently outstretched to dry and waited in this lordly stance for his boatman to take him back home to his cove.

Kissy changed with extreme propriety into her brown kimono and dried herself inside it. She announced that their haul was sixty-five *awabi*, which was quite wonderful. Of these Bond was responsible for ten, which was a very honourable first catch. Ridiculously pleased with himself, Bond took a vague bearing on the island which, because of the drifting of the boat, was now only a speck on the horizon, and gradually worked himself into the slow, unlaboured sweep of a Scottish gillie.

His hands were sore, his back ached as if he had been thrashed with a wooden truncheon, and his shoulders were beginning to sting with sunburn, but he comforted himself with the reflection that he was only doing what he would have had to do anyway — get into training for the swim and the climb and what would come afterwards, and he rewarded himself from time to time with a smile into Kissy's eyes. They never left him and the low sun shone into them and turned the soft brown to gold. And the speck became a lump, and the lump an island and at last they were home.

15

THE SIX GUARDIANS

THE NEXT DAY was as golden as the first and the haul of *awabi* went up to sixty-eight, largely thanks to Bond's improved diving.

The evening before, Kissy had come back from selling her shells at the market and had found Bond writhing on the floor of his room with cramps in his stomach muscles and her mother clucking helplessly over him. She had shooed her mother away, spread the soft *futon* on the floor beside him and had pulled off his bathing pants and rolled him on to the *futon* face downwards. Then she had stood upright on his back and had walked softly up and down his spine from his buttocks to his neck, and the ache had slowly gone. She told him to lie still and brought him warm milk. Then she led him into the tiny bathhouse and poured hot and then tepid water over him from an *awabi* tub until all the salt was out of his skin and hair. She dried him softly, rubbed warm milk into his sunburn and his chafed hands, and led him back to his room, telling him with gentle sternness to go to sleep and to call her if he awoke in the night and needed anything. She blew out his candle and left him, and he went out, to the night-song of the cricket in its cage, like a light.

In the morning, nothing remained of his aches except the soreness of the hands, and Kissy gave him the rare treat of an egg beaten up in his rice and bean curd and he apologized for his bad manners of the night before. She said, 'Todoroki-san, you have the spirit of ten *samurai*, but you have the body of only one. I should have known that I had asked too much of that single body. It was the pleasure of the day. It made me forget everything else. So it is I who apologize, and today we will not go so far. Instead, we will keep close to the cliffs of the island and see what we can find. I will do the rowing, for it is a small distance, but you will be able to do more diving because the place that I know of, which I haven't visited for many weeks, is inshore and the water is, at the most, twenty feet deep.'

And so it had been, and Bond had worn a shirt to protect him from the sun and his tally of shells had gone up to twenty-one, and the solitary shadow on the day had been the clear view he had had of the black fortress across the straits and the chunky yellow-and-black warning balloon that flew the column of black ideograms above it.

During one of their rests, Bond casually asked Kissy what she knew of the castle, and he was surprised by the way her face darkened. 'Todoroki-san, we do not usually talk about that place. It is almost a forbidden subject on Kuro. It is as if hell had suddenly opened its mouth half a mile away across the sea from our home. And my people, the Ama, are like what I have read about your gypsies. We are very superstitious. And we believe the devil himself has come to live over there.' She didn't look at the fortress, but gestured with her head. 'Even the *kannushi-san* does not deny our fears, and our elders say that the *gaijins* have always been bad for Japan and that this one is the incarnation of all the evil in the West. And there is already a legend that has grown up on the island. It is that our six *Jizo* Guardians will send a man from across the sea to slay this "King of Death", as we call him.'

'Who are these Guardians?'

'*Jizo* is the god who protects children. He is, I think, a Buddhist god. On the other side of the island, on the foreshore, there are five statues. The sixth has been mostly washed away. They are rather frightening to see. They squat there in a line. They have rough bodies of stone and round stones for heads and they wear white shirts that are changed by the people every month. They were put there centuries ago by our ancestors. They sit on the line of low tide, and as the tide comes up it covers them completely and they keep watch under the surface of the sea and protect us, the Ama, because we are known as "The Children of the Sea". At the beginning of every June, when the sea is warm after the winter and the diving begins, every person on the island forms into a procession and we go to the Six Guardians and sing to them to make them happy and favourable towards us.'

'And this story of the man from Kuro. Where did it come from?'

'Who knows? It could have come from the sea or the air and thus into the minds of the people. Where do stories like that come from? It is widely believed.'

'*Ah, so desu ka!*' said Bond, and they both laughed and got on with the work.

On the third day, when Bond was as usual eating his breakfast on the doorstep, Kissy came to the doorway and said softly, 'Come inside, Todoroki-san.' Mystified, he went in and she shut the door behind him.

She said in a low voice, 'I have just heard from a messenger from the *kannushi-san* that there were people here yesterday in a boat from the mainland. They brought *presentos* — cigarettes and sweets. They were asking about the visit of the police boat. They said it came with three visitors and left with only two. They wanted to know what had happened to the third visitor. They said they were guards from the castle and it was their duty to prevent trespassers. The elders accepted the *presentos*, but they showed *shiran-kao*, which is "the face of him who knows nothing", and referred the man to the *kannushi-san* who said that the third visitor was in charge of fishing licences. He had felt sick on the way to the island and had perhaps lain down in the boat on the way back. Then he dismissed the men and sent a boy to the top of the High Place to see where the boat went, and the boy reported that it went to the bay beside the castle and was put back into the boat-house that is there. The *kannushi-san* thought that you should know these things.' She looked at him piteously. 'Todoroki-san, I have a feeling of much friendship for you. I feel that there are secret things between you and the *kannushi-san*, and that they concern the castle. I think you should tell me enough to put me out of my unhappiness.'

Bond smiled. He went up to her and took her face in both his hands and kissed her on the lips. He said, 'You are very beautiful and kind, Kissy. Today we will not take the boat out because I must have some rest. Lead me up to the High Place from which I can take a good look at this castle and I will tell you what I can. I was going to anyway, for I shall need your help. Afterwards, I would like to visit the Six Guardians. They interest me — as an anthropologist.'

Kissy collected their usual lunch in a small basket, put on her brown kimono and rope-soled shoes and they set off along a small footpath that zigzagged up the peak behind the crouching grey cluster of the village. The time of the camellia was almost past, but here there were occasional bushes of wild camellias in red and white, and there was a profusion of these round a small grove of dwarf maples, some of which already wore their flaming autumn colours. The grove was directly above Kissy's house. She led him in and showed him the little Shinto shrine behind a rough stone *torii*. She said, 'Behind the shrine there is a fine cave, but the people of Kuro are afraid of it as it is full of ghosts. But I explored it once and if there are ghosts there they are friendly ones.' She clapped her hands before the shrine, bent her head for a moment, and clapped them again. Then they went on up the path to the top of the thousand-foot peak. A brace of gorgeous copper pheasants with golden tails fled squawking over the brow and down to a patch of bushes on the southern cliff as they approached. Bond told Kissy to stay out of sight while he went and stood behind the tall cairn of stones on the summit and gazed circumspectly round it and across the straits.

He could see over the high fortress wall and across the park to the towering black-and-gold donjon of the castle. It was ten o'clock. There were figures in blue peasant dress with high boots and long staves moving busily about the grounds. They occasionally seemed to prod into the bushes with their staves. They wore black *maskos* over their mouths. It crossed Bond's mind that they might be doing the morning rounds looking for overnight prey. What did they do when they found some half-blinded creature, or a pile of clothes beside one of the fumaroles whose little clouds of steam rose here and there in the park? Take them to the Doctor? And, in the case of the living, what happened then? And when he, Bond, got up that wall tonight, where was he going to hide from the guards? Well, sufficient unto the day! At least the straits were calm and it was cloudless weather. It looked as if he would get there all right. Bond turned away and went back to Kissy and sat with her on the sparse turf. He gazed across the harbour to where the Ama fleet lay sprawled across the middle distance.

He said, 'Kissy, tonight I have to swim to the castle and climb the wall and get inside.'

She nodded. 'I know this. And then you are going to kill this man and perhaps his wife. You are the man who we believe was to come to Kuro from across the sea and do these things.' She continued to gaze out to sea. She said dully, 'But why have you been chosen? Why should it not be another, a Japanese?'

'These people are *gaijins*. I am a *gaijin*. It will cause less trouble for the State if the whole matter is presented as being trouble between foreigners.'

'Yes, I see. And has the *kannushi-san* given his approval?'

'Yes.'

'And if . . . And after. Will you come back and be my boatman again?'

'For a time. But then I must go back to England.'

'No. I believe that you will stay for a long time on Kuro.'

'Why do you believe that?'

'Because I prayed for it at the shrine. And I have never asked for such a big thing before. I am sure it will be granted.' She paused. 'And I shall be swimming with you tonight.' She held up a hand. 'You will need company in the dark and I know the currents. You would not get there without me.'

Bond took the small dry paw in his. He looked at the childish, broken nails. His voice was harsh. He said, 'No. This is man's work.'

She looked at him. The brown eyes were calm and serious. She said, and she used his first name, 'Taro-san, your other name may mean thunder, but I am not frightened of thunder. I have made up my mind. And I shall come back every night, at midnight exactly, and wait among the rocks at the bottom of the wall. I shall wait for one hour in case you need my help in coming home. These people may harm you. Women are much stronger in the water than men. That is why it is the Ama girls who dive and not the Ama men. I know the waters round Kuro as a peasant knows the fields round his farm, and I have as little fear of them. Do not be stiff-necked in this matter. In any case, I shall hardly sleep until you come back. To feel that I am close to you for a time and that you may need me will give me some peace. Say yes, Taro-san.'

'Oh, all right, Kissy,' said Bond gruffly. 'I was only going to ask you to row me to a starting point down there somewhere.'

He gestured to the left across the straits. 'But if you insist on being an extra target for the sharks . . .'

'The sharks never trouble us. The Six Guardians look after that. We never come to any harm. Years ago, one of the Amas caught her rope in a rock under water, and the people have talked of the accident ever since. The sharks just think we are big fish like themselves.' She laughed happily. 'Now it is all settled and we can have something to eat and then I will take you down to see the Guardians. The tide will be low by then and they will want to inspect you.'

They followed another little path from the summit. It went over the shoulder of the peak and down to a small protected bay to the east of the village. The tide was far out and they could wade over the flat black pebbles and rocks and round the corner of the promontory. Here, on a stretch of flat stony beach, five people squatted on a square foundation of large rocks and gazed out towards the horizon. Except that they weren't people. They were, as Kissy had described, stone pedestal bodies with large round boulders cemented to their tops. But rough white shirts were roped round them, and they looked terrifyingly human as they sat in immobile judgment and guardianship over the waters and what went on beneath them. Of the sixth, only the body remained. His head must have been destroyed by a storm.

They walked round in front of the five and looked up at the smooth blank faces and Bond, for the first time in his life, had a sensation of deep awe. So much belief, so much authority seemed to have been invested by the builders in these primitive, faceless idols, guardians of the blithe, naked Ama girls, that Bond had a ridiculous urge to kneel and ask for their blessing as the Crusaders had once done before their God. He brushed the impulse aside, but he did bow his head and briefly ask for good fortune to accompany his enterprise. And then he stood back and watched with a pull at his heartstrings while Kissy, her beautiful face strained and pleading, clapped to attract their attention and then made a long and impassioned speech in which his name recurred. At the end, when she again clapped her hands, did the round boulderheads briefly nod? Of course not! But, when Bond took Kissy's hand and they walked away, she said happily, 'It is all right, Todoroki-san. You saw them nod their heads?'

'No,' said Bond firmly, 'I did not.'

They crept round the eastern shore of Kuro and pulled the boat up into a deep cleft in the black rocks. It was just after eleven o'clock and the giant moon rode high and fast through wisps of mackerel cloud. They talked softly, although they were out of sight of the fortress and half a mile away from it. Kissy took off her brown kimono and folded it neatly and put it in the boat. Her body glowed in the moonlight. The black triangle between her legs beckoned, and the black string round her waist that held the piece of material was an invitation to untie it. She giggled provocatively. 'Stop looking at my Black Cat!'

'Why is it called that?'

'Guess!'

Bond carefully pulled on his *ninja* suit of black cotton. It was comfortable enough and would give warmth in the water. He left the head-shroud hanging down his back and pushed the goggles that belonged to Kissy's father up his forehead. The small floating pack he was to tow behind him rode jauntily in the waters of the creek, and he tied its string firmly to his right wrist so that he would always know it was there.

He smiled at Kissy and nodded.

She came up to him and threw her arms round his neck and kissed him full on the lips.

Before he could respond, she had pulled down her goggles and had dived into the quiet, mercury sea.

16

THE LOVESOME SPOT

KISSY'S CRAWL WAS steady and relaxed and Bond had no difficulty in following the twinkling feet and the twin white mounds of her behind, divided excitingly by the black cord. But he was glad he had donned flippers because the tug of his floating container against the wrist was an irritating brake and, for the first half of the swim, they were heading diagonally against the easterly current through the straits. But then Kissy slightly changed her direction and now they could paddle lazily in towards the soaring wall that soon became their whole horizon.

There were a few tumbled rocks at its base, but Kissy stayed in the water, clinging to a clump of seaweed, in case the moon might betray her gleaming body to a sentry or a chance patrol, though Bond guessed that the guards kept clear of the grounds during the night so that the suicides would have free entry. Bond pulled himself up on the rocks and unzipped the container and extracted the packet of iron pitons. Then he climbed up a few feet so that he could stow his flippers away in a crack between the granite blocks above high water mark, and he was ready to go. He blew a kiss to the girl. She replied with the sideways wave of the hand that is the Japanese sign of farewell and then was off across the sea again, a luminous white torpedo that merged quickly into the path of the moon.

Bond put her out of his thoughts. He was getting chilled in his soaking black camouflage and it was time to get moving. He examined the fitting of the giant stone blocks and found that the cracks between them were spacious, as in the case of Tiger's training castle, and would probably provide adequate toeholds. Then he pulled down his black cowl and, towing the black container behind him, began his climb.

It took him twenty minutes to cover the two hundred feet of the slightly inclined wall, but he only had to use his pitons twice when he came to cracks that were too narrow to give a hold to his aching toes. And then he was at one of the gun-ports, and he slithered quietly across its six feet of flat masonry and cautiously looked over the edge into the park. As he had expected, there were stone steps down from the gun-port, and he crept down these into the dark shadows at its base and stood up against the inside of the wall panting quietly. He waited for his breath to calm down and then slipped back his cowl and listened. Not a wisp of wind stirred in the trees, but from somewhere came the sound of softly running water and, in the background, a regular, glutinous burping and bubbling. The fumaroles! Bond, a black shadow among the rest, edged along the wall to his right. His first task was to find a hideout, a base camp where he could bivouac in emergency and where he could leave his container. He reconnoitred various groves and clumps of bushes, but they were all damnably well-kept and the undergrowth had been meticulously cleared from their roots. And many of them exuded a sickly-sweet, poisonous night-smell. Then, up against the wall, he came upon a lean-to shed, its rickety door ajar. He listened and then inched the door open. As he had expected, there was a shadowy jumble of gardeners' tools, wheelbarrows and the like, and the musty smell of such places. Moving carefully, and helped by shafts of moonlight through the wide cracks in the planked walls, he got to the back of the hut where there was an untidy mound of used sacking. He reflected for a moment, and decided that though this place would be often visited, it had great promise. He untied the cord of the container from his wrist and proceeded methodically to move some of the sacks forward so as to provide a nest for himself behind them. When it was finished, and final touches of artistic disarray added, he parked his container behind the barrier and crept out again into the park to continue what he planned should be a first quick survey of the whole property.

Bond kept close to the boundary wall, flitting like a bat across the open spaces between clumps of bushes and trees. Although his hands were covered with the black material of the *ninja* suit, he avoided contact with the vegetation, which emitted a continually changing variety of strong odours and scents amongst which he recognized, as a result of ancient adventures in the Caribbean, only the sugary perfume of dogwood. He came to the lake, a wide silent shimmer of silver from which rose the thin cloud of steam he remembered from the aerial photograph. As he stood and watched it, a large leaf from one of the surrounding trees came wafting down and settled on the surface near him. At once a quick, purposeful ripple swept down on the leaf from the surrounding water and immediately subsided. There were some kind of fish in the lake and they would be carnivores. Only carnivores would be excited like that at the hint of a prey. Beyond the lake, Bond came on the first of the fumaroles, a sulphurous, bubbling pool of mud that constantly shuddered and spouted up little fountains. From yards away, Bond could feel its heat. Jets of stinking steam puffed out and disappeared, wraithlike, towards the sky. And now the jagged silhouette of the castle, with its winged turrets, showed above the tree-line, and Bond crept forward with added caution, alert for the moment when he would come upon the treacherous gravel that surrounded it. Suddenly, through a belt of trees, he was facing it. He stopped in the shelter of the trees, his heart hammering under his rib-cage.

Close to, the soaring black-and-gold pile reared monstrously over him, and the diminishing curved roofs of the storeys were like vast bat-wings against the stars. It was even bigger than Bond had imagined, and the supporting wall of black granite blocks more formidable. He reflected on the seemingly impossible problem of entry. Behind would be the main entrance, the lowish wall and the open countryside. But didn't castles always have an alternative entrance low down for a rearward escape? Bond stole cautiously forward, laying his feet flat down so that the gravel barely stirred. The many eyes of the castle, glittering white in the moonlight, watched his approach with the indifference of total power. At any moment, he expected the white shaft of a searchlight or the yellow-and-blue flutter of gunfire. But he reached the base of the wall without incident and followed it along to the left, remembering from ancient schooling that most castles had an exit at moat level beneath the drawbridge.

And so it was with the castle of Doctor Shatterhand — a small nail-studded door, arched and weather-beaten. Its hinges and lock were cracked and rusty, but a new padlock and chain had been stapled into the woodwork and the stone frame. No moonlight filtered down to this corner of what must once have been a moat, but was now grassed over. Bond felt carefully with his fingers. Yes! The chain and lock would yield to the file and jemmy in his conjurer's pockets. Would there be bolts on the inner side? Probably not, or the padlock would not have been thought necessary. Bond softly retraced his steps across the gravel, stepping meticulously in his previous footmarks. That door would be his target for tomorrow!

Now, keeping right-handed, but still following the boundary wall, he crept off again on his survey. Once, something slithered away from his approaching feet and disappeared with a heavy rustle into the fallen leaves under a tree. What snakes were there that really went for a man? The king-cobra, black mamba, the saw-scaled viper, the rattlesnake and the fer de lance. What others? The remainder were inclined to make off if disturbed. Were snakes day or night hunters? Bond didn't know. Among so many hazards, there weren't even the odds of Russian Roulette. When all the chambers of the pistol were loaded, there was not even a one in six chance to bank on.

Bond was now on the castle side of the lake. He heard a noise and edged behind a tree. The distant crashing in the shrubbery sounded like a wounded animal, but then, down the path, came staggering a man, or what had once been a man. The brilliant moonlight showed a head swollen to the size of a football, and only small slits remained where the eyes and mouth had been. The man moaned softly as he zigzagged along, and Bond could see that his hands were up to his puffed face and that he was trying to prise apart the swollen skin round his eyes so that he could see out. Every now and then he stopped and let out one word in an agonizing howl to the moon. It was not a howl of fear or of pain, but of dreadful supplication. Suddenly he stopped. He seemed to see the lake for the first time. With a terrible cry, and holding out his arms as if to meet a loved one, he made a quick run to the edge and threw himself in. At once there came the swirl of movement Bond had noticed before, but this time it involved a great area of water and there was a wild boiling of the surface round the vaguely threshing body. A mass of small fish were struggling to get at the man, particularly at the naked hands and face, and their six-inch bodies glittered and flashed in the moonlight. Once the man raised his head and let out a single, terrible scream and Bond saw that his face was encrusted with pendent fish as if with silvery locks of hair. Then his head fell back into the lake and he rolled over and over as if trying to rid himself of his attackers. But slowly the black stain spread and spread around him and finally, perhaps because his jugular had been pierced, he lay still, face downwards in the water, and his head jigged slightly with the ceaseless momentum of the attack.

James Bond wiped the cold sweat off his face. Piranha! The South American fresh-water killer whose massive jaws and flat, razor-sharp teeth can strip a horse down to the bones in under an hour! And this man had been one of the suicides who had heard of this terrible death! He had come searching for the lake and had got his face poisoned by some pretty shrub. The Herr Doktor had certainly provided a feast for his victims. Unending dishes for their delectation! A true banquet of death!

James Bond shuddered and went on his way. All right, Blofeld, he thought, that's one more notch on the sword that is already on its way down to your neck. Brave words! Bond hugged the wall and kept going. Gunmetal was showing in the east.

But the Garden of Death hadn't quite finished the display of its wares.

All over the park, a slight smell of sulphur hung in the air, and many times Bond had had to detour round steaming cracks in the ground and the quaking mud of fumaroles, identified by a warning circle of white-painted stones. The Doctor was most careful lest anyone should fall into one of these liquid furnaces by mistake! But now Bond came to one the size of a circular tennis court, and here there was a rough shrine in the grotto at the back of it and, dainty touch, a vase with flowers in it — chrysanthemums, because it was now officially winter and therefore the chrysanthemum season. They were arranged with some sprigs of dwarf maple, in a pattern which no doubt spelled out some fragrant message to the initiates of Japanese flower arrangement. And opposite the grotto, behind which Bond in his ghostly black uniform crouched in concealment, a Japanese gentleman stood in rapt contemplation of the bursting mudboils that were erupting genteelly in the simmering soup of the pool. James Bond thought 'gentleman' because the man was dressed in the top hat, frock coat, striped trousers, stiff collar and spats of a high government official — or of the father of the bride. And the gentleman held a carefully rolled umbrella between his clasped hands, and his head was bowed over its crook as if in penance. He was speaking, in a soft compulsive babble, like someone in a highly ritualistic church, but he made no gestures and just stood, humbly, quietly, either confessing or asking one of the gods for something.

Bond stood against a tree, black in the blackness. He felt he should intervene in what he knew to be the man's purpose. But how to do so knowing no Japanese, having nothing but his 'deaf and dumb' card to show? And it was vital that he should remain a 'ghost' in the garden, not get involved in some daft argument with a man he didn't know, about some ancient sin he could never understand. So Bond stood, while the trees threw long black arms across the scene, and waited, with a cold, closed, stone face, for death to walk on stage.

The man stopped talking. He raised his head and gazed up at the moon. He politely lifted his shining top hat. Then he replaced it, tucked his umbrella under one arm and sharply clapped his hands. Then walking, as if to a business appointment, calmly, purposefully, he took the few steps to the edge of the bubbling fumarole, stepped carefully over the warning stones and went on walking. He sank slowly in the glutinous grey slime and not a sound escaped his lips until, as the tremendous heat reached his groin, he uttered one rasping 'Arghh!', and the gold in his teeth showed as his head arched back in the rictus of death. Then he was gone and only the top hat remained, tossing on a small fountain of mud that spat intermittently into the air. Then the hat slowly crumpled with the heat and disappeared, and a great belch was uttered from the belly of the fumarole and a horrible stench of cooking meat overcame the pervading stink of sulphur and reached Bond's nostrils.

Bond controlled his rising gorge. Honourable salary-man had gone to honourable ancestors — his unknown sin expiated as his calcined bones sank slowly down into the stomach of the world. And one more statistic would be run up on Blofeld's abacus of death. Why didn't the Japanese air-force come and bomb this place to eternity, set the castle and the poison garden ablaze with napalm? How could this man continue to have protection from a bunch of botanists and scientists? And now here was he, Bond, alone in this hell to try and do the job with almost no weapon but his bare hands. It was hopeless! He was scarcely being given a chance in a million. Tiger and his Prime Minister were certainly exacting their pound of flesh in exchange for their precious MAGIC 44 — one hundred and eighty-two pounds of it to be exact!

Cursing his fate, cursing Tiger, cursing the whole of Japan, Bond went on his way, while a small voice whispered in his ear, 'But don't you want to kill Blofeld? Don't you want to avenge Tracy? Isn't this a God-given chance? You have done well tonight. You have penetrated his defences and spied out the land. You have even found a way into his castle and probably up to his bedroom. Kill him in his sleep tomorrow! And kill her too, while you're about it! And then back into Kissy's arms and, in a week or two, back over the Pole to London and to the applause of your Chief. Come on! Somewhere in Japan, a Japanese is committing suicide every thirty minutes all through the year. Don't be squeamish because you've just seen a couple of numbers ticked off on a sheet in the Ministry of Health, a couple of points added to a graph. Snap out of it! Get on with the job!'

And Bond listened to the whisper and went on round the last mile of wall and back to the gardeners' hut.

He took a last look round before going in. He could see a neck of the lake about twenty yards away. It was now gunmetal in the approaching dawn. Some big insects were flitting and darting through the softly rising steam. They were pink dragonflies. Pink ones. Dancing and skimming. But of course! The *haiku* of Tiger's dying agent! That was the last nightmarish touch to this obscenity of a place. Bond went into the hut, picked his way carefully between the machines and wheelbarrows, pulled some sacks over himself and fell into a shallow sleep full of ghosts and demons and screams.

17

SOMETHING EVIL COMES THIS WAY

THE DREAMED SCREAMS had merged into real ones when, four hours later, Bond awoke. There was silence in the hut. Bond got cautiously to his knees and put his eye to a wide crack in the rickety planking. A screaming man, from his ragged blue cotton uniform a Japanese peasant, was running across his line of vision along the edge of the lake. Four guards were after him, laughing and calling as if it were a game of hide-and-seek. They were carrying long staves, and now one of them paused and hurled his stave accurately after the man so that it caught in his legs and brought him crashing to the ground. He scrambled to his knees and held supplicating hands out towards his pursuers. Still laughing, they gathered round him, stocky men in high rubber boots, their faces made terrifying by black *maskos* over their mouths, black leather nose-pieces and the same ugly black leather soup-plate hats as the agent on the train had worn. They poked at the man with the ends of their staves, at the same time shouting harshly at him in voices that jeered. Then, as if at an order, they bent down and, each man seizing a leg or an arm, picked him off the ground, swung him once or twice and tossed him out into the lake. The ghastly ripple surged forward and the man, now screaming again, beat at his face with his hands and floundered as if trying to make for the shore, but the screams rapidly became weaker and finally ceased as the head went down and the red stain spread wider and wider.

Doubled up with laughter, the guards on the bank watched the show. Now, satisfied that the fun was over, they turned away and walked towards the hut, and Bond could see the tears of their pleasure glistening on their cheeks.

He got back under cover and heard their boisterous voices and laughter only yards away as they came into the hut and pulled out their rakes and barrows and dispersed to their jobs, and for some time Bond could hear them calling to each other across the park. Then, from the direction of the castle, came the deep tolling of a bell, and the men fell silent. Bond glanced at the cheap Japanese wrist-watch Tiger had provided. It was nine o'clock. Was this the beginning of the official working day? Probably. The Japanese usually get to their work half an hour early and leave half an hour late in order to gain face with their employer and show keenness and gratitude for their jobs. Later, Bond guessed, there would be an hour's luncheon break. Work would probably cease at six. So it would only be from six thirty on that he would have the grounds to himself. Meanwhile, he must listen and watch and find out more about the guards' routines, of which he had presumably witnessed the first — the smelling out and final dispatch of suicides who had changed their minds or turned faint-hearted during the night. Bond softly unzipped his container and took a bite at one of his three slabs of pemmican and a short draught from his water-bottle. God, for a cigarette!

An hour later, Bond heard a brief shuffling of feet on the gravel path on the other side of the lake. He looked through the slit. The four guards had lined up and were standing rigidly to attention. Bond's heart beat a little faster. This would be for some form of inspection. Might Blofeld be doing his rounds, getting his reports of the night's bag?

Bond strained his eyes to the right, towards the castle, but his view was obstructed by an expanse of white oleanders, that innocent shrub with its attractive clusters of blossom that is used as a deadly fish poison in many parts of the tropics. Dear, pretty bush! Bond thought. I must remember to keep clear of you tonight.

And then, following the path on the other side of the lake, two strolling figures came into his line of vision and Bond clenched his fists with the thrill of seeing his prey.

Blofeld, in his gleaming chain armour and grotesquely spiked and winged helmet of steel, its visor closed, was something out of Wagner, or, because of the Oriental style of his armour, a Japanese *Kabuki* play. His armoured right hand rested easily on a long naked *samurai* sword while his left was hooked into the arm of his companion, a stumpy woman with the body and stride of a wardress. Her face was totally obscured by a hideous bee-keeper's hat of dark green straw with a heavy pendent black veil reaching down over her shoulders. But there could be no doubt! Bond had seen that dumpy silhouette, now clothed in a plastic rainproof above tall rubber boots, too often in his dreams. That was her! That was Irma Bunt!

Bond held his breath. If they came round the lake to his side, one tremendous shove and the armoured man would be floundering in the water! But could the piranhas get at him through chinks in the armour? Unlikely! And how would he, Bond, get away? No, that wouldn't be the answer.

The two figures had almost reached the line of four men, and at this moment the guards dropped to their knees in unison and bowed their foreheads down to the ground. Then they quickly jumped up and stood again at attention.

Blofeld raised his visor and addressed one of the men, who answered with deference. Bond noticed for the first time that this particular guard wore a belt round his waist with a holstered automatic. Bond couldn't hear the language they were speaking. It was impossible that Blofeld had learned Japanese. English or German? Probably the latter as a result of some wartime liaison job. The man laughed and pointed towards the lake, where a collapsed balloon of blue clothing was jigging softly with the activities of the horde of feasting piranhas within it. Blofeld nodded his approval and the men again went down on their knees. Blofeld raised a hand in brief acknowledgment, lowered his visor and the couple moved regally on.

Bond watched carefully to see if the file of guards, when they got to their feet, registered any private expressions of scorn or hilarity once The Master's back was turned. But there was no hint of disrespect. The men broke ranks and hurried off about their tasks with disciplined seriousness, and Bond was reminded of Dikko Henderson's illustration of the automatic, ant-like subservience to discipline and authority of the Japanese that had resulted in one of the great crimes of the century. If only dear Dikko were here now. What a tremendous boost his fists and his surging zest would add to this lunatic operation!

The crime had concerned, said Dikko, a modest suburban branch of the Imperial Bank. It had been a normal day of business, when a man wearing an official-looking arm-band had presented himself to the manager of the bank. He was from the Ministry of Health. An outbreak of typhus was feared and he would be obliged if the manager would line up his staff in the courtyard so that he could administer the official antidote. The manager bowed and complied, and, after everything had been locked up, the fourteen staff assembled and listened carefully to the short lecture on health delivered by the man with the armband. Then everyone had bowed in acknowledgment of the wisdom of the Ministry of Health, and the official had bent to his small suitcase and produced fifteen glasses into which he measured medicine from a bottle. He handed a glass to each person and advised them to swallow the mixture at one gulp as otherwise it might damage their teeth. 'Now,' he had said, according to Dikko's version. 'All together! One. Two. Three!' And down went the honourable medicine and down fell the honourable local manager and staff of the Imperial Bank of Japan. The medicine had been neat cyanide.

The 'Ministry of Health official' had removed the keys from the trouser-pocket of the prone manager, had loaded up his car with two hundred and fifty million yen, and had driven cheerfully from the scene of what was to become known as the 'Teigin case' after the suburb in which it took place.

And here, Bond reflected, was the same total obedience to authority, but in this case the tacit approval and sympathy of the Black Dragon philosophy was operating. Blofeld told them to do such things as he had witnessed a couple of hours before. He was invested with power from certain departments of State. He had dressed for the part. His orders were obeyed. And there was honourable job to be done. Honourable job which resulted in much publicity in the newspapers. And this was a powerful *gaijin* who had powerful squeeze in high places and 'a wide face'. And if people wanted to kill themselves, why worry? If the Castle of Death, with perhaps an occasional extra push, was not available, they would choose the railways or the trams. Here was a public service. Almost a sub-department of the Ministry of Health! So long as their *maskos* and nose-pieces protected them from the poisons in the garden, the main thing was to do their jobs conscientiously and perhaps, one day, they would get a Minister of Self-Destruction appointed in the Diet! Then the great days of the Black Dragon *Kōan* would come again to save the Country of the Rising Sun from the creeping paralysis of *demokorasu*!

And now the two strolling figures were coming back into Bond's line of vision, but this time from the left. They had rounded the end of the lake and were on their way back, perhaps to visit other groups of guards and get their reports. Tiger had said there were at least twenty guards and that the property covered five hundred acres. Five working parties of four guards each? Blofeld's visor was up and he was talking to the woman. They were now only twenty yards away. They stopped at the edge of the lake and contemplated, with relaxed curiosity, the still turbulent mass of fish round the floating doll of blue cloth. They were talking German. Bond strained his ears.

Blofeld said, 'The piranhas and the volcanic mud are useful housekeepers. They keep the place tidy.'

'The sea and the sharks are also useful.'

'But often the sharks do not complete the job. That spy we put through the Question Room. He was almost intact when his body was found down the coast. The lake would have been a better place for him. We don't want that policeman from Fukuoka coming here too often. He may have means of learning from the peasants how many people are crossing the wall. That will be many more, nearly double the number the ambulance comes for. If our figures go on increasing at this rate, there is going to be trouble. I see from the cuttings Kono translates for me that there are already mutterings in the papers about a public inquiry.'

'And what shall we do then, lieber Ernst?'

'We shall obtain massive compensation and move on. The same pattern can be repeated in other countries. Everywhere there are people who want to kill themselves. We may have to vary the attractions of the opportunities we offer them. Other people have not the profound love of horror and violence of the Japanese. A really beautiful waterfall. A handy bridge. A vertiginous drop. These might be alternatives. Brazil, or somewhere else in South America, might provide such a site.'

'But the figures would be much smaller.'

'It is the concept that matters, liebe Irma. It is very difficult to invent something that is entirely new in the history of the world. I have done that. If my bridge, my waterfall, yields a crop of only perhaps ten people a year, it is simply a matter of statistics. The basic idea will be kept alive.'

'That is so. You are indeed a genius, lieber Ernst. You have already established this place as a shrine to death for evermore. People read about such fantasies in the works of Poe, Lautréamont, de Sade, but no one has ever created such a fantasy in real life. It is as if one of the great fairy tales has come to life. A sort of Disneyland of Death. But of course,' she hastened to add, 'on an altogether grander, more poetic scale.'

'In due course I shall write the whole story down. Then perhaps the world will acknowledge the type of man who has been living among them. A man not only unhonoured and unsung, but a man' — Blofeld's voice rose almost to a scream — 'whom they hunt down and wish to shoot like a mad dog. A man who has to use all his wiles just to stay alive! Why, if I had not covered my tracks so well, there would be spies on their way even now to kill us both or to hand us over for official murder under their stupid laws! Ah well, liebe Irma,' the voice was more rational, quieter, 'we live in a world of fools in which true greatness is a sin. Come! It is time to review the other detachments.'

They turned away and were about to continue along the lake when Blofeld suddenly stopped and pointed like a dog directly at Bond. 'That hut among the bushes. The door is open! I have told the men a thousand times to keep such places locked. It is a perfect refuge for a spy or a fugitive. I will make sure.'

Bond shivered. He huddled down, dragging sacks from the top of his barrier to give extra protection. The clanking steps approached, entered the hut. Bond could feel the man, only yards away, could feel his questing eyes and nostrils. There came a clang of metal and the wall of sacks shook at great thrusts from Blofeld's sword. Then the sword slashed down again and again and Bond winced and bit his lip as a hammer-blow crashed across the centre of his back. But then Blofeld seemed to be satisfied and the iron steps clanged away. Bond let out his breath in a quiet hiss. He heard Blofeld's voice say, 'There is nothing, but remind me to reprimand Kono on our rounds tomorrow. The place must be cleared out and a proper lock fitted.' Then the sound of the steps vanished in the direction of the oleander clump, and Bond gave a groan and felt his back. But, though many of the sacks above him had been sliced through, his protection had been just deep enough and the skin across his spine wasn't broken.

Bond got to his knees and rearranged the hideout, massaging his aching back as he did so. Then he spat the dust from the sacking out of his mouth, took a swallow from the water-bottle, assured himself through his slit that there was no movement outside and lay down and let his mind wander back over every word that Blofeld had uttered.

Of course the man was mad. A year earlier, the usual quiet tones that Bond remembered so well would never have cracked into that lunatic, Hitler scream. And the coolness, the supreme confidence that had always lain behind his planning? Much of that seemed to have seeped away, perhaps, Bond hoped, partly because of the two great failures he, Bond, had done much to bring about in two of Blofeld's most grandiose conspiracies. But one thing was clear — the hideout was blown. Tonight would have to be the night. Ah, well! Once again Bond ran over the hazy outline of his plan. If he could gain access to the castle, he felt pretty confident of finding a means to kill Blofeld. But he was also fairly certain that he himself would die in the process. *Dulce et decorum est* . . . and all that jazz! But then he thought of Kissy, and he wasn't so sure about not fearing for himself. She had brought a sweetness back into his life that he thought had gone for ever.

Bond dropped off into an uneasy, watchful sleep that was once again peopled by things and creatures out of nightmare-land.

18

OUBLIETTE

AT SIX O'CLOCK in the evening, the deep bell tolled briefly from the castle and dusk came like the slow drawing of a violet blind over the day. Crickets began to zing in a loud chorus and geckos chuckled in the shrubbery. The pink dragonflies disappeared and large horned toads appeared in quantities from their mud holes on the edge of the lake and, so far as Bond could see through his spy-hole, seemed to be catching gnats attracted by the shining pools of their eyes. Then the four guards reappeared, and there came the fragrant smell of a bonfire they had presumably lit to consume the refuse they had collected during the day. They went to the edge of the lake and raked in the tattered scraps of blue clothing and, amidst delighted laughter, emptied long bones out of the fragments into the water. One of them ran off with the rags, presumably to add them to the bonfire, and Bond got under cover as the others pushed their wheelbarrows up the slope and stowed them away in the hut. They stood chattering happily in the dusk until the fourth arrived and then, without noticing the slashed and disarrayed sacks in the shadows, they filed off in the direction of the castle.

After an interval, Bond got up and stretched and shook the dust out of his hair and clothes. His back still ached, but his overwhelming sensation was the desperate urge for a cigarette. All right. It might be his last. He sat down and drank a little water and munched a large wedge of the highly flavoured pemmican, then took another swig at the water-bottle. He took out his single packet of Shinsei and lit up, holding the cigarette between cupped hands and quickly blowing out the match. He dragged the smoke deep down into his lungs. It was bliss! Another drag and the prospect of the night seemed less daunting. It was surely going to be all right! He thought briefly of Kissy who would now be eating her bean curd and fish and preparing the night's swim in her mind. A few hours more and she would be near him. But what would have happened in those few hours? Bond smoked the cigarette until it burned his fingers, then crushed out the stub and pushed the dead fragments down through a crack in the floor. It was seven thirty and already some of the insect noises of sundown had ceased. Bond went meticulously about his preparations.

At nine o'clock he left the hideout. Again the moon blazed down and there was total silence except for the distant burping and bubbling of the fumaroles and the occasional sinister chuckle of a gecko from the shrubbery. He took the same route as the night before, came through the same belt of trees and stood looking up at the great bat-winged donjon that towered up to the sky. He noticed for the first time that the warning balloon with its advertisement of danger was tethered to a pole on the corner of the balustrade surrounding what appeared to be the main floor — the third, or centre one of the five. Here, from several windows, yellow light shone faintly, and Bond guessed that this would be his target area. He let out a deep sigh and strode quietly off across the gravel and came without incident to the tiny entrance under the wooden bridge.

The black *ninja* suit was as full of concealed pockets as a conjurer's tail-coat. Bond took out a pencil flashlight and a small steel file and set to work on a link of the chain. Occasionally he paused to spit into the deepening groove to lessen the rasp of metal on metal, but then there came the final crack of parting steel and, using the file as a lever, he bent the link open and quietly removed the padlock and chain from its stanchions. He pressed lightly and the door gave inwards. He took out his flashlight and pushed further, probing the darkness ahead with his thin beam. It was as well he did so. On the stone floor where his first step past the open door would have taken him, lay a yawning man-trap, its rusty iron jaws, perhaps a yard across, waiting for him to step on the thin covering of straw that partially concealed it. Bond winced as, in his imagination, he heard the iron clang as the saw-teeth bit into his leg below the knee. There would be other such booby traps — he must keep every sense on the alert!

Bond closed the door softly behind him, stepped round the trap and swept the beam of his torch ahead and around him.

Nothing but velvety blackness. He was in some vast underground cellar where no doubt the food supplies for a small army had once been stored. A shadow swept across the thin beam of light and another and another, and there was a shrill squeaking from all around him. Bond didn't mind bats or believe the Victorian myth that they got caught in your hair. Their radar was too good. He crept slowly forward, watching only the rough stone flags ahead of him. He passed one or two bulky arched pillars, and now the great cellar seemed to narrow because he could just see walls to right and left of him and above him an arched, cobwebby roof. Yes, here were the stone steps leading upwards! He climbed them softly and counted twenty of them before he came to the entrance, a wide double door with no lock on his side. He pushed gently and could feel and hear the resistance of a rickety-sounding lock. He took out a heavy jemmy and probed. Its sharp jaws notched round some sort of a cross-bolt, and Bond levered hard sideways until there came the tearing sound of old metal and the tinkle of nails or screws on stone. He pushed softly on the crack and, with a hideously loud report, the rest of the lock came away and half the door swung open with a screech of old hinges. Beyond was more darkness. Bond stepped through and listened, his torch doused. But he was still deep in the bowels of the castle and there was no sound. He switched on again. More stone stairs leading up to a modern door of polished timber. He went up them and carefully turned the metal door handle. No lock this time! He softly pushed the door open and found himself in a long stone corridor that sloped on upwards. At the end was yet another modern door, and beneath it showed a thin strip of light!

Bond walked noiselessly up the incline and then held his breath and put his ear to the keyhole. Dead silence! He grasped the handle and inched the door open and then, satisfied, went through and closed the door behind him, leaving it on the latch. He was in the main hall of the castle. The big entrance door was on his left, and a well-used strip of red carpet stretched away from it and across the fifty feet of hall into the shadows that were not reached by the single large oil lamp over the entrance. The hall was not embellished in any way, save for the strip of carpet, and its roof was a maze of longitudinal and cross beams interspersed with latticed bamboo over the same rough plaster-work as covered the walls. There was still the same castle-smell of cold stone.

Bond kept away from the carpet and hugged the shadows of the walls. He guessed that he was now on the main floor and that somewhere straight ahead was his quarry. He was well inside the citadel. So far so good!

The next door, obviously the entrance to one of the public rooms, had a simple latch to it. Bond bent and put his eye to the keyhole. Another dimly lit interior. No sound! He eased up the latch, inched the door ajar, and then open, and went through. It was a second vast chamber, but this time one of baronial splendour — the main reception room, Bond guessed, where Blofeld would receive visitors. Between tall red curtains, edged with gold, fine set-pieces of armour and weapons hung on the white plaster walls, and there was much heavy antique furniture arranged in conventional groupings on a vast central carpet in royal blue. The rest of the floor was of highly polished boards, which reflected back the lights from two great oil lanterns that hung from the high, timbered roof, similar to that of the entrance hall, but here with the main beams decorated in a zigzag motif of dark red. Bond, looking for places of concealment, chose the widely spaced curtains and, slipping softly from one refuge to the next, reached the small door at the end of the chamber that would, he guessed, lead to the private apartments.

He bent down to listen, but immediately leaped for cover behind the nearest curtains. Steps were approaching! Bond undid the thin chain from around his waist, wrapped it round his left fist and took the jemmy in his right hand and waited, his eyes glued to a chink in the dusty-smelling material.

The small door opened halfway to show the back of one of the guards. He wore a black belt with a holster. Would this be Kono, the man who translated for Blofeld? He had probably had some job with the Germans during the war — in the Kempeitai, perhaps. What was he doing? He appeared to be fiddling with some piece of apparatus behind the door. A light switch? No, there was no electric light. Apparently satisfied, the man backed out, bowed deeply to the interior and closed the door. He wore no *masko* and Bond caught a brief glimpse of a surly, slit-eyed brownish face as he passed Bond's place of concealment and walked on across the reception chamber. Bond heard the click of the far door and then there was silence. He waited a good five minutes before gently shifting the curtain so that he could see down the room. He was alone.

And now for the last lap!

Bond kept his weapons in his hands and crept back to the door. This time no sound came from behind it. But the guard had bowed. Oh well! Probably out of respect for the aura of The Master. Bond quietly but firmly thrust the door open and leaped through, ready for the attacking sprint.

A totally empty, totally featureless length of passageway yawned at his dramatics. It stretched perhaps twenty feet in front of him. It was dimly lit by a central oil lamp and its floor was of the usual highly polished boards. A 'nightingale floor'? No. The guard's footsteps had uttered no warning creaks. But from behind the facing door at the end came the sound of music. It was Wagner, the 'Ride of the Valkyries', being played at medium pitch. Thank you, Blofeld! thought Bond. Most helpful cover! And he crept softly forward down the centre of the passage.

When it came, there was absolutely no warning. One step across the exact halfway point of the flooring and, like a seesaw, the whole twenty feet of boards swivelled noiselessly on some central axis and Bond, arms and legs flailing and hands scrabbling desperately for a grip, found himself hurtling down into a black void. The guard! The fiddling about behind the door! He had been adjusting the lever that set the trap, the traditional oubliette of ancient castles! And Bond had forgotten! As his body plunged off the end of the inclined platform into space, an alarm bell, triggered by the mechanism of the trap, brayed hysterically. Bond had a fractional impression of the platform, relieved of his weight, swinging back into position above him, then he crashed shatteringly into unconsciousness.

Bond swam reluctantly up through the dark tunnel towards the blinding pinpoint of light. Why wouldn't someone stop hitting him? What had he done to deserve it? He had got two *awabis*. He could feel them in his hands, sharp-edged and rough. That was as much as Kissy could expect of him. 'Kissy,' he mumbled, 'stop it! Stop it, Kissy!'

The pinpoint of light expanded, became an expanse of straw-covered floor on which he was crouching while the open hand crashed sideways into his face. Piff! Paff! With each slap the splitting pain in his head exploded into a thousand separate pain fragments. Bond saw the edge of the boat above him and desperately raised himself to grasp at it. He held up the *awabis* to show that he had done his duty. He opened his hands to drop them into the tub. Consciousness flooded back and he saw the two handfuls of straw dribble to the ground. But the blows had stopped. And now he could see, indistinctly, through a mist of pain. That brown face! Those slit eyes! Kono, the guard. And someone else was holding a torch for him. Then it all came back. No *awabis*! No Kissy! Something dreadful had happened! Everything had gone wrong! *Shimata!* I have made a mistake! Tiger! The clue clicked and total realization swept through Bond's mind. Careful, now. You're deaf and dumb. You're a Japanese miner from Fukuoka. Get the record straight. To hell with the pain in your head. Nothing's broken. Play it cool. Bond put his hands down to his sides. He realized for the first time that he was naked save for the brief vee of the black cotton *ninja* underpants. He bowed deeply and straightened himself. Kono, his hand at his open holster, fired furious Japanese at him. Bond licked at the blood that was trickling down his face and looked blank, stupid. Kono took out his small automatic, gestured. Bond bowed again, got to his feet, and, with a brief glance round the straw-strewn oubliette into which he had fallen, followed the unseen guard with the torch out of the cell.

There were stairs and a corridor and a door. Kono stepped forward and knocked.

And then Bond was standing in the middle of a small, pleasant, library-type room and the second guard was laying out on the floor Bond's *ninja* suit and the appallingly incriminating contents of his pockets. Blofeld, dressed in a magnificent black silk kimono across which a golden dragon sprawled, stood leaning against the mantelpiece beneath which a Japanese brazier smouldered. It was him all right. The bland, high forehead, the pursed purple wound of a mouth, now shadowed by a heavy grey-black moustache that drooped at the corners, on its way, perhaps, to achieving mandarin proportions, the mane of white hair he had grown for the part of Monsieur le Comte de

Bleuville, the black bullet-holes of the eyes. And beside him, completing the picture of a homely couple at ease after dinner, sat Irma Bunt, in the full regalia of a high-class Japanese lady, the petit point of a single chrysanthemum lying in her lap waiting for those pudgy hands to take it up when the cause of this unseemly disturbance had been ascertained. The puffy, square face, the tight bun of mousy hair, the thin wardress mouth, the light brown, almost yellow eyes! By God, thought Bond dully, here they are! Within easy reach! They would both be dead by now but for his single criminal error. Might there still be some way of turning the tables? If only the pain in his head would stop throbbing!

Blofeld's tall sword stood against the wall. He picked it up and strode out into the room. He stood over the pile of Bond's possessions and picked them over with the tip of the sword. He hooked up the black suit. He said in German, 'And what is this, Kono?'

The head guard replied in the same language. His voice was uneasy and his eye-slits swivelled with a certain respect towards Bond and away again. 'It is a *ninja* suit, Herr Doktor. These are people who practise the secret arts of *ninjutsu*. Their secrets are very ancient and I know little of them. They are the art of moving by stealth, of being invisible, of killing without weapons. These people used to be much feared in Japan. I was not aware that they still existed. This man has undoubtedly been sent to assassinate you, my lord. But for the magic of the passage, he might well have succeeded.'

'And who is he?' Blofeld looked keenly at Bond. 'He is tall for a Japanese.'

'The men from the mines are often tall men, my lord. He carries a paper saying that he is deaf and dumb. And other papers, which appear to be in order, stating that he is a miner from Fukuoka. I do not believe this. His hands have some broken nails, but they are not the hands of a miner.'

'I do not believe it either. But we shall soon find out.' Blofeld turned to the woman. 'What do you think, my dear? You have a good nose for such problems — the instincts of a woman.'

Irma Bunt rose and came and stood beside him. She looked piercingly at Bond and then walked slowly round him, keeping her distance. When she came to the left profile she said softly, with awe, '*Du lieber Gott!*' She went back to Blofeld. She said in a hoarse whisper, still staring, almost with horror, at Bond, 'It cannot be! But it is! The scar down the right cheek! The profile! And the eyebrows have been shaved to give that upward tilt!' She turned to Blofeld. She said decisively, 'This is the English agent. This is the man Bond, James Bond, the man whose wife you killed. The man who went under the name of Sir Hilary Bray.' She added fiercely, 'I swear it! You have got to believe me, lieber Ernst!'

Blofeld's eyes had narrowed. 'I see a certain resemblance. But how has he got here? How has he found me? Who sent him?'

'The Japanese Geheimdienst. They will certainly have relations with the British Secret Service.'

'I cannot believe it! If that was so, they would have come with warrants to arrest me. There are too many unknown factors in this business. We must proceed with great circumspection and extract the whole truth from this man. We must at once find out if he is deaf and dumb. That is the first step. The Question Room should settle that. But first of all he must be softened up.' He turned to Kono. 'Tell Kazama to get to work.'

19

THE QUESTION ROOM

THERE WERE NOW ten guards in the room. They stood lined up against the wall behind Kono. They were all armed with their long staves. Kono fired an order at one of them. The man left his stave in an angle of the wall and came forward. He was a great, box-like man with a totally bald, shining head like a ripe fruit and hands like hams. He took up his position in front of Bond, his legs straddled for balance and his lips drawn back in a snarling smile of broken black teeth. Then he swung his right hand sideways at Bond's head and slapped him with tremendous force exactly on the bruise of Bond's fall. Bond's head exploded with fire. Then the left hand came at him and Bond rocked sideways. Through a mist of blood he could see Blofeld and his woman. Blofeld was merely interested, as a scientist, but the woman's lips were parted and wet.

Bond took ten blows and knew that he must act while he still had the purpose and the strength. The straddled legs offered the perfect target. So long as the man had not practised the *sumo* trick! Through a haze, Bond took aim and, as another giant blow was on its way, kicked upwards with every ounce of force left to him. His foot slammed home. The man gave an animal scream and crashed to the ground, clasping himself and rolling from side to side in agony. The guards made a concerted rush forward, their staves lifted, and Kono had his gun out. Bond leaped for the protection of a tall chair, picked it up and hurled it at the snarling pack of guards. One of the legs caught a man in the teeth and there was the sound of splintering bone. The man went down clutching his face.

'Halt!' It was the Hitlerian scream Bond had heard before. The men stood stock still and lowered their staves. 'Kono. Remove those men.' Blofeld pointed down at the two casualties. 'And punish Kazama for his incompetence. Get new teeth for the other one. And enough of this. The man will not speak with ordinary methods. If he can hear, he will not withstand the pressure of the Question Room. Take him there. The rest of the guards can wait in the audience chamber. *Also! Marsch!*'

Kono fired off orders to which the guards reacted at the double. Then Kono gestured to Bond with his gun, opened a small doorway beside the bookcase and pointed down a narrow stone passage. Now what? Bond licked the blood from the corners of his mouth. He was near the end of his tether. Pressure? He couldn't stand much more of it. And what was this Question Room? He mentally shrugged. There might still be a chance to get at Blofeld's throat. If only he could take that one with him! He went ahead down the passage, was deaf to the order from Kono to open the rough door at the end, had it opened for him by the guard while the pistol pressed into his spine, and walked forward into a bizarre room of roughly hewn stone that was very hot and stank disgustingly of sulphur.

Blofeld and the woman entered, the door was closed and they took their places in two wooden armchairs beneath an oil lamp and a large kitchen clock whose only unusual feature was that, at each quarter, the figures were underlined in red. The hands stood at just after eleven and now, with a loud iron tick, the minute hand dropped one span. Kono gestured for Bond to advance the twelve paces to the far end of the room where there was a raised stone pedestal-seat with arms. It dripped with drying grey mud and there was the same volcanic filth on the floor all round it. Above the stone seat, in the ceiling, there was a wide circular opening through which Bond could see a patch of dark sky and stars. Kono's rubber boots squelched after him and Bond was gestured to sit down on the stone throne. In the centre of the seat there was a large round hole. Bond did as he was told, his skin flinching at the hot sticky surface of the mud. He rested his forearms wearily on the stone arms of the throne and waited, his belly crawling with the knowledge of what this was all about.

Blofeld spoke from the other end of the room. He spoke in English. He said, in a loud voice that boomed round the naked walls, 'Commander Bond, or number 007 in the British Secret Service if you prefer it, this is the Question Room, a device of my invention that has the almost inevitable effect of making silent people talk. As you know, this property is highly volcanic.

You are now sitting directly above a geyser that throws mud, at a heat of around one thousand degrees Centigrade, a distance of approximately one hundred feet into the air. Your body is now at an elevation of approximately fifty feet directly above its source. I had the whimsical notion to canalize this geyser up a stone funnel above which you now sit. This is what is known as a periodic geyser. This particular example is regulated to erupt volcanically at exactly the fifteenth minute in every hour.' Blofeld looked behind him and turned back. 'You will therefore observe that you have exactly eleven minutes before the next eruption. If you cannot hear me, or the translation that will follow, if you are a deaf and dumb Japanese as you maintain, you will not move from that chair and, at the fifteenth minute past eleven, you will suffer a most dreadful death by the incineration of your lower body. If, on the other hand, you leave the seat before the death moment, you will have demonstrated that you can hear and understand and you will then be put to further tortures which will inevitably make you answer my questions. These questions will seek to confirm your identity, how you come to be here, who sent you and with what purpose, and how many people are involved in the conspiracy. You understand? You would not prefer to give up this play-acting? Very well. On the off chance that your papers are perhaps partially correct, my chief guard will now briefly explain the purpose of this room in the Japanese language.' He turned to the guard. '*Kono, sag' ihm auf japanisch den Zweck dieses Zimmers.*'

Kono had taken up his position by the door. He now harangued Bond in sharp Japanese sentences. Bond paid no attention. He concentrated on regaining his strength. He sat relaxed and gazed nonchalantly round the room. He had remembered the final 'hell' at Beppu and he was looking for something. Ah yes! There it was! A small wooden box in the corner to the right of his throne. There was no keyhole to it. Inside that box would undoubtedly be the regulating valve for the geyser. Could that bit of knowledge be put to some use? Bond tucked it away and racked his tired brain for some kind of a plan. If only the agonizing pulse in his head would stop. He rested his elbows on his knees and gently lowered his bruised face into his hands. At least that guard would now be in even worse agony than he!

Kono stopped talking. The clock uttered a deep iron tick.

It ticked nine times more. Bond looked up at the black-and-white clockwork face. It said 11.14. A deep, angry grumble sounded from deep down beneath him. It was followed by a hard buffet of very hot breath. Bond got to his feet and walked slowly away from the stinking stone vent until he reached the area of the floor that was not wet with mud. Then he turned and watched. The grumble had become a faraway roar. The roar became a deep howl that swelled up into the room like an express train coming out of a tunnel. Then there was a mighty explosion and a solid jet of grey mud shot like a gleaming grey piston out of the hole Bond had just left and exactly penetrated the wide aperture in the ceiling. The jet continued, absolutely solid, for perhaps half a second, and searing heat filled the room so that Bond had to wipe the sweat from his forehead. Then the grey pillar collapsed back into the hole and mud pattered on to the roof of the place and splashed down into the room in great steaming gobbets. A deep bubbling and burping came up the pipe and the room steamed. The stench of sulphur was sickening. In the total silence that followed, the tick of the clock to 11.16 was as loud as a gong-stroke.

Bond turned and faced the couple under the clock. He said cheerfully, 'Well, Blofeld, you mad bastard. I'll admit that your effects man down below knows his stuff. Now bring on the twelve she-devils and if they're all as beautiful as Fräulein Bunt, we'll get Noël Coward to put it to music and have it on Broadway by Christmas. How about it?'

Blofeld turned to Irma Bunt. 'My dear girl, you were right! It is indeed the same Britischer. Remind me to buy you another string of the excellent Mr Mikimoto's grey pearls. And now let us be finished with this man once and for all. It is beyond our bedtime.'

'Yes indeed, lieber Ernst. But first he must speak.'

'Of course, Irmchen. But that can be quickly done. We have already broken his first reserves. The second line of defence will be routine. Come!'

Back up the stone passage! Back into the library! Irma Bunt back to her petit point, Blofeld back to his stance by the mantelpiece, his hand resting lightly on the boss of his great sword. It was just as if they had returned after taking part in some gracious after-dinner entertainment: a game of billiards, a look at the stamp albums, a dull quarter of an hour with the home movies. Bond decided: to hell with the Fukuoka miner! There was a writing-desk next to the bookshelves. He pulled out its chair and sat down. There were cigarettes and matches. He lit up and sat back, inhaling luxuriously. Might as well make oneself comfortable before one went for The Big Sleep! He tapped his ash on to the carpet and crossed one knee over the other.

Blofeld pointed to the pile of Bond's possessions on the floor. 'Kono, take those away. I will examine them later. And you can wait with the guards in the outer hall. Prepare the blowlamp and the electrical machine for further examination in case it should be necessary.' He turned to Bond. 'And now — talk and you will receive an honourable and quick death by the sword. Have no misgivings. I am expert with it and it is razor-sharp. If you do not talk, you will die slowly and horribly and you will talk just the same. You know from your profession that this is so. There is a degree of prolonged suffering that no human can withstand. Well?'

Bond said easily, 'Blofeld, you were never stupid. Many people in London and Tokyo know of my presence here tonight. At this moment, you might argue your way out of a capital charge. You have a lot of money and you could engage the best lawyers. But, if you kill me, you will certainly die.'

'Mister Bond, you are not telling the truth. I know the ways of officialdom as well as you do. Therefore I dismiss your story in its entirety and without hesitation. If my presence here was officially known, a small army of policemen would have been sent to arrest me. And they would have been accompanied by a senior member of the C.I.A. on whose WANTED list I certainly feature. This is an American sphere of influence. You might have been allowed to interview me subsequent to my arrest, but an Englishman would not have featured in the initial police action.'

'Who said this was police action? When, in England, I heard rumours about this place, I thought the whole project smelled of you. I obtained permission to come and have a look. But my whereabouts is known and retribution will result if I do not return.'

'That does not follow, Mister Bond. There will be no trace of your ever having seen me, no trace of your entry into the property. I happen to have certain information that fits in with your presence here. One of my agents recently reported that the Head of the Japanese Secret Service, the *Kōan-Chōsa-Kyōku*, a certain Tanaka, came down in this direction accompanied by a foreigner dressed as a Japanese. I now see that your appearance tallies with my agent's description.'

'Where is this man? I would like to question him.'

'He is not available.'

'Very convenient.'

A red fire began to burn deep in the black pools of Blofeld's eyes. 'You forget that it is not I who am being interrogated, Mister Bond. It is you. Now, I happen to know all about this Tanaka. He is a totally ruthless man, and I will hazard a guess that fits the facts and that is made almost into a certitude by your crude evasions. This man Tanaka has already lost one senior agent whom he sent down here to investigate me. You were available, on some business concerned with your profession, perhaps, and, for a consideration, or in exchange for a favour, you agreed to come here and kill me, thus tidying up a situation which is causing some embarrassment to the Japanese Government. I do not know or care when you learned that Doctor Guntram Shatterhand was in fact Ernst Starvo Blofeld. You have your private reasons for wanting to kill me, and I have absolutely no doubt that you kept your knowledge to yourself and passed it on to no one for fear that the official action I have described would take the place of your private plans for revenge.' Blofeld paused. He said softly, 'I have one of the greatest brains in the world, Mister Bond. Have you anything to say in reply? As the Americans say, "It had better be good." '

Bond took another cigarette and lit it. He said composedly, 'I stick to the truth, Blofeld. If anything happens to me, you, and probably the woman as an accessory, will be dead by Christmas.'

'All right, Mister Bond. But I am so sure of my facts that I am now going to kill you with my own hands and dispose of your body without more ado. On reflection, I would rather do it myself than have it done slowly by the guards. You have been a thorn in my flesh for too long. The account I have to settle with you is a personal one. Have you ever heard the Japanese expression "*kirisute gomen*"?'

Bond groaned. 'Spare me the Lafcadio Hearn, Blofeld!'

'It dates from the time of the *samurai*. It means literally "killing and going away". If a low person hindered the *samurai*'s passage along the road or failed to show him proper respect, the *samurai* was within his rights to lop off the man's head. I regard myself as a latter-day *samurai*. My fine sword has not yet been blooded. Yours will be an admirable head to cut its teeth on.' He turned to Irma Bunt. 'You agree, mein Liebchen?'

The square wardress face looked up from its petit point. 'But of course, lieber Ernst. What you decide is always correct. But be careful. This animal is dangerous.'

'You forget, mein Liebchen. Since last January he has ceased to be an animal. By a simple stroke of surgery on the woman he loved, I reduced him to human dimensions.'

The dominant, horrific figure stood away from the mantelpiece and took up his sword.

'Let me show you.'

20

BLOOD AND THUNDER

BOND DROPPED HIS lighted cigarette and left it to smoulder on the carpet. His whole body tensed. He said, 'I suppose you know you're both mad as hatters.'

'So was Frederick the Great, so was Nietzsche, so was Van Gogh. We are in good, in illustrious company, Mister Bond. On the other hand, what are you? You are a common thug, a blunt instrument wielded by dolts in high places. Having done what you are told to do, out of some mistaken idea of duty or patriotism, you satisfy your brutish instincts with alcohol, nicotine and sex while waiting to be dispatched on the next misbegotten foray. Twice before, your Chief has sent you to do battle with me, Mister Bond, and, by a combination of luck and brute force, you were successful in destroying two projects of my genius. You and your government would categorize these projects as crimes against humanity, and various authorities still seek to bring me to book for them. But try and summon such wits as you possess, Mister Bond, and see them in a realistic light and in the higher realm of my own thinking.'

Blofeld was a big man, perhaps six foot three, and powerfully built. He placed the tip of the *samurai* sword, which has almost the blade of the scimitar, between his straddled feet, and rested his sinewy hands on its boss. Looking up at him from across the room, Bond had to admit that there was something larger than life in the looming, imperious figure, in the hypnotically direct stare of the eyes, in the tall white brow, in the cruel downward twist of the thin lips. The square-cut, heavily draped kimono, designed to give the illusion of bulk to a race of smallish men, made something huge out of the towering figure, and the golden dragon embroidery, so easily to be derided as a childish fantasy, crawled menacingly across the black silk and seemed to spit real fire from over the left breast. Blofeld had paused in his harangue. Waiting for him to continue, Bond took the measure of his enemy. He knew what would be coming — justification. It was always so. When they thought they had got you where they wanted you, when they knew they were decisively on top, before the knock-out, even to an audience on the threshold of extinction, it was pleasant, reassuring to the executioner, to deliver his apologia — purge the sin he was about to commit. Blofeld, his hands relaxed on the boss of his sword, continued. The tone of his voice was reasonable, self-assured, quietly expository.

He said, 'Now, Mister Bond, take Operation Thunderball, as your government dubbed it. This project involved the holding to ransom of the Western World by the acquisition by me of two atomic weapons. Where lies the crime in this, except in the Erewhon of international politics? Rich boys are playing with rich toys. A poor boy comes along and takes them and offers them back for money. If the poor boy had been successful, what a valuable by-product might have resulted for the whole world. These were dangerous toys which, in the poor boy's hands, or let us say, to discard the allegory, in the hands of a Castro, could lead to the wanton extinction of mankind. By my action, I gave a dramatic example for all to see. If I had been successful and the money had been handed over, might not the threat of a recurrence of my attempt have led to serious disarmament talks, to an abandonment of these dangerous toys that might so easily get into the wrong hands? You follow my reasoning? Then this recent matter of the bacteriological warfare attack on England. My dear Mister Bond, England is a sick nation by any standards. By hastening the sickness to the brink of death, might Britain not have been forced out of her lethargy into the kind of community effort we witnessed during the war? Cruel to be kind, Mister Bond. Where lies the great crime there? And now this matter of my so-called "Castle of Death".' Blofeld paused and his eyes took on an inward look. He said, 'I will make a confession to you, Mister Bond. I have come to suffer from a certain lassitude of mind which I am determined to combat. This comes in part from being a unique genius who is alone in the world, without honour — worse, misunderstood. No doubt much of the root cause of this accidie is physical — liver, kidneys, heart, the usual weak points of the middle-aged. But there has developed in me a certain mental lameness, a disinterest in humanity and its future, an utter boredom with the affairs of mankind. So, not unlike the gourmet, with his jaded palate, I now seek only the highly spiced, the sharp impact on the taste buds, mental as well as physical, the tickle that is truly exquisite. And so, Mister Bond, I came to devise this useful and essentially humane project — the offer of free death to those who seek release from the burden of being alive. By doing so, I have not only provided the common man with a solution to the problem of whether to be or not to be, I have also provided the Japanese Government, though for the present they appear to be blind to my magnanimity, with a tidy, out-of-the-way charnel-house which relieves them of a constant flow of messy occurrences involving the trains, the trams, the volcanoes and other unattractively public means of killing yourself. You must admit that, far from being a crime, this is a public service unique in the history of the world.'

'I saw one man being disgustingly murdered yesterday.'

'Tidying up, Mister Bond. Tidying up. The man came here wishing to die. What you saw done was only helping a weak man to his seat on the boat across the Styx. But I can see that we have no contact. I cannot reach what serves you for a mind. For your part, you cannot see further than the simple gratification of your last cigarette. So enough of this idle chatter. You have already kept us from our beds far too long. Do you want to be hacked about in a vulgar brawl, or will you offer your neck in the honourable fashion?' Blofeld took a step forward and raised his mighty sword in both hands and held it above his head. The light from the oil lamps shimmered on the blade and showed up the golden filigree engraving.

Bond knew what to do. He had known as soon as he had been led back into the room and had seen the wounded guard's stave still standing in the shadowed angle of the wall. But there was a bell-push near the woman. She would have to be dealt with first! Had he learned enough of the thrusts and parries of *bojutsu* from the demonstration at the *ninja* training camp? Bond hurled himself to the left, seized the stave and leaped at the woman whose hand was already reaching upwards.

The stave thudded into the side of her head and she sprawled grotesquely forward off her chair and lay still. Blofeld's sword whistled down, inches from his shoulder. Bond twisted and lunged to his full extent, thrusting his stave forward in the groove of his left hand almost as if it had been a billiard cue. The tip caught Blofeld hard on the breast-bone and flung him against the wall, but he hurtled back and came inexorably forward, swishing his sword like a scythe. Bond aimed at his right arm, missed and had to retreat. He was concentrating on keeping his weapon as well as his body away from the whirling steel, or his stave would be cut like a matchstick, and its extra length was his only hope of victory. Blofeld suddenly lunged, expertly, his right knee bent forward. Bond feinted to the left, but he was inches too slow and the tip of the sword flicked his left ribs, drawing blood. But before Blofeld could withdraw, Bond had slashed two-handed, sideways, at his legs. His stave met bone. Blofeld cursed, and made an ineffectual stab at Bond's weapon. Then he advanced again and Bond could only dodge and feint in the middle of the room and make quick short lunges to keep the enemy at bay. But he was losing ground in front of the whirling steel, and now Blofeld, scenting victory, took lightning steps and thrust forward like a snake. Bond leaped sideways, saw his chance and gave a mighty sweep of his stave. It caught Blofeld on his right shoulder and drew a curse from him. His main sword arm! Bond pressed forward, lancing again and again with his weapon and scoring several hits to the body, but one of Blofeld's parries caught the stave and cut off that one vital foot of extra length as if it had been a candle-end. Blofeld saw his advantage and began attacking, making furious forward jabs that Bond could only parry by hitting at the flat of the sword to deflect it. But now the stave was slippery in the sweat of his hands and for the first time he felt the cold breath of defeat at his neck. And Blofeld seemed to smell it, for he suddenly executed one of his fast running lunges to get under Bond's guard. Bond guessed the distance of the wall behind him and leaped backwards against it. Even so he felt the sword-point fan across his stomach. But, hurled back by his impact with the wall, he counter-lunged, swept the sword aside with his stave and, dropping his weapon, made a dive for Blofeld's neck and got both hands to it. For a moment the two sweating faces were almost up against each other. The boss of Blofeld's sword battered into Bond's side. Bond hardly felt the crashing blows. He pressed with his thumbs, and pressed and pressed and heard the sword clang to the floor and felt Blofeld's fingers and nails tearing at his face, trying to reach his eyes. Bond whispered through his gritted teeth, 'Die, Blofeld! Die!' And suddenly the tongue was out and the eyes rolled upwards and the body slipped down to the ground. But Bond followed it and knelt, his hands cramped round the powerful neck, seeing nothing, hearing nothing, in the terrible grip of blood lust.

Bond slowly came to himself. The golden dragon's head on the black silk kimono spat flame at him. He unclasped his aching hands from round the neck and, not looking again at the purple face, got to his feet. He staggered. God, how his head hurt! What remained to be done? He tried to cast his mind back. He had had a clever idea. What was it? Oh yes, of course! He picked up Blofeld's sword and sleep-walked down the stone passage to the torture room. He glanced up at the clock. Five minutes to midnight. And there was the wooden box, mud-spattered, down beside the throne on which he had sat, days, years before. He went to it and hacked it open with one stroke of the sword. Yes, there was the big wheel he had expected! He knelt down and twisted and twisted until it was finally closed. What would happen now? The end of the world? Bond ran back up the passage. Now he must get out, get away from this place! But his line of retreat was closed by the guards! He tore aside a curtain and smashed the window open with his sword. Outside there was a balustraded terrace that seemed to run round this storey of the castle. Bond looked around for something to cover his nakedness. There was only Blofeld's sumptuous kimono. Coldly, Bond tore it off the corpse, put it on and tied the sash. The interior of the kimono was cold, like a snake's skin. He looked down at Irma Bunt. She was breathing heavily with a drunken snore. Bond went to the window and climbed out, minding his bare feet among the glass splinters.

But he had been wrong! The balustrade was a brief one, closed at both ends. He stumbled from end to end of it, but there was no exit. He looked over the side. A sheer hundred-foot drop to the gravel. A soft fluted whistle above him caught his ear. He looked up. Only a breath of wind in the moorings of that bloody balloon! But then a lunatic idea came to him, a flashback to one of the old Douglas Fairbanks films when the hero had swung across a wide hall by taking a flying leap at the chandelier. This helium balloon was strong enough to hold taut fifty feet of framed cotton strip bearing the warning sign! Why shouldn't it be powerful enough to bear the weight of a man?

Bond ran to the corner of the balustrade to which the mooring line was attached. He tested it. It was taut as a wire! From somewhere behind him there came a great clamour in the castle. Had the woman woken up? Holding on to the straining rope, he climbed on to the railing, cut a foothold for himself in the cotton banner and, grasping the mooring rope with his right hand, chopped downwards below him with Blofeld's sword and threw himself into space.

It worked! There was a light night breeze and he felt himself wafted gently away over the moonlit park, over the glittering, steaming lake, towards the sea. But he was rising, not falling! The helium sphere was not in the least worried by his weight! Then blue-and-yellow fire fluttered from the upper storey of the castle and an occasional angry wasp zipped past him. Bond's hands and feet were beginning to ache with the strain of holding on. Something hit him on the side of the head, the same side that was already sending out its throbbing message of pain. And that finished him. He knew it had! For now the whole black silhouette of the castle swayed in the moonlight and seemed to jig upwards and sideways and then slowly dissolve like an ice-cream cone in sunshine. The top storey crumbled first, then the next, and the next, and then, after a moment, a huge jet of orange fire shot up from hell towards the moon and a buffet of hot wind, followed by an echoing crack of thunder, hit Bond and made his balloon sway violently.

What was it all about? Bond didn't know or care. The pain in his head was his whole universe. Punctured by a bullet, the balloon was fast losing height. Below, the softly swelling sea offered a bed. Bond let go with hands and feet and plummeted down towards peace, towards the rippling feathers of some childhood dream of softness and escape from pain.

21

OBIT:

THE TIMES

COMMANDER JAMES BOND, C.M.G., R.N.V.R.

M writes:—

As your readers will have learned from earlier issues, a senior officer of the Ministry of Defence, Commander James Bond, C.M.G., R.N.V.R., is missing, believed killed, while on an official mission to Japan. It grieves me to have to report that hopes of his survival must now be abandoned. It therefore falls to my lot, as the Head of the Department he served so well, to give some account of this officer and of his outstanding services to his country.

James Bond was born of a Scottish father, Andrew Bond of Glencoe, and a Swiss mother, Monique Delacroix, from the Canton de Vaud. His father being a foreign representative of the Vickers armaments firm, his early education, from which he inherited a first-class command of French and German, was entirely abroad. When he was eleven years of age, both his parents were killed in a climbing accident in the Aiguilles Rouges above Chamonix, and the youth came under the guardianship of an aunt, since deceased, Miss Charmian Bond, and went to live with her at the quaintly named hamlet of Pett Bottom near Canterbury in Kent. There, in a small cottage hard by the attractive Duck Inn, his aunt, who must have been a most erudite and accomplished lady, completed his education for an English public school, and, at the age of twelve or thereabouts, he passed satisfactorily into Eton, for which College he had been entered at birth by his father. It must be admitted that his career at Eton was brief and undistinguished and, after only two halves, as a result, it pains me to record, of some alleged trouble with one of the boys' maids, his aunt was requested to remove him. She managed to obtain his transfer to Fettes, his father's old school. Here the atmosphere was somewhat Calvinistic, and both academic and athletic standards were rigorous. Nevertheless, though inclined to be solitary by nature, he established some firm friendships among the traditionally famous athletic circles at the school. By the time he left, at the early age of seventeen, he had twice fought for the school as a light-weight and had, in addition, founded the first serious judo class at an English public school. By now it was 1941 and, by claiming an age of nineteen and with the help of an old Vickers colleague of his father, he entered a branch of what was subsequently to become the Ministry of Defence. To serve the confidential nature of his duties, he was accorded the rank of lieutenant in the Special Branch of the R.N.V.R., and it is a measure of the satisfaction his services gave to his superiors that he ended the war with the rank of Commander. It was about this time that the writer became associated with certain aspects of the Ministry's work, and it was with much gratification that I accepted Commander Bond's post-war application to continue working for the Ministry in which, at the time of his lamented disappearance, he had risen to the rank of Principal Officer in the Civil Service.

The nature of Commander Bond's duties with the Ministry, which were, incidentally, recognized by the appointment of C.M.G. in 1954, must remain confidential, nay secret, but his colleagues at the Ministry will allow that he performed them with outstanding bravery and distinction, although occasionally, through an impetuous strain in his nature, with a streak of the foolhardy that brought him in conflict with higher authority. But he possessed what almost amounted to 'The Nelson Touch' in moments of the highest emergency, and he somehow contrived to escape more or less unscathed from the many adventurous paths down which his duties led him. The inevitable publicity, particularly in the foreign press, accorded some of these adventures, made him, much against his will, something of a public figure, with the inevitable result that a series of popular books came to be written around him by a personal friend and former colleague of James Bond. If the quality of these books, or their degree of veracity, had been any higher, the author would certainly have been prosecuted under the Official Secrets Act. It is a measure of the disdain in which these fictions are held at the Ministry, that action has not yet — I emphasize the qualification — been taken against the author and publisher of these high-flown and romanticized caricatures of episodes in the career of an outstanding public servant.

It only remains to conclude this brief *in memoriam* by assuring his friends that Commander Bond's last mission was one of supreme importance to the State. Although it now appears that, alas, he will not return from it, I have the authority of the highest quarters in the land to confirm that the mission proved one hundred per cent successful. It is no exaggeration to pronounce unequivocally that, through the recent valorous efforts of this one man, the Safety of the Realm has received mighty reassurance.

James Bond was briefly married in 1962, to Teresa, only daughter of Marc-Ange Draco, of Marseilles. The marriage ended in tragic circumstances that were reported in the Press at the time. There was no issue of the marriage and James Bond leaves, so far as I am aware, no relative living.

M.G. writes:

I was happy and proud to serve Commander Bond in a close capacity during the past three years at the Ministry of Defence. If indeed our fears for him are justified, may I suggest these simple words for his epitaph? Many of the junior staff here feel they represent his philosophy: 'I shall not waste my days in trying to prolong them. I shall use my time.'

22

SPARROWS' TEARS

WHEN KISSY SAW the figure, black-winged in its kimono, crash down into the sea, she sensed that it was her man, and she covered the two hundred yards from the base of the wall as fast as she had ever swum in her life. The tremendous impact with the water had at first knocked all the wind out of Bond, but the will to live, so nearly extinguished by the searing pain in his head, was revived by the new but recognizable enemy of the sea and, when Kissy got to him, he was struggling to free himself from the kimono.

At first he thought she was Blofeld and tried to strike out at her.

'It's Kissy,' she said urgently, 'Kissy Suzuki! Don't you remember?'

He didn't. He had no recollection of anything in the world but the face of his enemy and of the desperate urge to smash it. But his strength was going and finally, cursing feebly, he allowed her to manhandle him out of the kimono and paid heed to the voice that pleaded with him.

'Now follow me, Taro-san. When you get tired I will pull you with me. We are all trained in such rescue work.'

But, when she started off, Bond didn't follow her. Instead he swam feebly round and round like a wounded animal, in ever-increasing circles. She almost wept. What had happened to him? What had they done to him at the Castle of Death? Finally she stopped him and talked softly to him and he docilely allowed her to put her arms under his armpits and, with his head cradled between her breasts, she set off with the traditional backward leg-stroke.

It was an amazing swim for a girl — half a mile with currents to contend with and only the moon and an occasional glance over her shoulder to give her a bearing, but she achieved it and finally hauled Bond out of the water in her little cove and collapsed on the flat stones beside him.

She was awoken by a groan from Bond. He had been quietly sick and now sat with his head in his hands, looking blankly out to sea with the glazed eyes of a sleep-walker. When Kissy put an arm round his shoulders, he turned vaguely towards her. 'Who are you? How did I get here? What is this place?' He examined her more carefully. 'You're very pretty.'

Kissy looked at him keenly. She said, and a sudden plan of great glory blazed across her mind, 'You cannot remember anything? You do not remember who you are and where you came from?'

Bond passed a hand across his forehead, squeezed his eyes. 'Nothing,' he said wearily. 'Nothing except a man's face. I think he was dead. I think he was a bad man. What is your name? You must tell me everything.'

'My name is Kissy Suzuki and you are my lover. Your name is Taro Todoroki. We live on this island and go fishing together. It is a very good life. But can you walk a little? I must take you to where you live and get you some food and a doctor to see you. You have a terrible wound on the side of your head and there is a cut on your ribs. You must have fallen while you were climbing the cliffs after seagulls' eggs.' She stood up and held out her hands.

Bond took them and staggered to his feet. She held him by the hand and gently guided him along the path towards the Suzuki house. But she passed it and went on and up to the grove of dwarf maples and camellia bushes. She led him behind the Shinto shrine and into the cave. It was large and the earth floor was dry. She said, 'This is where you live. I live here with you. I had put away our bed things. I will go and fetch them and some food. Now lie down, my beloved, and rest and I will look after you. You are ill, but the doctor will make you well again.'

Bond did as he was told and was instantly asleep, the pain-free side of his head cradled on his arm.

Kissy ran off down the mountain, her heart singing. There was much to be done, much to be arranged, but now she had got her man back she was desperately determined to keep him.

It was almost dawn and her parents were awake. She whispered to them excitedly as she went about warming some milk and putting together a bundle of *futon*, her father's best kimono and a selection of Bond's washing things — nothing to remind him of his past. Her parents were used to her whims and her independence. Her father merely commented mildly that it would be all right if the *kannushi-san* gave his blessing, then, having washed the salt off herself and dressed in her own simple brown kimono, she scampered off up the hill to the cave.

Later, the Shinto priest received her gravely. He almost seemed to be expecting her. He held up his hand and spoke to the kneeling figure. 'Kissy-chan, I know what I know. The spawn of the devil is dead. So is his wife. The Castle of Death has been totally destroyed. These things were brought about as the Six Guardians foretold, by the man from across the sea. Where is he now?'

'In the cave behind the shrine, *kannushi-san*. He is gravely wounded. I love him. I wish to keep him and care for him. He remembers nothing of the past. I wish it to remain so, so that we may marry and he may become a son of Kuro for all time.'

'That will not be possible, my daughter. In due course he will recover and go off across the world to where he came from. And there will be special inquiries for him, from Fukuoka, perhaps even from Tokyo, for he is surely a man of renown in his own country.'

'But *kannushi-san*, if you so instruct the elders of Kuro, they will show these people *shiran-kao*, they will say they know nothing, that this man Todoroki left, swimming for the mainland, and has not been heard of since. Then the people will go away. All I want to do is to care for him and keep him for myself as long as I can. If the day comes when he wishes to leave, I will not hinder him. I will help him. He was happy here fishing with me and my David-bird. He told me so. When he recovers, I will see that he continues to be happy. Should not Kuro cherish and honour this hero who was brought to us by the gods? Would not the Six Guardians wish to keep him for a while? And have I not earned some small token for my humble efforts to help Todoroki-san and save his life?'

The priest sat silent for a while with his eyes closed. Then he looked down at the pleading face at his feet. He smiled. 'I will do what is possible, Kissy-chan. And now bring the doctor to me and then take him up to the cave so that he can tend this man's wounds. Then I will speak to the elders. But for many weeks you must be very discreet and the *gaijin* must not show himself. When all is quiet again, he may move back into the house of your parents and allow himself to be seen.'

The doctor knelt beside Bond in the cave and spread out on the ground a large map of the human head with the sections marked with figures and ideograms. His gentle fingers probed Bond's wound for signs of fracture, while Kissy knelt beside him and held one of Bond's sweating hands in both of hers. The doctor bent forward and, lifting the eyelids one by one, gazed deeply into the glazed eyes through a large reading-glass. On his instructions, Kissy ran for boiling water, and the doctor proceeded to clean the cut made by the bullet across the terrible swelling of the first wound caused by Bond's crash into the oubliette. Then he tapped sulpha dust into the wound and bound up the head neatly and expertly, put surgical plaster over the cut across the ribs and stood up and took Kissy outside the cave. 'He will live,' he said, 'but it may be months, even years before he regains his memory. It is particularly the temporal lobe of his brain, where the memory is stored, that has been damaged. For this, much education will be necessary. You will endeavour all the time to remind him about past things and places. Then isolated facts that he will recognize will turn into chains of association. He should undoubtedly be taken to Fukuoka for an X-ray, but I think there is no fracture and in any case the *kannushi-san* has ordained that he is to remain under your care and his presence on the island to be kept secret. I shall of course observe the instructions of the honourable *kannushi-san* and only visit him by different routes and at night. But there is much you will have to attend to for he must not be moved in any way for at least a week. Now listen carefully,' said the doctor, and gave her minute instructions which covered every aspect of feeding and nursing and left her to carry them out.

And so the days ran into weeks and the police came again and again from Fukuoka, and the official called Tanaka came from Tokyo and later a huge man who said he was from Australia arrived and he was the most difficult of all for Kissy to shake off. But the face of *shiran-kao* remained of stone and the island of Kuro kept its secret. James Bond's body gradually mended and Kissy took him out for walks at night. They also went for an occasional swim in the cove, where they played with David and she told him all the history of the Ama and of Kuro and expertly parried all his questions about the world outside the island.

Winter came, and the Ama had to stay ashore and turn their hands to mending nets and boats and working on the small-holdings on the mountain side, and Bond came back into the house and made himself useful with carpentry and odd jobs and with learning Japanese from Kissy. The glazed look went from his eyes, but they remained remote and faraway and every night he was puzzled by dreams of a quite different world of white people and big cities and half-remembered faces. But Kissy assured him that these were just nightmares such as she had, and that they had no meaning, and gradually Bond came to accept the little stone-and-wood house and the endless horizon of sea as his finite world. Kissy was careful to keep him away from the south coast of the island, and dreaded the day when fishing would begin again at the end of May and he would see the great black wall across the straits and memory might come flooding back.

The doctor was surprised by Bond's lack of progress and resigned himself to the conclusion that Bond's amnesia was total, but soon there was no cause for further visits because Bond's physical health and his apparently complete satisfaction with his lot showed that in every other respect he was totally recovered.

But there was one thing that greatly distressed Kissy. From the first night in the cave she had shared Bond's *futon* and, when he was well and back in the house, she waited every night for him to make love to her. But, while he kissed her occasionally and often held her hand, his body seemed totally unaware of her however much she pressed herself against him and even caressed him with her hands. Had the wound made him impotent? She consulted the doctor, but he said there could be no connection, although it was just possible that he had forgotten how to perform the act of love.

So one day Kissy Suzuki announced that she was going to take the weekly mailboat to Fukuoka to do some shopping and, in the big city, she found her way to the local sex-shop, called The Happy Shop, that is a feature of all self-respecting Japanese towns, and told her problem to the wicked-looking old greybeard behind the innocent counter containing nothing more viciously alluring than tonics and contraceptives. He asked her if she possessed five thousand yen, which is a lot of money, and when she said she did, he locked the street door and invited her to the back of the shop.

The sex merchant bent down and pulled out from beneath a bench what looked like a small wired rabbit-hutch. He put this on the bench and Kissy saw that it contained four large toads on a bed of moss. Next he produced a metal contraption that had the appearance of a hot-plate with a small wire cage in the middle. He carefully lifted out one of the toads and placed it inside the cage so that it squatted on the metal surface. Then he hauled a large car battery on to the bench, put it alongside the 'hot-plate' and attached wires from one to the other. Then he spoke some encouraging endearments to the toad and stood back.

The toad began to shiver slightly, and the crosses in its dark red eyes blazed angrily at Kissy as if it knew it was all her fault. The sex merchant, his head bent over the little cage, watched anxiously and then rubbed his hands with satisfaction as heavy beads of sweat broke out all over the toad's warty skin. He reached for an iron teaspoon and a small phial, gently raised the wire cage and very carefully scraped the sweat-beads off the toad's body and dripped the result into the phial. When he had finished, the phial contained about half a teaspoon of clear liquid. He corked it up and handed it to Kissy, who held it with reverence and great care as if it had been a fabulous jewel. Then the sex merchant disconnected the wires and put the toad, which seemed none the worse for its experience, back in its hutch and closed the top.

He turned to Kissy and bowed. 'When this valuable product is desired by a sincere customer I always ask them to witness the process of distillation. Otherwise they might harbour the unworthy thought that the phial contained only water from the tap. But you have now seen that this preparation is the authentic sweat of a toad. It is produced by giving the toad a mild electric shock. The toad suffered only temporary discomfort and it will be rewarded this evening with an extra portion of flies or crickets. And now,' he went to a cupboard and took out a small pill-box, 'here is powder of dried lizard. A combination of the two, inserted in your lover's food at the evening meal, should prove infallible. However, to excite his mind as well as his senses, for an extra thousand yen I can provide you with a most excellent pillow-book.'

'What is a pillow-book?'

The sex merchant went back to his cupboard and produced a cheaply bound and printed paper book with a plain cover. Kissy opened it. Her hand went to her mouth and she blushed furiously. But then, being a careful girl who didn't want to be cheated, she turned some more of the pages. They all contained outrageously pornographic close-up pictures, most faithfully engraved, of the love-act portrayed from every possible aspect. 'Very well,' she whispered. She handed back the book. 'Please wrap up everything carefully.' She took out her purse and began counting out the notes.

Out in the shop, the wicked-faced old man handed her the parcel and, bowing deeply, unlocked the door. Kissy gave a perfunctory bob in return and darted out of the shop down the street as if she had just made a pact with the devil. But by the time she went to catch the mailboat back to Kuro, she was hugging herself with excitement and pleasure and making up a story to explain away her acquisition of the book.

Bond was waiting for her on the jetty. It was the first day she had been away from him and he had missed her painfully. They talked happily as they walked hand-in-hand along the foreshore among the nets and boats, and the people smiled to see them, but looked through them instead of greeting them for had not the priest decreed that their *gaijin* hero did not officially exist? And the priest's edict was final.

Back at the house, Kissy went happily about preparing a highly spiced dish of *sukiyaki*, the national dish of beef stew. This was not only a great treat, for they seldom ate meat, but Kissy didn't know if her love-potions had any taste and it would be wise not to take any chances. When it was ready, with a trembling hand, she poured the brown powder and the liquid into Bond's portion and stirred it well. Then she brought the dishes in to where the family awaited, squatting on the *tatami* before the low table.

She watched surreptitiously as Bond devoured every scrap of his portion and wiped his plate clean with a pinch of rice and then, after warm compliments on her cooking, drank his tea and retired to their room. In the evenings, he usually sat mending nets or fishing-lines before going to bed. As she helped her mother wash up she wondered if he were doing so now!

Kissy spent a long time doing her hair and making herself pretty before, her heart beating like a captured bird, she joined him.

He looked up from the pillow-book and laughed. 'Kissy, where in God's name did you get this?'

She giggled. 'Oh that! I forgot to tell you. Some dreadful man tried to make up to me in one of the shops. He pressed that into my hand and made an assignation for this evening. I agreed just to get rid of him. It is what we call a pillow-book. Lovers use them. Aren't the pictures exciting?'

Bond threw off his kimono. He pointed to the soft *futon* on the floor. He said fiercely, 'Kissy, take off your clothes and lie down there. We'll start at page one.'

Winter slid into spring and fishing began again, but now Kissy dived naked like the other girls and Bond and the bird dived with her and there were good days and bad days. But the sun shone steadily and the sea was blue and wild irises covered the mountain side and everyone made a great fuss as the sprinkling of cherry trees burst into bloom, and Kissy wondered what moment to choose to tell Bond that she was going to have a baby and whether he would then propose marriage to her.

But one day, on the way down to the cove, Bond looked preoccupied and, when he asked her to wait before they put the boat out as he had something serious to talk to her about, her heart leaped and she sat down beside him on a flat rock and put her arms round him and waited.

Bond took a crumpled piece of paper out of his pocket and held it out to her, and she shivered with fear and knew what was coming. She took her arms from round him and looked at the paper. It was one of the rough squares of newspaper from the spike in the little lavatory. She always tore these squares herself and discarded any that contained words in English — just in case.

Bond pointed. 'Kissy, what is this word "Vladivostok"? What does it mean? It has some kind of a message for me. I connect it with a very big country. I believe the country is called Russia. Am I right?'

Kissy remembered her promise to the priest. She put her face in her hands. 'Yes, Taro-san. That is so.'

Bond pressed his fists to his eyes and squeezed. 'I have a feeling that I have had much to do with this Russia, that a lot of my past life was concerned with it. Could that be possible? I long so terribly to know where I came from before I came to Kuro. Will you help me, Kissy?'

Kissy took her hands from her face and looked at him. She said quietly, 'Yes, I will help you, my beloved.'

'Then I must go to this place Vladivostok, and perhaps it will awaken more memories and I can work my way back from there.'

'If you say so, my love. The mailboat goes to Fukuoka tomorrow. I will put you on a train there and give you money and full directions. It is advertised that one can go from the northern island, Hokkaido, to Sakhalin which is on the Russian mainland. Then you can no doubt make your way to Vladivostok. It is a great port to the south of Sakhalin. But you must take care, for the Russians are not friendly people.'

'Surely they would do no harm to a fisherman from Kuro?'

Kissy's heart choked her. She got up and walked slowly down to the boat. She pushed the boat down the pebbles into the water and waited, at her usual place in the stern, for him to get in and for his knees to clasp hers as they always did.

James Bond took his place and unshipped the oars, and the cormorant scrambled on board and perched imperiously in the bows. Bond measured where the rest of the fleet lay on the horizon and began to row.

Kissy smiled into his eyes and the sun shone on his back and, so far as James Bond was concerned, it was a beautiful day just like all the other days had been — without a cloud in the sky.

But then, of course, he didn't know that his name was James Bond. And, compared with the blazing significance to him of that single Russian word on the scrap of paper, his life on Kuro, his love for Kissy Suzuki, were, in Tiger's phrase, of as little account as sparrows' tears.

THE MAN WITH THE GOLDEN GUN

'. . . 007 was a good agent once. There's no reason why he shouldn't be a good agent again. Within limits, that is. After lunch, give me the file on Scaramanga. If we can get him fit again, that's the right-sized target for 007.'

The Chief of Staff protested, 'But that's suicide, sir! Even 007 could never take him.'

M. said coldly, 'What would 007 get for this morning's bit of work? Twenty years? As a minimum, I'd say. Better for him to fall on the battlefield. If he brings it off, he'll have won his spurs back again and we can all forget the past. Anyway, that's my decision.'

There was a knock on the door and the duty Medical Officer came into the room. M. bade him good afternoon and turned stiffly on his heel and walked out through the open door.

The Chief of Staff looked at the retreating back. He said under his breath, 'You cold-hearted bastard!'

I

'CAN I HELP YOU?'

THE SECRET SERVICE holds much that is kept secret even from very senior officers in the organization. Only M. and his Chief of Staff know absolutely everything there is to know. The latter is responsible for keeping the Top Secret record known as 'The War Book' so that, in the event of the death of both of them, the whole story, apart from what is available to individual Sections and Stations, would be available to their successors.

One thing that James Bond, for instance, didn't know was the machinery at Headquarters for dealing with the public, whether friendly or otherwise — drunks, lunatics, bona fide applications to join the Service, and enemy agents with plans for penetration or even assassination.

On the cold, clear morning in November he was to see the careful cog-wheels in motion.

The girl at the switchboard at the Ministry of Defence flicked the switch to 'Hold' and said to her neighbour, 'It's another nut who says he's James Bond. Even knows his code number. Says he wants to speak to M. personally.'

The senior girl shrugged. The switchboard had had quite a few such calls since, a year before, James Bond's death on a mission to Japan had been announced in the Press. There had even been one pestiferous woman who, at every full moon, passed on messages from Bond from Uranus where it seemed he had got stuck while awaiting entry into heaven. She said, 'Put him through to Liaison, Pat.'

The Liaison Section was the first cog in the machine, the first sieve. The operator got back on the line: 'Just a moment, sir. I'll put you on to an officer who may be able to help you.'

James Bond, sitting on the edge of his bed, said, 'Thank you.'

He had expected some delay before he could establish his identity. He had been warned to expect it by the charming

'Colonel Boris' who had been in charge of him for the past few months after he had finished his treatment in the luxurious Institute on the Nevsky Prospekt in Leningrad. A man's voice came on the line. 'Captain Walker speaking. Can I help you?'

James Bond spoke slowly and clearly. 'This is Commander James Bond speaking. Number 007. Would you put me through to M., or his secretary, Miss Moneypenny. I want to make an appointment.'

Captain Walker pressed two buttons on the side of his telephone. One of them switched on a tape recorder for the use of his department, the other alerted one of the duty officers in the Action Room of the Special Branch at Scotland Yard that he should listen to the conversation, trace the call, and at once put a tail on the caller. It was now up to Captain Walker, who was in fact an extremely bright ex-prisoner-of-war interrogator from Military Intelligence, to keep the subject talking for as near five minutes as possible. He said, 'I'm afraid I don't know either of these two people. Are you sure you've got the right number?'

James Bond patiently repeated the Regent number which was the main outside line for the Secret Service. Together with so much else, he had forgotten it, but Colonel Boris had known it and had made him write it down among the small print on the front page of his forged British passport that said his name was Frank Westmacott, company director.

'Yes,' said Captain Walker sympathetically. 'We seem to have got that part of it right. But I'm afraid I can't place these people you want to talk to. Who exactly are they? This Mr Em, for instance. I don't think we've got anyone of that name at the Ministry.'

'Do you want me to spell it out? You realize this is an open line?'

Captain Walker was rather impressed by the confidence in the speaker's voice. He pressed another button and, so that Bond would hear it, a telephone bell rang. He said, 'Hang on a moment, would you? There's someone on my other line.' Captain Walker got on to the head of his Section. 'Sorry, sir. I've got a chap on who says he's James Bond and wants to talk to M. I know it sounds crazy and I've gone through the usual motions with the Special Branch and so on, but would you mind listening for a minute? Thank you, sir.'

Two rooms away a harassed man, who was the Chief Security Officer for the Secret Service, said 'Blast!' and pressed a switch. A microphone on his desk came to life. The Chief Security Officer sat very still. He badly needed a cigarette, but his room was now 'live' to Captain Walker and to the lunatic who called himself 'James Bond'. Captain Walker's voice came over at full strength. 'I'm so sorry. Now then. This man Mr Em you want to talk to. I'm sure we needn't worry about security. Could you be more specific?'

James Bond frowned. He didn't know that he had frowned and he wouldn't have been able to explain why he had done so. He said, and lowered his voice, again inexplicably, 'Admiral Sir Miles Messervy. He is head of a department in your Ministry. The number of his room used to be twelve on the eighth floor. He used to have a secretary called Miss Moneypenny. Good-looking girl. Brunette. Shall I give you the Chief of Staff's name? No? Well let's see, it's Wednesday. Shall I tell you what'll be the main dish on the menu in the canteen? It should be steak-and-kidney pudding.'

The Chief Security Officer picked up the direct telephone to Captain Walker. Captain Walker said to James Bond, 'Damn! There's the other telephone again. Shan't be a minute.' He picked up the green telephone. 'Yes, sir?'

'I don't like that bit about the steak-and-kidney pudding. Pass him on to the Hard Man. No. Cancel that. Make it the Soft. There was always something odd about 007's death. No body. No solid evidence. And the people on that Japanese island always seemed to me to be playing it pretty close to the chest. The Stone Face act. It's just possible. Keep me informed, would you?'

Captain Walker got back to James Bond. 'Sorry about that. It's being a busy day. Now then, this inquiry of yours. Afraid I can't help you myself. Not my part of the Ministry. The man you want is Major Townsend. He should be able to locate this man you want to see. Got a pencil? It's No. 44 Kensington Cloisters. Got that? Kensington double five double five. Give me ten minutes and I'll have a word with him and see if he can help. All right?'

James Bond said dully, 'That's very kind of you.' He put down the telephone. He waited exactly ten minutes and picked up the receiver and asked for the number.

James Bond was staying at the Ritz Hotel. Colonel Boris had told him to do so. Bond's file in the K.G.B. Archive described him as a high-liver, so, on arrival in London, he must stick to the K.G.B. image of the high life. Bond went down in the lift to the Arlington Street entrance. A man at the news-stand got a good profile of him with a buttonhole Minox. When Bond went down the shallow steps to the street and asked the commissionaire for a taxi, a canonflex with a telescopic lens clicked away busily from a Red Roses laundry van at the neighbouring goods entrance and, in due course, the same van followed Bond's taxi while a man inside the van reported briefly to the Action Room of the Special Branch.

No. 44 Kensington Cloisters was a dull Victorian mansion in grimy red brick. It had been chosen for its purpose because it had once been the headquarters of the Empire League for Noise Abatement, and its entrance still bore the brass plate of this long-defunct organization, the empty shell of which had been purchased by the Secret Service through the Commonwealth Relations Office. It also had a spacious old-fashioned basement, re-equipped as detention cells, and a rear exit into a quiet mews.

The Red Roses laundry van watched the front door shut behind James Bond and then moved off at a sedate speed to its garage not far from Scotland Yard while the process of developing the canonflex film went on in its interior.

'Appointment with Major Townsend,' said Bond.

'Yes. He's expecting you, sir. Shall I take your raincoat?' The powerful-looking doorman put the coat on a coat-hanger and hung it up on one of a row of hooks beside the door. As soon as Bond was safely closeted with Major Townsend, the coat would go swiftly to the laboratory on the first floor where its provenance would be established from an examination of the fabric. Pocket dust would be removed for more leisurely research. 'Would you follow me, sir?'

It was a narrow corridor of freshly painted clapboard with a tall, single window which concealed the Fluoroscope triggered automatically from beneath the ugly patterned carpet. The findings of its X-ray eye would be fed into the laboratory above the passage. The passage ended in two facing doors marked 'A' and 'B'. The doorman knocked on Room B and stood aside for Bond to enter.

It was a pleasant, very light room, close-carpeted in dove-grey Wilton. The military prints on the cream walls were expensively framed. A small, bright fire burned under an Adam mantelpiece which bore a number of silver trophies and two photographs in leather frames — one of a nice-looking woman and the other of three nice-looking children. There was a central table with a bowl of flowers and two comfortable club chairs on either side of the fire. No desk or filing cabinets, nothing official-looking. A tall man, as pleasant as the room, got up from the far chair, dropped *The Times* on the carpet beside it, and came forward with a welcoming smile. He held out a firm, dry hand.

This was the Soft Man.

'Come in. Come in. Take a pew. Cigarette? Not the ones I seem to remember you favour. Just the good old Senior Service.'

Major Townsend had carefully prepared the loaded remark — a reference to Bond's liking for the Morland Specials with the three gold rings. He noted Bond's apparent lack of comprehension. Bond took a cigarette and accepted a light. They sat down facing one another. Major Townsend crossed his legs comfortably. Bond sat up straight. Major Townsend said, 'Well now. How can I help you?'

Across the corridor, in Room A, a cold Office-of-Works cube with no furniture but a hissing gas fire, an ugly desk with two facing wooden chairs under the naked neon, Bond's reception by the Hard Man, the ex-police superintendent ('ex' because of a brutality case in Glasgow for which he had taken the rap), would have been very different. There, the man who went under the name of Mr Robson would have given him the full intimidation treatment — harsh, bullying interrogation, threats of imprisonment for false representation and God knows what else, and, perhaps, if he had shown signs of hostility or developing a nuisance value, a little judicious roughing-up in the basement.

Such was the ultimate sieve which sorted out the wheat from the chaff from those members of the public who desired access to 'The Secret Service'. There were other people in the building who dealt with the letters. Those written in pencil or in multi-coloured inks, and those enclosing a photograph, remained unanswered. Those which threatened or were litigious were referred to the Special Branch. The solid, serious ones were passed, with a comment from the best graphologist in the business, to the Liaison Section at Headquarters for 'further action'. Parcels went automatically, and fast, to the Bomb Disposal Squad at Knightsbridge Barracks. The eye of the needle was narrow. On the whole, it discriminated appropriately. It was an expensive set-up, but it is the first duty of a Secret Service to remain not only secret but secure.

There was no reason why James Bond, who had always been on the operative side of the business, should know anything about the entrails of the Service, any more than he should have understood the mysteries of the plumbing or electricity supply of his flat in Chelsea, or the working of his own kidneys. Colonel Boris, however, had known the whole routine. The secret services of all the great powers know the public face of their opponents, and Colonel Boris had very accurately described the treatment that James Bond must expect before he was 'cleared' and was allowed access to the office of his former chief.

So now James Bond paused before he replied to Major Townsend's question about how he could be of help. He looked at the Soft Man and then into the fire. He added up the accuracy of the description he had been given of Major Townsend's appearance and, before he said what he had been told to say, he gave Colonel Boris ninety out of a hundred. The big, friendly face, the wide-apart, pale brown eyes, bracketed by the wrinkles of a million smiles, the military moustache, the rimless monocle dangling from a thin black cord, the brushed-back, thinning sandy hair, the immaculate double-breasted blue suit, stiff white collar and Brigade tie — it was all there. But what Colonel Boris hadn't said was that the friendly eyes were as cold and steady as gun barrels and that the lips were thin and scholarly.

James Bond said patiently: 'It's really quite simple. I'm who I say I am. I'm doing what I naturally would do, and that's report back to M.'

'Quite. But you must realize' (a sympathetic smile) 'that you've been out of contact for nearly a year. You've been officially posted as "missing believed killed". Your obituary has even appeared in *The Times*. Have you any evidence of identity? I admit that you look very much like your photographs, but you must see that we have to be very sure before we pass you on up the ladder.'

'A Miss Mary Goodnight was my secretary. She'd recognize me all right. So would dozens of other people at H.Q.'

'Miss Goodnight's been posted abroad. Can you give me a brief description of H.Q., just the main geography?'

Bond did so.

'Right. Now, who was a Miss Maria Freudenstadt?'

'Was?'

'Yes, she's dead.'

'Thought she wouldn't last long. She was a double, working for K.G.B. Section 100 controlled her. I wouldn't get any thanks for telling you any more.'

Major Townsend had been primed with this very secret top question. He had been given the answer, more or less as Bond had put it. This was the clincher. This *had* to be James Bond. 'Well, we're getting on fine. Now, it only remains to find out where you've come from and where you've been all these months and I won't keep you any longer.'

'Sorry. I can only tell that to M. personally.'

'I see.' Major Townsend put on a thoughtful expression. 'Well, just let me make a telephone call or two and I'll see what can be done.' He got to his feet. 'Seen today's *Times*?' He picked it up and handed it to Bond. It had been specially treated to give good prints. Bond took it. 'Shan't be long.'

Major Townsend shut the door behind him and went across the passage and through the door marked 'A' where he knew that 'Mr Robson' would be alone. 'Sorry to bother you, Fred. Can I use your scrambler?' The chunky man behind the desk grunted through the stem of his pipe and remained bent over the midday *Evening Standard* racing news.

Major Townsend picked up the green receiver and was put through to the Laboratory. 'Major Townsend speaking. Any comment?' He listened, carefully, said 'thank you', and got through to the Chief Security Officer at Headquarters. 'Well, sir, I think it must be 007. Bit thinner than his photographs. I'll be giving you his prints as soon as he's gone. Wearing his usual rig — dark blue single-breasted suit, white shirt, thin black knitted silk tie, black casuals — but they all look brand new. Raincoat bought yesterday from Burberry's. Got the Freudenstadt question right, but says he won't say anything about himself except to M. personally. But whoever he is, I don't like it much. He fluffed on his special cigarettes. He's got an odd sort of glazed, sort of far-away look, and the "Scope" shows that he's carrying a gun in his right-hand coat pocket — curious sort of contraption, doesn't seem to have got a butt to it. I'd say he's a sick man. I wouldn't personally recommend that M. should see him, but I wouldn't know how we're to get him to talk unless he does.' He paused. 'Very good, sir. I'll stay by the telephone. I'm on Mr Robson's extension.'

There was silence in the room. The two men didn't get on well together. Major Townsend gazed into the gas fire, wondering about the man next door. The telephone burred. 'Yes, sir? Very good, sir. Would your secretary send along a car from the pool? Thank you, sir.'

Bond was sitting in the same upright posture, *The Times* still unopened in his hand. Major Townsend said cheerfully, 'Well, that's fixed. Message from M. that he's tremendously relieved you're all right and he'll be free in about half an hour. Car should be here in ten minutes or so. And the Chief of Staff says he hopes you'll be free for lunch afterwards.'

James Bond smiled for the first time. It was a thin smile which didn't light up his eyes. He said, 'That's very kind of him. Would you tell him I'm afraid I shan't be free.'

2

ATTENTAT!

THE CHIEF OF STAFF stood in front of M.'s desk and said firmly, 'I really wouldn't do it, sir. I can see him, or someone else can. I don't like the smell of it at all. I think 007's round the bend. There's no doubt it's him all right. The prints have just been confirmed by Chief of Security. And the pictures are all right — and the recording of his voice. But there are too many things that don't add up. This forged passport we found in his room at the Ritz, for instance. All right. So he wanted to come back into the country quietly. But it's too good a job. Typical K.G.B. sample. And the last entry is West Germany, day before yesterday. Why didn't he report to Station B or W? Both those Heads of Station are friends of his, particularly 016 in Berlin. And why didn't he go and have a look at his flat? He's got some sort of a housekeeper there, Scots woman called May, who's always sworn he was still alive and has kept the place going on her savings. The Ritz is sort of "stage" Bond. And these new clothes. Why did he have to bother? Doesn't matter what he was wearing when he came in through Dover. Normal thing, if he was in rags, would have been to give me a ring — he had my home number — and get me to fix him up. Have a few drinks and run over his story and then report here. Instead of that we've got this typical penetration approach and Security worried as hell.'

The Chief of Staff paused. He knew he wasn't getting through. As soon as he had begun, M. had swivelled his chair sideways and had remained, occasionally sucking at an unlighted pipe, gazing moodily out through the window at the jagged skyline of London. Obstinately, the Chief of Staff concluded, 'Do you think you could leave this one to me, sir? I can get hold of Sir James Molony in no time and have 007 put into The Park for observation and treatment. It'll all be done very gently. V.I.P. handling and so on. I can say you've been called to the

Cabinet or something. Security says 007's looking a bit thin. Build him up. Convalescence and all that. That can be the excuse. If he cuts up rough, we can always give him some dope. He's a good friend of mine. He won't hold it against us. He obviously needs to be got back in the groove — if we can do it, that is.'

M. slowly swivelled his chair round. He looked up at the tired, worried face that showed the strain of being the equivalent of Number Two in the Secret Service for ten years and more. M. smiled. 'Thank you, Chief of Staff. But I'm afraid it's not as easy as all that. I sent 007 out on his last job to shake him out of his domestic worries. You remember how it all came about. Well, we had no idea that what seemed a fairly peaceful mission was going to end up in a pitched battle with Blofeld. Or that 007 was going to vanish off the face of the earth for a year. Now we've got to know what happened during that year. And 007's quite right. I sent him out on that mission and he's got every right to report back to me personally. I know 007. He's a stubborn fellow. If he says he won't tell anyone else, he won't. Of course I want to hear what happened to him. You'll listen in. Have a couple of good men at hand. If he turns rough, come and get him. As for his gun' — M. gestured vaguely at the ceiling — 'I can look after that. Have you tested the damned thing?'

'Yes, sir. It works all right. But . . .'

M. held up a hand. 'Sorry, Chief of Staff. It's an order.' A light winked on the intercom. 'That'll be him. Send him straight in, would you?'

'Very good, sir.' The Chief of Staff went out and closed the door.

James Bond was standing smiling vaguely down at Miss Moneypenny. She looked distraught. When James Bond shifted his gaze and said 'Hullo, Bill' he still wore the same distant smile. He didn't hold out his hand. Bill Tanner said, with a heartiness that rang with a terrible falsity in his ears, 'Hullo, James. Long time no see.' At the same time, out of the corner of his eye, he saw Miss Moneypenny give a quick, emphatic shake of the head. He looked her straight in the eyes. 'M. would like to see 007 straight away.'

Miss Moneypenny lied desperately: 'You know M.'s got a Chiefs of Staff meeting at the Cabinet Office in five minutes?'

'Yes. He says you must somehow get him out of it.' The Chief of Staff turned to James Bond. 'Okay, James. Go ahead. Sorry you can't manage lunch. Come and have a gossip after M.'s finished with you.'

Bond said, 'That'll be fine.' He squared his shoulders and walked through the door over which the red light was already burning.

Miss Moneypenny buried her face in her hands. 'Oh, Bill!' she said desperately. 'There's something wrong with him. I'm frightened.'

Bill Tanner said, 'Take it easy, Penny. I'm going to do what I can.' He walked quickly into his office and shut the door. He went over to his desk and pressed a switch. M.'s voice came into the room: 'Hullo, James. Wonderful to have you back. Take a seat and tell me all about it.'

Bill Tanner picked up the office telephone and asked for Head of Security.

James Bond took his usual place across the desk from M. A storm of memories whirled through his consciousness like badly cut film on a projector that had gone crazy. Bond closed his mind to the storm. He must concentrate on what he had to say, and do, and on nothing else.

'I'm afraid there's a lot I still can't remember, sir. I got a bang on the head' (he touched his right temple) 'somewhere along the line on that job you sent me to do in Japan. Then there's a blank until I got picked up by the police on the waterfront at Vladivostok. No idea how I got there. They roughed me up a bit and in the process I must have got another bang on the head because suddenly I remembered who I was and that I wasn't a Japanese fisherman which was what I thought I was. So then of course the police passed me on to the local branch of the K.G.B. — it's a big grey building on the Morskaya Ulitsa facing the harbour near the railway station, by the way — and when they belinographed my prints to Moscow there was a lot of excitement and they flew me there from the military airfield just north of the town at Vtoraya Rechka and spent weeks interrogating me — or trying to, rather, because I couldn't remember anything except when they prompted me with something they knew themselves and then I could give them a few hazy details to add to their knowledge. Very frustrating for them.'

'Very,' commented M. A small frown had gathered between

his eyes. 'And you told them everything you could? Wasn't that rather, er, generous of you?'

'They were very nice to me in every way, sir. It seemed the least I could do. There was this Institute place in Leningrad. They gave me V.I.P. treatment. Top brain-specialists and everything. They didn't seem to hold it against me that I'd been working against them for most of my life. And other people came and talked to me very reasonably about the political situation and so forth. The need for East and West to work together for world peace. They made clear a lot of things that hadn't occurred to me before. They quite convinced me.' Bond looked obstinately across the table into the clear blue sailor's eyes that now held a red spark of anger. 'I don't suppose you understand what I mean, sir. You've been making war against someone or other all your life. You're doing so at this moment. And for most of my adult life you've used me as a tool. Fortunately that's all over now.'

M. said fiercely, 'It certainly is. I suppose among other things you've forgotten is reading reports of our P.O.W.s in the Korean war who were brainwashed by the Chinese. If the Russians are so keen on peace, what do they need the K.G.B. for? At the last estimate, that was about one hundred thousand men and women "making war" as you call it against us and other countries. This is the organization that was so charming to you in Leningrad. Did they happen to mention the murder of Horcher and Stutz in Munich last month?'

'Oh yes, sir.' Bond's voice was patient, equable. 'They have to defend themselves against the secret services of the West. If you would demobilize all this,' Bond waved a hand, 'they would be only too delighted to scrap the K.G.B. They were quite open about it all.'

'And the same thing applies to their two hundred divisions and their U-boat fleet and their I.C.B.M.s, I suppose?' M.'s voice rasped.

'Of course, sir.'

'Well, if you found these people so reasonable and charming, why didn't you stay there? Others have. Burgess is dead, but you could have chummed up with Maclean.'

'We thought it more important that I should come back and fight for peace here, sir. You and your agents have taught me certain skills for use in the underground war. It was explained to me how these skills could be used in the cause of peace.'

James Bond's hand moved nonchalantly to his right-hand coat pocket. M., with equal casualness, shifted his chair back from his desk. His left hand felt for the button under the arm of the chair.

'For instance?' said M. quietly, knowing that death had walked into the room and was standing beside him and that this was an invitation for death to take his place in the chair.

James Bond had become tense. There was a whiteness round his lips. The blue-grey eyes still stared blankly, almost unseeingly at M. The words rang out harshly, as if forced out of him by some inner compulsion. 'It would be a start if the warmongers could be eliminated, sir. This is for number one on the list.'

The hand, snub-nosed with black metal, flashed out of the pocket, but, even as the poison hissed down the barrel of the bulb-butted pistol, the great sheet of Armourplate glass hurtled down from the baffled slit in the ceiling and, with a last sigh of hydraulics, braked to the floor. The jet of viscous brown fluid splashed harmlessly into its centre and trickled slowly down, distorting M.'s face and the arm he had automatically thrown up for additional protection.

The Chief of Staff had burst into the room, followed by the Head of Security. They threw themselves on James Bond. Even as they seized his arms, his head fell forward on his chest and he would have slid from his chair to the ground if they hadn't supported him. They hauled him to his feet. He was in a dead faint. The Head of Security sniffed. 'Cyanide,' he said curtly. 'We must all get out of here. And bloody quick!' (The emergency had snuffed out Headquarters 'manners'.) The pistol lay on the carpet where it had fallen. He kicked it away. He said to M., who had walked out from behind his glass shield, 'Would you mind leaving the room, sir? Quickly. I'll have this cleaned up during the lunch hour.' It was an order. M. went to the open door. Miss Moneypenny stood with her clenched hand up to her mouth. She watched with horror as James Bond's supine body was hauled out and, the heels of its shoes leaving tracks on the carpet, taken into the Chief of Staff's room.

M. said sharply, 'Close that door, Miss Moneypenny. Get the duty M.O. up right away. Come along, girl! Don't just stand there gawking! And not a word of this to anyone. Understood?'

Miss Moneypenny pulled herself back from the edge of hysterics. She said an automatic 'Yes, sir', pulled the door shut and reached for the inter-office telephone.

M. walked across and into the Chief of Staff's office and closed the door. Head of Security was on his knees beside Bond. He had loosened his tie and collar button and was feeling his pulse. Bond's face was white and bathed in sweat. His breathing was a desperate rattle, as if he had just run a race. M. looked briefly down at him and then, his face hidden from the others, at the wall beyond the body. He turned to the Chief of Staff. He said briskly, 'Well, that's that. My predecessor died in that chair. Then it was a simple bullet, but from much the same sort of a crazed officer. One can't legislate against the lunatic. But the Office of Works certainly did a good job with that gadget. Now then, Chief of Staff. This is of course to go no further. Get Sir James Molony as soon as you can and have 007 taken down to The Park. Ambulance, surreptitious guard. I'll explain things to Sir James this afternoon. Briefly, as you heard, the K.G.B. got hold of him. Brainwashed him. He was already a sick man. Amnesia of some kind. I'll tell you all I know later. Have his things collected from the Ritz and his bill paid. And put something out to the Press Association. Something on these lines: "The Ministry of Defence is pleased," no, say delighted, "to announce that Commander James Bond etc., who was posted as missing, believed killed while on a mission to Japan last November, has returned to this country after a hazardous journey across the Soviet Union which is expected to yield much valuable information. Commander Bond's health has inevitably suffered from his experiences and he is convalescing under medical supervision." ' M. smiled frostily. 'That bit about information'll give no joy to Comrade Semichastny and his troops. And add a "D" Notice to editors: "It is particularly requested, for security reasons, that the minimum of speculation or comment be added to the above communiqué and that no attempts be made to trace Commander Bond's whereabouts." All right?'

Bill Tanner had been writing furiously to keep up with M. He looked up from his scratch pad, bewildered. 'But aren't you going to make any charges, sir? After all, treason and attempted murder . . . I mean, not even a court martial?'

'Certainly not.' M.'s voice was gruff. '007 was a sick man.

Not responsible for his actions. If one can brainwash a man, presumably one can un-brainwash him. If anyone can, Sir James can. Put him back on half pay for the time being, in his old Section. And see he gets full back pay and allowances for the past year. If the K.G.B. has the nerve to throw one of my best men at me, I have the nerve to throw him back at them. 007 was a good agent once. There's no reason why he shouldn't be a good agent again. Within limits, that is. After lunch, give me the file on Scaramanga. If we can get him fit again, that's the right-sized target for 007.'

The Chief of Staff protested, 'But that's suicide, sir! Even 007 could never take him.'

M. said coldly, 'What would 007 get for this morning's bit of work? Twenty years? As a minimum, I'd say. Better for him to fall on the battlefield. If he brings it off, he'll have won his spurs back again and we can all forget the past. Anyway, that's my decision.'

There was a knock on the door and the duty Medical Officer came into the room. M. bade him good afternoon and turned stiffly on his heel and walked out through the open door.

The Chief of Staff looked at the retreating back. He said, under his breath, 'You cold-hearted bastard!' Then, with his usual minute thoroughness and sense of duty, he set about the tasks he had been given. His not to reason why!

3

'PISTOLS' SCARAMANGA

At Blades, M. ate his usual meagre luncheon — a grilled Dover sole followed by the ripest spoonful he could gouge from the club Stilton. And as usual he sat by himself in one of the window seats and barricaded himself behind *The Times*, occasionally turning a page to demonstrate that he was reading it, which, in fact, he wasn't. But Porterfield commented to the head waitress, Lily, a handsome, much-loved ornament of the club, that 'there's something wrong with the old man today. Or maybe not exactly wrong, but there's something up with him.' Porterfield prided himself on being something of an amateur psychologist. As head waiter, and father confessor to many of the members, he knew a lot about all of them and liked to think he knew everything, so that, in the tradition of incomparable servants, he could anticipate their wishes and their moods. Now, standing with Lily in a quiet moment behind the finest cold buffet on display at that date anywhere in the world, he explained himself. 'You know that terrible stuff Sir Miles always drinks? That Algerian red wine that the wine committee won't even allow on the wine list. They only have it in the club to please Sir Miles. Well, he explained to me once that in the navy they used to call it "The Infuriator" because if you drank too much of it, it seems that it used to put you into a rage. Well now, in the ten years that I've had the pleasure of looking after Sir Miles, he's never ordered more than half a carafe of the stuff.' Porterfield's benign, almost priestly countenance assumed an expression of theatrical solemnity as if he had read something really terrible in the tea leaves. 'Then what happens today?' Lily clasped her hands tensely and bent her head fractionally closer to get the full impact of the news. 'The old man says, "Porterfield. A bottle of Infuriator. You understand? A full bottle!" So of course I didn't say anything but went off and brought it to him. But you mark my words, Lily,' he noticed a lifted hand down the long room and moved off, 'there's something hit Sir Miles hard this morning and no mistake.'

M. sent for his bill. As usual he paid, whatever the amount of the bill, with a five-pound note for the pleasure of receiving in change crisp new pound notes, new silver and gleaming copper pennies, for it is the custom at Blades to give its members only freshly minted money. Porterfield pulled back his table and M. walked quickly to the door, acknowledging the occasional greeting with a preoccupied nod and a brief lifting of the hand. It was two o'clock. The old black Phantom Rolls took him quietly and quickly northwards through Berkeley Square, across Oxford Street and via Wigmore Street into Regent's Park. M. didn't look out at the passing scene. He sat stiffly in the back, his bowler hat squarely set on the middle of his head, and gazed unseeing at the back of the chauffeur's head with hooded, brooding eyes.

For the hundredth time, since he had left his office that morning, he assured himself that his decision was right. If James Bond could be straightened out, and M. was certain that that supreme neurologist, Sir James Molony, could bring it off, it would be ridiculous to reassign him to normal staff duties in the Double-O Section. The past could be forgiven, but not forgotten — except with the passage of time. It would be most irksome for those in the know to have Bond moving about Headquarters as if nothing had happened. It would be doubly embarrassing for M. to have to face Bond across that desk. And James Bond, if aimed straight at a known target — M. put it in the language of battleships — was a supremely effective firing-piece. Well, the target was there and it desperately demanded destruction. Bond had accused M. of using him as a tool. Naturally. Every officer in the Service was a tool for one secret purpose or another. The problem on hand could only be solved by a killing. James Bond would not possess the Double-O prefix if he had not high talents, frequently proved, as a gunman. So be it! In exchange for the happenings of that morning, in expiation of them, Bond must prove himself at his old skills. If he succeeded, he would have regained his previous status. If he failed, well, it would be a death for which he would be honoured. Win or lose, the plan would solve a vast array of problems. M. closed his mind once and for all on his decision. He got out of the car and went up in the lift to the eighth floor and along the corridor, smelling the smell of some unknown disinfectant more and more powerfully as he approached his office.

Instead of using his key to the private entrance at the end of the corridor M. turned right through Miss Moneypenny's door. She was sitting in her usual place, typing away at the usual routine correspondence. She got to her feet.

'What's this dreadful stink, Miss Moneypenny?'

'I don't know what it's called, sir. Head of Security brought along a squad from Chemical Warfare at the War Office. He says your office is all right to use again but to keep the windows open for a while. So I've turned on the heating. Chief of Staff isn't back from lunch yet, but he told me to tell you that everything you wanted done is under way. Sir James is operating until four but will expect your call after that. Here's the file you wanted, sir.'

M. took the brown folder with the red Top Secret star in its top right-hand corner. 'How's 007? Did he come round all right?'

Miss Moneypenny's face was expressionless. 'I gather so, sir. The M.O. gave him a sedative of some kind and he was taken off on a stretcher during the lunch hour. He was covered up. They took him down in the service lift to the garage. I haven't had any inquiries.'

'Good. Well, bring me in the signals, would you. There's been a lot of time wasted today on all these domestic excitements.' Bearing the file M. went through the door into his office. Miss Moneypenny brought in the signals and stood dutifully beside him while he went through them, occasionally dictating a comment or a query. She looked down at the bowed, iron-grey head with the bald patch polished for years by a succession of naval caps and wondered, as she had wondered so often over the past ten years, whether she loved or hated this man. One thing was certain. She respected him more than any man she had known or had read of.

M. handed her the file. 'Thank you. Now just give me a quarter of an hour, and then I'll see whoever wants me. The call to Sir James has priority of course.'

M. opend the brown folder, reached for his pipe and began absent-mindedly filling it as he glanced through the list of subsidiary files to see if there was any other docket he immediately needed. Then he set a match to his pipe and settled back in his chair and read:

'FRANCISCO (PACO) "PISTOLS" SCARAMANGA.' And underneath, in lower-case type, 'Free-lance assassin mainly under K.G.B. control through D.S.S., Havana, Cuba, but often as an independent operator for other organizations, in the Caribbean and Central American states. Has caused widespread damage, particularly to the S.S., but also to C.I.A. and other friendly services, by murder and scientific maiming, since 1959, the year when Castro came to power and which seems also to have been the trigger for Scaramanga's operations. Is widely feared and admired in said territory throughout which he appears, despite police precautions, to have complete freedom of access. Has thus become something of a local myth and is known in his "territory" as "The Man with the Golden Gun" — a reference to his main weapon which is a gold-plated, long-barrelled, single-action Colt. 45. He uses special bullets with a heavy, soft (24 ct) gold core jacketed with silver and cross-cut at the tip, on the dum-dum principle, for maximum wounding effect. Himself loads and artifices this ammunition. Is responsible for the death of 267 (British Guiana), 398 (Trinidad), 943 (Jamaica) and 768 and 742 (Havana) and for the maiming and subsequent retirement from the S.S., of 098, Area Inspection Officer, by bullet wounds in both knees. (See above references in Central Records for Scaramanga's victims in Martinique, Haiti and Panama.)

'DESCRIPTION: Age about 35. Height 6 ft. 3 in. Slim and fit. Eyes, light brown. Hair reddish in a crew cut. Long sideburns. Gaunt, sombre face with thin "pencil" moustache, brownish. Ears very flat to the head. Ambidextrous. Hands very large and powerful and immaculately manicured. Distinguishing marks: a third nipple about two inches below his left breast. (N.B. in Voodoo and allied local cults this is considered a sign of invulnerability and great sexual prowess.) Is an insatiable but indiscriminate womanizer who invariably has sexual intercourse shortly before a killing in the belief that it improves his "eye". (N.B. a belief shared by many professional lawn tennis players, golfers, gun and rifle marksmen and others.)

'ORIGINS: A relative of the Catalan family of circus managers of the same name with whom he spent his youth. Self-educated. At the age of 16, after the incident described below, emigrated illegally to the United States where he lived a life of petty crime on the fringes of the gangs until he graduated as a full-time gunman for the "Spangled Mob" in Nevada with the cover of pit-boy in the casino of the Tiara Hotel in Las Vegas where in fact he acted as executioner of cheats and other transgressors within and outside "The Mob". In 1958 was forced to flee the States as the result of a famous duel against his opposite number for the Detroit Purple Gang, a certain Ramon "The Rod" Rodriguez, which took place by moonlight on the third green of the Thunderbird golf course at Las Vegas. (Scaramanga got two bullets into the heart of his opponent before the latter had fired a shot. Distance 20 paces.) Believed to have been compensated by "The Mob" with 100,000 dollars. Travelled the whole Caribbean area investing fugitive funds for various Las Vegas interests and later, as his reputation for keen and successful dealing in real estate and plantations became consolidated, for Trujillo of Dominica and Batista of Cuba. In 1959 settled in Havana and, seeing the way the wind blew, while remaining ostensibly a Batista man, began working undercover for the Castro party and, after the revolution, obtained an influential post as foreign "enforcer" for the D.S.S. In this capacity, on behalf, that is, of the Cuban Secret Police, he undertook the assassinations mentioned above.

'PASSPORTS: Various, including Cuban diplomatic.

'DISGUISES: None. They are not necessary. The myth surrounding this man, the equivalent, let us say, of that surrounding the most famous film star, and the fact that he has no police record, have hitherto given him complete freedom of movement and indemnity from interference in "his" territory. In most of the islands and mainland republics which constitute this territory, he has groups of admirers (e.g. the Rastafari in Jamaica) and commands powerful pressure groups who give him protection and succour when called upon to do so. Moreover, as the ostensible purchaser, and usually the legal front, for the "hot money" properties mentioned above, he has legitimate access, frequently supported by his diplomatic status, to any part of his territory.

'RESOURCES: Considerable but of unknown extent. Travels

on various credit cards of the Diners' Club variety. Has a numbered account with the Union des Banques de Crédit, Zürich, and appears to have no difficulty in obtaining foreign currency from the slim resources of Cuba when he needs it.

'MOTIVATION: (Comment by C.C.) —' M. refilled and relit his pipe, which had died. What had gone before was routine information which added nothing to his basic knowledge of the man. What followed would be of more interest. 'C.C.' covered the identity of a former Regius Professor of History at Oxford who lived a — to M. — pampered existence at Headquarters in a small and, in M.'s opinion, over-comfortable office. In between, again in M.'s opinion, over-luxurious and over-long meals at the Garrick Club, he wandered, at his ease, into Headquarters, examined such files as the present one, asked questions and had signals of inquiry sent, and then delivered his judgment. But M., for all his prejudices against the man, his haircut, the casualness of his clothes, what he knew of his way of life, and the apparently haphazard processes of his ratiocination, appreciated the sharpness of the mind, the knowledge of the world, that C.C. brought to his task and, so often, the accuracy of his judgments. In short, M. always enjoyed what C.C. had to say and he now picked up the file again with relish.

'I am interested in this man,' wrote C.C., 'and I have caused inquiries to be made on a somewhat wider front than usual, since it is not common to be confronted with a secret agent who is at once so much of a public figure and yet appears to be infinitely successful in the difficult and dangerous field of his choice — that of being, in common parlance, "a gun for hire". I think I may have found the origin of this partiality for killing his fellow men in cold blood, men against whom he has no personal animosity but merely the reflected animosity of his employers, in the following bizarre anecdote from his youth. In the travelling circus of his father, Enrico Scaramanga, the boy had several roles. He was a most spectacular trick shot, he was a stand-in strong man in the acrobatic troop, often taking the place of the usual artiste as bottom man in the "human pyramid" act, and he was the mahout, in gorgeous turban, Indian robes, etc., who rode the leading elephant in a troupe of three. This elephant, by the name of Max, was a male and it is a peculiarity of the male elephant, which I have learned with much interest and verified with eminent zoologists, that, at intervals during the year, they go "on heat" sexually. During these periods, a mucous deposit forms behind the animals' ears and this needs to be scraped off since otherwise it causes the elephant intense irritation. Max developed this symptom during a visit of the circus to Trieste, but, through an oversight, the condition was not noticed and given the necessary treatment. The "Big Top" of the circus had been erected on the outskirts of the town adjacent to the coastal railway line and, on the night which was, in my opinion, to determine the future way of life of the young Scaramanga, Max went berserk, threw the youth and, screaming horrifically, trampled his way through the auditorium, causing many casualties, and charged off across the fairground and on to the railway line down which (a frightening spectacle under the full moon which, as newspaper cuttings record, was shining on that night) he galloped at full speed. The local carabiniere were alerted and set off in pursuit by car along the main road that flanks the railway line. In due course they caught up with the unfortunate monster, which, its frenzy expired, stood peacefully facing back the way it had come. Not realizing that the elephant, if approached by its handler, could now be led peacefully back to its stall, the police opened rapid fire and bullets from their carbines and revolvers wounded the animal superficially in many places. Infuriated afresh, the miserable beast, now pursued by the police car from which the hail of fire continued, charged off again along the railway line. On arrival at the fairground, the elephant seemed to recognize its "home", the "Big Top", and, turning off the railway line, lumbered back through the fleeing spectators to the centre of the deserted arena and there, weakened by loss of blood, pathetically continued with its interrupted act. Trumpeting dreadfully in its agony, the mortally wounded Max endeavoured again and again to raise itself and stand upon one leg. Meanwhile the young Scaramanga, now armed with his pistols, tried to throw a lariat over the animal's head while calling out the "elephant talk" with which he usually controlled him. Max seems to have recognized the youth and — it must have been a truly pitiful sight — lowered its trunk to allow the youth to be hoisted to his usual seat behind the elephant's head. But at this moment the police burst into the sawdust ring and their captain, approaching very close, emptied his revolver into the elephant's right eye at a range of a few feet, upon which Max fell dying to the ground. Upon this, the young Scaramanga who, according to the Press, had a deep devotion for his charge, drew one of his pistols and shot the policeman through the heart and fled off into the crowd of bystanders pursued by the other policemen who could not fire because of the throng of people. He made good his escape, found his way south to Naples and thence, as noted above, stowed away to America.

'Now, I see in this dreadful experience a possible reason for the transformation of Scaramanga into the most vicious gunman of recent years. In him was, I believe, born on that day a cold-blooded desire to avenge himself on all humanity. That the elephant had run amok and trampled many innocent people, that the man truly responsible was his handler and that the police were only doing their duty, would be, psychopathologically, either forgotten or deliberately suppressed by a youth of hot-blooded stock whose subconscious had been so deeply lacerated. At all events, Scaramanga's subsequent career requires some explanation, and I trust I am not being fanciful in putting forward my own prognosis from the known facts.'

M. rubbed the bowl of his pipe thoughtfully down the side of his nose. Well, fair enough! He turned back to the file.

'I have comment,' wrote C.C., 'to make on this man's alleged sexual potency when seen in relation to his profession. It is a Freudian thesis, with which I am inclined to agree, that the pistol, whether in the hands of an amateur or of a professional gunman, has significance for the owner as a symbol of virility — an extension of the male organ — and that excessive interests in guns (e.g. gun collections and gun clubs) is a form of fetishism. The partiality of Scaramanga for a particularly showy variation of weapon, and his use of silver and gold bullets, clearly point, I think, to his being a slave to this fetish and, if I am right, I have doubts about his alleged sexual prowess, for the lack of which his gun fetish would be either a substitute or a compensation. I have also noted, from a "profile" of this man in *Time* magazine, one fact which supports my thesis that Scaramanga may be sexually abnormal. In listing his accomplishments, *Time* notes, but does not comment upon, the fact that this man cannot whistle. Now it may only be myth, and it is certainly not medical science, but there is a popular theory that a man who cannot whistle has homosexual tendencies. (At this point, the reader may care to experiment and, from his self-knowledge, help to prove or disprove this item of folklore! C.C.)' (M. hadn't whistled since he was a boy. Unconsciously his mouth pursed and a clear note was emitted. He uttered an impatient 'tchah!' and continued with his reading.) 'So I would not be surprised to learn that Scaramanga is not the Casanova of popular fancy. Passing to the wider implications of gunmanship, we enter the realms of the Adlerian power urge as compensation for the inferiority complex, and here I will quote some well-turned phrases of a certain Mr Harold L. Peterson in his preface to his finely illustrated *The Book of the Gun*, published by Paul Hamlyn. Mr Peterson writes: "In the vast array of things man has invented to better his condition, few have fascinated him more than the gun. Its function is simple; as Oliver Winchester said, with nineteenth-century complacency, 'A gun is a machine for throwing balls.' But its ever-increasing efficiency in performing this task, and its awesome ability to strike home from long range, have given it tremendous psychological appeal.

' "For possession of a gun and the skill to use it enormously augments the gunner's personal power, and extends the radius of his influence and effect a thousand times beyond his arm's length. And since strength resides in the gun, the man who wields it may be less than strong without being disadvantaged. The flashing sword, the couched lance, the bent longbow performed to the limit of the man who held it. The gun's power is inherent and needs only to be released. A steady eye and an accurate aim are enough. Wherever the muzzle points the bullet goes, bearing the gunner's wish or intention swiftly to the target . . . Perhaps more than any other implement, the gun has shaped the course of nations and the destiny of men." '

C.C. commented: 'In the Freudian thesis, "his arm's length" would become the length of the masculine organ. But we need not linger over these esoterica. The support for my premise is well expressed in Mr Peterson's sinewy prose and, though I would substitute the printing press for the gun in his concluding paragraph, his points are well taken. The subject, Scaramanga, is, in my opinion, a paranoiac in subconscious revolt against the father figure (i.e. the figure of authority) and a sexual fetishist with possible homosexual tendencies. He has other qualities which are self-evident from the earlier testimony. In conclusion, and having regard to the damage he has already wrought upon the personnel of the S.S., I conclude that his career should be terminated with the utmost dispatch — if necessary by the inhuman means he himself employs, in the unlikely event an agent of equal courage and dexterity can be made available.' Signed 'C.C.'

Beneath, at the end of the docket, the Head of the Caribbean and Central American Section had minuted 'I concur', signed 'C.A.', and the Chief of Staff had added, in red ink, 'Noted. C.O.S.'

M. gazed into space for perhaps five minutes. Then he reached for his pen and, in green ink, scrawled the word 'Action?' followed by the italic, authoritative '*M.*'.

Then he sat very still for another five minutes and wondered if he had signed James Bond's death warrant.

4
THE STARS FORETELL

THERE ARE FEW less prepossessing places to spend a hot afternoon than Kingston International Airport in Jamaica. All the money has been spent on lengthening the runway out into the harbour to take the big jets and little is left over for the comfort of transit passengers. James Bond had come in an hour before on a B.W.I.A. flight from Trinidad and there were two hours to go before his connection with a Cuban Airways flight for Havana. He had taken off his coat and tie and now sat on a hard bench gloomily surveying the contents of the In-Bond shop with its expensive scents, liquor and piles of over-decorated native ware. He had had luncheon on the plane, it was the wrong time for a drink and it was too hot and too far to take a taxi into Kingston even had he wanted to. He wiped his already soaking handkerchief over his face and neck and cursed softly and fluently.

A cleaner ambled in and, with the exquisite languor of such people throughout the Caribbean, proceeded to sweep very small bits of rubbish hither and thither, occasionally dipping a boneless hand into a bucket to sprinkle water over the dusty cement floor. Through the slatted jalousies a small breeze, reeking of the mangrove swamps, briefly stirred the dead air and then was gone. There were only two other passengers in the 'lounge', Cubans perhaps, with jippa-jappa luggage. A man and a woman. They sat close together against the opposite wall and stared fixedly at James Bond, adding minutely to the oppression of the atmosphere. Bond got up and went over to the shop. He bought a *Daily Gleaner* and returned to his place. Because of its inconsequence and occasionally bizarre choice of news the *Gleaner* was a favourite paper of Bond's. Almost the whole of that day's front page was taken up with new ganja laws to prevent the consumption, sale and cultivation of this local version of marijuana. The fact that de Gaulle had just sensationally announced his recognition of Red China was boxed well down the page. Bond read the whole paper — 'country newsbits' and all — with the minute care bred of desperation. His horoscope said: 'CHEER UP! Today will bring a pleasant surprise and the fulfilment of a dear wish. But you must earn your good fortune by watching closely for the golden opportunity when it presents itself and then seizing it with both hands.' Bond smiled grimly. He would be unlikely to get on the scent of Scaramanga on his first evening in Havana. It was not even certain that Scaramanga was there. This was a last resort. For six weeks, Bond had been chasing his man round the Caribbean and Central America. He had missed him by a day in Trinidad and by only a matter of hours in Caracas. Now he had rather reluctantly taken the decision to try and ferret him out on his home ground, a particularly inimical home ground, with which Bond was barely familiar. At least he had fortified himself in British Guiana with a diplomatic passport and he was now 'Courier' Bond with splendidly engraved instructions from Her Majesty to pick up the Jamaican diplomatic bag in Havana and return with it. He had even borrowed an example of the famous Silver Greyhound, the British Courier's emblem for three hundred years. If he could do his job and then get a few hundred yards' start, this would at least give him sanctuary in the British Embassy. Then it would be up to the F.O. to bargain him out. If he could find his man. If he could carry out his instructions. If he could get away from the scene of the shooting. If, if, if . . . Bond turned to the advertisements on the back page. At once an item caught his eye. It was so typically 'old' Jamaica. This is what he read:

FOR SALE BY AUCTION

AT 77 HARBOUR STREET, KINGSTON,
At 10.30 a.m. on WEDNESDAY,
28th MAY

under Powers of Sale contained in a mortgage from Cornelius Brown *et ux*

No. 3½ LOVE LANE, SAVANNAH LA MAR.

Containing the substantial residence and all that parcel of land by measurement on the Northern Boundary three chains and five perches, on the Southern Boundary five chains and one perch, on the Eastern Boundary two chains exactly and on the Western Boundary four chains and two perches be the same in each case and more or less and butting Northerly on No. 4 Love Lane.

THE C. D. ALEXANDER CO. LTD.

77 HARBOUR STREET KINGSTON
PHONE 4897.

James Bond was delighted. He had had many assignments in Jamaica and many adventures on the island. The splendid address and all the stuff about chains and perches and the old-fashioned abracadabra at the end of the advertisement brought back all the authentic smell of one of the oldest and most romantic of former British possessions. For all her new-found 'Independence' he would bet his bottom dollar that the statue of Queen Victoria in the centre of Kingston had not been destroyed or removed to a museum as similar relics of an historic infancy had been in the resurgent African states. He looked at his watch. The *Gleaner* had consumed a whole hour for him. He picked up his coat and brief-case. Not much longer to go! In the last analysis, life wasn't all that dismal. One must forget the bad and remember the good. What were a couple of hours of heat and boredom in this island compared with memories of Beau Desert and Honeychile Wilder and his survival against the mad Dr No? James Bond smiled to himself as the dusty pictures clicked across his brain. How long ago it all was! What had happened to her? She never wrote. The last he had heard, she had had two children by the Philadelphia doctor she had married. He wandered off into the grandly named 'Concourse' where the booths of many airlines stood empty, and promotion folders and little company flags on their counters gathered the dust blown in with the mangrove breeze.

There was the customary central display-stand holding messages for incoming and outgoing passengers. As usual, Bond wondered whether there would be something for him. In all his life there never had been. Automatically he ran his eye over the scattered envelopes, held, under tape, beneath each parent letter. Nothing under 'B' and nothing under his alias 'H' for 'Hazard, Mark' of the 'Transworld Consortium', successor to the old 'Universal Export', that had recently been discarded as cover for the Secret Service. Nothing. He ran a bored eye over the other envelopes. He suddenly froze. He looked around him, languidly, casually. The Cuban couple were out of sight. Nobody else was looking. He reached out a quick hand, wrapped in his handkerchief, and pocketed the buff envelope that said, 'Scaramanga. B.O.A.C. passenger from Lima'. He stayed where he was for a few minutes and then wandered slowly off to the door marked 'Men'.

He locked the door and sat down. The envelope was not sealed. It contained a B.W.I.A. message form. The neat B.W.I.A. writing said 'Message received from Kingston at 12.15: the samples will be available at No. 3½ S.L.M. as from midday tomorrow.' There was no signature. Bond uttered a short bark of laughter and triumph. S.L.M. — Savannah La Mar. Could it be? It must be! At last the three red stars of a jackpot had clicked into line. What was it his *Gleaner* horoscope had said? Well he would go nap on this clue from outer space — seize it with both hands as the *Gleaner* had instructed. He read the message again and carefully put it back in the envelope. His damp handkerchief had left marks on the buff envelope. In this heat they would dry out in a matter of minutes. He went out and sauntered over to the stand. There was no one in sight. He slipped the message back into its place under 'S' and walked over to the Cuban Airlines booth and cancelled his reservation. He then went to the B.O.A.C. counter and looked through the timetable. Yes, the Lima flight for Kingston, New York and London was due in at 13.15 the next day. He was going to need help. He remembered the name of Head of Station J. He went over to the telephone booth and got through to the High Commissioner's Office. He asked for Commander Ross. After a moment a girl's voice came on the line. 'Commander Ross's assistant. Can I help you?'

There was something vaguely familiar in the lilt of the voice. Bond said, 'Could I speak to Commander Ross? This is a friend from London.'

The girl's voice became suddenly alert. 'I'm afraid Commander Ross is away from Jamaica. Is there anything I can do?' There was a pause. 'What name did you say?'

'I didn't say any name. But in fact it's . . .'

The voice broke in excitedly, 'Don't tell me. It's James!'

Bond laughed. 'Well I'm damned! It's Goodnight! What the hell are you doing here?'

'More or less what I used to do for you. I heard you were back, but I thought you were ill or something. How absolutely marvellous! But where are you talking from?'

'Kingston Airport. Now listen, darling. I need help. We can talk later. Can you get cracking?'

'Of course. Wait till I get a pencil. Right.'

'First I need a car. Anything that'll go. Then I want the name of the top man at Frome, you know, the WISCO estate beyond Savannah La Mar. Large-scale survey map of that area, a hundred pounds in Jamaican money. Then be an angel and ring up Alexander's the auctioneers and find out anything you can about a property that's advertised in today's *Gleaner*. Say you're a prospective buyer. Three and a half Love Lane. You'll see the details. Then I want you to come out to Morgan's Harbour where I'm going in a minute, be staying the night there, and we'll have dinner and swop secrets until the dawn steals over the Blue Mountains. Can do?'

'Of course. But that's the hell of a lot of secrets. What shall I wear?'

'Something that's tight in the right places. Not too many buttons.'

She laughed. 'You've established your identity. Now I'll get on with all this. See you about seven. 'Bye.'

Gasping for air, James Bond pushed his way out of the little sweat box. He ran his handkerchief over his face and neck. He'd be damned! Mary Goodnight, his darling secretary from the old days in the OO Section! At Headquarters they had said she was abroad. He hadn't asked any questions. Perhaps she had opted for a change when he had gone missing. Anyway, what a break! Now he'd got an ally, someone he knew. Good old *Gleaner*! He got his bag from the Cuban Airlines booth and went out and hailed a taxi and said 'Morgan's Harbour' and sat back and let the air from the open windows begin to dry him.

The romantic little hotel is on the site of Port Royal at the tip of the Palisadoes. The proprietor, an Englishman who had once been in Intelligence himself and who guessed what Bond's job was, was glad to see him. He showed Bond to a comfortable air-conditioned room with a view of the pool and the wide mirror of Kingston harbour. He said, 'What is it this time? Cubans or smuggling? They're the popular targets these days.'

'Just on my way through. Got any lobsters?'

'Of course.'

'Be a good chap and save two for dinner. Broiled with melted butter. And a pot of that ridiculously expensive foie gras of yours. All right?'

'Wilco. Celebration? Champagne on the ice?'

'Good idea. Now I must get a shower and some sleep. That Kingston Airport's murder.'

James Bond awoke at six. At first he didn't know where he was. He lay and remembered. Sir James Molony had said that his memory would be sluggish for a while. The E.C.T. treatment at The Park, a discreet so-called 'convalescent home' in a vast mansion in Kent, had been fierce. Twenty-four bashes at his brain from the black box in thirty days. After it was over, Sir James had confessed that, if he had been practising in America, he wouldn't have been allowed to administer more than eighteen. At first, Bond had been terrified at the sight of the box and of the two cathodes that would be cupped to each temple. He had heard that people undergoing shock treatment had to be strapped down, that their jerking, twitching bodies, impelled by the volts, often hurtled off the operating-table. But that, it seemed, was old hat. Now there was the longed-for needle with the pentathol, and Sir James said there was no movement of the body when the current flashed through except a slight twitching of the eyelids. And the results had been miraculous. After the pleasant, quiet-spoken analyst had explained to him what had been done to him in Russia, and after he had passed through the mental agony of knowing what he had nearly done to M., the old fierce hatred of the K.G.B. and all its works had been reborn in him and, six weeks after he had entered The Park, all he wanted was to get back at the people who had invaded his brain for their own murderous purposes. And then had come his physical rehabilitation and the inexplicable amount of gun practice he had had to do at the Maidstone police range. And then the day arrived when the Chief of Staff had come down and explained about the gun practice and had spent the day with him and given him his orders, the scribble of green ink, signed 'M.', that wished him luck, and then the excitement of the ride to London Airport on his way across the world.

Bond took another shower and dressed in shirt, slacks and sandals and wandered over to the little bar on the waterfront and ordered a double Walker's de Luxe Bourbon on the rocks and watched the pelicans diving for their dinner. Then he had another drink with a water chaser to break it down and wondered about 3½ Love Lane and what the 'samples' would consist of and how he would take Scaramanga. This had been worrying him since he had been given his orders. It was all very fine to be told to 'eliminate' the man, but James Bond had never liked killing in cold blood and to provoke a draw against a man who was possibly the fastest gun in the world was suicide. Well, he would just have to see which way the cards fell. The first thing to do was to clean up his cover. The diplomatic passport he would leave with Goodnight. He would now be 'Mark Hazard' of the 'Transworld Consortium', the splendidly vague title which could cover almost any kind of human activity. His business would have to be with the West Indies Sugar Company because that was the only business, apart from Kaiser Bauxite, that existed in the comparatively deserted western districts of Jamaica. There was also the Negril project for developing one of the most spectacular beaches in the world, beginning with the building of the Thunderbird Hotel. He could be a rich man looking around for a building site. If his hunch was right, and the childish predictions of his horoscope, and if he came up with Scaramanga at the romantic Love Lane address, it would be a question of playing it by ear.

The prairie fire of the sunset raged briefly in the west and the molten sea cooled off into moonlit gunmetal.

A naked arm smelling of Chanel No. 5 snaked round his neck and warm lips kissed the corner of his mouth. As he reached up to hold the arm where it was, a breathless voice said, 'Oh, James! I'm sorry. I just had to! It's so wonderful to have you back.'

Bond put his hand under the soft chin and lifted up her mouth and kissed her full on the half-open lips. He said, 'Why didn't we ever think of doing that before, Goodnight? Three years with only that door between us! What must we have been thinking of?'

She stood away from him. The golden bell of hair fell back to embrace her neck. She hadn't changed. Still only the faintest trace of make-up, but now the face was golden with sunburn from which the wide-apart blue eyes, now ablaze with the moon, shone out with that challenging directness that had disconcerted him when they had argued over some office problem. Still the same glint of health over the good bones and the broad uninhibited smile from the full lips that, in repose, were so exciting. But now the clothes were different. Instead of the severe shirt and skirt of the days at Headquarters, she was wearing a single string of pearls and a one-piece short-skirted frock in the colour of a pink gin with a lot of bitters in it — the orangey-pink of the inside of a conch shell. It was all tight against the bosom and the hips. She smiled at his scrutiny. 'The buttons are down the back. This is standard uniform for a tropical Station.'

'I can just see Q Branch dreaming it up. I suppose one of the pearls has a death pill in it.'

'Of course. But I can't remember which. I'll just have to swallow the whole string. Can I have a daiquiri, please, instead?'

Bond gave the order. 'Sorry, Goodnight. My manners are slipping. I was dazzled. It's so tremendous finding you here. And I've never seen you in your working clothes before. Now then, tell me the news. Where's Ross? How long have you been here? Have you managed to cope with all that junk I gave you?'

Her drink came. She sipped it carefully. Bond remembered that she rarely drank and didn't smoke. He ordered another for himself and felt vaguely guilty that this was his third double and that she wouldn't know it and when it came wouldn't recognize it as a double. He lit a cigarette. Nowadays he was trying to keep to twenty and failing by about five. He stabbed the cigarette out. He was getting near to his target and the rigid training rules that had been drilled into him at The Park must from now on be observed meticulously. The champagne wouldn't count. He was amused by the conscience this girl had awakened in him. He was also surprised and impressed.

Mary Goodnight knew that the last question was the one he would want answered first. She reached into a plain straw handbag on a gold metal chain and handed him a thick envelope. She said, 'Mostly in used singles. A few fivers. Shall I debit you direct or put it in as expenses?'

'Direct, please.'

'The car's outside. You remember Strangways? Well it's his old Sunbeam Alpine. The Station bought it and now I use it. The tank's full and it goes like a bird. The top man at Frome is a man called Tony Hugill. Ex-navy. Nice man. Nice wife. Nice children. Does a good job. Has a lot of trouble with cane burning and other small sabotage — mostly with thermite bombs brought in from Cuba. Cuba's sugar crop is Jamaica's chief rival and with Hurricane Flora and all the rains they've been having over there, the Cuban crop is going to be only about three million tons this year, compared with a Batista level of about seven, and very late, because the rains have played havoc with the sucrose content.' She smiled her wide smile. 'No secrets. Just reading the *Gleaner*. So it's worth Castro's trouble to try and keep the world price up by doing as much damage as he can to rival crops so that he's in a better position to bargain with Russia. He's only got his sugar to sell and he wants food badly. This wheat the Americans are selling to Russia. A lot of that will find its way back to Cuba, in exchange for sugar, to feed the Cuban sugar croppers.' She smiled again. 'Pretty daft business, isn't it? I don't think Castro can hold out much longer. The missile business in Cuba must have cost Russia about a billion pounds. And now they're having to pour money into Cuba, money and goods, to keep the place on its feet. I can't help thinking they'll pull out soon and leave Castro to go the way Batista went. It's a fiercely Catholic country and Hurricane Flora was considered as the final judgment from heaven. It sat over the island and simply whipped it, day after day, for five days. No hurricane in history has ever behaved like that. The church-goers don't miss an omen like that. It was a straight indictment of the regime.'

Bond said with admiration, 'Goodnight, you're a treasure. You've certainly been doing your homework.'

The direct blue eyes looked straight into his, dodging the compliment. 'This is the stuff I live with here. It's built into the Station. But I thought you might like some background to Frome and what I've said explains why WISCO are getting these cane fires. At least we think it is. Apparently there's a tremendous chess game going on all over the world in sugar — in what they call sugar futures, that's sort of buying the stuff forward for delivery dates later in the year. Washington's trying to keep the price down, to upset Cuba's economy, but there's increased world consumption and a shortage largely due to Flora and the tremendous rains we've been having here after Flora which have delayed the Jamaican crop. I don't understand it all, but it's in Cuba's interest to do as much damage as possible to the Jamaican crop and this place Frome you're interested in produces about a quarter of Jamaica's total output.' She took a sip at her drink. 'Well, that's all about sugar. The top man there is this man Hugill. We've had a lot to do with him, so he'll be friendly. He was in Naval Intelligence during the war, sort of commando job, so he knows the score. The car's a bit aged but it's still pretty fast and it won't let you down. It's rather bashed about so it won't be conspicuous. I've put the survey map in the glove compartment.'

'That's fine. Now, last question and then we'll go and have dinner and tell each other our life stories. But, by the way, what's happened to your chief, Ross?'

Mary Goodnight looked worried. 'To tell you the truth, I don't exactly know. He went off last week on some job to Trinidad. It was to try and locate a man called Scaramanga. He's a local gunman of some sort. I don't know much about him. Apparently Headquarters want him traced for some reason.' She smiled ruefully. 'Nobody ever tells me anything that's interesting. I just do the donkey work. Well, Commander Ross was due back two days ago and he hasn't turned up. I've had to send off a Red Warning, but I've been told to give him another week.'

'Well, I'm glad he's out of the way. I'd rather have his Number Two. Last question. What about this 3½ Love Lane? Did you get anywhere?'

Mary Goodnight blushed. 'Did I not! That was a fine question to get me mixed up with. Alexander's were non-committal and I finally had to go to the Special Branch. I shan't be able to show my face there for weeks. Heaven knows what they must think of you. That place is a, is a, er —' She wrinkled her nose. 'It's a famous disorderly house in Sav' La Mar.'

Bond laughed out loud at her discomfiture. He teased her with malicious but gentle sadism. 'You mean it's a whorehouse?'

'James! For heaven's sake! Must you be so crude?'

5

NO. 3½ LOVE LANE

THE SOUTH COAST of Jamaica is not as beautiful as the north, and it is a long 120-mile hack over very mixed road surfaces from Kingston to Savannah La Mar. Mary Goodnight had insisted on coming along, 'to navigate and help with the punctures'. Bond had not demurred.

Spanish Town, May Pen, Alligator Pond, Black River, Whitehouse Inn, where they had luncheon — the miles unrolled under the fierce sun until, around four in the afternoon, a stretch of good straight road brought them among the sprucc little villas, each with its patch of brownish lawn, bougainvillaea, and single bed of canna lilies and crotons, which make up the 'smart' suburbs of the modest little coastal township that is, in the vernacular, Sav' La Mar.

Except for the old quarter on the waterfront, it is not a typically Jamaican town, nor a very attractive one. The villas, built for the senior staff of the Frome sugar estates, are drably respectable, and the small straight streets smack of a most un-Jamaican bout of town planning around the 1920s. Bond stopped at the first garage, took in petrol and put Mary Goodnight into a hired car for the return trip. He had told her nothing of his assignment and she had asked no questions when Bond told her vaguely that it was 'something to do with Cuba'. Bond said he would keep in touch when he could, and get back to her when his job was done and then, businesslike, she was off back down the dusty road and Bond drove slowly down to the waterfront. He identified Love Lane, a narrow street of broken-down shops and houses that meandered back into the town from the jetty. He circled the area to get the neighbouring geography clear in his mind and parked the car in a deserted area near the spit of sand on which fishing canoes were drawn up on raised stilts. He locked the car and sauntered back and into Love Lane. There were a few people about, poor people of the fisherman class. Bond bought a packet of Royal Blend at a small general store that smelled of spices. He asked where No. 3½ was and got a look of polite curiosity. 'Further up de street. Mebbe a chain. Big house on de right.' Bond moved over to the shady side and strolled on. He slit open the packet with his thumb-nail and lit a cigarette to help the picture of an idle tourist examining a corner of old Jamaica. There was only one big house on the right. He took some time lighting the cigarette while he examined it.

It must once have had importance, perhaps as the private house of a merchant. It was of two storeys with balconies running all the way round and it was wooden built with silvering shingles, but the gingerbread tracery beneath the eaves was broken in many places and there was hardly a scrap of paint left on the jalousies that closed off all the upstairs windows and most of those below. The patch of 'yard' bordering the street was inhabited by a clutch of vulturine-necked chickens that pecked at nothing and three skeletal Jamaican black-and-tan mongrels. They gazed lazily across the street at Bond and scratched and bit at invisible flies. But, in the background, there was one very beautiful *lignum vitae* tree in full blue blossom. Bond guessed that it was as old as the house — perhaps fifty years. It certainly owned the property by right of strength and adornment. In its delicious black shade a girl in a rocking chair sat reading a magazine. At the range of about thirty yards she looked tidy and pretty. Bond strolled up the opposite side of the street until a corner of the house hid the girl. Then he stopped and examined the house more closely.

Wooden steps ran up to an open front door, over whose lintel, whereas few of the other buildings in the street bore numbers, a big enamelled metal sign announced '3½' in white on dark blue. Of the two broad windows that bracketed the door, the left-hand one was shuttered, but the right-hand one was a single broad sheet of rather dusty glass through which tables and chairs and a serving-counter could be seen. Over the door a swinging sign said 'Dreamland Café in sun-bleached letters, and round this window were advertisements for Red Stripe beer, Royal Blend, Four Aces cigarettes and Coca-Cola. A hand-painted sign said 'SNAX' and, underneath, 'Hot Cock Soup Fresh Daily'.

Bond walked across the street and up the steps and parted the bead curtain that hung over the entrance. He walked over to the counter and was inspecting its contents, a plate of dry-looking ginger cakes, a pile of packeted banana crisps, and some sweet jars, when he heard quick steps outside. The girl from the garden came in. The beads clashed softly behind her. She was an octoroon, pretty as, in Bond's imagination, the word octoroon suggested. She had bold, brown eyes, slightly uptilted at the corners, beneath a fringe of silken black hair. (Bond reflected that there would be Chinese blood somewhere in her past.) She was dressed in a short frock of shocking pink which went well with the coffee and cream of her skin. Her wrists and ankles were tiny. She smiled politely. The eyes flirted. 'Evenin'.'

'Good evening. Could I have a Red Stripe?'

'Sure.' She went behind the counter. She gave him a quick glimpse of fine bosoms as she bent to the door of the icebox — a glimpse not dictated by the geography of the place. She nudged the door shut with a knee, deftly uncapped the bottle and put it on the counter beside an almost clean glass. 'That'll be one and six.'

Bond paid. She rang the money into the cash register. Bond drew up a stool to the counter and sat down. She rested her arms on the wooden top and looked across at him. 'Passing through?'

'More or less. I saw this place was for sale in yesterday's *Gleaner*. I thought I'd take a look at it. Nice big house. Does it belong to you?'

She laughed. It was a pity, because she was a pretty girl, but the teeth had been sharpened by munching raw sugar cane. 'What a hope! I'm sort of, well sort of manager. There's the café' (she pronounced it caif) 'and mebbe you heard we got other attractions.'

Bond looked puzzled. 'What sort?'

'Girls. Six bedrooms upstairs. Very clean. It only cost a pound. There's Sarah up there now. Care to meet up with her?'

'Not today, thanks. It's too hot. But do you only have one at a time?'

'There's Lindy, but she's engaged. She's a big girl. If you like them big, she'll be free in half an hour.' She glanced at a kitchen clock on the wall behind her. 'Around six o'clock. It'll be cooler then.'

'I prefer girls like you. What's your name?'

She giggled. 'I only do it for love. I told you I just manage the place. They call me Tiffy.'

'That's an unusual name. How did you come by it?'

'My momma had six girls. Called them all after flowers. Violet, Rose, Cherry, Pansy and Lily. Then when I came, she couldn't think of any more flower names so she called me "Artificial".' Tiffy waited for him to laugh. When he didn't, she went on. 'When I went to school they all said it was a wrong name and laughed at me and shortened it to Tiffy and that's how I've stayed.'

'Well, I think it's a very pretty name. My name's Mark.'

She flirted. 'You a saint too?'

'No one's ever accused me of it. I've been up at Frome doing a job. I like this part of the island and it crossed my mind to find some place to rent. But I want to be closer to the sea than this. I'll have to look around a bit more. Do you rent rooms by the night?'

She reflected. 'Sure. Why not? But you may find it a bit noisy. There's sometimes a customer who's taken some drinks too many. And there's not too much plumbing.' She leaned closer and lowered her voice. 'But I wouldn't have advised you to rent the place. The shingles are in bad shape. Cost you mebbe five hunnerd, mebbe a thousand to get the roof done.'

'It's nice of you to tell me that. But why's the place being sold? Trouble with the police?'

'Not so much. We operate a respectable place. But in the *Gleaner*, after Mr Brown, that's my boss, you read that "et ux"?'

'Yes.'

'Well, seems that means "and his wife". And Mistress Brown, Mistress Agatha Brown, she was Church of England, but she just done gone to the Catholics. And it seems they don't hold with places like 3½, not even when they're decently run. And their church here, just up the street, seems that needs a new roof like here. So Mistress Brown figures to kill two birds with the same stone and she goes on at Mr Brown to close the place down and sell it and with her portion she goin' fix the roof for the Catholics.'

'That's a shame. It seems a nice quiet place. What's going to happen to you?'

'Guess I'll move to Kingston. Live with one of my sisters and mebbe work in one of the big stores — Issa's mebbe, or Nathan's.

Sav' La Mar is sort of quiet.' The brown eyes became introspective. 'But I'll sure miss the place. Folks have fun here and Love Lane's a pretty street. We're all friends up and down the Lane. It's got sort of, sort of . . .'

'Atmosphere.'

'Right. That's what it's got. Like sort of old Jamaica. Like it must have been in the old days. Everyone's friends with each other. Help each other when they have trouble. You'd be surprised how often the girls do it for free if the man's a good feller, regular customer sort of, and he's short.' The brown eyes gazed inquiringly at Bond to see if he understood the strength of the evidence.

'That's nice of them. But it can't be good for business.'

She laughed. 'This ain't no business, Mister Mark. Not while I'm running it. This is a public service, like water and electricity and health and education and . . .' She broke off and glanced over her shoulder at the clock which said 5.45. 'Hell! You got me talking so much I've forgot Joe and May. It's their supper.' She went to the café window and wound it down. At once, from the direction of the *lignum vitae* tree, two large black birds, slightly smaller than a raven, whirled in, circled the interior of the café amidst a metallic clangour of song unlike the song of any other bird in the world, and untidily landed on the counter within reach of Bond's hand. They strutted up and down imperiously, eyeing Bond without fear from bold, golden eyes, and went through a piercing repertoire of tinny whistles and trills, some of which required them to ruffle themselves up to almost twice their normal size.

Tiffy went back behind the bar, took two pennies out of her purse, rang them up on the register and took two ginger cakes out of the flyblown display case. She broke off bits and fed the two birds, always the smaller of the two, the female, first, and they greedily seized the pieces from her fingers, and, holding the scraps to the wooden counter with a claw, tore them into smaller fragments and devoured them. When it was all over, and Tiffy had chided them both for pecking her fingers, they made small, neat white messes on the counter and looked pleased with themselves. Tiffy took a cloth and cleaned up the messes. She said, 'We call them kling-klings but learned folk call them Jamaican grackles. They're very friendly folk. The Doctor Bird, the humming bird with the streamer tail, is the Jamaican national bird, but I like these best. They're not so beautiful, but they're the friendliest birds and they're funny besides. They seem to know it. They're like naughty black thieves.' The kling-klings eyed the cake stand and complained stridently that their supper was over. James Bond produced twopence and handed it over. 'They're wonderful. Like mechanical toys. Give them a second course from me.'

Tiffy rang up the money and took out two more cakes. 'Now listen, Joe and May. This nice gemmun's been nice to Tiffy and he's now being nice to you. So don't you peck my fingers and make messes or mebbe he won't visit us again.' She was half-way through feeding the birds when she cocked an ear. There was the noise of creaking boards somewhere overhead and then the sound of quiet footsteps treading stairs. All of a sudden Tiffy's animated face became quiet and tense. She whispered to Bond: 'That's Lindy's man. Important man. He's a good customer here. But he don't like me because I won't go with him. So he can talk rough sometimes. And he don't like Joe and May because he reckons they make too much noise.' She shooed the birds in the direction of the open window, but they saw there was half their cake to come and they just fluttered into the air and then down to the counter again. Tiffy appealed to Bond. 'Be a good friend and just sit quiet whatever he says. He likes to get people mad. And then . . .' She stopped. 'Will you have another Red Stripe, mister?'

Bead curtains swished in the shadowy back of the room.

Bond had been sitting with his chin propped on his right hand. He now dropped the hand to the counter and sat back. The Walther PPK inside the waistband of his trousers to the left of his flat stomach signalled its presence to his skin. The fingers of his right hand curled slightly, ready to receive its butt. He moved his left foot off the rail of the stool on to the floor. He said, 'That'd be fine.' He unbuttoned his coat with his left hand and then, with the same hand, took out his handkerchief and wiped his face with it. 'It always gets extra hot around six before the Undertaker's Wind has started to blow.'

'Mister, the undertaker's right here. You care to feel his wind?'

James Bond turned his head slowly. Dusk had crept into the big room and all he could see was a pale, tall outline. The man was carrying a suitcase. He put it down on the floor and came forward. He must have been wearing rubber-soled shoes for his feet made no sound. Tiffy moved nervously behind the counter and a switch clicked. Half a dozen low-voltage bulbs came to life in rusty brackets around the walls.

Bond said easily, 'You made me jump.'

Scaramanga came up and leant against the counter. The description in Records was exact, but it had not caught the cat-like menace of the big man, the extreme breadth of the shoulders and the narrow waist, or the cold immobility of the eyes that now examined Bond with an expression of aloof disinterest. He was wearing a well-cut, single-breasted tan suit and 'co-respondent' shoes in brown and white. Instead of a tie, he wore a high stock in white silk secured by a gold pin the shape of a miniature pistol. There should have been something theatrical about the get-up but, perhaps because of the man's fine figure, there wasn't.

He said, 'I sometimes make 'em dance. Then I shoot their feet off.' There was no trace of a foreign accent underneath the American.

Bond said, 'That sounds rather drastic. What do you do it for?'

'The last time it was five thousand dollars. Seems like you don't know who I am. Didn't the cool cat tell you?'

Bond glanced at Tiffy. She was standing very still, her hands by her sides. The knuckles were white.

Bond said, 'Why should she? Why would I want to know?'

There was a quick flash of gold. The small black hole looked directly at Bond's navel. 'Because of this. What are you doing here, stranger? Kind of a coincidence finding a city slicker at 3½. Or at Sav' La Mar for the matter of that. Not by any chance from the police? Or any of their friends?'

'Kamerad!' Bond raised his hands in mock surrender. He lowered them and turned to Tiffy. 'Who is this man? A one-man takeover bid for Jamaica? Or a refugee from a circus? Ask him what he'd like to drink. Whoever he is, it was a good act.' James Bond knew that he had very nearly pulled the trigger of the gun. Hit a gunman in his vanity . . . He had a quick vision of himself writhing on the floor, his right hand without the power to reach for his own weapon. Tiffy's pretty face was no longer pretty. It was a taut skull. She stared at James Bond. Her mouth opened but no sound came from the gaping lips. She liked him and she knew he was dead. The kling-klings, Joe and May, smelled the same electricity. With a tremendous din of metallic squawks, they fled for the open window like black thieves escaping into the night.

The explosions from the Colt .45 were deafening. The two birds disintegrated against the violet back-drop of the dusk, the scraps of feathers and pink flesh blasting out of the yellow light of the café into the limbo of the deserted street like shrapnel.

There was a moment of deafening silence. James Bond didn't move. He sat where he was, waiting for the tension of the deed to relax. It didn't. With an inarticulate scream, that was half a filthy word, Tiffy took James Bond's bottle of Red Stripe off the counter and clumsily flung it. There came a distant crash of glass from the back of the room. Then, having made her puny gesture, Tiffy fell to her knees behind the counter and went into sobbing hysterics.

James Bond drank down the rest of his beer and got slowly to his feet. He walked towards Scaramanga and was about to pass him when the man reached out a languid left arm and caught him at the biceps. He held the snout of his gun to his nose, sniffing delicately. The expression in the dead brown eyes was far-away. He said, 'Mister, there's something quite extra about the smell of death. Care to try it?' He held out the glittering gun as if he was offering James Bond a rose.

Bond stood quite still. He said, 'Mind your manners. Take your hand off me.'

Scaramanga raised his eyebrows. The flat, leaden gaze seemed to take in Bond for the first time.

He released his grip.

James Bond went on round the edge of the counter. When he came opposite the other man, he found the eyes were now looking at him with faint, scornful curiosity. Bond stopped. The sobbing of the girl was the crying of a small dog. Somewhere down the street a 'Sound System' — a loudspeaker record player — began braying calypso.

Bond looked the man in the eye. He said, 'Thanks. I've tried it. I recommend the Berlin vintage. 1945.' He smiled a friendly, only slightly ironical smile. 'But I expect you were too young to be at that tasting.'

6

THE EASY GRAND

BOND KNELT DOWN beside Tiffy and gave her a couple of sharp slaps on the right cheek. Then on the left. The wet eyes came back into focus. She put her hand up to her face and looked at Bond with surprise. Bond got to his feet. He took a cloth and wetted it at the tap, then leant down and put his arm round her and wiped the cloth gently over her face. Then he lifted her up and handed her her bag that was on a shelf behind the counter. He said, 'Come on, Tiffy. Make up that pretty face again. Business'll be warming up soon. The leading lady's got to look her best.'

Tiffy took the bag and opened it. She looked past Bond and saw Scaramanga for the first time since the shooting. The pretty lips drew back in a snarl. She whispered fiercely so that only Bond could hear, 'I'm goin' fix that man, but good. There's Mother Edna up Orange Hill way. She's an obeah top woman. I'll go up there tomorrow. Come a few days, he won't know what hit him.' She took out a mirror and began doing up her face. Bond reached into his hip pocket and counted out five one-pound notes. He stuffed them into her open bag.

'You forget all about it. This'll buy you a nice canary in a cage to keep you company. Anyway, another pair of klings'll come along if you put some food out.' He patted her shoulder and moved away. When he came up with Scaramanga he stopped and said, 'That may have been a good circus act' (he used the word again on purpose) 'but it was rough on the girl. Give her some money.'

Scaramanga said, 'Shove it,' out of the corner of his mouth. He said suspiciously, 'And what's all this yack about circuses?' He turned to face Bond. 'Just stop where you are, Mister, and answer a few questions. Like I said, are you from the police? You've sure got the smell of cops around you. If not, what are you doing hereabouts?'

Bond said, 'People don't tell me what to do. I tell them.' He walked on into the middle of the room and sat down at a table. He said. 'Come and sit down and stop trying to lean on me. I'm unleanable-on.'

Scaramanga shrugged. He took two long strides, picked up one of the metal chairs, twirled it round and thrust it between his legs and sat bassackwards, his left arm lying along the back of the chair. His right arm rested on his thigh, inches from the ivory pistol butt that showed above the waistband of his trousers. Bond recognized that it was a good working position for a gunman, the metal back of the chair acting as a shield for most of the body. This was certainly a most careful and professional man.

Bond, both hands in full view on the table top, said cheerfully, 'No. I'm not from the police. My name's Mark Hazard. I'm from a company called "Transworld Consortium". I've been doing a job up at Frome, the WISCO sugar place. Know it?'

'Sure I know it. What you been doing there?'

'Not so fast, my friend. First of all, who are you and what's your business?'

'Scaramanga. Francisco Scaramanga. Labour relations. Ever heard of me?'

Bond frowned. 'Can't say I have. Should I have?'

'Some people who hadn't are dead.'

'A lot of people who haven't heard of me are dead.' Bond leaned back. He crossed one leg over the other, above the knee, and grasped the ankle in a clubman pose. 'I do wish you'd stop talking in heroics. For instance, seven hundred million Chinese have certainly heard of neither of us. You must be a frog in a very small pool.'

Scaramanga did not rise to the jibe. He said reflectively, 'Yeah. I guess you could call the Caribbean a pretty small pool. But there's good pickin's to be had from it. "The man with the golden gun." That's what they call me in these parts.'

'It's a handy tool for solving labour problems. We could do with you up at Frome.'

'Been having trouble up there?' Scaramanga looked bored.

'Too many cane fires.'

'Was that your business?'

'Sort of. One of the jobs of my company is insurance investigation.'

'Security work. I've come across guys like you before. Thought I could smell the cop-smell.' Scaramanga looked satisfied that his guess had been right. 'Did you get anywhere?'

'Picked up a few Rastafari. I'd have liked to get rid of the lot of them. But they went crying to their union that they were being discriminated against because of their religion so we had to call a halt. So the fires'll begin again soon. That's why I say we could do with a good enforcer up there.' Bond added blandly, 'I take it that's another name for your profession?'

Again Scaramanga dodged the sneer. He said, 'You carry a gun?'

'Of course. You don't go after the Rastas without one.'

'What kind of a gun?'

'Walther PPK. 7.65 millimetre.'

'Yes, that's a stopper all right.' Scaramanga turned towards the counter. 'Hey, cool cat. Couple of Red Stripes, if you're in business again.' He turned back and the blank eyes looked hard at Bond. 'What's your next job?'

'Don't know. I'll have to contact London and find out if they've got any other problems in the area. But I'm in no hurry. I work for them more or less on a free-lance basis. Why? Any suggestions?'

The other man sat quiet while Tiffy came out from behind the counter. She came over to the table and placed the tin tray with the bottles and glasses in front of Bond. She didn't look at Scaramanga. Scaramanga uttered a harsh bark of laughter. He reached inside his coat and took out an alligator-skin billfold. He extracted a hundred-dollar bill and threw it on the table. 'No hard feelings, cool cat. You'd be okay if you didn't always keep your legs together. Go buy yourself some more birds with that. I like to have smiling people around me.'

Tiffy picked up the note. She said, 'Thanks, Mister. You'd be surprised what I'm going to spend your money on.' She gave him a long, hard look and turned on her heel.

Scaramanga shrugged. He reached for a bottle of beer and a glass and both men poured and drank. Scaramanga took out an expensive cigar case, selected a pencil-thin cheroot and lit it with a match. He let the smoke dribble out between his lips and inhaled the thin stream up his nostrils. He did this several times with the same mouthful of smoke until the smoke was dissipated. All the while he stared across the table at Bond, seeming to weigh up something in his mind. He said, 'Care to earn yourself a grand — a thousand bucks?'

Bond said, 'Possibly.' He paused and added, 'Probably.' What he meant was, 'Of course! If it means staying close to you, my friend.'

Scaramanga smoked a while in silence. A car stopped outside and two laughing men came quickly up the steps. When they came through the bead curtains, working-class Jamaicans, they stopped laughing and went quietly over to the counter and began whispering to Tiffy. Then they both slapped a pound note on the counter and, making a wide detour away from the white men, disappeared through the curtains at the back of the room. Their laughter began again as Bond heard their footsteps on the stairs.

Scaramanga hadn't taken his eyes from Bond's face. Now he said, keeping his voice low, 'I got myself a problem. Some partners of mine, they've taken an interest in this Negril development. Far end of the property. Place called Bloody Bay. Know it?'

'I've seen it on the map. Just short of Green Island Harbour.'

'Right. So I've got some shares in the business. So we start building a hotel and get the first storey finished and the main living-rooms and restaurant and so on. So then the tourist boom slackens off — Americans get frightened of being so close to Cuba or some such crap. And the banks get difficult and money begins to run short. Follow me?'

'So you're a stale bull of the place?'

'Right. So I came over a few days ago and I'm staying at the Thunderbird and I've got a half-dozen of the main stockholders to fly in for a meeting on the spot. Sort of look the place over and get our heads together and figure what to do next. Now, I want to give these guys a good time so I've got a smart combo over from Kingston, calypso singers, limbo, plenty of girls — all the jazz. And there's swimming and one of the features of the place is a small-scale railway that used to handle the sugar cane. Runs to Green Island Harbour where I gotta forty-foot Chriscraft Roamer. Deep-sea fishing. That'll be another outing. Get me? Give the fellers a real good time.'

'So that they'll get all enthusiastic and buy out your share of the stock?'

Scaramanga frowned angrily. 'I'm not paying you a grand to get the wrong ideas. Or any ideas for the matter of that.'

'What for then?'

For a moment or two Scaramanga went through his smoking routine, the little pillars of smoke vanishing again and again into the black nostrils. It seemed to calm him. His forehead cleared. He said, 'Some of these men are kind of rough. We're all stockholders, of course, but that don't necessarily mean we're friends. Understand? I'll be wanting to hold some meetings, private meetings, with mebbe only two or three guys at a time, sort of sounding out the different interests. Could be that some of the other guys, the ones not invited to a particular meeting, might get it into their heads to bug a meeting or try and get wise to what goes on in one way or another. So it jes' occurs to me that you being live to security and such, that you could act as a kind of guard at these meetings, clean the room for mikes, stay outside the door and see that no one comes nosing around, see that when I want to be private I git private. D'you get the photo?'

Bond had to laugh. He said, 'So you want to hire me as a kind of personal bodyguard. Is that it?'

The frown was back. 'And what's so funny about that, Mister? It's good money, ain't it? Three, mebbe four days in a luxury joint like the Thunderbird. A thousand bucks at the end of it? What's so screwy about that proposition, eh?' Scaramanga mashed out the butt of his cigar against the underside of the table. A shower of sparks fell. He let them lie.

Bond scratched the back of his head as if reflecting. Which he was — furiously. He knew that he hadn't heard the full story. He also knew that it was odd, to say the least of it, for this man to hire a complete stranger to do this job for him. The job itself stood up, but only just. It made sense that Scaramanga would not want to hire a local man, an ex-policeman for instance, even if one could be found. Such a man might have friends in the hotel business who would be interested in the speculative side of the Negril development. And, of course, on the plus side, Bond would be achieving what he had never thought possible — he would have got right inside Scaramanga's guard. Or would he? There was the strong smell of a trap. But, assuming that Bond had not, by some obscure bit of ill luck, been blown, he couldn't for the life of him see what the trap could be. Well, clearly, he must make the gamble. In so many respects it was a chance in a million.

Bond lit a cigarette. He said, 'I was only laughing at the idea of a man of your particular skills wanting protection. But it all sounds great fun. Of course I'll come along. When do we start? I've got a car at the bottom of the road.'

Scaramanga thrust out an inside wrist and looked at a thin gold watch on a two-coloured gold bracelet. He said, '6.32. My car'll be outside.' He got up. 'Let's go. But don't forget one thing, Mister Whoosis. I rile mighty easy. Get me?'

Bond said easily, 'I saw how annoyed you got with those inoffensive birds.' He stood up. 'I don't see any reason why either of us should get riled.'

Scaramanga said indifferently, 'Okay, then.' He walked to the back of the room and picked up his suitcase, new-looking but cheap, strode to the exit and clashed through the bead curtain and down the steps.

Bond went quickly over to the counter. 'Goodbye, Tiffy. Hope I'll be coming by again one day. If anyone should ask after me, say I'm at the Thunderbird Hotel at Bloody Bay.'

Tiffy reached out a hand and timidly touched his sleeve. 'Go careful over there, Mister Mark. There's gangster money in that place. And watch out for yourself.' She jerked her head towards the exit: 'That's the worstest man I ever heard tell of.' She leaned forward and whispered, 'That's a thousand pound worth of ganja he's got in that bag. Rasta left it for him this morning. So I smelled the bag.' She drew quickly back.

Bond said, 'Thanks, Tiffy. See Mother Edna puts a good hex on him. I'll tell you why some day. I hope. 'Bye!' He went quickly out and down into the street where a red Thunderbird convertible was waiting, its exhaust making a noise like an expensive motor-boat. The chauffeur was a Jamaican, smartly dressed, with a peaked cap. A red pennant on the wireless aerial said 'The Thunderbird Hotel' in gold. Scaramanga was sitting beside the chauffeur. He said impatiently, 'Get in the back. Lift you down to your car. Then follow along. It gets a good road after a while.'

James Bond got into the car behind Scaramanga and wondered whether to shoot the man now, in the back of the head — the old Gestapo-K.G.B. point of puncture. A mixture of reasons prevented him — the itch of curiosity, an inbuilt dislike of cold murder, the feeling that this was not the predestined moment, the likelihood that he would have to murder the chauffeur also — these, combined with the softness of the night and the fact that the 'Sound System' was now playing a good recording of one of his favourites, 'After You've Gone', and that cicadas were singing from the *lignum vitae* tree, said 'No'. But at that moment, as the car coasted down Love Lane towards the bright mercury of the sea, James Bond knew that he was not only disobeying orders, or at best dodging them, he was also being a bloody fool.

7

UN-REAL ESTATE

WHEN HE ARRIVES AT a place on a dark night, particularly in an alien land which he has never seen before — a strange house, perhaps, or an hotel — even the most alert man is assailed by the confused sensations of the meanest tourist.

James Bond more or less knew the map of Jamaica. He knew that the sea had always been close to him on his left and, as he followed the twin red glares of the leading car through an impressive entrance gate of wrought iron and up an avenue of young royal palms, he heard the waves scrolling into a beach very close to his car. The fields of sugar cane would, he guessed from the approach, come close up against the new high wall that surrounded the Thunderbird property, and there was a slight smell of mangrove swamp coming down from below the high hills whose silhouette he had occasionally glimpsed under a scudding three-quarter moon on his right. But otherwise he had no clue to exactly where he was or what sort of a place he was now approaching and, particularly for him, the sensation was an uncomfortable one.

The first law for a secret agent is to get his geography right, his means of access and exit, and assure his communications with the outside world. James Bond was uncomfortably aware that, for the past hour, he had been driving into limbo and that his nearest contact was a girl in a brothel thirty miles away. The situation was not reassuring.

Half a mile ahead, someone must have seen the approaching lights of the leading car and pressed switches, for there was a sudden blaze of brilliant yellow illumination through the trees and a final sweep of the drive revealed the hotel. With the theatrical lighting and the surrounding blackness to conceal any evidence of halted construction work, the place made a brave show. A vast pale pink and white pillared portico gave the hotel an aristocratic frontage and, when Bond drew up behind the other car at the entrance, he could see through the tall Regency windows a vista of black and white marble flooring beneath blazing chandeliers. A bell captain and his Jamaican staff in red jackets and black trousers hurried down the steps and, after showing great deference to Scaramanga, took his suitcase and Bond's, then the small cavalcade moved into the entrance hall where Bond wrote 'Mark Hazard' and the Kensington address of Transworld Consortium in the register.

Scaramanga had been talking to a man who appeared to be the manager, a young American with a neat face and a neat suit. He turned to Bond. 'You're in Number 24 in the West Wing. I'm close by in Number 20. Order what you want from Room Service. See you about ten in the morning. The guys'll be coming in from Kingston around midday. Okay?' The cold eyes in the gaunt face didn't mind whether it was or not. Bond said it was. He followed one of the bell boys with his suitcase across the slippery marble floor and through an archway on the left of the hall and down a long white corridor with a close-fitted carpet in royal blue Wilton. There was a smell of new paint and Jamaican cedar. The numbered doors and the light fittings were in good taste. Bond's room was almost at the end on the left. No. 20 was opposite. The bell hop unlocked No. 24 and held the door for Bond. Air-conditioned air gushed out. It was a pleasant modern double bedroom and bath in grey and white. When he was alone, Bond went to the air-conditioning control and turned it to zero. Then he drew back the curtains and wound down the two broad windows to let in real air. Outside, the sea whispered softly on an invisible beach and the moonlight splashed the black shadows of palms across trim lawns. To his left, where the yellow light of the entrance showed a corner of the gravel sweep, Bond heard his car being started up and driven away, presumably to a parking lot which would, he guessed, be at the rear so as not to spoil the impact of the façade. He turned back into his room and inspected it minutely. The only objects of suspicion were a large picture on the wall above the two beds and the telephone. The picture was a Jamaican market scene painted locally. Bond lifted it off its nail, but the wall behind was innocent. He then took out a pocket knife, laid the telephone carefully, so as not to shift the receiver, upside down on a bed, and very quietly and carefully unscrewed the bottom plate. He smiled his satisfaction. Behind the plate was a small microphone joined by leads to the main cable inside the cradle. He screwed back the plate with the same care and put the telephone quietly back on the night table. He knew the gadget. It would be transistorized and of sufficient power to pick up a conversation in normal tones anywhere in the room. It crossed his mind to say very devout prayers out loud before he went to bed. That would be a fitting prologue for the central recording device!

James Bond unpacked his few belongings and called Room Service. A Jamaican voice answered. Bond ordered a bottle of Walker's de Luxe Bourbon, three glasses, ice and, for nine o'clock, Eggs Benedict. The voice said, 'Sure, sir.' Bond then took off his clothes, put his gun and holster under a pillow, rang for the valet and had his suit taken away to be pressed. By the time he had taken a hot shower followed by an ice-cold one and pulled on a fresh pair of Sea Island cotton underpants the bourbon had arrived.

The best drink in the day is just before the first one (the Red Stripe didn't count). James Bond put ice in the glass and three fingers of the bourbon and swilled it round the glass to cool it and break it down with the ice. He pulled a chair up to the window, put a low table beside it, took *Profiles in Courage* by Jack Kennedy out of his suitcase, happened to open it at Edmund G. Ross ('I looked down into my open grave'), then went and sat down, letting the scented air, a compound of sea and trees, breathe over his body, naked save for the underpants. He drank the bourbon down in two long draughts and felt its friendly bite at the back of his throat and in his stomach. He filled up his glass again, this time with more ice to make it a weaker drink, and sat back and thought about Scaramanga.

What was the man doing now? Talking long distance with Havana or the States? Organizing things for tomorrow? It would be interesting to see these fat, frightened stockholders! If Bond knew anything, they would be a choice bunch of hoods, the type that had owned the Havana hotels and casinos in the old Batista days, the men that held the stock in Las Vegas, that looked after the action in Miami. And whose money was Scaramanga representing? There was so much hot money drifting around the Caribbean that it might be any of the syndicates, any of the banana dictators from the islands or the mainland. And the man himself? It had been damned fine shooting that had killed the two birds swerving through the window of 3½. How in hell was Bond going to take him? On an impulse, Bond went over to his bed and took the Walther from under the pillow. He slipped out the magazine and pumped the single round on to the counterpane. He tested the spring of the magazine and of the breech and drew a quick bead on various objects round the room. He found he was aiming an inch or so high. But that would be because the gun was lighter without its loaded magazine. He snapped the magazine back and tried again. Yes, that was better. He pumped a round into the breech, put up the safety and replaced the gun under the pillow. Then he went back to his drink and picked up the book and forgot his worries in the high endeavours of great men.

The eggs came and were good. The mousseline sauce might have been mixed at Maxim's. Bond had the tray removed, poured himself a last drink and prepared for bed. Scaramanga would certainly have a master key. Tomorrow, Bond would whittle himself a wedge to jam the door. For tonight, he upended his suitcase just inside the door and balanced the three glasses on top of it. It was a simple booby trap but it would give him all the warning he needed. Then he took off his shorts and got into bed and slept.

A nightmare woke him, sweating, around two in the morning. He had been defending a fort. There were other defenders with him, but they seemed to be wandering around aimlessly, ineffectively, and when Bond shouted to rally them they seemed not to hear him. Out on the plain, Scaramanga sat bassackwards on the café chair beside a huge golden cannon. Every now and then, he put his long cigar to the touch-hole and there came a tremendous flash of soundless flame. A black cannon ball, as big as a football, lobbed up high in the air and crashed down into the fort with a shattering noise of breaking timber. Bond was armed with nothing but a longbow, but even this he could not fire because, every time he tried to fit the notch of the arrow into the gut, the arrow slipped out of his fingers to the ground. He cursed his clumsiness. Any moment now and a huge cannon ball would land on the small open space where he was standing! Out on the plain, Scaramanga reached his cigar to the touch-hole. The black ball soared up. It was coming straight for Bond! It landed just in front of him and came rolling very slowly towards him, getting bigger and bigger, smoke and sparks coming from its shortening fuse. Bond threw up an arm to protect himself. Painfully, the arm crashed into the side of the night table and Bond woke up.

Bond got out of bed, gave himself a cold shower and drank a glass of water. By the time he was back in bed, he had forgotten the nightmare and he went quickly to sleep and slept dreamlessly until 7.30 in the morning. He put on swimming trunks, removed the barricade from in front of the door and went out into the passage. To his left, a door into the garden was open and sun streamed in. He went out and was walking over the dewy grass towards the beach when he heard a curious thumping noise from among the palms to his right. He walked over. It was Scaramanga, in trunks, attended by a good-looking young Negro holding a flame-coloured terry-cloth robe, doing exercises on a trampoline. Scaramanga's body gleamed with sweat in the sunshine as he hurled himself high in the air from the stretched canvas and bounded back, sometimes from his knees or his buttocks and sometimes even from his head. It was an impressive exercise in gymnastics. The prominent third nipple over the heart made an obvious target! Bond walked thoughtfully down to the beautiful crescent of white sand fringed with gently clashing palm trees. He dived in and, because of the other man's example, swam twice as far as he had intended.

James Bond had a quick and small breakfast in his room, dressed, reluctantly because of the heat, in his dark blue suit, armed himself and went for a walk round the property. He quickly got the picture. The night, and the lighted façade, had covered up a half-project. The East Wing on the other side of the lobby was still lath and plaster. The body of the hotel — the restaurant, night club and living-rooms that were the tail of the T-shaped structure, were mock-ups — stages for a dress rehearsal hastily assembled with the essential props, carpets, light fixtures and a scattering of furniture, but stinking of fresh paint and wood shavings. Perhaps fifty men and women were at work, tacking up curtains, Hoovering carpets, fixing the electricity, but no one was employed on the essentials, the big cement mixers, the drills, the ironwork, that lay about behind the hotel like the abandoned toys of a giant. At a guess, the place would need another year and another five million dollars to become what the plans had said it was to be. Bond saw Scaramanga's problem. Someone was going to complain about this. Others would want to get out. But then again, others would want to buy in, but cheaply, and use it as a tax-loss to set against more profitable enterprises elsewhere. Better to have a capital asset, with the big tax concessions that Jamaica gave, than pay the money to Uncle Sam, Uncle Fidel, Uncle Trujillo, Uncle Leoni of Venezuela. So Scaramanga's job would be to blind his guests with pleasure, send them back half drunk to their syndicates. Would it work? Bond knew such people and he doubted it. They might go to bed drunk with a pretty coloured girl, but they would awake sober or they wouldn't have their jobs, they wouldn't be coming here with their discreet brief-cases.

He walked farther back on the property. He wanted to locate his car. He found it on a deserted lot behind the West Wing. The sun would get at where it was so he drove it forward and into the shade of a giant ficus tree. He checked the petrol and pocketed the ignition key. There were not too many small precautions he could take.

On the parking lot, the smell of the swamps was very strong. While it was still comparatively cool, he decided to walk farther. He soon came to the end of the young shrubs and guinea grass the landscaper had laid on. Behind these was desolation — a great area of sluggish streams and swampland from which the hotel land had been recovered. Egrets, shrikes and Lousiana herons rose and settled lazily, and there were strange insect noises and the call of frogs and geckos. On what would probably be the border of the property a biggish stream meandered towards the sea, its muddy banks pitted with the holes of land crabs and water rats. As Bond approached, there was a heavy splash and a man-sized alligator left the bank and showed its snout before submerging. Bond smiled to himself. No doubt, if the hotel got off the ground, all this area would be turned into an asset. There would be native boatmen, suitably attired as Arawak Indians, a landing-stage and comfortable boats, with fringed shades, from which the guests could view the 'tropical jungle' for an extra ten dollars on the bill.

Bond glanced at his watch. He strolled back. To the left, not yet screened by the young oleanders and crotons that had been planted for this eventual purpose, were the kitchens and laundry and staff quarters, the usual back quarters of a luxury hotel, and music, the heartbeat thump of Jamaican calypso, came from their direction — presumably the Kingston combo rehearsing. Bond walked round and under the portico into the main lobby. Scaramanga was at the desk talking to the manager. When he heard Bond's footsteps on the marble, he turned and looked and gave Bond a curt nod. He was dressed as on the previous day, and the high white cravat suited the elegance of the hall. He said 'Okay, then' to the manager and, to Bond, 'Let's go take a look at the conference room.'

Bond followed him through the restaurant door and then through another door to the right that opened into a lobby, one of whose walls was taken up with the glasses and plates of a buffet. Beyond this was another door. Scaramanga led the way through into what would one day perhaps be a card room or writing-room. Now there was nothing but a round table in the centre of a wine-red carpet and seven white leatherette armchairs with scratch pads and pencils in front of them. The chair facing the door, presumably Scaramanga's, had a white telephone in front of it.

Bond went round the room and examined the windows and the curtains and glanced at the wall brackets of the lighting. He said, 'The brackets could be bugged. And of course there's the telephone. Like me to go over it?'

Scaramanga looked at Bond stonily. He said, 'No need to. It's bugged all right. By me. Got to have a record of what's said.'

Bond said, 'All right, then. Where do you want me to be?'

'Outside the door. Sitting reading a magazine or something. There'll be the general meeting this afternoon around four. Tomorrow there'll mebbe be one or two smaller meetings, mebbe just me and one of the guys. I want all these meetings not to be disturbed. Got it?'

'Seems simple enough. Now, isn't it about time you told me the names of these men and more or less who they represent and which ones, if any, you're expecting trouble from?'

Scaramanga said, 'Take a chair and a paper and pencil.' He strolled up and down the room. 'First there's Mr Hendriks.

Dutchman. Represents the European money, mostly Swiss. You needn't bother with him. He's not the arguing type. Then there's Sam Binion from Detroit.'

'The Purple Gang?'

Scaramanga stopped in his stride and looked hard at Bond. 'These are all respectable guys, Mister Whoosis.'

'Hazard is the name.'

'All right. Hazard, then. But respectable, you understand. Don't go getting the notion that this is another Apalachian. These are all solid businessmen. Get me? This Sam Binion, for instance. He's in real estate. He and his friends are worth mebbe twenty million bucks. See what I mean? Then there's Leroy Gengerella. Miami. Owns Gengerella Enterprises. Big shot in the entertainment world. He may cut up rough. Guys in that line of business like quick profits and a quick turnover. And Ruby Rotkopf, the hotel man from Vegas. He'll ask the difficult questions because he'll already know most of the answers from experience. Hal Garfinkel from Chicago. He's in labour relations, like me. Represents a lot of Teamster Union funds. He shouldn't be any trouble. Those unions have got so much money they don't know where to put it. That makes five. Last comes Louie Paradise from Phoenix, Arizona. Owns Paradise Slots, the biggest people in the one-armed-bandit business. Got casino interests too. I can't figure which way he'll bet. That's the lot.'

'And who do you represent, Mr Scaramanga?'

'Caribbean money.'

'Cuban?'

'I said Caribbean. Cuba's in the Caribbean, isn't it?'

'Castro or Batista?'

The frown was back. Scaramanga's right hand balled into a fist. 'I told you not to rile me, Mister. So don't go prying into my affairs or you'll get hurt. And that's for sure.' As if he could hardly control himself longer, the big man turned on his heel and strode brusquely out of the room.

James Bond smiled. He turned back to the list in front of him. A strong reek of high gangsterdom rose from the paper. But the name he was most interested in was Mr Hendriks who represented 'European money'. If that was his real name, and he was a Dutchman, so, James Bond reflected, was he.

He tore off three sheets of paper to efface the impression of his pencil and walked out and along into the lobby. A bulky man was approaching the desk from the entrance. He was sweating mightily in his unseasonable wooden-looking suit. He might have been anybody — an Antwerp diamond merchant, a German dentist, a Swiss bank manager. The pale, square-jowled face was totally anonymous. He put a heavy brief-case on the desk and said in a thick Central European accent, 'I am Mr Hendriks. I think it is that you have a room for me, isn't it?'

8

PASS THE CANAPÉS!

THE CARS BEGAN rolling up. Scaramanga was in evidence. He switched a careful smile of welcome on and off. No hands were shaken. The host was greeted either as 'Pistol' or 'Mr S' except by Mr Hendriks, who called him nothing.

Bond stood within earshot of the desk and fitted the names to the men. In general appearance they were all much of a muchness. Dark-faced, clean-shaven, around five feet six, hard-eyed above thinly smiling mouths, curt of speech to the manager. They all held firmly on to their brief-cases when the bell boys tried to add them to the luggage on the rubber-tyred barrows. They dispersed to their rooms along the East Wing. Bond took out his list and added hat-check notations to each one except Hendriks who was clearly etched in Bond's memory. Gengerella became 'Italian origin, mean, pursed mouth'; Rotkopf, 'Thick neck, totally bald, Jew'; Binion, 'Bat ears, scar down left cheek, limp'; Garfinkel, 'The toughest. Bad teeth, gun under right armpit'; and, finally, Paradise, 'Showman type, cocky, false smile, diamond ring.'

Scaramanga came up. 'What you writing?'

'Just notes to remember them by.'

'Gimme.' Scaramanga held out a demanding hand.

Bond gave him the list.

Scaramanga ran his eyes down it. He handed it back. 'Fair enough. But you needn't have mentioned the only gun you noticed. They'll all be protected. Except Hendriks, I guess. These kinda guys are nervous when they move abroad.'

'What of?'

Scaramanga shrugged. 'Mebbe the natives.'

'The last people who worried about the natives were the redcoats, perhaps a hundred and fifty years ago.'

'Who cares? See you in the bar around twelve. I'll be introducing you as my Personal Assistant.'

'That'll be fine.'

Scaramanga's brows came together. Bond strolled off in the direction of his bedroom. He proposed to needle this man, and go on needling until it came to a fight. For the time being the other man would probably take it because it seemed he needed Bond. But there would come a moment, probably on an occasion when there were witnesses, when his vanity would be so sharply pricked that he would draw. Then Bond would have a small edge, for it would be he who had thrown down the glove. The tactic was a crude one, but Bond could think of no other.

Bond verified that his room had been searched at some time during the morning — and by an expert. He always used a Hoffritz safety razor patterned on the old-fashioned heavy-toothed Gillette type. His American friend Felix Leiter had once bought him one in New York to prove that they were the best, and Bond had stayed with them. The handle of a safety razor is a reasonably sophisticated hideout for the minor tools of espionage — codes, microdot developers, cyanide and other pills. That morning Bond had set a minute nick on the screw base of the handle in line with the 'Z' of the maker's name engraved on the shaft. The nick was now a millimetre to the right of the 'Z'. None of his other little traps, handkerchiefs with indelible dots in particular places arranged in a certain order, the angle of his suitcase with the wall of the wardrobe, the semi-extracted lining of the breast pocket of his spare suit, the particular symmetry of certain dents in his tube of Maclean's toothpaste, had been bungled or disturbed. They all might have been by a meticulous servant, a trained valet. But Jamaican servants, for all their charm and willingness, are not of this calibre. No. Between nine and ten, when Bond was doing his rounds and was well away from the hotel, his room had received a thorough going-over by someone who knew his business.

Bond was pleased. It was good to know that the fight was well and truly joined. If he found a chance of making a foray into No. 20, he hoped that he would do better. He took a shower. Afterwards, as he brushed his hair, he looked at himself in the mirror with inquiry. He was feeling a hundred per cent fit, but he remembered the dull, lacklustre eyes that had looked back at him when he shaved after first entering The Park — the tense, preoccupied expression on his face. Now the grey-blue eyes looked back at him from the tanned face with the brilliant glint of suppressed excitement and accurate focus of the old days. He smiled ironically back at the introspective scrutiny that so many people make of themselves before a race, a contest of wits, a trial of some sort. He had no excuses. He was ready to go.

The bar was through a brass-studded leather door opposite the lobby to the conference room. It was — in the fashion — a mock-English public-house saloon bar with luxury accessories. The scrubbed wooden chairs and benches had foam-rubber squabs in red leather. Behind the bar, the tankards were of silver, or simulated silver, instead of pewter. The hunting prints, copper and brass hunting horns, muskets and powder horns, on the walls could have come from the Parker Galleries in London. Instead of tankards of beer, bottles of champagne in antique coolers stood on the tables and, instead of yokels, the hoods stood around in what looked like Brooks Brothers 'tropical' attire and carefully sipped their drinks while 'Mine Host' leant against the polished mahogany bar and twirled his golden gun round and round on the first finger of his right hand like the snide poker cheat out of an old Western.

As the door closed behind Bond with a pressurized sigh, the golden gun halted in mid-whirl and sighted on Bond's stomach. 'Fellers,' said Scaramanga, mock boisterous, 'meet my Personal Assistant, Mr Mark Hazard, from London, England. He's come along to make things run smoothly over this weekend. Mark, come over and meet the gang and pass round the canapés.' He lowered the gun and shoved it into his waistband.

James Bond stitched a Personal Assistant smile on his face and walked up to the bar. Perhaps because he was an Englishman, there was a round of handshaking. The red-coated barman asked him what he would have and he said, 'Some pink gin. Plenty of bitters. Beefeater's.' There was desultory talk about the relative merits of gins. Everyone else seemed to be drinking champagne except Mr Hendriks who stood away from the group and nursed a Schweppes Bitter Lemon. Bond moved among the men. He made small talk about their flight, the weather in the States, the beauties of Jamaica. He wanted to fit the voices to the names. He gravitated towards Mr Hendriks. 'Seems we're the only two Europeans here. Gather you're from

Holland. Often passed through. Never stayed there long. Beautiful country.'

The very pale blue eyes regarded Bond unenthusiastically. 'Sank you.'

'What part do you come from?'

'Den Haag.'

'Have you lived there long?'

'Many, many years.'

'Beautiful town.'

'Sank you.'

'Is this your first visit to Jamaica?'

'No.'

'How do you like it?'

'It is a beautiful place.'

Bond nearly said 'Sank you'. He smiled encouragingly at Mr Hendriks as much as to say, 'I've made all the running so far. Now you say something.'

Mr Hendriks looked past Bond's right ear at nothing. The pressure of the silence built up. Mr Hendriks shifted his weight from one foot to the other and finally broke down. His eyes shifted and looked thoughtfully at Bond. 'And you. You are from London, isn't it?'

'Yes. Do you know it?'

'I have been there, yes.'

'Where do you usually stay?'

There was hesitation. 'With friends.'

'That must be convenient.'

'Pliss?'

'I mean it's pleasant to have friends in a foreign town. Hotels are so much alike.'

'I have not found this. Excuse pliss.' With a Germanic bob of the head Mr Hendriks moved decisively away from Bond and went up to Scaramanga, who was still lounging in solitary splendour at the bar. Mr Hendriks said something. His words acted like a command on the other man. Mr Scaramanga straightened himself and followed Mr Hendriks into a far corner of the room. He stood and listened with deference as Mr Hendriks talked rapidly in a low tone.

Bond, joining the other men, was interested. It was his guess that no other man in the room could have buttonholed

Scaramanga with so much authority. He noticed that many fleeting glances were cast in the direction of the couple apart. For Bond's money, this was either the Mafia or K.G.B. Probably even the other five wouldn't know which, but they would certainly recognize the secret smell of 'The Machine' which Mr Hendriks exuded so strongly.

Luncheon was announced. The Jamaican head waiter hovered between two richly prepared tables. There were place cards. Bond found that, while Scaramanga was host at one of them, he himself was at the head of the other table between Mr Paradise and Mr Rotkopf. As he expected, Mr Paradise was the better value of the two and, as they went through the conventional shrimp cocktail, steak, fruit salad of the Americanized hotel abroad, Bond cheerfully got himself involved in an argument about the odds at roulette when there are one zero or two. Mr Rotkopf's only contribution was to say, through a mouthful of steak and French fried, that he had once tried three zeros at the Black Cat Casino in Miami but that the experiment had failed. Mr Paradise said that so it should have. 'You got to let the suckers win sometimes, Ruby, or they won't come back. Sure, you can squeeze the juice out of them, but you oughta leave them the pips. Like with my slots. I tell the customers, don't be too greedy. Don't set 'em at thirty per cent for the house. Set 'em at twenty. You ever heard of Mr J. B. Morgan turning down a net profit of twenty per cent? Hell, no! So why try and be smarter than guys like that?'

Mr Rotkopf said sourly, 'You got to make big profits to put against a bum steer like this.' He waved a hand. 'If you ask me,' he held up a bit of steak on his fork, 'you're eating the only money you're going to see out of this dump at this minute.'

Mr Paradise leaned across the table and said softly, 'You know something?'

Mr Rotkopf said, 'I always told my money that the bindweed would get this place. The dam' fools wouldn't listen. And look where we are in three years! Second mortgage nearly run out and we've only got one storey up. What I say is . . .'

The argument went off into the realms of high finance. At the next-door table there was not even this amount of animation. Scaramanga was a man of few words. There were clearly none available for social occasions. Opposite him, Mr Hendriks exuded a silence as thick as Gouda cheese. The three hoods addressed an occasional glum sentence to anyone who would listen. James Bond wondered how Scaramanga was going to electrify this unpromising company into 'having a good time'.

Luncheon broke up and the company dispersed to their rooms. James Bond wandered round to the back of the hotel and found a discarded shingle on a rubbish dump. It was blazing hot under the afternoon sun, but the Doctor's wind was blowing in from the sea. For all its air-conditioning, there was something grim about the impersonal grey and white of Bond's bedroom. Bond walked along the shore, took off his coat and tie and sat in the shade of a bush of sea grapes and watched the fiddler crabs about their minuscule business in the sand while he whittled two chunky wedges out of the Jamaican cedar. Then he closed his eyes and thought about Mary Goodnight. She would now be having her siesta in some villa on the outskirts of Kingston. It would probably be high up in the Blue Mountains for the coolness. In Bond's imagination, she would be lying on her bed under a mosquito net. Because of the heat, she would have nothing on, and one could see only an ivory and gold shape through the fabric of the net. But one would know that there were small beads of sweat on her upper lip and between her breasts and the fringes of the golden hair would be damp. Bond took off his clothes and lifted up the corner of the mosquito net, not wanting to wake her until he had fitted himself against her thighs. But she turned, in half sleep, towards him and held out her arms. 'James . . .'

Under the sea-grape bush, a hundred and twenty miles away from the scene of the dream, James Bond's head came up with a jerk. He looked quickly, guiltily, at his watch. 3.30. He went off to his room and had a cold shower, verified that his cedar wedges would do what they were meant to do, and strolled down the corridor to the lobby.

The manager with the neat suit and neat face came out from behind his desk. 'Er, Mr Hazard.'

'Yes.'

'I don't think you've met my assistant, Mr Travis.'

'No, I don't think I have.'

'Would you care to step into the office for a moment and shake him by the hand?'

'Later perhaps. We've got this conference on in a few minutes.'

The neat man came a step closer. He said quietly, 'He particularly wants to meet you, Mr — er — Bond.'

Bond cursed himself. This was always happening in his particular trade. You were looking in the dark for a beetle with red wings. Your eyes were focused for that particular pattern on the bark of the tree. You didn't notice the moth with cryptic colouring that crouched quietly near by, itself like a piece of the bark, itself just as important to the collector. The focus of your eyes was too narrow. Your mind was too concentrated. You were using 1 × 100 magnification and your 1 × 10 was not in focus. Bond looked at the man with the recognition that exists between crooks, between homosexuals, between secret agents. It is the look common to men bound by secrecy — by common trouble. 'Better make it quick.'

The neat man stepped behind his desk and opened a door. Bond went in and the neat man closed the door behind them. A tall, slim man was standing at a filing cabinet. He turned. He had a lean, bronzed Texan face under an unruly mop of straight fair hair, and, instead of a right hand, a bright steel hook. Bond stopped in his tracks. His face split into a smile broader than he had smiled for what? Was it three years or four? He said, 'You goddamned lousy crook. What in hell are you doing here?' He went up to the man and hit him hard on the biceps of the left arm.

The grin was slightly more creased than Bond remembered, but it was just as friendly and ironical. Mr Travis said, 'The name is Leiter, Mr Felix Leiter. Temporary accountant on loan from Morgan Guarantee Trust to the Thunderbird Hotel. We're just checking up on your credit rating, Mr Hazard. Would you kindly, in your royal parlance, extract your finger, and give me some evidence that you are who you claim to be?'

9

MINUTES OF THE MEETING

JAMES BOND, ALMOST light-headed with pleasure, picked up a handful of travel literature from the front desk, said 'Hi!' to Mr Gengerella, who didn't reply, and followed him into the conference room lobby. They were the last to show. Scaramanga, beside the open door to the conference room, looked pointedly at his watch and said to Bond, 'Okay, feller. Lock the door when we're all settled and don't let anyone in even if the hotel catches fire.' He turned to the barman behind the loaded buffet. 'Get lost, Joe. I'll call for you later.' He said to the room, 'Right. We're all set. Let's go.' He led the way into the conference room and the six men followed. Bond stood by the door and noted the seating order round the table. He closed the door and locked it and quickly also locked the exit from the lobby. Then he picked up a champagne glass from the buffet, pulled over a chair and sited the chair very close to the door of the conference room. He placed the bowl of the champagne glass as near as possible to a hinge of the door and, holding the glass by the stem, put his left ear up against its base. Through the crude amplifier, what had been the rumble of a voice became Mr Hendriks speaking, '. . . and so it is that I will now report from my superiors in Europe . . .' The voice paused and Bond heard another noise, the creak of a chair. Like lightning he pulled his chair back a few feet, opened one of the travel folders on his lap and raised the glass to his lips. The door jerked open and Scaramanga stood in the opening, twirling his pass key on a chain. He examined the innocent figure on the chair. He said, 'Okay, feller. Just checking,' and kicked the door shut. Bond noisily locked it and took up his place again. Mr Hendriks said, 'I have one most important message for our Chairman. It is from a sure source. There is a man that is called James Bond that is looking for him in this territory. This is a man who is from the British Secret Service. I have no informations or descriptions of this man but it seems that he is highly rated by my superiors. Mr Scaramanga, have you heard of this man?'

Scaramanga snorted. 'Hell, no! And should I care? I eat one of their famous secret agents for breakfast from time to time. Only ten days ago, I disposed of one of them who came nosing after me. Man called Ross. His body is now very slowly sinking to the bottom of a pitch lake in eastern Trinidad — place called La Brea. The oil company, the Trinidad Lake Asphalt people, will obtain an interesting barrel of crude one of these days. Next question, please, Mr Hendriks.'

'Next I am wishing to know what is the policy of The Group in the matter of cane sabotage. At our meeting six months ago in Havana, against my minority vote, it was decided, in exchange for certain favours, to come to the aid of Fidel Castro and assist in maintaining and indeed increasing the world price of sugar to offset the damage caused by Hurricane Flora. Since this time there have been very numerous fires in the cane fields of Jamaica and Trinidad. In this connection, it has come to the ears of my superiors that individual members of The Group, notably,' there was the rustle of paper, 'Messrs Gengerella, Rotkopf and Binion, in addition to our Chairman, have engaged in extensive purchasing of July sugar futures for the benefit of private gain . . .'

There came an angry murmur from round the table. 'Why shouldn't we . . .? Why shouldn't they . . .?' The voice of Gengerella dominated the others. He shouted, 'Who in hell said we weren't to make money? Isn't that one of the objects of The Group? I ask you again, Mr Hendriks, as I asked you six months ago, who in hell is it among your so-called "superiors" who wants to keep the price of raw sugar down? For my money, the most interested party in such a gambit would be Soviet Russia. They're selling goods to Cuba, including, let me say, the recently abortive shipment of missiles to fire against my homeland, in exchange for raw sugar. They're sharp traders, the Reds. In their double-dealing way, even from a friend and ally, they would want more sugar for fewer goods. Yes? I suppose,' the voice sneered, 'one of your superiors, Mr Hendriks, would not by any chance be in the Kremlin?'

The voice of Scaramanga cut through the ensuing hubbub. 'Fellers! Fellers!' A reluctant silence fell. 'When we formed this

Co-operative, it was agreed that the first object was to co-operate with one another. Okay, then. Mr Hendriks. Let me put you more fully in the picture. So far as the total finances of The Group are concerned, we have a fine situation coming up. As an investment group, we have good bets and bad bets. Sugar is a good bet and we should ride that bet even though certain members of The Group have chosen not to be on the horse. Get me? Now hear me through. There are six ships controlled by The Group at this moment riding at anchor outside New York and other U.S. harbours. These ships are loaded with raw sugar. These ships, Mr Hendriks, will not dock and unload until sugar futures, July futures, have risen another ten cents. In Washington, the Department of Agriculture and the Sugar Lobby know this. They know that we have them by the balls. Meantimes the liquor lobby is leaning on them — let alone Russia. The price of molasses is going up with sugar and the rum barons are kicking up hell and want our ships let in before there's a real shortage and the price goes through the roof. But there's another side to it. We're having to pay our crews and our charter bills and so on, and squatting ships are dead ships, dead losses. So something's going to give. In the business, the situation we've developed is called the Floating Crop Game — our ships lying offshore, lined up against the Government of the United States. All right. So now four of us stand to win or lose ten million bucks or so — us and our backers. And we've got this little business of the Thunderbird on the red side of the sheet. So what do you think, Mr Hendriks? Of course we burn the crops where we can get away with it. I got a good in with the Rastafaris — that's a beat sect here that grows beards and smokes ganja and mostly lives on a bit of land outside Kingston called the Dungle — the Dunghill — and believes it owes allegiance to the King of Ethiopia, this King Zog or what-have-you, and that that's their rightful home. So I've got a man in there, a man who wants the ganja for them, and I keep him supplied in exchange for plenty fires and troubles on the cane lands. So all right, Mr Hendriks. You just tell your superiors that what goes up must come down and that applies to the price of sugar like anything else. Okay?'

Mr Hendriks said, 'I will pass on your saying, Mr Scaramanga. It will not cause pleasure. Now there is this business of the hotel. How is she standing, if you pliss? I think we are all wishing to know the true situation, isn't it?'

There was a growl of assent.

Mr Scaramanga went off into a long dissertation which was only of passing interest to Bond. Felix Leiter would in any case be getting it all on the tape in a drawer of his filing cabinet. He had reassured Bond on this score. The neat American, Leiter had explained, filling him in with the essentials, was in fact a certain Mr Nick Nicholson of the C.I.A. His particular concern was Mr Hendriks who, as Bond had suspected, was a top man of the K.G.B. The K.G.B. favours oblique control — a man in Geneva being the Resident Director for Italy, for instance — and Mr Hendriks at The Hague was in fact Resident Director for the Caribbean and in charge of the Havana centre. Leiter was still working for Pinkertons, but was also on the reserve of the C.I.A. who had drafted him for this particular assignment because of his knowledge, gained in the past mostly with James Bond, of Jamaica. His job was to get a breakdown of The Group and find out what they were up to. They were all well-known hoods who would normally have been the concern of the F.B.I., but Gengerella was a Capo Mafiosi and this was the first time the Mafia had been found consorting with the K.G.B. — a most disturbing partnership which must at all costs be quickly broken up, by physical elimination if need be. Nick Nicholson, whose 'front' name was Mr Stanley Jones, was an electronics expert. He had traced the main lead to Scaramanga's recording device under the floor of the central switch room and had bled off the microphone cable to his own tape recorder in the filing cabinet. So Bond had not much to worry about. He was listening to satisfy his own curiosity and to fill in on anything that might transpire in the lobby or out of range of the bug in the telephone on the conference room table. Bond had explained his own presence. Leiter had given a long low whistle of respectful apprehension. Bond had agreed to keep well clear of the other two men and to paddle his own canoe, but they had arranged an emergency meeting place and a postal 'drop' in the uncompleted and 'Out of Order' men's room off the lobby. Nicholson had given him a pass key for this place and all other rooms and then Bond had had to hurry off to his meeting. James Bond was immensely reassured by finding these unexpected reinforcements. He had worked with Leiter on some of his most hazardous assignments. There was no man like him when the chips were down. Although Leiter had only a steel hook instead of a right arm — a memento of one of those assignments — he was one of the finest left-handed one-armed shots in the States and the hook itself could be a devastating weapon at close quarters.

Scaramanga was finishing his exposition. 'So the net of it is, gentlemen, that we need to find ten million bucks. The interests I represent, which are the majority interests, suggest that this sum should be provided by a Note issue, bearing interest at ten per cent and repayable in ten years, such an issue to have priority over all other loans.'

The voice of Mr Rotkopf broke in angrily. 'The hell it will! Not on your life, Mister. What about the seven per cent second mortgage put up by me and my friends only a year back? What do you think I'd get if I went back to Vegas with that kind of parley? The old heave-ho! And at that I'm being optimistic.'

'Beggars can't be choosers, Ruby. It's that or close. What do you other fellers have to say?'

Hendriks said, 'Ten per cent on a first charge is good pizzness. My friends and I will take one million dollars. On the understanding, it is natural, that the conditions of the issue are, how shall I say, more substantial, less open to misunderstandings, than the second mortgage of Mr Rotkopf and his friends.'

'Of course. And I and my friends will also take a million. Sam?'

Mr Binion said reluctantly, 'Okay, okay. Count us in for the same. But by golly this has got to be the last touch.'

'Mr Gengerella?'

'It sounds a good bet. I'll take the rest.'

The voices of Mr Garfinkel and Mr Paradise broke in excitedly, Garfinkel in the lead. 'Like hell you will! I'm taking a million.'

'And so am I,' shouted Mr Paradise. 'Cut the cake equally. But dammit. Let's be fair to Ruby. Ruby, you oughta have first pick. How much do you want? You can have it off the top.'

'I don't want a damned cent of your phoney Notes. As soon as I get back, I'm going to reach for the best damned lawyers in the States — all of them. You think you can scrub a mortgage just by saying so, you've all got another think coming.'

There was silence. The voice of Scaramanga was soft and deadly. 'You're making a big mistake, Ruby. You've just got yourself a nice fat tax-loss to put against your Vegas interests. And don't forget that when we formed this Group we all took an oath. None of us was to operate against the interests of the others. Is that your last word?'

'It dam' is.'

'Would this help you change your mind? They've got a slogan for it in Cuba — *Rapido! Seguro! Economico!* This is how the system operates.'

The scream of terror and the explosion were simultaneous. A chair crashed to the floor and there was a moment's silence. Then someone coughed nervously. Mr Gengerella said calmly, 'I think that was the correct solution of an embarrassing conflict of interests. Ruby's friends in Vegas like a quiet life. I doubt if they will even complain. It is better to be a live owner of some finely engraved paper than to be a dead holder of a second mortgage. Put them in for a million, Pistol. I think you behaved with speed and correctness. Now then, can you clean this up?'

'Sure, sure.' Mr Scaramanga's voice was relaxed, happy. 'Ruby's left here to go back to Vegas. Never heard of again. We don't know nuthen'. I've got some hungry crocs out back there in the river. They'll give him free transportation to where he's going — and his baggage if it's good leather. I shall need some help tonight. What about you, Sam? And you, Louie?'

The voice of Mr Paradise pleaded. 'Count me out, Pistol. I'm a good Catholic.'

Mr Hendriks said, 'I will take his place. I am not a Catholic person.'

'So it be then. Well, fellers, any other business? If not, we'll break up the meeting and have a drink.'

Hal Garfinkel said nervously, 'Just a minute, Pistol. What about that guy outside the door? That limey feller? What's he going to say about the fireworks and all?'

Mr Scaramanga's chuckle was like the dry chuckle of a gecko. 'Just don't you worry your tiny head about the limey, Hal. He'll be looked after when the weekend's over. Picked him up in a bordello in a village near by. Place where I go get my weed and a bit of black tail. Got only temporary staff here to see you fellers have a good time over the weekend. He's the temporariest of the lot. Those crocs have a big appetite. Ruby'll be the main dish, but they'll need a dessert. Jes' you leave him to me. For all I know he may be this James Bond man Mr Hendriks has told us about. I should worry. I don't like limeys. Like some good yankee once said, "For every Britisher that dies, there's a song in my heart." Remember the guy? Around the time of the Israeli war against them. I dig that viewpoint. Stuck-up bastards. Stuffed shirts. When the time comes, I'm going to let the stuffing out of this one. Jes' you leave him to me. Or let's jes' say leave him to this.'

Bond smiled a thin smile. He could imagine the golden gun being produced and twirled round the finger and stuck back in the waistband. He got up and moved his chair away from the door and poured champagne into the useful glass and leant against the buffet and studied the latest hand-out from the Jamaica Tourist Board.

The click of Scaramanga's pass key sounded in the lock. Scaramanga looked at Bond from the doorway. He ran a finger along the small moustache. 'Okay, feller. I guess that's enough of the house champagne. Cut along to the manager and tell him Mr Ruby Rotkopf'll be checking out tonight. I'll fix the details. And say a major fuse blew during the meeting and I'm going to seal off this room and find out why we're having so much bad workmanship around the place. 'Kay? Then drinks and dinner and bring on the dancing girls. Got the photo?'

James Bond said that he had. He weaved slightly as he went to the lobby door and unlocked it. 'E. & O.E. — Errors and omissions excepted' as the financial prospectuses say, he thought that he had indeed now 'got the photo'. And it was an exceptionally clear print in black and white without 'fuzz'.

10

BELLY-LICK, ETC.

IN THE BACK office, James Bond went quickly over the highlights of the meeting. Nick Nicholson and Felix Leiter agreed they had enough on the tape, supported by Bond, to send Scaramanga to the chair. That night, one of them would do some snooping while the body of Rotkopf was being disposed of and try and get enough evidence to have Garfinkel and, better still, Hendriks indicted as accessories. But they didn't at all like the outlook for James Bond. Felix commanded him, 'Now don't you move an inch without that old equalizer of yours. We don't want to have to read that obituary of yours in *The Times* all over again. All that crap about what a splendid feller you are nearly made me throw up when I saw it reprinted in the American blatts. I dam' nearly fired off a piece to the *Trib* putting the record straight.'

Bond laughed. He said, 'You're a fine friend, Felix. When I think of all the trouble I've been to to set you a good example all these years.' He went off to his room, swallowed two heavy slugs of bourbon, had a cold shower and lay on his bed and looked at the ceiling until it was 8.30 and time for dinner. The meal was less stuffy than luncheon. Everyone seemed satisfied with the way the business of the day had gone and all except Scaramanga and Mr Hendriks had obviously had plenty to drink. Bond found himself excluded from the happy talk. Eyes avoided his and replies to his attempts at conversation were monosyllabic. He was bad news. He had been dealt the death card by the boss. He was certainly not a man to be pally with. While the meal moved sluggishly on — the conventional 'expensive' dinner of a cruise ship, desiccated smoked salmon with a thimbleful of small-grained black caviar, fillets of some unnamed native fish, possibly silk fish, in a cream sauce, 'poulet suprême', a badly roasted broiler with a thick gravy, and *bombe surprise*, was as predictable as such things are — the dining-room was being turned into a 'tropical jungle' with the help of potted plants, piles of oranges and coconuts and an occasional stem of bananas, as a back-drop for the calypso band which, in wine-red and gold-frilled shirts, in due course assembled and began playing 'Linstead Market' too loud. The tune closed. An acceptable but heavily clad girl appeared and began singing 'Belly-Lick' with the printable words. She wore a false pineapple as a head-dress. Bond saw a 'cruise ship' evening stretching ahead. He decided that he was either too old or too young for the worst torture of all, boredom, and got up and went to the head of the table. He said to Mr Scaramanga, 'I've got a headache. I'm going to bed.'

Mr Scaramanga looked up at him under lizard eyelids. 'No. If you figure the evening's not going so good, make it go better. That's what you're being paid for. You act as if you know Jamaica. Okay. Get these people off the pad.'

It was many years since James Bond had accepted a 'dare'. He felt the eyes of The Group on him. What he had drunk had made him careless — perhaps wanting to show off, like the man at the party who insists on playing the drums. Stupidly, he wanted to assert his personality over this bunch of tough guys who rated him insignificant. He didn't stop to think that it was bad tactics, that he would be better off being the ineffectual limey. He said, 'All right, Mr Scaramanga. Give me a hundred-dollar bill and your gun.'

Scaramanga didn't move. He looked up at Bond with surprise and controlled uncertainty. Louie Paradise shouted thickly, 'C'mon, Pistol! Let's see some action! Mebbe the guy can produce.'

Scaramanga reached for his hip pocket, took out his billfold and thumbed out a note. Next he slowly reached to his waistband and took out his gun. The subdued light from the spot on the girl glowed on its gold. He laid the two objects on the table side by side. James Bond, his back to the cabaret, picked up the gun and hefted it. He thumbed back the hammer and twirled the cylinder with a flash of his hands to verify that it was loaded. Then he suddenly whirled, dropped on his knee so that his aim would be above the shadowy musicians in the background and, his arm at full length, let fly. The explosion was deafening in the confined space. The music died. There was a tense silence. The remains of the false pineapple hit something in the dark background with a soft thud. The girl stood under the spot and put her hands up to her face and slowly folded to the dance floor like something graceful out of *Swan Lake*. The maître d'hôtel came running from among the shadows.

As chatter broke out among The Group, James Bond picked up the hundred-dollar note and walked out into the spotlight. He bent down and lifted the girl up by her arm. He pushed the dollar bill down into her cleavage. He said, 'That was a fine act we did together, sweetheart. Don't worry. You were in no danger. I aimed for the top half of the pineapple. Now run off and get ready for your next turn.' He turned her round and gave her a sharp pat on the behind. She gave him a horrified glance and scurried off into the shadows.

Bond strolled on and came up with the band. 'Who's in charge here? Who's in command of the show?'

The guitarist, a tall, gaunt Negro, got slowly to his feet. The whites of his eyes showed. He squinted at the golden gun in Bond's hand. He said uncertainly, as if signing his own death warrant, 'Me, sah.'

'What's your name?'

'King Tiger, sah.'

'All right then, King. Now listen to me. This isn't a Salvation Army fork-supper. Mr Scaramanga's friends want some action. And they want it hot. I'll be sending plenty of rum over to loosen things up. Smoke weed if you like. We're private here. No one's going to tell on you. And get that pretty girl back, but with only half the clothes on, and tell her to come up close and sing "Belly-Lick" very clearly with the blue words. And, by the end of the show, she and the other girls have got to end up stripped. Understand? Now get cracking or the evening'll fold and there'll be no tips at the end. Okay? Then let's go.'

There was nervous laughter and whispered exhortation to King Tiger from the six-piece combo. King Tiger grinned broadly. 'Okay, Captain, sah.' He turned to his men. 'Give 'em "Iron Bar", but hot. An' I'll go get some steam up with Daisy and her friends.' He strode to the service exit and the band crashed into its stride.

Bond walked back and laid the pistol down in front of Scaramanga, who gave Bond a long, inquisitive look and slid it back into his waistband. He said flatly, 'We must have a shooting match one of these days, Mister. How about it? Twenty paces and no wounding?'

'Thanks,' said Bond, 'but my mother wouldn't approve. Would you have some rum sent over to the band? These people can't play dry.' He went back to his seat. He was hardly noticed. The five men, or rather four of them because Hendriks sat impassively through the whole evening, were straining their ears to catch the lewd words of the Fanny Hill version of 'Iron Bar' that were coming across clearly from the soloist. Four girls, plump, busty little animals wearing nothing but white sequined G-strings, ran out on to the floor, and, advancing towards the audience, did an enthusiastic belly dance that brought sweat to the temples of Louie Paradise and Hal Garfinkel. The number ended amidst applause, the girls ran off and the lights were dowsed, leaving only the circular spot in the middle of the floor. The drummer, on his calypso box, began a hasty beat like a quickened pulse. The service door opened and shut and a curious object was wheeled into the circle of light. It was a huge hand, perhaps six feet tall at its highest point, upholstered in black leather. It stood, half open on its broad base, with the thumb and fingers outstretched as if ready to catch something. The drummer hastened his beat. The service door sighed. A glistening figure slipped through and, after pausing in the darkness, moved into the pool of light round the hand with a strutting jerk of belly and limbs. There was Chinese blood in her and her body, totally naked and shining with palm oil, was almost white against the black hand. As she jerked round the hand she caressed its outstretched fingers with her hands and arms and then, with well-acted swooning motions, climbed into the palm of the hand and proceeded to perform languorous, but explicit and ingenious acts of passion with each of the fingers in turn. The scene, the black hand, now shining with her oil and seeming to clutch at the squirming white body, was of an incredible lewdness, and Bond, himself aroused, noticed that even Scaramanga was watching with rapt attention, his eyes narrow slits. The drummer had now worked up to his crescendo. The girl, in well-simulated ecstasy, mounted the thumb, slowly expired upon it and then, with a last grind of her rump, slid down it and vanished through the exit. The act was over.

The lights came on and everyone, including the band, applauded loudly. The men came out of their separate animal trances. Scaramanga clapped his hand for the band leader, took a note out of his case and said something to him under his breath. The chieftain, Bond suspected, had chosen his bride for the night!

After this inspired piece of sexual dumb crambo, the rest of the cabaret was an anti-climax. One of the girls, only after her G-string had been slashed off with a cutlass by the band leader, was able to squirm under a bamboo balanced just eighteen inches off the floor on the top of two beer bottles. The first girl, the one who had acted as an unwitting pineapple-tee to Bond's William Tell act, came on and combined an acceptable strip-tease with a rendering of 'Belly-Lick' that got the audience straining its ears again, and then the whole team of six girls, less the Chinese beauty, came up to the audience and invited them to dance. Scaramanga and Hendriks refused with adequate politeness and Bond stood the two left-out girls glasses of champagne and learned that their names were Mabel and Pearl while he watched the four others being almost bent in half by the bear-like embraces of the four sweating hoods as they clumsily cha-cha'd round the room to the now riotous music of the half-drunk band. The climax to what could certainly class as an orgy was clearly in sight. Bond told his two girls that he must go to the men's room and slipped away when Scaramanga was looking elsewhere, but, as he went, he noted that Hendriks's gaze, as cool as if he had been watching an indifferent film, was firmly on him as he made his escape.

When Bond got to his room, it was midnight. His windows had been closed and the air-conditioning turned on. He switched it off and opened the windows half-way and then, with heartfelt relief, took a shower and went to bed. He worried for a while about having shown off with the gun, but it was an act of folly which he couldn't undo and he soon went to sleep to dream of three black-cloaked men dragging a shapeless bundle through dappled moonlight towards dark waters that were dotted with glinting red eyes. The gnashing white teeth and the crackling bones resolved themselves into a persistent scrabbling noise that brought him suddenly awake. He looked at the luminous dial of his watch. It said 3.30. The scrabbling became a quiet tapping from behind the curtains. James Bond slid quietly out of bed, took his gun from under his pillow and crept softly along the wall to the edge of the curtains. He pulled them aside with one swift motion. The golden hair shone almost silver in the moonlight. Mary Goodnight whispered urgently, 'Quick, James! Help me in!'

Bond cursed softly to himself. What the hell? He laid his gun down on the carpet and reached for her outstretched hands and half dragged, half pulled her over the sill. At the last moment, her heel caught in the frame and the window banged shut with a noise like a pistol shot. Bond cursed again, softly and fluently, under his breath. Mary Goodnight whispered penitently, 'I'm terribly sorry, James.'

Bond shushed her. He picked up his gun and put it back under his pillow and led her across the room and into the bathroom. He turned on the light and, as a precaution, the shower, and, simultaneously with her gasp, remembered he was naked. He said, 'Sorry, Goodnight,' and reached for a towel and wound it round his waist and sat down on the edge of the bath. He gestured to the girl to sit down on the lavatory seat and said, with icy control, 'What in hell are you doing here, Mary?'

Her voice was desperate. 'I had to come. I had to find you somehow. I got on to you through the girl at that, er, dreadful place. I left the car in the trees down the drive and just sniffed about. There were lights on in some of the rooms and I listened and, er,' she blushed crimson, 'I gathered you couldn't be in any of them and then I saw the open window and I just somehow knew you would be the only one to sleep with his window open. So I just had to take the chance.'

'Well, we've got to get you out of here as quick as we can. Anyway, what's the trouble?'

'A "Most Immediate" in Triple-X came over this evening. I mean yesterday evening. It was to be passed to you at all costs. H.Q. thinks you're in Havana. It said that one of the K.G.B. top men who goes under the name of Hendriks is in the area and that he's known to be visiting this hotel. You're to keep away from him. They know from "a delicate but sure source" ' (Bond smiled at the old euphemism for cipher-breaking) 'that among his other jobs is to find you and, er, well, kill you. So I put two and two together, and, what with you being in this corner of the island and the questions you asked me, I guessed that you might be already on his track but that you might be walking into an ambush, sort of. Not knowing, I mean, that while you were after him, he was after you.'

She put out a tentative hand, as if for reassurance that she had done the right thing. Bond took it and patted it absent-mindedly while his mind chewed on this new complication. He said, 'The man's here all right. So's a gunman called Scaramanga. You might as well know, Mary, that Scaramanga killed Ross. In Trinidad.' She put her hand up to her mouth. 'You can report it as a fact, from me. If I can get you out of here, that is. As for Hendriks, he's here all right, but he doesn't seem to have identified me for certain. Did H.Q. say whether he was given a description of me?'

'You were simply described as "the notorious secret agent, James Bond". But this doesn't seem to have meant much to Hendriks because he asked for particulars. That was two days ago. He may get them cabled or telephoned here at any minute. You do see why I had to come, James?'

'Yes, of course. And thanks, Mary. Now, I've got to get you out of that window and then you must just make your own way. Don't worry about me. I think I can handle the situation all right. Besides, I've got help.' He told her about Felix Leiter and Nicholson. 'You just tell H.Q. you've delivered the message and that I'm here and about the two C.I.A. men. H.Q. can get the C.I.A. angles from Washington direct. Okay?' He got to his feet.

She stood up beside him and looked up at him. 'But you will take care?'

'Sure, sure.' He patted her shoulder. He turned off the shower and opened the bathroom door. 'Now, come on. We must pray for a stroke of luck.'

A silken voice from the darkness at the end of the bed said, 'Well, the Holy Man jes' ain't running for you today, Mister. Step forward both of you. Hands clasped behind the neck.'

11

BALLCOCK, AND OTHER, TROUBLE

SCARAMANGA WALKED TO the door and turned the lights on. He was naked save for his shorts and the holster below his left arm. The golden gun remained trained on Bond as he moved.

Bond looked at him incredulously, then to the carpet inside the door. The wedges were still there, undisturbed. He could not possibly have got through the window unaided. Then he saw that his clothes cupboard stood open and that light showed through into the next room. It was the simplest of secret doors — just the whole of the back of the cupboard, impossible to detect from Bond's side of the wall and, on the other, probably, in appearance, a locked communicating door.

Scaramanga came back into the centre of the room and stood looking at them both. His mouth and eyes sneered. He said, 'I didn't see this piece of tail in the line-up. Where you been keeping it, buster? And why d'you have to hide it away in the bathroom? Like doing it under the shower?'

Bond said, 'We're engaged to be married. She works in the British High Commissioner's Office in Kingston. Cipher clerk. She found out where I was staying from that place you and I met. She came out to tell me that my mother's in hospital in London. Had a bad fall. Her name's Mary Goodnight. What's wrong with that and what do you mean coming busting into my room in the middle of the night waving a gun about? And kindly keep your foul tongue to yourself.' Bond was pleased with his bluster and decided to take the next step towards Mary Goodnight's freedom. He dropped his hands to his sides and turned to the girl. 'Put your hands down, Mary. Mr Scaramanga must have thought there were burglars about when he heard that window bang. Now, I'll get some clothes on and take you out to your car. You've got a long drive back to Kingston. Are you sure you wouldn't rather stay here for the rest of the night? I'm sure Mr Scaramanga could find us a spare room.'

He turned back to Mr Scaramanga. 'It's all right, Mr Scaramanga, I'll pay for it.'

Mary Goodnight chipped in. She had dropped her hands. She picked up her small bag from the bed where she had thrown it, opened it and began busying herself with her hair in a fussy, feminine way. She chattered, falling in well with Bond's bland piece of very British 'Now-look-here-my-man-manship'. 'No, honestly, darling, I really think I'd better go. I'd be in terrible trouble if I was late at the office and the Prime Minister, Sir Alexander Bustamante, you know he's just had his eightieth birthday, well he's coming to lunch and you know His Excellency always likes me to do the flowers and arrange the place cards and as a matter of fact,' she turned charmingly towards Mr Scaramanga, 'it's quite a day for me. The party was going to make up thirteen so His Excellency has asked me to be the fourteenth. Isn't that marvellous? But heaven knows what I'm going to look like after tonight. The roads really are terrible in parts aren't they, Mr — er — Scramble. But there it is. And I do apologize for causing all this disturbance and keeping you from your beauty sleep.' She went towards him like the Queen Mother opening a bazaar, her hand outstretched. 'Now you run along off back to bed again and my fiancé' (Thank God she hadn't said James! The girl was inspired!) ' 'll see me safely off the premises. Goodbye, Mr, er . . .'

James Bond was proud of her. It was almost pure Joyce Grenfell. But Scaramanga wasn't going to be taken by any double talk, limey or otherwise. She almost had Bond covered from Scaramanga. He moved swiftly aside. He said, 'Hold it, lady. And you, Mister, stand where you are.' Mary Goodnight let her hand drop to her side. She looked inquiringly at Scaramanga as if he had just rejected the cucumber sandwiches. Really! These Americans! The Golden Gun didn't go for polite conversation. It held dead steady between the two of them. Scaramanga said to Bond, 'Okay, I'll buy it. Put her through the window again. Then I've got something to say to you.' He waved his gun at the girl. 'Okay, bimbo. Get going. And don't come trespassing on other people's lands again. Right? And you can tell His friggin' Excellency where to shove his place cards. His writ don't run over the Thunderbird. Mine does. Got the photo? Okay. Don't bust your stays getting through the window.'

Mary Goodnight said icily, 'Very good, Mr, er . . . I will deliver your message. I'm sure the High Commissioner will take more careful note than he has done of your presence on the island. And the Jamaican Government also.'

Bond reached out and took her arm. She was on the edge of overplaying her role. He said, 'Come on, Mary. And please tell mother that I'll be through here in a day or two and I'll be telephoning her from Kingston.' He led her to the window and helped, or rather bundled her out. She gave a brief wave and ran off across the lawn. Bond came away from the window with considerable relief. He hadn't expected the ghastly mess to sort itself out so painlessly.

He went and sat down on his bed. He sat on the pillow. He was reassured to feel the hard shape of his gun against his thighs. He looked across at Scaramanga. The man had put his gun back in the shoulder holster. He leant up against the clothes cupboard and ran his finger reflectively along the black line of his moustache. He said, 'High Commissioner's Office. That also houses the local representative of your famous Secret Service. I suppose, Mister Hazard, that your real name wouldn't be James Bond? You showed quite a turn of speed with the gun tonight. I seem to have read somewhere that this man Bond fancies himself with the hardware. I also have information to the effect that he's somewhere in the Caribbean and that he's looking for me. Funny coincidence department, eh?'

Bond laughed easily. 'I thought the Secret Service packed up at the end of the war. Anyway, 'fraid I can't change my identity to suit your book. All you've got to do in the morning is ring up Frome and ask for Mr Tony Hugill, the boss up there, and check on my story. And can you explain how this Bond chap could possibly have tracked you down to a brothel in Sav' La Mar? And what does he want from you anyway?'

Scaramanga contemplated him silently for a while. Then he said, 'Guess he may be lookin' for a shootin' lesson. Be glad to oblige him. But you've got something about Number 3½. That's what I figgered when I hired you. But coincidence doesn't come in that size. Mebbe I should have thought again. I said from the first I smelled cops. That girl may be your fiancée or she may not, but that ploy with the shower bath. That's an old hood's trick. Probably a Secret Service one too. Unless, that is, you were screwin' her.' He raised one eyebrow.

'I was. Anything wrong with that? What have you been doing with the Chinese girl? Playing mahjongg?' Bond got to his feet. He stitched impatience and outrage on his face in equal quantities. 'Now look here, Mr Scaramanga. I've had just about enough of this. Just stop leaning on me. You go around waving that damned gun of yours and acting like God Almighty and insinuating a lot of tommyrot about the Secret Service and you expect me to kneel down and lick your boots. Well, my friend, you've come to the wrong address. If you're dissatisfied with the job I'm doing, just hand over the thousand dollars and I'll be on my way. Who in hell d'you think you are anyway?'

Scaramanga smiled his thin, cruel smile. 'You may be getting wise to that sooner than you think, shamus.' He shrugged. 'Okay, okay. But just you remember this, Mister. If it turns out you're not who you say you are, I'll blow you to bits. Get me? And I'll start with the little bits and go on to the bigger ones. Just so it lasts a heck of a long time. Right? Now you'd better get some shut-eye. I've got a meeting with Mr Hendriks at ten in the conference room. And I don't want to be disturbed. After that the whole party goes on an excursion on the railroad I was tellin' you about. It'll be your job to see that that gets properly organized. Talk to the manager first thing. Right? Okay, then. Be seeing ya.' Scaramanga walked into the clothes cupboard, brushed Bond's suit aside and disappeared. There came a decisive click from the next room. Bond got to his feet. He said 'Phew!' at the top of his voice and walked off into the bathroom to wash the last two hours away in the shower.

He awoke at 6.30, by arrangement with that curious extrasensory alarm clock that some people keep in their heads and that always seems to know the exact time. He put on his bathing trunks and went out to the beach and did his long swim again. When at 7.15 he saw Scaramanga come out of the East Wing followed by the boy carrying his towel, he made for the shore. He listened for the twanging thump of the trampoline and then, keeping well out of sight of it, entered the hotel by the main entrance and moved quickly down the corridor to his room. He listened at his window to make sure the man was still exercising, then he took the master key Nick Nicholson had given him and slipped across the corridor to No. 20 and was quickly inside. He left the door on the latch. Yes, there was his target, lying on the dressing-table. He strode across the room, picked up the gun and slipped out the round in the cylinder that would next come up for firing. He put the gun down exactly as he had found it, got back to the door, listened, and then was out and across the corridor and into his own room. He went back to the window and listened. Yes. Scaramanga was still at it. It was an amateurish ploy that Bond had executed, but it might gain him just that fraction of a second that, he felt it in his bones, was going to be life or death for him in the next twenty-four hours. In his mind, he smelled that slight whiff of smoke that indicated that his cover was smouldering at the edges. At any moment 'Mark Hazard of the Transworld Consortium' might go up in flames like some clumsy effigy on Guy Fawkes Night and James Bond would stand there, revealed, with nothing between him and a possible force of six other gunmen but his own quick hand and the Walther PPK. So every shade of odds that he could shift to his side of the board would be worthwhile. Undismayed by the prospect, in fact rather excited by it, he ordered a large breakfast, consumed it with relish and after pulling the connecting pin out of the ballcock in his lavatory went along to the manager's office.

Felix Leiter was on duty. He gave a thin managerial smile and said, 'Good morning, Mr Hazard. Can I help you?' Leiter's eyes were looking beyond Bond, over his right shoulder. Mr Hendriks materialized at the desk before Bond could answer.

Bond said, 'Good morning.'

Mr Hendriks replied with his little Germanic bow. He said to Leiter, 'The telephone operator is saying that there is a long-distance call from my office in Havana. Where is the most private place to take it, pliss?'

'Not in your bedroom, sir?'

'Is not sufficiently private.'

Bond guessed that he too had bowled out the microphone.

Leiter looked helpful. He came out from behind his desk. 'Just over here, sir. The lobby telephone. The box is soundproof.'

Mr Hendriks looked stonily at him. 'And the machine. That also is soundproof?'

Leiter looked politely puzzled. 'I'm afraid I don't understand, sir. It is connected directly with the operator.'

'Is no matter. Show me, pliss.' Mr Hendriks followed Leiter to the far corner of the lobby and was shown into the booth. He carefully closed the leather-padded door and picked up the receiver and talked into it. Then he stood waiting, watching Leiter come back across the marble floor and speak deferentially to Bond. 'You were saying, sir?'

'It's my lavatory. Something wrong with the ballcock. Is there anywhere else?'

'I'm so sorry, sir. I'll have the house engineer look at it at once. Yes, certainly. There's the lobby toilet. The decoration isn't completed and it's not officially in use, but it's in perfectly good working order.' He lowered his voice. 'And there's a connecting door with my office. Leave it for ten minutes while I run back the tape of what this bastard's saying. I heard the call was coming through. Don't like the sound of it. May be your worry.' He gave a little bow and waved Bond towards the central table with magazines on it. 'If you'll just take a seat for a few moments, sir, and then I'll take care of you.'

Bond nodded his thanks and turned away. In the booth, Hendriks was talking. His eyes were fixed on Bond with a terrible intensity. Bond felt the skin crawl at the base of his stomach. This was it all right! He sat down and picked up an old *Wall Street Journal*. Surreptitiously he tore a small piece out of the centre of page one. It could have been a tear at the cross-fold. He held the paper up at page two and watched Hendriks through the little hole.

Hendriks watched the back of the paper and talked and listened. He suddenly put down the receiver and came out of the booth. His face gleamed with sweat. He took out a clean white handkerchief and ran it over his face and neck and walked rapidly off down the corridor.

Nick Nicholson, as neat as a pin, came across the lobby and, with a courtly smile and a bow for Bond, took up his place behind the desk. It was 8.30. Five minutes later, Felix Leiter came out from the inner office. He said something to Nicholson and came over to Bond. There was a pale, pinched look round his mouth. He said, 'And now, if you'll follow me, sir.' He led the way across the lobby, unlocked the men's room door, followed

Bond in and locked the door behind him. They stood among the carpentry work by the wash-basins. Leiter said tensely, 'I guess you've had it, James. They were talking Russian, but your name and number kept on cropping up. Guess you'd better get out of here just as quickly as that old jalopy of yours'll carry you.'

Bond smiled thinly. 'Forewarned is forearmed, Felix. I knew it already. Hendriks has been told to rub me. Our old friend at K.G.B. headquarters, Semichastny, has got it in for me. I'll tell you why one of these days.' He told Leiter of the Mary Goodnight episode of the early hours. Leiter listened gloomily. Bond concluded, 'So there's no object in getting out now. We shall hear all the dope and probably their plans for me at this meeting at ten. Then they've got this excursion business afterwards. Personally I guess the shooting match'll take place somewhere out in the country where there are no witnesses. Now, if you and Nick could work out something that'd upset the Away Engagement, I'll make myself responsible for the home pitch.'

Leiter looked thoughtful. Some of the cloud lifted from his face. He said, 'I know the plans for this afternoon. Off on this miniature train through the cane fields, picnic, then the boat out of Green Island Harbour, deep-sea fishing and all that. I've reconnoitred the route for it all.' He raised the thumb of his left hand and pinged the end of his steel hook thoughtfully. 'Ye-e-e-s. It's going to mean some quick action and a heap of luck and I'll have to get the hell up to Frome for some supplies from your friend Hugill. Will he hand over some gear on your say-so? Okay, then. Come into my office and write him a note. It's only a half-hour's drive and Nick can hold the front desk for that time. Come on.' He opened a side door and went through into his office. He beckoned Bond to follow and shut the door behind him. At Leiter's dictation, Bond took down the note to the manager of the WISCO sugar estates and then went out and along to his room. He took a strong nip of straight bourbon and sat on the edge of his bed and looked unseeingly out of the window and across the lawn to the sea's horizon. Like a dozing hound chasing a rabbit in its dreams, or like the audience at an athletics meeting that lifts a leg to help the high-jumper over the bar, every now and then his right hand twitched involuntarily. In his mind's eye, in a variety of imagined circumstances, it was leaping for his gun.

Time passed and James Bond still sat there, occasionally smoking half-way through a Royal Blend and then absent-mindedly stubbing it out in the bed-table ash-tray. An observer would have made nothing of his thoughts. The pulse in his left temple was beating a little fast. There was some tension, but perhaps only the concentration applied to his thinking, in the slightly pursed lips, but the brooding, blue-grey eyes that saw nothing were relaxed, almost sleepy. It would have been impossible to guess that James Bond was contemplating the possibility of his own death later that day, feeling the soft-nosed bullets tearing into him, seeing his body jerking on the ground, his mouth perhaps screaming. Those were certainly part of his thoughts, but the twitching right hand was evidence that, in much of the whirring film of his thoughts, the enemy's fire was not going unanswered — perhaps had even been anticipated.

James Bond gave a deep relaxed sigh. His eyes came back into focus. He looked at his watch. It said 9.50. He got up, ran both hands down his lean face with a scrubbing motion, and went out and along the corridor to the conference room.

12

IN A GLASS, VERY DARKLY

THE SET-UP WAS the same. Bond's travel literature was on the buffet table where he had left it. He went through into the conference room. It had only been cursorily tidied. Scaramanga had probably said it was not to be entered by the staff. The chairs were roughly in position, but the ash-trays had not been emptied. There were no stains on the carpet and no signs of the carpet having been washed. It had probably been a single shot through the heart. With Scaramanga's soft-nosed bullets, the internal damage would be devastating, but the fragments of the bullet would stay in the body and there would be no bleeding. Bond went round the table, ostentatiously positioning the chairs more accurately. He identified the one where Ruby Rotkopf must have sat, across the table from Scaramanga, because it had a cracked leg. He dutifully examined the windows and looked behind the curtains, doing his job. Scaramanga came into the room followed by Mr Hendriks. He said roughly, 'Okay, Mr Hazard. Lock both doors like yesterday. No one to come in. Right?'

'Yes.' As Bond passed Mr Hendriks he said cheerfully, 'Good morning, Mr Hendriks. Enjoy the party last night?'

Mr Hendriks gave his usual curt bow. He said nothing. His eyes were granite marbles.

Bond went out and locked the doors and took up his position with the brochures and the champagne glass. Immediately, Hendriks began talking, quickly and urgently, fumbling for the English words. 'Mister S. I have bad troubles to report. My Zentrale in Havana spoke with me this morning. They have heard direct from Moscow. This man' — he must have made a gesture towards the door — 'this man is the British secret agent, the man Bond. There is no doubt. I am given the exact descriptions. When he goes swimming this morning, I am examining his body through glasses. The wounds on his body are clearly to be seen. The scar down the right side of the face leaves no doubt. And his shooting last night! The ploddy fool is proud of his shooting. I would like to see a member of my organization behave in zees stupid fashions! I would have him shot immediately.' There was a pause. The man's tone altered, became slightly menacing. His target was now Scaramanga. 'But, Mister S. How can this have come about? How can you possibly have let it arrive? My Zentrale is dumbfounded at the mistake. The man might have done much damage but for the watchfulness of my superiors. Please explain, Mister S. I must be making the very full report. How is it that you are meeting this man? How is that you are then carrying him efen into the centre of The Group? The details, pliss, Mister. The full accounting. My superiors will be expressing sharp criticism of the lack of vigilance against the enemy.'

Bond heard the rasp of a match against a box. He could imagine Scaramanga sitting back and going through the smoking routine. The voice, when it came, was decisive, uncowed. 'Mr Hendriks, I appreciate your outfit's concern about this and I congratulate them on their sources of information. But you tell your Central this: I met this man completely by accident, at least I thought so at the time, and there's no use worrying about how it happened. It hasn't been easy to set up this conference and I needed help. I had to get two managers in a hurry from New York to handle the hotel people. They're doing a good job, right? The floor staff and all the rest I had to get from Kingston. But what I really needed was a kind of personal assistant who could be around to make sure that everything went smoothly. Personally, I just couldn't be bothered with all the details. When this guy dropped out of the blue he looked all right to me. So I picked him up. But I'm not stupid. I knew that when this show was over I'd have to get rid of him, just in case he'd learned anything he shouldn't have. Now you say he's a member of the Secret Service. I told you at the beginning of this conference that I eat these people for breakfast when I have a mind to. What you've told me changes just one thing: he'll die today instead of tomorrow. And here's how it's going to happen.' Scaramanga lowered his voice. Now Bond could only hear disjointed words. The sweat ran down from his ear as he pressed it to the base of the champagne glass. 'Our train trip . . . rats in the cane . . . unfortunate accident . . . before I do it . . . one hell of a shock . . . details to myself . . . promise you a big laugh'. Scaramanga must have sat back again. Now his voice was normal. 'So you can rest easy. There'll be nothing left of the guy by this evening. Okay? I could get it over with now by just opening the door. But two blown fuses in two days might stir up gossip around here. And this way there'll be a heap of fun for everyone on the picnic.'

Mr Hendriks's voice was flat and uninterested. He had carried out his orders and action was about to follow, definitive action. There could be no complaint of delay in carrying out orders. He said, 'Yes. What you are proposing will be satisfactory. I shall observe the proceedings with much amusement. And now to other business. Plan Orange. My superiors are wishing to know that everything is in order.'

'Yes. Everything's in order at Reynolds Metal, Kaiser Bauxite and Alumina of Jamaica. But your stuff's plenty — what do they call it? — volatile. Got to be replaced in the demolition chambers every five years. Hey,' there was a dry chuckle, 'I sure snickered when I saw that the how-do-it labels on the drums were in some of these African languages as well as English. Ready for the big black uprising, huh? You better warn me about The Day. I hold some pretty vulnerable stocks on Wall Street.'

'Then you will lose a lot of money,' said Mr Hendriks flatly. 'I shall not be told the date. I do not mind. I hold no stocks. You would be wise to keep your money in gold or diamonds or rare postage stamps. And now the next matter. It is of interest to my superiors to be able to place their hands on a very great quantity of narcotics. You have a source for the supply of ganja, or marijuana as we call it. You are now receiving your supplies in pound weight. I am asking whether you can stimulate your sources of supply to providing the weed by the hundredweight. It is suggested that you then run shipments to the Pedro Cays. My friends can arrange for collection from there.'

There was a brief silence. Scaramanga would be smoking his thin cheroot. He said, 'Yeah, I think we could swing that. But they've just put some big teeth into these ganja laws. Real rough jail sentences, see? So the goddam price has up and gone through the roof. The going price today is £16 an ounce. A hundredweight of the stuff could cost thousands of pounds. And it's darned bulky in those quantities. My fishing boat could probably only ship one hundredweight at a time. Anyway, where's it for? You'll be lucky to get those quantities ashore. A pound or two is difficult enough.'

'I am not being told the destinations. I assume it is for America. They are the largest consumers. Arrangements have been made to receive this and other consignments initially off the coast of Georgia. I am being told that this area is full of small islands and swamps and is already much favoured by smugglers. The money is of no importance. I have instructions to make an initial outlay of a million dollars, but at keen market prices. You will be receiving your usual ten per cent commission. Is it that you are interested?'

'I'm always interested in a hundred thousand dollars. I'll have to get in touch with my growers. They have their plantations in thc Maroon country. That's in the centre of the island. This is going to take time. I can give you a quotation in about two weeks — a hundredweight of the stuff f.o.b. the Pedro Cays. Okay?'

'And a date? The Cays are very flat. This is not stuff to be left lying about, isn't it?'

'Sure. Sure. Now then. Any other business? Okay. Well, I've got something I'd like to bring up. This casino lark. Now, this is the picture. The government are tempted. They think it'll stimulate the tourist industry. But the Heavies — the boys who were kicked out of Havana, the Vegas machine, the Miami jokers, Chicago — the whole works, didn't take the measure of these people before they put the heat on. And they overplayed the slush fund approach — put too much money in the wrong pockets. Guess they should have employed a public relations outfit. Jamaica looks small on the map, and I guess the Syndicates thought they could hurry through a neat little operation like the Nassau job. But the Opposition party got wise, and the Church, and the old women, and there was talk of the Mafia taking over in Jamaica, the old "Cosa Nostra" and all that crap, and the spiel flopped. Remember we were offered an "in" coupla years back? That was when they saw it was a bust and wanted to unload their promotion expenses, coupla million bucks or so, on to The Group. You recall I advised against and gave my reasons. Okay. So we said no. But things have changed. Different party in power, bit of a tourist slump last year, and a certain Minister has been in touch with me. Says the climate's changed. Independence has come along and they've got out from behind the skirts of Aunty England. Want to show that Jamaica's with it. Got oomph and all that. So this friend of mine says he can get gambling off the pad here. He told me how and it makes sense. Before, I said stay out. Now I say come in. But it's going to cost money. Each of us'll have to chip in with a hundred thousand bucks to give local encouragement. Miami'll be the operators and get the franchise. The deal is that they'll put us in for five per cent — but off the top. Get me? On these figures, and they're not loaded, our juice should have been earned in eighteen months. After that it's gravy. Get the photo? But your, er, friends, don't seem too keen on these, er, capitalist enterprises. How do you figure it? Will they ante up? I don't want for us to go outside for the green. And, as from yesterday, we're missing a shareholder. Come to think of it, we've got to think of that too. Who we goin' to rope in as Number Six? We're short of a game for now.'

James Bond wiped his ear and the bottom of the glass with his handkerchief. It was almost unbearable. He had heard his own death sentence pronounced, the involvement of the K.G.B. with Scaramanga and the Caribbean spelled out, and such minor dividends as sabotage of the bauxite industry, massive drug smuggling into the States and gambling politics thrown in. It was a majestic haul in area Intelligence. He had the ball! Could he live to touch down with it? God, for a drink! He put his ear back to the hot base of the glass.

There was silence. When it came, the voice of Hendriks was cautious, indecisive. He obviously wanted to say 'I pass' — with the corollary, 'until I've talked to my Zentrale, isn't it?'

He said, 'Mister S. Is difficult pizzness, yes? My superiors are not disliking the profitable involvements but, as you will be knowing, they are most liking the pizzness that has the political objective. It was on these conditions that they instructed me to ally myself with your Group. The money, that is not the problem. But how am I to explain the political objective of opening casions in Jamaica? This I am wondering.'

'It'll almost certainly lead to trouble. The locals'll want to play — they're terrific gamblers here. There'll be incidents. Coloured people'll be turned away from the doors for one reason or another. Then the Opposition party'll get hold of that and raise hell about colour bars and so on. With all the money flying about, the unions'll push wages through the roof. It can all add up to a fine stink. The atmosphere's too damn peaceful around here. This'll be a cheap way of raising plenty of hell. That's what your people want, isn't it? Give the islands the hot foot one after another?'

There was another brief silence. Mr Hendriks obviously didn't like the idea. He said so, but obliquely: 'What you are saying, Mister S., is very interesting. But is it not that these troubles you envisage will endanger our monies? However, I will report your inquiry and inform you at once. It is possible that my superiors will be sympathetic. Who can be telling? Now there is this question of a new Number Six. Are you having anyone in mind?'

'I think we want a good man from South America. We need a guy to oversee our operations in British Guiana. We oughta get smartened up in Venezuela. How come we never got further with that great scheme for blocking the Maracaibo Bar? Like robbing a blind man, given a suitable block ship. Just the threat of it would make the oil companies shell out — that's a joke by the way — and go on shelling by way of protection. Then, if this narcotics spiel is going to be important, we can't do without Mexico. How about Mr Arosio of Mexico City?'

'I am not knowing this gentleman.'

'Rosy? Oh, he's a great guy. Runs the Green Light Transportation System. Drugs and girls into L.A. Never been caught yet. Reliable operator. Got no affiliates. Your people'll know about him. Why not check with them and then we'll put it up to the others? They'll go along with our say-so.'

'Is good. And now, Mister S. Have you anything to report about your own employer? On his recent visit to Moscow, I understand that he expressed satisfaction with your efforts in this area. It is a matter for gratification that there should be such close co-operation between his subversive efforts and our own. Both our chiefs are expecting much in the future from our union with the Mafia. Myself I am doubting. Mr Gengerella is undoubtedly a valuable link, but it is my impression that these people are only being activated by money. What is it that you are thinking?'

'You've said it, Mr Hendriks. In the opinion of my chief, the Mafia's first and only consideration is the Mafia. It has always been so and it always will be so. My Mister C. is not expecting great results in the States. Even the Mafia can't buck the anti-Cuban feeling there. But he thinks we can achieve plenty in the Caribbean by giving them odd jobs to do. They can be very effective. It would certainly oil the wheels if your people would use the Mafia as a pipeline for this narcotics business. They'll turn your million-dollar investment into ten. They'll grab the nine out of it of course. But that's not peanuts, and it'll tie them in to you. Think you could arrange that? It'll give Leroy G. some good news to report when he gets home. As for Mister C., he seems to be going along all right. Flora was a bodyblow but, largely thanks to the Americans leaning on Cuba the way they do, he's kept the country together. If the Americans once let up on their propaganda and needling and so forth, perhaps even make a friendly gesture or two, all the steam'll go out of the little man. I don't often see him. He leaves me alone. Likes to keep his nose clean, I guess. But I get all the co-operation I need from the D.S.S. Okay? Well, let's go see if the folks are ready to move. It's eleven thirty and the Bloody Bay Belle is due to be on her way at twelve. Guess it's going to be quite a fun day. Pity our chiefs aren't going to be along to see the limey eye get his chips.'

'Ha!' said Mr Hendriks noncommittally.

James Bond moved away from the door. He heard Mr Scaramanga's pass key in the lock. He looked up and yawned.

Mr Scaramanga and Mr Hendriks looked down at him. Their expressions were vaguely interested and reflective. It was as if he were a bit of steak and they were wondering whether to have it done rare or medium rare.

13

HEAR THE TRAIN BLOW!

AT TWELVE O'CLOCK they all assembled in the lobby. Scaramanga had added a broad-brimmed white Stetson to his immaculate tropical attire. He looked like the smartest plantation owner in the South. Mr Hendriks wore his usual stuffy suit, now topped with a grey Homburg. Bond thought that he should have grey suede gloves and an umbrella. The four hoods were wearing calypso shirts outside their slacks. Bond was pleased. If they were carrying guns in their waistbands, the shirts would hinder the draw. Cars were drawn up outside with Scaramanga's Thunderbird in the lead. Scaramanga walked up to the desk. Nick Nicholson was standing washing his hands in invisible soap and looking helpful. 'All set? Everything loaded on the train? Green Harbour been told? Okay, then. Where's that sidekick of yours, that man Travis? Haven't seen him around today.'

Nick Nicholson looked serious. 'He got an abscess in his tooth, sir. Real bad. Had to send him in to Sav' La Mar to have it out. He'll be okay by this afternoon.'

'Too bad. Dock him half a day's pay. No room for sleepers on this outfit. We're short-handed as it is. Should have had his snappers attended to before he took the job on. 'Kay?'

'Very good, Mr Scaramanga. I'll tell him.'

Mr Scaramanga turned to the waiting group. 'Okay, fellers. Now this is the spiel. We drive a mile down the road to the station. We get aboard this little train. Quite an outfit that. Feller by the name of Lucius Beebe had it copied for the Thunderbird company from the engine and rolling stock on the little old Denver, South Park and Pacific line. Okay. So we steam along this old cane-field line about twenty miles to Green Island Harbour. Plenty birds, bush rats, crocs in the rivers. Mebbe we get a little hunting. Have some fun with the hardware. All you guys got your guns with you? Fine, fine. Champagne lunch at Green Island and the girls and the music'll be there to keep us happy.

After lunch we get aboard the *Thunder Girl*, big Chriscraft, and take a cruise along to Lucea, that's a little township down the coast, and see if we can catch our dinner. Those that don't want to fish can play stud. Right? Then back here for drinks. Okay? Everyone satisfied? Any suggestions? Then let's go.'

Bond was told to get in the back of the car. They set off. Once again that offered neck! Crazy not to take him now! But it was open country with no cover and there were four guns riding behind. The odds simply weren't good enough. What was the plan for his removal? During the 'hunting' presumably. James Bond smiled grimly to himself. He was feeling happy. He wouldn't have been able to explain the emotion. It was a feeling of being keyed up, wound taut. It was the moment, after twenty passes, when you got a hand you could bet on — not necessarily win, but bet on. He had been after this man for over six weeks. Today, this morning perhaps, was to come the pay-off he had been ordered to bring about. It was win or lose. The odds? Foreknowledge was playing for him. He was more heavily forearmed than the enemy knew. But the enemy had the big battalions on their side. There were more of them. And, taking only Scaramanga, perhaps more talent. Weapons? Again leaving out the others, Scaramanga had the advantage. The long-barrelled Colt.45 would be a fraction slower on the draw, but its length of barrel would give it more accuracy than the Walther automatic. Rate of fire? The Walther should have the edge — and the first empty chamber of Scaramanga's gun, if it hadn't been discovered, would be an additional bonus. The steady hand? The cool brain? The sharpness of the lust to kill? How did they weigh up? Probably nothing to choose on the first two. Bond might be a shade trigger-happy — of necessity. That he must watch. He must damp down the fire in his belly. Get ice-cold. In the lust to kill, perhaps he was the strongest. Of course. He was fighting for his life. The other man was just amusing himself — providing sport for his friends, displaying his potency, showing off. That was good! That might be decisive! Bond said to himself that he must increase the other man's unawareness, his casual certitude, his lack of caution. He must be the P. G. Wodehouse Englishman, the limey of the cartoons. He must play easy to take. The adrenalin coursed into James Bond's bloodstream. His pulse rate began to run a fraction high. He felt it on his wrist. He breathed deeply and slowly to bring it down. He found that he was sitting forward, tensed. He sat back and tried to relax. All of his body relaxed except his right hand. This was in the control of someone else. Resting on his right thigh, it still twitched slightly from time to time like the paw of a sleeping dog chasing rabbits. He put it into his coat pocket and watched a turkey buzzard a thousand feet up, circling. He put himself into the mind of the 'John Crow', watching out for a squashed toad or a dead bush rat. The circling buzzard had found its offal. It came lower and lower. Bond wished it 'bon appétit'. The predator in him wished the scavenger a good meal. He smiled at the comparison between them. They were both following a scent. The main difference was that the John Crow was a protected bird. No one would shoot back at it when it made its final dive. Amused by his thoughts, Bond's right hand came out of his pocket and lit a cigarette for him, quietly and obediently. It had stopped going off chasing rabbits on its own.

The station was a brilliant mock-up from the Colorado narrow-gauge era — a low building in faded clapboard ornamented with gingerbread along its eaves. Its name 'Thunderbird Halt' was in old-style ornamental type, heavily seriffed. Advertisements proclaimed 'Chew Roseleaf Fine Cut Warranted Finest Virginia Leaf', 'Trains Stop for all Meals', 'No Checks Accepted'. The engine, gleaming in black and yellow varnish and polished brass, was a gem. It stood, panting quietly in the sunshine, a wisp of black smoke curling up from the tall stack behind the big brass headlight. The engine's name, 'The Belle', was on a proud brass plate on the gleaming black barrel and its number, 'No.1', on a similar plate below the headlight. There was one carriage, an open affair with padded foam-rubber seats and a daffodil Surrey roof of fringed canvas to keep off the sun, and then the brake van, also in black and yellow, with a resplendent gilt-armed chair behind the conventional wheel of the brake. It was a wonderful toy even down to the old-fashioned whistle which now gave a sharp admonitory blast.

Scaramanga was in ebullient form. 'Hear the train blow, folks! All aboard!' There was an anti-climax. To Bond's dismay he took out his golden pistol, pointed it at the sky and pressed the trigger. He hesitated only momentarily and fired again. The deep boom echoed back from the wall of the station and the station-master, resplendent in old-fashioned uniform, looked nervous. He pocketed the big silver turnip watch he had been holding and stood back obsequiously, the green flag now drooping at his side. Scaramanga checked his gun. He looked thoughtfully at Bond and said, 'All right, my friend. Now then, you get up front with the driver.'

Bond smiled happily. 'Thanks. I've always wanted to do that since I was a child. What fun!'

'You've said it,' said Scaramanga. He turned to the others. 'And you, Mr Hendriks. In the first seat behind the coal-tender, please. Then Sam and Leroy. Then Hal and Louie. I'll be up back in the brake van. Good place to watch out for game. 'Kay?'

Everybody took their seats. The station-master had recovered his nerve and went through his ploy with the watch and the flag. The engine gave a triumphant hoot and, with a series of diminishing puffs, got under way and they bowled off along the three-foot-gauge line that disappeared, as straight as an arrow, into a dancing shimmer of silver.

Bond read the speed gauge. It said twenty. For the first time he paid attention to the driver. He was a villainous-looking Rastafari in dirty khaki overalls with a sweat rag round his forehead. A cigarette drooped from between the thin moustache and the straggling beard. He smelled quite horrible. Bond said, 'My name's Mark Hazard. What's yours?'

'Rass, man! Ah doan talk wid buckra.'

The expression 'rass' is Jamaican for 'shove it'. 'Buckra' is a tough colloquialism for 'white man'.

Bond said equably, 'I thought part of your religion was to love thy neighbour.'

The Rasta gave the whistle halyard a long pull. When the shriek had died away, he simply said 'Sheeit', kicked the furnace door open and began shovelling coal.

Bond looked surreptitiously round the cabin. Yes. There it was! The long Jamaican cutlass, this one filed to an inch blade with a deadly point. It was on a rack by the man's hand. Was this the way he was supposed to go? Bond doubted it. Scaramanga would do the deed in a suitably dramatic fashion and one that would give him an alibi. Second executioner would be Hendriks. Bond looked back over the low coal-tender. Hendriks's eyes, bland and indifferent, met his. Bond shouted above the iron clang of the engine, 'Great fun, what?' Hendriks's eyes looked away and back again. Bond stooped so that he could see under the top of the Surrey. All the other four men were sitting motionless, their eyes also fixed on Bond. Bond waved a cheerful hand. There was no response. So they had been told! Bond was a spy in their midst and this was his last ride. In mobese, he was 'going to be hit'. It was an uncomfortable feeling having those ten enemy eyes watching him like ten gun barrels. Bond straightened himself. Now the top half of his body, like the iron 'man' in a pistol range, was above the roof of the Surrey and he was looking straight down the flat yellow surface to where Scaramanga sat on his solitary throne, perhaps twenty feet away, with all his body in full view. He also was looking down the little train at Bond — the last mourner in the funeral cortège behind the cadaver that was James Bond. Bond waved a cheery hand and turned back. He opened his coat and got a moment's reassurance from the cool butt of his gun. He felt in his trouser pocket. Three spare magazines. Ah well! He'd take as many of them as he could with him. He flipped down the co-driver's seat and sat on it. No point in offering a target until he had to. The Rasta flicked his cigarette over the side and lit another. The engine was driving herself. He leant against the cabin wall and looked at nothing.

Bond had done his homework on the 1:50,000 Overseas Survey map that Mary had provided and he knew exactly the route the little cane line took. First there would be five miles of the cane fields between whose high green walls they were now travelling. Then came Middle River, followed by the vast expanse of swamplands, now being slowly reclaimed, but still shown on the map as 'The Great Morass'. Then would come Orange River leading into Orange Bay, and then more sugar and mixed forest and agricultural smallholdings until they came to the little hamlet of Green Island at the head of the excellent anchorage of Green Island Harbour.

A hundred yards ahead, a turkey buzzard rose from beside the line and, after a few heavy flaps, caught the inshore breeze and soared up and away. There came the boom of Scaramanga's gun. A feather drifted down from the great right-hand wing of the big bird. The turkey buzzard swerved and soared higher. A second shot rang out. The bird gave a jerk and began to tumble untidily down out of the sky. It jerked again as a third bullet hit it before it crashed into the cane. There was applause from under the yellow Surrey. Bond leant out and called to Scaramanga, 'That'll cost you five pounds unless you've squared the Rasta. That's the fine for killing a John Crow.'

A shot whistled past Bond's head. Scaramanga laughed. 'Sorry. Thought I saw a rat.' And then, 'Come on, Mr Hazard. Let's see some gun play from you. There's some cattle grazing by the line up there. See if you can hit a cow at ten paces.'

The hoods guffawed. Bond put his head out again. Scaramanga's gun was on his lap. Out of the corner of his eye he saw that Mr Hendriks, perhaps ten feet behind him, had his right hand in his coat pocket. Bond called, 'I never shoot game that I don't eat. If you'll eat the whole cow, I'll shoot it for you.'

The gun flashed and boomed as Bond jerked his head under cover of the coal-tender. Scaramanga laughed harshly. 'Watch your lip, limey, or you'll end up without it.' The hoods haw-hawed.

Beside Bond, the Rasta gave a curse. He pulled hard on the whistle lanyard. Bond looked down the line. Far ahead, across the rails, something pink showed. Still whistling, the driver pulled on a lever. Steam belched from the train's exhaust and the engine began to slow. Two shots rang out and the bullets clanged against the iron roof over his head. Scaramanga shouted angrily, 'Keep steam up, damn you to hell!'

The Rasta quickly pushed up the lever and the speed of the train gathered back to 20 m.p.h. He shrugged. He glanced at Bond. He licked his lips wetly. 'Dere's white trash across de line. Guess mebbe it's some frien' of de boss.'

Bond strained his eyes. Yes! It was a naked pink body with golden blonde hair! A girl's body!

Scaramanga's voice boomed against the wind. 'Folks. Jes' a little surprise for you all. Something from the good old Western movies. There's a girl on the line ahead. Tied across it. Take a look. And you know what? It's the girl friend of a certain man we've been hearing of called James Bond. Would you believe it? An' her name's Goodnight, Mary Goodnight. It sure is goodnight for her. If only that fellow Bond was aboard now, I guess we'd be hearing him holler for mercy.'

14
THE GREAT MORASS

JAMES BOND LEAPED for the accelerator lever and tore it downwards. The engine lost a head of steam but there was only a hundred yards to go and now the only thing that could save the girl was the brakes under Scaramanga's control in the brake van. The Rasta already had his cutlass in his hand. The flames from the furnace glinted on the blade. He stood back like a cornered animal, his eyes red with ganja and fear of the gun in Bond's hand. Nothing could save the girl now! Bond, knowing that Scaramanga would expect him from the right side of the tender, leaped to the left. Hendriks had his gun out. Before it could swivel, Bond put a bullet between the man's cold eyes. The head jerked back. For an instant, steel-capped back teeth showed in the gaping mouth. Then the grey Homburg fell off and the dead head slumped. The golden gun boomed twice. A bullet whanged round the cabin. The Rasta screamed and fell to the ground, clutching at his throat. His hand was still clenched round the whistle lanyard and the little train kept up its mournful howl of warning. Fifty yards to go! The golden hair hung forlornly forward, obscuring the face. The ropes on the wrists and ankles showed clearly. The breasts offered themselves to the screaming engine. Bond ground his teeth and shut his mind to the dreadful impact that would come any minute now. He leaped to the left again and got off three shots. He thought two of them had hit, but then something slammed a great blow into the muscle of his left shoulder and he spun across the cab and crashed to the iron floor, his face over the edge of the footplate. And it was from there, only inches away, that he saw the front wheels scrunch through the body on the line, saw the blonde head severed from the body, saw the china-blue eyes give him a last blank stare, saw the fragments of the showroom dummy disintegrate with a sharp crackling of plastic and the pink splinters shower down the embankment.

James Bond choked back the sickness that rose from his stomach into the back of his throat. He staggered to his feet, keeping low. He reached up for the accelerator lever and pushed it upwards. A pitched battle with the train at a standstill would put the odds even more against him. He hardly felt the pain in his shoulder. He edged round the right-hand side of the tender. Four guns boomed. He flung his head back under cover. Now the hoods were shooting, but wildly because of the interference of the Surrey top. But Bond had had time to see one glorious sight. In the brake van, Scaramanga had slid from his throne and was down on his knees, his head moving to and fro like a wounded animal. Where in hell had Bond hit him? And now what? How was he going to deal with the four hoods, just as badly obscured from him as he was from them?

Then a voice from the back of the train, it could only be from the brake van, Felix Leiter's voice, called out above the shriek of the engine's whistle, 'Okay, you four guys. Toss your guns over the side. Now! Quick!' There came the crack of a shot. 'I said quick. There's Mr Gengerella gone to meet his maker. Okay, then. And now hands behind your heads. That's better. Right. Okay, James. The battle's over. Are you okay? If so show yourself. There's still the final curtain and we've got to move quick.'

Bond rose carefully. He could hardly believe it! Leiter must have been riding on the buffers behind the brake van. He wouldn't have been able to show himself earlier for fear of Bond's gunfire. Yes! There he was! His fair hair tousled by the wind, a long-barrelled pistol using his upraised steel hook as a rest, standing astride the now supine body of Scaramanga beside the brake wheel. Bond's shoulder had begun to hurt like hell. He shouted, with the anger of tremendous relief, 'God damn you, Leiter. Why in hell didn't you show up before? I might have got hurt.'

Leiter laughed. 'That'll be the day! Now listen, shamus. Get ready to jump. The longer you wait, the farther you've got to walk home. I'm going to stay with these guys for a while and hand them over to the law in Green Harbour.' He shook his head to show this was a lie. 'Now get goin'. It's The Morass. The landing'll be soft. Stinks a bit, but we'll give you an eau-de-Cologne spray when you get home. Right?'

The train ran over a small culvert and the song of the wheels changed to a deep boom. Bond looked ahead. In the distance was the spidery ironwork of the Orange River bridge. The still shrieking train was losing steam. The gauge said 19 m.p.h. Bond looked down at the dead Rasta. In death, his face was as horrible as it had been in life. The bad teeth, sharpened from eating sugar cane from childhood, were bared in a frozen snarl. Bond took a quick glance under the Surrey. Hendriks's slumped body lolled with the movement of the train. The sweat of the day still shone on the doughy cheeks. Even as a corpse he didn't ask for sympathy. In the seat behind him, Leiter's bullet had torn through the back of Gengerella's head and removed most of his face. Next to him, and behind him, the three gangsters gazed up at James Bond with whipped eyes. They hadn't expected all this. This was to have been a holiday. The calypso shirts said so. Mr Scaramanga, the undefeated, the undefeatable, had said so. Until minutes before, his golden gun had backed up his word. Now, suddenly, everything was different. As the Arabs say when a great sheikh has gone, has removed his protection, 'Now there is no more shade!' They were covered with guns from the front and the rear. The train stretched out its iron stride towards nowhere they had ever heard of before. The whistle moaned. The sun beat down. The dreadful stink of The Great Morass assailed their nostrils. This was abroad. This was bad news, really bad. The Tour Director had left them to fend for themselves. Two of them had been killed. Even their guns were gone. The tough faces, as white moons, gazed in supplication up at Bond. Louie Paradise's voice was cracked and dry with terror. 'A million bucks, Mister, if you get us out of this. Swear on my mother. A million.'

The faces of Sam Binion and Hal Garfinkel lit up. Here was hope! 'And a million.'

'And another! On my baby son's head!'

The voice of Felix Leiter bellowed angrily. There was a note of panic in it. 'Jump, damn you, James! Jump!'

James Bond stood up in the cabin, not listening to the voices supplicating from under the yellow Surrey. These men had wanted to watch him being murdered. They had been prepared to murder him themselves. How many dead men had each one of them got on his tally-sheet? Bond got down on the step of the cabin, chose his moment and threw himself clear of the clinker track and into the soft embraces of a stinking mangrove pool.

His explosion into the mud released the stench of hell. Great bubbles of marsh gas wobbled up to the surface and burst glutinously. A bird screeched and clattered off through the foliage. James Bond waded out on to the edge of the embankment. Now his shoulder was really hurting. He knelt down and was as sick as a cat.

When he raised his head it was to see Leiter hurl himself off the brake van, now a good two hundred yards away. He seemed to land clumsily. He didn't get up. And now, within yards of the long iron bridge over the sluggish river, another figure leaped from the train into a clump of mangrove. It was a tall, chocolate-clad figure. There was no doubt about it! It was Scaramanga! Bond cursed feebly. Why in hell hadn't Leiter put a finishing bullet through the man's head? Now there was unfinished business. The cards had only been reshuffled. The end game had still to be played!

The screaming progress of the driverless train changed to a roar as the track took to the trestles of the long bridge. Bond watched it vaguely, wondering when it would run out of steam. What would the three gangsters do now? Take to the hills? Get the train under control and go on to Green Harbour and try and take the *Thunder Girl* across to Cuba? Immediately the answer came! Half-way across the bridge, the engine suddenly reared up like a bucking stallion. At the same time there came a crash of thunder and a vast sheet of flame and the bridge buckled downwards in the centre like a bent leg. Chunks of torn iron sprayed upwards and sideways and there was a splintering crash as the main stanchions gave and slowly bowed down towards the water. Through the jagged gap, the beautiful Belle, a smashed toy, folded upon itself and, with a giant splintering of iron and woodwork and a volcano of spray and steam, thundered into the river.

A deafening silence fell. Somewhere behind Bond, a wakened tree frog tinkled uncertainly. Four white egrets flew down and over the wreck, their necks outstretched inquisitively. In the distance, black dots materialized high up in the sky and circled lazily closer. The sixth sense of the turkey buzzards had told them that the distant explosion was disaster — something that might yield a meal. The sun hammered down on the silver rails and, a few yards away from where Bond lay, a group of yellow butterflies danced in the shimmer. Bond got slowly to his feet and, parting the butterflies, began walking slowly but purposefully up the line towards the bridge. First Felix Leiter and then after the big one that had got away.

Leiter lay in the stinking mud. His left leg was at a hideous angle. Bond went down to him, his finger to his lips. He knelt beside him and said softly, 'Nothing much I can do for now, pal. I'll give you a bullet to bite on and get you into some shade. There'll be people coming before long. Got to get on after that bastard. He's somewhere up there by the bridge. What made you think he was dead?'

Leiter groaned, more in anger with himself than from the pain. 'There was blood all over the place.' The voice was a halting whisper between clenched teeth. 'His shirt was soaked in it. Eyes closed. Thought if he wasn't cold he'd go with the others on the bridge.' He smiled faintly. 'How did you dig the River Kwai stunt? Go off all right?'

Bond raised a thumb. 'Fourth of July. The crocs'll be sitting down to table right now. But that damned dummy! Gave me a nasty turn. Did you put her there?'

'Sure. Sorry, boy. Mr S. told me to. Made an excuse to spike the bridge this morning. No idea your girl friend was a blonde or that you'd fall for the spiel.'

'Bloody silly of me, I suppose. Thought he'd got hold of her last night. Anyway, come on. Here's your bullet. Bite the lead. The story-books say it helps. This is going to hurt, but I must haul you under cover and out of the sun.' Bond got his hands under Leiter's armpits and, as gently as he could, dragged him to a dry patch under a big mangrove bush above swamp level. The sweat of pain poured down Leiter's face. Bond propped him up against the roots. Leiter gave a groan and his head fell back. Bond looked thoughtfully down at him. A faint was probably the best thing that could have happened. He took Leiter's gun out of his waistband and put it beside his left, and only, hand. Bond still might get into much trouble. If he did, Scaramanga would come after Felix.

Bond crept off along the line of mangroves towards the bridge. For the time being he would have to keep more or less in the open. He prayed that, nearer the river, the swamp would yield to drier land so that he could work down towards the sea and then cut back towards the river and hope to pick up the man's tracks.

It was 1.30 and the sun was high. James Bond was hungry and very thirsty and his shoulder wound throbbed with his pulse. The wound was beginning to give him a fever. One dreams all day as well as all night, and now, as he stalked his prey, he found, quizzically, that much of his mind was taken up with visualizing the champagne buffet waiting for them all, the living and the dead, at Green Harbour. For the moment, he indulged himself. The buffet would be laid out under the trees, as he saw it, adjoining the terminal station, which would probably be on the same lines as Thunderbird Halt. There would be long trestle tables, spotless tablecloths, rows of glasses and plates and cutlery and great dishes of cold lobster salad, cold meat cuts, and mounds of fruit — pineapple and such — to make the décor look Jamaican and exotic. There might be a hot dish, he thought. Something like roast stuffed sucking-pig with rice and peas — too hot for the day, decided Bond, but a feast for most of Green Harbour when the rich 'tourists' had departed. And there would be drink! Champagne in frosted silver coolers, rum punches, Tom Collinses, whisky sours, and, of course, great beakers of iced water that would only have been poured when the train whistled its approach to the gay little station. Bond could see it all. Every detail of it under the shade of the great ficus trees. The white-gloved, uniformed coloured waiters enticing him to take more and more; beyond, the dancing waters of the harbour, in the background the hypnotic throb of the calypso band, the soft, enticing eyes of the girls. And, ruling, ordering all, the tall, fine figure of the gracious host, a thin cigar between his teeth, the wide white Stetson tilted low over his brow, offering Bond just one more goblet of iced champagne.

James Bond stumbled over a mangrove root, threw out his right hand for support from the bush, missed, tripped again and fell heavily. He lay for a moment, measuring the noise he must have made. It wouldn't have been much. The inshore wind from the sea was feathering the swamp. A hundred yards away the river added its undertone of sluggish turbulence. There were cricket and bird noises. Bond got to his knees and then to his feet. What in hell had he been thinking of? Come on, you bloody fool! There's work to be done! He shook his head to clear it. Gracious host! God damn it! He was on his way to kill the gracious host! Goblets of iced champagne? That'd be the day! He shook his head angrily. He took several very deep slow breaths. He knew the symptoms. This was nothing worse than acute nervous exhaustion with — he gave himself that amount of grace — a small fever added. All he had to do was to keep his mind and his eyes in focus. For God's sake no more day-dreaming! With a new, sharpened resolve he kicked the mirages out of his mind and looked to his geography.

There were perhaps a hundred yards to go to the bridge. On Bond's left, the mangroves were sparser and the black mud was dry and cracked. But there were still soft patches. Bond put up the collar of his coat to hide the white shirt. He covered another twenty yards beside the rail and then struck off left into the mangroves. He found that if he kept close to the roots of the mangroves the going wasn't too bad. At least there were no dry twigs or leaves to crack and rustle. He tried to keep as nearly as possible parallel with the river, but thick patches of bushes made him make small detours and he had to estimate his direction by the dryness of the mud and the slight rise of the land towards the river bank. His ears were pricked like an animal's for the smallest sound. His eyes strained into the greenery ahead. Now the mud was pitted with the burrows of land crabs and there were occasional remnants of their shells, victims of big birds or mongoose. For the first time, mosquitoes and sand-flies began to attack him. He could not slap them off but only dab at them softly with his handkerchief that was soon soaked with the blood they had sucked from him and wringing with the white man's sweat that attracted them.

Bond estimated that he had penetrated two hundred yards into the swamp when he heard the single, controlled cough.

15
CRAB-MEAT

THE COUGH SOUNDED about twenty yards away, towards the river. Bond dropped to one knee, his senses questing like the antennae of an insect. He waited five minutes. When the cough was not repeated, he crept forwards on hands and knees, his gun gripped between his teeth.

In a small clearing of dried, cracked black mud, he saw the man. He stopped in his tracks, trying to calm his breathing.

Scaramanga was lying stretched out, his back supported by a clump of sprawling mangrove roots. His hat and his high stock had gone and the whole of the right-hand side of his suit was black with blood upon which insects crawled and feasted. But the eyes in the controlled face were still very much alive. They swept the clearing at regular intervals, questing. Scaramanga's hands rested on the roots beside him. There was no sign of a gun.

Scaramanga's face suddenly pointed, like a retriever's, and the roving scrutiny held steady. Bond could not see what had caught his attention, but then a patch of the dappled shadow at the edge of the clearing moved and a large snake, beautifully diamonded in dark and pale brown, zigzagged purposefully across the black mud towards the man.

Bond watched, fascinated. He guessed it was a boa of the *Epicrates* family, attracted by the smell of blood. It was perhaps five feet long and quite harmless to man. Bond wondered if Scaramanga would know this. He was immediately put out of his doubt. Scaramanga's expression had not changed, but his right hand crept softly down his trouser leg, gently pulled up the cuff and removed a thin, stiletto-style knife from the side of his short Texan boot. Then he waited, the knife held ready across his stomach, not clenched in his fist, but pointed in the flick-knife fashion. The snake paused for a moment a few yards from the man and raised its head high to give him a final inspection. The forked tongue licked out inquisitively, again and again, then, still with its head held above the ground, it moved slowly forward.

Not a muscle moved in Scaramanga's face. Only the eyes were dead steady, watchful slits. The snake came into the shadow of his trouser leg and moved slowly up towards the glistening shirt. Suddenly the tongue of steel that lay across Scaramanga's stomach came to life and leaped. It transfixed the head of the snake exactly in the centre of the brain and pierced through it, pinning it to the ground and holding it there while the powerful body thrashed wildly, seeking a grip on the mangrove roots, on Scaramanga's arm. But immediately, when it had a grip, its convulsions released its coils which flailed off in another direction.

The death struggles diminished and finally ceased altogether. The snake lay motionless. Scaramanga was careful. He ran his hand down the full length of the snake. Only the tip of the tail lashed briefly. Scaramanga extracted the knife from the head of the snake, cut off its head with a single hard stroke and threw it, after reflection, accurately towards a crab hole. He waited, watching, to see if a crab would come out and take it. None did. The thud of the arrival of the snake's head would have kept any crab underground for many minutes, however enticing the scent of what had made the thud.

James Bond, kneeling in the bush, watched all this, every nuance of it, with the most careful attention. Each one of Scaramanga's actions, every fleeting expression on his face, had been an index of the man's awareness of his aliveness. The whole episode of the snake was as revealing as a temperature chart or a lie-detector. In Bond's judgment, Mr Scaramanga, for all his blood-letting and internal injuries, was still very much alive. He was still a most formidable and dangerous man.

Scaramanga, his task satisfactorily completed, minutely shifted his position, and, once again, foot by foot, made his penetrating examination of the surrounding bush.

As Scaramanga's gaze swept by him without a flicker, Bond blessed the darkness of his suit — a black patch of shadow among so many others. In the sharp blacks and whites from the midday sun, Bond was well camouflaged.

Satisfied, Scaramanga picked up the limp body of the snake, laid it across his stomach and carefully slit it down its underside as far as the anal vent. Then he scoured it and carefully etched the skin away from the red-veined flesh with the precise flicks and cuts of a surgeon. Every scrap of unwanted reptile he threw towards crab holes and, with each throw, a flicker of annoyance crossed the granite face that no one would come and pick up the crumbs from the rich man's table. When the meal was ready, he once again scanned the bush and then, very carefully, coughed and spat into his hand. He examined the results and flung his hand sideways. On the black ground, the sputum made a bright pink scrawl. The cough didn't seem to hurt him or cause him much effort. Bond guessed that his bullet had hit Scaramanga in the right chest and had missed a lung by a fraction. There was haemorrhage and Scaramanga was a hospital case, but the blood-soaked shirt was not telling the whole truth.

Satisfied with his inspection of his surroundings, Scaramanga bit into the body of the snake and was at once, like a dog with its meal, absorbed by his hunger and thirst for the blood and juices of the snake.

Bond had the impression that, if he now came forward from his hiding-place, Scaramanga, like a dog, would bare his teeth in a furious snarl. He got quietly up from his knees, took out his gun and, his eyes watching Scaramanga's hands, strolled out into the centre of the little clearing.

Bond was mistaken. Scaramanga did not snarl. He barely looked up from the cut-off length of snake in his two hands and, his mouth full of meat, said, 'You've been a long while coming. Care to share my meal?'

'No thanks. I prefer my snake grilled with hot butter sauce. Just keep on eating. I like to see both hands occupied.'

Scaramanga sneered. He gestured at his bloodstained shirt. 'Frightened of a dying man? You limeys come pretty soft.'

'The dying man handled that snake quite efficiently. Got any more weapons on you?' As Scaramanga moved to undo his coat, 'Steady! No quick movements. Just show your belt, armpits, pat the thighs inside and out. I'd do it myself only I don't want what the snake got. And while you're about it, just toss the knife into the trees. Toss. No throwing, if you don't mind. My trigger-finger's been getting a bit edgy today. Seems to want to go about its business on its own. Wouldn't like it to take over. Yet, that is.'

Scaramanga, with a flick of his wrist, tossed the knife into the air. The sliver of steel spun like a wheel in the sunshine. Bond had to step aside. The knife pierced the mud where Bond had been standing and stood upright. Scaramanga gave a harsh laugh. The laugh turned into a cough. The gaunt face contorted painfully. Too painfully? Scaramanga spat red, but not all that red. There could be only slight haemorrhage. Perhaps a broken rib or two. Scaramanga could be out of hospital in a couple of weeks. Scaramanga put down his piece of snake and did exactly as Bond had told him, all the while watching Bond's face with his usual cold, arrogant stare. He finished and picked up the piece of snake and began gnawing it. He looked up. 'Satisfied?'

'Sufficiently.' Bond squatted down on his heels. He held his gun loosely, aiming somewhere half-way between the two of them. 'Now then, let's talk. 'Fraid you haven't got too much time, Scaramanga. This is the end of the road. You've killed too many of my friends. I have the licence to kill you and I am going to kill you. But I'll make it quick. Not like Margesson. Remember him? You put a shot through both of his knees and both of his elbows. Then you made him crawl and kiss your boots. You were foolish enough to boast about it to your friends in Cuba. It got back to us. As a matter of interest, how many men have you killed in your life?'

'With you, it'll make the round fifty.' Scaramanga had gnawed the last segment of backbone clean. He tossed it towards Bond. 'Eat that, scum, and get on with your business. You won't get any secrets out of me, if that's your spiel. An' don't forget. I've been shot at by experts an' I'm still alive. Mebbe not precisely kicking but I've never heard of a limey who'd shoot a defenceless man who's badly wounded. They ain't got the guts. We'll just sit here, chewing the fat, until the rescue team comes. Then I'll be glad to go for trial. What'll they get me for eh?'

'Well, just for a start, there's that nice Mr Rotkopf with one of your famous silver bullets in his head in the river back of the hotel.'

'That'll match with the nice Mr Hendriks with one of your bullets somewhere behind his face. Mebbe we'll serve a bit of time together. That'd be nice, wouldn't it? They say the jail at Spanish Town has all the comforts. How about it, limey? That's where you'll be found with a shiv in your back in the sack-sewing department. An' by the same token, how d'you know about Rotkopf?'

'Your bug was bugged. Seems you're a bit accident-prone these days, Scaramanga. You hired the wrong security men. Both your managers were from the C.I.A. The tape'll be on the way to Washington by now. That's got the murder of Ross on it too. See what I mean? You've got it coming from every which way.'

'Tape isn't evidence in an American court. But I see what you mean, shamus. Mistakes seem to have got made. So okay,' Scaramanga made an expansive gesture of the right hand. 'Take a million bucks and call it quits?'

'I was offered three million on the train.'

'I'll double that.'

'No. Sorry.' Bond got to his feet. The left hand behind his back was clenched with the horror of what he was about to do. He forced himself to think of what the broken body of Margesson must have looked like, of the others that this man had killed, of the ones he would kill afresh if Bond weakened. This man was probably the most efficient one-man death-dealer in the world. James Bond had him. He had been instructed to take him. He must take him — lying down wounded, or in any other position. Bond assumed casualness, tried to make himself the enemy's cold equal. 'Any messages for anyone, Scaramanga? Any instructions? Anyone you want looking after? I'll take care of it if it's personal. I'll keep it to myself.'

Scaramanga laughed his harsh laugh, but carefully. This time the laugh didn't turn into the red cough. 'Quite the little English gentleman! Just like I spelled it out. S'pose you wouldn't like to hand me your gun and leave me to myself for five minutes like in the books? Well, you're right, boyo! I'd crawl after you and blast the back of your head off.' The eyes still bored into Bond's with the arrogant superiority, the cold superman quality that had made him the greatest pro gunman in the world — no drinks, no drugs — the impersonal trigger man who killed for money and, by the way he sometimes did it, for the kicks.

Bond examined him carefully. How could Scaramanga fail to break when he was going to die in minutes? Was there some last trick the man was going to spring? Some hidden weapon? But the man just lay there, apparently relaxed, propped up against the mangrove roots, his chest heaving rhythmically, the granite of his face not crumbling even minutely in defeat. On his forehead, there was not as much sweat as there was on Bond's. Scaramanga lay in dappled black shadow. For ten minutes, James Bond had stood in the middle of the clearing in blazing sunshine. Suddenly he felt the vitality oozing out through his feet into the black mud. And his resolve was going with it. He said, and he heard his voice ring out harshly, 'All right, Scaramanga, this is it.' He lifted his gun and held it in the two-handed grip of the target man. 'I'm going to make it as quick as I can.'

Scaramanga held up a hand. For the first time his face showed emotion. 'Okay, feller.' The voice, amazingly, supplicated. 'I'm a Catholic, see? Jes' let me say my last prayer. Okay? Won't take long, then you can blaze away. Every man's got to die some time. You're a fine guy as guys go. It's the luck of the game. If my bullet had been an inch, mebbe two inches, to the right, it'd be you that's dead in place of me. Right? Can I say my prayer, Mister?'

James Bond lowered his gun. He would give the man a few minutes. He knew he couldn't give him more. Pain and heat and hunger and thirst. It wouldn't be long before he lay down himself, right there on the hard cracked mud, just to rest. If someone wanted to kill him, they could. He said, and the words came out slowly, tiredly, 'Go ahead, Scaramanga. One minute only.'

'Thanks, pal.' Scaramanga's hands went up to his face and covered his eyes. There came a drone of Latin which went on and on. Bond stood there in the sunshine, his gun lowered, watching Scaramanga, but at the same time not watching him, the edge of his focus dulled by the pain and the heat and the hypnotic litany that came from behind the shuttered face and the horror of what Bond was going to have to do — in one minute, perhaps two.

The fingers of Scaramanga's right hand crawled imperceptibly sideways across his face, inch by inch, centimetre by centimetre. They got to his ear and stopped. The drone of the Latin prayer never altered its slow, lulling tempo.

And then the hand leaped behind the head and the tiny golden Derringer roared and James Bond spun round as if he had taken a right to the jaw and crashed to the ground.

At once Scaramanga was on his feet and moving forward like

a swift cat. He snatched up the discarded knife and held it forward like a tongue of silver flame.

But James Bond twisted like a dying animal on the ground and the iron in his hand cracked viciously again and again — five times, and then fell out of his hand on to the black earth as his gun-hand went to the right side of his belly and stayed there, clutching at the terrible pain.

The big man stood for a moment and looked up at the deep blue sky. His fingers opened in a spasm and let go the knife. His pierced heart stuttered and limped and stopped. He crashed flat back and lay, his arms flung wide, as if someone had thrown him away.

After a while, the land crabs came out of their holes and began nosing at the scraps of the snake. The bigger offal could wait until the night.

16

THE WRAP-UP

THE EXTREMELY SMART policeman from the wrecking squad on the railway came down the river bank at the normal, dignified gait of a Jamaican constable on his beat. No Jamaican policeman ever breaks into a run. He has been taught that this lacks authority. Felix Leiter, now put under with morphine by the doctor, had said that a good man was after a bad man in the swamp and that there might be shooting. Felix Leiter wasn't more explicit than that, but, when he said he was from the F.B.I. — a legitimate euphemism — in Washington, the policeman tried to get some of the wrecking squad to come with him and, when he failed, sauntered cautiously off on his own, his baton swinging with assumed jauntiness.

The boom of the guns and the explosion of screeching marsh birds gave him an approximate fix. He had been born not far away, at Negril, and, as a boy, he had often used his gins and his slingshot in these marshes. They held no fears for him. When he came to the approximate point on the river bank, he turned left into the mangrove and, conscious that his black and blue uniform was desperately conspicuous, stalked cautiously from clump to clump into the morass. He was protected by nothing but his nightstick and the knowledge that to kill a policeman was a capital offence without the option. He only hoped that the good man and the bad man knew this too.

With all the birds gone, there was dead silence. The constable noticed that the tracks of bush rats and other small animals were running past him on a course that converged with his target area. Then he heard the rattling scuttle of the crabs and, in a moment, from behind a thick mangrove clump, he saw the glint of Scaramanga's shirt. He watched and listened. There was no movement and no sound. He strolled, with dignity, into the middle of the clearing, looked at the two bodies and the guns and took out his nickel police whistle and blew three long blasts. Then he sat down in the shade of a bush, took out his report pad, licked his pencil and began writing in a laborious hand.

A week later, James Bond regained consciousness. He was in a green-shaded room. He was under water. The slowly revolving fan in the ceiling was the screw of a ship that was about to run him down. He swam for his life. But it was no good. He was tied down, anchored to the bottom of the sea. He screamed at the top of his lungs. To the nurse at the end of the bed it was the whisper of a moan. At once she was beside him. She put a cool hand on his forehead. While she took his pulse, James Bond looked up at her with unfocused eyes. So this was what a mermaid looked like! He muttered 'You're pretty,' and gratefully swam back down into her arms.

The nurse wrote ninety-five on his sheet and telephoned down to the ward sister. She looked in the dim mirror and tidied her hair in preparation for the R.M.O. in charge of this apparently Very Important Patient.

The Resident Medical Officer, a young Jamaican graduate from Edinburgh, arrived with the matron, a kindly dragon on loan from King Edward VII's. He heard the nurse's report. He went over to the bed and gently lifted Bond's eyelids. He slipped a thermometer under Bond's armpit and held Bond's pulse in one hand and a pocket chronometer in the other and there was silence in the little room. Outside, the traffic tore up and down a Kingston road.

The doctor released Bond's pulse and slipped the chronometer back into the trouser pocket under the white smock. He wrote figures on the chart. The nurse held the door open and the three people went out into the corridor. The doctor talked to the matron. The nurse was allowed to listen. 'He's going to be all right. Temperature well down. Pulse a little fast but that may have been the result of his waking. Reduce the antibiotics. I'll talk to the floor sister about that later. Keep on with the intravenous feeding. Dr Macdonald will be up later to attend to the dressings. He'll be waking again. If he asks for something to drink, give him fruit juice. He should be on soft foods soon. Miracle really. Missed the abdominal viscera. Didn't even shave a kidney. Muscle only. That bullet was dipped in enough poison to kill a horse. Thank God that man at Sav' La Mar recognized the symptoms of snake venom and gave him those massive anti-snake-bite injections. Remind me to write to him, matron. He saved the man's life. Now then, no visitors of course, for at least another week. You can tell the police and the High Commissioner's Office that he's on the mend. I don't know who he is, but apparently London keep on worrying us about him. Something to do with the Ministry of Defence. From now on, put them and all other inquiries through to the High Commissioner's Office. They seem to think they're in charge of him.' He paused. 'By the way, how's his friend getting on in Number Twelve? The one the American Ambassador and Washington have been on about. He's not on my list, but he keeps on asking to see this Mr Bond.'

'Compound fracture of the tibia,' said the matron. 'No complications.' She smiled. 'Except that he's a bit fresh with the nurses. He should be walking with a stick in ten days. He's already seen the police. I suppose it's all to do with that story in the *Gleaner* about those American tourists being killed when the bridge collapsed near Green Island Harbour. But the Commissioner's handling it all personally. The story in the *Gleaner*'s very vague.'

The doctor smiled. 'Nobody tells me anything. Just as well. I haven't got the time to listen to them. Well, thank you, matron. I must get along. Multiple crash at Halfway Tree. The ambulances'll be here any minute.' He hurried away. The matron went about her business. The nurse, excited by all this high-level talk, went softly back into the green-shaded room, tidied the sheet over the naked right shoulder of her patient where the doctor had pulled it down, and went back to her chair at the end of the bed and her copy of *Ebony*.

Ten days later, the little room was crowded. James Bond, propped up among extra pillows, was amused by the galaxy of officialdom that had been assembled. On his left was the Commissioner of Police, resplendent in his black uniform with silver insignia. On his right was a Judge of the Supreme Court in full regalia accompanied by a deferential clerk. A massive figure, to whom Felix Leiter, on crutches, was fairly respectful, had been introduced as 'Colonel Bannister' from Washington. Head of

Station C, a quiet civil servant called Alec Hill, who had been flown out from London, stood near the door and kept his appraising eyes unwaveringly on Bond. Mary Goodnight, who was to take notes of the proceedings but also, on the matron's strict instructions, watch for any sign of fatigue in James Bond and have absolute authority to close the meeting if he showed strain, sat demurely beside the bed with a shorthand pad on her knees. But James Bond felt no strain. He was delighted to see all these people and know that at last he was back in the great world again. The only matters that worried him were that he had not been allowed to see Felix Leiter before the meeting to agree their stories and that he had been rather curtly advised by the High Commissioner's Office that legal representation would not be necessary.

The Police Commissioner cleared his throat. He said, 'Commander Bond, our meeting here today is largely a formality, but it is held on the Prime Minister's instructions and with your doctor's approval. There are many rumours running around the island and abroad and Sir Alexander Bustamante is most anxious to have them dispelled for the sake of justice and of the island's good name. So this meeting is in the nature of a judicial inquiry having Prime Ministerial status. We very much hope that, if the conclusions of the meeting are satisfactory, there need be no more legal proceedings whatever. You understand?'

'Yes,' said Bond, who didn't.

'Now.' The Commissioner spoke weightily. 'The facts as ascertained are as follows. Recently there took place at the Thunderbird Hotel in the Parish of Westmoreland a meeting of what can only be described as foreign gangsters of outstanding notoriety, including representatives of the Soviet Secret Service, the Mafia, and the Cuban Secret Police. The objects of this meeting were, inter alia, sabotage of Jamaican installations in the cane industry, stimulation of illicit ganja-growing in the island and purchase of the crop for export, the bribery of a high Jamaican official with the object of installing gangster-run gambling in the island and sundry other malfeasances deleterious to law and order in Jamaica and to her international standing. Am I correct, Commander?'

'Yes,' said Bond, this time with a clear conscience.

'Now.' The Commissioner spoke with even greater emphasis.

'The intentions of this subversive group became known to the Criminal Investigation Department of the Jamaican Police and the facts of the proposed assembly were placed before the Prime Minister in person by myself. Naturally the greatest secrecy was observed. A decision then had to be reached as to how this meeting was to be kept under surveillance and penetrated so that its intentions might be learned. Since friendly nations, including Britain and the United States, were involved, secret conversations took place with the representatives of the Ministry of Defence in Britain and of the Central Intelligence Agency in the United States. As a result, expert personnel in the shape of yourself, Mr Nicholson and Mr Leiter were generously made available, at no cost to the Jamaican Government, to assist in unveiling these secret machinations against Jamaica held on Jamaican soil.' The Commissioner paused and looked round the room to see if he had stated the position correctly. Bond noticed that Felix Leiter nodded his head vigorously with the others, but, in his case, in Bond's direction.

Bond smiled. He had at last got the message. He also nodded his agreement.

'Accordingly,' continued the Commissioner, 'and working throughout under the closest liaison and direction of the Jamaican C.I.D., Messrs Bond, Nicholson and Leiter carried out their duties in exemplary fashion. The true intentions of the gangsters were unveiled, but alas, in the process, the identity of at least one of the Jamaica-controlled agents was discovered and a battle royal took place during the course of which the following enemy agents — here there will be a list — were killed, thanks to the superior gunfire of Commander Bond and Mr Leiter, and the following — another list — by the destruction by Mr Leiter's ingenious use of explosive of the Orange River Bridge on the Lucea–Green Island Harbour railway, now converted for tourist use. Unfortunately, two of the Jamaica-controlled agents received severe wounds from which they are now recovering in the Memorial Hospital. It remains to mention the names of Constable Percival Sampson of the Negril Constabulary who was first on the scene of the final battlefield, and Dr Lister Smith of Savannah La Mar who rendered vital first aid to Commander Bond and Mr Leiter. On the instructions of the Prime Minister, Sir Alexander Bustamante, a judicial inquiry was held this day at the bedside of Commander Bond and in the presence of Mr Felix Leiter to confirm the above facts. These, in the presence of Justice Morris Cargill of the Supreme Court, are now and hereby confirmed.'

The Commissioner was obviously delighted with his rendering of all this rigmarole. He beamed at Bond. 'It only remains', he handed Bond a sealed packet, a similar one to Felix Leiter and one to Colonel Bannister, 'to confer on Commander Bond of Great Britain, Mr Felix Leiter of the United States and, in absentia, Mr Nicholas Nicholson of the United States, the immediate award of the Jamaican Police Medal for gallant and meritorious services to the Independent State of Jamaica.'

There was muted applause. Mary Goodnight went on clapping after the others had stopped. She suddenly realized the fact, blushed furiously and stopped.

James Bond and Felix Leiter made stammered acknowledgments. Justice Cargill rose to his feet and, in solemn tones, asked Bond and Leiter in turn, 'Is this a true and correct account of what occurred between the given dates?'

'Yes, indeed,' said Bond.

'I'll say it is, Your Honour,' said Felix Leiter fervently.

The Judge bowed. All except Bond rose and bowed. Bond just bowed. 'In that case, I declare this inquiry closed.' The bewigged figure turned to Miss Goodnight. 'If you will be kind enough to obtain all the signatures, duly witnessed, and send them round to my chambers? Thank you so much.' He paused and smiled. 'And the carbon, if you don't mind?'

'Certainly, my lord.' Mary Goodnight glanced at Bond. 'And now, if you will forgive me, I think the patient needs a rest. Matron was most insistent . . .'

Goodbyes were said. Bond called Leiter back. Mary Goodnight smelled private secrets. She admonished, 'Now, only a minute!' and went out and closed the door.

Leiter leant over the end of the bed. He wore his most quizzical smile. He said, 'Well, I'll be goddamned, James. That was the neatest wrap-up job I've ever lied my head off at. Everything clean as a whistle and we've even collected a piece of lettuce.'

Talking starts with the stomach muscles. Bond's wounds were beginning to ache. He smiled, not showing the pain. Leiter was due to leave that afternoon. Bond didn't want to say goodbye to him. Bond treasured his men friends and Felix Leiter was a great slice of his past. He said, 'Scaramanga was quite a guy. He should have been taken alive. Maybe Tiffy really did put the hex on him with Mother Edna. They don't come like that often.'

Leiter was unsympathetic. 'That's the way you limeys talk about Rommel and Dönitz and Guderian. Let alone Napoleon. Once you've beaten them, you make heroes out of them. Don't make sense to me. In my book, an enemy's an enemy. Care to have Scaramanga back? Now, in this room, with his famous golden gun on you — the long one or the short one? Standing where I am? One bets you a thousand you wouldn't. Don't be a jerk, James. You did a good job. Pest control. It's got to be done by someone. Going back to it when you're off the orange juice?' Felix Leiter jeered at him. 'Of course you are, lamebrain. It's what you were put into the world for. Pest control, like I said. All you got to figure is how to control it better. The pests'll always be there. God made dogs. He also made their fleas. Don't let it worry your tiny mind. Right?' Leiter had seen the sweat on James Bond's forehead. He limped towards the door and opened it. He raised a hand briefly. The two men had never shaken hands in their lives. Leiter looked into the corridor. He said, 'Okay, Miss Goodnight. Tell matron to take him off the danger list. And tell him to keep away from me for a week or two. Every time I see him a piece of me gets broken off. I don't fancy myself as The Vanishing Man.' Again he raised his only hand in Bond's direction and limped out.

Bond shouted, 'Wait, you bastard!' But, by the time Leiter had limped back into the room, Bond, no effort left in him to fire off the volley of four-letter words that were his only answer to his friend, had lapsed into unconsciousness.

Mary Goodnight shooed the remorseful Leiter out of the room and ran off down the corridor to the floor sister.

17

ENDIT

A WEEK LATER, James Bond was sitting up in a chair, a towel round his waist, reading Allen Dulles on *The Craft of Intelligence* and cursing his fate. The hospital had worked miracles on him, the nurses were sweet, particularly the one he called 'The Mermaid', but he wanted to be off and away. He glanced at his watch. Four o'clock. Visiting time. Mary Goodnight would soon be there and he would be able to let off his pent-up steam on her. Unjust perhaps, but he had already tongue-lashed everyone in range in the hospital and, if she got into the field of fire, that was just too bad!

Mary Goodnight came through the door. Despite the Jamaican heat, she was looking fresh as a rose. Damn her! She was carrying what looked like a typewriter. Bond recognized it as the Triple-X deciphering machine. Now what?

Bond grunted surly answers to her inquiries after his health. He said, 'What in hell's that for?'

'It's an "Eyes Only". Personal from M.,' she said excitedly. 'About thirty groups.'

'Thirty groups! Doesn't the old bastard know I've only got one arm that's working? Come on, Mary. You get cracking. If it sounds really hot, I'll take over.'

Mary Goodnight looked shocked. 'Eyes Only' was a top-sacred prefix. But Bond's jaw was jutting out dangerously. Today was not a day for argument. She sat on the edge of the bed, opened the machine and took a cable form out of her bag. She laid her shorthand book beside the machine, scratched the back of her head with her pencil to help work out the setting for the day — a complicated sum involving the date and the hour of dispatch of the cable — adjusted the setting on the central cylinder and began cranking the handle. After each completed word had appeared in the little oblong window at the base of the machine, she recorded it in her book.

James Bond watched her expression. She was pleased. After a few minutes she read out: 'M PERSONAL FOR 007 EYES ONLY STOP YOUR REPORT AND DITTO FROM TOP FRIENDS [a euphemism for the C.I.A.] RECEIVED STOP YOU HAVE DONE WELL AND EXECUTED A DIFFICULT AND HAZARDOUS OPERATION TO MY ENTIRE REPEAT ENTIRE SATISFACTION STOP TRUST YOUR HEALTH UNIMPAIRED [Bond gave an angry snort] STOP WHEN WILL YOU BE REPORTING FOR FURTHER DUTY QUERY.'

Mary Goodnight smiled delightedly. 'I've never seen him be so complimentary! Have you, James? That repeat of ENTIRE! It's tremendous!' She looked hopefully for a lifting of the black clouds from Bond's face.

In fact Bond was secretly delighted, but he certainly wasn't going to show it to Mary Goodnight. Today she was one of the wardresses confining him, tying him down. He said grudgingly, 'Not bad for the old man. But all he wants is to get me back to that bloody desk. Anyway, it's a lot of jazz so far. What comes next?' He turned the pages of his book, pretending as the little machine whirred and clicked not to be interested.

'Oh, James!' Mary Goodnight exploded with excitement. 'Wait! I'm almost finished. It's tremendous!'

'I know,' commented Bond sourly. 'Free luncheon vouchers every second Friday. Key to M.'s personal lavatory. New suit to replace the one that's somehow got full of holes.' But he kept his eyes fixed on the flitting fingers, infected by Mary Goodnight's excitement. What in hell was she getting so steamed up about? And all on his behalf! He examined her with approval. Perched there, immaculate in her white tussore shirt and tight beige skirt, one neat foot curled round the other in concentration, the golden face under the shortish fair hair incandescent with pleasure, she was, thought Bond, a girl to have around always. As a secretary? As what? Mary Goodnight turned, her eyes shining, and the question went, as it had gone for weeks, without an answer.

'Now, just listen to this, James.' She shook the notebook at him. 'And for heaven's sake stop looking so curmudgeonly.'

Bond smiled at the word. 'All right, Mary. Go ahead. Empty the Christmas stocking on the floor. Hope it's not going to bust any stitches.' He put his book down on his lap.

Mary Goodnight's face became portentous. She said seriously, 'Just listen to this!' She read very carefully: IN VIEW OF THE OUTSTANDING NATURE OF THE SERVICES REFERRED TO ABOVE AND THEIR ASSISTANCE TO THE ALLIED CAUSE COMMA WHICH IS PERHAPS MORE SIGNIFICANT THAN YOU IMAGINE COMMA THE PRIME MINISTER PROPOSES TO RECOMMEND TO HER MAJESTY QUEEN ELIZABETH THE IMMEDIATE GRANT OF A KNIGHTHOOD STOP THIS TO TAKE THE FORM OF THE ADDITION OF A KATIE AS PREFIX TO YOUR CHARLIE MICHAEL GEORGE. [James Bond uttered a defensive, embarrassed laugh. 'Good old cipherines. They wouldn't think of just putting KCMG — much too easy! Go ahead, Mary. This is good!'] IT IS COMMON PRACTICE TO INQUIRE OF PROPOSED RECIPIENT WHETHER HE ACCEPTS THIS HIGH HONOUR BEFORE HER MAJESTY PUTS HER SEAL UPON IT STOP WRITTEN LETTER SHOULD FOLLOW YOUR CABLED CONFIRMATION OF ACCEPTANCE PARAGRAPH THIS AWARD NATURALLY HAS MY SUPPORT AND ENTIRE APPROVAL AND EYE SEND YOU MY PERSONAL CONGRATULATIONS ENDIT MAILEDFIST.'

James Bond again hid himself behind the throwaway line. 'Why in hell does he always have to sign himself "Mailedfist" for "M."? There's a perfectly good English word "Em". It's a measure used by printers. But of course it's not dashing enough for the Chief. He's romantic at heart like all the silly bastards who get mixed up with the Service.'

Mary Goodnight lowered her eyelashes. She knew that Bond's reflex concealed his pleasure — a pleasure he wouldn't for the life of him have displayed. Who wouldn't be pleased, proud? She put on a businesslike expression. 'Well, would you like me to draft something for you to send? I can be back with it at six and I know they'll let me in. I can check up the right sort of formula with the High Commissioner's staff. I know it begins with "I present my humble duty to Her Majesty". I've had to help with the Jamaica honours at New Year and her birthday. Everyone seems to want to know the form.'

James Bond wiped his forehead with his handkerchief. Of course he was pleased! But above all pleased with M.'s commendation. The rest, he knew, was not in his stars. He had never been a public figure and he did not wish to become one.

He had no prejudice against letters after one's name, or before it. But there was one thing above all he treasured. His privacy. His anonymity. To become a public person, a person, in the snobbish world of England, of any country, who would be called upon to open things, lay foundation stones, make after-dinner speeches, brought the sweat to his armpits. 'James Bond'! No middle name. No hyphen. A quiet, dull, anonymous name. Certainly he was a Commander in the Special Branch of the R.N.V.R., but he rarely used the rank. His C.M.G. likewise. He wore it perhaps once a year, together with his two rows of 'lettuce', because there was a dinner for the 'Old Boys' — the fraternity of ex-Secret Service men that went under the name of 'The Twin Snakes Club' — a grisly reunion held in the banqueting hall at Blades that gave enormous pleasure to a lot of people who had been brave and resourceful in their day but now had old men's and old women's diseases and talked about dusty triumphs and tragedies which, since they would never be recorded in the history books, must be told again that night, over the Cockburn '12, when 'The Queen' had been drunk, to some next-door neighbour such as James Bond who was only interested in what was going to happen tomorrow. That was when he wore his 'lettuce' and the C.M.G. below his black tie — to give pleasure and reassurance to the 'Old Children' at their annual party. For the rest of the year, until May polished them up for the occasion, the medals gathered dust in some secret repository where May kept them.

So now James Bond said to Mary Goodnight, avoiding her eyes, 'Mary, this is an order. Take down what follows and send it tonight. Right? Begins, quote MAILEDFIST EYES ONLY' [Bond interjected, I might have said PROMONEYPENNY. When did M. last touch a cipher machine?] YOUR [Put in the number, Mary] ACKNOWLEDGED AND GREATLY APPRECIATED STOP AM INFORMED BY HOSPITAL AUTHORITIES THAT EYE SHALL BE RETURNED LONDONWARDS DUTIABLE IN ONE MONTH STOP REFERRING YOUR REFERENCE TO A HIGH HONOUR EYE BEG YOU PRESENT MY HUMBLE DUTY TO HER MAJESTY AND REQUEST THAT EYE MAY BE PERMITTED COMMA IN ALL HUMILITY COMMA TO DECLINE THE SIGNAL FAVOUR HER MAJESTY IS GRACIOUS ENOUGH TO PROPOSE TO CONFER UPON HER HUMBLE AND OBEDIENT SERVANT BRACKET

ENDIT

TO MAILEDFIST PLEASE PUT THIS IN THE APPROPRIATE WORDS TO THE PRIME MINISTER STOP MY PRINCIPAL REASON IS THAT EYE DONT WANT TO PAY MORE AT HOTELS AND RESTAURANTS BRACKET.'

Mary Goodnight broke in, horrified. 'James. The rest is your business, but you really can't say that last bit.'

Bond nodded. 'I was only trying it on you, Mary. All right, let's start again at the last STOP. Right. EYE AM A SCOTTISH PEASANT AND EYE WILL ALWAYS FEEL AT HOME BEING A SCOTTISH PEASANT AND EYE KNOW COMMA SIR COMMA THAT YOU WILL UNDERSTAND MY PREFERENCE AND THAT EYE CAN COUNT ON YOUR INDULGENCE BRACKET LETTER CONFIRMING FOLLOWS IMMEDIATELY END IT OHOHSEVEN.'

Mary Goodnight closed her book with a snap. She shook her head. The golden hair danced angrily. 'Well really, James! Are you sure you don't want to sleep on it? I knew you were in a bad mood today. You may have changed your mind by tomorrow. Don't you want to go to Buckingham Palace and see the Queen and the Duke of Edinburgh and kneel and have your shoulder touched with a sword and the Queen to say "Arise, Sir Knight" or whatever it is she does say?'

Bond smiled. 'I'd like all those things. The romantic streak of the S.I.S. — and of the Scot, for the matter of that. I just refuse to call myself Sir James Bond. I'd laugh at myself every time I looked in the mirror to shave. It's just not my line, Mary. The thought makes me positively shudder. I know M.'ll understand. He thinks much the same way about these things as I do. Trouble was, he had to more or less inherit his K with the job. Anyway, there it is and I shan't change my mind so you can buzz that off and I'll write M. a letter of confirmation this evening. Any other business?'

'Well, there is one thing, James.' Mary Goodnight looked down her pretty nose. 'Matron says you can leave at the end of the week, but that there's got to be another three weeks' convalescence. Had you got any plans where to go? You have to be in reach of the hospital.'

'No ideas. What do you suggest?'

'Well, er, I've got this little villa up by Mona dam, James.' Her voice hurried. 'It's got quite a nice spare room looking out over Kingston harbour. And it's cool up there. And if you don't mind sharing a bathroom.' She blushed. 'I'm afraid there's no chaperone, but you know, in Jamaica, people don't mind that sort of thing.'

'What sort of thing?' said Bond, teasing her.

'Don't be silly, James. You know, unmarried couples sharing the same house and so on.'

'Oh that sort of thing! Sounds pretty dashing to me. By the way, is your bedroom decorated in pink, with white jalousies, and do you sleep under a mosquito net?'

She looked surprised. 'Yes. How did you know?' When he didn't answer, she hurried on. 'And James, it's not far from the Liguanea Club and you can go there and play bridge, and golf when you get better. There'll be plenty of people for you to talk to. And then of course I can cook and sew buttons on for you and so on.'

Of all the doom-fraught graffiti a woman can write on the wall, those are the most insidious, the most deadly.

James Bond, in the full possession of his senses, with his eyes wide open, his feet flat on the linoleum floor, stuck his head blithely between the mink-lined jaws of the trap. He said, and meant it, 'Goodnight. You're an angel.'

At the same time, he knew, deep down, that love from Mary Goodnight, or from any other woman, was not enough for him. It would be like taking 'a room with a view'. For James Bond, the same view would always pall.

OCTOPUSSY
AND
THE LIVING DAYLIGHTS

For, only a couple of hours earlier, Major Dexter Smythe's already dismal life had changed very much for the worse. So much for the worse that he would be lucky if, in a few weeks' time — time for the sending of cables from Government House to the Colonial Office, to be relayed to the Secret Service and thence to Scotland Yard and the Public Prosecutor, and for Major Smythe's transportation to London with a police escort — he got away with a sentence of imprisonment for life.

And all this because of a man called Bond, Commander James Bond, who had turned up at ten thirty that morning in a taxi from Kingston.

OCTOPUSSY

'YOU KNOW WHAT?' said Major Dexter Smythe to the octopus. 'You're going to have a real treat today if I can manage it.'

He had spoken aloud and his breath had steamed up the glass of his Pirelli mask. He put his feet down to the sand beside the nigger-head and stood up. The water reached to his armpits. He took off the mask and spat into it, rubbed the spit round the glass, rinsed it clean and pulled the rubber band of the mask back over his head. He bent down again.

The eye in the mottled brown sack was still watching him carefully from the hole in the coral, but now the tip of a single small tentacle wavered hesitatingly an inch or two out of the shadows and quested vaguely with its pink suckers uppermost. Dexter Smythe smiled with satisfaction. Given time, perhaps one more month on top of the two during which he had been chumming up with the octopus, and he would have tamed the darling. But he wasn't going to have that month. Should he take a chance today and reach down and offer his hand, instead of the expected lump of raw meat on the end of his spear, to the tentacle — shake it by the hand, so to speak? No, Pussy, he thought. I can't quite trust you yet. Almost certainly other tentacles would whip out of the hole and up his arm. He only needed to be dragged down less than two feet, the cork valve on his mask would automatically close and he would be suffocated inside it or, if he tore it off, drowned. He might get in a quick lucky jab with his spear, but it would take more than that to kill Pussy. No. Perhaps later in the day. It would be rather like playing Russian roulette, and at about the same five-to-one odds. It might be a quick, a whimsical way out of his troubles! But not now. It would leave the interesting question unsolved. And he had promised that nice Professor Bengry at the Institute. Dexter Smythe swam leisurely off towards the reef, his eyes questing for one shape only, the squat sinister wedge of a scorpion fish, or, as Bengry would put it, *Scorpaena plumieri*.

Major Dexter Smythe, OBE, Royal Marines (Retd), was the remains of a once brave and resourceful officer and of a handsome man who had made easy sexual conquests all his military life and particularly among the Wrens and Wracs and ATS who manned the communications and secretariat of the very special task force to which he had been attached at the end of his service career. Now he was fifty-four, slightly bald and his belly sagged in the Jantzen trunks. And he had had two coronary thromboses. His doctor, Jimmy Greaves (who had been one of their high poker game at Queen's Club when Dexter Smythe had first come to Jamaica), had half-jocularly described the later one, only a month before, as 'the second warning'. But, in his well-chosen clothes, his varicose veins out of sight and his stomach flattened by a discreet support belt behind an immaculate cummerbund, he was still a fine figure of a man at a cocktail party or dinner on the North Shore, and it was a mystery to his friends and neighbours why, in defiance of the two ounces of whisky and ten cigarettes a day to which his doctor had rationed him, he persisted in smoking like a chimney and going to bed drunk, if amiably drunk, every night.

The truth of the matter was that Dexter Smythe had arrived at the frontier of the death-wish. The origins of this state of mind were many and not all that complex. He was irretrievably tied to Jamaica, and tropical sloth had gradually riddled him so that while outwardly he appeared a piece of fairly solid hardwood, under the varnished surface the termites of sloth, self-indulgence, guilt over an ancient sin and general disgust with himself had eroded his once hard core into dust. Since the death of Mary two years before, he had loved no one. He wasn't even sure that he had really loved her, but he knew that, every hour of the day, he missed her love of him and her gay, untidy, chiding and often irritating presence, and though he ate their canapés and drank their martinis, he had nothing but contempt for the international riff-raff with whom he consorted on the North Shore. He could perhaps have made friends with the soldier elements, the gentleman-farmers inland, or the plantation owners on the coast, the professional men and the politicians, but that would mean regaining some serious purpose in life which his sloth, his spiritual accidie, prevented, and cutting down on the bottle, which he was definitely unwilling to do. So Major Smythe was bored, bored to death, and, but for one factor in his life, he would long ago have swallowed the bottle of barbiturates he had easily acquired from a local doctor. The lifeline that kept him clinging to the edge of the cliff was a tenuous one. Heavy drinkers veer towards an exaggeration of their basic temperaments, the classic four — Sanguine, Phlegmatic, Choleric and Melancholic. The Sanguine drunk goes gay to the point of hysteria and idiocy. The Phlegmatic sinks into a morass of sullen gloom. The Choleric is the fighting drunk of the cartoonists who spends much of his life in prison for smashing people and things, and the Melancholic succumbs to self-pity, mawkishness and tears. Major Smythe was a Melancholic who had slid into a drooling fantasy woven around the birds and insects and fish that inhabited the five acres of Wavelets (the name he had given his small villa is symptomatic), its beach and the coral reef beyond. The fish were his particular favourites. He referred to them as 'people' and, since reef fish stick to their territories as closely as do most small birds, after two years he knew them all intimately, 'loved' them and believed that they loved him in return.

They certainly knew him, as the denizens of zoos know their keepers, because he was a daily and a regular provider, scraping off algae and stirring up the sand and rocks for the bottom-feeders, breaking up sea eggs and urchins for the small carnivores and bringing out scraps of offal for the larger ones, and now, as he swam slowly and heavily up and down the reef and through the channels that led out to deep water, his 'people' swarmed around him fearlessly and expectantly, darting at the tip of the three-pronged spear they knew only as a prodigal spoon, flirting right up to the glass of the Pirelli and even, in the case of the fearless, pugnacious demoiselles, nipping softly at his feet and legs.

Part of Major Smythe's mind took in all these brilliantly coloured little 'people', but today he had a job to do and while he greeted them in unspoken words — 'Morning, Beau Gregory' to the dark blue demoiselle sprinkled with bright blue spots, the 'jewel fish' that exactly resembles the starlit fashioning of a bottle of Worth's 'Vol de Nuit'; 'Sorry. Not today, sweetheart,' to a fluttering butterfly fish with false black 'eyes' on its tail and, 'You're too fat anyway, Blue Boy,' to an indigo parrot fish that must have weighed a good ten pounds — his eyes were searching for only one of his 'people' — his only enemy on the reef, the only one he killed on sight, a scorpion fish.

Scorpion fish inhabit most of the southern waters of the world, and the 'rascasse' that is the foundation of *bouillabaisse* belongs to the family. The West Indian variety runs up to only about twelve inches long and perhaps a pound in weight. It is by far the ugliest fish in the sea, as if nature were giving warning. It is a mottled brownish grey with a heavy, wedge-shaped shaggy head. It has fleshy pendulous 'eyebrows' that droop over angry red eyes and a coloration and broken silhouette that are perfect camouflage on the reef. Though a small fish, its heavily toothed mouth is so wide that it can swallow whole most of the smaller reef fishes, but its supreme weapon lies in its erectile dorsal fins, the first few of which, acting on contact like hypodermic needles, are fed by poison glands containing enough tetrodotoxin to kill a man if they merely graze him in a vulnerable spot — in an artery, for instance, or over the heart or in the groin. They constitute the only real danger to the reef swimmer, far more dangerous than barracuda or shark, because, supremely confident in their camouflage and armoury, they flee before nothing except the very close approach of a foot or actual contact. Then they flit only a few yards on wide and bizarrely striped pectorals and settle again watchfully either on the sand, where they look like a lump of overgrown coral, or amongst the rocks and seaweed, where they virtually disappear. And Major Smythe was determined to find one, spear it and give it to his octopus to see if it would take or spurn it, see if one of the ocean's great predators would recognize the deadliness of another, know of its poison. Would the octopus consume the belly and leave the spines? Would it eat the lot and, if so, would it suffer from the poison? These were the questions Bengry at the Institute wanted answered and today, since it was going to be the beginning of the end of Major Smythe's life at Wavelets and though it might mean the end of his darling Octopussy, Major Smythe had decided to find out the answers and leave one tiny memorial to his now futile life in some dusty corner of the Institute's marine biological files.

For, only a couple of hours earlier, Major Dexter Smythe's already dismal life had changed very much for the worse. So much for the worse that he would be lucky if, in a few weeks' time — time for the sending of cables from Government House to the Colonial Office, to be relayed to the Secret Service and thence to Scotland Yard and the Public Prosecutor, and for Major Smythe's transportation to London with a police escort — he got away with a sentence of imprisonment for life.

And all this because of a man called Bond, Commander James Bond, who had turned up at ten thirty that morning in a taxi from Kingston.

The day had started normally. Major Smythe had awoken from his Seconal sleep, swallowed a couple of Panadols (his heart condition forbade him aspirin), showered and skimped his breakfast under the umbrella-shaped sea-almonds and spent an hour feeding the remains of his breakfast to the birds. He then took his prescribed doses of anti-coagulant and blood-pressure pills and killed time with the *Daily Gleaner* until he could have his elevenses which, for some months now, he had advanced to ten thirty. He had just poured himself the first of two stiff brandies and ginger ales, 'the drunkard's drink', when he heard the car coming up the drive.

Luna, his coloured housekeeper, came out into the garden and announced, 'Gemmun to see you, Major.'

'What's his name?'

'Him doan say, Major. Him say to tell you him come from Govment House.'

Major Smythe was wearing nothing but a pair of old khaki shorts and sandals. He said, 'All right, Luna. Put him in the living-room and say I won't be a moment,' and went round the back way into his bedroom and put on a white bush shirt and trousers and brushed his hair. Government House! Now what the hell?

As soon as he had walked through into the living-room and seen the tall man in the dark blue tropical suit standing at the picture window looking out to sea, Major Smythe had somehow sensed bad news. Then, when the man had turned slowly to look at him with watchful, serious blue-grey eyes, he had known that this was officialdom, and when his cheery smile was not returned, inimical officialdom. A chill had run down Major Smythe's spine. 'They' had somehow found out.

'Well, well. I'm Smythe. I gather you're from Government House. How's Sir Kenneth?'

There was somehow no question of shaking hands. The man said, 'I haven't met him. I only arrived a couple of days ago. I've been out round the island most of the time. My name's Bond, James Bond. I'm from the Ministry of Defence.'

Major Smythe remembered the hoary euphemism for the Secret Service. He said, with forced cheerfulness, 'Oh. The old firm?'

The question had been ignored. 'Is there somewhere we can talk?'

'Rather. Anywhere you like. Here or in the garden? What about a drink?' Major Smythe clinked the ice in the glass he still held in his hand. 'Rum and ginger's the local poison. I prefer the ginger by itself.' The lie came out with the automatic smoothness of the alcoholic.

'No thanks. And here would be fine.' The man leaned negligently against the wide mahogany window-sill.

Major Smythe sat down and threw a jaunty leg over the low arm of one of the comfortable planters' chairs he had had copied from an original by the local cabinet-maker. He pulled out the drink coaster from the other arm, took a deep pull at his glass and slid it, with a consciously steady hand, down into the hole in the wood. 'Well,' he said cheerily, looking the other man straight in the eyes, 'what can I do for you? Somebody been up to some dirty work on the North Shore and you need a spare hand? Be glad to get into harness again. It's been a long time since those days, but I can still remember some of the old routines.'

'Do you mind if I smoke?' The man had already got his cigarette case in his hand. It was a flat gunmetal one that would hold a round fifty. Somehow this small sign of a shared weakness comforted Major Smythe.

'Of course, my dear fellow.' He made a move to get up, his lighter ready.

'It's all right, thanks.' James Bond had already lit his cigarette. 'No, it's nothing local. I want to, I've been sent out to ask you to recall your work for the Service at the end of the war.' James Bond paused and looked down at Major Smythe carefully. 'Particularly the time when you were working with the Miscellaneous Objectives Bureau.'

Major Smythe laughed sharply. He had known it He had known it for absolutely sure. But when it came out of this man's mouth, the laugh had been forced out of Major Smythe like the scream of a hit man. 'Oh Lord, yes. Good old MOB. That was a lark all right.' He laughed again. He felt the anginal pain, brought on by the pressure of what he knew was coming, build up across his chest. He dipped his hand into his trouser pocket, tilted the little bottle into the palm of his hand and slipped the white TNT pill under his tongue. He was amused to see the tension coil up in the other man, the way the eyes narrowed watchfully. It's all right, my dear fellow. This isn't a death pill. He said, 'You troubled with acidosis? No? It slays me when I go on a bender. Last night. Party at Jamaica Inn. One really ought to stop thinking one's always twenty-five. Anyway, let's get back to MOB Force. Not many of us left, I suppose.' He felt the pain across his chest withdraw into its lair. 'Something to do with the Official History?'

James Bond looked down at the tip of his cigarette. 'Not exactly.'

'I expect you know I wrote most of the chapter on the Force for the War Book. It's a long time ago now. Doubt if I'd have much to add today.'

'Nothing more about that operation in the Tyrol — place called Ober Aurach, about a mile east of Kitzbühel?'

One of the names he had been living with for all these years forced another harsh laugh out of Major Smythe. 'That was a piece of cake! You've never seen such a shambles. All those Gestapo toughs with their doxies. All of 'em hog-drunk. They'd kept their files all tickety-boo. Handed them over without a murmur. Hoped that'd earn 'em easy treatment, I suppose. We gave the stuff a first going-over and shipped all the bods off to the Munich camp. Last I heard of them. Most of them hanged for war crimes, I expect. We handed the bumph over to HQ at Salzburg. Then we went on up the Mittersill valley after another hideout.' Major Smythe took a good pull at his drink and lit a cigarette. He looked up. 'That's the long and the short of it.'

'You were Number 2 at the time, I think. The CO was an American, a Colonel King from Patton's army.'

'That's right. Nice fellow. Wore a moustache, which isn't like an American. Knew his way among the local wines. Quite a civilized chap.'

'In his report about the operation he wrote that he handed you all the documents for a preliminary run-through as you were the German expert with the unit. Then you gave them all back to him with your comments?' James Bond paused. 'Every single one of them?'

Major Smythe ignored the innuendo. 'That's right. Mostly lists of names. Counter-Intelligence dope. The CI people in Salzburg were very pleased with the stuff. Gave them plenty of new leads. I expect the originals are lying about somewhere. They'll have been used for the Nuremberg Trials. Yes, by Jove!' Major Smythe was reminiscent, pally. 'Those were some of the jolliest months of my life, haring around the country with MOB Force. Wine, women and song! And you can say that again!'

Here, Major Smythe was saying the whole truth. He had had a dangerous and uncomfortable war until 1945. When the Commandos were formed in 1941 he had volunteered and been seconded from the Royal Marines to Combined Operations Headquarters under Mountbatten. There his excellent German (his mother had come from Heidelberg) had earned him the unenviable job of being advanced interrogator on Commando operations across the Channel. He had been lucky to get away from two years of this work unscathed and with the OBE (Military), which was sparingly awarded in the last war. And then, in preparation for the defeat of Germany, the Miscellaneous Objectives Bureau had been formed jointly by the Secret Service and Combined Operations, and Major Smythe had been given the temporary rank of Lieutenant-Colonel and told to form a unit whose job would be the cleaning up of Gestapo and Abwehr hideouts when the collapse of Germany came about. The OSS got to hear of the scheme and insisted on getting into the act to cope with the American wing of the front, and the result was the creation of not one but six units that went into operation in Germany and Austria on the day of surrender. They were units of twenty men, each with a light armoured car, six jeeps, a wireless truck and three lorries, and they were controlled by a joint Anglo-American headquarters in SHAEF, which also fed them with targets from the army intelligence units and from the SIS and OSS. Major Smythe had been Number 2 of 'A' Force which had been allotted the Tyrol — an area full of good hiding places with easy access to Italy and perhaps out of Europe — that was known to have been chosen as funk-hole number 1 by the people MOB Force was after. And, as Major Smythe had just told Bond, they had had themselves a ball. All without firing a shot — except, that is, two fired by Major Smythe.

James Bond said casually, 'Does the name of Hannes Oberhauser ring a bell?'

Major Smythe frowned, trying to remember. 'Can't say it does.' It was eighty degrees in the shade, but he shivered.

'Let me refresh your memory. On the same day as those documents were given to you to look over, you made inquiries at the Tiefenbrunner Hotel, where you were billeted, for the best mountain guide in Kitzbühel. You were referred to Oberhauser. The next day you asked your CO for a day's leave which was granted. Early next morning you went to Oberhauser's chalet, put him under close arrest and drove him away in your jeep. Does that ring a bell?'

That phrase about 'refreshing your memory'. How often had Major Smythe himself used it when he was trying to trap a German liar? Take your time! You've been ready for something like this for years. Major Smythe shook his head doubtfully. 'Can't say it does.'

'A man with greying hair and a gammy leg. Spoke some English as he'd been a ski-instructor before the war.'

Major Smythe looked candidly into the cold, clear eyes. 'Sorry. Can't help you.'

James Bond took a small blue leather notebook out of his inside pocket and turned the leaves. He stopped turning them. He looked up. 'At that time, as side-arms, you were carrying a regulation Webley & Scott .45 with the serial number 8967/362.'

'It was certainly a Webley. Damned clumsy weapon. Hope they've got something more like the Luger or the heavy Beretta these days. But I can't say I ever took a note of the number.'

'The number's right enough,' said James Bond. 'I've got the date of its issue to you by HQ and the date when you turned it in. You signed the book both times.'

Major Smythe shrugged. 'Well then, it must have been my

gun. But' — he put rather angry impatience into his voice — 'what, if I may ask, is all this in aid of?'

James Bond looked at him almost with curiosity. He said, and now his voice was not unkind, 'You know what it's all about, Smythe.' He paused and seemed to reflect. 'Tell you what. I'll go out into the garden for ten minutes or so. Give you time to think things over. Give me a hail.' He added seriously, 'It'll make things so much easier for you if you come out with the story in your own words.' He walked to the door into the garden. He turned round. 'I'm afraid it's only a question of dotting the i's and crossing the t's. You see I had a talk with the Foo brothers in Kingston yesterday.' He stepped out on to the lawn.

Something in Major Smythe was relieved. Now at least the battle of wits, the trying to invent alibis, the evasions, were over. If this man Bond had got to the Foos, to either of them, they would have spilled the beans. The last thing they wanted was to get in bad with the government, and anyway there was only about six inches of the stuff left.

Major Smythe got briskly to his feet, went to the loaded sideboard and poured himself out another brandy and ginger ale, almost fifty-fifty. He might as well live it up while there was still time! The future wouldn't hold many more of these for him. He went back to his chair and lit his twentieth cigarette of the day. He looked at his watch. It said eleven thirty. If he could be rid of the chap in an hour, he'd have plenty of time with his 'people'. He sat and drank and marshalled his thoughts. He could make the story long or short, put in the weather and the way the flowers and pines had smelled on the mountain, or he could cut it short. He would cut it short.

Up in that big double bedroom in the Tiefenbrunner, with the wads of buff and grey paper spread out on the spare bed, he hadn't been looking for anything special, just taking samples here and there and concentrating on the ones marked in red KOMMANDOSACHE, HOECHST VERTRAULICH. There weren't many of these, and they were mostly confidential reports on German top brass, intercepts of broken Allied ciphers and the whereabouts of secret dumps. Since these were the main targets of 'A' Force, Major Smythe had scanned them with particular excitement — food, explosives, guns, espionage records, files of Gestapo personnel — a tremendous haul! And then, at the bottom of the packet, there had been the single envelope sealed with red wax and the notation ONLY TO BE OPENED IN FINAL EMERGENCY. The envelope contained one single sheet of paper. It was unsigned and the few words were written in red ink. The heading said VALUTA, and beneath was written WILDE KAISER. FRANZISKANER HALT. 100 M. OESTLICH STEINHÜGEL. WAFFENKISTE. ZWEI BAR 24 KT and then a list of measurements in centimetres. Major Smythe held his hands apart as if telling a story about a fish he had caught. Each bar would be nearly as big as a couple of bricks. And one single English sovereign of only eighteen-carat was selling nowadays for two to three pounds! This was a bloody fortune! Forty, fifty thousand pounds' worth! Maybe even a hundred! He had no idea, but, quite coolly and speedily, in case anyone should come in, he put a match to the paper and the envelope, ground the ashes to powder and swilled them down the lavatory. Then he took out his large-scale Austrian Ordnance map of the area and in a moment had his finger on the Franziskaner Halt. It was marked as an uninhabited mountaineers' refuge on a saddle just below the highest of the easterly peaks of the Kaiser mountains, that awe-inspiring range of giant stone teeth that give Kitzbühel its threatening northern horizon. And the cairn of stones would be about there, his fingernail pointed, and the whole bloody lot was only ten miles and perhaps a five hours' climb away!

The beginning had been as this fellow Bond had described. He had gone to Oberhauser's chalet at four in the morning, had arrested him and had told his weeping, protesting family that he, Smythe, was taking him to an interrogation camp in Munich. If the guide's record was clean, he would be back home within a week. If the family kicked up a fuss it would only make trouble for Oberhauser. Smythe had refused to give his name and had had the forethought to shroud the numbers on his jeep. In twenty-four hours, 'A' Force would be on its way and, by the time the military government got to Kitzbühel, the incident would already be buried under the morass of the occupation tangle.

Oberhauser had been a nice enough chap once he had recovered from his fright, and when Smythe talked knowingly about skiing and climbing, both of which he had done before the war, the pair, as Smythe intended, became quite pally. Their route lay along the bottom of the Kaiser range to Kufstein, and Smythe drove slowly, making admiring comments on the peaks that were now flushed with the pink of dawn. Finally, below the Peak of Gold, as he called it to himself, he slowed to a halt and pulled off the road into a grassy glade. He turned in his seat and said candidly, 'Oberhauser, you are a man after my own heart. We share many interests together and from your talk and from the man I think you to be, I am sure you did not cooperate with the Nazis. Now I will tell you what I will do. We will spend the day climbing on the Kaiser and I will then drive you back to Kitzbühel and report to my commanding officer that you have been cleared at Munich.' He grinned cheerfully. 'Now. How about that?'

The man had been near to tears of gratitude. But could he have some kind of paper to show that he was a good citizen? Certainly. Major Smythe's signature would be quite enough. The pact was made, the jeep was driven up a track and well hidden from the road and they were off at a steady pace, climbing up through the pine-scented foot-hills.

Smythe was well dressed for the climb. He had nothing on under his bush jacket, shorts and a pair of the excellent rubber-soled boots issued to American parachutists. His only burden was the Webley & Scott and, tactfully, for Oberhauser was after all one of the enemy, Oberhauser didn't suggest that he leave it behind some conspicuous rock. Oberhauser was in his best suit and boots, but that didn't seem to bother him and he assured Major Smythe that ropes and pitons would not be needed for their climb and that there was a hut directly up above them where they could rest. It was called the Franziskaner Halt.

'Is it indeed?' said Major Smythe.

'Yes, and below it there is a small glacier. Very pretty, but we will climb round it. There are many crevasses.'

'Is that so?' said Major Smythe thoughtfully. He examined the back of Oberhauser's head, now beaded with sweat. After all, he was only a bloody Kraut, or at any rate of that ilk. What would one more or less matter? It was all going to be as easy as falling off a log. The only thing that worried Major Smythe was getting the bloody stuff down the mountain. He decided that he would somehow sling the bars across his back. After all, he could slide it most of the way in its ammunition box or whatnot.

It was a long, dreary hack up the mountain and when they were above the tree line the sun came up and it was very hot. And now it was all rock and scree, and their long zigzags sent boulders and rubble rumbling and crashing down the slope that got ever steeper as they approached the final crag, grey and menacing, that lanced away into the blue above them. They were both naked to the waist and sweating so that the sweat ran down their legs into their boots, but, despite Oberhauser's limp, they kept up a good pace, and when they stopped for a drink and a swab down at a hurtling mountain stream Oberhauser congratulated Major Smythe on his fitness. Major Smythe, his mind full of dreams, said curtly and untruthfully that all English soldiers were fit, and they went on.

The rock face wasn't difficult. Major Smythe had known that it wouldn't be or the climbers' hut couldn't have been built on the shoulder. Toe holds had been cut in the face and there were occasional iron pegs hammered into crevices. But he couldn't have found the more difficult traverses alone and he congratulated himself on deciding to bring a guide.

Once, Oberhauser's hand, testing for a grip, dislodged a great slab of rock, loosened by years of snow and frost, and sent it crashing down the mountain. Major Smythe suddenly thought about noise. 'Many people around here?' he asked as they watched the boulder hurtle down into the tree line.

'Not a soul until you get near Kufstein,' said Oberhauser. He gestured along the arid range of high peaks. 'No grazing. Little water. Only the climbers come here. And since the beginning of the war . . .' He left the phrase unfinished.

They skirted the blue-fanged glacier below the final climb to the shoulder. Major Smythe's careful eyes took in the width and depth of the crevasses. Yes, they would fit! Directly above them, perhaps a hundred feet up under the lee of the shoulder, were the weather-beaten boards of the hut. Major Smythe measured the angle of the slope. Yes, it was almost a straight dive down. Now or later? He guessed later. The line of the last traverse wasn't very clear.

They were up at the hut in five hours flat. Major Smythe said he wanted to relieve himself and wandered casually along the shoulder to the east, paying no heed to the beautiful panoramas of Austria and Bavaria that stretched away on either side of him perhaps fifty miles into the heat haze. He counted his paces carefully. At exactly 120 there was the cairn of stones, a loving memorial, perhaps, to some long-dead climber. Major Smythe, knowing differently, longed to tear it apart there and then. Instead he took out his Webley & Scott, squinted down the barrel and twirled the cylinder. Then he walked back.

It was cold up there at ten thousand feet or more, and Oberhauser had got into the hut and was busy preparing a fire. Major Smythe controlled his horror at the sight. 'Oberhauser,' he said cheerfully, 'come out and show me some of the sights. Wonderful view up here.'

'Certainly, Major.' Oberhauser followed Major Smythe out of the hut. Outside he fished in his hip pocket and produced something wrapped in paper. He undid the paper to reveal a hard, wrinkled sausage. He offered it to the Major. 'It is only what we call a "Soldat",' he said shyly. 'Smoked meat. Very tough but good.' He smiled. 'It is like what they eat in Wild West films. What is the name?'

' "Biltong",' said the Major. Then — and later this had slightly disgusted him — he said, 'Leave it in the hut. We will share it later. Come over here. Can we see Innsbruck? Show me the view on this side.'

Oberhauser bobbed into the hut and out again. The Major fell in just behind him as he talked, pointing out this or that distant church spire or mountain peak.

They came to the point above the glacier. Major Smythe drew his revolver and, at a range of two feet, fired two bullets into the base of Hannes Oberhauser's skull. No muffing! Dead on!

The impact of the bullets knocked the guide clean off his feet and over the edge. Major Smythe craned over. The body hit twice only and then crashed on to the glacier. But not on to its fissured origin. Half-way down and on a patch of old snow! 'Hell!' said Major Smythe.

The deep boom of the two shots that had been batting to and fro among the mountains died away. Major Smythe took one last look at the black splash on the white snow and hurried off along the shoulder. First things first!

He started on the top of the cairn, working as if the devil was after him, throwing the rough, heavy stones indiscriminately down the mountain to right or left. His hands began to bleed, but he hardly noticed. Now there were only two feet or so left, and nothing! Bloody nothing! He bent to the last pile, scrabbling feverishly. And then! Yes! The edge of a metal box. A few more rocks away and there was the whole of it! A good old grey Wehrmacht ammunition box with the trace of some lettering still on it. Major Smythe gave a groan of joy. He sat down on a hard piece of rock and his mind went orbiting through Bentleys, Monte Carlo, pent-house flats, Cartier's, champagne, caviare and, incongruously, but because he loved golf, a new set of Henry Cotton irons.

Drunk with his dreams, Major Smythe sat there looking at the grey box for a full quarter of an hour. Then he glanced at his watch and got briskly to his feet. Time to get rid of the evidence. The box had a handle at each end. Major Smythe had expected it to be heavy. He had mentally compared its probable weight with the heaviest thing he had ever carried — a forty-pound salmon he had caught in Scotland just before the war — but the box was more than double that weight, and he was only just able to heave it out of its last bed of rocks on to the thin alpine grass. He slung his handkerchief through one of the handles and dragged it clumsily along the shoulder to the hut. Then he sat down on the stone doorstep, and, his eyes never leaving the box, tore at Oberhauser's smoked sausage with his strong teeth and thought about getting his fifty thousand pounds — for that was the figure he put it at — down the mountain and into a new hiding place.

Oberhauser's sausage was a real mountaineer's meal — tough, well fatted and strongly garlicked. Bits of it stuck uncomfortably between Major Smythe's teeth. He dug them out with a sliver of matchstick and spat them on the ground. Then his intelligence-wise mind came into operation and he meticulously searched among the stones and grass, picked up the scraps and swallowed them. From now on he was a criminal — as much a criminal as if he had robbed a bank and shot the guard. He was a cop turned robber. He *must* remember that! It would be death if he didn't — death instead of Cartier's. All he had to do was to take infinite pains. He would take those pains, and by God they would be infinite! Then, for ever after, he would be rich and happy. After taking ridiculously minute trouble to eradicate any sign of entry into the hut, he dragged the ammunition box to the edge of the last rock face and, aiming it away from the glacier, tipped it, with a prayer, into space.

The grey box, turning slowly in the air, hit the first steep slope below the rock face, bounded another hundred feet and landed with an iron clang in some loose scree and stopped. Major Smythe couldn't see if it had burst open. He didn't mind one way or the other. The mountain might as well do it for him!

With a last look round, he went over the edge. He took great care at each piton, tested every handhold and foothold before he put weight on them. Coming down, he was a much more valuable life than he had been climbing up. He made for the glacier and trudged across the melting snow to the black patch on the icefield. There was nothing to be done about footprints. It would only take a few days for them to be melted down by the sun. He got to the body. He had seen many corpses during the war, and the blood and broken limbs meant nothing to him. He dragged the remains of Oberhauser to the nearest deep crevasse and toppled it in. Then he went carefully round the lip of the crevasse and kicked the snow overhang down on top of the body. Satisfied with his work, he retraced his steps, placing his feet exactly in his old footprints, and made his way on down the slope to the ammunition box.

Yes, the mountain had burst open the lid for him. Almost casually he tore away the cartridge-paper wrappings. The two great hunks of metal glittered up at him under the sun. There were the same markings on each — the swastika in a circle below an eagle, and the date, 1943 — the mint marks of the Reichsbank. Major Smythe gave a nod of approval. He replaced the paper and hammered the crooked lid half-shut with a rock. Then he tied the lanyard of his Webley round one of the handles and moved on down the mountain, dragging his clumsy burden behind him.

It was now one o'clock and the sun beat fiercely down on his naked chest, frying him in his own sweat. His reddened shoulders began to burn. So did his face. To hell with them! He stopped at the stream from the glacier, dipped his handkerchief in the water and tied it across his forehead. Then he drank deeply and went on, occasionally cursing the ammunition box as it caught up with him and banged at his heels. But these discomforts, the sunburn and the bruises, were nothing compared with what he would have to face when he got down to the valley and the going levelled out. For the time being he had gravity on his side. There would come at least a mile when he would have to carry the blasted stuff. Major Smythe winced at the thought of the havoc it would wreak on his burned back. 'Oh well,' he said to himself almost light-headedly, 'il faut souffrir pour être millionaire!'

When he got to the bottom and the time had come he sat and rested on a mossy bank under the firs. Then he spread out his bush shirt and heaved the two bars out of the box and on to its centre, tying the tails of the shirt as firmly as he could to where the sleeves sprang from the shoulders. After digging a shallow hole in the bank and burying the empty box, he knotted the two cuffs of the sleeves firmly together, knelt down and slipped his head through the rough sling, got his hands on either side of the knot to protect his neck, and staggered to his feet, crouching far forward so as not to be pulled over on his back. Then, crushed under half his own weight, his back on fire under the contact with his burden, and his breath rasping through his constricted lungs, coolie-like, he shuffled slowly off down the little path through the trees.

To this day he didn't know how he had made it to the jeep. Again and again the knots gave under the strain and the bars crashed down on the calves of his legs, and each time he had sat with his head in his hands and then started all over again. But finally, by concentrating on counting his steps and stopping for a rest at every hundredth, he got to the blessed little car and collapsed beside it. And then there had been the business of burying his hoard in the wood, amongst a jumble of big rocks that he would be sure to find again, and of cleaning himself up as best he could and getting back to his billet by a circuitous route that avoided the Oberhauser chalet. And then it was all done and he had got drunk by himself on a bottle of cheap schnapps, eaten and gone to bed and to a stupefied sleep. The next day, MOB 'A' Force had moved off up the Mittersill valley on a fresh trail, and six months later Major Smythe was back in London and his war was over.

But not his problems. Gold is difficult stuff to smuggle, certainly in the quantity available to Major Smythe, and it was now essential to get his two bars across the Channel and into a new hiding place. So he put off his demobilization and clung to the privileges of his temporary rank, particularly to his Military Intelligence passes, and soon got himself sent back to Germany as a British representative at the Combined Interrogation Centre in Munich. There he did a scratch job for six months during which he collected his gold and stowed it away in a battered suitcase in his quarters. Then on two weekend leaves he flew to England, each time carrying one of the bars in a bulky briefcase. The walk across the tarmac at Munich and Northolt and the handling of his case as if it contained only papers required two benzedrine tablets and a will of iron; but at last he had his fortune safe in the basement of an aunt's flat in Kensington and could get on with the next phase of his plans at leisure. He resigned from the Royal Marines, got himself demobilized and married one of the many girls he had slept with at MOB Force Headquarters, a charming blonde Wren called Mary Parnell from a solid middle-class family. He got passages for them both in one of the early banana boats sailing from Avonmouth to Kingston, Jamaica, which they both agreed would be a paradise of sunshine, good food and cheap drink and a glorious haven from the gloom, restrictions and Labour Government of post-war England. Before they sailed, Major Smythe showed Mary the gold bars, from which he had chiselled away the mint marks of the Reichsbank. 'I've been clever, darling,' he said. 'I just don't trust the pound these days, so I've sold out all my securities and swapped the lot for gold. There'll be over twenty thousand pounds' worth there if I play it right. That should give us a fair slice of the good life, just cutting off a chunk now and then and selling it.'

Mary Parnell was not familiar with the ramifications of the currency laws. She knelt down and ran her hands lovingly over the gleaming bars. Then she got up and threw her arms round Major Smythe's neck and kissed him. 'You're a wonderful, wonderful man,' she said, almost in tears. 'Frightfully clever and handsome and brave and now you're rich as well. I'm the luckiest girl in the world.'

'Well anyway we're rich,' said Major Smythe. 'But promise me you won't breathe a word or we'll have all the burglars in Jamaica round our ears. Promise?'

'Cross my heart.'

Prince's Club, in the foot-hills above Kingston, was indeed a paradise. Pleasant enough members, wonderful servants, unlimited food and cheap drink, and all in the wonderful setting of the tropics that neither of them had known before. They were a popular couple and Major Smythe's war record earned them the entrée to Government House society, after which their life was one endless round of parties, with tennis for Mary and golf (with the Henry Cotton irons!) for Major Smythe. In the evenings there was bridge for her and the high poker game for him. Yes, it was paradise all right, while, in their homeland, people munched their spam, fiddled in the black market, cursed the government and suffered the worst winter weather for thirty years.

The Smythes met all their initial expenditure from their combined cash reserves, swollen by wartime gratuities, and it took Major Smythe a full year of careful sniffing around before he decided to do business with the Messrs Foo, import and export merchants. The brothers Foo, highly respected and very rich, were the acknowledged governing junta of the flourishing Chinese community in Jamaica. Some of their trading was suspected to be devious in the Chinese tradition, but all Major Smythe's casually meticulous inquiries confirmed that they were utterly trustworthy. The Bretton Woods Convention, fixing a controlled world price for gold, had been signed and it had already become common knowledge that in Tangier and Macao — two free ports which, for different reasons, had escaped the Bretton Woods net — a price of at least one hundred dollars per ounce of gold, ninety-nine fine, could be obtained compared with the fixed world price of thirty-five dollars per ounce. And, conveniently, the Foos had just begun to trade again with a resurgent Hong Kong, already the entrepôt for gold-smuggling into the neighbouring Macao. The whole set-up was, in Major Smythe's language, tickety-boo. He had a most pleasant meeting with the Foo brothers. No questions were asked until it came to examining the bars. At this point the absence of mint marks resulted in a polite inquiry as to the original provenance of the gold.

'You see, Major,' said the older and blander of the brothers behind the big, empty, mahogany desk, 'in the bullion market the mint marks of all respectable national banks and responsible dealers are accepted without question. Such marks guarantee the fineness of the gold. But of course there are other banks and dealers whose methods of refining,' his benign smile widened a fraction, 'are perhaps not quite, shall we say, so accurate.'

'You mean the old gold brick swindle,' said Major Smythe with a twinge of anxiety. 'Hunk of lead covered with gold plating?'

Both brothers tee-heed reassuringly. 'No, no, Major. That of course is out of the question. But,' the smiles held constant, 'if you cannot recall the provenance of these fine bars, perhaps you would have no objection if we were to undertake an assay. There are methods of determining the exact fineness of such bars. My brother and I are competent in these methods. If you would care to leave these with us and perhaps come back after lunch?'

There had been no alternative. Major Smythe had to trust the Foos utterly now. They could cook up any figure and he would just have to accept it. He went over to the Myrtle Bank and had one or two stiff drinks and a sandwich that stuck in his throat. Then he went back to the cool office of the Foos.

The setting was the same — the two smiling brothers, the two bars of gold, the briefcase, but now there was a piece of paper and a gold Parker pen in front of the elder brother.

'We have solved the problem of your fine bars, Major,' ('Fine'! Thank God, thought Major Smythe) 'and I am sure you will be interested to know their probable history.'

'Yes indeed,' said Major Smythe, with a brave show of enthusiasm.

'They are German bars, Major. Probably from the wartime Reichsbank. This we have deduced from the fact that they contain ten per cent of lead. Under the Hitler régime, it was the foolish habit of the Reichsbank to adulterate their gold in this manner. This fact became rapidly known to dealers and the price of German bars, in Switzerland, for instance, where many of them found their way, was adjusted downwards accordingly. So the only result of the German foolishness was that the national bank of Germany lost a reputation for honest dealing it had earned over the centuries.' The Chinaman's smile didn't vary. 'Very bad business, Major. Very stupid.'

Major Smythe marvelled at the omniscience of these two men so far from the great commercial channels of the world, but he also cursed it. Now what? He said, 'That's very interesting, Mr Foo. But it is not very good news for me. Are these bars not "good delivery", or whatever you call it in the bullion world?'

The elder Foo made a slight throwaway gesture with his right hand. 'It is of no importance, Major. Or rather, it is of very small importance. We will sell your gold at its true mint value, let us say, eighty-nine fine. It may be re-fined by the ultimate purchaser, or it may not. That is not our business. We shall have sold a true bill of goods.'

'But at a lower price.'

'That is so, Major. But I think I have some good news for you. Have you any estimates as to the worth of these two bars?'

'I had thought around twenty thousand pounds.'

The elder Foo gave a dry chuckle. 'I think, if we sell wisely and slowly, you should receive more than one hundred thousand dollars, Major — subject, that is, to our commission, which will include shipping and incidental charges.'

'How much would that be?'

'We were thinking about a figure of ten per cent, Major. If that is satisfactory to you.'

Major Smythe had an idea that bullion brokers received a fraction of one per cent. But what the hell? He had already as good as made ten thousand pounds since lunch. He said 'Done' and got up and reached his hand across the desk.

From then on, every quarter, he would visit the office of the Foos, carrying an empty suitcase. There would be five hundred new Jamaican pounds in neat bundles on the broad desk and the two gold bars, that diminished inch by inch, together with a typed slip showing the amount sold and the price obtained in Macao. It was all very simple and friendly and highly business-like, and Major Smythe didn't think that he was being submitted to any form of squeeze other than the duly recorded ten per cent. In any case he didn't particularly care. Two thousand net a year was good enough for him, and his only worry was that the income tax people would get after him and ask him what he was living on. He mentioned this possibility to the Foos. But they said he was not to worry and, for the next two quarters, there was only four hundred pounds instead of five on the table and no comment was made by either side. 'Squeeze' had been administered in the right quarter.

And so the lazy, sunshiny days passed by and stretched out into years. The Smythes both put on weight and Major Smythe had the first of his two coronaries and was told by his doctor to cut down on his alcohol and cigarettes and take life more easily. He was also to avoid fats and fried food. At first Mary Smythe tried to be firm with him; then, when he took to secret drinking and to a life of petty lies and evasions, she tried to back-pedal on her attempts to control his self-indulgence. But she was too late. She had already become the symbol of the janitor to Major Smythe and he took to avoiding her. She berated him with not loving her any more and, when the resultant bickering became too much for her simple nature, she became a sleeping-pill addict. Then, after one flaming, drunken row, she took an overdose 'just to show him'. It was too much of an overdose and it killed her. The suicide was hushed up, but the resultant cloud did Major Smythe no good socially and he returned to the North Shore which, although only some three miles across the island from the capital, is, even in the small society of Jamaica, a different world. And there he had settled in Wavelets and, after his second coronary, was in the process of drinking himself to death when this man called Bond arrived on the scene with an alternative death warrant in his pocket.

Major Smythe looked at his watch. It was a few minutes after twelve o'clock. He got up and poured himself another stiff brandy and ginger ale and went out on to the lawn. James Bond was sitting under the sea-almonds, gazing out to sea. He didn't look up when Major Smythe pulled up another aluminium garden chair and put his drink on the grass beside him. When Major Smythe had finished telling his story, Bond said unemotionally, 'Yes, that's more or less the way I figured it.'

'Want me to write it all out and sign it?'

'You can if you like. But not for me. That'll be for the court martial. Your old Corps will be handling all that. I've got nothing to do with the legal aspects. I shall put in a report to my own Service of what you've told me and they'll pass it on to the

Royal Marines. Then I suppose it'll go to the Public Prosecutor via Scotland Yard.'

'Could I ask a question?'

'Of course.'

'How did they find out?'

'It was a small glacier. Oberhauser's body came out at the bottom of it earlier this year. When the spring snows melted. Some climbers found it. All his papers and everything were intact. The family identified him. Then it was just a question of working back. The bullets clinched it.'

'But how did you get mixed up in the whole thing?'

'MOB Force was a responsibility of my, er, Service. The papers found their way to us. I happened to see the file. I had some spare time on my hands. I asked to be given the job of chasing up the man who did it.'

'Why?'

James Bond looked Major Smythe squarely in the eyes. 'It just happened that Oberhauser was a friend of mine. He taught me to ski before the war, when I was in my teens. He was a wonderful man. He was something of a father to me at a time when I happened to need one.'

'Oh, I see.' Major Smythe looked away. 'I'm sorry.'

James Bond got to his feet. 'Well, I'll be getting back to Kingston.' He held up a hand. 'No, don't bother. I'll find my way to the car.' He looked down at the older man. He said abruptly, almost harshly — perhaps, Major Smythe thought, to hide his embarrassment — 'It'll be about a week before they send someone out to bring you home.' Then he walked off across the lawn and through the house and Major Smythe heard the iron whirr of the self-starter and the clatter of the gravel on the unkempt drive.

Major Smythe, questing for his prey along the reef, wondered what exactly those last words of the Bond man had meant. Inside the Pirelli his lips drew mirthlessly back from the stained teeth. It was obvious, really. It was just a version of the corny old act of leaving the guilty officer alone with his revolver. If the Bond man had wanted to, he could have telephoned Government House and had an officer of the Jamaica Regiment sent over to take Major Smythe into custody. Decent of him, in a way. Or was it? A suicide would be much tidier, save a lot of paper-work and tax-payers' money. Should he oblige the Bond man and be tidy? Join Mary in whatever place suicides go to? Or go through with it — the indignity, the dreary formalities, the headlines, the boredom and drabness of a life sentence that would inevitably end with his third coronary? Or should he defend himself — plead wartime, a struggle with Oberhauser on the Peak of Gold, prisoner trying to escape, Oberhauser knowing of the gold cache, the natural temptation of Smythe to make away with the bullion, he, a poor officer of the Commandos confronted with sudden wealth? Should he dramatically throw himself on the mercy of the court? Suddenly Major Smythe saw himself in the dock, a splendid, upright figure, in the fine bemedalled blue and scarlet of the ceremonial uniform which was the traditional rig for courts martial. (Had the moths got into the japanned box in the spare room at Wavelets? Had the damp? Luna would have to look to it. A day in the sunshine if the weather held. A good brushing. With the help of his corset, he could surely still get his forty-inch waist into the thirty-four-inch trousers Gieves had built for him twenty, thirty years ago.) And, down on the floor of the court, at Chatham probably, the Prisoners' Friend, some staunch fellow, at least of colonel's rank in deference to his own seniority, would be pleading his cause. And there was always the possibility of appeal to a higher court. Why, the whole affair might become a *cause célèbre*. He would sell his story to the papers, write a book . . . Major Smythe felt the excitement mounting in him. Careful, old boy! Careful! Remember what the good old snip-cock had said! He put his feet to the ground and had a rest amidst the dancing waves of the nor'-east trades that kept the North Shore so delightfully cool until the torrid months, August, September, October, of the hurricane season. After his two pink gins, skimpy lunch and happily sodden siesta, he would have to give all this more careful thought. And then there were cocktails with the Arundels and dinner at the Shaw Park Beach Club with the Marchesis. Then some high bridge and home to his Seconal sleep. Cheered by the prospect of the familiar routine, the black shadow of Bond retreated into the background. Now then, scorp, where are you? Octopussy's waiting for her lunch! Major Smythe put his head down and, his mind freshly focused and his eyes questing, continued his leisurely swim along the shallow valley between the coral clumps that led out towards the white-fringed reef.

Almost at once he saw the two spiny antennae of a lobster, or rather of its cousin, the West Indian langouste, weaving inquisitively towards him, towards the turbulence he was creating, from a deep fissure under a nigger-head. From the thickness of the antennae it would be a big one, three or four pounds! Normally, Major Smythe would have put his feet down and delicately stirred up the sand in front of the lair to bring the lobster farther out, for they are an inquisitive family. Then he would have speared it through the head and taken it back for lunch. But today there was only one prey in his mind, one shape to concentrate on – the shaggy, irregular silhouette of a scorpion fish. And ten minutes later, he saw a clump of seaweedy rock on the white sand that just wasn't a clump of seaweedy rock. He put his feet softly down and watched the poison spines erect themselves along the back of the thing. It was a good-sized one, perhaps three-quarters of a pound. He got his three-pronged spear ready and inched forward. Now the red angry eyes of the fish were wide open and watching him. He would have to make a single quick lunge from as nearly the vertical as possible, otherwise, he knew from experience, the barbed prongs, needle sharp though they were, would almost certainly bounce off the horny head of the beast. He swung his feet up off the ground and paddled forward very slowly, using his free hand as a fin. Now! He lunged forwards and downwards. But the scorpion fish had felt the tiny approaching shockwave of the spear. There was a flurry of sand and it had shot up in a vertical take-off and whirred, in almost bird-like flight, under Major Smythe's belly.

Major Smythe cursed and twisted round in the water. Yes, it had done what they so often do, gone for refuge to the nearest algae-covered rock and there, confident in its superb camouflage, gone to ground on the seaweed. Major Smythe had only to swim a few feet, lunge down again, this time more accurately, and he had it, flapping and squirming on the end of his spear.

The excitement and the small exertion had caused Major Smythe to pant and he felt the old pain across his chest lurking, ready to come at him. He put his feet down and, after driving his spear all the way through the fish, held it, still flapping desperately, out of the water. Then he slowly made his way back across the lagoon on foot and walked up the sand of his beach to the wooden bench under the sea-grape. Then he dropped the spear with its jerking quarry on the sand beside him and sat down to rest.

It was perhaps five minutes later that Major Smythe felt a curious numbness more or less in the region of his solar plexus. He looked casually down and his whole body stiffened with horror and disbelief. A patch of his skin, about the size of a cricket ball, had turned white under his tan and, in the centre of the patch, there were three descending punctures topped by little beads of blood. Automatically, Major Smythe wiped away the blood. The holes were only the size of pinpricks, but Major Smythe remembered the rising flight of the scorpion fish and he said aloud, with awe in his voice, but without animosity, 'You got me, you bastard! By God, you got me!'

He sat very still, looking down at his body and remembering what it said about scorpion fish stings in the book he had borrowed from the Institute and had never returned — *Dangerous Marine Animals*, an American publication. He delicately touched and then prodded the white area round the punctures. Yes, the skin had gone totally numb and now a pulse of pain began to throb beneath it. Very soon this would become a shooting pain. Then the pain would begin to lance all over his body and become so intense that he would throw himself on the sand, screaming and thrashing about, to rid himself of it. He would vomit and foam at the mouth and then delirium and convulsions would take over until he lost consciousness. Then, inevitably in his case, there would ensue cardiac failure and death. According to the book the whole cycle would be complete in about a quarter of an hour — that was all he had left — fifteen minutes of hideous agony! There were cures, of course — procaine, antibiotics and anti-histamines — if his weak heart would stand them. But they had to be near at hand and, even if he could climb the steps up to the house and supposing Jimmy Greaves had these modern drugs, the doctor couldn't possibly get to Wavelets in under an hour.

The first jet of pain seared into Major Smythe's body and bent him over double. Then came another and another, radiating through his stomach and limbs. Now there was a dry, metallic taste in his mouth and his lips were prickling. He gave a groan and toppled off the seat on to the beach. A flapping on the sand beside his head reminded him of the scorpion fish. There came a lull in the spasms of pain. Instead his whole body felt as if it was on fire but, beneath the agony, his brain cleared. But of course! The experiment! Somehow, somehow he must get out to Octopussy and give her her lunch!

'Oh, Pussy, my Pussy, this is the last meal you'll get.'

Major Smythe mouthed the jingle to himself as he crouched on all fours, found his mask and somehow forced it over his face. Then he got hold of his spear, tipped with the still flapping fish, and, clutching his stomach with his free hand, crawled and slithered down the sand and into the water.

It was fifty yards of shallow water to the lair of the octopus in the coral cranny and Major Smythe, screaming all the while into his mask, somehow, mostly on his knees, made it. As he came to the last approach and the water became deeper, he had to get to his feet and the pain made him jiggle to and fro, as if he was a puppet manipulated by strings. Then he was there and, with a supreme effort of will, held himself steady as he dipped his head down to let some water into his mask and clear the mist of his screams from the glass. Then, blood pouring from his bitten lower lip, he bent carefully down to look into Octopussy's house. Yes! the brown mass was still there. It was stirring excitedly. Why? Major Smythe saw the dark strings of his blood curling lazily down through the water. Of course! The darling was tasting his blood. A shaft of pain hit Major Smythe and sent him reeling. He heard himself babbling deliriously into his mask. Pull yourself together, Dexter, old boy! You've got to give Pussy her lunch! He steadied himself and, holding the spear well down the shaft, lowered the fish down towards the writhing hole.

Would Pussy take the bait, the poisoned bait that was killing Major Smythe, but to which an octopus might be immune? If only Bengry could be here to watch! Three tentacles, weaving excitedly, came out of the hole and wavered round the scorpion fish. Now there was a grey mist in front of Major Smythe's eyes. He recognized it as the edge of unconsciousness and feebly shook his head to clear it. And then the tentacles leapt!

But not at the fish! At Major Smythe's hand and arm. Major Smythe's torn mouth stretched in a grimace of pleasure. Now he and Pussy had shaken hands! How exciting! How truly wonderful!

But then the octopus, quietly, relentlessly, pulled downwards and terrible realization came to Major Smythe. He summoned his dregs of strength and plunged his spear down. The only effect was to push the scorpion fish into the mass of the octopus and offer more arm to the octopus. The tentacles snaked upwards and pulled more relentlessly. Too late Major Smythe scrabbled away his mask. One bottled scream burst out across the empty bay, then his head went under and down and there was an explosion of bubbles to the surface. Then Major Smythe's legs came up and the small waves washed his body to and fro while the octopus explored his right hand with its buccal orifice and took a first tentative bite at a finger with its beak-like jaws.

The body was found by two young Jamaicans spinning for needle fish from a canoe. They speared the octopus with Major Smythe's spear, killed it in the traditional fashion by turning it inside out and biting its head off, and brought the three corpses home. They turned Major Smythe's body over to the police and had the scorpion fish and the 'sea-cat' for supper. The local correspondent of the *Daily Gleaner* reported that Major Smythe had been killed by an octopus, but the paper translated this into 'found drowned' so as not to frighten the tourists.

Later, in London, James Bond, privately assuming 'suicide', wrote the same verdict of 'found drowned', together with the date, on the last page and closed the bulky file.

It is only from the notes of Dr Greaves, who performed the autopsy, that it has been possible to construct some kind of a postscript to the bizarre and pathetic end of a once valuable officer of the Secret Service.

THE PROPERTY OF A LADY

IT WAS, EXCEPTIONALLY, a hot day in early June. James Bond put down the dark grey chalk pencil that was the marker for the dockets routed to the Double-O Section and took off his coat. He didn't bother to hang it over the back of his chair, let alone take the trouble to get up and drape the coat over the hanger Mary Goodnight had suspended, at her own cost (damn women!), behind the Office of Works' green door of his connecting office. He dropped the coat on the floor. There was no reason to keep the coat immaculate, the creases tidy. There was no sign of any work to be done. All over the world there was quiet. The In and Out signals had, for weeks, been routine. The daily top secret SITREP, even the newspapers, yawned vacuously — in the latter case scratchings at domestic scandals for readership, for bad news, the only news that makes such sheets readable, whether top secret or on sale for pennies.

Bond hated these periods of vacuum. His eyes, his mind, were barely in focus as he turned the pages of a jaw-breaking dissertation by the Scientific Research Section on the Russian use of cyanide gas, propelled by the cheapest bulb-handled children's water pistol, for assassination. The spray, it seemed, directed at the face, took instantaneous effect. It was recommended for victims from twenty-five years upwards, on ascending stairways or inclines. The verdict would then probably be heart-failure.

The harsh burr of the red telephone sprayed into the room so suddenly that James Bond, his mind elsewhere, reached his hand automatically towards his left armpit in self-defence. The edges of his mouth turned down as he recognized the reflex. On the second burr he picked up the receiver.

'Sir?'

'Sir.'

He got up from his chair and picked up his coat. He put on the coat and at the same time put on his mind. He had been dozing in his bunk. Now he had to go up on the bridge. He walked through into the connecting office and resisted the impulse to ruffle up the inviting nape of Mary Goodnight's golden neck.

He told her 'M' and walked out into the close-carpeted corridor and along, between the muted whizz and zing of the Communications Section, of which his Section was a neighbour, to the lift and up to the eighth.

Miss Moneypenny's expression conveyed nothing. It usually conveyed something if she knew something — private excitement, curiosity, or, if Bond was in trouble, encouragement or even anger. Now the smile of welcome showed disinterest. Bond registered that this was going to be some kind of a routine job, a bore, and he adjusted his entrance through that fateful door accordingly.

There was a visitor — a stranger. He sat on M's left. He only briefly glanced up as Bond came in and took his usual place across the red leather-topped desk.

M said, stiffly, 'Dr Fanshawe, I don't think you've met Commander Bond of my Research Department.'

Bond was used to these euphemisms.

He got up and held out his hand. Dr Fanshawe rose, briefly touched Bond's hand and sat quickly down as if he had touched paws with a Gila monster.

If he looked at Bond, inspected him and took him in as anything more than an anatomical silhouette, Bond thought that Dr Fanshawe's eyes must be fitted with a thousandth of a second shutter. So this was obviously some kind of an expert — a man whose interests lay in facts, things, theories — not in human beings. Bond wished that M had given him some kind of a brief, hadn't got this puckish, rather childishly malign desire to surprise — to spring the jack-in-a-box on his staff. But Bond, remembering his own boredom of ten minutes ago, and putting himself in M's place, had the intuition to realize that M himself might have been subject to the same June heat, the same oppressive vacuum in his duties, and, faced by the unexpected relief of an emergency, a small one perhaps, had decided to extract the maximum effect, the maximum drama, out of it to relieve his own tedium.

The stranger was middle-aged, rosy, well-fed, and clothed

rather foppishly in the neo-Edwardian fashion — turned-up cuffs to his dark blue, four-buttoned coat, a pearl pin in a heavy silk cravat, spotless wing collar, cuff links formed of what appeared to be antique coins, pince-nez on a thick black ribbon. Bond summed him up as something literary, a critic perhaps, a bachelor — possibly with homosexual tendencies.

M said, 'Dr Fanshawe is a noted authority on antique jewellery. He is also, though this is confidential, adviser to HM Customs and to the CID on such things. He has in fact been referred to me by our friends at MI5. It is in connexion with our Miss Freudenstein.'

Bond raised his eyebrows. Maria Freudenstein was a secret agent working for the Soviet KGB in the heart of the Secret Service. She was in the Communications Department, but in a watertight compartment of it that had been created especially for her, and her duties were confined to operating the Purple Cipher — a cipher which had also been created especially for her. Six times a day she was responsible for encoding and dispatching lengthy SITREPS in this cipher to the CIA in Washington. These messages were the output of Section 100 which was responsible for running double agents. They were an ingenious mixture of true fact, harmless disclosures and an occasional nugget of the grossest misinformation. Maria Freudenstein, who had been known to be a Soviet agent when she was taken into the Service, had been allowed to steal the key to the Purple Cipher with the intention that the Russians should have complete access to these SITREPS — be able to intercept and decipher them — and thus, when appropriate, be fed false information. It was a highly secret operation which needed to be handled with extreme delicacy, but it had now been running smoothly for three years and, if Maria Freudenstein also picked up a certain amount of canteen gossip at Headquarters, that was a necessary risk, and she was not attractive enough to form liaisons which could be a security risk.

M turned to Dr Fanshawe. 'Perhaps, Doctor, you would care to tell Commander Bond what it is all about.'

'Certainly, certainly.' Dr Fanshawe looked quickly at Bond and then away again. He addressed his boots. 'You see, it's like this, er, Commander. You've heard of a man called Fabergé, no doubt. Famous Russian jeweller.'

'Made fabulous Easter eggs for the Czar and Czarina before the revolution.'

'That was indeed one of his specialities. He made many other exquisite pieces of what we may broadly describe as objects of vertu. Today, in the sale rooms, the best examples fetch truly fabulous prices — £50,000 and more. And recently there entered this country the most amazing specimen of all — the so-called Emerald Sphere, a work of supreme art hitherto known only from a sketch by the great man himself. This treasure arrived by registered post from Paris and it was addressed to this woman of whom you know, Miss Maria Freudenstein.'

'Nice little present. Might I ask how you learned of it, Doctor?'

'I am, as your Chief has told you, an adviser to HM Customs and Excise in matters concerning antique jewellery and similar works of art. The declared value of the package was £100,000. This was unusual. There are methods of opening such packages clandestinely. The package was opened — under a Home Office Warrant, of course — and I was called in to examine the contents and give a valuation. I immediately recognized the Emerald Sphere from the account and sketch of it given in Mr Kenneth Snowman's definitive work on Fabergé. I said that the declared price might well be on the low side. But what I found of particular interest was the accompanying document which gave, in Russian and French, the provenance of this priceless object.' Dr Fanshawe gestured towards a photostat of what appeared to be a brief family tree that lay on the desk in front of M. 'That is a copy I had made. Briefly, it states that the Sphere was commissioned by Miss Freudenstein's grandfather directly from Fabergé in 1917 — no doubt as a means of turning some of his roubles into something portable and of great value. On his death in 1918 it passed to his brother and thence, in 1950, to Miss Freudenstein's mother. She, it appears, left Russia as a child and lived in White Russian *émigré* circles in Paris. She never married, but gave birth to this girl, Maria, illegitimately. It seems that she died last year and that some friend or executor, the paper is not signed, has now forwarded the Sphere to its rightful owner, Miss Maria Freudenstein. I had no reason to question this girl, although as you can imagine my interest was most lively, until last month Sotheby's announced that they would auction the piece, described as "the property of a lady", in a week from today. On behalf of the British Museum and, er, other interested parties, I then made discreet inquiries and met the lady, who, with perfect composure, confirmed the rather unlikely story contained in the provenance. It was then that I learned that she worked for the Ministry of Defence and it crossed my rather suspicious mind that it was, to say the least of it, odd that a junior clerk, engaged presumably on sensitive duties, should suddenly receive a gift to the value of £100,000 or more from abroad. I spoke to a senior official in MI5 with whom I have some contact through my work for HM Customs and I was in due course referred to this, er, department.' Dr Fanshawe spread his hands and gave Bond a brief glance. 'And that, Commander, is all I have to tell you.'

M broke in. 'Thank you, Doctor. Just one or two final questions and I won't detain you any further. You have examined this emerald ball thing and you pronounce it genuine?'

Dr Fanshawe ceased gazing at his boots. He looked up and spoke to a point somewhere above M's left shoulder. 'Certainly. So does Mr Snowman of Wartski's, the greatest Fabergé experts and dealers in the world. It is undoubtedly the missing masterpiece of which hitherto Carl Fabergé's sketch was the only record.'

'What about the provenance? What do the experts say about that?'

'It stands up adequately. The greatest Fabergé pieces were nearly always privately commissioned. Miss Freudenstein says that her grandfather was a vastly rich man before the revolution — a porcelain manufacturer. Ninety-nine per cent of all Fabergé's output has found its way abroad. There are only a few pieces left in the Kremlin — described simply as "pre-revolutionary examples of Russian jewellery". The official Soviet view has always been that they are merely capitalist baubles. Officially they despise them as they officially despise their superb collection of French Impressionists.'

'So the Soviet still retain some examples of the work of this man Fabergé. Is it possible that this emerald affair could have lain secreted somewhere in the Kremlin through all these years?'

'Certainly. The Kremlin treasure is vast. No one knows what

they keep hidden. They have only recently put on display what they have wanted to put on display.'

M drew on his pipe. His eyes through the smoke were bland, scarcely interested. 'So that, in theory, there is no reason why this emerald ball should not have been unearthed from the Kremlin, furnished with a faked history to establish ownership, and transferred abroad as a reward to some friend of Russia for services rendered?'

'None at all. It would be an ingenious method of greatly rewarding the beneficiary without the danger of paying large sums into his, or her, bank account.'

'But the final monetary reward would of course depend on the amount realized by the sale of the object — the auction price for instance?'

'Exactly.'

'And what do you expect this object to fetch at Sotheby's?'

'Impossible to say. Wartski's will certainly bid very high. But of course they wouldn't be prepared to tell anyone just how high — either on their own account for stock, so to speak, or acting on behalf of a customer. Much would depend on how high they are forced up by an underbidder. Anyway, not less than £100,000 I'd say.'

'Hm.' M's mouth turned down at the corners. 'Expensive hunk of jewellery.'

Dr Fanshawe was aghast at this bare-faced revelation of M's philistinism. He actually looked M straight in the face. 'My dear sir,' he expostulated, 'do you consider the stolen Goya, sold at Sotheby's for £140,000, that went to the National Gallery, just an expensive hunk, as you put it, of canvas and paint?'

M said placatingly, 'Forgive me, Dr Fanshawe. I expressed myself clumsily. I have never had the leisure to interest myself in works of art nor, on a naval officer's pay, the money to acquire any. I was just registering my dismay at the runaway prices being fetched at auction these days.'

'You are entitled to your views, sir,' said Dr Fanshawe stuffily.

Bond thought it was time to rescue M. He also wanted to get Dr Fanshawe out of the room so that they could get down to the professional aspects of this odd business. He got to his feet. He said to M, 'Well, sir, I don't think there is anything else I need to know. No doubt this will turn out to be perfectly straightforward (like hell it would!) and just a matter of one of your staff turning out to be a very lucky woman. But it's very kind of Dr Fanshawe to have gone to so much trouble.' He turned to Dr Fanshawe. 'Would you care to have a staff car to take you wherever you're going?'

'No thank you, thank you very much. It will be pleasant to walk across the park.'

Hands were shaken, goodbyes said and Bond showed the doctor out. Bond came back into the room. M had taken a bulky file, stamped with the top secret red star, out of a drawer and was already immersed in it. Bond took his seat again and waited. The room was silent save for the riffling of paper. This also stopped as M extracted a foolscap sheet of blue cardboard used for Confidential Staff Records and carefully read through the forest of close type on both sides.

Finally he slipped it back in the file and looked up. 'Yes,' he said and the blue eyes were bright with interest. 'It fits all right. The girl was born in Paris in 1935. Mother very active in the Resistance during the war. Helped run the Tulip Escape Route and got away with it. After the war, the girl went to the Sorbonne and then got a job in the Embassy, in the Naval Attaché's office, as an interpreter. You know the rest. She was compromised — some unattractive sexual business — by some of her mother's old Resistance friends who by then were working for the NKVD, and from then on she has been working under Control. She applied, no doubt on instruction, for British citizenship. Her clearance from the Embassy and her mother's Resistance record helped her to get that by 1959, and she was then recommended to us by the FO. But it was there that she made her big mistake. She asked for a year's leave before coming to us and was next reported by the Hutchinson network in the Leningrad espionage school. There she presumably received the usual training and we had to decide what to do about her. Section 100 thought up the Purple Cipher operation and you know the rest. She's been working for three years inside headquarters for the KGB and now she's getting her reward — this emerald ball thing worth £100,000. And that's interesting on two counts. First it means that the KGB is totally hooked on the Purple Cipher or they wouldn't be making this fantastic payment. That's good news. It means that we can hot up the material we're passing over — put across some Grade 3 deception material and perhaps even move up to Grade 2. Secondly, it explains something we've never been able to understand — that this girl hasn't hitherto received a single payment for her services. We were worried by that. She had an account at Glyn, Mills that only registered her monthly pay cheque of around £50. And she's consistently lived within it. Now she's getting her pay-off in one large lump sum via this bauble we've been learning about. All very satisfactory.'

M reached for the ashtray made out of a twelve-inch shell base and rapped out his pipe with the air of a man who has done a good afternoon's work.

Bond shifted in his chair. He badly needed a cigarette, but he wouldn't have dreamed of lighting one. He wanted one to help him focus his thoughts. He felt that there were some ragged edges to this problem — one particularly. He said, mildly, 'Have we ever caught up with her local Control, sir? How does she get her instructions?'

'Doesn't need to,' said M impatiently, busying himself with his pipe. 'Once she'd got hold of the Purple Cipher all she needed to do was hold down her job. Damn it, man, she's pouring the stuff into their lap six times a day. What sort of instructions would they need to give her? I doubt if the KGB men in London even know of her existence — perhaps the Resident Director does, but as you know we don't even know who he is. Give my eyes to find out.'

Bond suddenly had a flash of intuition. It was as if a camera had started grinding in his skull, grinding out a length of clear film. He said quietly, 'It might be that this business at Sotheby's could show him to us — show us who he is.'

'What the devil are you talking about, 007? Explain yourself.'

'Well, sir,' Bond's voice was calm with certainty, 'you remember what this Dr Fanshawe said about an underbidder — someone to make these Wartski merchants go to their very top price. If the Russians don't seem to know or care very much about Fabergé, as Dr Fanshawe says, they may have no very clear idea what this thing's really worth. The KGB wouldn't be likely to know about such things anyway. They may imagine it's only worth its break-up value — say ten or twenty thousand pounds for the emerald. That sort of sum would make more sense than the small fortune the girl's going to get if Dr Fanshawe's right. Well, if the Resident Director is the only man who knows about this girl, he will be the only man who knows she's been paid. So he'll be the underbidder. He'll be sent to Sotheby's and told to push the sale through the roof. I'm certain of it. So we'll be able to identify him and we'll have enough on him to have him sent home. He just won't know what's hit him. Nor will the KGB. If I can go to the sale and bowl him out and we've got the place covered with cameras, and the auction records, we can get the FO to declare him persona non grata inside a week. And Resident Directors don't grow on trees. It may be months before the KGB can appoint a replacement.'

M said, thoughtfully, 'Perhaps you've got something there.' He swivelled his chair round and gazed out of the big window towards the jagged skyline of London. Finally he said, over his shoulder, 'All right, 007. Go and see the Chief of Staff and set the machinery up. I'll square things with Five. It's their territory, but it's our bird. There won't be any trouble. But don't go and get carried away and bid for this bit of rubbish yourself. I haven't got the money to spare.'

Bond said, 'No, sir.' He got to his feet and went quickly out of the room. He thought he had been very clever and he wanted to see if he had. He didn't want M to change his mind.

Wartski has a modest, ultra-modern frontage at 138 Regent Street. The window, with a restrained show of modern and antique jewellery, gave no hint that these were the greatest Fabergé-dealers in the world. The interior — grey carpet, walls panelled in sycamore, a few unpretentious vitrines — held none of the excitement of Cartier's, Boucheron or Van Cleef, but the group of framed Royal Warrants from Queen Mary, the Queen Mother, the Queen, King Paul of Greece and the unlikely King Frederick IX of Denmark, suggested that this was no ordinary jeweller.

James Bond asked for Mr Kenneth Snowman. A good-looking, very well-dressed man of about forty rose from a group of men sitting with their heads together at the back of the room and came forward.

Bond said quietly, 'I'm from the CID. Can we have a talk? Perhaps you'd like to check my credentials first. My name's

James Bond. But you'll have to go direct to Sir Ronald Vallance or his PA. I'm not directly on the strength at Scotland Yard. Sort of liaison job.'

The intelligent, observant eyes didn't appear even to look him over. The man smiled. 'Come on downstairs. Just having a talk with some American friends — sort of correspondents really. From "Old Russia" of Fifth Avenue.'

'I know the place,' said Bond. 'Full of rich-looking icons and so on. Not far from the Pierre.'

'That's right.' Mr Snowman seemed even more reassured. He led the way down a narrow, thickly carpeted stairway into a large and glittering showroom which was obviously the real treasure house of the shop. Gold and diamonds and cut stones winked from lit cases round the walls.

'Have a seat. Cigarette?'

Bond took one of his own. 'It's about this Fabergé piece that's coming up at Sotheby's tomorrow — this Emerald Sphere.'

'Ah, yes.' Mr Snowman's clear brow furrowed anxiously. 'No trouble about it I hope?'

'Not from your point of view. But we're very interested in the actual sale. We know about the owner, Miss Freudenstein. We think there may be an attempt to raise the bidding artificially. We're interested in the underbidder — assuming, that is, that your firm will be leading the field, so to speak.'

'Well, er, yes,' said Mr Snowman with rather careful candour. 'We're certainly going to go after it. But it'll sell for a huge price. Between you and me, we believe the V and A are going to bid, and probably the Metropolitan. But is it some crook you're after? If so you needn't worry. This is out of their class.'

Bond said, 'No. We're not looking for a crook.' He wondered how far to go with this man. Because people are very careful with the secrets of their own business doesn't mean that they'll be careful with the secrets of yours. Bond picked up a wood and ivory plaque that lay on the table. It said:

> It is naught, it is naught, saith the buyer.
> But when he is gone his way, he boasteth.
>
> – Proverbs XX, 14

Bond was amused. He said so. 'You can read the whole history of the bazaar, of the dealer and the customer, behind that quotation,' he said. He looked Mr Snowman straight in the eyes. 'I need that sort of nose, that sort of intuition in this case. Will you give me a hand?'

'Certainly. If you'll tell me how I can help.' He waved a hand. 'If it's secrets you're worried about, please don't worry. Jewellers are used to them. Scotland Yard will probably give my firm a clean bill in that respect. Heaven knows we've had enough to do with them over the years.'

'And if I told you that I'm from the Ministry of Defence?'

'Same thing,' said Mr Snowman. 'You can naturally rely absolutely on my discretion!'

Bond made up his mind. 'All right. Well, all this comes under the Official Secrets Act, of course. We suspect that the underbidder, presumably to you, will be a Soviet agent. My job is to establish his identity. Can't tell you any more, I'm afraid. And you don't actually need to know any more. All I want is to go with you to Sotheby's tomorrow night and for you to help me spot the man. No medals, I'm afraid, but we'd be extremely grateful.'

Mr Kenneth Snowman's eyes glinted with enthusiasm. 'Of course. Delighted to help in any way. But,' he looked doubtful, 'you know it's not necessarily going to be all that easy. Peter Wilson, the head of Sotheby's, who'll be taking the sale, would be the only person who could tell us for sure — that is, if the bidder wants to stay secret. There are dozens of ways of bidding without making any movement at all. But if the bidder fixes his method, his code so to speak, with Peter Wilson before the sale, Peter wouldn't think of letting anyone in on the code. It would give the bidder's game away to reveal his limit. And that's a close secret, as you can imagine, in the rooms. And a thousand times not if you come with me. I shall probably be setting the pace. I already know how far I'm going to go — for a client by the way — but it would make my job vastly easier if I could tell how far the underbidder's going to go. As it is, what you've told me has been a great help. I shall warn my man to put his sights even higher. If this chap of yours has got a strong nerve, he may push me very hard indeed. And there will be others in the field of course. It sounds as if this is going to be quite a night. They're putting it on television and asking all the millionaires and dukes and duchesses for the sort of gala performance Sotheby's do rather well. Wonderful publicity of course. By Jove, if they knew there was cloak-and-dagger stuff mixed up with the sale, there'd be a riot! Now then, is there anything else to go into? Just spot this man and that's all?'

'That's all. How much do you think this thing will go for?'

Mr Snowman tapped his teeth with a gold pencil. 'Well now, you see that's where I have to keep quiet. I know how high I'm going to go, but that's my client's secret.' He paused and looked thoughtful. 'Let's say that if it goes for less than £100,000 we'll be surprised.'

'I see,' said Bond. 'Now then, how do I get into the sale?'

Mr Snowman produced an elegant alligator-skin notecase and extracted two engraved bits of pasteboard. He handed one over. 'That's my wife's. I'll get her one somewhere else in the rooms. B5 — well placed in the centre front. I'm B6.'

Bond took the ticket. It said:

Sotheby & Co.

Sale of

A Casket of Magnificent Jewels
and
A Unique Object of Vertu by Carl Fabergé

The Property of a Lady
Admit one to the Main Sale Room
Tuesday, 20 June, at 9.30 pm precisely

ENTRANCE IN ST GEORGE STREET

'It's not the old Georgian entrance in Bond Street,' commented Mr Snowman. 'They have an awning and red carpet out from their back door now that Bond Street's one-way. Now,' he got up from his chair, 'would you care to see some Fabergé? We've got some pieces here my father bought from the Kremlin around 1927. It'll give you some idea what all the fuss is about, though of course the Emerald Sphere's incomparably finer than anything I can show you by Fabergé apart from the Imperial Easter Eggs.'

Later, dazzled by the diamonds, the multi-coloured gold, the silken sheen of translucent enamels, James Bond walked up and out of the Aladdin's Cave under Regent Street and went off to spend the rest of the day in drab offices around Whitehall planning drearily minute arrangements for the identification and photographing of a man in a crowded room who did not yet possess a face or an identity but who was certainly the top Soviet spy in London.

Through the next day, Bond's excitement mounted. He found an excuse to go into the Communications Section and wander into the little room where Miss Maria Freudenstein and two assistants were working the cipher machines that handled the Purple Cipher dispatches. He picked up an *en clair* file — he had freedom of access to most material at headquarters — and ran his eye down the carefully edited paragraphs that, in half an hour or so, would be spiked, unread, by some junior CIA clerk in Washington and, in Moscow, be handed, with reverence, to a top-ranking officer of the KGB. He joked with the two junior girls, but Maria Freudenstein only looked up from her machine to give him a polite smile and Bond's skin crawled minutely at this proximity to treachery and at the black and deadly secret locked up beneath the frilly white blouse. She was an unattractive girl with a pale, rather pimply skin, black hair and a vaguely unwashed appearance. Such a girl would be unloved, make few friends, have chips on her shoulder — more particularly in view of her illegitimacy — and a grouse against society. Perhaps her only pleasure in life was the triumphant secret she harboured in that flattish bosom — the knowledge that she was cleverer than all those around her, that she was, every day, hitting back against the world — the world that despised, or just ignored her, because of her plainness — with all her might. One day they'd be sorry! It was a common neurotic pattern — the revenge of the ugly duckling on society.

Bond wandered off down the corridor to his own office. By tonight that girl would have made a fortune, been paid her thirty pieces of silver a thousandfold. Perhaps the money would change her character, bring her happiness. She would be able to afford the best beauty specialists, the best clothes, a pretty flat. But M had said he was now going to hot up the Purple Cipher

Operation, try a more dangerous level of deception. This would be dicey work. One false step, one incautious lie, an ascertainable falsehood in a message, and KGB would smell a rat. One more, and they would know they were being hoaxed and probably had been ignominiously hoaxed for three years. Such a shameful revelation would bring quick revenge. It would be assumed that Maria Freudenstein had been acting as a double agent, working for the British as well as the Russians. She would inevitably and quickly be liquidated — perhaps with a cyanide pistol Bond had been reading about only the day before.

James Bond, looking out of the window across the trees in Regent's Park, shrugged. Thank God it was none of his business. The girl's fate wasn't in his hands. She was caught in the grimy machine of espionage and she would be lucky if she lived to spend a tenth of the fortune she was going to gain in a few hours in the auction rooms.

There was a line of cars and taxis blocking George Street behind Sotheby's. Bond paid off his taxi and joined the crowd filtering under the awning and up the steps. He was handed a catalogue by the uniformed commissionaire who inspected his ticket, and went up the broad stairs with the fashionable, excited crowd and along a gallery and into the main auction room that was already thronged. He found his seat next to Mr Snowman, who was writing figures on a pad on his knee, and looked round him.

The lofty room was perhaps as large as a tennis court. It had the look and the smell of age and the two large chandeliers, to fit in with the period, blazed warmly in contrast to the strip lighting along the vaulted ceiling whose glass roof was partly obscured by a blind, still half-drawn against the sun that would have been blazing down on the afternoon's sale. Miscellaneous pictures and tapestries hung on the olive-green walls and batteries of television and other cameras (amongst them the MI5 cameraman with a press pass from the *Sunday Times*) were clustered with their handlers on a platform built out from the middle of a giant tapestried hunting scene. There were perhaps a hundred dealers and spectators sitting attentively on small gilt chairs. All eyes were focused on the slim, good-looking auctioneer talking quietly from the raised wooden pulpit. He was dressed in an immaculate dinner jacket with a red carnation in the buttonhole. He spoke unemphatically and without gestures.

'Fifteen thousand pounds. And sixteen.' A pause. A glance at someone in the front row. 'Against you, sir.' The flick of a catalogue being raised. 'Seventeen thousand pounds I am bid. Eighteen. Nineteen. I am bid twenty thousand pounds.' And so the quiet voice went, calmly, unhurriedly on while down among the audience the equally impassive bidders signalled their responses to the litany.

'What is he selling?' asked Bond, opening his catalogue.

'Lot 40,' said Mr Snowman. 'That diamond rivière the porter's holding on the black velvet tray. It'll probably go for about twenty-five. An Italian is bidding against a couple of Frenchmen. Otherwise they'd have got it for twenty. I only went to fifteen. Liked to have got it. Wonderful stones. But there it is.'

Sure enough, the price stuck at twenty-five thousand and the hammer, held by its head and not by its handle, came down with soft authority. 'Yours, sir,' said Mr Peter Wilson and a sales clerk hurried down the aisle to confirm the identity of the bidder.

'I'm disappointed,' said Bond.

Mr Snowman looked up from his catalogue. 'Why is that?'

'I've never been to an auction before and I always thought the auctioneer banged his gavel three times and said going, going, gone, so as to give the bidders a last chance.'

Mr Snowman laughed. 'You might still find that operating in the Shires or in Ireland, but it hasn't been the fashion at London sale rooms since I've been attending them.'

'Pity. It adds to the drama.'

'You'll get plenty of that in a minute. This is the last lot before the curtain goes up.'

One of the porters had reverently uncoiled a glittering mass of rubies and diamonds on his black velvet tray. Bond looked at the catalogue. It said 'Lot 41' which the luscious prose described as:

A PAIR OF FINE AND IMPORTANT RUBY AND DIAMOND BRACELETS, the front of each in the form of an elliptical cluster composed of one larger and two smaller rubies within a border of cushion-shaped diamonds, the sides and back formed of simpler clusters alternating with diamond openwork scroll motifs springing from single-stone ruby centres millegriffe-set in gold, running between chains of rubies and diamonds linked alternately, the clasp also in the form of an elliptical cluster.

*According to family tradition, this lot was formerly the property of Mrs Fitzherbert (1756–1837) whose marriage to the Prince of Wales afterwards Geo. IV was definitely established when in 1905 a sealed packet deposited at Coutts Bank in 1833 and opened by Royal permission disclosed the marriage certificate and other conclusive proofs.

These bracelets were probably given by Mrs Fitzherbert to her niece, who was described by the Duke of Orleans as 'the prettiest girl in England'.

While the bidding progressed, Bond slipped out of his seat and went down the aisle to the back of the room where the overflow audience spread out into the New Gallery and the Entrance Hall to watch the sale on closed-circuit television. He casually inspected the crowd, seeking any face he could recognize from the 200 members of the Soviet Embassy staff whose photographs, clandestinely obtained, he had been studying during the past days. But amidst an audience that defied classification — a mixture of dealers, amateur collectors and what could be broadly classified as rich pleasure-seekers — was not a feature, let alone a face, that he could recognize except from the gossip columns. One or two sallow faces might have been Russian, but equally they might have belonged to half a dozen European races. There was a scattering of dark glasses, but dark glasses are no longer a disguise. Bond went back to his seat. Presumably the man would have to divulge himself when the bidding began.

'Fourteen thousand I am bid. And fifteen. Fifteen thousand.' The hammer came down. 'Yours, sir.'

There was a hum of excitement and a fluttering of catalogues. Mr Snowman wiped his forehead with a white silk handkerchief. He turned to Bond. 'Now I'm afraid you are more or less on your own. I've got to pay attention to the bidding and anyway for some unknown reason it's considered bad form to look over one's shoulder to see who's bidding against you — if you're in the trade that's to say — so I'll only be able to spot him if he's somewhere up front here, and I'm afraid that's unlikely. Pretty well all dealers, but you can stare around as much as you like. What you've got to do is to watch Peter Wilson's eyes and then try and see who he's looking at, or who's looking at him. If you can spot the man, which may be quite difficult, note any movement he makes, even the very smallest. Whatever the man does — scratching his head, pulling at the lobe of his ear or whatever, will be a code he's arranged with Peter Wilson. I'm afraid he won't do anything obvious like raising his catalogue. Do you get me? And don't forget that he may make absolutely no movement at all until right at the end when he's pushed me as far as he thinks I'll go, then he'll want to sign off. Mark you,' Mr Snowman smiled, 'when we get to the last lap I'll put plenty of heat on him and try and make him show his hand. That's assuming of course that we are the only two bidders left in.' He looked enigmatic. 'And I think you can take it that we shall be.'

From the man's certainty, James Bond felt pretty sure that Mr Snowman had been given instructions to get the Emerald Sphere at any cost.

A sudden hush fell as a tall pedestal draped in black velvet was brought in with ceremony and positioned in front of the auctioneer's rostrum. Then a handsome oval case of what looked like white velvet was placed on top of the pedestal and, with reverence, an elderly porter in grey uniform with wine-red sleeves, collar and back belt, unlocked it and lifted out Lot 42, placed it on the black velvet and removed the case. The cricket ball of polished emerald on its exquisite base glowed with a supernatural green fire and the jewels on its surface and on the opalescent meridian winked their various colours. There was a gasp of admiration from the audience and even the clerks and experts behind the rostrum and sitting at the tall counting-house desk beside the auctioneer, accustomed to the Crown jewels of Europe parading before their eyes, leaned forward to get a better look.

James Bond turned to his catalogue. There it was, in heavy type and in prose as stickily luscious as a butterscotch sundae:

THE TERRESTRIAL GLOBE
DESIGNED IN 1917 BY CARL FABERGÉ FOR

A RUSSIAN GENTLEMAN AND NOW THE PROPERTY OF HIS GRANDDAUGHTER
42 A VERY IMPORTANT FABERGÉ TERRESTRIAL GLOBE.

A sphere carved from an extraordinarily large piece of Siberian emerald matrix weighing approximately one thousand three hundred carats and of a superb colour and vivid translucence, represents a terrestrial globe supported upon an elaborate *rocaille* scroll mount finely chased in *quatre-couleur* gold and set with a profusion of rose-diamonds and small emeralds of intense colour, to form a table-clock.

Around this mount six gold *putti* disport themselves among cloud-forms which are naturalistically rendered in carved rock-crystal finished matt and veined with fine lines of tiny rose-diamonds.

The Globe itself, the surface of which is meticulously engraved with a map of the world with the principal cities indicated by brilliant diamonds embedded within gold collets, rotates mechanically on an axis controlled by a small clock-movement, by *G. Moser*, signed, which is concealed in the base, and is girdled by a fixed gold belt enamelled opalescent oyster along a reserved path in *champlevé* technique over a moiré *guillochage* with painted Roman numerals in pale sepia enamel serving as the dial of the clock, and a single triangular pigeon-blood Burma ruby of about five carats set into the surface of the orb, pointing the hour.

Height: 7½ in. *Workmaster, Henrik Wigström*. In the original double-opening white velvet, satin-lined, oviform case with the gold key fitted in the base.

*The theme of this magnificent sphere is one that had inspired Fabergé some fifteen years earlier, as evidenced in the miniature terrestrial globe which forms part of the Royal Collection at Sandringham. (See plate 280 in *The Art of Carl Fabergé*, by A. Kenneth Snowman.)

After a brief and searching glance round the room, Mr Wilson banged his hammer softly. 'Lot 42 — an object of vertu by Carl Fabergé.' A pause. 'Twenty thousand pounds I am bid.'

Mr Snowman whispered to Bond, 'That means he's probably got a bid of at least fifty. This is simply to get things moving.'

Catalogues fluttered. 'And thirty, forty, fifty thousand pounds I am bid. And sixty, seventy, and eighty thousand pounds. And ninety.' A pause and then: 'One hundred thousand pounds I am bid.'

There was a rattle of applause round the room. The cameras had swivelled to a youngish man, one of three on a raised platform to the left of the auctioneer who were speaking softly into telephones. Mr Snowman commented, 'That's one of Sotheby's young men. He'll be on an open line to America. I should think that's the Metropolitan bidding, but it might be anybody. Now it's time for me to get to work.' Mr Snowman flicked up his rolled catalogue.

'And ten,' said the auctioneer. The man spoke into his telephone and nodded. 'And twenty.'

Again a flick from Mr Snowman.

'And thirty.'

The man on the telephone seemed to be speaking rather more words than before into his mouthpiece — perhaps giving his estimate of how much further the price was likely to go. He gave a slight shake of his head in the direction of the auctioneer and Peter Wilson looked away from him and round the room.

'One hundred and thirty thousand pounds I am bid,' he repeated quietly.

Mr Snowman said, softly, to Bond, 'Now you'd better watch out. America seems to have signed off. It's time for your man to start pushing me.'

James Bond slid out of his place and went and stood amongst a group of reporters in a corner to the left of the rostrum. Peter Wilson's eyes were directed towards the far right-hand corner of the room. Bond could detect no movement, but the auctioneer announced, 'And forty thousand pounds.' He looked down at Mr Snowman. After a long pause Mr Snowman raised five fingers. Bond guessed that this was part of his process of putting the heat on. He was showing reluctance, hinting that he was near the end of his tether.

'One hundred and forty-five thousand.' Again the piercing glance towards the back of the room. Again no movement. But again some signal had been exchanged. 'One hundred and fifty thousand pounds.'

There was a buzz of comment and some desultory clapping. This time Mr Snowman's reaction was even slower and the auctioneer twice repeated the last bid. Finally he looked directly at Mr Snowman. 'Against you, sir.' At last Mr Snowman raised five fingers.

'One hundred and fifty-five thousand pounds.'

James Bond was beginning to sweat. He had got absolutely nowhere and the bidding must surely be coming to an end. The auctioneer repeated the bid.

And now there was the tiniest movement. At the back of the room, a chunky-looking man in a dark suit reached up and unobtrusively took off his dark glasses. It was a smooth, nondescript face — the sort of face that might belong to a bank manager, a member of Lloyd's, or a doctor. This must have been the prearranged code with the auctioneer. So long as the man wore his dark glasses he would raise in tens of thousands. When he took them off, he had quit.

Bond shot a quick glance towards the bank of cameramen. Yes, the MI5 photographer was on his toes. He had also seen the movement. He lifted his camera deliberately and there was the quick glare of a flash. Bond got back to his seat and whispered to Snowman, 'Got him. Be in touch with you tomorrow. Thanks a lot.' Mr Snowman only nodded. His eyes remained glued on the auctioneer.

Bond slipped out of his place and walked swiftly down the aisle as the auctioneer said for the third time, 'One hundred and fifty-five thousand pounds I am bid,' and then softly brought down his hammer. 'Yours, sir.'

Bond got to the back of the room before the audience had risen, applauding, to its feet. His quarry was hemmed in amongst the gilt chairs. He had now put on his dark glasses again and Bond put on a pair of his own. He contrived to slip into the crowd and get behind the man as the chattering crowd streamed down the stairs. The hair grew low down on the back of the man's rather squat neck and the lobes of his ears were pinched in close to his head. He had a slight hump, perhaps only a bone deformation, high up on his back. Bond suddenly remembered. This was Piotr Malinowski, with the official title on the Embassy staff of 'Agricultural Attaché'. So!

Outside, the man began walking swiftly towards Conduit Street. James Bond got unhurriedly into a taxi with its engine running and its flag down. He said to the driver, 'That's him. Take it easy.'

'Yes, sir,' said the MI5 driver, pulling away from the kerb.

The man picked up a taxi in Bond Street. The tail in the

mixed evening traffic was easy. Bond's satisfaction mounted as the Russian's taxi turned up north of the Park and along Bayswater. It was just a question whether he would turn down the private entrance into Kensington Palace Gardens, where the first mansion on the left is the massive building of the Soviet Embassy. If he did, that would clinch matters. The two patrolling policemen, the usual Embassy guards, had been specially picked that night. It was their job just to confirm that the occupant of the leading taxi actually entered the Soviet Embassy.

Then, with the Secret Service evidence and the evidence of Bond and of the MI5 cameraman, there would be enough for the Foreign Office to declare Comrade Piotr Malinowski persona non grata on the grounds of espionage activity and send him packing. In the grim chess game that is secret service work, the Russians would have lost a queen. It would have been a very satisfactory visit to the auction rooms.

The leading taxi *did* turn in through the big iron gates.

Bond smiled with grim satisfaction. He leant forward.

'Thanks, driver. Headquarters please.'

THE LIVING DAYLIGHTS

JAMES BOND LAY at the five-hundred-yard firing point of the famous Century Range at Bisley. The white peg in the grass beside him said 4.4 and the same number was repeated high up on the distant butt above the single six-foot-square target that, to the human eye and in the late summer dusk, looked no larger than a postage stamp. But Bond's lens, an infra-red Sniperscope fixed above his rifle, covered the whole canvas. He could even clearly distinguish the pale blue and beige colours into which the target was divided, and the six-inch semicircular bull looked as big as the half moon that was already beginning to show low down in the darkening sky above the distant crest of Chobham Ridges.

James Bond's last shot had been an inner left — not good enough. He took another glance at the yellow and blue wind flags. They were streaming across range from the east rather more stiffly than when he had begun his shoot half an hour before, and he set two clicks more to the right on the wind gauge and traversed the cross-wires on the Sniperscope back to the point of aim. Then he settled himself, put his trigger finger gently inside the guard and on to the curve of the trigger, shallowed his breathing and very, very softly squeezed.

The vicious crack of the shot boomed across the empty range. The target disappeared below ground and at once the 'dummy' came up in its place. Yes, the black panel was in the bottom right-hand corner this time, not in the bottom left: a bull.

'Good,' said the voice of the Chief Range Officer from behind and above him. 'Stay with it.'

The target was already up again and Bond put his cheek back to its warm patch on the chunky wooden stock and his eye to the rubber eyepiece of the 'scope. He wiped his gun hand down the side of his trousers and took the pistol grip that jutted sharply down below the trigger guard. He splayed his legs an inch more. Now there were to be five rounds rapid. It would be interesting to see if that would produce 'fade'. He guessed not. This extraordinary weapon the Armourer had somehow got his hands on gave one the feeling that a standing man at a mile would be easy meat. It was mostly a .308 calibre International Experimental Target rifle built by Winchester to help American marksmen at World Championships, and it had the usual gadgets of super-accurate target weapons — a curled aluminium 'hand' at the back of the butt that extended under the armpit and held the stock firmly into the shoulder, and an adjustable pinion below the rifle's centre of gravity to allow the stock to be 'nailed' into its grooved wooden rest. The Armourer had had the usual single-shot bolt action replaced by a five-shot magazine, and he had assured Bond that if he would allow only two seconds between shots to steady the weapon there would be no fade even at five hundred yards. For the job that Bond had to do, he guessed that two seconds might be a dangerous loss of time if he missed with his first shot. Anyway, M had said that the range would be not more than three hundred yards. Bond would cut it down to one second — almost continuous fire.

'Ready?'

'Yes.'

'I'll give you a count-down from five. Now! Five, four, three, two, one. Fire!'

The ground shuddered slightly and the air sang as the five whirling scraps of cupro-nickel spat off into the dusk. The target went down and quickly rose again decorated with four small white discs closely grouped on the bull. There was no fifth disc — not even a black one to show an inner or an outer.

'The last round was low,' said the Range Officer lowering his night-glasses. 'Thanks for the contribution. We sift the sand on those butts at the end of every year. Never get less than fifteen tons of good lead and copper scrap out of them. Good money.'

Bond had got to his feet. Corporal Menzies from the Armourers' section appeared from the pavilion of the Gun Club and knelt down to dismantle the Winchester and its rest. He looked up at Bond. He said with a hint of criticism, 'You were taking it a bit fast, sir. Last round was bound to jump wide.'

'I know, Corporal. I wanted to see how fast I *could* take it. I'm not blaming the weapon. It's the hell of a fine job. Please tell the Armourer so from me. Now I'd better get moving. You're finding your own way back to London, aren't you?'

'Yes. Good night, sir.'

The Chief Range Officer handed Bond a record of his shoot — two sighting shots and then ten rounds at each hundred yards up to five hundred. 'Damned good firing with this visibility. You ought to come back next year and have a bash at the Queen's Prize. It's open to all comers nowadays — British Commonwealth, that is.'

'Thanks. Trouble is, I'm not all that much in England. And thanks for spotting for me.' Bond glanced at the distant Clock Tower. On either side, the red danger flag and the red signal drum were coming down to show that firing had ceased. The hands stood at nine fifteen. 'I'd like to have bought you a drink, but I've got an appointment in London. Can we hold it over until that Queen's Prize you were talking about?'

The Range Officer nodded noncommittally. He had been looking forward to finding out more about this man who had appeared out of the blue after a flurry of signals from the Ministry of Defence and had then proceeded to score well over ninety per cent at all distances, and that after the range was closed for the night and visibility was poor to bad. And why had he, who only officiated at the annual July meeting, been ordered to be present? And why had he been told to see that Bond had a six-inch bull at 500 instead of the regulation fifteen-inch? And why this flummery with the danger flag and signal drum that were only used on ceremonial occasions? To put pressure on the man? To give an edge of urgency to the shoot? Bond. Commander James Bond. The NRA would surely have a record of anyone who could shoot like that. He'd remember to give them a call. Funny time to have an appointment in London. Probably a girl. The Range Officer's undistinguished face assumed a disgruntled expression. Sort of fellow who got all the girls he wanted.

The two men walked through the handsome façade of Club Row behind the range to Bond's car that stood opposite the bullet-pitted iron reproduction of Landseer's famous 'Running Deer'. 'Nice-looking job,' commented the Range Officer. 'Never seen a body like that on a Continental. Have it made specially?'

'Yes. The Sports Saloons are really only two-seaters. And damned little luggage space. So I got Mulliner's to make it into a real two-seater with plenty of boot. Selfish car, I'm afraid. Well, good night. And thanks again.' The exhaust boomed healthily and the back wheels briefly spat gravel.

The Chief Range Officer watched the ruby lights vanish up King's Avenue towards the London road. He turned on his heel and went to find Corporal Menzies on a search for information that was to prove fruitless. The corporal remained as wooden as the big mahogany box he was in the process of loading into a khaki Land-Rover without military symbols. The Range Officer was a major. He tried pulling his rank without success. The Land-Rover hammered away in Bond's wake. The major walked moodily off to the offices of the National Rifle Association to try and find out what he wanted in the library under 'Bond, J.'.

James Bond's appointment was not with a girl. It was with a BEA flight to Hanover and Berlin. As he bit off the miles to London Airport, pushing the big car hard so as to have plenty of time for a drink, three drinks, before the take-off, only part of his mind was on the road. The rest was re-examining, for the umpteenth time, the sequence that was now leading him to an appointment with an aeroplane. But only an interim appointment. His final rendezvous on one of the next three nights in Berlin was with a man. He had to see this man and infallibly shoot him dead.

When, at around two thirty that afternoon, James Bond had gone in through the double-padded doors and had sat down opposite the turned-away profile on the other side of the big desk, he had sensed trouble. There was no greeting. M's head was sunk into his stiff turned-down collar in a Churchillian pose of gloomy reflection, and there was a droop of bitterness at the corners of his lips. He swivelled his chair round to face Bond, gave him an appraising glance as if, Bond thought, to see that his tie was straight and his hair properly brushed, and then began speaking, fast, clipping off his sentences as if he wanted to be rid of what he was saying, and of Bond, as quickly as possible.

'Number 272. He's a good man. You won't have come across him. Simple reason that he's been holed up in Novaya Zemlya since the war. Now he's trying to get out — loaded with stuff. Atomic and rockets. And their plan for a whole new series of tests. For 1961. To put the heat on the West. Something to do with Berlin. Don't quite get the picture but the FO say if it's true it's terrific. Makes nonsense of the Geneva Conference and all this blether about nuclear disarmament the Communist bloc are putting out. He's got as far as East Berlin. But he's got practically the whole of the KGB on his tail — and the East German security forces of course. He's holed up somewhere in the city and he got one message over to us — that he'd be coming across between six and seven pm on one of the next three nights — tomorrow, next day, or the day after. He gave the crossing point. Trouble is,' the downward curve of M's lips became even more bitter, 'the courier he used was a double. Station WB bowled him out yesterday. Quite by chance. Had a lucky break with one of the KGB codes. The courier'll be flown out for trial, of course. But that won't help. The KGB know that 272 will be making a run for it. They know when. They know where. They know just as much as we do and no more. Now, the code we cracked was a one-day-only setting on their machines. But we got the whole of that day's traffic and that was good enough. They plan to shoot him on the run. At this street crossing between East and West Berlin he gave us in his message. They're mounting quite an operation — Operation "Extase" they call it. Put their best sniper on the job. All we know about him is that his code name is the Russian for "Trigger". Station WB guess he's the same man they've used before for sniper work. Long-range stuff across the frontier. He's going to be guarding this crossing every night and his job is to get 272. Of course they'd obviously prefer to do a smoother job with machine-guns and what have you. But it's quiet in Berlin at the moment and apparently the word is it's got to stay so. Anyway,' M shrugged, 'they've got confidence in this "Trigger" operator and that's the way it's going to be!'

'Where do I come in, sir?' James Bond had guessed the answer, guessed why M was showing his dislike of the whole business. This was going to be dirty work and Bond, because he belonged to the Double-O Section, had been chosen for it. Perversely, Bond wanted to force M to put it in black and white. This was going to be bad news, dirty news, and he didn't want to hear it from one of the Section officers, or even from the Chief of Staff. This was to be murder. All right. Let M bloody well say so.

'Where do you come in, 007?' M looked coldly across the desk. 'You know where you come in. You've got to kill this sniper. And you've got to kill him before he gets 272. That's all. Is that understood?' The clear blue eyes remained cold as ice. But Bond knew that they remained so only with an effort of will. M didn't like sending any man to a killing. But, when it had to be done, he always put on this fierce, cold act of command. Bond knew why. It was to take some of the pressure, some of the guilt, off the killer's shoulders.

So now Bond, who knew these things, decided to make it easy and quick for M. He got to his feet. 'That's all right, sir. I suppose the Chief of Staff has got all the gen. I'd better go and put in some practice. It wouldn't do to miss.' He walked to the door.

M said quietly, 'Sorry to have to hand this to you. Nasty job. But it's got to be done well.'

'I'll do my best, sir.' James Bond walked out and closed the door behind him. He didn't like the job, but on the whole he'd rather have it himself than have the responsibility of ordering someone else to go and do it.

The Chief of Staff had been only a shade more sympathetic. 'Sorry you've bought this one, James,' he had said. 'But Tanqueray was definite that he hadn't got anyone good enough on his Station, and this isn't the sort of job you can ask a regular soldier to do. Plenty of top marksmen in the BAOR, but a live target needs another kind of nerve. Anyway, I've been on to Bisley and fixed a shoot for you tonight at eight fifteen when the ranges will be closed. Visibility should be about the same as you'll be getting in Berlin around an hour earlier. The Armourer's got the gun — a real target job, and he's sending it down with one of his men. You'll find your own way. Then you're booked on a midnight BEA charter flight to Berlin. Take a taxi to this address.' He handed Bond a piece of paper. 'Go up to the fourth floor and you'll find Tanqueray's Number 2 waiting for you. Then I'm afraid you'll just have to sit it out for the next three days.'

'How about the gun? Am I supposed to take it through the German customs in a golf bag or something?'

The Chief of Staff hadn't been amused. 'It'll go over in the FO bag. You'll have it by tomorrow midday.' He had reached for a signal pad. 'Well, you'd better get cracking. I'll just let Tanqueray know everything's fixed.'

James Bond glanced down at the dim blue face of the dashboard clock. Ten fifteen. With any luck by this time tomorrow it would all be finished. After all, it was the life of this man 'Trigger' against the life of 272. It wasn't *exactly* murder. Pretty near it, though. He gave a vicious blast on his triple windhorns at an inoffensive family saloon, took the roundabout in a quite unnecessary dry skid, wrenched the wheel harshly to correct it and pointed the nose of the Bentley towards the distant glow that was London Airport.

The ugly six-storey building at the corner of Kochstrasse and the Wilhelmstrasse was the only one standing in a waste of empty bombed space. Bond paid off his taxi and got a brief impression of waist-high weeds and half-tidied rubble walls stretching away to a big deserted crossroads lit by a central cluster of yellowish arc lamps, before he pushed the bell for the fourth floor and at once heard the click of the door-opener. The door closed itself behind him and he walked over the uncarpeted cement floor to the old-fashioned lift. The smell of cabbage, cheap cigar smoke and stale sweat reminded him of other apartment houses in Germany and Central Europe. Even the sigh and faint squeal of the slow lift were part of a hundred assignments when he had been fired off by M, like a projectile, at some distant target where a problem waited for his coming, waited to be solved by him. At least this time the reception committee was on his side. This time there was nothing to fear at the top of the stairs.

Number 2 of Secret Service Station WB was a lean, tense man in his early forties. He wore the uniform of his profession — well-cut, well-used, lightweight tweeds in a dark green herringbone, a soft white silk shirt and an old school tie — in his case Wykehamist. At the sight of the tie, and while they exchanged conventional greetings in the small musty lobby of the apartment, Bond's spirits, already low, sank another degree. He knew the type: backbone of the Civil Service; over-crammed and underloved at Winchester; a good second in PPE at Oxford; the war, staff jobs he would have done meticulously; perhaps an OBE; Allied Control Commission in Germany where he had been recruited into the I Branch and thence — because he was the ideal staff man and A1 with Security and because he thought he would find life, drama, romance, the things he had never had — into the Secret Service. A sober, careful man had been needed to chaperon Bond on this ugly business. Captain Paul Sender, late of the Welsh Guards, had been the obvious choice. He had bought it. Now, like a good Wykehamist, he concealed his distaste for the job beneath careful, trite conversation as he showed Bond the layout of the apartment and the arrangements that had been made for the executioner's preparedness and, to a modest extent, his comfort.

The flat consisted of a large double bedroom, a bathroom, and a kitchen containing tinned food, milk, butter, eggs, tea, bacon, bread and one bottle of Dimple Haig. The only odd feature in the bedroom was that one of the double beds was angled up against the curtains covering the single broad window and was piled high with three mattresses below the bedclothes.

Captain Sender said, 'Care to have a look at the field of fire? Then I can explain what the other side have in mind.'

Bond was tired. He didn't particularly want to go to sleep with the picture of the battlefield on his mind. He said, 'That'd be fine.'

Captain Sender switched off the lights. Chinks from the street light at the intersection showed round the curtains. 'Don't want to draw the curtains,' said Captain Sender. 'Unlikely, but they may be on the look-out for a covering party for 272. If you'd just lie on the bed and get your head under the curtains, I'll brief you about what you'll be looking at. Look to the left.'

It was a sash window and the bottom half was open. The mattress, by design, gave only a little and James Bond found himself more or less in the firing position he had been in on the Century Range, but now staring across broken, thickly weeded bombed ground towards the bright river of the Zimmerstrasse — the border with East Berlin. It looked about a hundred and fifty yards away. Captain Sender's voice from above him and behind the curtain began reciting. It reminded Bond of a spiritualist séance.

'That's bombed ground in front of you. Plenty of cover. A hundred and thirty yards of it up to the frontier. Then the frontier — the street — and then a big stretch of more bombed ground on the enemy side. That's why 272 chose this route. It's one of the few places in the town which is broken land — thick weeds, ruined walls, cellars — on both sides of the frontier. He will sneak through that mess on the other side and make a dash across the Zimmerstrasse for the mess on our side. Trouble is, he'll have thirty yards of brightly lit frontier to sprint across. That'll be the killing ground. Right?'

Bond said, 'Yes.' He said it softly. The scent of the enemy, the need to take care, already had him by the nerves.

'To your left, that big new ten-storey block is the Haus der Ministerien, the chief brain-centre of East Berlin. You can see the lights are still on in most of the windows. Most of those'll stay on all night. These chaps work hard — shifts all round the clock. You probably won't need to worry about the lighted ones. This "Trigger" chap'll almost certainly fire from one of the dark windows. You'll see there's a block of four together on the corner above the intersection. They've stayed dark last night and tonight. They've got the best field of fire. From here, their range varies from three hundred to three hundred and ten yards. I've got all the figures and so on when you want them. You needn't worry about much else. That street stays empty during the night — only the motorized patrols about every half an hour — light armoured car with a couple of motor-cycles as escort. Last night, which I suppose is typical, between six and seven when this thing's going to be done, there were a few people that came and went out of that side door. Civil servant types. Before that nothing out of the ordinary — usual flow of people in and out of a busy government building — except, of all things, a whole damned women's orchestra. Made the hell of a racket in some concert hall they've got in there. Part of the block is the Ministry of Culture. Otherwise nothing — certainly none of the KGB people we know, nor any signs of preparation for a job like this. But there wouldn't be. They're careful chaps, the opposition. Anyway, have a good look. Don't forget it's darker than it will be tomorrow around six. But you can get the general picture.'

Bond got the general picture and it stayed with him long after the other man was asleep and snoring softly with a gentle regular clicking sound — a Wykehamist snore, Bond reflected irritably.

Yes, he had got the picture — the picture of a flicker of movement among the shadowy ruins on the other side of the gleaming river of light, a pause, then the wild zigzagging sprint of a man in the full glare of the arcs, the crash of gunfire and either a crumpled, sprawling heap in the middle of the wide street or the noise of his onward dash through the weeds and rubble of the Western Sector — sudden death or a home run. The true gauntlet! How much time would Bond have to spot the Russian sniper in one of those dark windows? And kill him? Five seconds? Ten? When dawn edged the curtains with gunmetal, Bond capitulated to his fretting mind. It had won. He went softly into the bathroom and surveyed the ranks of medicine bottles that a thoughtful Secret Service had provided to keep its executioner in good shape. He selected the Tuinal, chased down two of the ruby and blue depth-charges with a glass of water and went back to bed. Then, pole-axed, he slept.

He awoke at midday. The flat was empty. Bond drew the curtains to let in the grey Prussian day and, standing well back from the window, gazed out at the drabness of Berlin and listened to the tram noises and to the distant screeching of the U-Bahn as it took the big curve into the Zoo station. He gave a quick, reluctant glance at what he had examined the night before, noted that the weeds among the bomb rubble were much the same as the London ones — rose-bay willow-herb, dock and bracken — and then went into the kitchen. There was a note propped against a loaf of bread: 'My friend [a Secret Service euphemism which in this context meant Sender's chief] says it's all right for you to go out. But to be back by 1700 hours. Your gear [double-talk for Bond's rifle] has arrived and the batman will lay it out this pm. P. Sender.'

Bond lit the gas cooker, burned the message with a sneer at his profession, and then brewed himself a vast dish of scrambled eggs and bacon which he heaped on buttered toast and washed down with black coffee into which he had poured a liberal tot of whisky. Then he bathed and shaved, dressed in the drab, anonymous, middle-European clothes he had brought over for the purpose, looked at his disordered bed, decided to hell with it, and went down in the lift and out of the building.

James Bond had always found Berlin a glum, inimical city varnished on the Western side with a brittle veneer of gimcrack polish, rather like the chromium trim on American motor-cars. He walked to the Kurfürstendamm, sat in the Café Marquardt, drank an espresso and moodily watched the obedient queues of pedestrians waiting for the 'Go' sign on the traffic lights while the shiny stream of cars went through their dangerous quadrille at the busy intersection. It was cold outside and the sharp wind from the Russian steppes whipped at the girls' skirts and at the waterproofs of the impatient hurrying men each with the inevitable briefcase tucked under his arm. The infra-red wall heaters in the café glared redly down and gave a spurious glow to the faces of the café-squatters consuming their traditional 'one cup of coffee and ten glasses of water', reading the free newspapers and periodicals in their wooden racks or earnestly bent over business documents. Bond, closing his mind to the evening, debated with himself about ways to spend the afternoon. It finally came down to a choice between a visit to that respectable-looking brownstone house in the Clausewitzstrasse, known to all concierges and taxi-drivers, or a trip to the Wannsee and a strenuous walk in the Grünewald. Virtue triumphed. Bond paid for his coffee, went out into the cold and took a taxi to the Zoo station.

The pretty young trees round the long lake had already been touched by the breath of autumn and there was occasional gold amongst the green. Bond walked hard for two hours along the leafy paths, then chose a restaurant with a glassed-in veranda above the lake and greatly enjoyed a high tea consisting of a double portion of matjes herrings smothered in cream and onion rings, and two 'Molle mit Korn', the Berlin equivalent of a 'boiler-maker and his assistant' — schnapps, doubles, washed down with draught Löwenbräu. Then, feeling more encouraged, he took the S-Bahn back into the city.

Outside the apartment house, a nondescript young man was tinkering with the engine of a black Opel Kapitan. He didn't take his head out from under the bonnet when Bond passed close by him and went up to the door and pressed the bell.

Captain Sender was reassuring. It was a 'friend' — a corporal from the transport section of Station WB. He had fixed up some bad engine trouble on the Opel. Each night, from six to seven, he would be ready to produce a series of multiple backfires when a signal on a walkie-talkie operated by Sender told him to do so. This would give some kind of cover for the noise of Bond's shooting. Otherwise the neighbourhood might alert the police and there would be a lot of untidy explaining to be done. Their hideout was in the American Sector and, while their American 'friends' had given Station WB clearance for this operation, the 'friends' were naturally anxious that it should be a clean job and without repercussions.

Bond was suitably impressed by the car gimmick, as he was by the very workmanlike preparations that had been made for him in the living-room. Here, behind the head of his high bed, giving a perfect firing position, a wood and metal stand had been erected against the broad window-sill and along it lay the Winchester, the tip of its barrel just denting the curtains. The wood and all the metal parts of the rifle and Sniperscope had been painted a dull black and, laid out on the bed like sinister evening clothes, was a black velvet hood stitched to a waist-length shirt of the same material. The hood had wide slits for the eyes and mouth. It reminded Bond of old prints of the Spanish Inquisition, or of the anonymous operators on the guillotine platform during the French Revolution. There was a similar hood on Captain Sender's bed, and on his section of the window-sill there lay a pair of night-glasses and the microphone for the walkie-talkie.

Captain Sender, his face worried and tense with nerves, said there was no news at the Station, no change in the situation as they knew it. Did Bond want anything to eat? Or a cup of tea? Perhaps a tranquillizer — there were several kinds in the bathroom?

Bond stitched a cheerful, relaxed expression on his face and said no thanks, and gave a light-hearted account of his day while an artery near his solar plexus began thumping gently as tension built up inside him like a watch-spring tightening. Finally his small talk petered out and he lay down on his bed with a German thriller he had bought on his wanderings, while Captain Sender moved fretfully about the flat, looking too often at his watch and chain-smoking Kent filter-tips through (he was a careful man) a Dunhill filter holder.

James Bond's choice of reading matter, prompted by a spectacular jacket of a half-naked girl strapped to a bed, turned out to have been a happy one for the occasion. It was called *Verderbt, Verdammt, Verraten.* The prefix '*ver*' signified that the girl had not only been ruined, damned and betrayed, but that she had suffered these misfortunes most thoroughly. James Bond temporarily lost himself in the tribulations of the heroine, Gräfin Liselotte Mutzenbacher, and it was with irritation that he heard Captain Sender say that it was five thirty and time to take up their positions.

Bond took off his coat and tie, put two sticks of chewing gum in his mouth and donned the hood. The lights were switched off by Captain Sender and Bond lay along the bed, got his eye to the eyepiece of the Sniperscope and gently lifted the bottom edge of the curtain back and over his shoulders.

Now dusk was approaching, but otherwise the scene, a year later to become famous as 'Checkpoint Charlie', was like a well-remembered photograph — the waste-land in front of him, the bright river of the frontier road, the farther waste-land and, on the left, the ugly square block of the Haus der Ministerien with its lit and dark windows. Bond scanned it all slowly, moving the Sniperscope, with the rifle, by means of the precision screws on the wooden base. It was all the same except that now there was a trickle of personnel leaving and entering the Ministry through the door on to the Wilhelmstrasse. Bond looked along at the four dark windows — dark again tonight — that he agreed with Sender were the enemy's firing points. The curtains were drawn back and the sash windows were wide open at the bottom. Bond's 'scope could not penetrate into the rooms, but there was no sign of movement within the four oblong, black, gaping mouths.

Now there was extra traffic in the street below. The women's orchestra came trooping down the pavement towards the entrance — twenty laughing, talking girls carrying their instruments — violin and wind instrument cases, satchels with their scores, and four of them with the drums — a gay, happy little crocodile. Bond was reflecting that some people still seemed to find life fun in the Soviet Sector, when his glasses picked out and stayed on the girl carrying the 'cello. Bond's masticating jaws stopped still and then reflectively went on with their chewing as he twisted the screw to depress the Sniperscope and keep her in its centre.

The girl was taller than the others and her long, straight fair hair, falling to her shoulders, shone like molten gold under the arcs at the intersection. She was hurrying along in a charming, excited way, carrying the 'cello case as if it were no heavier than a violin. Everything was flying — the skirt of her coat, her feet, her hair. She was vivid with movement and life and, it seemed, with gaiety and happiness as she chattered to the two girls who flanked her and laughed back at what she was saying. As she turned in at the entrance amidst her troupe, the arcs momentarily caught a beautiful, pale profile. And then she was gone and, it seemed to Bond, with her disappearance a stab of grief lanced into his heart. How odd! How very odd! This had not happened to him since he was young. And now this single girl, seen only indistinctly and far away, had caused him to suffer this sharp pang of longing, this thrill of animal magnetism! Morosely, Bond glanced down at the luminous dial of his watch. Five fifty. Only ten minutes to go. No transport arriving at the entrance. None of those anonymous black Zik saloons he had half expected. He closed as much of his mind as he could to the girl and sharpened his wits. Get on, damn you! Get back to your job!

From somewhere inside the Ministry there came the familiar sounds of an orchestra tuning up — the strings tuning their instruments to single notes on the piano, the sharp blare of individual woodwinds — then a pause and then the collective crash of melody as the whole orchestra threw itself competently, so far as Bond could judge, into the opening bars of what even to James Bond was vaguely familiar.

'The Polovtsian Dances from *Prince Igor*,' said Captain Sender succinctly. 'Anyway, six o'clock coming up,' and then, urgently, 'Hey! Right-hand bottom of the four windows! Watch out!'

Bond minutely depressed the Sniperscope. Yes, there was movement inside the black cave. Now, from the interior, a thick black object, a weapon, had slid out. It moved firmly, minutely, swivelling down and sideways so as to cover the stretch of the Zimmerstrasse between the two waste-lands of rubble. Then the unseen operator in the room behind seemed satisfied and the weapon remained still, fixed obviously to a stand such as Bond had beneath his rifle.

'What is it? What sort of gun?' Captain Sender's voice was

more breathless than it should have been. Take it easy, dammit! thought Bond. It's me who's supposed to have the nerves.

He strained his eyes, taking in the squat flash eliminator at the muzzle, the telescopic sight and thick downward chunk of magazine. Yes, that would be it! Absolutely for sure — and the best they had!

'Kalashnikov,' he said curtly. 'Sub-machine-gun. Gas-operated. Thirty rounds in 7.62 millimetre. Favourite with the KGB. They're going to do a saturation job after all. Perfect for range. We'll have to get him pretty quick or 272'll end up not just dead but strawberry jam. You keep an eye out for any movement over there in the rubble. I'll have to stay married to that window and the gun. He'll have to show himself to fire. Other chaps are probably spotting behind him — perhaps from all four windows. Much the sort of set-up we expected, but I didn't think they'd use a weapon that's going to make all the racket this one will. Should have known they would. A running man would be hard to get in this light with a single-shot job.'

Bond fiddled minutely with the traversing and elevating screws at his fingertips and got the fine lines of the 'scope exactly intersected, just behind where the butt of the enemy gun merged into the blackness behind. Get the chest — don't bother about the head!

Inside the hood, Bond's face began to sweat and his eye socket was slippery against the rubber of the eyepiece. That didn't matter. It was only his hands, his trigger finger, that must stay bone dry. As the minutes ticked by, he frequently blinked his eyes to rest them, shifted his limbs to keep them supple, listened to the music to relax his mind.

The minutes slouched on leaden feet. How old would she be? Early twenties — say, twenty-three. With that poise and insouciance, the hint of authority in her long easy stride, she would come of good racy stock — one of the old Prussian families probably, or from similar remnants in Poland or even Russia. Why in hell did she have to choose the 'cello? There was something almost indecent in the idea of that bulbous, ungainly instrument between her splayed thighs. Of course Suggia had managed to look elegant, and so did that girl Amaryllis somebody. But they should invent a way for women to play the damned thing side-saddle.

At his side Captain Sender said, 'Seven o'clock. Nothing's stirred on the other side. Bit of movement on our side, near a cellar close to the frontier; that'll be our reception committee — two good men from the Station. Better stay with it until they close down. Let me know when they take that gun in.'

'All right.'

It was seven thirty when the KGB sub-machine-gun was gently drawn back into the black interior. One by one the bottom sashes of the four windows were closed. The cold-hearted game was over for the night. 272 was still holed up. Two more nights to go!

Bond softly drew the curtain over his shoulders and across the muzzle of the Winchester. He got up, pulled off his cowl and went into the bathroom and stripped and had a shower. Then he had two large whiskies on the rocks in quick succession, while he waited, his ears pricked, for the now muffled sound of the orchestra to stop. When at eight o'clock it did (with the expert comment from Sender, 'Borodin's *Prince Igor*, Choral Dance Number 17, I think,') he said to Sender, who had been getting off his report in garbled language to the Head of Station, 'Just going to have another look. I've rather taken to that tall blonde with the 'cello.'

'Didn't notice her,' said Sender, uninterested. He went into the kitchen. Tea, guessed Bond. Or perhaps Horlicks. Bond donned his cowl, went back to his firing position and depressed the Sniperscope to the doorway of the Ministry. Yes, there they went, not so gay and laughing now. Tired, perhaps. And now here she came, less lively but still with that beautiful careless stride. Bond watched the blown golden hair and the fawn raincoat until it had vanished into the indigo dusk up the Wilhelmstrasse. Where did she live? In some miserable, flaked room in the suburbs? Or in one of the privileged apartments in the hideous, lavatory-tiled Stalinallee?

Bond drew himself back. Somewhere, within easy reach, that girl lived. Was she married? Did she have a lover? Anyway to hell with it! She was not for him.

The next day, and the next night-watch, were duplicates, with small variations, of the first. James Bond had two more brief rendezvous, by Sniperscope, with the girl, and the rest was a killing of time and a tightening of the tension that, by the time the third and final day came, was like a fog in the small room.

James Bond crammed the third day with an almost lunatic programme of museums, art galleries, the zoo and a film, hardly perceiving anything he looked at, his mind's eye divided between the girl and those four black squares and the black tube and the unknown man behind it — the man he was now certainly going to kill tonight.

Back in the apartment punctually at five, Bond narrowly averted a row with Captain Sender, because he had poured himself a stiff whisky before putting on the hideous cowl that now stank of his sweat. Captain Sender had tried to prevent him and, when he failed, had threatened to call up Head of Station and report Bond for breaking training.

'Look, my friend,' said Bond wearily, 'I've got to commit a murder tonight. Not you. Me. So be a good chap and stuff it, would you? You can tell Tanqueray anything you like when it's over. Think I like this job? Having a Double-O number and so on? I'd be quite happy for you to get me sacked from the Double-O Section. Then I could settle down and make a snug nest of papers as an ordinary Staffer. Right?' Bond drank down his whisky, reached for his thriller, now arriving at an appalling climax, and threw himself on the bed.

Captain Sender, icily silent, went off into the kitchen to brew, from the sounds, his inevitable cuppa.

Bond felt the whisky beginning to melt the coiled nerves in his stomach. Now then, Liselotte, how in hell are you going to get out of this fix?

It was exactly six five when Sender, at his post, began talking excitedly. 'Bond, there's something moving way back over there. Now he's stopped — wait, no, he's on the move again, keeping low. There's a bit of broken wall there. He'll be out of sight of the opposition. But thick weeds, yards of them, ahead of him. Christ! He's coming through the weeds. And they're moving. Hope to God they think it's only the wind. Now he's through and gone to ground. Any reaction?'

'No,' said Bond tensely. 'Keep on telling me. How far to the frontier?'

'He's only got about fifty yards to go.' Captain Sender's voice was harsh with excitement. 'Broken stuff, but some of it's open. Then a solid chunk of wall right up against the pavement. He'll have to get over it. They can't fail to spot him then. Now! Now he's made ten yards, and another ten. Got him clearly then. Blackened his face and hands. Get ready! Any moment now he'll make the last sprint.'

James Bond felt the sweat pouring down his face and neck. He took a chance and quickly wiped his hands down his sides and then got them back to the rifle, his finger inside the guard, just lying along the curved trigger. 'There's something moving in the room behind the gun. They must have spotted him. Get that Opel working.'

Bond heard the code word go into the microphone, heard the Opel in the street below start up, felt his pulse quicken as the engine leaped into life and a series of ear-splitting cracks came from the exhaust.

The movement in the black cave was now definite. A black arm with a black glove had reached out and under the stock.

'Now!' ejaculated Captain Sender. 'Now! He's run for the wall! He's up it! Just going to jump!'

And then, in the Sniperscope, Bond saw the head of 'Trigger' — the purity of the profile, the golden bell of hair — all laid out along the stock of the Kalashnikov! She was dead, a sitting duck! Bond's fingers flashed down to the screws, inched them round and, as yellow flame fluttered at the snout of the sub-machine-gun, squeezed the trigger.

The bullet, dead on at three hundred and ten yards, must have hit where the stock ended up the barrel, might have got her in the left hand, but the effect was to tear the gun off its mountings, smash it against the side of the window-frame and then hurl it out of the window. It turned several times on its way down and crashed into the middle of the street.

'He's over!' shouted Captain Sender. 'He's over! He's done it! My God, he's done it!'

'Get down!' said Bond sharply, and threw himself sideways off the bed as the big eye of a searchlight in one of the black windows blazed on, swerving up the street towards their block and their room. Then gunfire crashed and the bullets howled into their window, ripping the curtains, smashing the woodwork, thudding into the walls.

Behind the roar and zing of the bullets, Bond heard the Opel race off down the street and, behind that again, the fragmentary whisper of the orchestra. The combination of the two background noises clicked. Of course! The orchestra had probably raised an infernal din throughout the Haus der Ministerien, having been used, like the backfiring Opel on this side, to provide some cover for a sharp burst of fire, on their side by 'Trigger'. Had she carried her weapon to and fro every day in that 'cello case? Was the whole orchestra composed of KGB women? Had the other instrument cases contained only equipment — the big drum perhaps the searchlight — while the real instruments were available in the concert hall? Too elaborate? Too fantastic? Probably. But there had been no doubt about the girl. In the Sniperscope, Bond had even been able to see one wide, heavily lashed, aiming eye. Had he hurt her? Almost certainly her left arm. There would be no chance of seeing her, seeing how she was, if she left with the orchestra. Now he would never see her again. Their window would be a death trap. To underline the fact, a stray bullet smashed into the mechanism of the Winchester, already overturned and damaged, and hot lead splashed down on Bond's hand, burning the skin. On Bond's emphatic oath, abruptly the firing stopped and silence sang in the room.

Captain Sender emerged from beside his bed, brushing glass out of his hair. They crunched across the floor and through the splintered door into the kitchen. Here, because it faced away from the street, it was safe to switch on the light.

'Any damage?' asked Bond.

'No. You all right?' Captain Sender's pale eyes were bright with the fever that comes in battle. They also, Bond noticed, held a sharp glint of accusation.

'Yes. Just get an Elastoplast for my hand. Caught a splash from one of the bullets.' Bond went into the bathroom. When he came out, Captain Sender was sitting by the walkie-talkie he had fetched from the sitting-room. He was speaking into it. Now he said into the microphone, 'That's all for now. Fine about 272. Hurry the armoured car, if you would. Be glad to get out of here, and 007 will need to write his version of what happened. Okay? Then OVER and OUT.'

Captain Sender turned to Bond. Half accusing, half

embarrassed, he said, 'Afraid Head of Station needs your reasons in writing for not getting that chap. I had to tell him I'd seen you alter your aim at the last second. Gave "Trigger" time to get off a burst. Damned lucky for 272 he'd just begun his sprint. Blew chunks off the wall behind him. What was it all about?'

James Bond knew he could lie, knew he could fake a dozen reasons why. Instead he took a deep pull at the strong whisky he had poured for himself, put the glass down and looked Captain Sender straight in the eye.

' "Trigger" was a woman.'

'So what? KGB have got plenty of women agents — and women gunners. I'm not in the least surprised. The Russian women's team always does well in the World Championships. Last meeting, in Moscow, they came first, second and third against seven countries. I can even remember two of their names — Donskaya and Lomova, terrific shots. She may even have been one of them. What did she look like? Records'll probably be able to turn her up.'

'She was a blonde. She was the girl who carried the 'cello in that orchestra. Probably had her gun in the 'cello case. The orchestra was to cover up the shooting.'

'Oh!' said Captain Sender slowly. 'I see. The girl you were keen on?'

'That's right.'

'Well, I'm sorry, but I'll have to put that in my report too. You had clear orders to exterminate "Trigger".'

There came the sound of a car approaching. It pulled up somewhere below. The bell rang twice. Sender said, 'Well, let's get going. They've sent an armoured car to get us out of here.' He paused. His eyes flicked over Bond's shoulder, avoiding Bond's eyes. 'Sorry about the report. Got to do my duty, y'know. You should have killed that sniper whoever it was.'

Bond got up. He suddenly didn't want to leave the stinking little smashed-up flat, leave the place from which, for three days, he had had this long-range, one-sided romance with an unknown girl — an unknown enemy agent with much the same job in her outfit as he had in his. Poor little bitch! She would be in worse trouble now than he was! She'd certainly be court-martialled for muffing this job. Probably be kicked out of the

KGB. He shrugged. At least they'd stop short of killing her — as he himself had done.

James Bond said wearily, 'Okay. With any luck it'll cost me my Double-O number. But tell Head of Station not to worry. That girl won't do any more sniping. Probably lost her left hand. Certainly broke her nerve for that kind of work. Scared the living daylights out of her. In my book, that was enough. Let's go.'